Thomas Longueville

A Life of Archbishop Laud

Thomas Longueville

A Life of Archbishop Laud

ISBN/EAN: 9783743336414

Manufactured in Europe, USA, Canada, Australia, Japa

Cover: Foto ©Raphael Reischuk / pixelio.de

Manufactured and distributed by brebook publishing software
(www.brebook.com)

Thomas Longueville

A Life of Archbishop Laud

GVLL: QVONDAM ARCH: CANT:

Lend me but one poore teare, when thou dost see,
This wretched Pourtraict of just miserie,
I was Great Innovator, Tyran, Foe
To Church, & State, all Times shall call me so.
But since, I'm Thunder-striken to the Ground
Learne how to stand, insult not ore my wound.

W: M: sculp:

A LIFE OF
ARCHBISHOP LAUD

BY

"A ROMISH RECUSANT."

" Laud, who stands upon the historic stage halfway between culprit
and martyr."

Romanes Lecture, 1892,
By the Right Hon. W. E. Gladstone, M.P.

WITH PORTRAIT FROM A RARE ENGRAVING BY W. MARSHALL, PREFIXED
TO "THE RECANTATION OF THE PRELATE OF CANTERBURY,"
PRINTED IN 1641.

LONDON
KEGAN PAUL, TRENCH, TRÜBNER & CO., LTD.
PATERNOSTER HOUSE, CHARING CROSS ROAD.
1894

The Author wishes it to be distinctly understood that his unqualified application of the word Archbishop, and other ecclesiastical titles, to the clergy of the Established Church of England, in no way implies any recognition on his part of the· validity of Anglican orders.

PREFACE.

I VENTURE to claim for the following biography that it is one of the least original ever written. A great, if not the greater, part of it consists of extracts from the writings of others, chiefly contemporaries of its subject, and bearing directly or indirectly upon his history. Where I felt so disposed, I have written on my own account, and written freely; in other places, I have introduced my authorities and stood by while they told their own story in their own words. I hesitated long as to whether I should call this book a "Life of Laud," or "Materials for a Life of Laud," and it was only the clumsiness of the latter title which deterred me from making use of it.

In making quotations from old books or manuscripts, it is a question whether the better course is to give them as they stand, or in modern spelling and phraseology. Some critics object to the former as wearisome, others to the latter as too commonly inaccurate. I have adopted both; but, for the most part, I have given the literal rendering; partly because the English of the period with which I had to deal was not so different from our own as to present difficulties, or prove unpalatable to the modern reader, and partly because a moderniser, like a translator, rarely succeeds in leaving all its original freshness and force in the work which he manipulates.

I anticipate accusations from my critics of having gone too far afield in my attempts to throw side-lights upon the career of Laud. It may be that on this count I am guilty. If so, my excuse must be that I have sinned in an honest endeavour to illustrate his life and character by recalling to the minds of my readers the times in which he lived and the people with whom he was brought into contact.

All this has been easy to say: I must now tread upon more delicate ground. A life of a Protestant Archbishop written by a Catholic and a convert is likely to be looked upon by the majority of English readers as an attack from the enemy; moreover, an idea still largely prevails in this country that Catholics are never to be trusted when they deal with historical subjects, and that converts are invariably bitter. As to the two last mentioned imputations, while I should be sorry to think it necessary to reply to the first of them, I have something to say about the second. A convert from the Anglican to the Catholic Church may regard the establishment which he has repudiated in one of two lights. He may either look at it with feelings of resentment as an heretical body which long kept him away from what he believes to be the true Church, by counterfeiting its authority, its doctrines, and its ceremonies; or he may see in it an heretical body, it is true, but one retaining many valuable vestiges, traditions, and principles of the ancient Church, to which, by the grace of God, they led him when followed to their logical conclusions, and he may reflect that whither they have led him, they may also lead others.

In attacking what they consider the errors of Anglicanism, Catholics, like other combatants, cannot fight in silken gloves; the weapons they use, be they logic, invective, or even satire, may be sharp and may cause pain; but in order to prove that the feelings of Catholics towards Anglicans need not necessarily be bitter, I will copy some words used by the head of the Catholic Church upon earth. I have already said that much of this book will be found to consist of quotations; let the first be from the writings of the Holy Father.[1]

In a letter to the English Bishops, dated 27th November 1885, Pope Leo XIII. says :—

---

[1] If any quotation should appear on the title page and it should be objected that it took precedence of the Pope's, I would reply that usually, and certainly in the present instance, the title page is not the first to be written, but absolutely the last.

"In your country of Great Britain we know that besides yourselves very many of your nation are not a little anxious about religious education. They do not in all things agree with us; nevertheless, they see how important, for the sake of society and of men individually, is the preservation of that Christian wisdom which your forefathers received through St Augustine from our predecessor, St Gregory the Great; which wisdom the violent tempests that came afterwards have not entirely scattered. There are, as we know, at this day many of an excellent disposition of mind who are diligently striving to retain what they can of the ancient faith, and who bring forth many and great fruits of charity. As often as we think of this so often are we deeply moved, for we love with a paternal charity that island, which was not undeservedly called the Mother of Saints, and we see in the disposition of mind of which we have spoken the greatest hope, and as it were a pledge, of the welfare and prosperity of the British people."

From the writings of a Pope I will turn to those of a Prince of the Church and an honoured Englishman. In 1890, Cardinal Vaughan (then Bishop of Salford) wrote in *England's Conversion by the Power of Prayer* (pp. 8, 9) that the Anglican Establishment had "changed its temper and attitude. Its bishops, ministers, and people are busily engaged in ignoring or denouncing those very articles which were drawn up to be their eternal protest against the Old Religion." "Societies are formed, tracts and books are written, lectures are delivered all over the country, to prove to the people that the past three hundred years have been a dismal mistake." "In a word, Catholic doctrines and practices are being reinstated all over the land, and the old heresies cast out. The arch has been turned, the keystone alone is wanting. When a sick man is in a crisis of suffering, we pray the more for him, because he is near to death or to a cure." "While some of us have been straining our minds and hearts in one direction, shaking our heads and lamenting because the conversions are so few,—behold, the whole country has become half converted without observation. I do not say that half the people, or any considerable section of the people, are yet *converted;* but I say that the decay of prejudice, the advance of truth, the change in sentiment and policy, and in faith and practice, justify us in saying that England is half converted from what she was during the last three centuries,—and this both within the Establishment and without."

Surely the words of this Pope and of this Cardinal, here quoted, may, in the first place, dispose Catholics to look back with some interest to the earlier history of the Establishment, including that of Laud, and, in the second, lead Anglicans to hope that Catholic writers, in dealing with their Church and Churchmen, may not be altogether ungenerous foes.

And well may converts look with a kindly spirit upon their Anglican neighbours; for, if they consider it an inestimable privilege to have been received into the Holy Catholic Church, it behoves at least the less distinguished in virtues and attainments to reflect with modesty and gratitude upon the extraordinary miracle of mercy which selected them—so few out of so many—to see the " Kindly Light" and to follow it, while the vast majority of their former co-religionists, some of them immensely their superiors in mental ability, in the extent of their studies, and even, perhaps, in heroic works of charity and self-denial, have not had this grace given to them.

CONTENTS.

CHAPTER I.

Principal events from 1573 to 1589.

CHAPTER II.

1589 to early in seventeenth century.

CHAPTER III.

Late in sixteenth century to 1605.

CHAPTER IV.

1606 and various periods.

CHAPTER V.

1607—1615.

CHAPTER VI.

1616—1621.

CHAPTER VII.

1621—1624.

Contents.

CHAPTER XXX.

1638—1640.

CHAPTER XXXI.

Very varying dates.

CHAPTER XXXII.

1639—1640.

CHAPTER XXXIX.

1644.

CHAPTER XL.

1644—1645.

CHAPTER XLI.

1645.

CHAPTER XLII.

1645.

LIST OF ABBREVIATIONS.

HIST.—The History of the Troubles and Tryal of The Most Reverend Father In God, and Blessed Martyr, William Laud, Lord Archbishop of Canterbury. Wrote by Himselfe, during his Imprisonment in the Tower. Preface by Hen. Wharton. London, 1795.

DIARY—[To the above] is prefixed The Diary of His Own Life Faithfully and entirely Published from the Original Copy.

CYP. ANG.—Cyprianus Anglicanus, or The History of the Life and Death of The Most Reverend and Renowned Prelate William, By Divine Providence, Lord Archbishop of Canterbury, &c. By Peter Heylin.

BENSON—William Laud, some-time Archbishop of Canterbury. A Study. By A. C. Benson, B.A. London : Kegan Paul, Trench & Co., 1887.

CAL. STA. PA. DOM.—Calendar of State Papers, Domestic.

DIC. NAT. BIO.—A Dictionary of National Biography. By Sidney Lee.

HIST. REB.—The History of the Great Rebellion. By Edward Earl of Clarendon. Oxford : Printed at the Theater, 1707.

LAUD'S LAB.—Labyrinthus Cantuariensis, or Doctor Laud's Labyrinth, &c. By T. C. Paris, 1658.

LIB. ANG.-CATH. THEOL.—Library of Anglo-Catholic Theology. Oxford : John Henry Parker, 1846.

S. P. O.—State Paper Office.

ENG. UNIV.—The English Universities. From the German of V. A. Huber. Edited by F. W. Newman.

REC. ENG. PROV. S. J.—Records of the English Province of the Society of Jesus, &c. By Henry Foley, S. J. 1877.

ENCY. BRIT.—Encyclopædia Britannica. 8th Edition.

SCRINIA RESERATA—Scrinia Reserata : A Memorial offer'd of the Great Deservings of John Williams, D.D., &c., &c., Lord Archbishop of York. Written by John Hackett, late Bishop of Litchfield and Coventry. 1692.

PANZANI—Memoirs of Gregorio Panzani, Envoy from Rome to the English Clergy. Translated from the Italian Original by the Rev. Joseph Berington.

RUSHWORTH—Rushworth's Historical Recollections.

HIST. COLL.— Do. do.

CONF. WITH FISHER—A Relation of The Conference between William Laud, late Archbishop of Canterbury, and Mr Fisher the Jesuit, &c. With an Answer to such exceptions as A. C. takes against it. Oxford : At the University Press, 1839.

LIFE OF ARCHBISHOP LAUD.

CHAPTER I.

My hero was the son of a tailor. One of his bitter enemies, and he had many, describes him as a man of very low birth, "*E facce plebis*"; on the other hand, Heylin, who acted as his Boswell, says:—"If Laud's father was a tailor, he also kept not only many Lomes (looms) in his house, but many Weavers;"[1] and he adds that his mother was actually so aristocratic as to be "sister to a Lord Mayor of London." Moreover, we should remember that the scope of the tailor's art was much wider in the sixteenth century than it is in the nineteenth. Who has not read of that great tailor's son, of fiction, Sir Piercie Shafto? with his "murrey-coloured double-piled Genoa velvet, puffed out with ciprus," his "rich crimson silk doublet, slashed out and lined with cloth of gold, with baldric and trimmings to correspond," and his "four suits of as pure and elegant device as ever the fancy of a fair lady doated upon, every one having a treble and appropriate change of ribbons, trimmings, and fringes, which, in case of need, may, as it were, renew each of them, and multiply the four into twelve."[2] Obviously, a tailor, especially a tailor who was also a weaver, might not only have been a man of taste and skill, but also of at least very substantial means, in the sixteenth century. As a matter of fact, when Laud's father died, he left him £1200, the equivalent of a

[1] "Cyp. Angl.," p. 42.   [2] "The Monastery," by Sir Walter Scott.

A

very comfortable little capital in our own days, besides
his stock in trade, his house in Reading, and two houses
at Swallowfield.

"I was born Octob. 7, 1573, at *Reading*," says Laud in
his diary.[1]

He was the only child of a second marriage,[2] and a
delicate baby; for he says of himself:—"In my Infancy
I was in danger of Death by Sickness." There is a tradition that he was born in a house situated on the north
side of Broad Street, which was noticeable for "the semi-
circular termination of the brick front in the upper storey."[3]
Mr Coates, from whom I quote, attempts to prove, and
apparently with success, that Prynne's assertion that he
was born "at a cottage just against the Cage" is utterly
false. Broad Street was not very far from the modern
railway stations, on the northern side of the town. And
here it may be well to observe that the biographer of Laud
has frequently to balance his opinion somewhere between
the calumnies of Prynne, blended as they are with a certain
amount of truth, and the exaggerated panegyrics of Heylin,
and some of his other admirers, both contemporary and
modern.

Mr Bruce, in his interesting but unfinished essay, prefixed
to the "Life of Laud" in Dean Hook's *Lives of the Archbishops
of Canterbury*,[4] tells us that, at Reading School, Laud "so
distinguished himself, that his master foretold his fuuret
eminence, and expressed a hope, that when Laud should
become a great man, he would not forget how much he owed
to the training he received at Reading School [Lloyd's
'Memoires']. His master was severe in discipline, but came
to the conclusions just mentioned from observing the strange
dreams, witty speeches, generous spirit, great apprehension,
and notable performances of his pupil."

It is easy to imagine the sharp, intelligent boy, rendered,
perhaps, more precocious by the delicacy of his early childhood, his inability to join in ordinary children's games, and

[1] "Hist. W. L.," p. 1.   [2] Benson, p. 12.
[3] Coates's "History of Reading," p. 411.   [4] Vol. xi. p. 4.

his consequently increased intercourse with older people,
attracting the attention of the schoolmaster. Then, a clever
little boy, for William Laud was small in stature, is apt to
receive more credit than he deserves, when he excels much
bigger boys of his own age. His face, again, if never
handsome, was noticeable. His portraits show us bright,
piercing eyes, with remarkably high eyebrows, which give
a half-surprised, half-supercilious expression to his countenance, and we read that he had a high, harsh, irritable
voice, and a nervous, impetuous manner. A master might
well be both interested and amused with a lad of this
description.

If a pedagogue was considered "severe" in those days,
great indeed must have been his severity. The floggings of
the period were serious matters, judging from the fact that
early in the seventeenth century, a son of the Bishop of
Bristol committed suicide in order to avoid one.[1]

A use of the rod, considered excessive even at the latter
end of the sixteenth century, may have helped to produce in
Laud that stoical contempt for such corporal punishments
as the pillory, whippings, ear-croppings, and nose-slittings,
which he exhibited in the Court of High Commission and
the Star Chamber, in later years. At the same time, we
must remember that, even in his school-days, there was
something of a reaction from the brutal severity of peda-
gogues. In 1581, the headmaster of Merchant Taylor's
School wrote : — "For gentlenesse and curtesie towards
children, I do thinke it more nedefull than beatinge ;"[2] and,
somewhere near the same time, Brinsley, the author of
Pueriles Confabulatiunculæ, went so far as to suggest that
the birch-rod should be replaced by a " lytel twigge."

Already, too, books of the *Reading-without Tears* type
had begun to come into fashion. Four years before the
birth of Laud, a book was published, entitled *A delysious
Surupe newly claryfied for yonge scholars yᵗ thurste for the
swete lycore of Laten speche.* In the same year, William
Hayward wrote his *Grammer Warre*, in which *Amo*, king

[1] "Cal. Sta. Pa.," 1611-18, p. 120.   [2] Mulcaster's "Positives," Brit. Mus.

of the verbs, and *Poeta*, king of the nouns, have a battle,
and the pronouns are called in as allies. Very nearly at the
same date, if a trifle earlier, Roger Ascham published his
famous *Schoolemaister, or Plaine and perfyte way of teaching
children to understand writing and speakyng the Latin tong,
but specially purposed for the private Bringing up of youth in
Jentlemen's and Noblemen's houses;* and so long as forty
years before Laud's birth, an Eton master (Udall), had
written a book called *Floures of Latyn Spekynge.*[1] In respect
to religious instruction, it may be worth mentioning that
Dean Nowell of St Paul's, the successor of the famous Dean
Colet, published, three years before the birth of Laud, a
Catechism which became the standard work of its kind, and
remained so for many years.[2]

It is far from unlikely that Laud might have studied a
children's reading-book which was much in fashion in his
youth, entitled, *A Booke in Englyssh metre of the great mar-
chaunt man called Dyves Pragmaticus, very pretye for chyldren
to rede, wherby they may better and more readyer rede and
write Wares and Implements in this worlde contayned;* or
a book some thirty years older, *The Secret of Secrets of
Aristotle . . . very gode to teach children to read English;* or
a child's book of about the same period, Andrew Borde's
Introduction to Knowledge, in which run the lines :—

> " I am an Englishman, and naked I stand here,
>   Musing in my minde what raiment I shall were."

But one of the best known books for children, that
appeared immediately before Laud was born, was *The Schoole
of Vertue,* which was for long used as a lesson book and was
even reprinted in the early part of the present century. It
taught good manners and, with one or two of its fellows,
provoked a wicked writer to publish a sort of parody, called
The School of Slovenrie, the style of which may be judged
by the following couplet :—

> " When thou art set, devoure as much as thou with healthe canst eate,
>   Thou therefore wert to dinner bid, to help away his meate."

[1] See "The Child and his Book," by Mrs Field, p. 149.   [2] *Ib.* p. 143.

I mention these books to show that a great step had been made in juvenile literature just before Laud's birth and in his early childhood.

Among certain classes, a clerical career is regarded as an important social advancement. The smallest Scotch farmer hopes that his first-born son may some day "wag his pow" in the pulpit; the Irish cotter that his boy may live to be addressed as "yer riverence"; and in England, the burgher sets before himself the sending of his son to college and his subsequent "ordination," as the highest object of his ambition. What more natural, therefore, than that Laud, the tailor, should make up his mind to send his only child to Oxford, with a view to his becoming a clergyman, and his thoughts may have been directed towards churches and benefices by the duties of his office of churchwarden, an honour which he obtained only a couple of years before he sent his son to college.

At a time when public feeling was beginning to run high between the supporters of "Church and Queen" and the Puritans, even boys would place themselves on one side or the other; many of us have seen little lads giving and enduring bloody noses, for the sake of religious tenets which they but very partially understood; and it is probable that at a town like Reading the tendency was towards the school of thought then held to be orthodox by the loyal and the influential.

Of politics, again, much would no doubt be heard and said at Reading. When we consider how many roads converge on Reading on their way to London, it becomes evident that that town must have been an important local centre of news and gossip; although it must be admitted that the London road was then so bad near the town, and, owing to its low level, so subject to floods, as to be sometimes impassable for a month or six weeks together.[1] Even in the early years of the present century, my father's schoolmaster used, during an illness of the then reigning monarch, to go every day to the nearest post-town, await the arrival of the London coach at

---

[1] Coates's "History of Reading," p. 458.

the inn where the horses were changed, and call out in a
pompous voice, as it drew up ;—" Well, guard, and how is
poor king ? " Much more must coachmen and travellers have
been pestered for news, in days when newspapers had only
just been invented, and that scarcely more than in name, and
even stage-coaches and guards were yet things in the dim
future.

And here it may be worth inquiring what subjects of
common conversation are likely to have come within the
hearing of, and to have influenced, the boy in whose career
we are interesting ourselves ; for, if a dull, or even an ordinary, lad cares little as to what anybody, except himself and
his play-fellows, are doing, a sharp, thoughtful, imaginative
boy, such as Laud is represented to have been, would listen
with pricked ears to his elders retailing " the news." Fathers
in our time can learn what is going on all over the world, as
they sit in silence with their newspapers ; or impart their
ideas by writing to them ; when Laud was a boy, on the contrary, political information was chiefly obtained by hearing
and communicated by speaking.

Queen Elizabeth was reigning in her full glory. Laud's
historian would naturally like to imagine that he might have
seen her pass through Reading, accompanied by an imposing retinue, and consider the effect such a spectacle would
produce upon an excitable boy, engendering in him those
strong opinions upon the Divine Right of monarchs for which
he afterwards became so conspicuous ; but truth compels me
to say that the queen, after making some stay at Reading when
he was three years old, an age at which her appearance can
scarcely have made much impression upon him, did not visit
that town again, so far as I can ascertain, until he was nineteen
and probably at Oxford. Nevertheless, a regal sojourn at a
provincial town would leave many traditions behind it for
several years, and little William would be brought up in an
atmosphere of stories about his excellent and almost super-
human queen and " governess," as she was called. It is
pretty certain, too, that he would be congratulated on living
in the reign of good Queen Bess, so escaping the " fires of

Smithfield" and "Bloody Mary" by fifteen years. The very founder of the "Church of England, as by law established," of which he was to become so prominent a member, had been living within twenty-six years of his own time, and within twenty-seven, the great hero of the Reformation, Martin Luther himself. Laud was born only a year too late to be a contemporary of a man whose name became odious to him —the notorious John Knox, and he can scarcely have failed to hear a good deal concerning him in his boyhood. He would hear also of another man remarkable in the religious world, who had died seven years before his own birth ; I mean Saint Ignatius of Loyola, the Founder of the Society of Jesus. A lad then unknown to fame, but one who was destined to be celebrated in the history of the Church, Saint Francis of Sales, was six years older than Laud ; and a boy much nearer home, and three years yet older, whose name, William Shakespeare, was, if possible, even less known, was to become far more famous than the subject of my memoir.

A boy at a grammar school in the early years of Laud might possibly, I will not venture to say would probably, hear some strong expressions used concerning an event which had been brought to a conclusion just ten years before his birth. This was the great Council of Trent, of which he had much to say and to write as he grew older, and there is every reason for believing that he had been brought up to regard it with hatred and scorn.

In alluding to things ecclesiastical, it may be worth observing that, at the time of his birth, the occupant of the Archdiocese, to which he was one day to succeed, was Archbishop Parker, concerning the validity of whose orders there has been so much and such bitter wrangling.

Perhaps, at seven years old, Laud may not have been too young to at least partially comprehend the prevailing gossip about the persecution of the Puritans, which was then being carried on at the order of their fierce enemy, Queen Elizabeth. As a set-off against this, when he was eight, Father Campion, the Jesuit, was put to the torture. When he was twelve, the following Act of Parliament was

passed :—" 27 Eliz. cap. 2, sect. 3." I do not hesitate to
quote it at some length, as it was fraught with exceedingly
serious consequences.

"And be it further enacted by the Authority aforesaid,
that it shall not be Lawful to or for any Jesuit, Seminary
Priest, or other such Priest, Deacon, or Religious Ecclesiastical
Person whatsoever, being borne within this Realm, or any
other Her Majesty's Dominions, and heretofore since the
said Feast of the Nativity of *St John Baptist*, in the first
year of Her Majesty's Reign, made, ordained, or professed
or hereafter to be made, ordained, or professed, by any
Authority or Jurisdiction, derived, challenged, or pretended
from the See of *Rome*, by, or of what Name, Title, or Degree
so-ever, the same shall be called or known, to come into, be, or
remain in any part of this Realm, or any other Her Highness
Dominions, after the end of the same forty days, other than
in such special Cases, and upon such special Occasions only,
and for such time only, as is expressed in this Act ; and if
he do, then every such Offence shall be taken and adjudged
to be High Treason ; and every Person so offending, shall
for his Offence be adjudged a Trayter, and shall suffer, lose
and forfeit, as in case of High Treason. And every Person,
which after the end of the same forty days, and after such
time of departure, as is before limited and appointed, shall
wittingly, and willingly receive, relieve, comfort, aid, or
maintain, any such Jesuit, Seminary Priest, or other Priest,
Deacon or Religious or Ecclesiastical Person, as is aforesaid,
being at liberty, or out of hold, knowing him to be a
Jesuit, Seminary Priest, or other such Priest, Deacon, or
Religious or Ecclesiastical Person, as is aforesaid, shall also
for such offence be adjudged a Felon, without Benefit of
Clergy, and suffer Death, lose and forfeit, as in Case of one
Attainted of Felony."

A lad of twelve would hear his elders rejoicing over the
passing of this Act with awe and interest, and the tone of
their remarks would probably have much in common with a
passage in Sir Edward Coke's " Institutes,"[1] wherein he states

---

[1] Lib. 3. cap. 37.

that "these Jesuits and Romish Priests coming daily into and swarming within this Realm, instilling" "Poison into the Subjects Hearts," "Her Majesty made it Treason," for any Jesuit or priest to come into her kingdom, "Intending thereby to keep them out of the same, to the end, that they should not infect any other Subjects, with such Treasonable and Damnable Persuasions and Practises, as aforesaid."

Close at hand were monuments of the stern usage applied to the professors of these "Damnable Persuasions." Just thirty-four years before Laud's birth, the Lord Abbot of Reading Abbey—and a great Abbot was he, mitred and by right a peer of parliament, only ranking, it is said, after the Abbots of Glastonbury and St Albans,—was drawn, hanged, and quartered, with two of his monks to keep him company, at the pleasure of King Henry VIII., "for denying the king's supremacie." This martyrdom would, no doubt, be represented as a mete and decent "execution" to the boy, Laud. Had not the excellent Cromwell written to the very bishop of the diocese himself, when he had remonstrated :— "I can take your writing, or thys heate of your stomach, every whyt as well as I can, I trust, beware of flatterers." By King Henry VIII. and his admirers, it seems to have been somewhat reluctantly admitted, that the first power was the Almighty ; but they were equally certain that the second was the King's Gracious Majesty, and the third the bishops, subject to the pleasure of the king.

At Laud's birth, there were still living three of the old Catholic bishops who had resigned their sees—as they all had done, to a man—rather than adopt the new religion. These were Heath, Archbishop of York ; Watson, Bishop of Lincoln ; and Goldwell, Bishop of St Asaph. Only eleven years before Laud was born, Jewell wrote to Peter Martyr : "The Marian Bishops are still confined in the Tower."[1] The last of these bishops (Goldwell) died when Laud was twelve years old.

When Laud was fourteen, the national fury was stirred up

---

[1] "Queen Elizabeth and the Catholic Hierarchy." Bridgett and Knox, p. 40.

against the Catholics by the news that that very Catholic king, Philip of Spain, had sent a great Armada to take possession of England and depose its queen. When the English shores, with those of Scotland and Ireland, had been strewn with its helpless wreckage, although a mad joy took the place of frenzied terror, the popular animosity against the co-religionists of its author in no degree abated. In the opinion of most loyal Englishmen, the destruction of King Philip's great ships in the seas surrounding these islands was as much a divine judgment upon the wicked, as that of Pharaoh and his hosts in the Red Sea; and as Philip meant Popery (by the way, almost his first war had been against the Pope), it was also a divine judgment, nay, more, a divine decision and pronouncement upon the wickedness and falseness of that religion. So thought the English Protestants; and I would ask every fair-minded Catholic to make due allowances for my hero, if, at the impressionable age of fourteen, when he heard of the approach to his native land of a dreaded power, with the professed object of over-throwing its monarchy, government, and religion, in the name of a religion other than his own, he began to hate that religion, and if, when he heard of the utter rout of the enemy, he thought that, once crushed, it should never again be permitted to raise its head, and that every Englishman who professed it was a dangerous rebel.

Earlier in the same year, another blow had been struck at Catholicism in this country, in the execution of Mary, Queen of Scots. Popular feeling in our own days is, on the whole, rather in favour of that unfortunate queen; but it is highly improbable that much sympathy would be felt for her misfortunes in the unromantic home of an English burgher, loyal to Queen Elizabeth, in her own times. He would regard her as a traitorous rebel, who would upset the then ruling powers if she could, and any disturbance of the ruling powers might disorganise the woollen and tailoring trades, and lessen the profits of Mr William Laud. On the arrival of the news that her head had been severed from her body, the bells were rung, and bonfires were lighted in and about

London, nor is it likely that so happy an incident would escape public recognition at loyal Reading.

There was perhaps more heartfelt joy throughout the country in the following year, at the death of the queen's favourite, Leicester, who held, among others of greater importance, the post of Chancellor of Oxford, which many years later fell to the lot of Laud.

We now come to a very important period in Laud's life, his career at Oxford. Probably because the mayor and civic authorities had the right of nomination to a scholarship there, he was sent to St John's College. It was then a very new establishment, having been founded only thirty-four years earlier by Sir Thomas White; and it was just a year younger than Trinity. The spirit of these two new colleges was supposed to be rather in the direction of a variety of knowledge than of theology and the classics, and Sir Thomas Pope, who founded the last named, said :—" I remembre, when I was a young scholler at Eton, the Greek tongue was growing apace, the studie of which is now alate much decayed." When the advantage of a classical education was advocated, he replied :—" This purpose I will lyke; but I fear the tymes will not bear it now."

Laud's father would feel an additional interest in sending his son to St John's, because its founder had followed the same trade as himself in the same town of Reading. Having left it for London, of which city he became Lord Mayor, and in it distinguished himself for his services during the rebellion of Sir Thomas Wyatt, receiving knighthood as a reward from the hands of Queen Mary, Sir Thomas White amassed a large fortune, and is understood to have first intended to build a college at Reading, but afterwards to have decided to do so at either Oxford or Cambridge. I dwell upon some details here because the name of Laud is so intimately connected with St John's College, and if Sir Thomas White founded it, Laud did much for it in the way of building and adornment.

The story goes that White dreamed that he should build a college at a place where he should find two elms of equal height growing out of the same tree, and a third near them, of lower stature; that he went to Cambridge and failed to find them, but afterwards discovered them "without the North Gate of the City of Oxford," on the site of the present college of St John the Baptist.[1] Eventually he erected that college at which he gave elective scholarships to the towns of Reading, Coventry, Bristol, and Tunbridge.

[1] Coates's "Hist. of Reading."

CHAPTER II.

Laud was fortunate enough to escape being at Oxford under the chancellorship of Leicester, by two years; but that chancellor's works remained. As Huber says of him :—
" The character of this chancellor and his coterie is enough to explain even the worst phenomena of Oxford ; nor can we be surprised that as soon as he recognised in the University a useful tool, he used it unscrupulously. He bestowed upon his servants and creatures all academic influence and emoluments, without care for the rights and claims of men or things." [1]

It is difficult for us to realise the condition of Oxford at the end of the sixteenth and the early part of the seventeenth centuries. The author just quoted tells us that only in 1638 was the principle introduced "of a real examination as a preparation for the academic degree, the granting of which had until then depended upon a plurality of votes, although nominally upon the old scholastic exercises, which for a long time had become a practical nullity ; " and he adds in a footnote :—" Real examinations may have taken place in Oxford up to the thirteenth century ; but they had completely fallen into disuse at all events after the end of this century."

As to the discipline prevailing at Oxford, an undated document among the Domestic State Papers,[2] but assigned to the time of Laud's boyhood, may give some idea.

" 12 or 15 persones, most M^{rs} of Arte,"—Masters of Arts, and not undergraduates, be it observed — " of Christe's Church, standing in ye highwaye, there cam by them in God's peace and the Quene's, a pore myllner a horse backe,

[1] The " English Universities." From German of V. A. Huber. Ed. F. W. Newman.
[2] Vol. xxiv. 19.

wth five and six small gristes under him, whome they torned besides his horse, and threwe the same griste downe, some in one place and some in another, and some in wet and fowle places; and as many of them as could ryde on the said horse got uppone him, and rode up and downe ye towne; and the poore miller went after them, desyrenge them to have his horse agayne, for that he was a servaunt, and shold have blame for his long taryeinge." "Beinge also requested gentlye to delyver the poore myller his horse, by divers honest inhabytants of the towne, they gave them very evyll and opprobrious words, unmete to be repeated." "Havinge had their pleasure in rydeinge, they whipped the poore fellowe wth his own whippe." "Yet not so contente, they tooke his hat oute of his hand, and rent yt all in peeces, and so departed away, levinge the poore myller w^{th}out recompense for his injuries, being a very evill example." And further on—"No man's servant nor the M^r himself, can sit at their owen dores, nor goe about their busynes in the eveninge quietly, but he shalbe beaten, and havinge any thing in his hand, y^t shalbe taken awaye frome him, as wyne and wyne-pot. And yf a man goe wth a lanthorne to see his waye, yt shalbe smytten out of his hand and broken, and the party beaten." Moreover, "certeyne of the University," "wth swords and bucklers and clubs, and other weapons," "went up and downe the streats, misusinge both men and women, wth opprobryous words, they lienge in their beds, neythur thinckinge nor doinge any harm to them; and all (as y^t should seme) was to begynne a new ryot, or rather an insurrection."

The most violent town-and-gown rows of modern times were nothing to these, and it would be easy to multiply evidence that a spirit of wild and coarse lawlessness prevailed among the members of the university for many years after Leicester's chancellorship had ended. As time went on, and Laud himself became chancellor, strong measures were taken to repress this disgraceful condition of things.

In the days of Elizabeth, the old scholastic philosophy was tabooed at Oxford, as was everything that was supposed to have any Catholic tendency. Under Leicester's influence, Puritanical teaching was encouraged there, although his royal mistress would have had it otherwise; but it was difficult to regulate the religious tone of a university to the exact taste of a queen of whom De Silva could write:—"The Catholics hate her because she is not a Papist, the Protestants because she is less furious and violent in heresy than they would like to see her."[1]

Shortly before Laud's arrival at Oxford, there was a fierce contest as to the election of a successor to Leicester in the chancellorship. The champion of the Puritanical party in the Church of England was the Earl of Essex, that of the High Churchmen was Lord Chancellor Hatton. The latter obtained most votes in Convocation and was elected; but his reign was short, as he died in 1591, and Lord Treasurer Buckhurst became chancellor in his stead.

Either the religious views of Laud were greatly influenced by his tutor, or they were two men of singularly sympathetic ideas. Buckeridge belonged to a party, already in existence and gradually increasing in power and numbers, which endeavoured to take its stand midway between Puritanism and Catholicism, a party which, even in our own days shows no signs of failing; on the one hand, it declaimed against Calvinism, and on the other against "Popery." Each of its clerical members had, as it were, awakened with the sudden discovery, "Hullo! I am a priest!" The rest—the "sacramental grace," the "apostolical succession," the "power of absolution," the "branch-of-the-Catholic-Church" theory, and so on, followed as corollaries.

There had indeed been much to bring about a reaction from the state of things which had been tolerated by the indifference of the new Church. Queen Elizabeth wrote to Archbishop Parker of "the unclean and negligent order and spare keeping of the houses of prayer," a thing that "breedeth no small offence and scandal to see;" and of the "unmeet and unseemly tables with foul cloths, for the communion of the Sacrament;" and of "the place of prayer desolate of all cleanliness and of meet ornament for such a place, whereby

[1] Froude's "Hist. of Eng.," vol. xi. p. 292.

it might be known a place provided for divine service." I quote from Mr Froude. The same author tells us that the Bishop of London, a few years before Laud's time, complained of the Protestant exiles who came from other countries and leavened the newly-made Church of England, as "for the most part *facinorosi, ebriosi, et sectarii.*" And, about a year later, Lord Sussex wrote to Cecil:—"The people without discipline, utterly devoid of religion, come to service as to a May game ; the ministers for disability and greediness, be had in contempt ; and the wise fear more the impiety of the licentious professors than the superstitions of the erroneous Papists."

The bitterness of the Puritans, again, was in itself sufficient to awaken a reaction. Two black-letter fly-sheets [2] of about the year 1571, speak of "abolishinge and abhoringe all tradicions and inventions of man whatsoever," of "the fylthye cannon lawe," the "abominable" "reliques of Anti-Christe," "the filthyness and pollution of these detestable traditions," this "idolatrouse trash," and "them that have receaved these markes of the Romysh beast." The writer of one of them goes on to say :—"I will not beautifie with my presence those filthy ragges which bryng the heavenly worde of the Eternell our Lorde God into bondage, subjection, and slaverie." "They," the Episcopalians, "glad and strengthen the papists in their errour, and greve the godlie." "God geve us strength styl to stryve." A supplication to the queen, which accompanies them, beseeches her "now in the thirteenth year of her reign," to "imitate Jehosaphat, and cast down idolatry." Let her "cut down, root out, and utterly destroy all monuments of idolatry, as forked caps and tippets, surplices, copes, starch-cakes, godfathers, and godmothers," &c.

Nor was all the strong language used on the Calvinist side. One of the opposite party, when it got into full power, wrote :—"We" "have kept ourselves warm with the hopes of rubbing, fubbing, and scrubbing those scurvy, filthy, dirty, nasty, lousy, itchy, scabby," "stinking, slovenly," "logger-

---

[1] Froude's "Hist. of Eng.," vol. vii. p. 468.
[2] "Cal. Sta. Pap.," vol. xx. Nos. 107, 107 i., 107 ii.

headed, foolish, insolent, proud, beggarly, impertinent, absurd, grout-headed, villainous, barbarous, bestial, false, lying, roguish, devilish, long-eared, short-haired, damnable, atheistical, puritanical crew."[1] I have omitted the strongest adjectives.

No life of Laud would be complete without some notice of the position of the rival parties in the Church of England during his university career, and this must be my apology for dwelling upon it at some length.

It should be remembered that less than twenty years before Laud's time, one Anglican bishop, Ridley, who had died for his cause, had knocked down the altars in the churches of his diocese, and substituted tables in the middle of the buildings, which the Catholics called " oyster-boards " ; that Bishop Hooper, who had also been put to death, had for a long time refused altogether to wear any Episcopal vestments ; and that Bishop Ponet had wished that the title of bishop should be abandoned.[2] About a dozen years before the birth of Laud, Bishop Jewel showed his opinions pretty plainly in his letters. " We have exhibited," he says, " to the queen all our articles of religion and doctrine, and have not departed in the least degree from the confession of Zurich." This is pretty strong, considering the opinions at Zurich ! " As to your expressing a hope that our bishops will be consecrated without any superstitious and offensive ceremonies ; you mean, I suppose, without oil, without chrism, without the tonsure. And you are not mistaken ; for the sink would indeed have been emptied to no purpose if we had suffered these dregs to settle at the bottom. Those oily, shaven, portly hypocrites we have sent back to Rome, whence we first imported them."[3]

In a publication, entitled *A Retentive to Stay, &c.*, London, 1580, is to be found the following elegant profession of faith : —" With all our heart we abhore, defie, detest, and spit at your stinking, greasy, anti-Christian Orders." Nor must the opinions of the Anglican bishops shortly preceding Laud's days be overlooked. Archbishop Cranmer, having been

[1] " Cal. Sta. Pap.," vol. cccxxiv. No. 50.
[2] Macaulay's " Hist. of Eng.," vol. i. chap. i.   [3] " Zurich Letters," xxii.

B

asked a question by Henry VIII., replied :—" The civil magistrates under the King be Lord Chancellor, Lord Treasurer, admirals, sheriffs ; the ministers of God's Word under his Majesty be bishops, parsons, vicars, and such other priests as be appointed by his Highness to that ministration ; as for example, the Bishop of Canterbury, the Bishop of Durham, the Parson of Winwiche, &c., all the said officers be appointed, assigned, and elected in every place by the laws and orders of kings and princes. In the admission of many of these offices be divers comely ceremonies and solemnities, *and which be not of necessity, but only for a good order and seemly fashion ; for if such offices and ministrations were committed without such solemnity, they were nevertheless duly committed, and there is no more promise of God that grace is given in the committing of the ecclesiastical office than it is in the committing of the civil office.*"

When asked :—" Whether in the New Testament be required any consecration of a bishop or a priest, or only appointing to the office be sufficient ? " he answered :—" In the New Testament he that is appointed to be a bishop or a priest *needeth no consecration* by the Scripture, *for election or appointment is sufficient.*" And to the same question, Bishop Barlow, who is reputed to have consecrated Archbishop Parker, through whom all the Anglican clergy claim their orders, replied :—" Only the appointing."[1] Besides all this, Barlow, when he was Bishop of St David's, is reported to have said that " if the King's Grace, being Supreme Head of the Church of England, did choose, denominate, and elect any layman being learned to be a bishop, that he so chosen would be as good a Bishop as he is or the best in England."[2]

These quotations show that neither Cranmer nor Barlow believed in Apostolical succession, and it follows that they cannot have had the intention of imparting that which they not only claimed to have no power to impart, but did not even believe to exist. As Macaulay says :—" The founders

---

[1] Burnet, quoted by Fr. Gallwey, pp. 449, 450, 451, in his "Lectures on Ritualism."

[2] "Kennet Collection," vol. xlvi., quoted by Fr. Gallwey.

of the Anglican Church had retained episcopacy as an ancient, a decent, and a convenient ecclesiastical polity, but had not declared that form of church government to be of divine institution."

On the other hand, it is a mistake to dwell too much upon the High Church Orthodoxy of Laud, as if he had been the inventor, or originator of that school of religious thought and ceremony. Archbishop Bancroft, who occupied the See of Canterbury, had zealously "muzled" the "Puritan faction," as Heylin tells us ;[1] and if, as was undoubtedly the fact, many clergymen never used a surplice when they administered the communion at their "oyster-boards" in the middle of their churches, others "did in the ministration of the Sacraments bestir themselves in a White Vesture."[2]

If any single bishop can be justly called the founder of High Anglicanism, it should be rather Andrews than Laud. In his reply to Bellarmin, Bishop Andrews says :—" We acknowledge a presence as true and real as you do, but we determine nothing rashly as to the manner of it."[3] In his writings he affirms that to bishops were "transferred the chief part of the Apostolic function, the oversight of the Church ; and the power of commanding, correcting, and ordaining."[4] It is evident, however, that he considered these special powers to have been "transferred" to them more for the sake of discipline and convenience, and as a sort of afterthought under unexpected circumstances, than as having any supernatural character. Accordingly he proceeds to add :—" The occasion which caused the apostles to appoint bishops seemeth to have been schisms." It necessarily follows, of course, that without the schisms no bishops would have been required.

Heylin tells us that Andrews introduced the custom for the clergy of making an "obeysance towards the East, before they betook themselves to their seats" in church.[5] In *Canterburies Doome*, by Wm. Prynne, page 134, there is a description of Bishop Andrews' private chapel, with an

---

[1] " Cyp. Angl.," pp. 57-8. [2] *Ib.* p. 6. [3] *Ib.* p. 23.
[4] " Lib. of Angl. Cath. Theol. Andrews," p. 356. [5] " Cyp. Angl." p. 16.

elaborate plan. On the communion table, leaning against the wall, is a very large cushion, with a great alms-dish resting against it, an arrangement which still prevails, or till lately prevailed, in certain English cathedrals. On either side was a candle-stick and candle, although, be it observed, he states in his writings, that "the burning of tapers in their churches at noon-day is altogether a pagan custom."[1] At the north and south ends of the table were "stuffed kneeling stools." A few feet from the communion-rails, right in the middle of the chapel, and in front of the lectern, which was apparently the most honoured thing in the building, and was raised on three steps, stood a table "for music." On this music-table was a censer and incense boat, "wherein y* clarke putteth frankincense at y* reading of the first lesson." Among the other properties of the sanctuary was a silver-gilt canister for wafers. Possibly, like the candles, the wafer-canister and the censer were for ornament and not for use ; otherwise, Bishop Andrews was rather an advanced ritualist for his day. But, like not a few modern ritualists, he was very " low " in some respects. For instance, it is clear that he did not encourage weekly " celebrations," and would not tolerate them except on Sundays. " The sacraments," he says, " and discipline are for the Sabbath day, but not for *every* Sabbath.[2] Again, he would not admit that either the Catholics or the Easterns could possibly interpret Scripture aright. He says :—" And so both jointly and severally their grounds are false, and ours are the only true means of interpretation."[3] Like many of the loftiest of modern High-Churchmen, too, he hated Catholics, and especially Jesuits. " I conceive," he observes, that " the Jesuits " " resemble the heathen priests of the Indians, called brachmans, mentioned by Osorius ; he saith, 'these heathen clergy-priests also study philosophy and the mathematical arts, insomuch that by their learning and counterfeit holiness they continue all their lifetime the singular contrivers of all fraud and villany.' "[4]

---

[1] "Lib. of Angl. Cath. Theol. Andrews," p. 372.   [2] *Ib.* p. 163.
[3] *Ib.* p. 61.   [4] *Ib.* p. 373.

Besides his candlesticks and wafers, and censers and incense, he had taken a high flight in drawing up, and using with some ceremony, forms for the consecration of churches and chalices. Now I want the reader specially to bear in mind all these High-Church practices of Andrews. To say that Laud "revived," or introduced most of these things into the Church of England is a mistake. In all his life he never did anything "higher" than Andrews had done, unless it were the putting of a cross, and, in at least one instance, a crucifix, over a communion - table. Certainly he greatly spread and even enforced some of the ritualistic customs of Andrews, and, what was more, he was abused for them, and he suffered for them; but, so far as I have been able to ascertain, he never made a single step in advance of Bishop Andrews, or probably of one or two other bishops who preceded or were contemporaneous with him, either in doctrine or in ritual. Laud was energetic, determined, and thorough; but he was not remarkable for originality, nor can I find that he sought out Catholic usages and endeavoured to implant them in the new Anglican establishment. Early in the seventeenth century, he obtained the friendship of Andrews, became devotedly attached to him, and took his theology and ritual as his model. When impeached for high treason many years later, on account of teachings and practices which were said to be popish, his chief defence was that he had only taught and done things which Bishop Andrews had done and taught before him.

Another bishop, "high" as to the real-presence, was Bishop Morton. He says "that the question betwixt us and the Papists is not concerning the Real Presence, which the Protestants (as their own Jesuites witness) do also profess." [1] It must, indeed, have been puzzling for the faithful Anglican to know in which of his pastors to believe, when another bishop, Bishop Cooper, "in language remarkably clear and strong," maintained, "that no form of Church government is divinely ordained, that Protestant communities, in establish-

[1] "Cyp. Angl."

ing different forms, have only made a legitimate use of their Christian liberty; and that Episcopacy is peculiarly suited to England because the English constitution is monarchical."[1]

It may not be unnatural for outsiders to retort that there are even more dissensions in the Anglican Establishment now than there were then. This I do not deny; but, since then, three hundred years have given it a certain stability, dignity, and maturity, and time has proved to its rival schools that they can co-exist within it without shattering its fabric; moreover, not a few, nor they the least influential, of its members, pride themselves more upon its comprehensiveness than upon any other of its virtues. That particular virtue had not been discovered at the period of which I write.

[1] Macaulay's "Hist. of Eng.," vol. i. chap. i.

CHAPTER III.

IF Buckeridge, Laud's tutor at St John's, was "the leading controversialist in sacramental matters,"[1] on the High-Church side, other, and higher authorities in the university were of a very different stamp. Abbot, who afterwards became Archbishop of Canterbury, was Master of University College. As Mr Benson says of him [2] :—" His favourite tenet was the descent of the visible Church, not through the main unmistakable channel, but through by-waters and side-streams. That a man should have gravely held the truth to have passed through Berengarians, Albigenses, Wicklifites, Hussites, to Luther and Calvin, is nearly incredible ; yet this was the text of Abbot." Another strong Calvinist, and a correspondent of Calvin himself, was the President of Magdalen, Dr Lawrence Humphrey, the Regius Professor of Divinity, and a disciple of Zwinglius. When such a man was lecturing in the divinity schools, the theological tone at Oxford was not likely to be very Episcopalian. The President of Corpus Christi College, Dr Rainolds, was also a strong Puritan.

The year after his arrival, Laud obtained the coveted scholarship in his college. Learning and science were at this time beginning to make rapid strides, and to the very year in which Laud was elected a scholar, is commonly attributed the invention of one of the most important instruments of science—the microscope, although it was probably known in a primitive form before that date.

Of Laud's undergraduate life we know little. Wood describes him as "a very forward, confident, and zealous person." He was made a fellow of his college in his fourth year at Oxford, when he was a few months under twenty. Early in the following year, his father died, and although his

[1] Benson, p. 18.   [2] *Ib.* p. 19.

mother was to have the income of her husband's property for her life, his own fortune, if a small one, was assured, and he was in no danger of becoming one of the penurious clergy so common at that period.

> "A gentle squier would gladly entertaine,
> Into his house some trencher chaplaine :"
>
> "——he would contented be
> To give five markes and winter liverie."
> *Bishop Hall.*

Or as Peacham says in his *Complete Gentleman* :—" If they " (English gentlemen) "can procure some poure Bachelor of Arts from the Universities to teach their children to say grace, and serve the cure of an impropriation ; who, wanting means and friends, will be content upon the promise of £10 a yeare ; at his first coming to be pleased with £5." A modern writer says :—" Harrison admits, with a sigh, that the lower ecclesiastics were generally despised ; but he seeks to explain the fact, less by their ignorance, and immorality, than by their poverty."[1] Laud had the good fortune not to be one of these.

The mention of the clerics of the period, reminds me of one professing a different religion, who died the year after that of Laud's father's death. I am thinking of St Philip Neri, the founder of the Congregation of Oratorians. Everyone knows the story that whenever he met the students of the English College in the streets of Rome, he used to take off his hat and salute them. He could not but know that those among their number who should return as priests to their native shores would be in imminent danger of death ; that, in fact, such a return would of itself be a capital offence ; and many of them, as they returned his salute, might well have exclaimed :—" Morituri te salutant."

As Lingard says[2] :—" From the defeat of the Armada till the death of the queen, during the lapse of fourteen years, the Catholics groaned under the pressure of incessant persecution. Sixty-one clergymen, forty-seven laymen, and two

[1] Huber's " Eng Univ.," vol. i. p. 341.
[2] Lingard's " Hist. of Eng.," vol. vi. p. 257.

gentlewomen suffered capital punishment for some or other of the spiritual felonies and treasons which had been lately created." Besides these, many Catholics were imprisoned, or fined, or whipped, or had their ears bored with a hot iron, or were racked, or otherwise tortured for the sake of their religion. Yet in spite of all these persecutions, Mr Froude tells us that shortly before Laud's first arrival at Oxford, it was a nursery for Jesuits.[1] Father Edmund Campian, the Jesuit, had been a Fellow of Laud's own college, Father Parsons had been a Fellow of Balliol. I may observe, in passing, that Oxford has continued to be a " nursery for Jesuits "; at the present moment, one exceedingly able Jesuit Father is a Fellow of Laud's beloved St John's itself, and a good many others are, or have been, Fellows, or Masters or Bachelors of Arts at Oxford. But to proceed. "Oxford became a perpetual recruiting ground from which year after year flights of students passed over to Rheims or to another college which the Pope had erected at Rome."[2] Only three years before Laud went to St John's a correspondent of Walsingham's wrote :—" Those who are seminary priests learnt not their papistry abroad, but carried it with them from their colleges at Oxford."[3] Mr Froude says :—" The pupils whom Campian and his friends had trained at Oxford had caught and retained his spirit. They grew from boys to men. They took their degrees and became fellows, and Holt of Oriel, Arden of Trinity, Garnet, Bryant, Sherwin, Emerson, and many more, wandered together by Cherwell and Isis, brooding over their master's teaching, and resolving one by one to break the ties of home and kindred and devote their lives to the cause of the Catholic faith."

Laud took his degree of Bachelor of Arts when he was twenty-one. At twenty-three he had a serious illness, and the next year another. When he was twenty-five he took his Master's degree, and in the same year he was appointed " Grammar Reader," shortly after which he " fell into a great sickness." Possibly these three successive illnesses may

---

[1] Froude's "Hist. of Eng.," vol. xi. 308, 12.   [2] *Ib.*
[3] Domestic MSS., 1585.

have interfered with his theological studies, although the preparation for Anglican ordination was not a very serious matter in those days ; or it may be that he was engaged for some time in educating others ; at any rate, he was not made a deacon until he was twenty-seven, nor a " priest " until he was twenty-eight.

In the meantime, when he was twenty-five, Protestants throughout Europe were encouraged by the famous Edict of Nantes, by which Henry IV. of France granted toleration to his Protestant subjects. To Laud, this might appear a somewhat qualified blessing ; for, in France, Protestantism meant Calvinism, which he hated, and an edict which in that country threw open posts of trust, profit, and honour to Calvinists in France, might encourage men of their way of thinking in England. The horrible and detestable " massacre of St Bartholomew " had taken place in the year preceding Laud's birth, and perhaps he may have reflected that French guarantees of security and freedom to Protestants were not always to be trusted, especially as King Henry, who granted the edict, had abjured Protestantism and become a Catholic only five years earlier.

In the same year as that in which the Edict of Nantes was promulgated, a young man was elected to be one of his brother fellows, on whose career he was to exercise considerable influence.   This was Juxon, who became his intimate friend, and eventually succeeded him in the Presidency of St John's, the Bishopric of London, and the Archbishopric of Canterbury. Like Andrews, Juxon was an Anglican bishop who held very high views and had the good luck to suffer very little for them. Laud was made the scapegoat.

Laud's mother died the year that he was made deacon, so he then became possessed of the whole of his little fortune.

Both his deacon's and his priest's " orders " were received from the hands of Dr Young,. the Bishop of Rochester. That ecclesiastic " found his study raised above the system and opinions of the age, upon the noble foundation of the Fathers, Councils, and the ecclesiastical historians, and

presaged that, if he lived, he would be an instrument of
restoring the Church from the narrow and private principles
of modern times."[1]   That Laud had read considerably
among the works of the 'Fathers—in each of whom he
appears to have seen an Anglican—and that he had at
least dipped into the writings of more modern Catholics,
including those of a living theologian who was then
attracting considerable attention — Bellarmin—is evident
from his *Conferences with Fisher.*

The year in which Laud received Anglican priests' orders
the famous Earl of Essex was executed, and, in the next, a
beginning of many changes important to Laud was caused
by the death of Queen Elizabeth. But at that time, whatever his secret ambition or aspirations may have been, he
was not a courtier, and the death of a queen did not much
affect his daily life. Far more important events to him must
have appeared his appointment to the Divinity Lectureship
at St John's in the year the queen died, and to the Proctorship of the University of Oxford in the following year, when
he himself was thirty. In his divinity lectures, he publicly
displayed his colours. He lectured, says Heylin, on "the
perpetual Visibility of the Church of Christ, derived from
the Apostles to the Church of Rome, continued in that
Church (as in others of the east and south) till the Reformation."[2] Such a doctrine was certain to rouse the ire of
Abbott, the Vice-Chancellor, since, as the same author tells
us, he traced his Church " from the Berengarians to the Albigenses, from the Albigenses to the Wickliffists, from the
Wickliffists unto the Hussites, and from the Hussites unto
Luther and Calvin." Coming from so prominent a member
of the university as the Proctor of the year, Laud's lecture
would appear the more atrocious in Abbott's eyes, and the
two principal officers of Oxford were thus placed in violent
opposition to each other. To the enmity between Abbott
and Laud I shall have to refer presently. Nor was the
Vice-Chancellor his only opponent. Scarcely had his term

---

[1] A quotation (authority not mentioned) in Mozley's Essay on Laud.
[2] "Cyp. Angl.," p. 49.

of Proctorship ended before he was "shrewdly ratled by Dr Holland,"[1] for maintaining, when he "performed his exercise for Bachelor of Divinity," that "there could be no true Church without Diocesan Bishops." Evidently, Dr Holland thought that to follow the lead of the Vice-Chancellor was a very safe policy, and Laud found himself practising what a modern writer has called "the gentle art of making enemies."

Six months after he had been elected Proctor, Laud was appointed Chaplain to the Earl of Devonshire,—a man of quite a different family from the later Earls of Devonshire, and the present Duke,—who had but just received that title from King James I., together with the Garter. This nobleman had held a command in the fleet which opposed the Armada ; he had also been Lord Lieutenant of Ireland, and had put down a rebellion at the Battle of Kinsale.

To enter the service of so distinguished a man, was a step, and indeed the first, for Laud in a secular direction. The appointment to such a post would have an additional attraction to him, because his patron, if Camden is to be trusted, was nearly as eminent for learning as for valour, having in those respects, "no superior, and but few equals," and Moryson, his secretary, describes him as "beautiful in person, as well as valiant ; and learned, as well as wise." Unfortunately, his morals were not so unimpeachable as his bravery, his learning, or his wisdom. When a young man, he had fallen in love with the sister of no less a person than the great Earl of Essex, who was beheaded for high treason at the Tower three years before Laud obtained the chaplaincy ; he had asked her to marry him, and she had consented ; but her friends had forced her to marry Lord Rich, afterwards Earl of Warwick, as Lord Devonshire, or Charles Blount, as he was at that time, was only a younger son with no great prospects. While his wife, she had three sons and four daughters ; but it is to be feared that, owing to her guilty love for Blount, she was anything than faithful to him. Relations between the husband and wife became more and

[1] "Cyp. Angl."

more strained, and some four or five years after Lord Rich
had been present at the sacking of Cadiz, he divorced
Penelope—for that was her name.

Clergymen, who enjoy the patronage of influential and
clever magnates with loosish morals, sometimes find themselves placed in difficult positions. To Laud, who, by the way,
had lately been dignified by the title of Bachelor of Divinity,
Lord Devonshire one day presented himself, and asked him
to marry him to Lady Rich. This was a couple of years
after he had been appointed to the chaplaincy. Many
clergymen would have winced at such a request; but to a
High-Churchman it must have been exceptionally odious.
Some authorities maintain that Laud was threatened; that
he was what Americans call "cornered" in some way, is
almost certain. At any rate, "serving my ambition and
the sins of others," as he says, he gave way, and consented.
The thought that he was doing exceedingly wrong must
have sorely scared his conscience; but more excruciating
still must have been the reflection that his conduct could
only be justified on the most extreme Calvinistic grounds.
Would not people say :—" Is Saul also among the prophets ? "
Would not every good Churchman turn his back upon him,
and would not every Puritan chuckle on hearing what he had
done? Well might he write in his diary—" My cross about
the Earl of *Devon's* marriage, Decemb. 26, 1605, *die Jovis.*"
And at such a holy season, too, to commit such an act ! one
can almost hear him saying to himself in mournful tones.

If he sinned, he repented ! A well-known Jesuit author
writes to me :—" In the first editions of my * * * * I had
a note reflecting strongly on Laud for having married Lord
Devonshire to Lady Rich in the lifetime of her husband.
But when I found that he so regretted it in his after life,
and kept its anniversary as a fast day, I struck his name
out of the note on p. 101 of my third edition." It was
doubtless of this false step that Laud wrote :—" Lapidatus
non pro sed a peccato "—" Stoned not on account of a sin,
but *by* a sin "; for it was on St Stephen's day that this
particular sin was committed.

Nor was the offence without its temporal punishment. King James, the theologian, ecclesiastical lawyer, and pedant, was furious. The unfortunate earl wrote him an apology; but His Majesty's ire was so implacable as to cause the delinquent to die of "the spleen" within a year. As to Laud, it is probable that to this event must be attributed the slowness of his advancement during the next few years, so far as regal favour was concerned. Mr Benson in his brilliant "Study" of Laud, says :—"I came, the other day, upon the actual petition of Lord Rich for divorce, filed among the Lambeth papers." (The very mention of the Lambeth papers makes a biographer of Laud almost wish that, like Mr Benson, he were the son of an Archbishop of Canterbury!) 'And there is also a curious relic, attributed by tradition to the time of Laud, which has undoubtedly reference to the same event. This is a portrait, rather stiff and Flemish in style, which hangs in the great corridor of the palace, of a sweet-faced, gentle lady, her bunches of auburn hair standing out very strongly against a pale-green background. On the back, in large old letters, are traced the words, 'A Countess of Devonshire.' It cannot be doubted which."[1] If this portrait was brought to Lambeth by Laud, one would have thought that he might have hung many a pleasanter memento upon his walls.

Sixteen years after he had committed his fault, he performed a curious penance for it. It so happened that he had to preach before the court, in the very chapel in which the so-called marriage had been performed. The subject he chose for his sermon was the peace of the Church, and in the course of it he said :—"Yet will I do the people right; for though many of them are guilty of inexcusable sin, as sacrilege, so too many of us priests are guilty of other as great sins as sacrilege."[2] Perhaps he thought that his congregation would expect him to make what is called "some allusion in his sermon" to the incident which would naturally be in the minds of all his hearers, and he may have said this to satisfy them.

---

[1] Benson, p. 35.　　　　　　　[2] *Ib.*, p. 35, note.

It would seem that the Earl of Devonshire had printed a defence of his conduct, and at the same time aired his heterodox views upon the subject of divorce; for there is an entry in the Calendar of State Papers : — " Censures on the Earl of Devonshire's Tract touching Marriage and Divorce, by Wm. Laud."[1]   And the very next entry runs :— " Dissertation on Matrimony, Divorce, &c., from Matt. 19, v. 6; probably connected with the above." If the dates are correct, Laud's censure of his patron's tract must have been written only four months after the unlucky marriage ceremony.

He wrote a very good private prayer of contrition for the part he had taken in the unhappy business, and there can be no doubt that he was heartily ashamed of it, and heartily sorry for it.

Less than two months before Lord Devonshire's marriage, the whole of England had been excited by the discovery of the horrible gunpowder plot. It would be difficult to exaggerate the effect that is likely to have been produced upon Laud by such an incident at such a time. It should be remembered that he had only been four years in priest's " orders," that, at thirty-three, he was beginning to attain some celebrity, as one of the leading young clergymen of the High-Church School at Oxford ; and that he had just been Proctor, and had had the courage to brave the displeasure of the Vice-Chancellor himself for the sake of his advanced views. Placed in the forefront of the battle against Puritanism and Calvinism, he could scarcely help reflecting upon the source from which he had derived, if not stolen, his weapons : indeed, he boldly asserted that the Anglican Church had obtained her orders through Rome ; what would be more natural, therefore, than that he should be inclined to consider the claims of the Catholic Church ? Let us assume this to have been the case ; I make the assumption in no unfriendly spirit towards his memory ; let us suppose that he was beginning to think that, after all, Rome might not be quite so black as she was painted.

[1] " Cal. Sta. Pa.," 1603-10, 1606, April ? Nos. 53 and 54.

And then, what happened? News came to him that a most
diabolical conspiracy to destroy the whole Parliament by
means of the cowardly and dastardly medium of an
explosion of gunpowder had just been discovered; that
the object was the overthrow of the prevailing Protestant
powers and the introduction of Catholic powers; that the
conspirators were all what are termed "good Catholics;"
that one of them was the owner of large properties in three
of the midland counties; that another was not only a
knight of high character and great estates, but very highly
connected, and, worst of all, that two Jesuit priests had been
privy, and even consenting, to the plot. Here would be
a nice story for a man considering the attractions of the
Catholic Church.

We, of course, know that the gunpowder plot, although
undertaken by Catholics, was a freak as mad and as un-
authorised as it was wicked; that about four months before
its discovery, the General of the Jesuits himself, Father
Aquaviva, had written "very earnest letters" to the Jesuit
afterwards accused, Father Garnet, "wherein he saith that
he writeth *in mandato Papæ*, that we were expressly commanded by His Holiness to hinder by all possible means all
conspiracies of Catholics";[1] and that both this same Father
Garnet and Father Blackwell, the archpriest of England,
did all they could to make these wishes of the Pope's generally known among English Catholics. We also know that
Catesby had twisted the Pope's exhortation, of some five or
six years earlier, when the succession to the English Crown
was in dispute, to support the Catholic claimant, into a very
different thing, namely an exhortation to depose the Protestant monarch, when he was no longer a claimant but a king;
that he had asked Father Garnet "whether, in case it were
lawful to kill a person or persons, it were necessary to regard
the innocents which were present, lest they also should
perish withal," to which Father Garnet had replied that "in
all just wars it is practised and held lawful to beat down
houses and walls and castles, notwithstanding innocents were

[1] Hatfield MS.

in danger, so that such battering were necessary for the obtaining of victory,"[1] and that, in conversation with his accomplices, he had exaggerated this reply into the consent of a Jesuit to the gunpowder plot. We know that, a little later, he had revealed the plot to Father Greenway under seal of confession, giving him permission to inform Father Garnet also under seal of confession;[2] and that both these fathers had done all they could to dissuade him from his purpose without avail, and had suffered intense misery of mind in consequence, but had considered themselves bound by the inviolable seal of the confessional not to reveal the matter to others. We also know that while Father Greenway was undoubtedly bound by that seal, Father Garnet, after his arrest, wrote to the latter :—"To testify that I do and always did condemn the intention, and that indeed I might have revealed a general knowledge had of Mr Catesby out of confession, but hoping of the Pope's prevention, and being loth to hurt my friend, I acknowledge to have so far forth offended God and the King, and so ask forgiveness ";[3] the "Pope's prevention" referring to a letter he himself had written to the General, requesting him to beg the Pope to forbid all Catholics in England to take up arms against the Government, on pain of excommunication.[4] We know, too, that, instead of having confessed himself guilty, without reserve, as was given out, what Father Garnet really wrote was :—"I, Henry Garnet, of the Society of Jesus, priest, do here freely protest before God, that I hold the late intention of the powder action to have been altogether unlawful and most horrible, &c. &c. I also protest that I was ever of opinion, that it was unlawful to attempt any violence against the King's Majesty and Estates after he was once received by the realm. And I acknowledge that I was bound to reveal all knowledge that I had of this or any other treason out of the sacrament of confession. And

---

[1] Hatfield MS.

[2] Greenway's Relation, Stonyhurst MS., p. 109. I quote from "Father Henry Garnet and The Gunpowder Plot," by the Rev. J. H. Pollen, S.J.

[3] Hatfield MS., 115, fol. 154.

[4] Father Pollen's "Father Garnet and the Gunpowder Plot," p. 13.

whereas partly upon hope of prevention, partly for that I would not betray my friend, I did not reveal the general knowledge of Mr Catesby's intention, which I had by him, I do acknowledge myself highly guilty, to have offended God, the King's Majesty, and estate, and humbly ask of all forgiveness, exhorting all Catholics that they no way build upon my example."[1] We also know, as, for that matter, every Catholic knew then, that to profane the sacrament by receiving Holy Communion, with the intention of perpetrating an atrocious crime, would be a fearful sacrilege and to eat and drink damnation.

The opinion of the arch priest (the chief ecclesiastic of the Catholic Church at that time in England), on the gunpowder plot may be worth quoting. Dr Hook writes[2] that, on Nov. 28, he "published a letter to the English Papists, in which he condemned the late plot as 'a detestable and damnable practice, odious in the sight of God, horrible to the understanding of men.' He exhorted them 'not to attempt any practice or action, tending, in any degree, to the hurt or prejudice of the person of our sovereign lord the king, the prince, nobility, counsellors, and officers of state, but towards them, in their several places and degrees, to behave as becomes dutiful subjects and religious Catholics.'"[3]

But all that I have to do with this matter, on the present occasion, is to consider what the effect of the news of the horrible affair would be, or be likely to be, at the time, upon a man with some inclinations towards the Catholic Church, as I am assuming may have been the case with Laud. Let us endeavour to imagine the feelings with which high Anglicans would receive the news that a band of Catholics, containing some desperadoes, but also comprising two or three well-known country gentlemen, if not a peer or so, and a couple of the Jesuit fathers at Farm Street, had almost succeeded in blowing up with dynamite the principal Government buildings in London, with the intention of

---

[1] P. R. O. Dom. James I., xx. 12.
[2] "Lives of the Archbishops of Canterbury," vol. v. p. 226.
[3] Collier, vii. 320.

placing England under Irish rule. Would such news be conducive to conversions to the Catholic Church among respectable High-Church Anglicans ? I ask the question in order to do justice to the subject of my biography ; and it is only on his account, and with a view to a right understanding of his conduct, that I introduce the subject of the execrable gunpowder plot into my pages.

CHAPTER IV.

LAUD'S life was destined to be a stormy one. The tempest about the part he had taken in Lord Devonshire's marriage was still raging, when another burst forth about a different subject. This was a sermon. The notice of it in the Diary is as follows:—"*Anno* 1606. The Quarrel Dr *Ayry* picked with me about my Sermon at St Mary's, Oct. 21, 1606." He was now in hot water once more with a Vice-Chancellor, for Airy had succeeded Abbott. Heylin says that Dr Airy stigmatised the sermon for "'containing in it sundry scandalous and Popish passages'; the good man making all things to be matter of Popery, which were not held forth unto him in *Calvin's Institutes.*"[1] As Mr Gardiner says, Laud "escaped a public recantation; but became a marked man, as Popishly inclined."[2]

Not only was Laud attacked *for* sermons: he was also attacked *in* sermons. I may allude here, although chronologically it should be noticed rather later, to a virulent onslaught made upon him by Abbott's brother, in a sermon from the university pulpit. Having described Laud's teaching, he apostrophised the teacher of it, and staring straight at the place where Laud was sitting, he exclaimed:—"What art thou, ROMISH or ENGLISH? PAPIST or PROTESTANT? Or what art thou? A mungrel, or compound of both?"[3] And then he went on to call him "a Protestant by ordination; a Papist in point of free will and the like!" "A Protestant in receiving the sacrament; a Papist in the doctrine of the sacrament!" "What!" cried he, with passionate vehemence. "Do you think there are two heavens?" He was now pretending that our Lord was

[1] "Cyp. Angl."   [2] "Diction. of Nat. Bio.," *Laud.*
[3] "Cyp. Angl." pp. 57, 58.

speaking. " If there be, get you to the other, and place yourself there ; for into this, where I am, you shall never come ! "

So strong was the feeling against him, that "it was a heresy," he wrote, "to be seen in my company, to salute me in the street."

It may be well, at this stage, to consider how far Laud merited the accusation of " Popish inclinations." As I have already said, he did not "go further," to use a modern term, in his High-Churchism than Andrews, or several others of his contemporaries. Indeed, some of his pronouncements would be considered very moderate indeed by high Anglicans of our own days. " All sides agree," he says, in his *Conference with Fisher*, " in the faith of the Church of England, that in the most blessed sacrament the worthy receiver is by his faith made spiritually partaker of the true and real body and blood of Christ truly, and really, and of all the benefits of his passion. Your Roman Catholics add a manner of this his presence, transubstantiation, which many deny, and the Lutherans a manner of this presence, consubstantiation, which more deny." " It is safer communicating with the Church of England than with the Roman or Lutheran, because all agree in this truth, not in any other opinion." [1] Here he appears to claim a lower view, as to the real presence, for the Anglicans than for the Lutherans. Again he says :—" Protestants of all sorts maintain a true and real presence of Christ in the eucharist ; and then, where is any known or damnable heresy here ? [2] Surely this was making no high claim—to put his Church on the same footing with other Protestant Churches as to the eucharist ! In a note on the same page, he quotes the article xxviii. :—" The body of Christ is given, taken, and eaten in the supper (of the Lord) only after an heavenly and spiritual manner." On the following page he quotes Cranmer :—" If by this word *really* you understand *corporaliter*, corporally in his natural and organical body, under the forms of bread and wine, it is contrary to the holy word of God." Then he quotes Ridley,

---

[1] " Conf. with Fisher," Oxford, 1839, p. 241.   [2] *Ib.*, p. 247.

and says :—"And for Calvin, he comes no whit short of these."[1] He keeps harping on the point that Lutherans and Calvinists and Anglicans all hold variations of the same doctrine on the real presence, all of them being diametrically opposed to that of the Catholics. "As for the Lutherans, they neither deny nor doubt of his true and real presence there ; and they are Protestants. And as for the Calvinists, if they might be rightly understood, they also maintain a most true and real presence, though they cannot permit their judgment to be transubstantiated ; and they are Protestants too."[2] We are all Protestants, and our differences of opinion as to the real presence, are much the same as those 'twixt tweedledum and tweedledee ! he seems to say.

On the subject of purgatory, again, he is what the majority of my fellow-countrymen would call "very sound." The Primitive Church, says he, never did "acknowledge a purgatory in a side-part of hell."[3] He is equally "sound" on baptism ; for he continues, in the same sentence :—"nor make the intention of the priest of the essence of baptism." And, for all his talk about getting orders through the Church of Rome, he was at heart "sound" on the question of Apostolical succession. "Most evident it is," says he, "that the succession which the Fathers meant is not tied to place or person, but it is tied to the verity of doctrine."[4] And, again :—"For succession in the general I shall say this ; it is a great happiness where it may be had visible and continued, and a great conquest over the mutability of this present world. But I do not find any one of the ancient Fathers that makes local, personal, visible, and continued succession, a necessary sign or mark of the true Church in any one place."[5] It is quite clear, therefore, that Laud, who was naturally fond of ceremonial, decency, and order, and such like things, was of Cranmer's opinion, already quoted, that "In the admission of many of these offices be divers comely ceremonies and solemnities, and which be not of

---

[1] "Conference with Fisher," Oxford, 1839, p. 249.   [2] *Ib.*, p. 246.
[3] *Ib.*, p. 275.   [4] *Ib.*, p. 323.   [5] *Ib.*, p. 322.

necessity, but only for a good order and seemly fashion ; for
if such offices and ministrations were committed without
such solemnity, they were nevertheless duly committed."
And that "appoyntement whiche the Appostels by necessyte
made by common election and sometyme by their owne
several assignment, could not then be doon by Christen
princes, bicause at that tyme they were not ; and nowe at
these dayes appertayneth to Christian princes and rulers." [1]

Very strong evidence of his opinion on the question of
the necessity of consecration and Apostolical succession in
bishops is given on page 141 of his own *History*. He
writes :—" Neither *is Episcopacy in all the Parts and Powers
of it, that which it was in time of* Popery, and *still is in the*
Roman Church." (The italics are his own.) " *Nor is the
other Form of Government*" (*i.e.,* Presbytery) " *received, maintained, and Practised in all other* Reformed *Churches ;* unless
these men be so straightlaced, as not to admit the Churches
of *Sweden,* and *Denmark,* and indeed, all, or most of the
Lutherans, to be *Reformed* Churches. For in *Sweden* they
retain both the Thing and the Name; and the Governours
of their Churches are, and are called *Bishops.* And among
the other *Lutherans* the Thing is retained, though not the
Name. For instead of *Bishops,* they are called *Superintendents.* And yet even here too, these Names differ more
in sound than in sense. For *Bishop* is the same in *Greek,*
that *Superintendent* is in *Latin.* Nor is this change very
well liked by the Learned. Howsoever, *Luther,* since he
would change the Name, did yet very wisely, that he would
leave the Thing, and make choice of such a name as was not
altogether unknown to the Ancient Church." [2]

Here, therefore, we have it in black and white, in Laud's
own writing, that in their Superintendents, the Lutherans had
the Thing, Bishop. That the Thing had not been honoured
with the "divers comely ceremonies," commonly called consecration, that the Thing had no pretension to orders, made
no difference : it was Bishop, quite as much as the Anglican

---

[1] I quote from Estcourt's " Question of Anglican Ordination," pp. 70, 71.
[2] " Hist. of the Troub. and Tryal of Will. Laud," p. 141.

Archbishop of Canterbury was Bishop. If words mean anything, Laud's words mean this, and they show how far he believed in Apostolical succession, and in any orders, for that matter. When we add to this that he distinctly denied the necessity of intention for the validity of a sacrament; that he even denied the necessity of a "purpose to do therein as the Church doth,"[1] adding, "nor is the intention of either bishop or priest of absolute necessity to the essence of a sacrament," we begin to realise how far Laud was doctrinally a High-Churchman.

The Anglican position in his days is thus described by one of Laud's modern Anglican biographers:—"There is more in Episcopacy than a form of government. But this was not seen at first; the primary impression of many of the Reformers being that they were all, episcopal or otherwise, on an equal footing. This will account for the evident unwillingness on the part of the rulers of the English Church at the time of the Reformation to commit themselves to any statement on the subject of orders, which might have the effect of cutting off the foreigners from communion. This was only natural, for foreigners were invited and encouraged to come; it would have therefore been most unmannerly to have passed any enactment against them. The validity of orders conferred by the foreign consistories was therefore looked upon as an open question. Many who had received no other ordination were admitted to livings, and divines, sound in the main, were unwilling to pass any decided opinion. Even Hooker takes no higher ground than the lawfulness of episcopacy, and allows necessity as justification of ordination by Presbyters; while the more advanced in the new doctrine thought this an unnecessary limitation, and that under all circumstances Presbyters were equal to Bishops. Hence the uncertainty in which the question was enveloped in Queen Elizabeth's reign."[2] A few lines further on, he says that Cosin wrote:—"If a Minister so ordained in these French Churches came to incorporate himself with ours, and to

---

[1] "Conf. with Fisher," Oxford, 1839, p. 229.
[2] "Life of Laud" by the Rev. John Baines, p. 125.

receive a public charge or cure of souls among us in the
Church of England (as I have known some of them to have
done of late, and can instance many others before my time),
&c.," "nor did our laws require more of" them "than to
declare" their "consent to the religion received among us,
and to subscribe the Articles established." Bishop Cosin
was more than twenty years younger than Laud, and a
High-Churchman, who got into trouble for his extreme views.

Obviously, in the opinion of the most orthodox Anglican
divines of the time, it was the same in the case of the clergy
as in that of the bishops. If the foreign ministers had not
got the Name of priests, they had the Thing, and as to priest,
presbyter, and minister, "these names" differed "more in
sound than in sense."

When one asks oneself why Laud should have been
selected as the object of attack by the Puritanical party, one
can only reply that it was probably for the same reason that
one ritualist clergyman is chosen for prosecution by the
Church Association instead of another, in these days.
Chance, no doubt, has much to do with it; aggressiveness,
or at least self-assertion, may have more; personal distinction, in some cases, perhaps, most of all, while personal
charms may save many. The late Mr Machonochie was not
so "high" as certain of his unprosecuted fellow-clergy, and
Bishop Andrews, who used wafer-bread for communion, was
left in peace, while poor Archbishop Laud pleaded, without
avail, as he stood, a prisoner, at his trial—"For Wafers, I
neither gave, or received the Communion but in Ordinary
Bread." [1]

Much was made by Laud's enemies of his prayers for the
canonical hours; but these, which are given in his Devotions,
have practically nothing in common with the Divine Office
of the Catholic Church. Nor were any of his prayers of
a particularly Catholic tone, and it is a matter for surprise
that one who had such an inclination towards the Church's
ceremonies did not avail himself to a greater extent of her
devotions.

[1] " Hist. of the Trial and Troub. of Will. Laud," p. 342.

Perhaps Laud reached his "highest" point when he "approved Auricular Confession," as Heylin tells us.[1] In the nineteenth century, it strikes one as curious that his enemies dwelt less on this point, when accusing him of what are now termed "popish leanings," than on little ceremonies and ritual observances which are now practised in the most evangelical of churches.

The question of his attitude towards the Catholic Church itself will necessarily present itself from time to time, as we proceed ; and we shall find that it varied considerably at different periods of his life, more, perhaps, on account of political than religious causes ; therefore, in dealing with it in the present chapter, I will be somewhat brief.

First let his own Boswell speak for him. Having alluded to the question of a reconciliation of the Anglicans with Rome, he proceeds [2] :—"Admitting, as we may say, that no such Reconciliation was upon the Anvil," he "had some thoughts (and I have reason to believe it) by Conferences first, and if that failed, by the ordinary course of Ecclesiastical censures, of gaining *Papists* to the Church ; and therefore it concerned him in part of Prudence, to smooth the way, by removing all such Blocks and Obstacles which had been laid before them by the *Puritan* Faction." In another place he says [3] :—"Seeing the *Puritans* grown so strong even to endangering of our Peace both in Church and State, by the negligence and remissness of the former Government, he thought it necessary to show some countenance to the *Papists ;* that the ballance being kept even between the parties, the Church and State might be preserved (as indeed they were) in the greater safety." And again [4] :—"It was the Petulancy of the Puritans on the one side, and the Pragmaticalness of the Jesuites on the other, which made the breach wider than at first ; and had those hot spirits on both sides been calmed a while, moderate men might possibly have agreed upon such equal terms, as would have laid a sure foundation for the peace of Christendom."

An important witness to the staunchness of his Protes-

---

[1] " Cyp. Ang.," p. 390.   [2] *Ib.*, p. 391.   [3] *Ib.*, p. 386.   [4] *Ib.*, p. 388.

tantism is his friend, Lord Clarendon, who declares that " no
man was a greater or abler enemy to Popery."[1] Again, he
speaks of " the Protestant Religion" being " more advanced
against the Church of *Rome* (without prejudice to other useful
or godly labours) especially by those two Books of the late
Lord Arch-Bishop of *Canterbury* his Grace," *i.e.*, Laud, " and
of *Mr Chillingworth*, than it had been from the Reformation."
Yet he admits that Laud " was always maligned, and
persecuted by those who were of the *Calvinian* Faction,
which was then very powerful, and who, according to their
usual maxim, and practice, call every man they do not
love, Papist." [2]

Laud's great enemy, Prynne, is scarcely fair or accurate in
making out that he invariably tolerated priests and Jesuits,
although "he hath bin so carefull that a poore man could
not goe to a neighbour Parish to heare a Sermon, when he
had none at home, could not have a Sermon repeated, nor
prayer used in his own Family, but he was a fit subject for
the High Commission Court ; yet the other," that is to say
the toleration and encouragement of Catholics, " hath beene
done in all parts of the Realme, and no notice of it by any
Ecclesiasticall Judges or Courts." [3]

There is plenty of evidence on the other side. In the
Whiteway Diary, in the British Museum, there is an entry,
" 22 Oct. 1634. I heard Allison, a Coachman, and Robins,
an alderman of Yarmouth, censured in the Star Chamber for
slandering the present Archbishop of York, Dr Neile, as if
in the king's return from Scotland last year he should have
petitioned him for a toleration of Popery." Allison was
sentenced to be fined £1000 to the king, and £500 to the
archbishop, and to be whipped in the pillory at York,
Yarmouth, and Ipswich. In passing sentence, " Dr Lawde,
Archbishop of Canterbury, spoke wittily and bitterly."
We read in the same diary, on "4 Dec. 1623. At this
time a Popish lawyer about London was censured at the
Star Chamber, for saying that King Henry VIII. did . . .

---

[1] Clarendon's " Hist. of the Rebellion," book iv. p. 572.
[2] *Ib.* book i. p. 90.   [3] " Canterburies Doome," p. 30.

the Protestant religion [an indelicate expression] *to have his ears cut off, his nose split, his forehead marked with B for blasphemy, whipped about London, and fined £10,000 to the king.*" And again, "25 Feby. 163¾. The City of London was fined in the Star Chamber at £70,000, for suffering of Papists to plant in their plantation of Londonderry in Ireland," &c.[1]

I merely make these quotations in order to show that, in the Star Chamber, Catholics were not unduly favoured in Laud's time, and I may, for the same purpose, quote Lingard, who says that Laud published a letter, which was also signed by the Bishop of Rochester, "directing that not only Catholic priests and the harbourers of priests, but all persons in possession of papistical or heretical books, all who had been, or were suspected of having been, present at the celebration of mass, all whose children had been baptised or were taught by popish priests, or had been, or were about to be sent to popish seminaries, should be apprehended and brought before His Majesty's commissioners for ecclesiastical matters."[2]

From this it is obvious that Laud did not hesitate to persecute the Catholics; questions and instructions in his visitations, when a bishop, afford similar evidence; on the other hand, he seems to have taken more pleasure in persecuting the Puritan and "the precise."

Even on the scaffold, as the writer of the supplement to his History says, "his great care was to clear his Majesty and the Church of *England*, from any inclination to Popery."[3] In his speech, which had been written beforehand, the poor old man said :—"I have always lived in the Protestant Religion established in *England*, and in that I come now to Die."[4] Yet even then his stronger antipathy to the Puritans than to the Catholics came out, when he said :—

---

[1] I quote from "Records of The English Province S. J.," by Henry Foley, pp. 71, 72.

[2] Lingard's "Hist. of Eng.," vol. vii. p. 223.

[3] "Hist. of the Troubles and Tryal of Will. Laud," p. 446.

[4] *Ib.*, p. 450.

"The *Pope* never had such an Harvest in *England* since the Reformation, as he hath now upon the Sects and Divisions that are amongst us."[1]

As I have said before, it is in his *Conference with Fisher* that we can best judge of his feelings towards the Catholic Church. Here he says: — "Rome and other national churches are in this universal Catholic house as so many daughters." "Rome is an elder sister."[2] "The Protestants did not get that name by protesting against the Church of Rome, but by protesting against her errors and superstitions."[3] And again, "I heartily pray that he" (God) "will be pleased to give all of you" (Papists) "a light of his truth and a love to it, that you may no longer be made instruments of the Pope's boundless ambition, and this most unchristian brain-sick device, that in all controversies of the faith he is infallible."[4]

No. Whatever he may have been, William Laud was not a Catholic, and it is very doubtful whether he ever had much inclination towards Catholicism. Protestants, and perhaps Catholics also when judging Protestants, are apt to forget that a love of ceremonial and ecclesiastical pomp and power do not necessarily betoken any leaning towards the Church of Christ. Many excellent Catholics, nay, many great saints, have had no taste for music, architecture, or painting, have cared little for ceremonies, and have shunned all offers of power and place as if they were the plague.

---

[1] "Hist. of the Troubles and Tryal of Will. Laud.," p. 443.
[2] "Conf. with Fisher," Oxford, p. 262.   [3] *Ib.*, p. 111.   [4] *Ib.* p. 320.

CHAPTER V.

HAVING disposed of Laud's quarrel with Dr Airy, we come, in the next year, 1607, to his presentation and induction to his first benefice, "the Vicaridge of *Stanford* in *Northamptonshire*."

Five months later, he writes :—" The Advowson of *North-Kilworth* in *Leicestershire* given to me, *April* 1608." He now began "to get on," to use a modern phrase. " I proceeded Doctor in Divinity in the Act, *anno* 1608." He was then thirty-five. Almost more important, so far as his advancement was concerned, was his appointment in August, of the same year, as chaplain to Dr Neile, then Bishop of Rochester, a man of tact and amiability. Moreover, he had some influence with the king, and, by its use, he was enabled to direct the future of Laud into a new and most important channel.

In the same year was born the greatest ornament of the school of thought which Laud most detested. John Milton was as opposite to him in character as in creed ; but, whatever his influence upon his time, he will not figure much, if at all, in this biography.

Within fourteen months of his appointment to Dr Neile's chaplaincy, a great event occured in the life of Laud—his first sermon preached before the king. If he had what is called "a bad manner," he knew well enough how to act the courtier in the pulpit. In one of his sermons before the king, we find this passage, which may serve as a specimen of many others :—" And, Sir, as you were first up, and have sounded an alarum in the ears of your people ; not that they should ' fast and pray,' and ' serve God ' alone, but go with you into the house of the Lord ; so go on to serve your Preserver. Your merit, and the nobleness of your heart will

46

glue the hearts of the people to you. And your religious care of God's cause and service will make Him, I doubt not, ' arise,' and haste to the ' maintenance' of your cause, as of ' His own.' "

One of his latest, and, I might add, one of the best of his biographers, Mr Benson, says of his sermons in general that they "are curiously difficult reading ; they are closely argued, emphatically stated, but have not the quality of permanence. I know of no reading where the attention so persistently wanders and is so rarely enchained." [1] In truth, his style was not very exhilarating. For instance, he begins the sermon from which I have just made an extract :— " This psalm in the very letter is a complaint of the waste that was made upon the city of Jerusalem, and the profanation of the Temple that was in it. And these go together ; for when did any man see a kingdom, or a great city, wasted, and the mother church left standing in beauty? Sure I think never. For enemies when they have possessed a city seldom think themselves masters of their own possessions, till they have, as they think, plucked that god out of his house, which defended the city." And he ends with :—" As we have therefore now begun, so let us pray on as the prophet did, that God, even our gracious Father, will be no longer like unto one that sleeps " (and then he continues with " thats "—that he will do this, that he will do that, and that he will do the other, for about half a page, finally winding up with :—" That after the ' maintenance of His own cause ' here, we may in our several times be received up to Him in glory, through Jesus Christ our Lord, to whom, with the Father, &c." In short, it is impossible to read Laud's published sermons from end to end without being reminded of that barrel-organlike tone which characterised the preaching common in Anglican pulpits forty years ago. He was very fond of parading his knowledge of the Fathers, after this fashion :—" So the ancient Fathers, Justin, Tertullian, Origen, Athanasius, and the rest, are clear, and upon very good grounds, &c."

[1] " Archp. Laud," A. C. Benson, p. 199.

A court preacher, in those days, of course, would have been nothing if not quasi-astrological and classical; accordingly we find him saying things of this sort :—"Join them, and 'keep the unity of the Spirit,' and I will fear no danger though Mars were 'lord of the ascendant' in the very instant of his 'session' of Parliament, and 'in the second house,' or joined, or in aspect, with the 'lord of the second,' which yet Ptolemy thought brought much hurt to commonwealths." And, again :—"As you may see in that brag of the heathen in Minutius Felix."

In order "to be near my Ld. of Rochester," he exchanged his advowson of North Kilworth for West Tilbery in Essex, in the year in which he first preached before the king, and in the following, "My Ld. of *Rochester* gave me *Cuckstone* in *Kent*, Maii 25, 1610." About four months afterwards he resigned his Fellowship of St John's College. "Left Oxford," he says, "the 8th of the same month" (October 1610). And doubtless not a few of the authorities at Oxford would be heartily glad to get rid of him.

Less than a month after he had left Oxford, he wrote :— "I fell sick of a *Kentish* Ague, caught at my Benefice, Novemb. 5, 1610, which held me two months." Perhaps this made him anxious to quit so unhealthy a living, at any rate, before the month was out, or his fit of ague over, he "left *Kuckstone*, and was inducted in *Norton*, Novemb. 1610 by Proxy."

With the above, stands the entry, "In the midst of this Sickness, the Suit about the Presidentship of St John's began." His old tutor, Buckeridge, who had for some time held the presidentship, resigned it, and he was proposed in his stead. Party feeling ran very high on either side ; but he had many staunch friends in his old college, and in May he was elected. Whether by accident or design—it was said that one of the fellows tore it from the bursar's hand and burned it—the paper on which was written the result of the scrutiny was destroyed. Lord Chancellor Ellsmere, incited by Abbott, then Archbishop of Canterbury elect, objected to Laud's appointment, and appealed to the king.

In the Calendar of State Papers,[1] we find the Bishop of Winchester, Bilson, writing in June to King James, as to "illegal methods pursued in the election of Dr Laud as President of St John's College, Oxford," and a reply from the king, inquiring "whether the illegality in Dr Laud's election proceeded from faction or misconstruction of the Statutes," adding that, "the Council on both parties are to be re-heard for a final decision." In August, King James heard the case at Tichbourne, in person, sitting three hours over it, and confirmed the election. A few weeks later, we find him writing to the Bishop of Winchester, that he "considers the election of Dr Laud as President of St John's College, Oxford, was no further corrupt or partial than all elections are liable to be; therefore wishes it to stand, and clearer interpretations of the Statutes to be made for the future."[2]

According to Heylin, Laud felt no ill-will towards his opponents at his election. "To the other fellows," he says, "who had opposed him in his election, he always showed a fair and equal countenance, hoping to gain them by degrees; but if he found any to be intractable, and not easily to be gained by favours, he would find some handsome way or another to remove them out of the college, that others, not engaged either side, might succeed in their places." This is not exactly the disposition commonly assigned by historians to Laud; but it should be studied for what it is worth; nor should we forget that to "remove" his enemies "out of the college" was not unconducive to his own interests, or that unless this had been done in a "handsome way," the obnoxious fellows would have refused to go.

It was not so much to any of the fellows as to Abbott that he attributed the opposition to his election. On May 10, 1611, he wrote in his Diary:—"The Archbishop of *Canterbury* was the original cause of all my troubles."

Among the Stonyhurst MSS. (*Anglia*, vol. iii. n. 103) is a letter written during the same month by the Jesuit, Father Coffin or Cuffyn, *alias* Hatton, alluding to this same Arch-

---

[1] P. 43, June 14, 1611.   [2] *Ib.*, p. 76, Sept. 23, 1611.

bishop in the following terms :—" To Bancroft the pseudo
Archbishop of Canterbury succeeds George Abbot, a brutal
and fierce man, and a sworn enemy of the very name of
Catholic." And what follows shows the strong anti-
Catholic spirit then prevailing. " The King meditates the
extermination of all Catholics ; the prisons are everywhere
crammed ; the Catholics hide themselves in caves and holes
of the earth, and others fly before the face of the persecutors
into these parts. An infinite number of pursuivants riotously
pass through every county of England, and it is incredible to
tell how they harass and afflict the most innocent men ; for,
entering the houses and lands, they carry off everything
—beds, tables, covers, clothes, chests, trunks, and especially
money. If they find the master of the house they thrust the
infamous oath of supremacy upon him, and if he refuses to
take it, they carry him off to the nearest gaol, there in
poverty and chains, in darkness and squalor, in hunger and
nakedness,—*vel ducat vitam, vel animam agat.* The times
of Elizabeth, although most cruel, were the mildest and
happiest, in comparison of those of James."[1]

Another testimony to Abbott's persecution of Catholics
is to be found in the *Chronological Notes of the English
Congregation of the Order of St Benedict,*[2] by Dom Bennet
Weldon, O.S.B. of St Edmund's, Paris. He gives an account
of the martyrdom of Father Maurus, a Benedictine monk.
" He was banished and so went to Douay, from whence
returning to England, he was soon taken and pursued to
death by the aforementioned George Abbot, Titular Bishop
of London, to whom he was carried to be examined. The
chief proof of his priesthood urged against him was that as
he came by water from Graves End, that he might not be
discovered he flung into the Thames a little bag where his
Breviary, faculties, medals and crosses were, which a fisher-
man catching in his net, carried to George Abbot, Titular
Bishop of London (*now become*) Titular Archbishop of
Canterbury. As soon as Father Maurus heard the fatal
sentence, he answered with a loud voice, ' Thanks be to God,

[1] " Records of the Eng. Prov. S. J.," series 1, p. 70.　　[2] Chap. xxvii.

never any news did I ever more wish for, nor were there ever any so welcome to me, &c.' 'But be you all witness I pray you, that I have committed no crime against his Majesty or the country: I am only accused of Priesthood and for Priesthood condemned.' This said, he returned to prison as unconcerned as if nothing had been done against him, whereas the said Titular Bishop, George Abbot, who sat with the Judges to hear him condemned, withdrew from the company like a man possessed with Orestes' furies. R. F. Maurus gave up his life on Whitsun Eve on the 9th of June (1612) very courageously with Mr Newport a Secular Priest."

I dwell the more upon Abbott's persecution of Catholics; because I wish to show that Laud, when, in course of time, he succeeded Abbott in the archbishopric, although guilty of occasionally persecuting them, nevertheless to some extent curbed the zeal of the pursuivants, and that he even threatened one of them, who had made himself notoriously obnoxious, with a whipping.

It seems probable that the hearing of the appeal against Laud's election to the Presidentship of St John's raised him in King James's estimation; for, within little more than a couple of months, he made him one of his own royal chaplains. It is, more or less, from this date, that Laud's court life may be said to have begun. His presidentship, together with the inheritance which had befallen him on his mother's death, gave him tolerable wealth for a bachelor, and he had no reason to be afraid of the expenses which his visits to the royal palaces might entail upon him. Of the monarch at that time presiding over the court, it is not necessary that I should say much: everybody knows him to have been a clever fool, and an intolerable prig; everybody is aware that he was as ugly as he was vain, as shrewd as he was unpractical, as drunken as he was religious, and as bombastic as he was cowardly.

His finances were already in a low condition. Indeed, in the very year that he made Laud his chaplain (1611), he endeavoured to raise the wind by means of the ingenious device of a new dignity, which he offered, to the number of two hundred patents, to any gentlemen of good family, or possessed of clear annual incomes of £1000, who would provide him with the monetary equivalent of thirty soldiers for three years; that is to say, £1095. The dignity was to be termed a Baronetcy. This honour was not so greedily sought for as had been expected, and at the end of six years less than half of the two hundred patents had been sold, the amount thus realised being about £101,835.

Laud had not been many months President of St John's College, before a death occurred which made some stir in his university. Like Laud, Sir Thomas Bodley had been fellow of his college (Merton), had served the office of proctor, and had risen to royal favour; but, after being employed in several embassies, he had fallen into disgrace, and in 1597 retired into private life. He then set to work to restore the public library at Oxford, which he rebuilt. The first stone of this library, which now bears his name, was laid the year before Laud was made President of St John's, and the year afterwards Bodley died. It is merely to show that even great public benefactors have their detractors, and with no desire to lessen the credit of a celebrated name, that, in addition to the panegyric of Isaac Wake in a letter to Carleton, announcing the death of Sir Thomas Bodley—"leaving all lovers of learning sorrowful bemoners of their owne loss in his,"[1] I quote a few extracts from the State Calendar recounting letters from Chamberlain to Carleton, during the months succeeding his death:—"Death of Sir Thomas Bodley. Particulars of his will. He has left legacies to great people, £7000 to his library, and £200 to Merton College; but little to his brothers, his old servants, his friends, or the children of his wife, by whom he had all his wealth." "Sir Thomas Bodley's executors cannot excuse him of unthankfulness to many of his relatives and friends, he being 'so drunk with the applause and vanitie of his librarie, that he made no conscience to rob Peter to pay Paul.'" "The great funeral at Oxford is the last act of Sir Thomas Bodley's vanity, whose ambition appears in many

[1] "Cal. Sta. Pa. Dom.," 1611-18, p. 168.

ways." [1] Be all this, however, as it may, Bodley's example, and the sensation made by his death and imposing funeral, so soon after Laud had taken up his position as President of St John's, is not unlikely to have imbued the latter with an ambition to distinguish himself, as he subsequently did by adding to the literary treasures of his university.

A period at which Laud was rising in court favour may not be unfitting for a notice of a criticism by a foreign ambassador on that court and sundry other English matters. If Sir John Digby, writing from Madrid,[2] is to be trusted, the Spanish Ambassador sent home the following report of the English court :—" That the King grows too fat to be able to hunt comfortably ; spends much time in reading, especially religious works, and eats and drinks so recklessly that it is thought he will not be long lived ; he is obstinate in his religious opinions."   " That the Prince is a fine youth of sweet disposition, and, under good masters, might be easily trained to the religion his predecessors lived in."   " That Catholics are persecuted by the Archp. of Canterbury " (Laud's great enemy, Abbott) " and Bp. of London, and by the King, in hope to propitiate Parliament into granting subsidies, and that he may have their forfeitures to give to his servants."   Anti-Catholicism, therefore, would appear to have been the best method of rising in court favour at that particular time.   About the same period, Laud writes of more than one " unfortunateness " which he had with people whose names are only hinted at by initials.   It is just possible that these " unfortunatenesses " may have been the result of his refusing to join in the violent no-popery cry then evidently in repute at court.

In the court, as at Oxford, death carried away an important personage at the end of the year 1612.   Sir Thomas Lake wrote to Carleton,[3] in November, of the " death of the Prince of Wales in the pride of his years, on the anniversary of a memorable deliverance, and the eve of his sister's marriage.   The king, apprehending the

---

[1] " Cal. Sta. Pa. Dom.," various letters.   [2] *Ib.*, vol. lxxiv. No. 58.
[3] *Ib.*, vol. lxxi. No. 31.

worst, and not enduring to be so near the place, removed to Theobalds, and kept his bed." We see something of the character of James I. here. "The queen is at Somerset House. They have not seen each other 'for feare to refresh the sense of the wound.'"

The "sister's marriage" here spoken of was destined to give Laud some trouble in the future. Prince Frederick, Elector Palatine, had just come to England to marry the Princess Elizabeth, when Henry, Prince of Wales, was taken ill and died. This approaching marriage was eagerly encouraged by the Puritan and Calvinistic party in this country. To Laud's enemy, Abbott, it must have been especially grateful, and we find him feasting the bridegroom and all his followers. About seven weeks after the death of Prince Henry, the betrothal took place, and received Abbott's benediction, for which he in his turn received a present of plate from Prince Frederick, worth £1000.[1] On the fourteenth of the following February, he married the royal couple in the chapel at Whitehall.

Some notes, in Laud's handwriting, attributed to the same year, refer to, and are placed with, some satirical papers "relating to the foundation of a Mock College for Innocents or Fools, to be called Gotam College, Oxford."[2] His notes are indorsed upon a complimentary ode, addressed to himself.

Dr Neile, now Bishop of Lincoln, continued to patronise Laud. The year after the marriage of the Princess Elizabeth, that is to say in 1614, Laud being then forty-one, he gave him the Prebendary of Bugden. During the same year, Laud suffered from "a most fierce salt Rheume," in his "left Eye, like to have endangered it."[3] In the following year, he reached a higher ecclesiastical grade, being made Archdeacon of Huntingdon by the Bishop of Lincoln.

It was somewhere about this time that Abbott's brother, then Vice-Chancellor of Oxford, made the violent onslaught upon Laud, mentioned in a previous chapter, from the pulpit

---

[1] Howe's "Chron.," p. 1007.
[2] "Cal. Sta. Pa. Dom.," vol. lxxv., Nos. 56-66.
[3] Diary, p. 3.

of St Mary's, calling him a "mungrel," and asking him whether he was a Papist or a Protestant. The matter appears to have been referred to the king, for the following entry of a letter occurs in the Calendar of State Papers (Domestic) in June 1615.[1] "The King permits Dr Laud's return to Oxford, having made an end of all those matters, the Archbishop having acknowledged the error of his brother in it, and Dr Abbot having apologized by saying that all the University understood Dr Laud's remarks were meant for him. Imperfect. Indorsed [by Laud], 'What His Magistye sayd concerninge Dr Abbot's sermon against me.'"

To have wrung an apology from Archbishop Abbott, or at least an acknowledgment of the error of his brother, was a great triumph for Laud. Perhaps his patron, the Bishop of Lincoln, may have aided him ; nor is the latter unlikely to have been in the royal favour just at that time, as he was then engaged in pressing his clergy to furnish arms to the king. In the very same month he wrote to the following effect, to one, John Lambe. "The clergy of the diocese, being less forward than was hoped in the benevolence, they are no longer to enjoy exemption from providing arms for the musters. Requests him to search the old books, and give notice to them of what is required of each. Those whose livings are below £40 are to be spared ; those of £40 and £50 to be put two to a musket; of £60, two to a corslet; of £70 to £100, muskets ; £100 to £140, corslets ; £140 to £200, petronels ; and above £200, lances."[2] Abbott, however, wrote to Neile commending his action.

As court chaplain, Laud was summoned from Oxford to Woodstock, in 1616, to preach before King James ; and he "preached, with great applause" (sic) "from Miriam's leprosy, as a warning to detractors against Government."[3] Next to his God, Laud worshipped his king, and how far he did this on principle, and how far with a view to obtaining royal

---

[1] "Cal. Sta. Pa. Dom.," vol. lxxx., No. 124. [2] *Ib.*, vol. lxxx., No. 123.
[3] *Ib.*, vol. lxxxviii., No. 61.

patronage is a question upon which his various biographers have differed considerably. Without committing myself unconditionally to either opinion on the matter, I may say that I am inclined to think that his faith in the Divine Right of Kings, and especially of English kings, was almost as strong as his faith in Christianity.

CHAPTER VI.

In the year 1616—that of Shakespeare's death, by the way, an event probably of little interest to Laud, whose nature was anything but poetical—the subject of my story had so far advanced in royal favour as to be taken to Scotland by King James I. The feeling in that country towards anything like High-Church practices may be understood when I say that Laud gave great offence there, by once wearing a surplice at a funeral.[1] Chamberlain writes to Carleton :—" Exceptions taken by the Scotch at Dr Laud, for putting on a surplice at a funeral, and at the Dean of St Paul's for commending the soul of the deceased to God, which he was forced to retract. They are so averse to English customs, that a Scottish bishop, Dean of the King's chapel, refused to receive the sacrament with His Majesty, kneeling."[2]

The king, himself, did little to make Laud popular by telling the Scotch divines that " he had brought some English theologians to enlighten their minds."[3] As Mr Benson very truly says, " Had Laud known it, on this occasion was sown that vast unintermitting Scottish hatred of the man that was so great a factor in his fall."[4]

It was, to all intents and purposes, a religious republic that King James attempted to reform in Scotland. Without denying that King Charles was chiefly responsible for his own overthrow, it may be pretty safe to assert that James did much to prepare it by his treatment of ecclesiastical matters in the North. He began by selecting thirteen clergymen of what he considered orthodox views, and appointing them to the vacant Scottish bishoprics. For the moment, however, we will take our leave of Scotch affairs

[1] Nichol's Progresses.   [2] "Cal. Sta. Pa. Dom.," 1611-18, p. 473.
[3] Mozeley's "Essays," vol. i. p. 129.   [4] "Archp. Laud," Benson, p. 37.

57

to notice those of Laud. While he was yet in Scotland, the deanery of Gloucester fell vacant, and was bestowed upon him by the king.

This appointment showed what a step he had made in the king's graces. Only three or four years earlier he had apparently made so little progress, and was so little noticed by the king, that he was on the point of altogether retiring from court, and contenting himself with Oxford life, when his friend and patron, Neile, dissuaded him and induced him to make another trial. This was rewarded by the journey with the king to Scotland and the " Deanry " of Gloucester.

This deanery, however, was not found to be a bed of roses. The Bishop of Gloucester, Dr Miles Smith, was a great Hebrician, and a translator of the so-called " Bishop's Bible " ; but very Calvinistic in his views. One of the first things that his new dean did, was to remove the communion-table from the " middest of the quire " [1] and place it altarwise against the east wall.

The Bishop was furious. " No sooner had he heard what the new Dean had done about the Communion Table, but he expressed his dislike of it." " He is said to have protested unto the Dean, and some of the Prebends, that if the Communion Table were removed, or any such innovations brought into that Cathedral, he would never come more within those walls." [2] He deputed his chaplain to write about the matter to the chancellor of the diocese, acquainting him " with the strange Reports which were come unto them touching the situation of the Communion Table in the place where the High Altar stood before, and that low obeysances were made to it, assuring him how much the secret Papists would rejoyce." He went on to express his astonishment " that no man should have any spark of *Elias* Spirit to speak a word in God's behalf, and the Preachers should swallow down such things in silence, and that the Prebends should be so faint-hearted as to shrink in the first wetting, especially having the Law on their side against it." [3]

Whatever " the Law " may have been, Laud had a power-

---

[1] " Cyp. Ang." p. 63.   [2] *Ib.*, p. 64.   [3] *Ib.*

ful precedent for his treatment of the communion-table, in its
position in the king's own chapel, to say nothing of many
of the cathedrals, and he held his own against the bishop,
who is said never to have re-entered his own cathedral on
account of the objectionable situation of what he termed the
" Nehushtan." I do not suppose that Laud broke his heart
at his absence. It is often thrown in the teeth of ritualists
that, unlike the early High-Churchmen of the Anglican
Establishment, they refuse to obey their bishops when they
object to their advanced proceedings. In the conduct of
Laud towards the Bishop of Gloucester, they have a
valuable precedent. Among the state papers, is a letter
to Laud,[1] in which his correspondent complains of a libel,
in much the same tone as that expressed in the letter of
the bishop's chaplain already quoted, and advises that the
attention of the Court of High Commission should be called
to it, attributing the whole matter to " that scismaticall faction
of the Puritanes."

Laud had not long been Dean of Gloucester when another
living was given to him, that of Ibstock in Leicestershire.
The following year, he received a reminder that court
favourites did not invariably come to a happy end, in the
execution of Sir Walter Raleigh, whose courageous conduct
on the scaffold was, as it were, a sort of precursor of his
own.

About the same time, or a trifle earlier, arrived in England,
an ecclesiastic whose presence did a good deal to encourage
the king in his theological designs. Much as James, his son
Charles after him, and Laud also, desired to make the
Puritans "conformable," the great wish of their hearts was,
that the Catholics should acknowledge the Anglican Establishment to be the Catholic Church in England, and that
they should become, what Mr Froude terms, Catholics without the Pope. It is almost needless to say that the majority
of the Catholics in England, that is the majority of the
English people, had lost, or shall I say been robbed of, their
Catholicism and become Protestants in the days of Edward

---

[1] Domestic, vol. xc., No. 75.

VI. and Elizabeth; indeed, it was their tendency to go too far in this direction, which was the principal religious trouble of the Stuart kings; but what the latter most anxiously sought for, was that the remnant still faithful to their Catholicism should come to the Anglican churches, receive communion in them, and acknowledge the king as head of the Church in this country.

King James flattered himself that many English Catholics would be led to do this by the example of an illustrious Roman Catholic foreigner, Marco Antonio de Dominis, no less a personage than His Grace the Archbishop of Spalatro, who came to England and joined the Established Church of the country.

He had the reputation of being a good mathematician and man of science, and he is said to have been the first to promulgate the true theory of the rainbow. He was consecrated Bishop of Segni, and was afterwards raised to the Archbishopric of Spalatro. There the spirit of reform overcame him, and, having offended the Pope, he had to fly from his archdiocese. At Venice, he became acquainted with the Anglican Bishop Bedell, who was then acting as chaplain to the English Ambassador, Sir Henry Wotton. Bedell brought him to England, where he published a book and dedicated it to King James.[1]

So far as ecclesiastical rank was concerned, he was the richest "take" of any foreign convert since the establishment of the Anglican Church, and possibly the chief authorities in that body may have flattered themselves that if an Italian Archbishop had joined it, there were hopes that the Pope himself might follow him. To Laud and James his "conversion" must have been a matter of unqualified and intense satisfaction.

In the year 1618, Brent wrote a letter[2] to Carleton, beginning by saying that the king was in bed with the gout, and going on to inform him that the Archbishop of Spalatro had been made Master of the Savoy. He was "printing a book more strongly against Rome than ever." Nine days

---

[1] " Ency. Brit.," 8th Ed., vol. vii. p. 100.   [2] Dom., vol. xcvi. No. 51.

later,[1] the archbishop himself wrote to the receiver of the above letter, sending a copy of his book, and informing him that the king had made him not only Master of the Savoy, but also a Prebend of Canterbury, and Dean of Windsor.

The estimation among Catholics of the validity of Anglican orders is well known ; but a somewhat different complexion might be put upon the question, if this Catholic bishop actually consecrated any Anglican bishops, at any rate so far as their own individual successors are concerned.[2] Chamberlain wrote to Carleton, in Dec. 1617 :—" The Archbp. of Spalato assisted the Archbp. of Canterbury and other Bishops in laying hands on the new Bishops of Bristol and Lincoln, Drs Felton and Montaigne." [3]   Yet there is nothing in this to show that he was the consecrating bishop: the inference, indeed, would be exactly the contrary.

Nearly a year later, we find a letter between the same correspondents saying that the archbishop had "sunk in estimation, by intruding into a parsonage in the gift of the Dean and Chapter of Windsor."[4]   In fact, Laud's great friend, Montague, said that de Dominis was so greedy of preferment that he would "be circumcised and denie Jesus Christ, if the Grand Signior would make him chiefe Muftie."

This dignitary only affects my biography in so far as the joining the Anglican Church by so exalted a Catholic ecclesiastic was an important event during the life of Laud, and, although it obliges me to anticipate, I will dispose of him as shortly as I well can.

In March 1622, Locke wrote :[5]—" The Bishop of Spalato has resigned the Deanery of Windsor," and there is a document of a date but little later, of still greater importance.[6] It reports that the archbishop requested the king for his

---

[1] Dom., vol. xcvi. No. 62.

[2] The difficulty, however, would still remain, that " in the ordination of a priest or bishop," " *there was then no express mention made in the words of ordaining them, that it was for the one or other office.*   In both it was said, ' Receive the Holy Ghost, in the name of, &c.' " (Burnet's " Hist. of Ref." ii. b. i., p. 252, ed. Pocock).   It was not until 1662 (*see* Keeling's " Liturgiæ Britannicæ ") that the words, " Receive the Holy Ghost, for the office and work of a Bishop, &c.," were added.

[3] " Cal. Sta. Pa. Dom.," 1611-18, p. 504.   [4] *Ib.*, p. 595.

[5] *Ib.*, p. 366.   [6] *Ib.*, p. 367.

dismissal, when the Bishops of London and Durham, and the Dean of Winchester, were sent to him by His Majesty to accuse him of holding intercourse with the Pope. He denied that he had held direct intercourse; but he said that he wished to go to Rome in the hope of promoting "the good of England by persuading the Pope to allow of the Oath of Allegiance; also that he thought, as both Churches agreed on fundamentals, a reconciliation might be effected." "He said he desired the union of the two religions by mutually yielding; gave his opinion on transubstantiation, the worship of the Virgin, &c." A series of communications between the king and himself was carried on through letters and messengers. Then Abbott, Archbishop of Canterbury, went to him and censured him "for returning to a Church which he had called Babylon." He replied that Pope "Gregory XV. was a good man, and many things were now reformed, but he would always protest the Church of England to be orthodox in fundamentals. Then they told him that the King did not grant him leave to depart, but ordered him to begone from the realm in twenty days, never to return at his peril."[1] There is no evidence that Laud had anything to do with this peremptory dismissal; but it sounds rather in his style, and we know that he was at that time in favour at court.

A curious letter[2] exists from the Archbishop of Spalatro to Cyril, Patriarch of Alexandria. Protestant re-unionists then, as now, turned to the East, and apparently with as little success. The summary of the letter runs:—"Long groaned under the Egyptian bondage of the Church of Rome, but at last escaped a year before to Goschen, which is England, where, under a wise and pious King, true defender of the faith, the cause of Christ triumphs. Sends him a copy of the first part of his work on ecclesiastical republics. Vindicates therein the Eastern Church from the calumnies of Rome. Interests him to become an agent in healing the disunion between the Eastern Church and that of England, and to communicate any difficulties that he may see therein to the Archbp. of Canterbury or to himself."

[1] "Cal. Sta. Pa. Dom.," 1619-23, pp. 367-8.   [2] *Ib.*, p. 369.

In the same year, he returned to Rome and was reconciled to the Catholic Church. It is of this period, that, in his famous *Conference with Fisher*, Laud wrote to that Jesuit:— "When you had fooled the archbishop of Spalatro back to Rome, there you either made him say, or said it for him (for in print it is, and under his name), that since it is now defined by the Church, a man is as much bound to believe there is a purgatory, as that there is a trinity of persons in the Godhead, How far comes this short of blasphemy, to make the Trinity and purgatory things alike and equally credible." [1]

The archbishop, however, once again changed his mind, and wrote letters to England, recanting the recantation of his recantation. These epistles were intercepted, and the heretic was imprisoned in the Castle of St Angelo, where he died. [2] Shortly before that event, the then Rector of the English College at Rome is reported to have said of him to Sir Edward Sackvill :—" He was a Male-content Knave when he fled from us, a Railing Knave while he lived with you, and a Motley, parti-colour'd Knave now he is come again." [3]

Laud was a good deal at court during the years in which the king was so much interested in this archiepiscopal *protégé*, and the very unsatisfactory outcome of the whole business would not be likely to make him hope much for the future of the Anglican Establishment from renegade bishops of the Church of Rome.

We must now go back to the period of Laud's life at which we left it to consider the incident of the conversion to Anglicanism of this Sicilian dignitary.

Great changes and developments were beginning at Oxford, especially in the direction of natural science. These advancements were chiefly owed to the energy of Laud, Saville, Camden and Aldrich, and the first of them, the Professorship of Natural History, was founded in 1618. The need of increased knowledge of natural history in those days may be judged from a work that was published more than sixty years later. The whole book is full of curiosities; I can

---

[1] "Conf. with Fisher," Oxford, p. 298.
[2] "Ency. Brit.," 8th Ed., vol. viii. p. 100, and Beeton's "Ency.," vol. i.
[3] "Scrinia Reserata," by John Hackett, p. 104.

only give here a few specimens. It tells us that swallows in winter either "joyn bill to bill, wing to wing, and foot to foot, hanging together in a conglomerated mass," and sink into the sea, or else they go to warm "countreys" where "they have been found naked and without their feathers." "As for the Cameleopardus, he is begotten by a mixt generation between the Camel and Leopard, or Panther." "As for your mimick Dogs, it is supposed that they come from a commixtion of Dogs with Apes." The long streaming spiders' webs sometimes seen stretching from railings, are meteors, and not things "spun from the spider's bowels," according to the "fond opinion," "engrafted among the ignorant." Birds of Paradise "have no wings, neither do they fly, but are borne up in the air by the subtility of their plumes and lightness of their body." [1] At the same time, it is only fair to say that science was rapidly advancing, and that at about the very time of the establishment of the chair of Natural History at Oxford, Harvey made his great discovery concerning the circulation of the blood.

A Professorship of Geometry was founded at Oxford in 1619, one of Moral Philosophy in 1621, one of Ancient History in 1622, one of Anatomy in 1626, and one of Music in the same year; Botany followed in 1632, and Arabic four years later.

Laud was seldom long without an illness or seizure of some sort, and, in the year 1619, he says that he "fell suddenly dead for a time at Wickham," on his "return from London."

Laud was now, and had been for some little time, a courtier, and to courtiers this year, 1619, was a memorable one. First came the death of the queen, on the second of March. There were long delays before the funeral, which did not take place until May. On March 27th, Chamberlain writes to Carleton that the queen's funeral is "postponed, because the Master of the Wardrobe will not pay double prices, as are usually charged now, for want of ready money"; [2] and again, nearly a month later:—"The delay in the Queen's funeral causes remarks; the charge is to be more than three times that of Queen Elizabeth's, though money is so scarce

---

[1] *Speculum Mundi.*   [2] "Cal. Sta. Pa. Dom.," 1619-23, p. 27.

that her plate will have to be coined." Then he mentions
" contests for precedency among the Lady Mourners."[1]   And
when it is over, he writes, on May 14th :—" The procession
at the Queen's funeral was very dull."[2]   To Carleton, also,
Brent writes that the cost would be " more than £40,000."[3]

In the meantime, " the King had a violent attack of the
stone."[4]   Within a month of his wife's funeral, he returned
in state to Whitehall.   " He was gaily dressed and attended,
which will seem strange to the Ambassadors in mourning,
come to condole [on the Queen's death]."[5]   And Brent
writes :—" The Ambassador of Lorraine came in mourning
to condole, and found mourning cast off ; the King said he
should have come sooner."[6]

Another momentous event to the English court in 1619,
and one which indirectly affected Laud, was the coronation
of the Princess Elizabeth, the daughter of King James (who
had been married some few years previously to the Elector
Palatine Frederick) as Queen of Bohemia.   The Emperor
Ferdinand had not long been crowned, before he was
deposed, and the Elector Palatine was elected King of
Bohemia in his stead.

The coronation of his daughter gave James little, if any,
pleasure.   The great wish of his heart was that his son,
Charles, should marry the Infanta of Spain, and the Spanish
Ambassador persuaded him that the elevation of his daughter
and son-in-law to the throne of Bohemia was a skilfully contrived plot to oblige him to break off his attempted alliance
with Spain and go to war on behalf of his daughter, Elizabeth.

Archbishop Abbott urged him strongly to wage war for
his child and the Protestant faith ; but he refused even to
countenance his son-in-law's election and coronation ; saying that it was the " work of a faction ;—that his subjects
were as dear to him as his daughter, and therefore he could
not consent to embroil them in an unjust war."[7]

---

[1] "Cal. Sta. Pa. Dom.," 1619-23, p. 39.   [2] *Ib.*, p. 45.
[3] *Ib.*, p. 44.   [4] *Ib.*, p. 27.
[5] *Ib.*, p. 51, Chamberlain to Carleton.   [6] *Ib.*, p. 54.
[7] Green's " Lives of the Eng. Princesses," vol. v. p. 310 ; and Nichols,
vol. iii. p. 569.

This matter chiefly concerns my biography in its relation to Laud and his enemy, Abbott ; for, as will be seen by-and-bye, while Abbott was dead against the Spanish alliance, Laud favoured it.

The year after Frederick and Elizabeth had been crowned King and Queen of Bohemia, they were driven out of that country. On hearing the news, King James sent his daughter £20,000, asked subsidies for his son-in-law's restoration from Parliament, and talked about shedding his blood to that end, if necessary ; but when he heard that his dethroned daughter and her dethroned husband intended to pay him a visit in England, he sent instructions to his Ambassador to hint to them his " mislike of such a course," and that nothing could possibly " be more displeasing unto " him than to receive them as guests.

While her royal father was showing such scant affection, the ex-Queen of Bohemia left open in her reception-room, with the obvious intention that it should be read, a letter which she had received from Abbott, after writing to ask his advice as to the acceptance of the crown of Bohemia ; in this epistle, the archbishop not only replied in the affirmative, but advised that, even if King James refused his consent, it should be accepted, as he would be certain to support her when once the deed was done.[1] Abbott could scarcely have acted in a more dangerous manner than to write such a letter, for, if discovered, it would bring him into terrible disrepute with his king. On the other hand, Abbott's loss of favour proportionately exalted his rival, Laud, and the opposition to James's policy both in Bohemia and Spain by Abbott, and the encouragement of it by Laud, probably went far towards making the good fortune of the latter.

If Laud praised the king and all his doings, not so all other divines. Chamberlain writes that the king " has committed Shingleton, of Oxford, for declaiming against his court, and ridiculing his Latinities, in a sermon at Paul's Cross."

In 1621, we find the following entry in Laud's Diary :—" I

[1] Goodman's " Court of James I.," vol. i. p. 236.

was installed Prebendary of *Westminster*, Januar. 22, 1620, *comp. Angl.*, having had the Advowson of it Ten Years the *November* before."

Laud was now gradually attaining an advantage which was to have an immense influence on his career—his intimacy with Buckingham.   At this time that royal favourite, although not yet duke, was in the zenith of his power, so far as the reign of James I. was concerned, for, in the opinion of some people, including Clarendon, he fell somewhat in the estimation of that monarch after his expedition to Spain.

No more important friendship than that of Buckingham could have been contracted at the time of which I am writing.   His power was enormous ; his own ascent had been "so quick, that it seem'd rather a Flight than a growth, and he was such a Darling of Fortune, that he was at the Top, before he was well seen at the Bottom ; "[1] and his power was equalled by his zeal in furthering the interests of his friends ; " His Kindness, and Affection to his Friends was so vehement," says Clarendon, "that they were as so many marriages for better and worse, and so many leagues offensive and defensive ; as if he thought himself obliged to love all his Friends, and to make war upon all they were angry with, let the cause be what it would."[2]

It was not until a year after the time with which I am now dealing (1620-21), that Laud's great intimacy with Buckingham was thoroughly established, and it is difficult to ascertain exactly when their warm friendship first began. There is evidence, however, that in 1620 and 1621 they were already on at least good terms.

Early in June 1621, King James hinted to Laud that he intended to bring him to the front when opportunity should offer.   We find a memorandum in Laud's Diary :—" The King's Gracious Speech to me, *June* 3, 1621, concerning my long Service.   He was pleased to say : He had given me nothing but *Gloucester*, which he well knew was a Shell without a Kernel."   There were clearly better things coming !

---

[1] " Hist. of the Reb.," Clarendon, book i. p. 34.   [2] *Ib.*, pp. 31, 32.

CHAPTER VII.

I NOW come to a most important event in the history of Laud—his elevation to the Episcopal bench. It is said to have come about in a curious manner. As will be seen, by-and-bye, I say " said " advisedly.

Dr Williams, the Lord Keeper of the Privy Seal, was also Dean of Westminster. He had been nominated for the Bishopric of Lincoln, and he had good grounds for believing that if he should resign his deanery, it would be given to Laud. Now to Laud and his " views " he had an intense dislike, and he was most anxious that such a man should not be appointed to so influential a post as the Deanery of Westminster. Nevertheless, he could not conceal from himself the fact that the king was determined to push him on, and the best course appeared to be to induce His Majesty to give him high preferment in some place where he could do as little harm as possible. When, therefore, the Bishopric of St David's fell vacant a few weeks after the king had apologised to Laud for not having yet presented him to anything better than the Deanery of Gloucester, Dr Williams went to King James in order to induce him to dispose of Laud, once for all, by sending him to that out-of-the-way diocese. At any rate, this is one view of Williams' conduct.

According to Bishop Hacket's account of their interview,[1] the king was by no means disposed to go to the length of making Laud a bishop, although, judging from his late professions of good intentions, as reported by Laud himself, one feels inclined to suppose that Hacket's account of the conversation between King James and Dr Williams must be exaggerated, to say the least of it ; nor is it improbable that

[1] I quote from Mr Benson, pages 41 and following.

the exaggeration, if any, was originated by Dr Williams, who was given to fibbing,[1] in recounting the incident. On the other hand, it is possible that the king may have had his own reasons for pretending to be unwilling to advance Laud too hurriedly.

"'[2] Well,' said the king, 'I perceive whose attorney you are ; Stenny'" (Buckingham) "'hath set you on.'" "'Was there not a certain lady who forsook her husband, and married a Lord that was her paramour? Who knit that knot? Shall I make a man a Prelate, one of the angels of my Church, who hath a flagrant crime upon him?'"

"'Sir,' said Williams, 'you are a good master ; but who will dare serve you if you will not pardon one fault, though of a scandalous size, to him who is heartily penitent? I pawn my faith to you that he is heartily penitent ; and there is no other blot that hath sullied his good name.'"

"'You press well," replied the king, 'and I hear you with patience. Neither will I revive a trespass which repentance hath mortified and buried. And because I see that I shall not be rid of you, unless I tell you my unpublished cogitations, *the plain truth is, I keep Laud back from all place of rule and authority because I find he hath a restless spirit and cannot see when matters are well, but loves to toss and change, and to bring things to a pitch of reformation floating in his own brain,* which may endanger the steadfastness of that which, God be praised, is at a good pass. I speak not at random : he hath made himself known to me to be such an one. For when, three years past, I had obtained of the Assembly of Perth to consent to five articles of order and decency in a correspondence with this Church of England, I gave them promise that I would try their obedience no further anent ecclesiastical affairs. Yet this man hath pressed me to invite them to a nearer conjunction with the Liturgy and Canons of this nation ; but I sent him back again, with

---

[1] Clarendon's "Hist. of the Reb.," vol. iii. p. 345.

[2] I quote chiefly from Mr Benson's very ably modernised rendering of Hacket's account in "Scrinia Reserata," except where I specially mention that I refer to the original.

the frivolous draft that he had drawn. And now, your importunity hath compelled me to shrive myself thus unto you, I think you are at your furthest, and have no more to say for your client.' "

" ' May it please you, sir,' answered Williams, ' I will speak but this once. You have convicted your chaplain of an attempt very audacious and very unbecoming. My judgment goes quite against his : yet I submit this to your sacred judgment, that Dr Laud is of a great and tractable wit. He did not well see how he came into his error ; but he will presently see the way to come out of it. Some diseases, which are very acute, are quickly cured.' "

" ' And if,' said the king, ' there is no whoe ' (way) ' but you must carry it, then take him with you, but, by my soul, you will repent it.' " And so, the narrative informs us, he " went away in anger, using other words of fierce import, too tart to be repeated."

King James's opinion of Laud, as here quoted, has been generally accepted as genuine ; as to Williams's share in the conversation, historians differ, some going so far as to doubt whether he recommended Laud for the Bishopric of St David's at all.

The doubts as to the veracity of the account of the conversation between Williams and the king are chiefly based upon a sentence in Clarendon,[1] in which he speaks thus of the former :—" He had a faculty of making relations of things done in his own Presence, and discourses made to himself, or in his own hearing, with all the circumstances of answers, and replies, and upon Arguments of great moment ; all which, upon Examination, were still found to have nothing in them that was Real, but to be the pure effect of his own Invention."

And now, I will venture, with all humility, to give my own opinion on the question. It is that Williams neither recommended Laud to the king for the Bishopric of St David's, out of any goodwill towards him, nor to keep for himself the Deanery of Westminster, but solely in order to

---

[1] " Hist. of the Reb.," vol. iii., p. 345.

curry favour with Buckingham, who had urged him to do it. Buckingham wanted a rochet for his friend Laud, and, as I shall show, had found himself foiled in his own attempts to persuade James to bestow one, by the ill-offices of Archbishop Abbott ; he determined, therefore, to endeavour to turn the scale in favour of his own nominee by inducing a divine to recommend Laud, as if he were doing so spontaneously.

Here is Bishop Hacket's account, in his *Life of Williams :*— [1] Laud, he says, "a Learned Man, and a Lover of Learning," "had fasten'd on the Lord Marquess to be his Mediator, whom he had made sure by great Observances. But the Arch-Bishop of *Canterbury* had so opposed him, and represented him with suspicion (in my judgment improbably grounded) of Unsoundness in Religion, that the Lord Marquess was at a stand, and could not get the Royal Assent to that Promotion. His Lordship, as his Intimates know, was not wont to let a Suit fall, which he had undertaken ; in this he was the stiffer, because the Arch-Bishop's Contest in the King's Presence was sour and supercilious. Therefore he resolved to play his Game in another hand ; and conjures the Lord Keeper to commend Dr *Laud* strenuously and importunately to the King's good Opinion, to fear no Offence, neither to desist for a little Storm. Accordingly he watch'd when the King's Affections were most still and pacificous ; and besought his Majesty to think considerately of his Chaplain the Doctor, who deserved well when he was a young Man in his Zeal against the Millenary Petition ! And for his Incorruption in Religion, let his Sermons plead for him in the Royal Hearing, of which no Man could judge better than so great a Scolar as His Majesty."

Then followed the conversation given above, in the very first sentence of which, it will be remembered, James was sharp enough to tell Williams he was quite sure that Buckingham had put him on to plead Laud's cause.

The remarks made by Bishop Hacket, when he has ended his account of the conversation, may be worth giving. " So

[1] " Scrinia Reserata," p. 63.

the Lord Keeper procured to Dr *Laud* his first Rochet, and retained him in his Prebend of *Westminster*, a Kindness which then he mightily valued ; and gave him about a year after a Living of about £120 *per annum* in the Diocese of St *David's* to help his Revenue : Which being unsought, and brought to him at *Durham-House* by Mr William *Winn*, his expression was, ' Mr *Winn*, my Life will be too short to requite your Lord's Goodness.' But how those scores were paid, is known at home and abroad."

Laud's own account of his appointment is to be found in his Diary :—" June 29. His Majesty gave me the Grant of the Bishoprick of St David's, being St *Peter's* day. The general expectation in Court was, that I should then have been made Dean of *Westminster*, and not Bishop of St *David's*." This bears out the possibility of Williams's desire to prevent his obtaining it by getting him appointed to St David's. Laud then goes on to say :—" The King gave me leave to hold the Presidentship of St *John Baptist's* Colledge in *Oxon*, in my *Commendam* with the Bishoprick of St *Davids* : [But by Reason of the strictness of that Statute, which I will not violate, nor my Oath to it, under any colour, I am resolved before my Consecration to leave it.]" Accordingly, we find an entry in the Diary :—" *Octob.* 10. I was chosen Bishop of St *Davids*, *Octob.* 10, 1621. I resigned the Presidentship of St *Johns* in *Oxford*, *Novemb.* 17, 1621." Considering the pluralities of those days, to his credit be it spoken.

It was otherwise with Dr Williams. He need not have been so afraid that Laud would get his deanery of Westminster. In August there was issued a " Grant to John Williams, Dean of Westminster, Bp. Elect of Lincoln, and Keeper of the Great Seal, of licence to retain his Deanery in commendam, because the usual residence of the Chancellor being otherwise employed, he has no other residence near the Court ; also of dispensation from personal attention to the duties of the Bishopric and Deanery, as long as he holds the Great Seal, on condition of his taking care that they be not neglected."[1] The contrast between the conduct of Williams

[1] " Cal. Sta. Pa. Dom.," 1619-23, p. 283.

and my hero in these cases is remarkable, but requires no comment.

A later memorandum in Laud's Diary runs :—"I was consecrated Bishop of *St Davids, Novemb.* 18, 1621, at *London-House* Chappel, by the Reverend Fathers, the Lords Bishops of *London, Worcester, Chichester, Elye, Landaffe, Oxon.* The Arch-Bishop being thought Irregular for casual Homicide."[1]

As this case of "casual homicide" to a considerable extent crippled the power of one of Laud's greatest enemies, it merits some notice here. The fact is briefly recorded in a letter from Chamberlain to Carleton, July 28, 1621.[2] "The Archp. of Canterbury going into Hampshire to consecrate a chapel for Lord Zouch, has had the misfortune to kill his keeper, when shooting at a deer." And, again, on August 4, "The Archp. of Canterbury, immediately on his misfortune, sent to inform the King, who sent him a gracious answer, that such an accident might happen to anyone. The verdict on the coroner's inquest was, that [the Keeper died] 'per infortunium suæ propriæ culpæ.'"[3] On August 5th, the Archbishop himself wrote to Lord Zouch,[4] in whose park the accident took place :—"thanks for his entertainment at Bramsell. His counsel do not consider the verdict given on the coroner's inquest to be legally drawn up ; requests him to resummon the coroner and jury to supply all defects, the credit of his profession being involved, and the enemies of the gospel too ready to slander him." He wrote to him again, on the 29th, that [5] his "unhappy accident has been a bitter potion, on account of his conflict in his conscience, for what sin he is permitted to be the talk of men, to the rejoicing of the Papist and insulting the Puritan." About a week later, Locke wrote to Carleton[6] that the "Archbishop has kept secluded ever since the accident" ; but three days afterwards that "the Archbishop of Canterbury has attended the King to the sermon, for the first time since the accident" ; and in another four days that "Archbishop

---

[1] Diary, p. 4. [2] "Cal. Sta. Pa.," 1619-23, p. 279. [3] *Ib.*, p. 281.
[4] *Ib.*, same page. [5] *Ib.*, p. 285. [6] *Ib.*, p. 287.

Abbot has been again with the King, and it is hoped all will now go well with him."

From the time of the announcement of the accident itself, King James had taken a very kindly and sympathetic view of it. " His Majesty," says Bishop Hacket,[1] " who had the Bowels of a Lamb, censured the Mischance with these words of melting Clemency, That an Angel might have miscarried in that sort."

Early in the following month (October) a commission was given by the " King [2] to the Lord Keeper, Bps. of London, Winchester, and Rochester, and others. To inquire into the nature of the accidental killing of the keeper in Bramsell Park, by Geo. Abbot, Archp. of Canterbury, whether it amounts to an irregularity or otherwise, in a person of his rank in the church, and to consider the scandal that may have arisen thereon."

On one side it was argued that an archbishop had no right to be hunting at all, and that his offence consequently was murder, in the same manner that a poacher aiming at a stag, to which he had no right, and accidentally killing a keeper, would have technically committed that crime. The great legal authority, Coke, thought otherwise. An old book on the law relating to game says :—" Every Lord of Parliament, Spiritual or Temporal, sent for by the King, may in coming and returning kill a Deer or two in the *King's Forest*, Chase, or Park, through which he passeth." "And Sir *Edward Coke*, treating of this Law observes, That although Spiritual Persons are prohibited by the Canon Law to hunt Game ; yet by the Common Law of the Land for their Recreation, and to make them fitter for the Performance of their Office, they may use the Diversion and Exercise of Hunting." [3] In addition to this, "he dragged to light an immemorial statute that a bishop's *morte* of hounds was to escheat to the king on his decease, not to the natural heirs. Ergo, argued Coke, he may hunt with them while he is alive, if they are to pass to some one else on his death." [4]

---

[1] "Scrinia Reserata," p. 65.   [2] *Ib.*, p. 295.
[3] "The Game Law," pub. 1727, p. 3.   [4] Benson, p. 46.

On November 10th Chamberlain wrote to Carleton that "the Commissioners on the Archp. of Canterbury's case were equally divided, but the Bp. of Winchester, siding with the four lawyers so forcibly against the other five Bishops, turned the scale in his Grace's favour. The King absolved him; the new Bishops" (one of whom would be Laud) "are so unwilling to receive consecration from his hand, that he has commissioned three other Bishops to consecrate for him."[1]

In the same month we find a "Commission to the Bp. of Lincoln, Lord Keeper, the Bps. of London, Winchester, Norwich, Ely, Bath and Wells, and Chichester, to grant a dispensation to the Archp. of Canterbury, for the death of Peter Hawkins, casually slain by him."[2]

In spite of his dispensation, Abbott's power was on the wane; but I do not think that his disgrace was so much owing to his accidental homicide, as his opposition to the policy of King James, especially in the matter of the Spanish match and the crown of Bohemia, in both of which policies Laud supported the king. Part of Abbott's powers may have been put in commission; yet we find him performing many clerical and even episcopal acts; such as preaching before the king, and at Queen Anne's funeral, banishing Jesuits, and granting a dispensation to Sir Edward Conway, "for himself, his wife, and two others whom he may choose, to eat flesh at prohibited times, as fish does not agree with his health, on condition of his doing it privately, to avoid scandal, and paying 13s. 4d. a year to the poor of his parish;"[3] yet he remained out of favour at court, and without much influence, for the rest of his life. Nevertheless, he still retained the power of making himself disagreeable, as we shall see by-and-bye.

The first episcopal act of the new Bishop of St David's was a thankless one—the sending to his diocese of his own and the archbishop's letters demanding, at the king's order, a contribution from the clergy towards the expenses of the war in the Palatinate. He did not visit his diocese until

---

[1] "Cal. Sta. Pa. Dom.," 1619-23, p. 308.   [2] *Ib.*, p. 311.
[3] *Ib.*, 1623-5, p. 542.

seven or eight months after he had been made its bishop. In the meanwhile, we read in his Diary of his preaching before the king and going to an entertainment given by Count Swartzenbergh. Five months after he had become a bishop, "Being the Tuesday in Easter week, the King sent for me, and set me into a course about the Countess of *Buckingham*, who about that time was wavering in point of religion." [1]

Mr Edward Cardwell, in his preface to the 1839 edition of Laud's *Correspondence with Fisher* (the edition to which I refer throughout), after stating that although the king had denounced such crimes as exercising the office of a priest and "seducing his subjects from the religion established," his "real intentions were interpreted more from his acts of forbearance than from his threats of punishment," says [2] :— "Among the emissaries whom the Romanists employed at this time in England, one of the most active and intelligent was a Jesuit of the name of Piersey, who has been better known under the assumed appellation of Fisher. He had obtained admission to the countess, mother of Villiers, who was afterwards Duke of Buckingham, and had made some progress in converting her to the Romish faith, in the hope that through the influence of her son, she might be able to obtain further indulgences from the court in favour of the Roman Catholics."

A rather differently worded account of the matter is given in an old manuscript at Stonyhurst [3] :—"The Viscount de Purbeck, brother of the Marquis of Buckingham, having been converted to the Catholic faith, and reconciled to Holy Church, by Father John Perseus, S.J., betook himself to the Countess his mother, and gave her so good an account of the said Father, and of the consolation he had received of him, that she greatly desired to speak to him, and sending him to call the Father, she heard him discourse fully of the Catholic faith, asking of him also many doubts, and in the end she rested so entirely satisfied," &c.

She asked Fisher, as we will call Father John Percy, since

[1] Diary, p. 5.   [2] P. v.   [3] Stoneyhurst MS., Anglia., vol. vii.

that was the alias by which he was best known—" F. Fisher,
a notorious Jesuite "[1]—to write out for her the substance of
this conversation, and, on receiving it, she showed it to the
king, who determined to have it refuted in her presence by an
Anglican theologian, and for this purpose summoned a Dr
White (afterwards Bishop of Carlisle), as well as the Jesuit
himself to dispute the matter before his own royal presence
and that of the Countess.   White had Father Fisher's
document to study for ten days before the conference took
place.   "The minister," said Father Fisher, "only said a few
words, the King did nearly all the speaking,"[2] and, when it
was over, "the Countess complained that nothing had been
said respecting the claim which the Romanists make to a
visible and infallible church."[3]   A further controversy being,
therefore, necessary, "it was determined that a third conference should be held, and Dr Laud, then Bishop of St David's,
who was distinguished for his theological learning, and had
recently given the king evidence of his great skill in composition, was appointed to conduct the argument on the side
of protestantism."[4]

Laud's own account of this controversy was not published
until about two or three years later, in reply to one that had
been written by, or was at least attributed to, Fisher, under
the initials " A. C."; but it will be more convenient to us
to dispose of the subject altogether, now that we have
embarked upon it.

Of Laud's *Relation of the Conference*, Dean Hook writes:
—" He would be a bold man who at the present time should
engage in doctrinal controversy with Rome without first
perusing a work which has long occupied the first place in
the theological literature of England."[5]   Another Anglican,
Mr Benson, the son of no less a person than the present
Archbishop of Canterbury, takes a very different view of
this work.   He writes of it in one place as "a nearly unread-

[1] Gee's " List of Romish Priests and Jesuits about London."
[2] " Records of the Eng. Province S.J." series 1, p. 531.
[3] Laud's " Conf. with Fisher," Preface, p. vi.   [4] *Ib.*
[5] Hook's " Lives of the Archbishops of Canterbury," vol. xi. pp. 55, 56.

able folio,"[1] and in another as "justly forgotten."[2]　Where
two good Anglicans differ so greatly, it becomes an outsider
to stand respectfully silent; but it may be permitted to me
to say that if the book is wordy and heavy, and that if the
reader may smile when the author says that he leaves "all
gall out of his ink," it contains here and there some spirited,
if not exactly fine, passages.

I will quote part of a panegyric on the Bible, as an
instance in point:—"See the riches of natural knowledge
which are stored up there, as well as supernatural: consider
how things quite above reason consent with things reasonable: weigh it well, what majesty lies there hid under
humility! what depth there is, with a perspicuity unimi-
table! what delight it works in the soul that is devoutly
exercised in it! how the sublimest wits find in it enough to
amaze them, while the simplest want not enough to direct
them."[3]　And then he proceeds to draw an entirely false
conclusion from all this, but that is a matter on which I do
not intend to enter.

Nor have I either the space or the inclination to enter here
upon the question of the theological merits of either side in
this controversy; but I will venture to express my surprise
that none of the biographies of Laud that I have read take
any notice of an ably written reply which was published in
Paris, some thirty-six years after the actual controversy took
place.　It is called "Labyrinthus Cantvariensis or *Doctor
Laud's Labyrinth.*　Beeing an ansvver to the Late Archbishop of Canterbvries Relation of a conference between
Himselfe and Mr Fisher, &c.　*Wherein* the true grounds of
the *Roman Catholiqve* Religion are asserted, the principall
Controuersies betvvixt Catholiques and Protestants thoroughly
examined, and the Bishops Meandrick vvindings throughout
his vvhole vvorke layd open to publique vievv.　By T. C."

It seems that the book had been written some years before
it appeared; but at that particular time, the Anglican Church
was "in so bleeding a condition, that it might have been

---

[1] Benson, p. 95.　　　　　[2] *Ib.*, p. 200.
[3] Laud's " Conf. with Fisher," Oxford, 1839, p. 93.

thought unhandsome to impugne it." [1] The author found "in perusall of the Bishop's book," "many affected windings and artificiall meanders." [2]

It is but fair to say that Laud apparently held much the same opinion of Fisher's book. "A. C., having, as it seems, little new matter, is at the same again, and over and over it must go ; " and presently he says :—" To all which I have abundantly answered before. Marry then he infers, &c." And in another place :—" A. C. may ask everlastingly, if he will ask the same over and over again. For, I pray, wherein doth this differ from his first question, &c. ? " And yet again :—" Good God ! whither will not a strong bias carry even a learned judgment ! "

On the opposite side, the reply accuses Laud of " citing of nominatives without verbs," and thus evading the question " by a nimble turn."

Then Laud accuses his opponent of misquotation :—" So A. C. out of St Bernard. But St Bernard not so. For these last words, ' of all the Christian churches in the world,' are not in St Bernard."

A similar charge is brought against Laud by the author of the *Labyrinth*, as may be seen by looking at even the headings of the chapters, such as :—" Bellarmine miscited ; " " Vincentius Liringensis falsified thrice at least ; " " Occham, St Augustin, Canus, Almain and Gerson, either miscited, or their sense perverted by the Bishop; " "St Irænæus not rightly translated by the Bishop ; " " St Epiphanius miscited and mistaken by the Bishop." [3]

Per contra, Laud accuses Fisher of hoping " his cunning malice would not be discovered." [4] " There is a great deal of cunning," he says, " and as much malice in this passage, but I shall easily pluck the sting out of this wasp." [5] The author of the *Labyrinth* again appears to think Laud not altogether free from malice when he says that he makes " a pretty sleight to blast the credit of his adversary."

[1] Lab. Cant., Pref.   [2] *Ib.*

[3] " Laud's Lab.," several places.   [4] " Conf. with Fisher," Oxford, p. 316.

[5] *Ib.*, p. p. 314.

Laud constantly charges Fisher with a false, or at least an inaccurate, account of the actual verbal controversy which took place between them, and, towards the end of his book, he says, in well-feigned despair :—" What ! not one answer perfectly related ! " [1]

The writer of the *Labyrinth* uses very similar language about Laud's work. " Now in that whole place which I have perused very diligently, there are neither those cited words, nor anything like them. What is there then ? Marry, the quite contrary." [2]

I merely give these few quotations in order to show that if Laud's accusations of inaccuracy and cunning against Fisher are to be entertained, there is also another side to the question. To judge of the merits of the controversy itself, *A Relation of the Conference between William Laud and Mr Fisher the Jesuit* and *Laud's Labyrinth* should be read together.

---

[1] " Conf. with Fisher," Oxford, p. 236. [2] " Laud's Lab.," p. 78.

CHAPTER VIII.

I NOW come to one of the recognised landmarks in the life of Laud,—his friendship with Buckingham. In most respects, few men could have been more different. Laud, a rather plain, red-faced, clumsy-gaited little man, with a hard, harsh voice, blurting out his opinions with little respect of persons, was a strong contrast to the handsome, graceful, courteous and diplomatic Buckingham. The former, whatever may have been his failings, was at least a celibate, against whose purity of life no whisper of scandal is known to have been ever raised ; the latter was foul-tongued, a faithless husband, and an abandoned profligate. Laud was plain and modest in his attire, even for a clergyman ; as to Buckingham, " it was common with him at any ordinary dancing to have his cloaths trimmed with great diamond buttons, and to have diamond hat-bands, cockades and earings ; and to be yoked with great and manifold yokes of pearls."[1]

As I have already observed, it is difficult to assign an exact date to the commencement of the friendship between Laud and Buckingham ; and its origin remains a matter of surmise. On June 9, 1622, Laud writes in his Diary :— " Being *Whitsunday*, my Lord Marquess of Buckingham was pleased to enter into a near Respect to me. The particulars are not for paper." To rush to the conclusion that this was the occasion of the beginning of their great intimacy would be hasty ; for the two following entries sufficiently describe the cause of the " near Respect." " June 15. I became C." (confessor) "to my Lord of *Buckingham*. And June 16. Being *Trinity Sunday*, he Received the Sacrament at *Greenwich*." Probably their relations as confessor and penitent would increase their intimacy to a greater or less

[1] MS. Harleian Lib. B. II. 90, c. 7, fol. 642.

F

81

extent; although in the Catholic Church many penitents go
to confessors for years without any personal friendship:
indeed, it not uncommonly happens that they are un-
acquainted with each other outside the confessional. Of
course, where the confessor and penitent were already
personal friends, the case might be somewhat different,
although I think that many Catholics would bear me out in
saying that it is possible to be on friendly terms with a
confessor and chaplain, without necessarily becoming more
intimate or more friendly through the confessional; for in
confession only sins, and those the penitent's exclusively, need
be mentioned, and even in relation to these, no names of
persons should be given. Protestants are apt to forget that
the confessor cannot make the slightest allusion to anything
said in the confessional, when speaking to his penitent outside of it, unless the penitent gives him special and formal
leave to do so.

My own impression is that Laud's strong friendship
with Buckingham owed its rise to the conference with
Fisher. It may be that Buckingham himself had been half-
convinced by Father Fisher's arguments, and that he was
only too grateful to Laud for enabling him to persuade himself that in the Anglican Establishment he had "got everything," including confession, that he would be able to get
if he became a Catholic, and that it was quite unnecessary,
nay that it would be absolutely sinful, to take a step which
would be the ruin of his then proud position as the most
influential personage in the kingdom.

About a fortnight after King James had first spoken to
Laud about a conference with Fisher, Laud went to the
court at Greenwich, " and came back in Coach with the Lord
Marquess *Buckingham*. My promise then to give his
Lordship the Discourse he spake to me for." Their con-
versation during this drive was clearly on the question of
Anglicanism *versus* Catholicism; for, nine days afterwards,
he writes:—" I delivered my Lord Marquess *Buckingham*
the Paper concerning the difference between the Church of
England and *Rome*, in point of Salvation, &c." Five days

later "the Conference between Mr *Fisher*, a Jesuit and my self, before the Lord Marquess *Buckingham*, and the Countess his Mother" took place. Buckingham's first confession to Laud came off within a month, and this looks as if Laud had said to him: "If you only want to be a Roman Catholic in order to go to confession, why not come to me?" Until his mother became a Catholic, Buckingham does not appear to have shown any theological tastes or inclinations; and it may be worth noticing that now, as then, Anglicans who have never exhibited the slightest interest in their own Church, until one of their nearest relatives has left it for the Catholic Church, after that event, often suddenly discover that they love it with an ardour which puts filial affection to the blush, and overflow with a temporary zeal and short-lived piety.

If the smart courtier obtained spiritual advancement through their intimacy, the ecclesiastic obtained temporal. As Professor Mozley puts it :—"Laud wedged his passage further and further through this dense mass," *i.e.*, the difficulties and obstacles in the way of royal favour, "and found himself at last approaching something like a centre, and penetrating within the inner circle, in which stood the great man himself—the wielder of court power, the dispenser of court favours—Buckingham. The proximity once begun became rapidly closer, till the two fairly met, and Laud and Buckingham made a coalition."[1]

There has been considerable scoffing at poor Laud's prayer for a continuation of the good graces of Buckingham. It is headed "Pro Duce Buckinghamiæ," and contains the petition, "continue him a true-hearted friend to me thy poor Servant whom thou hast honoured in his eyes." This is considered by some people to be the prayer of a cringing toady; but, after all, the favour of such a man as Buckingham was a matter of immense importance to a man desiring promotion; and if prayers for temporal blessings are to be made at all, surely a prayer for his friendship was quite justifiable, on this score at least.

[1] Mozley's " Essay on Laud," p. 12).

Some historians regard Laud in the light of an ambitious character, whose sole object was to work his way to supreme power, not only in the State Church, but also in the State itself. This appears to me to be looking at his history from a false standpoint. I do not think that his nature was a selfish one. It is true that his greatest admirer cannot fairly defend him from the charge of having been self-opinionated; but that is a very different thing from being self-interested. Perhaps his greatest fault in the way of self-pleasing was his excessive love of power. Professor Mozley, whom I have so lately quoted, writes of his " natural turn for the exercise of power, for tactics, for managing—so strong a taste in a mind that feels itself to have it."[1] He might even have said "so strong a *passion.*"

The very influence obtained by means of his friendship with Buckingham, which we have just been considering, was not used solely for personal purposes. The treasury was then desperately empty, and it was sought to replenish it by alienating the lands belonging to the Charterhouse— already alienated, so far as that goes, from their rightful owners. Laud strongly opposed this second robbery, and induced Buckingham to prevent it.

Nothing could have been more unfair than Archbishop Abbott's remark—"There he" (Laud) "sits privately whole hours with Buckingham, feeding his humours with malice and spite."

Laud is said to have written out speeches for Buckingham. Dry indeed must they have been, if this be true! In a speech in Parliament, some four years later than the time of which I am writing, Buckingham "acknowledged how easy a thing it was to him in his younger years and inexperienced, to fall into thousands of errors, but still he hoped the fear of God, his sincerity in the true religion established in the Church of England (though accompanied with many weaknesses and imperfections, which he was not ashamed humbly to confess), &c." It was but natural that, when they heard this, his audience should look at each other with a smile and whisper—" Laud."

[1] Mozley's "Essay on Laud," p. 126.

But we must take leave of Buckingham to accompany Laud on his first visitation to his out-of-the-way diocese. On July 5th he "first entered Wales." Heylin calls St David's "a poor city, God wot." In the middle ages it had been one of some importance, owing to its enormous concourse of pilgrims—to say nothing of the famous shrine of St David himself, the whole neighbourhood was full of holy wells and chapels—and there had been a splendid bishop's palace ; but even in Laud's time, it had become the "decayed Episcopal city" that it has remained ever since. Nor would a bishop from London be over-eagerly welcomed, for there were few places in Wales where the distinction between the Welsh and the English were more jealously observed.

It may be interesting here to look at one or two of the "Articles to be inquired of in the first visitation of the Right Rev. Father in God, William Laud, Bishop of St Davids, 1622." [1]

"Have you a convenient and decent communion table, with a carpet of silk, or some other decent stuff, continually laid upon the table at the time of divine service, and a fair linen cloth upon the same, at the time of the receiving of Holy Communion ? And whether is the same table placed in convenient sort within the chancel, and whether is it so used out of divine service, as is not agreeable to the holy use of it, and by sitting on it, throwing hats upon it, writing on it, or is it abused to other profaner uses : and are the Ten Commandments set up on the east end of your church or chapel, where the people may best see and read them : and other sentences of holy Scripture written on the walls for that purpose ? "

It was the mark of a High-Churchman to have the commandments put up over his communion-table in Laud's days, be it observed !

Here is another interesting inquiry, intended for church-wardens.[2] "Doth your minister, being a preacher, endeavour

[1] "Lib. of Ang. Cath. Theol.," Part v., vol. vi. pp. 378 and foll.
[2] *Ib.*, p. 380.

and labour diligently to reclaim the popish recusants in his parish from their errors (if there be any such abiding in your parish)? Or whether is your parson, vicar, or curate, over-conversant with, or a favourer of recusants, whereby he is suspected not to be sincere in his religion?" Let it be remembered that the Welsh, unlike the English, had not, as a nation, accepted the newly-coined religion, and that they so far "dissented" from it as to remain in their old Catholic faith, although priestless, saying their Catholic prayers, and meeting in their huts or on the hill-sides, to worship together and sing psalms and hymns, as best they could. The days of the Wesleys and their Methodism were yet to come.

Laud began his "Visitation at the Colledge of *Brecknocke*." This would be Christ's College, of which the Bishop of St David's was, *ex officio*, dean. There he preached. A fortnight later he was at his cathedral city and preached there also. Ten days afterwards he "visited at *Camarthen*, and Preached. The Chancellor and " his " Commissioners visited at Emlyn, &c., July 16, 17, and at Haverford-West, July 19, 20. Aug. 15," he "set forward towards *England* from *Carmarthen*."

In a fortnight he was at Windsor, talking over his late conference with Father Fisher, "in the presence of the King, the Prince, the Lord Marquess *Buckingham*, his Lady, and his Mother." For the next two or three months, he occupied his leisure in writing, at the king's command, his *Relation* of the conference with Fisher. He seems to have been pleased at being able to write in his Diary, "I was three times with the King this *Christmas*," and he ended the year 1622 high in royal favour, as well as in that which was almost as important, the favour of Buckingham.

Early in 1623, he wrote:—"I ordained *Edmund Provant* a *Scot* Priest. He was my First-begotten in the Lord." Equally gratifying must it have been to be "instituted at *Peterborough* to the Parsonage of *Creeke*." This was by no means his "first begotten " piece of church-patronage.

We now come to an entry in his Diary of some moment:—
" *Febr.* 17, *Munday*, the Prince and the Marquess *Buckingham*

set forward very secretly for *Spain*." Laud was one of the few and select in the secret that Prince Charles and Buckingham, under the names of John and Thomas Smith, accompanied by only three attendants, had gone to Spain to try to bring about a match with the Infanta.

Not only had the King of Spain, but King James also, as well as Buckingham, sent messengers to Rome to induce the Pope (Gregory XV.) to grant a dispensation for the "mixed marriage." His holiness had refused to grant it unless the King of England would relieve the Catholics in his own country from the pressure of the penal laws. This James consented to do, and he gave orders to Lord Keeper Williams, Bishop of Lincoln, to grant pardons under the great seal to such Catholic recusants as should be able and willing to give security for their appearance if required. He also promised, on the word of a king, that, provided mass was said only in private houses, Catholics should practise their religion unmolested in his kingdom.

Unfortunately, King James had made use of an expression, in a certain theological treatise, which was not likely to incline the Holy Father to look very favourably upon the marriage of a Catholic princess with his son. He had called the Pope Antichrist! In this dilemma, Laud came to the rescue, by suggesting that James should excuse himself by pretending that he had merely used the term "argumentatively," "as a man might say."

When the Spanish expedition became known in England, it was commonly thought that it would lead to the conversion to the Catholic faith of the heir to the British throne. It was reported that Laud had been privy to the project of the expedition from the first, and that he had been the author of the king's quasi-retraction of his Pope-Antichrist theory. A strong feeling set in against him in consequence, and his list of enemies was greatly increased from that time.

The prince and Buckingham had not started more than four days before Laud wrote a letter to the latter, and, shortly afterwards, he received one from Buckingham. It is a little difficult to reconcile his exceeding Anglicanism with his

complacency at the proposed marriage of the heir apparent
to the English crown with a Papist, especially when we
consider that he aided and abetted it by attempting to
extricate the king from his difficulty about that unlucky
"Antichrist" remark.   Perhaps the fury of his enemy,
Abbott, on the other side may have had something to do
with his zeal in promoting it.   Indeed, nothing could well
have been stronger than Abbott's exhortation to the king, in
giving him advice directly opposite to that of Laud.

"By your act," he wrote, "you labour to set up that most
damnable and heretical doctrine of the church of Rome."
This was pretty strong language for a subject to use to a
monarch, nor very likely to please him! "You show yourself," he went on, "a patron of those doctrines which your
conscience tells yourself are superstitious, idolatrous, and
detestable.   Add to this what you have done in sending your
son into Spain, without the consent of your council or the
privity of your people" (and, still worse, with the consent
and the privity of that abominable Laud, he no doubt added
mentally).   "Believe it, sir, howsoever his return may be
safe, yet the drawers of him to that action will not pass
away unquestioned, unpunished."   (That Laud was in his
mind when he wrote this, can scarcely be doubted, and must
have been apparent to the king.)   "Besides," he continued,
"this toleration which you endeavour to set up by proclamation, it cannot be done without a parliament, unless your majesty will let your subjects see, that you will take to yourself
a liberty to throw down the laws of your land at pleasure."[1]

On reading such a letter as this, it would be only natural
in the king, to contrast the conduct of the two bishops in
the matter ; nor is it unlikely that he would show the angry
letter of the Archbishop of Canterbury to the Bishop of St
David's, and the scene that would then be likely to follow
can easily be imagined.

Uninfluenced by the tirade of his archbishop, King James
made Buckingham a duke during his absence, sent jewels,
officers, and chaplains (probably of Laud's choosing) to

---

[1] Rushworth, p. 85.

Prince Charles, and promised not only to keep the proceedings of the adventurers from the knowledge of his Council,
but to ratify any treaty they might make with the Spanish
minister.[1] " The king," wrote Chamberlain, " keeps all close,
and burns the letters as fast as he reads them." [2]   In another
letter he wrote to Carleton :—" The Prince's servants and
chaplains are to follow him with chapel furniture, Latin
prayer-books, &c. The service is to be performed in Latin, and
the Communion celebrated with wafer cakes and wine and
water."   Does not this sound very like a suggestion of
Laud's ? Most certainly it would not be Abbott's ! " But,"
goes on Chamberlain, " it will be to no purpose, as the
Spaniards will not come near." [3]   I hope I may not be thought
irrelevant in noticing an allusion in one of these two letters
to another marriage, as it is a curiosity.   " Sir Hen. Fiennes,
half-brother to the late Earl of Berkshire, is fined £2000, for
contracting a marriage, *de futuro*, before his wife's death."

There was one element which the king overlooked, or of
which he may have been ignorant, and that was the mutual
and extreme jealousy between Buckingham and Digby, Earl
of Bristol and English Ambassador at the court of Spain.
This did much to hamper the negotiations, which were further
complicated by the artifices of the Spanish Minister, Olivarez,
and delayed by the death of the Pope.

Nevertheless, an agreement that " the marriage should be
celebrated in Spain, and afterwards ratified in England ; that
the children should remain till the age of ten years under the
care of their mother ; that the infanta and her servants should
possess a church and chapel for the free use of their religion ;
and that her chaplains should be Spaniards living under
canonical obedience to their own bishop," [4] was eventually
signed by King James and the Lords of the Council, including
Archbishop Abbott, in spite of his letter.   " Now I must tell
you miracles," said the king ; " our great primate hath
behaved himself wonderfully well." [5] James alone signed, also,

---

[1] Hardwicke Papers, 410, 417, 419.   [2] " Cal. Sta. Pa.," 1619-23, p. 585.
[3] *Ib.*, p. 554.   [4] Lingard's " Hist. of Eng.," vol. vii. chap. iii.
[5] Har. Papers, i. 428.

a private treaty, in the house of the Spanish Ambassador, before four witnesses.

During his absence, Buckingham's enemies in England were not idle. Laud wrote to tell his friend that cabals were being formed against him. In Spain, his quarrels with both Bristol and Olivarez made his position odious. Political questions connected with the Palatinate, again, hindered the marriage, as James and Charles were asking the King of Spain to help to restore it to Frederick, and on the 5th of October, Prince Charles and Buckingham returned from their fruitless errand. "*Oct. 6, Munday*," wrote Laud, "they came to *London*. The greatest expression of Joy by all sorts of People, that I ever saw."

Weary of the delays and intrigues at the court of Spain, Prince Charles had left Madrid, and, on the point of setting sail from the coast of Spain, he had written a declaration to the effect that unless King Philip would make good terms with regard to the Palatinate, he would not become his son-in-law.[1] After his return, too, King James said that he "liked not to marry his son with a portion of his daughter's tears."

Laud continued to rise in the royal favour. On the other hand, we read, in a letter from Chamberlain, that "on Christmas Day, the Bishop of London's sermon, probably from its length, displeased the King, and he grew so loud that the Bishop was obliged to end abruptly."[2] In the meantime, King James had been putting a bridle on "the abuses and extravagances of preachers." "None below the degree of Dean" were "to enter on the deep points of election or universal redemption, &c." "None" were "to fall into invectives against either Puritans or Papists." "All transgressors of these directions to be suspended."[3] So arbitrary was the king to his clergy, that, when Prince Charles had gone to Spain, he imprisoned a clergyman for praying for his safe return as if there could possibly be any question, or need of prayers, on the subject.[4]

---

[1] Green's "Lives of the Princesses of Eng.," vol. v. p. 415.
[2] "Cal. Sta. Pa. Dom.," 1619-23, p. 479.　　　　[3] *Ib.*, pp. 436, 437.
[4] Green's "Eng. Princesses," vol. v. p. 405.

CHAPTER IX.

SHORTLY before the return to England of Prince Charles and Buckingham, Laud discovered that Williams, the Lord Keeper, was very jealous of his friendship with the last named, and that he had done him some "very ill offices."[1] A few days after the newly-made duke had come home, he wrote :—"I acquainted my Lord Duke of *Buckingham* with that which passed between the Lord Keeper and me." How much this quarrel preyed on his mind is shown by his mentioning in his Diary that he "did Dream" about it. Several entries follow concerning his disagreements with him, and early in the following year is one :—"My Lord Keeper met with me in the with-drawing-Chamber, and quarrelled me *gratis*."[2] This evidently depressed him ; for four days later, he wrote :—"It was *Sunday*. I was alone, and languishing with I know not what sadness. I was much concerned at the Envy and undeserved Hatred born to me by the Lord Keeper." Within a month, however, the quarrel was patched up. "*Februar.* 18, my Lord Duke of *Buckingham* told me of the Reconciliation and Submission of my Lord Keeper ; and that it was confessed unto him, that his Favour to me was a chief Cause. *Invidia quo tendis ? &c. At ille de novo fœdus pepigit.*" And a month later he wrote :—"Lord Keeper his Complementing with me."[3]

Williams's knowledge that he could ill afford to make enemies just at that particular time may have led him to make the reconciliation. Sir Francis Englefield had accused him of bribery. It is true that for this, Englefield had been fined £3000 in the Star Chamber ;[4] but it was not the only charge against him. There was also an

[1] Diary, p. 7. [2] *Ib.*, p. 8.
[3] *Ib.*, p. 10. [4] "Cal. Sta. Pa. Dom.," 1623-5, p. 165.

accusation of a false judgment in Chancery,[1] and Nethersole wrote that Lady Darcy's case was "embarrasing, the House being distracted what to do with the Lord Keeper."[2] Yet he was striving to the best of his ability to please James and Buckingham, and when efforts were being made to "rate the subsidies high, the Lord Keeper said, that for any man to disguise his wealth was to sin against the Holy Ghost, like Ananias and Sapphira."[3]

Laud's quarrel with Williams was scarcely made up before he got into another; indeed Williams was partly the cause of it.

The members of Convocation had been subsidising the king to the extent of one fifth of their incomes. On Holy Saturday, Laud went to his friend, Buckingham, and represented to him how terrible was this tax to many clergymen with small incomes, and he obtained from him a gracious promise of redress. Delighted at this, on Easter Monday he went to Williams and told him what he had said to Buckingham, and with how favourable a result. Williams replied that "it was the best Office that was done the Church this Seven Years. And so said my Lord of Durham."[4] Then Williams, and the Bishop of Durham also, persuaded Laud to go to Abbott and tell him the good news. Now, as after events proved, Williams loved Laud little better now than when they had been quarrelling, and it is not impossible that he may have suggested to him that he should do this, with a view to getting him into hot water. He was a shrewd, clever man, and he may have been already aware of Abbott's views on the subject. Here is Laud's own account of what actually happened. "His Grace was very angry. Asked, what I had to do to make any Suit for the Church. Told me, never any Bishop attempted the like at any time, nor would any but my self have done it. That I had given the Church such a wound, in speaking to any Lord of the Laity about it, as I could never make whole again. That if my Lord Duke did fully understand what I had done; he would

[1] "Cal. Sta. Pa. Dom.," 1623-5, p. 171.　　　[2] *Ib.*, p. 246.
[3] *Ib.*, p. 292. Chamberlain.　　　[4] Diary, p. 11.

never indure me to come near him again. I answered: I
thought I had done a very good Office for the Church;
and so did my Betters think. If his Grace thought otherwise, I was sorry I had offended him. And I hoped, being
done out of a good Mind, for the support of many poor
Vicars abroad in the Country, who must needs sink under
Three Subsidies in a Year, my Error (if it were one) was
pardonable."[1] The following addition is significant:—"I went
to my Lord Duke, and acquainted him with it; lest I might
have ill Offices done me for it, to the *King* and the *Prince.*"

Within a couple of months he was visiting Buckingham
for a very different purpose, namely to sit up with him during
an illness. This was apparently a sort of seizure, or succession of seizures, of some kind. One "was the first Fit, that
he could be perswaded to take orderly." Two days later,
"he took his Fit very orderly."[2] Another night, "My Lord
Duke of *Buckingham* missed his Fit." Perhaps one would
scarcely have expected a gay courtier like Buckingham to
have selected Laud for a sick nurse, highly as he seemed
to respect him as a confessor and a theologian; but the
weary nights thus spent together would greatly increase
their intimacy.

I may mention that, on the Good Friday of the same year,
Laud was much scandalised at Lord Mansfield's having
tilted on that day. "With the shock of the meeting, his
Horse, weaker or resty, tumbled over and over, and brake
his own neck in the place; the Lord had no great harm.
Should not this day have other Imployment?"[3] He, himself, also received a slight injury from a horse, a few months
later. "My Horse trod on my foot, and lamed me: which
stayed me in the Country a week longer than I intended."[4]
Less than three weeks earlier, he complains of something
worse—"My passion by Blood, and my fear of a Stone, &c."
In the same year, he also mentions a riding accident to
a greater person than either himself or Lord Mansfield:—
"Prince *Charles* his grievous fall, which he had in hunting."[5]

---

[1] Diary, p. 11.   [2] *Ib.*, p. 12.   [3] *Ib.*, p. 11.

            [4] *Ib.*   [5] *Ib.*, p. 13.

Reverting to his own ills, he writes in October:—"*Sunday,*
I fell at Night *in Passionem Iliacam;* which had almost put
me into a Fever. I continued ill fourteen days."[1] Shortly
before this he had gone "to lye and keep House, and Preach,"[2]
at the livings which he held *in commendam.*

Laud was not the only bishop accused of Popish inclinations and practices. In the same year "a complaint is made
against the Bp. of Norwich for forbidding all preaching on
Sunday forenoons in the 32 churches there, and confining
it to the cathedral, which will not hold a fourth of the
usual hearers, and for other things tending to Popery."[3]
And again, "Sir Edw. Coke reported the accusations brought
in the House of Commons against the Bp. of Norwich, viz.,"
"excommunication of persons for not turning their faces to
the east in praying, which is a usurpation of Papal power,"
"and his excommunication of seven persons for attending a
private catechetical meeting held by a clergyman, whom he
compelled to acknowledge himself wrong in holding it. He
is suspected of inclining to Popery."[4] It is well to observe
that this was before any evidence appears of similar stringency
on the part of Laud. Nor was this ecclesiastical policy
without royal favour. "The Lord Keeper will not have the
King's speech at the breaking up of Parliament published,
on account of some passages not very pleasing relative to
the Puritans, whom he accused of careless traducing of the
Bp. of Norwich."[5]

The conversation in the ante-chambers of great personages
was a not inconsiderable feature in political life in Laud's
days, as in later. Early in January 1625, Laud, while
waiting for an audience of the Duke of Buckingham, "fell
in speech with"[6] Secretary Calvert "about some differences
between the *Greek* and the *Roman* Church." As I have already
had occasion to remark, so long ago as this, Anglicans seem
to have looked for countenance, if not for intercommunion,
in the East. "Then also, and there," continues Laud, "a

---

[1] Diary.   [2] *Ib.*
[3] Nethersole to Carleton. "Cal. Sta. Pa. Dom.," 1623-5, p. 238.
[4] *Ib.*, p. 246.   [5] *Ib.*, p. 267. Locke to Carleton.   [6] Diary, p. 14.

Young Man, that took on him to be a *Frenchman*, fell into discourse about the Church of *England*. He grew at last earnest for the *Roman* Church ; but *Tibi dabo claves*, and *Pasce oves :* was all he said, save that he would shew this proposition in *St Augustin, Romana Ecclesia facta est caput omnium Ecclesiarum ab instante mortis Christi.* I believe he was a Priest ; but he wore a lock down to his shoulders." Evidently, the momentous passages quoted by this French-man conveyed little idea of their import to the mind of Laud.

One of the first things that would strike a casual reader of Laud's Diary would be the trouble he took to record his dreams and the importance which he attached to them. A specimen of these occurs in the Diary in the month from which I have just made a quotation. It runs :—"*Januar.* 30. *Sunday* Night, my Dream of my Blessed Lord and Saviour *Jesus Christ.* One of the most comfortable passages that ever I had in my Life." As a rule, on the contrary, his dreams were singularly devoid of " comfortable passages ;" things were always going wrong in them, from small ones, such as that he was going to marry someone and could not find the marriage service in his book, to regular howling nightmares. Indeed, on reading the frequent notices of horrible dreams in his Diaries, one wishes that peaceful sleep could have been invoked for the restless (and probably bilious) little bishop, in the words of his own contemporaries, Beaumont and Fletcher :—

> " Care-charming Sleep, thou easer of all woes,
> Brother to Death, sweetly thyself dispose,
> On this afflicted " (Laud). " Fall like a cloud
> In gentle showers ; give nothing that is loud
> Or painful to his slumbers ; easy, light,
> And as a purling stream thou son of night
> Pass by his troubled senses ; sing his pain,
> Like hollow-murmuring wind or silver rain !
> Into this " (Laud) " gently, oh gently slide,
> And kiss him into slumbers like a bride."

They might have written them on purpose for him !
There was certainly a strong element of superstition in

his character.   Some of the entries in his Diary incline
one to fancy that he may have even half-believed in
astrology.

" May 1, E. B. Marryed.   The Sign in Pisces." [1]

Some readers consider the following to have been looked
on as a mysterious and solemn portent :—" *Aug.* 25. *Friday*,
Two Robin red-breasts flew together through the Door into
my Study, as if one pursued the other.   That sudden motion
almost startled me.   I was then preparing a Sermon on
Ephes. 4, 30, and Studying." [2]   And in the year 1628 there
seems a suspicion of celestial augury in :—" January 30.
Wednesday, My Lord Duke of *Buckingham's* Son was born,
the Lord *George* : New Moon *die* 26."   In 1636 he wrote :—
" Octob. 14, *Friday* Night, I Dreamed marvelously, that the
King was offended with me, and would cast me off, and tell
me no cause why.   *Avertat Deus.*   For Cause I have given
none."   In October 1640, the only thing he thought worth
recording in his Diary for twelve days, was :—*Oct.* 27, *Tuesday*, *Simon* and *Jude's* Eve, I went into my upper Study, to
see some Manuscripts, which I was sending to *Oxford.*   In
that Study hung my Picture, taken by the Life ; and coming
in, I found it fallen down upon the Face, and lying on the
Floor, the String broken, by which it was hanged against the
Wall.   I am almost every day threatened with my Ruine in
Parliament.   God grant this be no Omen." [3]   In 1642, he
recorded a dream in which he thought he saw his old college
in ruins, and he added :—" God be merciful." [4]

It naturally strikes a Catholic as somewhat singular that
a religious-minded man, with a tendency to give credit to
supernatural agencies acting through the medium of natural
objects, especially a man living so near the times when his
own country was Catholic, and himself claiming many of the
practices and ceremonies of Catholics for his own Church, nay
even maintaining that that Church was identical with the
Church which had prevailed in England before the Reformation, should apparently have placed no faith in any efficacy
of relics, blessed objects, or communion with saints.   Accord-

[1] Diary, p. 12.   [2] *Ib.*, p. 35.   [3] *Ib.*, p. 39.   [4] *Ib.*, p. 64.

ing to him, the sign of pisces might possibly influence a
wedding, but not so the prayer of a saint in heaven; he
thinks much of a couple of cock-robins flying into his room,
yet pays no heed to guardian angels; and he regards the fall
of a picture, through the two very natural causes of the wearing away of a string by pressure and the force of gravitation
as a sign from heaven.

We now come to an historical event which had a considerable influence upon the career of Laud. "*Anno* 1625. *March
27. Midlent* Sunday, I Preached at *White-hall.* I ascended the
Pulpit, much troubled, and in a very melancholy moment;
the Report then spreading, that his Majesty King *James*, of
most Sacred Memory to me, was Dead. Being interrupted
with the dolours of the Duke of *Buckingham*, I broke off
my Sermon in the middle. The King died at *Theobalds*
about three quarters of an hour past Eleven in the forenoon. He breathed forth his Blessed Soul most Religiously,
and with great constancy of Faith, and Courage. . . .
The King fell Sick, *March* 4, on *Friday.* The Disease
appeared to be a Tertian Ague. But I fear it was the Gout,
which by the wrong application of Medicines, was driven
from his feet to his inward vital parts."[1] A *post-mortem*
was made with a view to ascertaining the true cause of
his death, and the verdict of the experts was that his head
" was very full of braines; but his blood was wonderfully
tainted with melancholy."[2]

It may, perhaps, be expected that I should say a good
deal concerning the monarch who first admitted Laud to his
court, and, to some extent also, to his intimacy; but I will
content myself by quoting the following description of him.
"He was of a middle stature, more corpulent throghe his
clothes than in his bodey, yet fatt enough: his clothes
ever being made large and easie, the doubletts quilted for
stiletto proofe, his breeches in grate pleits, and full stuffed.
He was naturally of a timorous disposition, which was
the gratest reasone of his quilted doublets. His eyes
large, ever roulling after any stranger cam in his presence,

---

[1] Diary, p. 15.　　　[2] Harleian MSS., 389; Ellis's " Letters," ccciv.

in so much as maney for shame have left the roome, as
being out of countenance. His beard was wercy thin ;
his toung too large for his mouthe, and made him drinke
wercy vncomlie, as if eatting his drinke, wich cam out into
the cupe in each syde of his mouthe. His skin vas als softe
as tafta sarsnet, wich felt so because he never washt his
hands, onlie rubb'd his fingers ends slightly vith the vett
end of a napkin. His legs wer vercy weake . . . he was
not able to stand at sevin zeires of age ; that weaknes made
him euer leaning on other men's shoulders." [1]

Although James brought Laud forward and made him a
bishop, it is doubtful whether he thoroughly trusted him.
It is difficult to know what value should be set upon his
conversation with Williams, recorded in a previous chapter ;
but it is certain that for a long time after he had made Laud
a royal chaplain, he did nothing further for him. King
James acted as if it was his place to teach and not to learn
from his clergy, and, fond as he was of indecent buffoonery,
he prided himself upon his knowledge of theology and canon
law. After a fashion, too, he was able and learned—"the
wisest fool in Europe," as the Duke of Sully called him.
His death rather helped than hindered both the ecclesiastical
and political progress of Laud, as we shall see in due course.
He may have been "of most sacred memory to" Laud ; but
so shrewd a man could scarcely have failed to form a fairly
accurate judgment of his far from noble character. Until
his acquaintance with Laud, James had held views which
were a mixture of High-Churchism with Calvinism, and
Laud partially succeeded in eliminating the latter element ;
in short, King James relinquished Calvinism and adopted a
sort of quasi-Arminianism.

Laud may not have found it a very arduous task to convince
King James of the error of the Calvinistic theory that "the
Church" is an independent body, having ample powers of
self-legislation, and yielding no privilege to princes except
that of protecting it. Equally easy would it be to persuade
a king, who loved the power of Church patronage, that the

[1] Balfour, ii. 108.

doctrine that all the clergy are of equal rank and authority is a heresy. James would be pretty certain to consider himself excepted from Calvin's dogma that no man can merit through his own works, although he might cordially approve of the doctrine that if the predestinated, such as himself for instance, fell into sin, they could not be damned. From a logical point of view, Laud might soon induce James, who was intelligent enough in many respects, to adopt the theory of Arminius that predestination consists in the foreknowledge of God, from the creation of the world, of the conduct of every individual that should ever be born ; as well as several other Arminian doctrines which had much in common with those of the Catholic Church ; such as that Christ died for all men ; but that only the faithful should be saved ; that all good works are attributable to the Holy Spirit, which nevertheless does not force men to perform them without their own free will ; and that God will give the truly faithful grace to resist sin.

It ought to be carefully remembered that the Arminian doctrines in the time of King James should not be confused with certain developments of Arminianism which began some five years after his death ; the latter chiefly took the direction of building the hope of salvation mainly on morality and good works ; the theory that everyone had a right to interpret Scripture for himself, even to the extent of what is now called free thought, and a denial of the necessity of any help from the Holy Spirit.

Laud was often called an Arminian, and in one sense he may have deserved the name ; for we should not forget that most modern High-Churchmen hold views which would have been called Arminian in the latter part of the reign of James I.; whereas a few years later, when he eagerly repudiated the title, Arminianism implied doctrines which most Anglicans would now condemn as heterodox. Due allowance for this fact is not, perhaps, always made by those who maintain that Laud introduced and encouraged Arminianism in this country, although in the sense of the teaching of Arminius himself, it may be true that "the Arminian system has very much prevailed in England since the time of Archbishop Laud."[1]

It may not be altogether unworthy of mention here that, in the very year of King James's death, died also Maurice, Prince of Orange, a great patron of the Calvinists, who had driven the Arminians out of Holland, and that after his decease they were readmitted and began to build churches in that country, as well as a college at Amsterdam.

To the English Puritans, everything that was not extreme Calvinism was Arminianism, and they were exceedingly jealous of the High-Church clergy, who held views opposed to their own, and yet enjoyed influential favour. When asked what the Arminians held, a divine replied :—" All the best bishoprics and deaneries in England."[2] The Calvinists went further, and asserted that the Catholics encouraged Arminianism among the English in order to draw them towards the Church ; but it is improbable that they took the trouble, and pretty certain that they had not the opportunity, of so doing ; although it is likely enough that they would prefer the increase of Arminian doctrines to that of Calvinistic ; much as modern Catholics, on the whole, are gratified at the spread of certain Catholic doctrines and practises among the Anglicans, because they hope that some of those who adopt them may be dissatisfied until they have accepted the whole teaching of the Catholic Church ; as has already happened in very many instances. In the well-known clumsy forgery called " A letter founde amongst some Jesuites, lately taken at Clerkenwell, London, directed to the Father Rector at Bruxelles," of which there are many copies, the writer is made to say :—" Nowe wee have planted that soveraigne drug Arminianisme, which wee hope will purge the Protestants from their heresie, and flourishe and beare fruyte in due season." By the Puritans, in fact, Catholicism and Arminianism were classed together ; thus we find an entry in the *Whiteway Diary*, in the British Museum :—" 20th Jany. 1629. This day the Parliament

---

[1] " Ency. Brit.," vol. iii. p. 617, 8th Ed.
[2] Macaulay's " Hist.," vol. i. chap. i.

met again at Westminster . . . The House resolved to settle religion and to provide for the Suppression of Popery and Arminianism before they could conclude any other business."

Except that the two words were without the convenient alliteration of Ritualism and Romanism, Arminianism and Catholicism were coupled together by the extreme Low-Church party in Laud's times quite as glibly as the same party couples the two former "isms" in our own—to the disgust of the professors of both ; but I have never been able to find, in any seventeenth century writings, traces of the better-be-one-thing-or-the-other tone, so often used by old-fashioned Protestants when speaking of Ritualists in these days ; nor have I met with the case of an Anglican in Laud's times, saying :—" Well, after all, I am glad he is a Catholic and not one of those damned Arminians," as I have known one to say in my own, with the last word altered for Ritualist.

CHAPTER X.

THERE can be little doubt that Mr Gardiner is correct in saying that with "the accession of Charles I., Laud's real predominance in the Church of England began." On the fourth day of the new reign, a command from the king was delivered by the Lord Chamberlain (Pembroke) to Laud, to prepare a sermon to be preached before his Majesty and the House of Lords, and, on the eighth, Laud delivered to Buckingham, at his request, "a Schedule, in which were wrote the Names of many Church-Men, marked with the Letters O. and P.," of which O. stood for Orthodox, and P. for Puritan. "The Duke of *Buckingham* had commanded to digest their Names in that method; that (as himself said) he might deliver them to King *Charles.*"[1] This, of course, would be with a view to future preferment and its contrary. All, however, was not secure; for the duke informed Laud that a certain person had "blackened" his name to the king, reminding him of the little bishop's former misdemeanour in going through the form of marriage between the Earl of Devonshire and a divorced woman twenty years earlier. Nevertheless, this blackening process seems to have done Laud no great harm; for, on the very day that he heard of it, he received a royal command to go to Andrews, Bishop of Winchester, "and learn from him, what he would have done in the Cause of the Church; and bring back his answer, especially in the matter of the *Five Articles, &c.*"[2] After fulfilling this order, he went with Andrews to the country-house "which *John* Lord Bishop of *Rochester* hath by *Bromley.*"[3] They "Dined there; and returned in the Evening." As I have already said, Andrews had at least

---

[1] Diary, p. 16.   [2] *Ib.*   [3] *Ib.*, p. 18.

as much claim to be considered the founder of modern
High-Churchism as Laud.

"Auricular confession," says D'Israeli, "however condemned as a point of Popery, was still adhered to by
many."[1]   And he goes on to say that "Bishop Andrews
would loiter in the aisles of Paul's to afford his spiritual
comfort to the unburtheners of their conscience."   Perhaps
no Anglican ecclesiastic was more of one mind with Laud,
and judging from the way in which he speaks of him, it is
probable that Laud was more influenced by Andrews than
by any other theologian except his first tutor at Oxford.
He calls him "*Lancelot Andrews*, the most worthy Bishop of
Winchester, the great Light of the *Christian* World."[2]

Three weeks after the accession of Charles I., a piece of
good fortune threw Laud into greater intimacy with him.
This was the fact of "the Bishop of *Durham* being Sick," on
which occasion, at that bishop's own desire, he was appointed
"to wait upon his Majesty in the quality of Clark of the
Closet," until his recovery.   In the meantime the grave and
the gay were being freely intermingled.

On "*May* 7. *Saturday*, we Celebrated the Funeral of King
James."[3]   On the 1st of that month, the Duke of Bucking-
ham had started " early in the morning " and " in great haste "
" towards the Sea-side, to pass over into *France* to meet
Queen *Mary ;* " and on the 11th, " the Marriage " (by proxy
of course) " was Celebrated at *Paris*, between his Majesty
King *Charles*, and the most Illustrious Princess *Henrietta
Maria* of *France*, Daughter of Henry IV."

" Sir George Goringe," says an old letter, " hath sent
her divers of our Common Prayer Books, in French, which
some suppose to give hope of her conversion ; but others
much doubt it, she having a Bishop and twenty-eight Priests,
resolute Papists, as are all her servants ? "[4]

Within three weeks, Laud tells us, " King *Charles* set
forward toward *Canterbury*, to meet the Queen," and twelve
days later still, " it was *Trinity Sunday*, Queen *Mary* cross-

[1] " Life and Reign of Charles I.," vol. i. p. 162.   [2] Diary, p. 36.
[3] *Ib.*, p. 17.   [4] Harleian MSS., 389 ; Ellis's " Letters," cccvii.

ing the Seas, Landed upon our Shore about Seven a Clock
in the Evening. God grant, that she may be an Evening
and an Happy Star to our Orb." He was never at his best
when he tried to be poetical!

Laud makes no mention of the facts that the marriage had
been celebrated by the Cardinal of Rochefoucault on a
platform before the large doors of the Cathedral of Paris,[1]
and that the contract was repeated in the great hall at
Canterbury; this arrangement would certainly annoy him,
as he would naturally wish the marriage to be performed
with the full rites of his own Church in the Cathedral at
Canterbury, if at Canterbury it was to be ; but he describes
the arrival in London with some detail.

"*June* 16. *Thursday,* the King and Queen came to *London.*
They arrived at Court at five a Clock. It was ill weather, and
the day cloudy." (There was a heavy thunderstorm, say other
writers.) "When they came by the *Tower* of *London* (for
they came by water instead of coach)," each in "green suits,"[2]
he might have added, "the King led out the Queen to the
outside of the Barge, that she might see the People and the
City. But at the same time, a violent shower of Rain falling
down, forced them both to return into the inward part of the
Barge. The shower continued, until they had entred *White-
Hall;* and then ceased."[3] Those of us who make hay know
only too well how it can rain in this country during "leafy
June;" but for that matter, so it can in Paris and its neighbourhood, therefore the new queen may not have been much
surprised at the "ill weather." Laud does not mention that
on the queen's entrance to London certain people got
drenched through another cause than rain, one of the barges
bearing spectators having been upset for want of ballast,
thus immersing above a hundred persons in the waters of
the Thames.

A couple of days after the royal entry, Laud mentions "the
Pestilence, which then began to be very rife," in consequence
of which "the King omitted the pomp usual upon" the day

[1] Somers's Tracts, iv. 95 ; and Balfour, ii. 119-25.

[2] Harleian MSS., 389 ; Ellis's "Letters," cccxiii.   [3] Diary, p. 19.

of the opening of Parliament, "lest the conflux of People
should be of ill consequence"; and Laud's sermon, which was
to have been "Preached in *Westminster* Abbey at the
beginning of this Session," was delivered instead on the
following day, "in the Chappel at *White-Hall.*" He writes
that at the opening of Parliament there was a French and, of
course, Catholic, Bishop, present, "who Attended the Queen."
It is almost impossible that Laud can have looked upon
him with other than jealous eyes.

In consequence of the pestilence, the king and queen left
London and went to Hampton Court, where they practically
passed their honeymoon. "The King," says Laud, "Commanded the Archbishop of *Canterbury*, with six other
Bishops, whom he Named, to advise together concerning a
Publick Fast, and a Form of Prayer, to implore the Divine
Mercy, now that the Pestilence began to spread, and the
extraordinary wet weather threatened a Famine."[1] Laud was
one of the bishops selected. He records that in one week
there died at "London 1222 Persons." No wonder, then,
that he was glad to get out of the plague-stricken city:
he writes, "I went into the Country, to the House of my
good Friend *Francis Windebank.*" This future Secretary of
State had become a favourite of Laud's when he was an
undergraduate at St John's, Oxford, and he was to owe to
Laud, in a great measure, the rapid advancement which
was so soon to fall to his share.

After a couple of days' stay with Windebank, Laud went
on to Windsor, "to perform some Businesses committed to"
his "trust by the Right Reverend Bishop of Durham."
"The Court was there at that time." He returned that night
to Windebank's, and went to Windsor again two days afterwards, and "stood by the King at Dinner-time; Some
Matters of Philosophy were the subject of the Discourse."
The same evening, he says:—"I Eat in the House of the
Bishop of *Gloucester.*" We saw lately that the queen had her
bishop with her, and the king may have thought it well to be
protected by bishops of his own! "The next day one of the

---

[1] Diary, p. 20.

Bishops Servants, who had waited at Table, was seized with the Plague. God be merciful to me and the rest." [1]   He was glad to go back to Windebank's that evening, having a swelled leg, as to the cause of which he was uncertain, but inclined to the opinion that it might have been brought about "by the biting of Buggs."   To find such fellow-visitors in a royal palace seemed hard ; but Laud would probably look with suspicion upon the members of the queen's French retinue, and think that the presence of the " Buggs " could easily be accounted for.   On the twentieth of July was the public fast, and Laud preached that day, and also on the following Sunday, at Windebank's parish church of Hurst.

If Laud experienced no sensations of jealousy at the presence of a real bishop and priests at the English court, he must have been more than human.   Most trying of all must it have been to him when the news reached him that King Charles had actually attended mass—if indeed he ever did so ; I quote from a small book [2] published in the middle of the seventeenth century—" He had been publickly seen at mass " it states, "at *Somerset* house thinking to have gul'd the world, when he was placed in the Queen's Lobby." "At length in comes the Earle of *Dorset* with a just indigna-tion, not reflecting on *None-Such Charles* as on a Prince ; and faining not to heed his quality kept his hat on, and hardly taking it off, hee said (as if it had bin to some indifferent person) *God save you Sir, you have this morning forfeited fifteen shillings : Why* Dorset, said the King, *doe you speake in such termes ?*   To which *Dorset* answered; *the fifteen shillings Sir, make three Crowns, which you have forfeited, and your three Kingdomes to boote, by your having been seen at Masse, where of there are a thousand witnesses : For that all the whole congregation saw you, and know it, and thus have you publickly transgressed against the Fundamentall Laws of your Land.*   For the which that Lord was put into the Courts black-book."

Everyone who could had left London, on account of the plague, and the Parliament was to meet at Oxford.   Laud

---

[1] Diary, p. 21.   [2] "None-Such Charles, his Character," p. 131.

also went thither from Windebank's, on the Friday. On the Sunday, he was in the parlour of the President's lodging at his old College of St John's, when he suddenly fell down, how he did not know, and hurt his left shoulder and hip. I think that a modern doctor would infer, from his own description of his tumble, that it must have been caused by a fainting fit, or a vertigo of some sort. At least one other fall that he had in after life also sounds as if it had proceeded from some such attack, and it seems not unlikely that if he had not been executed, he might have died of apoplexy.

Parliament was opened at Oxford the next day, and immediately "a great assault was made" in it against the Duke of Buckingham, a thing that would be highly displeasing, if not alarming, to Laud. In twelve days, however, "the Parliament was dissolved; the *Commons* not hearkening, as was expected, to the King's proposals." This was the beginning of discontent and troubles, but they were not to reach their climax for many years to come. Laud told the truth in saying that the Parliament was dissolved because it would not listen to the king's proposals, but the appearance of the pestilence at Oxford was made the ostensible pretext.

The session, which may be said to have begun in London and ended at Oxford, was rendered stormy by other causes besides the refusal of the Commons to grant the subsidies demanded by the king. One was "a pious petition" presented by the House to the king, imploring him to put into immediate execution the existing laws against all Catholic priests and recusants. As his Majesty had but just married a Catholic princess, such a petition, however pious, was neither graceful nor well-timed, especially as he had bound himself by a treaty to be indulgent within his realms to those of his wife's faith, and his palace was at that moment crowded with Catholic noblemen from France. He was prudent enough, however, to give as gracious an answer as circumstances permitted.

Another bone of contention in the House of Commons was a book written by Dr Montagu. As this was a matter in which Laud was mixed up, I shall dwell on it at some length, and, although it will oblige me to anticipate (and to look back, also, for that matter), I will dispose of it altogether while I am about it.

In the reign of James, Richard Montagu, Chaplain in Ordinary to the king, Fellow of Eton, and Canon of Windsor, had been also Rector of Stanford-Rivers in Essex. Not very far from his rectory, stood by itself in a lonely field a house which, after having been long un-occupied, was taken by a stranger of whom none of the neighbours seemed to know anything. By day, the building, to all appearances, might still have been untenanted, but at night figures were occasionally observed going to or from the house. By degrees, it was whispered that the mysterious old place had several residents, and that these were Jesuits, who were attempting to make converts in the surrounding country.[1]

Montagu, who was a High-Churchman and fond of con-troversy, by some means intimated to the inhabitants of the lonely grange that he knew who and what manner of men they were, and that he would be delighted to dispute with them about religion, adding that, if they could convince him, he would strike his flag and join their Church.

In a short time, a little pamphlet, entitled *A New Gag for an Old Gospel* was dropped in the night through his study window, with a note, begging for a reply, attached to it.

Finding that the pamphlet attacked, not the High-Church party to which he belonged, but Calvinism, or, at any rate the Calvinistic element in Anglicanism, and represented that Calvinistic element to be the orthodox religion of the Church of England as by law established, Montagu was as furious as a modern Puseyite might have been if a Catholic priest had attacked him for holding the most extreme evangelical views. He wrote a lengthy reply, which King James advised him to publish, and it appeared, in due course, under the title of *The Gagger Gagged.*

[1] Benson, p. 75.

Nothing could possibly have been more anti-Catholic. Its very title-page is enough to prove this. "A Gagg for a new Gospell? No: A new Gagg for an old Goose, who would needes undertake to stop all Protestant mouths for ever, with 276 places out of their owne English Bibles, or An Answer to a late Abridger of Countrouversies and Belyar of the Protestants Doctrine." He writes about the "jugling tricks" and the "puppet playes" at "Lauretto." "As for Miracles, Visions, and such Hobgoblin Stuffe, I am contented you appropriate for your owne." He addresses the author of the opposition pamphlet as "Silly Man," and tells him things which are "enough to shame you, if you be not past grace of shame." "I have discovered," he says, "your false play," "your cousening trick," and your "ridiculous interpretation"; and he politely adds:—"If I have any occasion hereafter to speake of learned and moderate men, I will except you and yours." As to the "Councels of Trent, of Florence, of Lateran," he considered them of no more authority than the "synods of Gapp and Dort."

Strange to say, it was not with the Catholics, but with the Puritans that this book was to get its author into trouble. His repudiation of Calvinist doctrines gave intense annoyance to their many ardent professors among the Anglicans, and, in his controversy with the Jesuits, he raised the wrath of the whole Puritan faction in his own Church, by defending the use of images, the sign of the cross, the use of the word altar, the real presence, confession, absolution, and, in a certain limited sense, apostolical succession and orders. Moreover, although "farre from the Iesuites fancie," on the subject, Montagu professes that he "agreeth in part with the Councell of Trent," and he thinks that "the markes of the Great Antichrist fit the Turkish Tyrannie every way as well as the Papacy."

There was a terrible outcry against the book, whereupon, Montagu wrote another which he called *Appello Cæsarem*, "A IVST APPEALE from Two Vniust Informers." Unfortunately for him, his patron, King James, died about that time, and the first Parliament under King Charles had not been opened many days before the Committee of Religion which had been immediately appointed, took in hand Dr Montagu's books and prepared a charge against him to be delivered to the House of Lords. He had committed the terrible crime of admitting that the Church of Rome, although in error, was nevertheless a true Church. At Oxford, on the 2nd of August, Laud, with two other Anglican bishops, wrote to King Charles pleading on Montagu's behalf.[1] It may easily be understood how Laud would sympathize with a High-Church clergyman, who, like himself, had written a book of controversy against a Jesuit. The Parliament, however, was bent on punishing him, and notwithstanding Laud's entreaties, the king refrained from any interference in the matter. Fortunately for Montagu, the sudden dissolution of the Parliament, recorded above, saved him for the moment from further trouble.

The matter, however, was not allowed to rest there. On one of the first days of the following year, Laud wrote in his Diary that, " by the King's Command, a Consultation was held, what was to be done in the Cause of *Richard Montague.* There were present, the Bishops of *London, Durham, Winchester, Rochester,* and *St Davids.*"[2] At the same time he, with the other four bishops, wrote to Buckingham, not only pleading in behalf of Montagu, but defending his books.[3]

The dispute over Montagu and his works went on, at intervals, for about three years. Finally, the House of Commons fined him £2000, and condemned him to imprisonment.[4] At this King Charles was offended. Montagu was one of his own royal chaplains, and he did not admit the right of the House of Commons to punish members of his household. One of the many unpleasant tiffs between the king and his Commons ensued. The latter were obdurate ; had not the affair, said they, been put into the hands of the Committee of Religion, and had not that Committee condemned Montagu and his writings ?

Laud now came to the rescue. He saw that the king's

[1] " Dic. Nat. Biog.," *Laud.*   By S. R. Gardiner.   [2] Diary, p. 26.
[3] " Dic. Nat. Biog.," *Laud.*   [4] Benson, p. 79.

dignity was hurt by the interference of the odious House of Commons with one of his own domestic officials ; so he eagerly seized the opportunity, and struck while the iron was hot. The See of Chichester happened to be vacant, and he persuaded the king to give it to Montagu, and thus, by making him a peer, place him above the reach of the Lower House. The Commons were furious ! Unquestionably, it was a very smart piece of strategy—if not of sharp practise— on the part of Laud, and a glorious victory over his enemies ; but it increased their spite against him, and probably their number also.

Having made a bishop of Montagu, the king thought it wise to pardon the new dignitary for his objectionable writings in a somewhat ostentatious manner, and he was prudent enough to have a pretty broad hint conveyed to him that he must be more careful for the future. The Attorney General was chosen for the purpose, and he fulfilled his errand by means of a letter. " As commanded by the King, he has prepared a pardon for the Bishop, but not having the customary warrant in writing, has not caused the bill to be engrossed. Haply this pardon may set him free in *foro civili*, but the Parliament may call things past in question, not-withstanding this pardon, nay perhaps, by the pardon, they will rather be stirred to question him. He is now a father of our Church, and as a father will tender its peace and quiet. Alas ! a little spot is seen upon that white garment, and a little fire, nay a spark, may inflame a great mass. We are bound in conscience to prevent occasions of strife. Suggests, therefore, that he should review his book, and take away the acrimony of the style, and explain things left doubtful, so that his own pen may remove all scandal, and a stop be given to this unhappy difference and jealousy, which otherwise may trouble the quiet of our Church, and occasion the disquiet of the commonwealth. Wishing that a clearing of these clouds may proceed from the Bishop, and then the pardon would seasonably follow."[1] In short, it would appear, that if the bishop should do what he was told, " then " the Attorney

[1] " Cal. Sta. Pa.," 1628-9, p. 346.

General would happen to have by him a copy of "the customary warrant in writing."

Perhaps Montagu did not act upon this good advice; for three months later we find a "Proclamation for suppressing the book written by Richard Montague, now Bishop of Chichester, then Bachelor of Divinity, entitled 'Appello Cæsarem, or An Appeal to Cæsar,' which was published in the year 1625, and was the first cause of those disputes which have since troubled the quiet of the Church." [*Coll. Procs., Car. I., No.* 99].[1] This was much as if the Pope had first made a man a bishop, and then promptly put his writings on the Index.

I have dwelt the longer on Montagu's books, because, not only did Laud take an active part in defending both the works themselves and the writer, but his countenance and even his possession of copies of them was eventually brought as a charge against him at his trial for high treason.

In his own account of his defence, he writes:—"The Fourth Charge, *To the Licensing of* Sales, *and other Books which had* Popery *in them, &c.* . . . The Sixth Instance was in Bishop *Montague's* Books, the *Gagg,* and the *Appeal.* Here they said, that *Dr* White *told Dr* Featly, *that five or six Bishops did allow these Books.* But he did not name me to be one of them. Then Mr *Pryn* urged upon his Oath, *that these Books were found in my Study.* And I cannot but bless myself at this Argument. For I have *Bellarmine* in my Study; Therefore I am a *Papist:* Or I have the *Alcaron* in my Study; Therefore I am a Turk, is as good an Argument as this: I have Bishop *Montague's* Books in my Study; Therefore I am an *Arminian.* May Mr *Pryn* have Books of all kinds in his Study, and may not the Archbishop of *Canterbury* have them in his? Yea, but he says, *there is a Letter of the Bishops to me, submitting his Books to my Censure.* This Letter hath no date, and so belike Mr *Pryn* thought he might be bold both with it and his Oath, and apply it to what Books he pleas'd. But as God would have it, there are Circumstances in it as good as a Date. For 'tis therein

[1] "Cal. Sta. Pa.," 1628-9,, p. 451.

expressed, that he was now ready to remove from *Chichester* to *Norwich*. Therefore he must needs speak of submitting those his Books to me, which were then ready to be set out, which were his *Origines Ecclesiastica*, not the *Gagg*, nor the *Appeal*, which are the Books Charged, and which were Printed divers Years before he was made a Bishop." [1]

Of course Laud knew well enough that he had defended Montagu with regard to both *The Gag* and *The Appeal;* but when he was on trial for his life, he was quite justified in endeavouring to evade the charge instead of admitting that he had approved of the books. I cannot understand any reasonable person blaming a prisoner, being tried on a capital charge, for resorting to such a mild evasion as this if the opportunity presented itself—unless the prisoner happened to be a Jesuit, in which case I know from experience that the average English reader of history would condemn such a proceeding as casuistry, falsehood, and, in the very worst sense, Jesuitism.

[1] " Hist. of the Troub. and Tryal of W. Laud," pp. 363-5.

CHAPTER XI.

In order to discuss the Montagu affair, we left Laud at Oxford, where we must now return to him. It will be remembered that on the 31st of July 1625 he had had a sudden attack of illness in the President's lodging at St John's College; the next day "Parliament began at Oxford,"[1] and, on the 12th of August, "the Parliament was dissolved." For August 15th, there stands the following entry[2]:—"My Relapse, I never was weaker in the judgment of the Phisician. It was *Munday*. The same day I began my journey towards Wales."

When we consider what the roads were like in those times, to start on a journey of more than two hundred miles, with a view to making a visitation of his diocese, says much for the determination and courage of a delicate man, on the very day that he had suffered a relapse and had been pronounced weaker than he had ever been in his life by his doctor; and his Oxford doctor would probably have had much experience of his constitution. Nevertheless, the journey seems to have done him more good than harm; for six days later, that is to say on the following Sunday, he "Preached at Brecnock," where he stayed a couple of days, "very busie in performing some business."[3] Although well enough to preach and work, either the fatigue of his long journey or the unwholesomeness of the food he obtained on it, disturbed his slumbers, and he describes his dreams, which appear to have been unpleasantly vivid.

The next Wednesday, he arrived safely ("thanks be to God") at his own house, or palace at "*Aberguille*," in spite of his coach having been "twice overturned that day"; the first time he "was in it; but the latter time it was empty."[4]

Since he had last visited his diocese, just three years

[1] Diary, p. 21.   [2] Ib.   [3] Ib., p. 22.   [4] Ib.

earlier, he had had a domestic chapel, or oratory, built at his palace, at his own expense, and it was now ready for use; he "named it the chappel of St *John Baptist* in grateful remembrance of St *John Baptist's* Colledge in *Oxford*," of which he had been "first Fellow, and afterwards President." Like not a few modern High-Church Anglicans, he just a little over-reached himself in his endeavours to be Popish; for, after his own fashion, he "consecrated" it. Even his hagiographer, Heylin, writes that "it was objected that neither Gratian, nor the Roman Pontifical, conceive such Consecrations necessary to a Private Chappel."[1] To be stormed at by Puritans, and to be laughed at by Catholics, for this performance, must have been very trying to the temper of the High-Church bishop, in his attempts to be ultra-orthodox. To make matters worse, after everything had been arranged for the consecration, he was "intent on prayer" the very evening before the Sunday on which it was to take place, when it suddenly struck him—with that peculiar force with which exterior things have a way of striking us, when we imagine ourselves to be praying—that it must be very near the date of the beheading of St John the Baptist; so "when Prayers were finished," he "consulted the Calendar." To his vexation he found that the beheading of St John the Baptist fell "upon *Munday*, to wit," and not upon Sunday as he "could have wished." In fact, the feast would come the day after the fair. He hoped that this would be "of no ill *Omen*," and he comforted himself by reflecting that the day on which he was to consecrate the chapel to St John the Baptist was the selfsame on which King James had sat "for three hours together at least," hearing his cause about his election to the Presidentship of St John's, and with very happy results; he appears to have considered that, after all, for practical purposes, James, the king, was of more service to him than John, the saint, and as he did not believe in the invocation of saints, this was natural enough.

Poor man, he had very bad nights in Wales, "*valde*

[1] "Cyp. Angl.," p. 88.

turbatus sum per insomnia," he writes, gloomily. In the course of his dreams, "all seemed to be out of order," as things, indeed, not uncommonly appear on such occasions. There is something truly pathetic in this, and who has not experienced that wretched sensation on a restless dreamy night? After describing his nocturnal miseries and nightmares, he writes devoutly : — "God grant better things." [1]

His description of the candidature for Anglican ordination in his diocese is grotesquely lamentable :—"One only Person desired to Receive Holy Orders from me ; and he found to be unfit, upon Examination." [2] "I sent him away with an Exhortation, not Ordaining." Small wonder, after the experience of examining this solitary Welsh aspirant for orders, that he dreamt worse than ever—of people "cloathed in flourishing green Garments," and of a bishop with "his Head and Shoulders covered with Linen."

One day, he "went on Horseback up to the Mountains," and so fine and warm was the weather for the time of year (October 10th) that when he returned, he and his "Company" picnicked "in the open Air" instead of dining in the country house of his Registrar, where he appears to have been staying.

A month later he started for England, after spending but little short of three months in his diocese. It took him ten days to get to "Honye-Lacye in Herefordshire," and four days after that he reached the house of his "great Friend Fr. Windebanke. There the Wife of my Friend (for himself was then at Court) immediately as soon as I came, told me, that the Duke of *Buckingham* (then negotiating for the Publick in the *Low-Countries*) had a Son born ; whom God bless with all the good things of Heaven and Earth." [3] I firmly believe that in writing this he was thoroughly sincere. Whatever may be said against him, he was capable of strong attachments, and he was exceedingly fond of Buckingham, Windebanke, and Strafford ; but with respect to the two kings, James I. and Charles I., while it is certain

---

[1] Diary, p. 23.   [2] *Ib.*   [3] *Ib.*, pp. 24-5.

that to each he was a faithful servant, the extent of his affection, apart from his loyal devotion, is not quite so easy to gauge; although, on the whole, I am inclined to think that it was very considerable in the case of Charles.

If Laud was open to the charge of being usually absent from his diocese, he certainly was not guilty of laziness about preaching. There are constant entries in his Diary as to sermons. "I Preached at *Carmarthen ;*" "I Preached at *Honye-Lacye ;*" "I Preached at *Hurst ;*" and, again, "I Preached at *Hurst* upon *Christmas* day;" and so on.

On the first day of 1626, he was at Hampton Court. Everything had not gone quite smoothly in the royal family since he had been last at court. And now it is my purpose to try to prove for him an *alibi*.

It is well known that Charles guaranteed to the queen the free practise of her religion, a chapel for her private use in the royal palaces, and the privilege of her attendant confessor, and chaplains : it is equally notorious, that within six weeks of her arrival in England, her confessor, the Abbé Sancy, was sent back to France by the king, and that the latter endeavoured to reduce her chapel and her religious privileges within the narrowest possible limits. At Whitehall, instead of a handsome room for her oratory, she was only allowed "the most retired chamber in the palace."[1] At her first mass, "the queen, at eleven o'clock, came out of her chamber in a petticoat, and with a veil over her head, supported by the Count de Filliers, her chamberlain, followed by six of her women, and the mass was mumbled over. Whilst they were at mass, the king gave orders that no Englishman or woman should come near the place."[2] The same authority tells us that when pressed for better accommodation, the king replied :—" If the queen's closet, where they now say mass, be not large enough, let them have it in the great chamber ; and if the great chamber be not wide enough, they may use the garden ; and if the garden were not spacious enough to serve their turn, then was the park the fittest place." It is, how-

---

[1] Strickland's "Lives of the Queens of Eng.," vol. viii. p. 32
Ellis's "Historical Letters."

ever, but fair to say, that among the State Papers [1] exists a
" Warrant to pay Daniel du Plessis, Bishope of Mende, chief
Almoner to the Queen, £2000 a year "—a large sum in those
times—"for charges incident to the Queen's chapel and
oratory, and all ecclesiastical persons and servitors belonging
to the same." The question is, Was it paid?

Charles, in fact, became very soon tired of the French
priests and all the Monsieurs, or " Monsers " as he called
them. He wrote to Buckingham, who was then abroad, of
"the maliciousness of the *monsers*, by making and fomenting
discontentments in my wife. I could tarry no longer from
advertising you that I mean to seek for no other grounds to
cashier my *monsers*. That you may (if you think good)
advertise the queen mother "—this, of course, was Marie de
Medicis—"of my intention."

Now it might not unnaturally be supposed that Laud,
being jealous of the presence of foreign and Catholic
ecclesiastics about the court, influenced the king against
them and induced him to send them all back to France,
Bishops, Confessors, " Monsers," " Bugges," and the whole
company ; but, with the exception of being presented to the
queen with the rest of the bishops who happened to be at the
time in London, and spending part of two days at Windsor,
and a few days at Oxford, he does not appear to have been
near the court for six months, and it is probable that when
he was at Oxford, the king would spend most of his time at
Woodstock. More than half of the first six months of the
king's married life was spent by Laud in Wales, or on his
journey to or from it ; about seven weeks of it he spent at
Windebank's, and part of it in London, while the royal
family were at Hampton Court. On the day that King
Charles wrote his angry letter to Buckingham, threatening
to cashier the "monsers," Laud was in Herefordshire. I
think this makes it pretty clear that to whatever extent
Charles may afterwards have been guided by Laud, he
acted independently of him for the first half-year of his
married life. Whether Laud encouraged the king in his

---

[1] "Domestic Sta. Pa.," vol. iv. July 20, 1625.

dislike of priests and French people, or not, is another
question ; but, to my mind, there is evidence, or to say the
least, an *alibi*, in support of the theory that he did not
engender it.

As to the queen herself, Laud was actually charged, at his
trial, of having been an instrument in her hands, instead of an
enemy.   All that he himself admitted was that:—" Upon
occasion of some Service done, she was graciously pleased to
give me leave to have immediate Access unto her, when I had
Occasion." [1]   Upon the whole, the queen and he appear to
have lived upon very good terms with each other.   Possibly
he might have been more popular if he had been less intimate with her.   From the first, Henrietta Maria and her
French retinue were looked on with suspicion, if not with
absolute dislike, by the majority of the English.   Chamberlain
wrote to Carleton [2] of "the Queen's train, poor pitiful women,
not worth looking after," and of one of them in particular,
the Duchess of Chevreuse, that she is " fair, but paints foully."
He then proceeds to say that "they begin to mutter about
religion, and the king having promised that he would never
marry with conditions derogatory to protestantism.   Complaints of ill management, &c."

One day after Laud had rejoined the court, Sunday, the
first of January 1626, he was named with other bishops to
consult together on the following Wednesday, at Whitehall,
concerning the ceremonies to be used at the approaching
coronation.   At the same time, he heard a piece of news that
did not please him, which was that "the bigger part of the
Bishop of *Durham's* House was appointed for the Residence
of the Ambassadour Extraordinary of *France*." [3]   Now Laud
" had abode as a Guest for Four Years compleat " at this
very house with his "good Friend the Bishop of *Durham*," and
the new arrangement not only obliged him to turn out, but
" forced " him " to make over much haste " in so doing.   On
the Tuesday he " fixed " himself at his " own House at Westminster " ; his servant having already brought all his things

[1] " Hist. of the Troub. and Tryal of W. Laud," p. 382.
[2] " Cal. Sta. Pa. Dom.," 1625-6, p. 48.   [3] Diary, p. 25.

there, " save only " his books, and the fetching of these, and placing "them in order in" his "Study" appears to have fussed and worried him not a little.

When the bishops met to arrange the ceremonies for the coronation, they examined the service-book used at that of King James, and "were fain to mend many slips of the Pen, to make Sense in some places, and good *English* in other. And the Book being trusted with me, I had Reason to do it with my own Hand."[1]   This afterwards gave rise to the accusation against Laud of having tampered with the coronation service and made it more Popish.

The same night, the Lord Chamberlain, Pembroke, came to Laud with an order from the king to preach a month later at the opening of Parliament.   There was another meeting of bishops about the ceremonial for the coronation, and Abbott, the archbishop, had the task—an ungrateful one to such an enemy of Laud's—of informing him that it was the king's wish that he should act at the ceremony instead of the Dean of Westminster, Williams, Bishop of Lincoln, whose presence on the occasion his Majesty refused to tolerate ; for, as I observed in a former chapter, Williams had got into disgrace when Lord Keeper.   The Duke of Buckingham took Laud to the king to show him the notes and alterations that had been made in the office for the consecration.   He says, himself :— "The other   Bishops sent me,   being Puny, to give the Account."   Whether puny or not, every private interview he had with the king gave him an opportunity of increasing his intimacy with, and influence over, him.

Two days before the coronation, the king not only summoned the bishops and peers that were to take part in the ceremony, but also had the regalia brought for his inspection.   Then they seem to have had a sort of private rehearsal.   Charles " put on St *Edward's* Tunicks," and made Laud "read the Rubricks of direction." [2]

Representing the Dean of Westminster, it fell to Laud to make all the arrangements in the abbey.   " Finding the old Crucifix among the *Regalia*, he caused it to be placed on

---

[1] " Hist. of Troub. and Tryal of W. Laud," p. 321.   [2] Diary, p. 27.

the Altar, as in former times;"[1] says Heylin, and this was urged against him by his enemies many years later, when he appears to have forgotten it. "They say," writes Laud, "there was a Crucifix among the Regalia, and that it stood upon the Altar at the Coronation, and that I did not except against it." "I remember not any there."[2] Laud was also accused of altering the coronation oath, by adding the words—"agreeable to the King's Prerogative," and omitting :—"which the People have chosen, or shall choose." To this he replied that if any alteration were made in it at all, it was certainly not made by him, and that the oath was tendered, not by himself, but by Abbott, then Archbishop of Canterbury.

The coronation of Charles I. was destined to bring trouble to another person besides Laud. This was the queen. Henrietta Maria refused to be crowned by an heretical archbishop. The bishop she had with her claimed the right of crowning her ; but this Abbott, Archbishop of Canterbury, would not allow.[3] Finding that she was not to be persuaded, the king tried to induce her to be present within the abbey, without taking part in the ceremony. When she refused this also, he begged her, at least, to attend in a latticed box,[4] so placed that she could not herself be seen ; but she positively refused to be present in the abbey at all. Instead of doing so, according to Miss Strickland, she watched the procession, both going and coming, from the bay window of the old gate-house, which formerly stood over the roadway leading from Whitehall to the abbey—Sir B. Rudyerd writes to Nethersole that she "stood in a window at Sir Abraham Williams's, to see the show";[5] but he may have lived in this part of Whitehall—and it was said that as the pompous procession took its stately way from the palace of Whitehall, the queen's French ladies-in-waiting were seen frisking and frolicing around her in the window from which they were, so

[1] "Cyp. Angl.," p. 148.   [2] "Hist. of Troub. and Tryal of W. L.," p. 318.
[3] "Cal. Sta. Pa. Dom.," 1625-6, p. 225.
[4] Strickland's "Queens of Eng.," vol viii. p. 37.
[5] "Cal. Sta. Pa. Dom.," 1625-6, p. 246.

to speak, watching the fun, with no outward signs of reverence. This was not calculated to send Charles to the great function in the best of tempers, or with the happiest of hearts.

Everything else, however, seems to have gone well. Here is the account of the ceremony in Laud's Diary :—" The King entred the Abby-Church a little before Ten a Clock ; and it was past Three, before he went out of it. It was a very Bright Sun-shining Day. The Solemnity being ended, in the great Hall at *Westminster*, when the King delivered into my hands the *Regalia*, which are kept in the Abby-Church of *Westminster*, he did (which had not before been done) deliver to me the Sword called *Curtana*, and two others, which had been carried before the King that day, to be Kept in the Church, together with the other *Regalia*. I returned, and Offered them Solemnly at the Altar in the Name of the King, and laid them up with the rest."

This was an opportunity for one of those little functions, not provided for in the Anglican Liturgy, which Laud so much enjoyed ; but the solemn offering of the sword " Curtana, and two others," was charged against him as a serious crime, some eighteen years afterwards.

" In so great a Ceremony," he continues, " and amidst an incredible concourse of People, nothing was lost, or broke, or disordered." And he presently adds, with evident, and perhaps justifiable, pride at his own good management, that he " heard some of the Nobility saying to the King in their return, that they never had seen any Solemnity, although much less, performed with so little Noise, and so great Order."

It must have been bitter to Williams, the Bishop of Lincoln, to hear how successfully his rival had filled his place at the king's coronation. A few days after it, he wrote to Charles, saying that " the King's gracious speeches to him when he took his leave, and his own conscious innocence, have comforted him in the affliction of being enjoined from his Majesty's presence—the only Heaven wherein his soul delights," [1] and he added that he had endured with patience

---

[1] " Cal. Sta. Pa. Dom.," 1625-6, p. 249.

"his sequestration from the coronation;" more abject still, and exceedingly impious, is a sentence in the same letter, in which he describes himself as "a poor Bishop who has ever honoured his Majesty's person above all objects in the world to come."

Williams must have been reminded that he was not the only Lord Keeper who had got into trouble, by the death, about that time, of Francis Bacon, Viscount St Albans, who had been sentenced to imprisonment and a fine of £40,000 for corruption and bribery while holding that very office, some half dozen years earlier. Of Bacon, Laud's biographer, Heylin, writes, that he was "a man of good and bad qualities equally compounded, one of a most strong brain, and a Chymical head."

CHAPTER XII.

As the year 1626 progressed, Laud was more and more with King Charles. Within a month of the coronation, he heard that the king had had an alarming fall :—" Feb. 27. *Munday, The Danger* which hapened to King *Charles* from his Horse ; which having broken the two Girts of the Saddle, and the Saddle together with the Rider fallen together under his Belly, stood trembling, until the King, having received no hurt, &c."[1] This does not say very much for the evenness of the balance of Charles I. in his saddle, and it reminds me of a criticism of his horsemanship to the effect that "he did not ride like a Prince but like a post-boy."[2]

If he was disposed to be guided by Laud, the king was not wholly bishop-ridden. In April he sent for all the bishops that were in London to come to him at four o'clock one afternoon. Fourteen came, and then, says Laud, "his Majesty chid us, that in this time of Parliament we were silent in the Cause of the Church, and did not make known to him what might be Useful, or was Prejudicial to the Church ; professing himself ready to promote the Cause of the Church."[3]

Very soon Charles had an opportunity of proving his good-will towards Laud, " *May* 4. Thursday, *Arthur Lake* Bishop of *Bath* and *Wells* Died at *London*."[4] The bishopric thus made vacant was much more valuable than St David's, and, on the 20th of June, Laud tells us " His Majesty King *harles* named me to be Bishop of *Bath* and *Wells*." Two months later he was " elected "; on the 18th of September,

---

[1] Diary, p. 29.
[2] " Life of Charles I.," vol. iii. p. 114. D'Israeli calls the man who said this " a coarse libeller."
[3] Diary, p. 32.   [4] *Ib.*, p. 33.

his election was confirmed, and the next day he swore homage to his Majesty "who there presently restored to me the *Temporalities*, from the death of my Predecessor." [1] Of these "temporalities" the Crown would get its share. Among the State Papers is a "grant to Bishop Laud of Bath and Wells, of the instalment of the first fruits of the said Bishopric, to be paid by him in four years." [2]

So far as I can ascertain, he never visited his diocese of Bath and Wells ; and he did not hold the bishopric for more than about eight months. Buckingham persuaded the king to appoint a man named Theophilus Field to St David's in the place of Laud, and the new bishop said, or wrote, to his predecessor, Laud, that the Duke of Buckingham behaved remarkably like the Almighty, who "very oft, as he passeth by and seems to turn from us, leaves a blessing behind." [3]

Laud's election to the bishopric of Bath and Wells had only been confirmed eight days, when another great post was offered to him. The Duke of Buckingham came to him on the last day of September, and told him that the king had determined to make him Dean of the Chapel Royal, in the place of the Bishop of Winchester. "It never rains, but it pours," and, a couple of days later, the duke hinted to him that, if Abbott should die, the king intended to make him Archbishop of Canterbury !

Laud was not deterred by the promise of royal favours from doing what he believed to be his duty, and within six weeks of his appointment to the Deanery of the Chapel Royal, he ventured to tutor King Charles in a style from which probably every other prelate in England would have flinched.

"Taking occasion," he says, "from the abrupt both beginning and ending of Publick Prayer on the fifth of *November*, I desired his Majesty King *Charles*, that he would please to be present at Prayers as well as Sermon every *Sunday ;* "—surely even most country squires would have objected to be lectured like this !—" and that at whatsoever part of the Prayers he came, the Priest then officiating

---

[1] Diary, p. 33.   [2] Domestic, Appendix, 1626, Nov. 8.
[3] "Cal. Sta. Pa. Dom.," 1627-8, Preface, p. 16.

might proceed to the end of the Prayers." Charles must
have taken the first suggestion very meekly, or Laud would
not have dared to proceed to the second. Nothing, however,
succeeds like success, as the saying goes, and "the most
Religious King not only assented to this Request; but also
gave me thanks." In short, he kissed the rod. "This had
not before been done from the beginning of K. *James's* Reign
to this day. Now, thanks be to God, it obtaineth."[1]

Laud's influence and importance, in the September of this
year, is demonstrated by a little incident recorded in the
Domestic State Papers.[2] The king had written to Abbott
and others, commissioning them "to require and collect a
loan for the King's use from persons able to lend, or dwelling
within the County of Middlesex," and it seems to have been
desired that Abbott should urge the other bishops to make
similar endeavours in their own dioceses. Abbott wrote
to Secretary Conway, and consulted him as to the king's
pleasure with regard to the method of communicating with
the bishops, as it would be undesirable that papers detailing
so delicate a matter should "fall into the hands of ill willers
as well as of those that wish well." The very next day,
Conway sent the archbishop's letter to the very last man to
whom he would have wished it to be referred, namely, Laud,
and asked his opinion of it. The same evening Laud sent
his answer. "Thinks the instructions, which are to be sent
to every minister, should be printed; that they should be in
the form of a little book; that a charge should be given to
the printer for secrecy, and the like to the ministers who
receive them, and to the officers who deliver them." When
Abbott asked Conway what was the "king's pleasure," he
most certainly did not intend to inquire what was Laud's
pleasure; but so far as the pleasure of the king was concerned,
it is difficult to believe that Conway would have referred the
matter to Laud, unless Charles had expressly desired that
he should do so. Curiously enough, Conway consulted him
on the very day that Buckingham informed him that he was
to be made Dean of the Chapel Royal.

[1] Diary, pp. 36-7. [2] Vol. xxxvi.

Laud's gratification at his own rapid advancement must have been qualified by the death of Lancelot Andrews, Bishop of Winchester, whom he succeeded as Dean of the Chapel Royal. It was in recording his death in his Diary, that he wrote of him as "the great Light of the *Christian* World." Indeed Laud may be said to have been rather a disciple of Andrews, than the originator of what are sometimes spoken of as "Laudian views."

Williams, Bishop of Lincoln, seems to have "pitifully, and to the great detriment of the Church of *England*, signified to the King"[1] that certain papers written by Andrews "concerning Bishops, that they are *Jure Divino*," ought not to be printed, and Laud went to Charles and persuaded him to the contrary.

If all was prospering now with Laud, not so with his friend, the Duke of Buckingham. There was bitter enmity between the latter and the Earl of Bristol, and both were accused of high treason in Parliament, each maintaining that the other was guilty of it. There were "perpetual Heats in the House;" and in May,[2] "King Charles came into the Parliament House; and made a short Speech to the Lords, concerning preserving the Honour of the Nobility against the vile and malicious Calumnies of those in the House of *Commons*, who had accused the Duke." Then he says that there were eight members "who in this matter chiefly appeared." "The Prologue, Sir *Dudley Digges*, the Epilogue, *John Elliot*, were this day by the King's Command committed to the *Tower*. They were both dismissed thence within a few days."

Laud's principal penitent had not of late been living in the odour of sanctity. When he had gone to Paris to bring the princess to England, Buckingham left his piety at home, appeared at the French court in a white velvet suit set all over with diamonds, said to be worth £80,000,[3] to say nothing of twenty-seven other very rich suits, and made love to the young queen, Anne of Austria.

Laud might well pray "pro Duce Buckinghamiæ," at this

[1] Diary, p. 38.   [2] *Ib*,. p. 33.   [3] Hardwicke Papers, i. 571 ; Ellis, iii. 189.

juncture. Nor does his penitence, if he pretended any, appear to have been very genuine; for he tried hard to get another invitation to the French court, and was actually appointed ambassador at Paris, but was objected to by Cardinal Richelieu.

It seems anomalous to read of one of the king's ministers being able to afford to wear eighty thousand pounds worth of diamonds at a time when the commissioners at Plymouth were writing to the Council of "soldiers forced to keep their beds for want of clothes."[1]

Buckingham, none the less, remained on intimate terms with his confessor, and we read of his showing to him a paper upon the *Invocation of Saints*,[2] which had been put into his hands by his Popish mother. He was made Chancellor of the University of Cambridge, and on going thither for that purpose, he took his favourite bishop with him.

Laud writes:[3]—"I was there incorporated; and so I was the first who was presented to the most Illustrious Duke, then sitting in the *Congregation* House. The Duke was treated by the University in an Academical manner, yet splendidly."

Within a fortnight, Buckingham's only son died—it will be remembered that he was born during Laud's second visitation at St David's—and Laud conducted the funeral "about mid-night" on "the Eve of *Palm-Sunday*."

Laud carefully avoids any mention in his Diary of the disputes between the king and queen regarding her French chaplains and attendants; possibly he may not have been consulted in the matter; but their expulsion can scarcely have failed to be gratifying to him. It is needless to repeat the well-known story, recounted by the king himself, of the family row and curtain-lecture, which took place one night when the royal couple were "a-bed;" or to describe how all the queen's French attendants were sent to Somerset House, and eventually to their native land. "Force them away,

---

[1] "Cal. Sta. Pa. Dom.," 1625-6, p. 227.
[2] Laud's Diary, p. 37. [3] *Ib.*, p. 39.

dryve them away, lyke so manie wylde beastes ; and so the devill goe with them " was the royal order.[1] Bassompierre, who came to England as ambassador extraordinary, smoothed down the ruffled feathers of both the king and the queen with wonderful tact, and it was arranged that Henrietta Maria should have a bishop, a confessor and his companion, and ten chaplains, provided they were neither Jesuits nor Oratorians (as a matter of fact they were Capuchins), and arrangements were made with regard to her chapels. Bassompierre also obtained the release of all the English priests, seventeen in number, who were at that time imprisoned for their religion in London. I may take this opportunity of saying that the English translation of the Bassompierre papers describing his experiences in this country, accompanied as it is by voluminous notes, forms an interesting and amusing little volume, which should be read by every student of the reign of Charles I.

Instead of being complimented for his skilful management, on his return to France, Bassompierre was very coldly received by Louis XIII., who intimated that he had compromised the dignity of his nation by not insisting upon the full performance of the articles of the marriage between Charles and Henrietta Maria, and it was even hinted among the courtiers that the ambassador had either been hoodwinked by the flatteries of Buckingham, or bribed by the presents of King Charles. Some historians, Lingard [2] among others, doubt whether Louis's displeasure was real or assumed ; it is certain that he did not repudiate the terms made by his envoy ; but when the latter requested that Buckingham might be allowed to return to Paris, he refused point blank, with haste and indignation.

The irritation felt by the French king at the dismissal, by his royal brother-in-law, of his sister's chaplains and servants was increased by Charles's ostentatious promises of protection to Louis the Thirteenth's Protestant subjects. It must not be forgotten, of course, that the English Parliament was very jealous of the admission of Catholic priests to the English

[1] Ellis, iii. p. 224.   [2] " Hist. of Eng.," vol. vii. chap. iv.

court and of the relaxation of the penal laws against English Catholics. It should also be remembered that Charles considered himself defrauded by the French of the alliance, defensive and offensive, which he had expected to be ratified after his marriage with the sister of the King of France. The ill-feeling continued on both sides, but it for the first time took a practical form when Charles declared himself the champion of the liberties of the Reformed Churches, and sent Buckingham in command of a fleet of forty-two ships of war, thirty-four transports, an army of seven regiments of nine hundred men each and a squadron of cavalry, to the coast of France.

On the eve of the start of this expedition, Laud accompanied " King *Charles* from *London* to *Southwick* by Portsmouth," and, with his Majesty, "dined a-board the Triumph."[1] To have his king and his confessor on board his ship must have inspirited Buckingham, before sailing with his fleet.

Not long before he went with the king to visit Buckingham on board ship, Laud had been made a Privy Councillor —a great step in power, and he himself writes of it :—" God grant, it may conduce to his Honour, and to the good of the Kingdom and the Church."[2]

But a still further advancement befell him while he was with the king at Southwick, superintending the despatch of the fleet and army. "The Bishoprick of *London* was granted me," he writes. With this appointment came a great increase in his influence, together with a proportionate addition to his unpopularity. He was now both feared and hated.

It is melancholy to find a letter from the Duchess of Buckingham to her husband, written only a few days before he sailed, begging him not to deceive her and to love her only. She tells him that it would be impossible for any woman to love a man more than she loves him.[3] He had promised her that he would not undertake the expedition at all, and when he had broken this promise, he made another to go and bid her farewell, which he also broke.

Here are a few modernised quotations from another letter

---

[1] Diary, p. 41. [2] *Ib.* [3] "Dom. Sta. Pa., Charles I.," vol. lxvii., No. 60.

which she wrote to her pious husband, just about the time
that he had got his confessor at the port from which he was
to embark, and in the ship in which he was to sail. " I have
been a very miserable woman hitherto, that could never keep
you at home. But now I will ever look to be so, until some
blessed occasion comes to draw you quite from the Court."
" God, of his mercy, give me patience, and if I were sure my
soul would be well, I could wish myself to be out of this
miserable world."   " Never whilst I live will I trust you
again, nor never will put you to your oath for anything again.
I wonder why you sent me word by Crow " (Treasurer of the
Navy, who had formerly been Keeper of the Privy Purse to
the Duke) " that you would see me shortly, to put me in new
hopes ; I pray God never woman may love a man as I have
done you, that none feel that which I have done for you."

Of course there was a P.S., in which, among other things,
she writes, " Burn this, for God's sake." What would have
been the poor woman's feelings had she known that, instead
of being burned, it would be docketted among the National
State Papers, where we find it more than two hundred and
sixty years after it was written, to say nothing of its being
printed and published in the Calendar ?

Before Buckingham's fleet weighed anchor, " We," the king
and Laud, " came to *London*," and two days later, Laud
received the royal command " to go all the Progress."   In
five days, " the Duke of *Buckingham* set forwards towards the
Isle of *Ree*," and in three more, " the Progress began to Oatlands." Laud accompanied the king, and mentions his losing
a jewel, worth £1000, out hunting.

On the seventh of July, he made the following curious
entry in his Diary :—" *Saturday-night*, I dreamed that I had
lost two Teeth. The Duke of *Buckingham* took the Isle of
Ree."

Presently four entries relating to the Duke and his expedition come in succession :—*July* 29. The first News came
from my Lord Duke of his Success : *Sunday, August* 12.
The second News came from my Lord Duke to Windsor :
Sunday, August 26. The third News came from my Lord

to Aldershot : *Sunday*, September. News came from my Lord Duke to *Theobalds :* The first fear of ill Success : "

Well might Laud have "fears of ill success" for his friend and patron ; for a French flotilla of fourteen ships had burst through the boom and revictualled the fortress, and Buckingham, having received a reinforcement, ordered a general assault, which failed.

To increase the despondency of Laud, the Dean of Canterbury not only said to an acquaintance of his (who repeated it to Laud), " that the business could not go well in the Isle of *Ree ;* " but added that " there must be a Parliament," and that " some must be sacrificed " to the popular discontent, and that, among these, Laud " was as like as any." Laud also heard that " Sir *Dudlye Diggs*," whom it will be remembered the king had lately sent to the Tower for censuring Buckingham in the House of Commons, had made a similar remark.

In October, Laud makes the melancholy entry :—" The Retreat out of the Isle of *Ree*."

Buckingham had determined to withdraw his troops. There was, however, a French corps between his own camp and the place of embarkation, and in order to reach the sea he was obliged to march along a narrow causeway across the marshes to a bridge, which connected the little island of Oie with the larger one of Rhé. He sent his small body of cavalry to cover his retreat; but it was broken up by the French, consequently the confusion and slaughter on the causeway was terrible. Buckingham, it was said, lost twelve hundred men in the course of the day; but he managed to embark the remains of his army, and he displayed considerable personal courage, being the last man to leave the shore.

Laud reports, " My Lord Duke's return to Court," if with sadness at the failure of his expedition, no doubt with joy at his return. His friend, patron, and penitent received a letter from his duchess after his arrival, beginning :—" My Lord, Since I heard the news of your landing, I have been still every hour looking for you, that I cannot now till I see you, sleep at nights, &c.," and ending with "your true loving and obedient wife." [1]   He also received a letter from his Romanist mother, who had tried to tempt his pure soul to Popery with a tract on the *Invocation of Saints.* She says, "at your departure from me, you told me you went to make peace, but it was not from your heart." You "embroil the whole Christian world in wars, and then declare it for religion." "You know the worthy King your Master never liked that way." "God hath blessed you with a virtuous wife and sweet daughter, with another son, I hope, if you do not destroy it by this way you take ; she cannot believe a word you speak, you have so much deceived her." [2]

So much for Laud's pious convert, saved from Fisher, his mother, and "Romanism." And this may be a favourable opportunity for quoting a curious entry from Laud's Diary, [3] especially as it was made during the period dealt with in this chapter. It runs :—*March* 8, *Thursday*, I came to *London.* The Night following I dreamed, that I was reconciled to the Church of *Rome.* This troubled me much ; and I wondered exceedingly, how it should happen. Nor was I aggrieved with my self only by Reason of the Errors of that Church, but also upon account of the Scandal, which from that my fall, would be cast upon many Eminent and Learned Men in the Church of *England.*"

---

[1] S.P.O. Dom. Charles I., vol. lxxxiv. No. 80.
[2] *Ib.*, vol. lxxxv. No. 22.   P. 39.

CHAPTER XIII.

LAUD and Abbott were destined to be ever in conflict. A certain Dr Sibthorpe preached a sermon at Northampton to prove the legality of a forced loan. This, of course, gave satisfaction in high places, and, in order to give it greater authority, the archbishop was asked to allow it to be printed with his special license. Laud, however, writes of "the *Exceptions*, which the Arch-Bishop of Canterbury had Exhibited against Doctor *Sibthorp's* Sermon." In fact, Abbott distinctly refused to give any sort of imprimatur to it. Laud, on the contrary, licensed it, to the great gratification of the king, who suspended and sequestrated the Archbishop of Canterbury for refusing to do so, and commissioned the Bishops of London, Durham, Rochester, Bath and Wells, and Oxford, to administer his archdiocese. Such an act on the part of Charles I. was high-handed to the last degree, and a biographer of Laud would naturally like to know whether he had any part in advising the king to follow such a course. We are aware that Buckingham was a bitter enemy of Abbott, and the sequestration might likely enough have been at his suggestion, had he not been away from England on his expedition to the Isle of Rhé, during the three months preceding the appointment of the Commission of the five bishops to execute archiepiscopal jurisdiction. Be this as it may, Abbott's refusal was a most uncourtierlike step, and practically ruined him.

Nor were the inferior clergy more delicately handled than their archbishop. An order was issued that no clergyman was to make any allusion to the ill-fated expedition to the Isle of Rhé, a thing odious to many of their parishioners.[1] One preacher, anxious to curry court favour, said in his

---

[1] D'Israeli's "Life of Charles I.," vol. ii. p. 76.

sermon that people ought not to complain at having to make any sacrifice for his Majesty, as all they had was "the King's by divine right." The sermon was approved of in the quarter desired, and it was published ; but the preacher's house was burnt down by his less loyal neighbours.

In January 1628, Lord Carleton wrote[1] to Laud from the Hague, apologising for having in "a previous letter congratulated him on some preferment which had been erroneously conferred upon him by rumour." Very possibly this may have been the Archbishopric of Canterbury, on a report that Abbott had resigned. He begs "him to accept the congratulation provisionally until the suggested preferment really falls upon him." Further on he says that Scottish ministers have been trying to introduce among the English regiments in Holland, a liturgy between the English and the Dutch ; and he adds that the Hague "has served as a refuge for ministers who would not conform, but it is noways fit that it should become a nursery for non-conformists." Anglican ecclesiastical matters in Holland were destined to give Laud some trouble, and I shall have occasion to refer to them by-and-bye.

Want of money induced Charles I. to summon a Parliament early in 1628. He restored Archbishop Abbott to the exercise of his authority in order that he might attend it, and he also set free Williams and the Earl of Bristol for the same purpose. Laud preached at the opening. Six weeks earlier he had had the misfortune to strain a back sinew of his right leg when he was with the king at Hampton Court. Of an accident which had taken place a few months earlier, he had written that, in getting out of his coach, "my foot stumbling, I fell headlong. I never had a more dangerous fall ; but by God's mercy, I escaped with a light bruise of my Hip only."[2] But this back-sinew affair was more serious. It was all he could do to make "a shift to go and Christen my Lord Duke's Son, the Lord *George*, at *Wallingford* House." This was the son whose expected arrival Buckingham's mother had hinted at in her letter quoted in the last

---

[1] "Cal. Sta. Pa. Dom.," 1627-8, p. 514.   [2] Diary, p. 41.

chapter. When he had to preach at the opening of Parliament, he "had much ado to stand," and he "continued lame long after" the accident.

The new Parliament not only censured Buckingham, but Laud, himself, also. " I was complained of by the House of *Commons*," he says, "for warranting Doctor *Mainwaring's* Sermons to the Press." The House of Lords had censured Dr Mainwaring for a sermon, which it pronounced to be "against the liberty and propriety of the subject." Williams was privately sent to Bishop Montaigne, who had licensed the sermon, to inquire whether any warrant or message had been sent on the subject from Laud ; but nothing could be discovered ; so Laud was eventually "acquitted in open Parliament."[1]

But the Commons had not yet done with him. Later on the very same day, they "were making their *Remonstrance* to the King," as he tells us, and one heading was "Innovation of Religion. Therein they Named my Lord Bishop of *Winchester* and my self." An honourable member then got up and said :—"Now we have named these persons, let us think of some causes why we did it." Whereupon, Sir Edward Coke replied :—"Have we not named my Lord of Buckingham without showing cause, and may we not be as bold with them ?"

The hostile spirit exhibited towards Laud by the Parliament may have induced him to use his influence with the king in favour of dispensing with it. The Commons were evidently bent on his ruin ; the king might possibly have remained on his throne if he had continued to summons a Parliament ; but Laud would have fallen. If the long interval, which presently followed, without a Parliament was chiefly owing to Laud, he certainly obtained for himself a lengthened period of power and prosperity ; he assured for himself, however, a terrible retribution at the end of it.

Laud also got into trouble about this time for the countenance he gave to *A Collection of Private Devotions, or The Hours of Prayer*, a book written by Dr Cozens, a Prebend

[1] "Hist. of the Troub. and Tryals of W. Laud," p. 238.

of Durham. It contained the "Seven Sacraments, Three Theological Virtues, Seven Gifts of the Holy Ghost, Seven Deadly Sins and their Contrary Virtues, Forms of Prayer for the 1st, 3rd, 6th, and 9th Hours, Vespers and Compline, Preparation for Holy Communion, &c." There could be no doubt from whence the "List of Contents" of such a book had been taken, whatever its interior might be. It was, in fact, the forerunner of many Anglican manuals of a kindred nature which have been published within the last quarter of a century. This book, like Dr Mainwaring's sermon, had been licensed by Bishop Montaigne, who might, therefore, have been expected to be an exceedingly High-Churchman, and orthodox and zealous to the backbone ; but Heylin describes him as "a man unactive and addicted to voluptuousness, and one that loved his ease too much to disturb himself in the concerns of the Church." [1]

This book of devotions was published in 1627, and in 1628 appeared a reply by Prynne, entitled *A Brief Survey and Censure of Cozens his Cozening Devotions*, declaring that book to have been framed in general according to the "Horaries and Primers of the Church of Rome," particularly "Our Lady's Primer or Office," and that it was "Popish trash and trumpery, taken out of Popish Primers and Catechisms." Before this reply came out, in September 1627, a document is entered among the State Papers, [2] containing "observations on Dr Cosin's Book of Hours of Prayer, principally with respect to the publication of a reprint of a first impression, which was called in, because it contained a prayer for a man after his soul is departed." It is indorsed, in Bishop Laud's hand, "Delivered to my Lord Conwaye, God knowes bye whome, and by his Lordship sent to his Majesty." It does not require much reading between the lines to conjecture from this that his Majesty was not over pleased about the matter, and that Laud wished that "God-knowes-whome" had not been so officious. Yet the king must have been pacified, for some time afterwards, when

[1] "Cyp. Ang.," p. 164.
[2] "Cal. Sta. Pa. Dom.," 1627-8, p. 342.

the Deanery of Peterborough was vacant, and Laud named four of the royal chaplains to him for the post, "the king pitched upon Dr Cozens," the reason given being that "he had but Forty Pounds a year by his Headship in Peter-House to maintain himself, his Wife and Children."

Cozen writes to Laud, in 1628,[1] complaining that "a son of Belial and a solicitor" had "invented an incredible slander" against him, "and informed it to Mr Attorney General." This seems to have been repeated to Charles I., for Cozen "is burdened with grief, that, while he labours to serve God and the King, his Majesty should be prejudiced against him, and he be reckoned among those offenders and spurners against authority whom he ever abhorred."

The recent mention of Bishop Mountain, or "Montaigne," Laud's predecessor in the See of London, reminds me of an expression of the "Nolo episcopari," or rather of the "nolo archiepiscopari," which may be worth quoting:[2]—"Bishop Montaigne, of London, to George Duke of Buckingham. Has received certain intelligence of the Archbishop of York's death. Reminds the Duke of the writer's earnest suit and of his gracious answer when the Duke did the writer the honour to see him, his sick servant, the last time at his house, which he shall never forget. It is the place and house where he was born. Besides, the world will see that he is still where he was by such an eminent favour, which he values far above the commodity and honour of the bishopric." That is to say, if words mean anything, that Montaigne valued the privilege of being a favoured servant of Buckingham "far above" that of being a favoured servant of God. We can now better understand why Heylin wrote of him as one who "loved his ease."

I must return to Cozen, to show that he and Laud were on friendly terms. Five weeks after the latter had been in actual possession of the Bishopric of London, Cozen wrote to him concerning a Dr Smart, a Prebend of Durham, who had preached a sermon in that cathedral which gave great offence. The dean and chapter had already written[3] to Laud about the

---

[1] "Cal. Sta. Pa.," 1628-9, p. 390.   [2] *Ib.*, p. 59.   [3] *Ib.*, p. 243.

matter to " crave his assistance and preservation from obloquy
and contempt ; " but Cozen wrote[1] privately at great length,
and added that " Smart preferred four indictments at the last
Assizes in Durham ; one that they placed the communion
table the wrong way ; another, that they stand up and sing
the creed after the Gospel "—there is plenty of evidence
that until very near the period of which I am writing, in the
reformed Anglican Church, it was usual to sit during the
creed—" a third that they use wax lights and tapers ; and
a fourth that Mr Burgoyne has set up an altar in his church
at Wearmouth,—all by Smart supposed to be superstitious
ceremonies, and contrary to the Act of Uniformity.   A great
noise there was about it."   The grand jury threw out the
bill, and the judge gave Dr Smart a lecture, " adding, that
the man deserved no small punishment who, in this un-
wonted sort, had gone about to disgrace the Church, and
dishonour the solemnity of God's service there, where he
himself had been an eye and ear witness that all things
were done in decency and in order."

This was all very well ; but, says Cozen, " Smart sticks
not to profess that he will fetch them all into higher courts."

It is impossible to read this without being reminded of
certain appeals, in ritual cases, from the Court of Arches to
the Privy Council, within comparatively recent memory, and
perhaps a smile may be excusable.

Laud's Diary in 1628 contains the usual memoranda of his
aches and pains.   One day, he has " a terrible salt Rheum
in " his left eye.   On another he " fell Sick," and " came Sick
from *Hampton-Court*."   On a third, he was " sore plucked "
with his sickness.   On a fourth, he was " forced to put on a
Truss " for the ailment generally requiring such a remedy,
although he did not know how it had been " occasioned,
unless it were with swinging of a Book for my Exercise in
private."   From this it appears that he was in the habit of
using a heavy volume as a dumb-bell.

A very short entry records a very momentous event :—
" August 23. *Saturday*, St *Bartholomew's* Eve, the Duke of

[1] "Cal. Sta. Pa. Dom.," 1628-9, p. 259.

Buckingham slain at *Portsmouth* by one *Felton* about Nine
in the Morning." [1]

The news reached Laud on the following day at Croydon,
where he, with three other bishops, was engaged in "the
Consecration of Bishop *Montague* for *Chichester*, with my
Lord's Grace." "My Lord" was evidently Buckingham,
so that Montague became Bishop of Chichester, not by the
Grace of God, but by the Grace of Buckingham. Indeed it is
impossible to study the history of Laud without perceiving
that to him Buckingham was "Very Duke of Very Dukes,"
as Lord Brougham said of a very different person.

It may surprise some people to read of Laud's threatening a prisoner with the rack. When Felton, who had
assassinated Buckingham, was called before the Council, he
was pressed [2] "to confess who had set him on work to do
such a bloody act, and if the Puritans had no hand therein :
he denied they had ; and so he did to the last, that no person
whatsoever knew any thing of his intentions, or purpose to
kill the duke, that he revealed it to none living. Dr Laud,
Bishop of London, being then at the Council-table, told him,
if he would not confess, he must go to the rack. Felton
replied, if it must be so, he could not tell whom he might
nominate (*sic*) the extremity of torture ; and if what he should
say then must go for truth, he could not tell whether his
lordship (meaning Laud), or which of their lordships, he
might name ; for torture might draw unexpected things from
him. After this he was asked no more questions, but sent
back to prison."

Within a month of his death, the following epitaph was
suggested for the Duke of Buckingham :—

> "Ænigma Mundi Minor,
> Omnia fui, nec quicquam habui ;
> Patriæ parens et Hostis audio ;
> Deliciæ idem et ludibrium Parlamenti ;
> Qui dum Papistis bellum infero, insimulor Papista ;
> Dum Protestantium partibus consulo, occidor a Protestante." [3]

[1] Diary, p. 43.

[2] Rushworth, vol. i. p. 638.   [3] S. P. O., Charles I., vol. cxvii. No. 29.

The last word alludes to the fact that his murderer,
Felton, was a Protestant. Laud wrote to Secretary Conway
that "he had the news of that accursed fact" (the death of
Buckingham) "to his great sorrow and grief of heart. It is
the saddest accident that ever befel him, and should be so for
all good Christians."[1]

Undoubtedly he must have grieved greatly over the death
of his friend, and the downfall of so important a patron,
especially at a time when his enemies were declaring themselves with greater and greater courage, would make him
nervous about his own future; but he evidently received
great consolation in the loss of his pet penitent and dear
ord, "from a very Gracious Message from his Majesty, upon
my Lord Duke's death," "very Gracious Letters from the
King's Majesty, written with his own Hand," and, on the first
occasion of his court, after Buckingham's death, "the Gracious
Speech, which that Night the King was pleased to use to
me." In short the death of Buckingham had the effect of
strengthening rather than of weakening Laud's power; as
it made the king depend more exclusively upon his advice ;
moreover, there had been of late a strong, and daily increasing, animus against the great royal favourite, and if the
Commons could have succeeded in effecting his overthrow, it
is probable that Laud also would have been crushed in the
ruin. As it was, Laud rose higher in the king's favour, and
the end of the year 1628 saw him becoming one of the most
powerful factors in the State.

The first quarter of 1629 showed that the Commons were
bitterly opposed to the Episcopal favourite. "The Parliament, which was broken up this *March* 10," he writes,
" laboured my ruin ; but, God be blessed for it, found nothing
against me." There were other signs, however, of his unpopularity. "*March* 29. *Sunday*, Two Papers were found in
the Dean of *Paul's* his Yard before his House. The one
was to this effect concerning my self; *Laud*, look to thy
self; be assured thy Life is sought. As thou art the Fountain
of all Wickedness, Repent thee of thy monstrous Sins, before

[1] "Cal. Sta. Pa. Dom.," 1628-9, p. 269.

thou be taken out of the World, &c. And assure thy self, neither God nor the World can endure such a vile Counccllor to live, or such a Whisperer ; or to this effect."[1]

Laud took this matter very seriously. "Mr Dean delivered both Papers to the King that Night. Lord I am a grievous Sinner ; but I beseech thee, deliver my Soul from them that hate me without a Cause."

The anti-Laudian spirit found its way into the pulpit. A certain Mr Salisbury, in a sermon on Matthew xxiv. 6, " deplored the changes introduced into the Church, and the unhappy dissensions in Parliament, and urged upon his hearers to suffer all things in a passing fortitude rather than permit the least impairing of the national liberties." Laud apparently sent notes of this sermon to Lord Chief Justice Hyde, and asked his advice. The reply came that " Lord Chief Justice Hyde has advised with the rest of his brethren, and they utterly condemn Mr Salisbury of much folly and indiscretion, and hold him worthy to be proceeded against, but advise that he should be convented before the Ecclesiastical Commissioners."[2]

If any proof were wanting that a strong and outspoken party existed in opposition to Laud, it would be found in the fact that a clergyman, and apparently one with something against his character, could venture to hint that he would threaten to join it unless Laud would give him preferment. Here is an instance in point[3]:—" John Traske to Bishop Laud, of London. Will not think so vilely of his venerableness as that he should be so implacably cruel against a man unseen, unheard, unknown, and never spoken with to this day. What if he once erred ? How long was it ? How long since relinquished ? Has confessed by authority in pulpit and in print. Can bring large testimony for his orthodox teaching. The late King gave charge for his preferment to the then Lord Chancellor. Is loath to be of that number who go railing up and down against bishops for bare maintenance. Knows no law to starve any, and he knows no way to live out of his callings."

[1] Diary, p. 44.   [2] " Cal. Sta. Pa. Dom.," 1628-9, p. 551.   [3] *Ib.*, p. 576.

As to what was " orthodox teaching," there was more than one opinion. Certainly the House of Commons held a very different one from that of Laud. In the already mentioned " Remonstrance," the House submitted that " some prelates near the king, having gotten the chief administration of ecclesiastical affairs under His Majesty, discountenance and hinder the preferment of those that are orthodox, and favour such as are contrary ;"[1] and then Laud is expressly mentioned, as also is the Bishop of Winchester. Threatening indeed were the clouds which were beginning to gather on Laud's horizon, although he was basking in the full sunshine of the royal patronage and pleasure.

So far as danger threatened Laud from the Parliament, it was destined to be held in suspense for a period of eleven years. Early in March 1629, while Holles was suggesting a protest in the House of Commons, the first section of which was " Whoever shall seek to bring in popery, Arminianism, or other opinions disagreeing from the true and orthodox church, shall be reputed a capital enemy to this kingdom and commonwealth," the king came into the House of Lords and sent for the sergeant-at-arms. The Commons would not allow him to obey. He then sent the usher of the black rod to deliver a message to it, and he was refused admission, whereupon he commanded the captain of the guard to break open the door ; but when he reached it he found that the Commons had adjourned till the tenth. On that day, the king went to the House of Lords, and, without even summoning the Commons, dissolved Parliament. The houses were not again convoked until 1640, the interval being the longest in the whole parliamentary history of this country.

[1] " Constitutional Documents of the Puritan Revolution, 1628-60," Gardiner, p. 1;.

CHAPTER XIV.

Two births, interesting to Laud, took place in the spring of the year 1629. The first was that of a posthumous son of his dear Lord Duke of Buckingham, which he christened when about three weeks old. The second was one of greater importance.

The queen was expecting to become a mother, and, anxious to know the result, she consulted a lady who professed to be a prophetess. This was Lady Eleanor, a daughter of the Earl of Castlehaven, and the wife of Sir John Davies, the Attorney General. Lady Eleanor seems to have been half-clever, half-mad. The foundation of her claim to prophetical powers was the discovery that the letters composing her names—her christian name and her maiden surname—twisted into an anagram, formed the words "Reveal, O Daniel," and this she interpreted to mean that the mantle of that prophet had descended upon her shoulders. She had the good luck to foretell her first husband's death [1] correctly, and this happy hit established her reputation. One day when she was in waiting, the queen asked her whether she should have a son, and her reply was that she should indeed have a son, but that it "would be born, christened, and buried all in one day!" I should not mention this matter were it not that I shall have to show, a little later, how Lady Eleanor Davies tried her hand at forecasting the future of Laud himself, and with what result. I should observe, here, that in venturing to prophesy to the queen, she greatly offended the king, who said to her:—"How now, Lady Eleanor; are not you the person who foretold your husband's death in three days before it happened? It was the next to breaking his heart."

[1] Ballard's "Celebrated Women."

On the thirteenth of May, writes Laud, "about Three of the Clock, the Queen was delivered before her time of a Son."[1]

Miss Strickland[2] tells us that "a contest took place between Charles I. and the queen's confessor, whether the heir of Great Britain should be baptized according to the church of England, or the church of Rome; but the king carried his point, and the boy was named Charles James, by Dr Webb, the chaplain in attendance." The child was in a very languid condition from the moment of its premature birth, and about an hour after its baptism it died. Laud describes these events as follows:—"He was Christened, and Died within short space, his Name *Charles:* This was *Ascension* Eve. The next Day being Maij 14. *Ascension* Day, *Paulò post mediam Noctem,* I Buried him at *Westminster.*" And then follows an atrocious pun. "If God repair not this loss; I much fear it was *Descension-day* to this State."

The year 1629 was not one of the most eventful in the life of Laud. During the latter half of it he was in ill-health. On the 14th of August, he says:—"I fell sick upon my way towards the Court at *Woodstock.* I took up my Lodging at my ancient Friend's House, Mr *Francis Windebank.* There I lay in a most grievous burning Fever, till *Munday Sep. 7;*" "On which Day I had my last Fit." He was "brought so low," as to be unable to return to his own house in London until the 29th of October. His first act on his recovery was to present his "humble Duty and Service to his Majesty at *Denmark-House.*" For some time after this he "had divers Plunges, and was not able to put" him "self into the service of" his "Place till *Palm-Sunday,* which was March 21" in the following year. This was one of the longest, indeed I think quite the longest, illness that Laud had in his whole life.

While the subject of our biography is lying in bed, we may notice some letters and documents written about that time, demonstrating the condition of his Church. One is an order by another bishop "to be affixed in all parish churches

---

[1] Diary, p. 44. [2] "Lives of the Queens of England," viii. p. 55.

K

within his jurisdiction, for reforming certain abuses."[1] "The abuses are :—That during Divine service young men, misled by the example of their elders, sit covered. That men walk up and down, and talk before and after Divine service, and keep ales and drinking within the Church, and write their rates upon the Communion Table, &c." The communion-table would, of course, be in the body of the church. In what part of the church the "ales and drinking" took place is not stated.

A proclamation was issued from Hampton Court, ordering that "fish days, and especially Lent, are to be duly observed, 'the ancient and laudable custom' of abstinence from suppers on Fridays and the 'eves of feasts commanded to be fasted' is ordered to be kept in all taverns and ordinaries."[2]

While Laud was still invalided, one of his clergy wrote to him complaining that the people were "over much addicted to 'hearing the word,' as they call it, to the neglect of God's service and worship,"[3] and recommending him to silence a Mr Hooker, whom, he says, Bishop Andrews had suppressed in his diocese. A few days later, Laud received a letter signed by forty-nine beneficed clergy, stating that they "esteem and know Mr Hooker to be for doctrine, orthodox, for life and conversation, honest, and for disposition, peaceable, no ways turbulent or factious. Recommend him to the Bishop's favour, and intreat his continuance."[4]

Worries came to him again, in his convalescence, from "the Inhabitants of Hammersmith, in the parish of Fulham," who wrote[5] begging "him to consider the length and foulness of the way between Fulham and that place, in winter most toilsome, sometimes over ploughed lands, and almost unpassable ;" and they ask leave to build a chapel of ease at Hammersmith. Edmund, Earl of Mulgrave, adds a letter supporting their cause. He had "thought to have attended him, to have moved him in that particular, and also to have congratulated him on his recovery from long

---

[1] "Cal. Sta. Pa. Dom.," 1629-31, p. 141.   [2] *Ib.*, p. 348.
[3] *Ib.*, p. 87.   [4] *Ib.*, p. 92.   [5] *Ib.*, p. 115.

sickness, but the Earl is himself suffering from dangerous disease."

Laud wrote in reply [1] that " the relics of his fearful disease have stuck so close, that he has not been able to visit his Lordship." " Shall look that the chapel be built as other churches are, east and west, without tricks." From this " without tricks," it would appear that Laud felt some doubts as to the orthodoxy of Lord Mulgrave and the people of Hammersmith, especially as he goes on to say that " some men under the title of ' able and conformable ministers,' bring in notorious disturbers of the peace of the church ; therefore, the Bishop suggests that the appointment of minister should be left to him."

Lord Mulgrave wrote in answer that " the chapel shall stand east and west, without tricks, as was ever intended." As to " the nomination of the minister, none of them distrust the Bishop, but who knows how he may be succeeded. Craves that some few of the inhabitants may present one or more to his approbation, who, giving him good testimony of life, doctrine, and conformableness, will, it is hoped, be as acceptable to the Bishop as if he had made the election. Suspects that some one has possessed the Bishop with an opinion that some of them aim to bring in some busy-headed or factious man."

Occasionally, Laud's letters were more cheering. A couple of months after his correspondence with Lord Mulgrave, a Dr Aylett wrote to him : [2]—" Was last Tuesday at Chelmsford lecture, where Mr South of Writtle preached, who spake so pertinently against the schism of inconformity, and so gently advised them to peace, that a lawyer said as he came out, ' A few such excellent sermons would bring again the people in love with conformity.' Was bold to thank the preacher in the Bishop's name." But he adds significantly : — " Saw there no conformity in hood or surplice. Offers to give a lecture if directed."

Almost simultaneously with Laud's complete recovery, occurred a convenient death :—" The Earl of *Pembroke*, Lord

[1] " Cal. Sta. Pa. Dom.," 1629-31, p. 118.   [2] *Ib.*, p. 197.

Steward, being Chancellor of the University of *Oxford*, died of an Apoplexie." This "apoplexie" cleared the way for Laud. Only two days after the death of Pembroke, "the University of *Oxford* chose me Chancellor; and word was brought me of it, the next Morning, *Munday*." Scarcely any post could have been more to his liking.

Every rose, however, has its thorn; nor was this particular rose an exception. "I was welcomed into my Chancellorship of Oxford," he says, "with two very ill accidents; in either sermon one."[1] "The first, I hear, was committed by one of Exeter College; who preached directly against all obeisance, or any devout gesture in receiving of the communion. And if this be true, we shall not kneel neither. I would not be too sour at my first coming in; and yet I would not have sermons of such ill-example lead the way into my government there."

Laud's influence at Oxford had been great for many years, and his election was the consequence of his concordance with the heads of the colleges. His chancellorship was remarkable for his personal interest in the affairs of the university and his management of them, even when absent from it, and one of the first things he did was to arrange that the vice-chancellor should send him a detailed account of what was going on at Oxford, twice a week.[2]

To his credit be it spoken, although he sought to advance his own ecclesiastical polity, as he conceived it to be his duty, he none the less introduced useful reforms both in discipline and in study, and he presented the university with nearly six hundred valuable manuscripts in Arabic, Hebrew, Greek, and Latin, during the first five years of his chancellorship.[3]

We must now return to the queen. Lady Eleanor Davies had prophesied again, foretelling that Henrietta Maria would have another son and a strong one, and bonfires were actually lighted in honour of the delivery of such a prophecy by that silly woman. It so happened that the prophetess

[1] "Libr. of Anglo-Cath. Theol.," vol. v. part i. p. 15.
[2] "Eng. Univ.," by Huber. Trans. F. W. Newman, vol. ii. part i. p. 43.
[3] *Ib.*, p. 45.

was again right. On the 29th of May 1630, a baby, and an
ugly baby, prince was born. The king sent a formal intima-
tion to Laud. "The King to Bishop Laud. It having
pleased God to vouchsafe unto the King a son, according to
the laudable custom of his royal progenitors, he makes known
the joyful tidings to him, as Bishop of London, by Sir William
Segar, Garter."[1] Laud tells us in his Diary that he had been
in the house three hours before the child was born, and that
he "had the Honour and the Happiness to see the Prince,
before he was full one hour old."

The very morning of its birth, the king rode in state to
Laud's own cathedral, St Paul's, to return thanks;[2] but
whether Laud was present does not appear.

Laud was commanded to christen the child in the king's—
not the queen's—chapel at St James's. A draft exists[3] of
the "Orders for the christening of the Prince. The chapel
and all rooms through which the procession was to pass
were to be hanged with tapestry; an organ was to be
brought into the chapel; a stage was to be erected in the
middle of the chapel and the font to be set thereon; after
the christening the infant to be carried to the King and
Queen to receive their blessing; the bishops and clergy to
attend in their copes; the mayor in his velvet, the aldermen
in their scarlet gowns; artillery to be shot off at the Tower,
and by the shipping, immediately after the christening, and
bonfires to be made at night."

Besides royal functions and attendances at court, Laud
had plenty of letters and episcopal work to occupy him
about this time. I may give a few specimens of his correspondence. The Bishop of Durham wrote to him concerning
the weary length of the services in his cathedral, one beginning
at eight A.M. and continuing till eleven, and suggesting "the
propriety of dividing the Sunday Morning service prescribed
by the Prayer Book into several parts to be read at different
hours in the forenoon."[4]

---

[1] "Cal. Sta. Pa. Dom.," 1629-31, p. 269.
[2] Strickland's "Lives of the Queens of Eng.," vol. viii. p. 58.
[3] "Cal. Sta. Pa. Dom.," 1629-31, p. 283. [4] *Ib.*, p. 541.

Lord Wentworth wrote to recommend his chaplain, who had been in his house nearly twenty years, for a vacant prebend at Durham. He was a man "infinitely happy in his conversation," and there was "not a learneder man on the north of Trent, nor a priest of better temper or life."[1]

The Council wrote to Laud, announcing that the proclamation regarding abstinence, referred to above, had been "much contemned in inns and such like places, as seems very strange to his Majesty and this Board;" and "it is his Majesty's pleasure that the ecclesiastical court shall take effectual order that the offenders be punished, &c."[2]

The very next entry in the Calendar of State Papers is a "List of the Master Printers of London, with a sum placed against each of their names in the handwriting of Bishop Laud, and headed 'To St Paul's;'—to the repair of St Paul's. The sums assessed run from" £6 up to £40.

Then there is a letter from Laud himself to a Dr Samuel Brooke, "respecting his intended tract on Predestination." Laud considers that "somewhat about those controversies is unmasterable in this life, neither can he think any expression can be so happy as to settle all these difficulties. Doubts whether the King will have these controversies further stirred, which now begin to be more at peace."[3] One cannot doubt that a "Theological paper indorsed by Bishop Laud, as containing 'Mr Mady's doctrine about election,'"[4] would be answered in a similar tone.

But in ecclesiastical matters, the person whose case interested Laud chiefly in the year 1630, was Dr Leighton, of whom Laud's biographer, Heylin, writes as follows.[5] "Leighton, a Scot by birth, a Doctor of Physic by Profession, a fiery Puritan in Faction, dedicated a most pestilent book unto them, called *Sion's Plea.* In this Book he incited them *to kill all the Bishops, and to smite them under the fifth Rib,* inveighing also against the Queen, whom he branded by the

---

[1] "Cal. Sta. Pa. Dom.," 1629-31, p. 354.　　[2] *Ib.*, p. 379.
[3] *Ib.*, p. 405.　　[4] *Ib.*, p. 528.　　[5] "Cyp. Angl.," p. 187.

name of an Idolatress, a Canaanite, and the Daughter of Heth."

At Laud's instigation,[1] Leighton was brought before the Star Chamber, where he was condemned to pay a fine of £10,000; to be publicly whipped; to be placed for two hours in the pillory, and to have an ear cut off, a nostril slit open, and a cheek branded with the letters S.S. (Sower of Sedition); and, a week later, to be again whipped, to be again put in the pillory, to lose the other ear, to have the other nostril slit, and to have the other cheek branded. When this extraordinarily severe sentence had been passed, Leighton gave "thanks to God, who had given him the victory over his enemies." It is said that from this trial dates the friendship of Laud and Wentworth. [2]

The notes in Laud's own Diary,[3] relating to Leighton, may be worthy of quotation here :—" *Novemb. 4. Thursday, Leighton* was degraded at the High Commission. *Novemb. 9. Tuesday,* That Night *Leighton* broke out of the *Fleet.* The Warden says, he got or was helped over the Wall; the Warden professes, he knew not this till *Wednesday* Noon. He told it not me till *Thursday* Night. He was taken again in *Bedfordshire,* and brought back to the *Fleet* within a Fortnight. *Novemb. 26. Friday,* Part of his Sentence was executed upon him at *Westminster.*"

Laud seems to have thought it necessary to counterbalance this severity upon a Puritan by a show of at least strictness towards Catholics; for it was probably at his advice that the king forbade any English Catholics to hear mass in the queen's chapels, enjoined the enforcement of the existing laws against the Jesuits, and offered a reward of £100 for the apprehension of a Catholic bishop known to be in London. [4] It is true that only one priest was martyred about the time of which I am now writing, and that this took place through the over-zealous haste of a certain judge; but many priests suffered long terms of imprisonment, a few dying while undergoing this treatment.

[1] Lingard, vol. vii. chap. iv. [2] "Dic. Nat. Biog.," *Laud,* by S. R. Gardiner.
[3] Diary, p. 45. [4] Lingard, vol. viii. chap. iv.

Five months after his recovery from his long illness, Laud
"was taken with an extream Cold and Lameness" and was
laid up for a week.   This was only about a fortnight before
the trial of Leighton, and, if the "Lameness" proceeded
from gout, it may help to account for the severity of the
sentence upon Leighton, especially if the "extream Cold"
drove it in.   He is, indeed, likely to have had the gout, if he
drank the "Metheglins" then so popular, or "a pleasant and
wholesome drink," composed of honey and "small Ale,"
recommended by his friend, Sir Kenelm Digby.[1]

The next year Laud again showed his zeal against the
Puritans.   This time, instead of letting his great admirer,
Heylin, tell the story, I will depute that office to Prynne, a
gentleman who regarded Laud and his policy from a some-
what different point of view.[2]   "In the year 1631, William
Beale, servant to Master Henry Gellibrand, Professor of
Mathematics at Gresham College, London, set forth an
Almanacke for that yeare, . . . agreeing with the Kalendar
before Master Fox his Acts and Monuments printed oft
times by publicke authority, without the least exception
both in Queen Elizabeth's, King James, and King Charles's
Reignes, in which Almanacke, the names of the Popish
Saints canonized by Popes and thrust into our Kalendars
were omitted, and the names of reall Saints and Martyrs
mentioned in the Booke of Martyrs, inserted, just as they are
in Master Fox his Kalendar."   And then, after saying something about Laud, he continues :—"This Prelate being then
Bishop of London taking great exception against this Almanacke, brought both Mr Gellibrand and his man into the
High Commission for compiling and publishing it, where he
prosecuted them with great violence."   He then describes
Gellibrand's defence, and says that, on its conclusion, Laud
"stood up in a great passion, and publicly informed the
Court, That the Queen her selfe sent for him, and specially
complained against this Almanacke, which gave great offence
to those of her religion ; and desired him to prosecute the

---

[1] "The Closet of the Eminently Learned Sir Kenelme Digbie, Knt. Opened."
[2] "Canterburies Doome," p. 186.

Author of it, and suppresse the Book ; and therefore he hoped
he should not passe unpunished in this court."

Strange to say, the court acquitted the prisoner ; whereupon Laud " stood up again in a fury, and said to Mr
Gellibrand, ' Sir, Remember that you have made Faction
in this court, for which you ought to be punished ; and
know that you are not yet discharged hence. I will sit in
your skirts, for I heare you keepe Conventicles at Gresham
College after your Lectures there.' Whereupon he gave
Order for a second prosecution against him in the High
Commission, which so affected this good man, that it put
him in a Feaver fit, whereof he died."

I will spare my readers Prynne's inferences and moralizings
upon these incidents.

Before ending this chapter, I will mention Laud's appointment, in the year 1630, of Peter Heylin, who was to become
his own biographer and the fierce opponent of Prynne, as one
of his private chaplains.   He had been appointed historical
lecturer, and had become a writer on geographical and historical subjects, soon after taking his degree, and later he
had studied theology, after which he had attracted the
attention of Laud, as well as that of many adverse critics, by
maintaining that " the Church of England came from the
Church of Rome, and not from the Waldenses, Wycliffites,
and Hussites,"[1] in opposition to the Regius Professor of
Divinity at Oxford, who took the opposite and, at that time,
more usual view.   A year after Laud had made him his
chaplain, Laud's enemy, Williams, Bishop of Lincoln, refused
to institute him to a living in his diocese, for which the king
had recommended him.   " The king retaliated by appointing
Heylin to a prebend of Westminster," " of which Williams
was dean.   From that time forward it was one of Heylin's
favourite occupations to annoy Williams, who was in disgrace
at Court, and make himself an instrument of the royal vengeance."[2]   In this pursuit he is not likely to have received
much discouragement from Laud.   Like his master, Heylin
was a strenuous advocate of the theory that communion-tables

[1] The Bishop of Peterborough's article on Heylin ; " Dic. Nat. Bio."   [2] *Ib.*

should be placed " altarwise," and he discovered, and anathe-
matized in a pamphlet, called *A Coal from the Altar*, a letter
written by Williams to one of his clergy, in which he said that
they should be placed " not altar-wise, but table-wise ; "
whereupon Williams, under the veil of " a Lincolnshire
clergyman," wrote a book in reply, entitled *The Holy Table,
Name, and Thing.* To this Heylin retorted with another book,
Antidotum Lincolniense, and so the game went merrily on,
until Williams was suspended and Heylin thereby made
happy.

CHAPTER XV

On the 16th of January 1631, Laud performed an act which afterwards brought him into trouble. "I Consecrated," he says, "*St Catherine Creed-Church* in *London.*"

Here is Rushworth's description of the beginning of the ceremony.[1] "At his approach to the West door of the church, some that were prepared for it, cry'd out, *Open, Open, ye everlasting Doors, that the King of Glory may enter in*, and presently the doors were opened; and the Bishop coming in and falling upon his Knees, with his Eyes lifted up, and his Arms spread abroad, uttered these words: This Place is holy, the ground is holy, &c." This was said by his enemies to have been taken from the Roman Pontifical; but Laud declared that he only used a form of consecration which had been practised by Bishop Andrews. At his trial, he said that one of the witnesses had accused him, on this occasion, of using "many Bowings and Cringings"; and he protested that "for my kneeling down at my entrance to begin with Prayer, and after to proceed with Reverence, I did but my Duty in that, let him scoffingly call it Cringing, or *Ducking*, or what he please."[2]

Whether Andrews or Laud drew up this form of consecration is not of much consequence; what is certain is that it was something of an adaptation of the Roman Ritual. "Lift up your gates, ye princes, and be ye lifted up, ye everlasting doors, and the King of Glory shall come in,"[3] are the words used when a Catholic bishop is at the threshold of a church which he is about to consecrate, and, if any one will take the trouble to compare Rushworth's description of

---

[1] "Hist. Coll.," vol. ii. p. 69.   [2] "Hist.," p. 340.
[3] "Order for the Dedication or Consecration of a Church." Manresa Press, Roehampton, p. 8.

Laud's proceedings on this occasion with the Roman rite,
he will find many other points of similarity. The going
through this performance, on the part of Laud, was surely
very like " playing at church " ; for it was quite unauthorized
by his own religious body.

Laud continues :—" The same witness said 'that at the
beginning I took up Dust, and threw it in the Air, and
after used divers Curses.' This witness had need look
well to his Oath ; for there was no throwing up of Dust,
no Curses used throughout the whole Action."

" Then it was urged at the Bar, *That a prayer which I used,
was like one that is in the Pontifical.* So in the *Missal* are
many Prayers like to the Collects used in the *English
Liturgy.*"

" Said Mr *Brown, but the Treason is, To seek, by these
Ceremonies, to overthrow the Religion Established.* Nor was
that ever sought by me : And God of his Mercy Preserve
the true *Protestant* Religion amongst us."

Continuing his defence for using certain old Catholic
prayers and ceremonies in the consecration of St Catherine's
Cree, he said, " We have separated the Chaff, shall we cast
away the Corn too ? If it come to that, let us take heed
we fall not upon the *Devil's Winnowing,* who labours to
beat down the Corn ; 'tis not the Chaff that Troubles him,
S. *Luc.* 22."

Exactly. And I have no doubt that it was on this
principle that I once saw a High-Church Anglican clergyman celebrating the communion service with a large copy of
the *Book of Common Prayer* on the desk on the communion-
table, and a very small copy of the *Garden of the Soul,*
opened at " The Ordinary of the Mass," lying beside it.
I asked him, afterwards, his reasons for this, and he said
that he read aloud the prescribed order for holy communion
out of the Anglican prayer book, and interposed, in a
whisper, such prayers out of the Roman Missal as he
thought good, adding that this was a common practice
among clergymen of his school. Like Laud, he probably
fancied that he was separating the chaff without casting

away the corn, and as to the " Devil's Winnowing," he
would say that, of the two books upon the communion-
table, " it is not the *Book of Common Prayer* 'that Troubles
him,' S. *Luc.* 22.' " Both Laud and my friend appear to
have forgotten that such Catholic corn as the Order for the
Consecration of Churches and the Ordinary of the Mass had
long ago been cast among the chaff by the Church to
which they belonged ; or it may have been that they were
uncomfortably conscious of the fact that the Anglican
winnowing machine was apt to scatter the grain indis-
criminately with the husk.

The intimacy between Laud and King Charles continued
to increase. " *March* 20. *Sunday*," he writes, " His Majesty
put his Great Case of Conscience to me, about &c. Which
I after answered." What the case of conscience was is not
recorded.

The king had granted Laud a quantity of timber from
Shotover to be used in enlarging the buildings at St John's
College, and into this work he threw his whole heart. This
project he " published " " to the Colledge about the end of
March " 1631, having " resolved on it in *November* last."
The President " and others " of St John's replied that " if
their gratitude were mute, the very stones of their college
would, like the statue of Memnon, commemorated by Taci-
tus, give forth music to his glory." [1] The first stone was laid
on the 26th of July, and the work appears to have gone on
apace, for just a year later, much had evidently been done
when Dr Juxon wrote to Laud, saying that [2] " if he please
to disburse £3200, the quadrangle of St John's will be
absolutely uniform, without the least eye-sore, more than
the tops of the tunnels of the chimneys in the east range
of the old quadrangle, the cloisters being of the largest
size that art can allow, and the pillars of the best stone,
under marble, growing (*sic*) in that part of England. The
cloister is of a form not yet seen in Oxford (for that
under Jesus College Library is a misfeatured thing), therefore he wishes a little extraordinary charge might be

[1] "Cal. Sta. Pa. Dom.," 1631-2, p. 11.   [2] *Ib.*, 1631-3, p. 287.

bestowed there, that that wherein they are singular might be eminent."

Laud had plenty of business to occupy him in London also. He received a letter from Bishop Hall of Exeter, who 'wrote last week to give information about a busy, ignorant schismatic, lurking in London. Now hears that there are eleven several congregations of separatists about the city, furnished with their idly-pretended pastors, who meet together in brew-houses every Sunday."[1] What would not a Bishop of London give in these days to know that there were only eleven congregations of separatists in the metropolis?

Judging from the letters existing from different parsons, begging Laud not to believe reports of their misbehaviour, he must have kept his clergy in very considerable awe. As to the laity, Laud sometimes wrote to them in a tone of ironical banter. Thus we find a letter from him in April 1631 to " Sir John Lambe at Rowell, co. Northampton," in which he stated that he " was confident without his promise, that Sir John would never call the writer *ad testificandum*, but if he had been ready for mirth, might have made good sport with he knows whom about it, ' for that 's the way to Winchester.' " (There was a rumour shortly afterwards that Laud was to be translated from London to that see. So, at least, says Nicholas in a letter to Pennington.) " Observes that he has become a great courtier of late. Green's Norton being in the King's gift, he can give the Bishop notice of the sickness of the incumbent; but Sudborough being in the poor Bishop of London's gift, and under Sir John's nose at Rowell, he can send him no word of it, though the parson be as dangerously sick as he of Green's Norton. To make amends, begs him to ride over to Sudborough, and if the living be void, to send exact word how far it is distant from Brackley."[2]

In the provinces, as well as in his diocese and at Oxford, Laud had his worries. His friend, Cozen, together with a Dr Lindsell, Dean of Lichfield, seems to have spoken his mind to Laud, at Fulham, about the Bishop of Durham, Cozen's

---

[1] " Cal. Sta. Pa. Dom.," 1631-3, p. 74.   [2] *Ib.*, p. 10.

bishop. Whereupon Laud wrote a letter to the latter on the subject; for Cozen informed Laud that the Bishop of Durham "declared his great displeasure against Dr Lindsell and the writer, for the speech they had with Bishop Laud at Fulham, which he calls 'Accusations and articles preferred against him,' and after answering them caused Bishop Laud's letter to be publicly read, calling it a libel and a saucy letter." [1] Cozen "hopes it will not offend Bishop Laud if he legally refuses Bishop Howson's censure, he having already declared himself against the writer."

Laud seems to have used his influence with the king on Cozen's behalf against his bishop; for the latter (the Bishop of Durham) wrote to Laud, saying that "his Majesty also required Bishop Howson to desist from his proceeding against Dr Lindsell and Dr Cozen, upon pretence of ordering the public prayers, wherein his Majesty has been misinformed." [2] He goes on to say that he "conceives that he has suffered more than ever was offered to a Bishop of Durham."

As the summer of 1631 advanced, there were "great disorders"[3] at Laud's beloved Oxford. An appeal was made by "Mr *Foord* of *Magdalen Hall*, and Mr *Thorne* of Baliol Colledge," against some decision given by Laud's own vice-chancellor, and the two proctors had actually had the effrontery to receive their appeal, "as if it had not been *perturbatio pacis, &c.*" This, of course, was very shocking, and the vice-chancellor appealed to the king. "The King with all the Lords of his Council then present, heard the Cause at *Woodstock*, Aug. 23, 1631, being *Tuesday* in the After-noon." Mr Foord, Mr Thorne, and a Mr Hodges of Exeter College, were "banished the University," and "both the Proctors were commanded to come into the Convocation House, and there resign their Office." Besides this, the Rector of Exeter and the Principal of Magdalen Hall "received a sharp admonition for their misbehaviour in this business." Therefore the Oxford Dons were given pretty clearly to understand that Laud intended to be obeyed and

---

[1] "Cal. Sta. Pa. Dom.," 1631-3, p. 152.   [2] *Ib.*, p. 190.
[3] Diary, p. 46.

respected, as their chancellor, and that the king would support him in all that he did.

On the fourth of November, the queen had another child, "the Lady *Mary*, Princess, born at *St James's, inter horas quintam and sextam matutinas.* It was thought, she was born three weeks before her time."[1] Laud baptized her, in the chapel at St James's.[2]

The court had worries about this time concerning the king's sister, the Queen of Bohemia. Her husband, the ex-king of that country, had not only lost his crown and kingdom, but also his own dominions in the Palatine. The terrible Thirty Years' War had begun, and Gustavus Adolphus, King of Sweden, was just at this time showing "himself one of the greatest leaders that ever commanded an army,"[3] at the head of the Protestant League. England had not yet joined in the war; but many Englishmen and Scotchmen were serving in the Swedish army, and there was a strong feeling in England in favour of the Protestant cause, which was increased by the interest which was felt in the fate of the Queen of Bohemia, sister to King Charles. Without formally joining in the war, Charles prevailed upon the Marquess of Hamilton to levy 6000 men, with which, at Charles's expense, he was to join the army of Gustavus Adolphus. Hamilton took an active part in the campaign terminating with the battle of Leipsic; but, not content with this, Gustavus Adolphus asked Charles to send to his assistance an English army of 20,000 foot and 5000 horse, a request with which he was unable to comply, very greatly to the annoyance of his sister, the Queen of Bohemia. Immediately after the birth of his thirteenth child,[4] the King of Bohemia set forth to join Gustavus Adolphus in the war: About this time Sir Henry Vane, as ambassador from King Charles, attempted to negotiate with Gustavus Adolphus for the restoration of the Palatinate to the King of Bohemia. Much unpleasantness resulted between Charles and his

[1] Diary, p. 46.   [2] Strickland, " Lives of the Eng. Queens," chap. viii. p. 61.
[3] Freeman's " General Sketch," p. 281.
[4] Green's " Princesses of Eng.," vol. v. p. 493.

sister as to the conditions offered. Charles wanted one thing and his sister another; the terms thought good enough by the former were considered very offensive by the latter. The foundation was thus laid for affairs into which Laud was to be drawn by-and-bye; and already, even in December 1631, the Queen of Bohemia had begun to enlist the services of Laud on her own behalf with her brother, King Charles; for Laud writes that he "has always been ready to do her service with the King his master. No brother can be fuller of kindness and care for her good and that of her children, and hopes she will have joy in the end for his wise and prudent and affectionate care of them."[1]

How far his correspondent appreciated her brother's "kindness and care for her good" may be inferred from a letter which she wrote in the same year to Sir Thomas Roe, whom she addresses as "Honest Tom." Speaking of her "dear brother," she says:—"we are not made acquainted with anything that he treats there though they say that it is for our good. You may judge what comfort that is to us" (that is to say her husband and herself), "to be used as little children that cannot keep counsel; for when we desire to know what is treated, we are answered that it is not fit, that such things should be divulged abroad."[2]

Laud was much interested in a more private matter nearer home. A godchild of his own, Chillingworth, a son of a mayor of Oxford, and a Fellow of Trinity, was employed by Laud as a spy and commissioned to send him a weekly budget of information from Oxford. It was by means of a letter from him that Laud obtained the conviction and the passing of a tremendous sentence upon Alexander Gill, an usher of St Paul's School, and a tutor of Milton's. Of this matter, even an admirer of Laud's like Mr Benson, says:—"It is rather a revolting story: it argues that if Chillingworth was nothing more than indiscreet in writing it, Laud was nothing less than unscrupulous in using it."[3]

About the year 1630, this pet instrument of Laud's

---

[1] "Cal. Sta. Pa. Dom.," 1631-3, p. 196.
[2] German Correspondence, 1631.   [3] Benson, p. 95.

greatly misbehaved himself. I will let Wood[1] describe what happened. "Being unsettled in his thoughts, he became acquainted with one who went by the name of John Fisher"— this was the Father Fisher with whom Laud had had his famous controversy—"a learned Jesuit and sophistical disputant, who was often conversant in these parts. [Oxford.] At length by his persuasions, and for the satisfaction of some doubts which he could not find among our great men at home, he went to the Jesuit College of St Omer, forsook his religion, and by these motives following, which he left among them under his own hand, became a Roman Catholic."

His "Ten Reasons" form no part of a Life of Laud; but he afterwards wrote a kind of *Apologia*, and to this Laud replied by personal letters, with the result of inducing him to return to Oxford. So, at least, says Mr Benson;[2] but Wood's account is "that he finding not that satisfaction from the Jesuits concerning various points of religion, or (as some say) not that respect which he expected (for the common report among his contemporaries in Trinity College was that the Jesuits, to try his temper and exercise his obedience, did put him upon servile duties far below him), he left them in the year 1631, returned to the Church of England (though the Presbyterians said not, but that he was always a Papist in his heart), and was kindly received by his godfather, Dr Laud, then Bishop of London."

Some light is thrown upon the subject by a letter written to Laud in March 1632, from which, by the way, it would appear that Chillingworth had not yet formally returned to the Church of England, by Dr Juxon, afterwards himself Bishop of London, and one who would not be likely to minimise the value of Chillingworth's restoration to Anglicanism if he could honestly avoid doing so. In his opinion, Chillingworth is "Ambitious to be Bishop Laud's convert; for," he thinks, "*all his motives are not spiritual, protest he never so much.*"[3]

Mr Benson admits that, after his return to Anglicanism,

---

[1] Wood's "Athen. Oxon.," vol. ii. pp. 40 and following, Ed. 1721.
[2] Benson, p. 95.   [3] "Cal. Sta. Pa. Dom.," 1631-3, p. 290.

"he had scruples about subscription"; but he states that "Laud overcame them, and made him Canon of Salisbury and master of a hospital at Leicester." The contemporary Jesuit, Father Knott, wrote of him, that "the profession of Catholic religion not suiting to his desires and designs, he fell upon Socinianism, that is no religion at all."[1]

In 1632, Laud received a letter which must have caused him scandal as well as annoyance.[2] It informed him that the vice-chancellor at the sister university had committed suicide. The letter is recorded thus:—"To Bishop Laud. Relates the history of the suicide of Dr Butts, Vice-Chancellor of Cambridge." "On Easter Sunday he lay in bed, but said he was well and cheerful, bade his wife go to church, and when she was gone, charged his servants to go down for half an hour, for he would take a rest. He then rose in his shirt, bolted the door, took the kerchief about his head and hanged himself."

In June 1632, to Laud's great delight, " Mr *Francis Windebancke* my Old Friend was sworn Secretary of State; which place I obtained for him of my Gracious Master King Charles."[3] Undoubtedly, Laud would not have obtained this post for him, could he have foreseen that he would become a Catholic. Windebank, however, had for a long time, been a great friend to Catholics,[4] and the very entry above quoted was brought in evidence against Laud at his trial. He was accused of "his familiarity and commerce with the Jesuits, priests, and those most affected to the Popish faction. The first was Secretary Windebank, the greatest and most visible protector of the priests."[5] Indeed, only three years after his appointment as Secretary of State, we find him giving a discharge for Laud's old enemy, Father Fisher, who was then imprisoned for being a Jesuit in Eng-

---

[1] "A Direction to N. N. being an admonition to Mr Chillingworth to attend to his own Arguments," by Father Edward Knott, S.J.

[2] "Cal. Sta. Pa. Dom.," 1631-4, p. 302. Also, partly in Masson's "Life of Milton."

[3] Diary, p. 47.

[4] "Records of the Eng. Prov. S.J." Series I, p. 252, Note.

[5] "Kingdom's Intelligencer." King's Pamphlets, No. 167. British Museum.

land. " Theis are to will and require you forthwith to enlarge and sett at liberty the body of John Peers [Percy, *als* Fisher, now prisoner in your charge, for wch this shall be y^r warrant.—FRAN. WINDEBANK." [1]

Within a month of his success in obtaining the Secretary-ship of State for Windebank, Laud had the satisfaction of writing as follows in his Diary. " Doctor *Juxon*, then Dean of *Worcester*, at my suit sworn Clark of his Majestie's Closet. That I might have one I might trust near his Majesty, if I grow weak or infirm ; as I must have a time."

Juxon was a man who had the good luck to live through troublous times without incurring much personal trouble, although a High-Churchman. He held several important offices, became Bishop of London, and attended Charles I. on the scaffold. Then, instead of being prosecuted or persecuted, he went quietly to an estate he possessed in Gloucestershire, and became a master of hounds. At the Restoration, he returned to London and was made Arch-bishop of Canterbury, eventually dying at the age of eighty-one.

In September 1632, a religious function took place in Laud's diocese, which can scarcely have failed to give him intense annoyance. This was the laying of the founda-tion stone of a Catholic church, in the tennis-courtyard of Somerset House.[2] Another Catholic church was begun at St James's, and, a year or two later, mass was said in these two chapels with more ceremony than had been possible in England for a long period ; but of this I will say more in due course.

The year 1632 closed quietly for Laud. It is true that the king had small-pox on the second of December ; but, Laud tells us, " he had a very gentle disease of it," and he was sufficiently recovered by Christmas day for Laud to preach to him. The court, however, was in mourning, the King of Bohemia having died in the previous month, and

---

[1] Dom. Charles I., vol. ccxcv. No. 57, 1635.
[2] Pery's " News Letter ; " Ellis's " Original Letters," New series, vol. iii., p. 271.

Laud wrote on the 27th of December : — "The Earl of *Arundel* set forward towards the *Low Countries*, to fetch the Queen of *Bohemia* and her children." On the whole, although there were incidents in plenty connected with Laud's affairs, they were not of any great or immediate importance to him-self, personally. It was very different in the year 1633.

CHAPTER XVI

In the spring of the year 1633, Charles I. started for Scotland, taking Laud with him. The ostensible object of his journey was to be crowned king of that country. He was attended by an imposing train of English noblemen, and the whole expedition was one great state progress. He had intended to make a triumphal entrance into the great northern city of York; but "the Day was extream Windy and Rainy, that he could not"; and here Laud makes one of his wretched attempts at a joke :—"I called it *York-Friday*."[1]

Even in passing through York, Laud had an eye to furthering his own ecclesiastical policy. A letter, written in the hand of his secretary, copied from one by the king to the Dean and Chapter of York immediately after his visit, can scarcely be doubted to have been the result of Laud's own suggestion. It may be, indeed, that this was the original draft written at Laud's dictation, for the king's approval and use. It says that[2] "the King, when lately in the Chapter of St Peter, in York, there to give God thanks for his safety thus far onward of his journey, observed" that houses were built against the very walls of the cathedral, and one inside it. "The King commands that the persons addressed neither build nor suffer any dwelling-house or stable to be erected within or without the cathedral; and that the house within the cross aisle be forthwith pulled down." He also observed "when he came into the quire," that, "there had been a removing of seats which were placed there for the use of the wives of deans and prebendaries, and other women of quality." These were to be taken away at once; "a fair seat" was "to be left or made upon the north side of the quire above the stalls, for the Lord President's lady and her

[1] Diary, p. 48.   [2] "Cal. Sta. Pa. Dom.," 1633-4, p. 72.

company, and no other." We have all been accustomed to hear that Cromwell made a stable in this church or the other; but, from the above, it would appear that precedents had been set for such desecrations under the monarchy.

On arriving at Edinburgh, the king received an enthusiastic welcome; but the Bishop of the Isles was injudicious enough to say to him at dinner, that the Scots were likely enough to imitate the Jews, and that their hosannas at his entry might be changed, by-and-bye, for "Away with him, crucify him," whereupon the king became very serious and ate no more.[1]

Of the coronation itself, Laud says :—"Tuesday after *Trinity-Sunday*, King *Charles* Crowned at *Holyrood-Church* in *Edinburgh*. I never saw more expressions of Joy than were after it." Of this memorandum in Laud's Diary, D'Israeli writes as follows[2] :—"Laud was too poor a politician, in the impetuosity of his temper, when on this very occasion he pushed aside one of the Scottish Bishops who would not be clad in the sacred vestments—to detect the serpent which was sleeping under the flowers." This is put strongly; but it is difficult to deny that there is a modicum of truth in it.

The coronation ceremony was performed by the Bishop of St Andrews, and there were no great obstacles in the way of carrying it out with some pomp and show of ecclesiastical order; for, although the cathedral churches of Scotland had fallen into neglect, "the King's own Chappel at *Holy-rood-House* had still been maintain'd with the comeliness of the Cathedral Service, and all other Decencies used in the Royal Chapel."[3]

The day after his coronation, the king opened the Scottish Parliament, in which friction soon began to make itself manifest. When the Parliament was asked to confirm the Statutes empowering the Crown to regulate the apparel of the clergy, a stout resistance was made. Pointing to a paper which he held in his hand, Charles said :—"Your names are

---

[1] MS. Letter of 1633, quoted by Lingard.
[2] "Life and Reign of Ch. I.," vol. iii. p. 207.
[3] Clarendon's "Hist. of the Reb.," vol. i. p. 82.

here! to-day I shall see who are willing to serve me." As D'Israeli points out, Laud may not have shown very delicate tact in his behaviour in Scotland ; but can more be said for his royal master ?

On his last Sunday in Edinburgh, Laud preached before the king "in the Chappel in *Holyrood-House.*" The next day he started for a tour through the country, visiting St Andrews, Dundee, Falkland, St Johnston, Dunblain, Stirling—in travelling to which town he had a "dangerous and cruel Journey, crossing part of the *Highlands* by Coach, which was a Wonder there,"—"Lithgow, and so to *Edinburgh*" again. Two days later he started for London.

In this expedition to Scotland, Charles, as Clarendon tells us,[1] "proposed nothing more to himself, than to Unite his three Kingdoms in one Form of God's Worship, and publick Devotions." "To that end, the then Bishop of *London*, Dr *Laud*, attended on his Majesty throughout that whole journey, which, as he was Dean of the Chapel, he was not obliged to do, and no doubt would have been excus'd from, if that Design had not been in view ; to accomplish which he was no less solicitous than the King himself, nor the King less solicitous for his advice. He Preach'd in the Royal Chapel at *Edenbourgh* (which scarce any *English*-man had ever done before in the King's presence) and principally upon the benefit of Conformity, and the reverend Ceremonies of the Church." Or as D'Israeli describes it :—"By the side of Charles stood his evil genius—the Kirk-party scowled, as the Bishop of London in his rochet preached on the benefit of Conformity and the sacredness of Ceremonies, from that pulpit, whence Knox had thundered on their eternal abolition."[2] All this was better received than might have been expected, and Clarendon remarks that "many Wise Men" were of opinion that "if the King had then propos'd the Liturgy of the Church of *England* to have been then receiv'd and practised by that Nation, it would have been submitted to without opposition." Instead of doing this, Charles

[1] "Hist. of the Rebellion," vol. i. p. 82.
[2] "Life and Reign of Ch. I.," vol. iii. p. 206.

hesitated. "Laud, indeed," says Lingard,[1] "laboured strenuously to establish at once the English liturgy; but his reasoning and influence were compelled to yield to the obstinacy of the Scottish bishops, who deemed it a disgrace to their country to owe either the service or the discipline of their Church to their English neighbours." The king, accordingly, assigned the task of compiling a new code of ecclesiastical law, as well as a liturgy, to four of the Scotch bishops, and their efforts were to be submitted for revision to Laud, and two other English bishops.

It took Laud a fortnight and a day to travel from Edinburgh to London: the king arrived there a day or two before him.

Eight days after Laud's return to Fulham, an event occurred of the greatest importance to him. He writes an account of it somewhat abruptly. "*Aug.* 4. *Sunday*, News came to Court of the Lord Arch-Bishop of *Canterbury's* Death; and the King resolved presently to give it to me. Which he did *Aug.* 6."

Clarendon describes this at great length.[2] After saying that Laud went to see the king on his return, he adds:— "His Majesty entertained him chearfully with this Compelation, *My Lord's Grace of* Canterbury, *you are very welcome*, and gave order the same day for the despatch of all the necessary forms for the Translation: so that within a Month or thereabouts after the death of the other Arch-Bishop, he was compleatly invested in that high Dignity, and settled in his Palace at *Lambeth*." A few lines further on, he says, "that his Promotion to Canterbury was long foreseen, and was expected; nor was it attended with any increase of envy or dislike." Perhaps he thought that there had been enough of each already.

The paragraphs which follow bear so much upon the subject of my biography that I shall venture to make a few quotations from them, and I shall do so the more readily, because the threshold of his greatest advancement in life seems a fitting occasion to consider his character.

[1] "Hist. of Eng.," vol. vii. chap. v.   [2] Vol. i. p. 89.

"He" (Laud) "was a Man of great Parts, and very exemplary Virtues, allay'd and discredited by some unpopular natural Infirmities; the greatest of which was (besides a hasty, sharp way of expressing himself) that he believ'd Innocence of Heart, and Integrity of Manners, was a guard strong enough to secure any Man in his Voyage through this World, in what Company soever he travell'd, and through what Ways soever he was to pass: and sure never Man was better supplied with that Provision." I beg my readers carefully to consider this criticism, as it is one to which my own studies of the history of Laud greatly incline me.

A little later he says:—"When he came into great Authority, it may be, he retain'd too keen a memory of Those who had so unjustly, and uncharitably Persecuted him before; and I doubt, was so far transported with the same Passions he had reason to complain of in his Adversaries, that, as they accus'd Him of Popery, because he had some doctrinal Opinions which they liked not, though they were nothing ally'd to Popery; so he entertain'd too much prejudice to some Persons, as if They were Enemies to the Discipline of the Church, because they concurr'd with Calvin in some doctrinal Points; when they abhorr'd his Discipline, and reverenced the Government of the Church, and pray'd for the peace of it with as much Zeal, and Fervency as any in the Kingdom; as they made manifest in their Lives, in their Sufferings with it, and for it."

I am afraid that there is some truth in what Clarendon says as to his having been "transported with the same Passions he had reason to complain of in his Adversaries." The natural man in Laud was good, straightforward, and honest; but he was sadly lacking in what Catholics term supernatural grace.

But to continue:—" He was a Man of great Courage and Resolution, and being most assur'd within himself, that he propos'd no end in all his actions and designs, but what was Pious and Just (as sure no man had ever a heart more entire to the King, the Church, or his Country) he never studied the easiest ways to those ends: he thought, it may be, that any art or industry that way would discredit, at least make the Integrity of the end suspected, let the cause be what it will. He did court Persons too little ; nor cared to make his designs, and purposes, appear as candid as they were, by showing them in any other dress than their own natural beauty, though perhaps in too rough a manner ; and did not consider enough what men said, or were like to say of him. If the faults, and Vices were fit to be look'd into, and discover'd, let the Persons be who they would that were guilty of them, they were sure to find no connivance of Favour from him. He intended the Discipline of the Church should be felt, as well as spoken of, and that it should be applied to the greatest and most splendid Transgressors, as well as to the punishment of smaller Offences, and meaner Offenders." And he goes on to say that " Persons of Honour, and great Quality, of the Court, and of the Country, were every day cited into the High-Commission Court, upon the fame of their Incontinence, or other Scandal in their lives, and were there prosecuted to their Shame, and Punishment : "—it is almost impossible to help reflecting how busy he would have been on this score, had he lived in the reign of Charles II., instead of in that of Charles I.—"and as the Shame (which they call'd an Insolent Triumph upon their Degree and Quality, and levelling Them with the common People) was never forgotten, but watch'd for revenge; so the Fines impos'd there were the more question'd, and repin'd against, because they were assign'd to the rebuilding, and repairing St *Paul's* Church ; and thought therefore to be the more Severely impos'd, and the less Compassionately reduc'd and excus'd : which likewise made the jurisdiction and rigour of the Star-Chamber more felt, and murmur'd against, and sharpen'd many men's humours against the Bishops, before they had any ill Intention towards the Church."

Some of my readers, whose clergymen are engaged in restoring their churches, may be able to sympathize with these people of "Quality," if they will try to imagine their parsons empowered to fine them, and devoting the fines so obtained to their building funds. Could anything be more galling ?

The contrast between these fines wrung from angry offenders, and the method by which funds were raised for the erection of many Catholic cathedrals is very great. I am referring to the so-called "sale of Indulgences!" The Church has, at times, published to her children, in her exercise of that power of the Keys given to Peter and his successors, that the temporal penalties, or canonical penances, due for their sins—these being first duly repented of and forgiven—were by her commuted, wholly or in part, for other works of piety, amongst the rest for alms given towards the building of a Church or Hospital. Surely voluntary penitential offerings of this kind were more likely to lead to the benefit of the souls of the sinners than Laud's fines !

Everybody was not of the king's opinion that Laud was the man best fitted to be appointed to the See of Canterbury. A certain Justinian Paget writes to his cousin :[1]— "You may be confident that Dr Laud is Archbishop of Canterbury ; for his *congé d' éslire* was returned the last week, and it is said the king hath given his royal assent; but it seems every man hath not ; for it is said that a preacher in London, in his prayer, prayed God not to send a Bonner or a persecutor of the Church among them ; as if he thought Dr Laud would be such an one."

The very day that fortune favoured Laud by the death of Abbott, he was offered, he tells us, a still greater honour than an archbishopric, namely, to be made a Prince of the Catholic Church. He writes :—"*Aug.* 4. That very Morning, at *Greenwich,* there came one to me, Seriously, and that avowed ability to perform it, and offered me to be a Cardinal : I went presently to the King, and acquainted him both with the Thing, and the Person."

It is one thing to avow that one can obtain a favour for a friend, and another to do so! Let me quote Laud's orthodox modern Anglican biographer, Dean Hook, on this in-

[1] " Court and Times of Charles I.," vol. ii. p. 227.

cident.[1] " It is difficult to believe that the person who made this offer acted with authority ; it was probably a trap to make the bishop, now almost expecting the primacy, commit himself to the contempt of the Romanists and to the increased malevolence of the Puritans."

In this I so far agree with Dean Hook that I cannot believe the offer of a cardinal's hat to have been made with authority. Very likely some Catholic—possibly, nay, not improbably, the queen herself may have said something of this sort :— " If you will become a Catholic, I have no doubt I can get the Pope to send you a Cardinal's biretta ! " His formal abjuration of the Anglican heresy would obviously have been a *sine quā non*.

Heylin quotes Andreas ab Habernfield to the effect that Con " had a command to make offer of a Cardinal's cap to the Lord Archbishop in the name of the Pope of Rome ; and that he should allure him also with higher promises,"—this he well might, by those of heaven and eternal happiness, which are much higher things than " Cardinals' caps "; but the only higher earthly honour could be the Popedom, which even the Pope himself would not have it in his power to offer —" that he might corrupt his sincere mind ; yet a fitting occasion was never offered whereby he might insinuate himself into the Lord Archbishop, &c." [2] All this, I think with Dean Hook, should be accepted with great reservation, if, indeed, with any credence whatever. The opinion of Lingard, as the principal Catholic English historian, is worth quoting on this question. After giving certain evidence on the subject, he winds up by saying [3] :—" I am inclined to think that the proposal of the cardinal's hat came to the new archbishop from Queen Henrietta, under the notion that there might be some truth in the reports, which had been so long current, of Laud's secret attachment to the Roman Catholic creed."

In considering this question, it should be borne in mind how apt foreign Catholics are to rush to the conclusion that

---

[1] Hook's " Lives of the Archps. of Cant.," vol. xi. pp. 231-2.
[2] " Cyp. Ang.," pp. 386 and foll.
[3] " Hist. of Eng.," vol. vii. chap. v., Footnote.

Anglican clergymen are on the very threshold of the Church, when they hear of their practising ceremonies not unlike our own, or using Catholic devotions ; we English Catholics know better; but most probably Henrietta Maria thought that Laud only wanted the touch of a feather, as it were, to turn him over, so delicately may she have believed him to have been balanced on the extreme edge of High-Church Anglicanism.

As to the Cardinal's hat itself, had Laud become a Catholic, he need not have been ordained priest in order to obtain it. How soon he might have been made a cardinal is another question altogether ; but when we reflect that Manning and Newman were made cardinals in the nineteenth century, it seems not improbable, that, had Laud become a Catholic, he would have been made a cardinal in the seventeenth.

The offer which had been made to Laud on August 4, was renewed, he tells us, on the 17th, "a serious offer to be made a cardinal," he calls it ; but, he adds that he answered, "something dwelt within me, which would not suffer that, till *Rome* were other than it is." In short, he could not make up his mind to become a Catholic. As Mr Benson says on this very point [1] :—" The answer was a very genuine one. Laud was hardly nearer Rome than he was to Calvinism. He was far too real an Erastian at heart, far too earnest a believer in the interdependence of Church and State to lie down either with the Pope or Luther." Herein Mr Benson has made an admirable criticism. Laud, and he might have added Laud's followers, even down to the present day, are, *in principle*, hardly nearer to Rome than to Calvinism, however "high " their views, or gorgeous their vestments ; their position is one of negation ; they will not lie down either with the Pope or Luther ! To an Englishman there is nothing so dear as the spirit of compromise, and they represent the theological incarnation of it.

It was in this year of 1633 that the king revived, as is always supposed at Laud's instigation, the famous Book o Sports. It is our pleasure, it enjoined :—" That the Bishop of

[1] Benson, p. 109.

the Diocese take the like strait order with all Puritans and Precisians within the same, either constraining them to conform themselves or to leave the country according to the laws of our kingdom and canons of our Church ; and so strike equally on both hands against the contemners of our authority and adversaries of our Church ; and as for our good people's recreation, our pleasure is, that after the end of the divine service our good people be not disturbed letted or discouraged from any lawful recreation, such as dancing, either men or women, the archery for men, leaping, vaulting, or any other harmless recreation, nor from having of May-games, Whitsun-ales, and Morris-dances ; and the setting of May-poles and other sports therewith used : so as the same be had in due and convenient time, without impediment or neglect of divine service," &c. Bear-baitings and bull-baitings, however, were forbidden.

It should be remembered that this publication had been provoked by " An Act for punishing divers abuses committed on the Lord's day called Sunday," and also by another, entitled an Act for " the further reformation of sundry abuses committed on the Lord's day commonly called Sunday."

Laud was no rigid Sabbatarian. Prynne tells us [1] that " this profane Archbishop," when Bishop of London, insisted upon the revocation of a sentence passed upon a poor old woman for selling apples in St Paul's churchyard on a Sunday, and also upon the withdrawal of a proclamation of the Lord Mayor of London against those " who profane the Sabbath Day by buying and selling ;" although it is but fair to say that he only took exception to the latter on the ground that it intruded upon his own episcopal jurisdiction.

Chief Justice Richardson, in defiance of the Book of Sports, issued an order for the suppression of Sunday games and popular festivals. This was a bold step, and immediately plunged him into hot water. He was summoned before the Council Board, where Laud not only required him instantly to withdraw his order, but gave him such a wigging, that, on meeting Lord Dorset when leaving the Board, and being

---

[1] " Canterburies Doome," p. 132.

asked how he had got on within it, he said, with tears in his eyes :—"Very ill, my Lord, for I have been choked with a pair of lawn sleeves."[1]

Laud, indeed, never hesitated to speak his mind about judges. A few months before he was made Archbishop, the judges in the Court of Common Pleas had offended him by " tendering two rules," of which he disapproved. They appear to have been withdrawn ; but Laud alluded to them in the Court of High Commission. Standing at the council table,[2] "' If this prohibition,' quoth he, ' had taken place, I hope my Lord's Grace of Canterbury ' " (Abbott) " ' would have excommunicated throughout his province all the judges who should have had a hand therein. For mine own part, I will assure you, if he would not, I would have done it in my diocese, and myself in person denounced it both in Paul's church and other churches of the same, against the authors of so enormous a scandal to our church and religion.' "

Occasionally he received from the judges " as good as he gave " ; Cottington, in particular, was fond of teasing him, so Laud may have been glad to seize an opportunity of letting their lordships know that a spiritual lord was greater than a legal.

[1] " Cyp. Ang.," p. 243.
[2] Rev. Joseph Mead to Sir M. Stuteville. "Court and Times of Chas. I.," vol. ii. p. 120.

CHAPTER XVII.

LAUD'S appointment to the archbishopric greatly increased his labours, and at the same time, his influence at court ; and the State Papers contain many of his letters, written " at the king's command," in which there is every appearance of his having rather "commanded the king." There had been some puritanical goings-on in the Inns of Court ; Laud, therefore, wrote to the "two Societies of the Temple that [1] " foreseeing that almost all young gentlemen spend part of their time in one or other of the Inns of Court, and afterwards, when they return to live in their several countries, steer themselves according to such principles as in those places are preached unto them, His Majesty therefore has commanded the writer to signify to the persons addressed that though he will not infringe any of their just and ancient privileges, nor have the writer to write this as if he should take it on him by his ordinary jurisdiction to intromit himself there, yet he requires them to take order that their minister do every Sunday and holiday, in his surplice and hood, morning and evening, read the whole entire service before the sermon, as it is ordered in the Common Prayer Book, and that the preacher also, once at least every quarter, read the whole divine service, in his surplice and hood, as is before required of the curate." As a matter of fact, Laud found considerable difficulty in inducing many clergymen to wear surplices, or " whites," as they were termed, at all.

Certain bishops had got into a lax habit of " laying hands " upon men who had no title. Laud procured a royal letter to all the bishops, intimating that "his Majesty would call into the High Commission Court every bishop who should presume to give orders to any man that had not a title." [2] Very odd

[1] " Cal. Sta. Pa. Dom.," 1633-4, p. 340. [2] *Ib.*, p. 21.

sort of men, indeed, were the parsons made by some of the bishops. We read that one of them, the Rev. Robert Revell, Vicar of Dronfield, Co. Derby, had been " convented " and enjoined public penance for a grave breach of morality. Besides this,[1] " being distempered with drink he drew a rapier and threatened Francis Bullock therewith ; " and " on Ascension Day, 1632, being at home drinking, he sent his son to bid the clerk read the prayers to the congregation, which he did."

In 1637, articles were exhibited against the churchwardens of Knotting, Co. Bedford.[2] " It is objected against them that " " in the chancel of the said church, in or about the sacred place where the Communion-Table stands, there were fighting-cocks brought thither and cock-fightings there held, and many persons assembled to behold the same, and to bet and lay wagers thereon ; and particularly they " (the churchwardens) " and Mr Alney, minister of Knotting, and some of his sons, and many others, both youths and men and others, were present as actors and spectators, and laughed and sported thereat, and most profanely abused the said consecrated place."

Here was plenty of opportunity for Laud's reforming energy. To remove the communion-table at all was bad enough, in his opinion ; but to remove it to make room for a cock-fight was going, as it is the fashion to say now, " a little too far." Yet, in the face of such facts as these, existing when the Anglican Church had been under weigh for many years, people talk of the low state into which the Catholic Church in England had sunk in the days of Henry VIII., and of " reforms " being necessary.

But I wish to be fair, nor to write of the lower depths into which the Established Church sank, as if they were its highest, or even its average, level.

In order to show that Laud brought about a better state of things, I will make a quotation from the writings of Father Cyprien, one of Henrietta Maria's chaplains.[3] Archbishop

[1] " Cal. Sta. Pa. Dom.," 1633-4, p. 203.   [2] *Ib.*, 1637, p. 508.
[3] " Memoirs of the Mission in England of the Capuchin Friars," Colburn's Ed., pp. 332-3.

Laud, " under the authority of the King, undertook to effect
a uniformity of the Protestant religion throughout Great
Britain, which comprises England and Scotland, resolved to
introduce the ceremonies into the Church, and ordered the
clergy to wear the surplice in the performance of their duty.
To back this prelate several ministers began to preach publicly quite the contrary of what had before been believed—
such as the following truths : that the Pope is not Anti-
Christ ; that ceremonies are necessary in the Church ; that
auricular confession is obligatory on every one who has
sinned ; that in the Christian religion there must be altars.
Nor content with proclaiming these truths from the pulpit,
they composed divers books, which were printed, published,
and distributed in all quarters, I leave you to conceive with
what consolation to the Catholics ; while the Puritans, that
is to say, the Calvinists, were inflamed with wrath, fury, and
rage. *Peccator videbit et irascetur ; dentibus suis fremet et
tabescet.* At that time we were much visited by Protestant
ministers, who conversed very familiarly with us, willingly
listened to the reasons of our belief, inquired concerning our
ceremonies, came to the queen's chapel to learn the practice
of them, admitted that the Catholic was the true Church, but,
withheld by the consideration of their benefices and their
wives, imagined that they could be saved in the Protestant
Church, having, they said, the same fundamental points as
the Church of Rome."

Substitute the word " vestments " for " surplice," and " Low-
Church people " for " Puritans " and " Calvinists," and we
have almost exactly what an Italian Capuchin, who had lived
for some years in England, once said to me, in my own house.
The following remarks of Father Cyprien's might also have
come from his mouth ; indeed he often said something very
like them :—" England is full of various sects opposed to one
another, and all hostile to the Catholics." They " all boast
of following the genuine doctrine of Jesus Christ, and which
nevertheless, attack, and are at irreconcilable enmity with
one another." And more than this, the religious differences,
he says, are not only between sect and sect ; but " between

family and family, between servant and servant, between sister and sister, between brother and brother, of the *same* sect."

To show how differently different people regard the same thing, after giving Father Cyprien's encomiums of Laud and his followers, I will quote another author who wrote shortly after Laud's death. [1] "Little *Hocus Pocus*" (a blasphemous parody of the words of consecration in the Mass, *Hoc est Corpus*), "Little *Hocus Pocus, Canterbury*, did most assiduously countenance the idolatrous stoopings, cringings, and papist-like, Chappell boysterous roarings out of Creed, and Prayers."

If Laud had been content simply "to raise the tone," as High-Churchmen say, of the doctrines and ceremonies of his Church, he might have escaped serious trouble ; unfortunately he insisted on hunting out and persecuting those who even secretly, or in semi-secrecy taught lower doctrines and practised a plainer form of worship than he approved. He would not allow proceedings of which he disapproved quietly to die out ; they must needs be *stamped* out. Even where two or three were gathered together in God's name, to worship in an "uncomformable" manner, there would he, in the person of his pursuivant, be in the midst of them.

A paper, dated Lambeth, [2] was probably suggested by its occupant (Laud), although it professed to emanate from the Commissioners of Ecclesiastical Causes. It is addressed to "all Justices of the Peace, Mayors, and other Officers of the Peace." "There remain in divers parts of the kingdom sundry sets of separatists, novalists [*sic*] and sectaries, as namely—Brownists, Anabaptists, Arians, Taskites, Familists, and some other sorts, who, upon Sundays and other festival days, under pretence of repetition of sermons, ordinarily use to meet together in great numbers in private houses and other obscure places, and there keep private conventicles and exercises of religion by law prohibited, to the corrupting of sundry his Majesty's good subjects, manifest contempt of his Highness's laws and disturbance of the church. For re-

[1] "None-such Charles," pp. 128-9. [2] "Cal. Sta. Pa. Dom.," 1637, p. 538.

formation whereof the persons addressed are to enter any house where they shall have intelligence that such conventicles are held, and every room thereof search for persons assembled and for all unlicensed books, and bring all such persons and books found before the Ecclesiastical Commission as shall be thought meet."

It will be observed that, under these instructions, an officer of the peace might enter any house in which he suspected that a few friends might be meeting together to read the Bible and pray, as used to be so common a few years ago in Evangelical families.

Among other matters to which Laud devoted great attention, was the press. The king's printers "had been faulty in the English print with which they" had been entrusted, so "his Majesty" had "resolved," writes Laud to them, [1] "to punish them"; and the king writes to Laud, probably at his own suggestion, to say that a fine of £300, which the High Commissioners had just imposed upon them for this offence ("base and corrupt printing of the Bible") should be spent in buying good Greek type. "Power is given to the Archbishop to mitigate the fine according to the printer's diligence in advancing the work."

"*Arch-Bishop* Laud's *Account of his Province* [2] *sent to the King for the Year* 1633, *with the King's Apostills, in the Margin*" throws some light on his doings. In his own diocese of Canterbury, he hears "of many things amiss" and that some of "my Peculiars in *London* are extreamly out of order." Before giving up his Bishopric of London, he had "proceeded against *Nathaniel Ward*, Parson of *Groudon* in *Essex*, to Excommunication and Deprivation, for refusing to subscribe to the Articles."

After describing the condition of three other dioceses, he comes to "Repon" where the Bishop of Coventry and Lichfield had suppressed a "Seditious Lecture," "and divers Monthly-Lectures, with a Fast and a Moderator," "as also a Running Lecture, so called because the Lecturer went from

---

[1] "Cal. Sta. Pa. Dom.," 1637, p. 423.
[2] "Hist. of the Troubles and Tryal of W. L.," p. 525.

Village to Village." "They say this Lecture was ordained to Illuminate the Dark Corners of that Diocese." The king has written in the margin of this "C. R. If there be Dark Corners in this Dioces; it were fitt a true Light should Illuminate it; and not this that is falce and uncertaine."

The happiest bishop noticed in this report is St Asaph, who "returns, that all is exceedingly well in his Diocess, save only that the Number and Boldness of some *Romish* Recusants increaseth much in many Places, and is incouraged by the Superstitions and frequent Concourse of some of that Party to *Holy-Well*, otherwise called *St Winifred's* Well." The poor Bishop of St Asaph of to-day finds that the Number and Boldness of the Romish Recusants "increaseth much" more; for he has two large Jesuit Colleges, one English, and one French, one Capuchin Monastery, several convents of nuns of various orders, at least three Jesuit Missions, and very many others under secular priests, within the limits of his diocese.

Now that I am noticing Laud's annual report for 1633 to the king, I may as well include one or two others.

In one, he reports that the Bishop of St Asaph "hath little to return"; and I am sure that I shall make the present Bishop of St Asaph's mouth water when I add that the occupant of his See, in Laud's days, reports that throughout his diocese "there is nothing but common Peace, and universal Conformity."[1] But this was before the days of the Wesleys and the Methodists; the Bishop, however, "heartily wishes, that" his people "might be as well acquitted of Superstition and Prophaneness." As a matter of fact, the Welsh people clung on to their "Popery" as best they could, without priests to guide them, until the followers of the Wesleys succeeded in inducing them to join their sects and branch sects.

Long after priests had disappeared in North Wales, the people, especially in retired places, continued to practise the religion that had been handed down to them from their forefathers, each generation being less and less instructed, and

---

[1] "Archp. Laud's History," p. 552.

their faith becoming vaguer and vaguer, until in many places a hazy Christianity, with a few devotions such as hymn-singing, the saying of a few familiar prayers, the invocation of certain saints, prayers in burial grounds for the dead, and visits to holy wells, were all that was left of it. Yet these people would have nothing to do with the State Church, and it was among these sheep without a shepherd that the Wesleys evangelized with such success.

One entry in the Annual Accounts, presented by Laud to King Charles, relates to "that wild Young Gentleman Mr *South,*" who had committed an atrocious crime and been summoned in consequence before the High Commission by Laud. Here Laud makes a bad pun, saying, "I hope your Majesty will give me leave to make *South* blow *West* for *St Paul's;*" and the king makes one still worse, by scribbling in the margin "C. R. The South-West Wind is commonly the best, therefore I will not hinder the blowing that way." One trembles at the thought of what Laud must have been in society, if he tried to be funny in the style which he sometimes adopted with his pen.

In Norwich, writes Laud, "one Mr *Bridge* rather than he would Conform, hath left his Lecture and two Cures, and is gone into Holland." Beside this, Charles puts a marginal note :—" C. R. Let him goe : Wee are well ridd of him."

In one account (1634), Laud writes :—" I conceive under favour, that the *Dutch* Churches in *Canterbury* and *Sandwich* are great Nurseries of Inconformity in those parts." Whereupon the king scribbles :—" Put mee in mynd of this at some convenient tyme, when I am at Council, and I shall redress it." In fact, Charles seems to have been ever ready to carry out Laud's wishes. On another matter Laud asks whether his Majesty approves, and there is a marginal note :—" C. R. I doe, and will express my Pleasure (if need be) what way you will."

The language used in the pulpit by some of the puritanical clergy shocked Laud, as well it might. He reports a curate to the king for having "used this base and Unchristian passage in the Pulpit, That God so loved the *world, that for it he sent his Son to live like a Slave, and dye like a Beast.*" King Charles caps this—as I grieve to say religious people usually do cap profane stories, whenever they are able—by writing in the margin :—" C. R. This is not much unlike that which was not longe since uttered elsewhere," and thereupon quotes something even more blasphemous and offensive.

Once more we have the Bishop of St Asaph and his holy well. He has reported that he has "no Complaint, but the usual." Lady Falkland "and her Company came as Pilgrims" to St Winifrid's Well, "who were the more observed, because they travelled on Foot, and Dissembled neither their quality, nor their Errand." Laud had already "complained of this in open Council" to the king, and he now begged that his Majesty would " be graciously pleased that the Order then resolved on for her confinement may be put in execution." Charles's note to this is laconic and to the point :—" Itt is done." It is needless to say that this was a case of pure and simple persecution of Catholics on Laud's part and also on Charles's. There was no excuse whatever for interference with this pious and inoffensive lady.

I must not forget to mention that on Laud's first going to Lambeth, the day before his " Translation," his " Coach, Horses, and Men sunk to the bottom of the Thames in the Ferry-Boat, which was overladen, but I Praise God for it, I lost neither Man nor Horse."

And now Lady Eleanor Davies reappears upon the scene, rousing the ire of Laud by prophesying "against me, that I should very few Days out-live the Fifth of November." It was all very well to prophesy evil things of kings and queens, but very dangerous to do so of archbishops ; at any rate of an archbishop of the type of Laud.

Some lines[1] among the State Papers reflecting upon Laud, are thought by Mr Bruce[2] to be perhaps " the rhapsodical compositions of Lady Eleanor Davies, who was called in question in November 1633, for prophesying that the arch-

[1] S. P. O. Dom., vol. ccxlviii. No. 93.
[2] " Cal. Sta. Pa. Dom.," 1633-4, p. 266.

bishop should outlive the 5th November but a very few days.
The lines are entitled, ' Handwriting, October 1633. *Exaudi
Deus.* Psalm 55,' and in the margin there is a deduction of the
same number 55 out of the name LAVD." He adds that
their exact meaning " is difficult to discover." The punctua-
tion is peculiar.

> " God of the Earth. Earth is England.
> out of Earth, Comes a Beaste,
> breed of the first, by the Sea Sand
> of Evils not the Least,
> two Horns like to a Lambe, not wilde
> like Yorke, & Lambeth Looke,
> oath giueth all, as Dragon milde
> righte Hand, bidds Laye on Booke.

> " Six Hundred-Sixtie-six, accounte
> the Beast, His number tolde.
> to fifftie five years, doo amounte.
> So many moneths, is olde
> Marke, Moneths, read of the Man of sinn
> Whose Howers Last doo runn
> Six Hundred-Sixtie, six beginn.
> to counte His Moneth, to come.

> even so come. Lord Jesus Amen."

Lady Eleanor Davies seems to have sent a sort of prophetical memorial to the king.[1] She wrote under her maiden
name of " Lady Eleanor Tuchet " (her father was the Earl
of Castlehaven), and she announced that " Early in the morning the B. [Bishop ?] beast ascended out of the bottomless
pit, with seven heads (seven years having made war), hath
overcome and killed them. Books sealed by the prophets, by
the Bishop of *Lambeth* are condemned to be burned at Paul's
Cross, where our Lord pictured was also crucified. This is
the third day their dead bodies throwed in loose sheets of
paper, lie in the streats of the great city, more cruel hard-
hearted than other tongues and nations, who will not suffer
them to be buried."

Instead of being treated like a lunatic, this poor woman

[1] S. P. O. Dom., vol. cclv. No. 20.

was fined £3000, and kept a close prisoner in the Gate-house. It was said that she was far more overwhelmed by a remark of the Dean of Arches, at her trial, than by her sentence. It will be remembered that she founded her claims to be a prophetess chiefly upon a discovery that the letters of her name, "Eleianor Audeley"—her father had been Baron Audley before being created Earl of Castlehaven—could be twisted into the anagram, "Reveale O Daniel." The dean was seen writing on a piece of paper, when he suddenly looked up to the prisoner and said :—"Madam, I see you build much on anagrams, and I have found one which I think will fit you —Never so Mad a Ladie." There was a roar of laughter in the court, and Heylin says that she afterwards either "grew wiser, or less regarded."

More sane antagonists, however, than Lady Eleanor attacked Laud, and he was obliged to "aduertise his Majesty of the Falsehood and Practise that was against him." But one other half-mad ill-wisher "came into the Court at St James's, with a great Sword by his Side, swearing, the King should do him Justice against me, or he wou'd take another course with me."

With his unpopularity among certain people, Laud's favour with the king seemed to increase. Charles's third son, or second living son, born on the 13th or 14th (see Evelyn) of October was christened James at St James's on the 24th of November, by the archbishop, and created Duke of York by the king.

Earlier in this chapter I have quoted from a letter written to Laud from Ireland. The condition of ecclesiastical matters in that country greatly distressed him, as well it might ; for the Anglican clergy were, and had for many years been, anything but a credit to their religion. Even at the close of the sixteenth century, Spenser gave the following opinion of them. [1] "Whatever disorders you see in the Church of England, you may find these, and many more [in Ireland], namely, gross simony, greedy covetousness, fleshly incontinency, careless sloth, and generally all dis-

---

[1] I quote from Baine's "Life of Laud," p. 150.

ordered life in the common clergymen. And besides all these, they have their particular enormities; for all the Irish Priests which now enjoy the church livings, they are in a manner mere laymen, saving that they have taken holy orders; but otherwise they go and live like laymen, follow all kinds of husbandry and other worldly affairs, as other Irishmen do. They neither read the Scriptures, nor preach to the people, nor administer the communion; but baptism they do, for they christen, yet after the Popish fashion."

Whether any improvement had been made in this condition of things thirty or forty years later, I do not know; but it seems pretty clear that the Protestant Church in Ireland was in a state very repugnant to the mind of Laud, and that he determined to remedy it. Fortunately, he had an instrument, on the spot, well qualified for that purpose. Lord Wentworth, who had been one of the most conspicuous members of the House of Commons in condemning the exactions of Charles, in that king's third Parliament, had since then been won over to the royalist cause, and in 1632 he was appointed Lord Deputy of Ireland. He had already become a warm friend of Laud's and consulted him as to the management of Church matters in the land which he was now to govern. It would take me too far afield to give even a rough sketch of his arbitrary rule over the Irish Parliament and people; moreover it is too well known to require description here; it may suffice to say that in the year 1634 he wrote to Laud saying that he had succeeded in making the king as absolute a monarch in Ireland, as any in the universe.[1] Laud thought it of the highest importance to have the Irish, as well as the Scottish Established Church, under exactly the same discipline as the English, greatly to the vexation of the Irish Protestant prelates, who considered their Church distinct and independent, and were perfectly satisfied with their own articles of religion, which were much too Calvinistic to be pleasing to Laud. Wentworth, guided by Laud, ordered Archbishop Usher to draw up a canon authorizing the English articles of religion, and when the canon did not

[1] Wentworth to Laud, 16th Dec. 1634.

satisfy him, he drew up another, himself, in its place, and
sent it to the House, with instructions that no debate should
be allowed upon it, and that if any members voted against
the measure, their names should be reported to him.

In one of his letters to Wentworth [1] Laud writes :—" I have
known the Bishop of Waterford long, and when he lived in
College ; he would have done any Thing, or sold any Man for
six Pence Profit." He " was ever full of Jests, and would at
any Time lose a Friend rather than spare it."

In another letter to Wentworth,[2] in 1634, he makes one
remark which is so excellent and so much to the purpose
that I cannot forbear to quote it :—" That the Divine Service
may be read throughout the Churches, be the Company that
vouchsafe to come never so few. Let God have his whole
Service with Reverence, and He will quickly send in more
to help to perform it."

It was not only through Wentworth that Laud interfered
with Church matters in Ireland. Bramhall, Wentworth's
chaplain, reported to him that the Earl of Cork had erected a
monument over his family vault, in St Patrick's Cathedral,
on the very place where the high altar had formerly stood, " as
if it were contrived to gain the worship and reverence which
the chapter and whole church are bound by special statute
to give towards the East." Lord Cork received an intima-
tion from Laud that he must forthwith pull it down, whereupon he wrote to Laud to say that his wife's family had for a
long time had the privilege of burying beneath the site of the
high altar, and that " in accomplishment of her dying desire
who was the mother of fifteene Children," he had " pro-
pounded unto the Lord Archbishop of Dublin, and the Deane
and Chapter of St Patrick's," to purchase the place for a
" Sellar," or family vault, and erect a tomb over it ; that,
until then, the floods and " raynes " had come into the
chancel and " anoyed withall," especially as the " flower "
(floor) of it was only of earth ; but that he had paved it and
drained it, so that the communion-table now stood " very dry
and gracefully " ; and he declared that the building of this

---

[1] " Strafford Papers," vol. i. p. 212, anno 1633.   [2] *Ib.*, p. 254.

monument, which was thirty feet high, and the paving and draining, had cost him at least a thousand pounds.

In support of Lord Cork, the Archbishop of Dublin wrote to Laud that the communion-table, which used to stand on a " floore of earth," and was often " drovvned vvith water " " in former times," was now, thanks to the earl, on a pavement of " faire hevven stones," and was placed with more decency ; and that " his Lordship has in hand to set up a faire Skrine of timber, somewhat distant from the monument," " in which skrine the Decalogue shal be fairely painted ; and the Com- munion Table shall bee placed close to the same, more decently then it has ever been," and that the earl had exhibited ex- emplary " meritts " and very great zeal in advancing the interests of true religion. (Observe, in passing, that the Arch- bishop of Dublin hoped to please Laud by this promise that the Decalogue " shal be fairely painted " in " the skrine." There is plenty of evidence that, in those times, to have the ten commandments painted above the communion-table was considered the summit of High-Church orthodoxy.)

To this letter, says Prynne,[1] " this Arch-Prelate returned this waspish insolent answer " :—" I am very glad to hear from your Lordship of his [Lord Cork's] zeale for the advance- ment of true religion : but I may not conceale from your Lordship that I have likewise heard from others that hee hath gotten into his hands no small proportion of the Church's means. And if that be so, any man may see his end in advancing true Religion. But such a Zeale that pore Church hath little need of." As for " the Tombe which occasioned all the rest," he said he could not judge without seeing it, and that the matter must be left to the decision of authorities who should be authorised to examine into the matter on the spot.

At first sight, the interference of an English archbishop in Irish ecclesiastical affairs may appear anomalous ; but it should be remembered that Laud had been made Chancellor of Dublin ; so that he was acting well within his rights. It almost appeared as if excuses were made to give him power

---

[1] " Canterburies Doome," p. 85.

wherever possible, and what he writes in jest to Wentworth, might have been said more seriously [1] :—" I was fain to write nine Letters yesterday into Scotland. I think you have a Plot to see, whether I will be a *Universalis Episcopus*, that you and your Brethren may take occasion to call me Anti-Christ."

[1] " Strafford Papers," vol. i. p. 271.

CHAPTER XVIII.

I HAVE been demonstrating that Laud, far from confining his proceedings to his own country, much less his own archdiocese, endeavoured to hold the reins of management, both of Scotland and Ireland; it will now be my business to show that he wished to extend his influence very widely beyond even those limits.

His scheme was to unite all Protestant bodies in one large Church, each sect to be more or less under the discipline of its own laws and canons, but federated to all the rest in certain points common to all; in short, he seems to have wished to oppose a more or less compact Protestant Church to the Catholic Church.

This scheme was put into shape by Sir Thomas Roe, formerly ambassador at Constantinople, and a man named John Durie, a clergyman of the Church of Scotland and an ardent re-unionist. Their project is described by Mr Bruce[1] as "a union of recognition and brotherhood among all Protestant Churches." Modern High-Church admirers of Laud may do well to make a note of this! "Durie, with the archbishop's concurrence, had drawn two letters, one proposed to be addressed by the Archbishop to the Lutheran, and the other to the Calvinistic Churches in Germany, as testifying Laud's desire to promote the scheme of union."[2]

That is to say, Archbishop Laud desired to promote a union between the Established Church of England and two German Churches, which repudiated orders and apostolical succession.

It was arranged that Durie should attend the Diet of Frankfort with a view to furthering this great Protestant amalgamation. Before he started, Laud gave him letters to

---

[1] Preface to "Cal. Sta. Pa. Dom.," 1633-4, p. xxxv. [2] Ib., p. xxxvi.

carry with him, which Durie declares he found "emphatical enough, and full of strong expressions of love towards the work"[1]—the work of a great Protestant union between the Anglican, Lutheran, and Calvinistic Churches!

It is quite clear that it was essentially a Protestant Union, and not a Union of all nominal Christians, whether Catholic or Protestant, that was aimed at ; nay more, that it was a Union of Protestants *versus* Catholics ; for, in his recapitulation, at his trial before the Lords, Laud says[2] :—" Lastly, there have been above Three-score Letters and other Papers, brought out of my Study into this Honourable House ; they are all about composing the Differences between *the Lutherans and the Calvinists in Germany.* Why they should be brought hither, but in hope to charge them upon me, I know not ; and then the Argument will be thus : I laboured to reconcile the *Protestants* in *Germany*, that they might unanimously set themselves against the *Papists ;* therefore I laboured to bring *Popery* into *England.*" It is true that nothing is said here of the union of the Anglicans with the rival Protestant sects abroad ; but it shows the spirit in which his "reconciliations" were proposed.

When it came to a question of paying Durie's expenses, Laud said :—" If I had been in this see twenty or twenty-two years, as my predecessor was, I could, perhaps, be able to allow you seven or eight score pounds a year, but now I am not able : therefore, if this which I am ready to do, can serve your turn, you may make use of it."[3] He then proceeded to make Durie the offer of a living in Devonshire, which was to provide him an income while he laboured to promote the great "Evangelical Alliance." When Durie objected that he could not, at the same time, be at his "cure and abroad," Laud replied, "You may have a curate." Durie found, however, that, after paying a curate out of the emoluments of the living offered, the balance would be very small.

King Charles does not appear to have entered into the

---

[1] Preface to "Cal. Sta. Pa. Dom.," 1633-4, p. xxvii.   [2] "Hist.," p. 419.
[3] "Cal. Sta. Pa. Dom.," 1633-4, p. xxxviii.

scheme with quite so much cordiality as Laud ; for the latter writes to Sir Thomas Roe[1] that " His Majesty has been acquainted with the business Roe writ of, and has given a very pious and a prudent answer, though it reach not home in all circumstances to that which is desired."

Nevertheless, in a measure he encouraged it ; for we find Roe writing[2] some months later to Windebank that :—" His Majesty has declared his liking, [for the project] the Archbishop of Canterbury has taken the direction, the foreign churches seek to him, and will obey him." He declares that " the work is far improved above hope, above the means, above the exquisite skill and labour of princes and learned men in the former age, and Roe must conclude that it is Gods only blessing [*sic*] and that he will perfect it, if they be worthy of the blessing." Further on he says that " the peace of the reformed church can never be secure while it is divided and the enemy concur in one end and head. Unity will prevail."

Later, again, there seemed to be difficulties with the king. Durie wrote to Roe,[3] that he had been to see Archbishop Laud, who had told him that he might " come when he would and should always be welcome." He added, however, " that, as for the king, he found not that he was willing to declare himself as yet, for causes which he kept to himself, and that Durie had done well in writing hitherto nothing unto them, lest in writing before things be resolved upon, he should be forced to retract ; that between this and spring things would frame themselves otherwise in those parts, and according to their state a course may be taken."

About the same time Roe wrote to the Bishop of Durham,[4] " how Durie, a Scotch minister, was employed into Germany for the reconciliation of the Lutheran and Calvinistic Churches." " He has come home with many letters to the Archbishop of Canterbury, signifying the desire of the Germans, and imploring his Majesty's assistance as mediator. Now it depends on what we will do here. Fears we shall rather quit

---

[1] "Cal. Sta. Pa. Dom.," 1833-4, p. 197.   [2] *Ib.*, p. 403.
[3] *Ib.*, p. 406.   [4] *Ib.*, p. 430.

it with shame than prosecute it with zeal. The Archbishop
has promised to assist, but he is so cautelous, and refers to
his Majesty, that it is a doubt it will perish by being in hands
that cannot intend it [*i.e.*, attend to it]." Roe prays the
Almighty "to show his Majesty in a true light what is fit
for him, his church, and people." The project "has already
cost £400, and they must seek help of good men." Sad
to say, good men helped but little, and, to use a modern
phrase, the grand scheme for a Protestant Union eventually
"languished for want of funds."

A few months later than the date of the letter quoted
above, Roe wrote [1] to Baron Oxenstiern urging him "to press
forward the project for union of the churches, with respect to
which the king waits to engage himself until he is informed
of the concurrence of the Lord Chancellor Oxenstiern." And
when, in 1634, the Diet was sitting at Frankfort, he wrote [2]
from Bulwick to Archbishop Laud, begging him "to take
care that some instructions be given to the king's representative there to avow Durie's person or the negotiation.
Durie is confident that God will give His church peace,
that this is the time and that the Archbishop may have
the honour."

Then came a letter [3] from Laud himself to Roe, mentioning
the project as "so good a cause." "That it succeeded not
was no fault of the Archbishop." "Concerning Durie's
return to the Diet, the Archbishop's letters have lain by him
long since, one to such Lutherans, and the other to such
Calvinists, as wrote to him. In those letters the Archbishop
has expressed himself so far as it can be anyways fit, and
Durie has free leave to go to the Diet to be held in May.
His success there the Archbishop wishes may be happy."
This proves Laud's personal sympathy with the undertaking.
" The writer has moved his Majesty several times, but though
the king highly approves the work, yet will he not publicly
avow either Durie or his negotiation ; neither doth he hold
it fit so to do, where the Princes upon the place have not

---

[1] "Cal. Sta. Pa. Dom.," 1833-4, p, 320.   [2] *Ib.*, p. 544.
[3] *Ib.*, p. 562.

publicly declared themselves." "He has spoken his mind to his Majesty in private, and that is all he can do."

Laud still continued to further the cause by sending, with another, two letters[1] to Durie, "one to be showed to the Reformed and the other to the Lutheran churches." In a letter to Roe,[2] Durie says that Laud had written him letters which he found "emphatical enough, and full of strong expressions of love to the work, and some commendation of Durie's labours."

There can be no question of Laud's desire for the promotion of the scheme, nor is it unlikely that he may have conceived the idea of one day becoming, himself, a sort of Protestant Pope over all the Reformed Churches of the world !

Even later than any of the letters already quoted on the subject, Laud wrote to Durie,[3] acknowledging the receipt of "letters directed to him from brothers in Christ in the Palatinate, Biponto, Hesse, and elsewhere in Germany "—surely these must have been the forefathers of the "dear, dissenting brothers " talked of by modern Evangelicals—"from which he understands how diligently Durie has prosecuted the business of restoring the peace of the Church. Urges him to proceed, assures him of his prayers, and his aid at the proper time. Meanwhile he is pressed by many burdens, but wishes Durie to salute for him all who are solicitous for the peace of the Church, and especially the distinguished theologians who have written to him, but whose letters he is unable to answer on account of the pressure of other business."

It is interesting, at the present time, to consider what Laud's ideal great Protestant Church would be like now, if his wishes had been realised. Anglicans when on the Continent could not in that case be going, as they frequently do now, to high masses, vespers, benedictions, and other functions in Catholic cathedrals and churches, but would have to content themselves with those Lutheran, French Protestant, Vaudois, and such like Reformed conventicles with which they would be legally allied.

---

[1] "Cal. Sta. Pa. Dom.," 1833-4, p. 566.　　[2] *Ib.*, p. 309.
[3] *Ib.*, 1634-5, p. 148.

So seldom, at present, do high Anglicans attend services in Lutheran churches, that it may be well to call their attention to Laud's consistency in inclining towards that body. In its churches, the altars stood "as of old" much more than in the highest of the High Anglican; for they were not only placed "altarwise," but at least so far as the substructure was concerned, consisted, I believe, of the actual altars themselves, and not, as in England, of mere communion-tables placed where the altars formerly stood; moreover, the very side-altars, in many cases, were left standing. A fine example of this may be seen at the present day in the Lutheran Church at Nuremberg. It is true that the Lutheran clergy did not "wear whites"; but, if they wore blacks instead, they left the crucifixes on the altars and lighted the candles. As to the absence of bishops, it has already been shown that, in Laud's opinion, bishops were actually present in the Lutheran Church, under another name.

Before dismissing the subject of the Universal Protestant Church, which Laud so much desired, it may be well to give a quotation from Heylin which bears upon it.[1] In reply to some assertions that Laud inclined rather towards Catholicism than Protestantism, he says:—" Had he directed his endeavours to suppress the Protestants, he would not have given so much countenance to *Dury*, a *Scot*, who entertained him with some hopes of working an Accord betwixt the *Lutheran* and *Calvinian* Churches. In which service, as he wasted a great deal of time to little purpose; so he received as much encouragement from *Canterbury* as he had reason to expect. Welcome at all times to his Table, and speaking honourably to him upon all occasions, till the times were changed, when either finding the impossibility of his Undertaking, or wanting the supply of that Oyl which maintained his Lamp, he proved a true *Scot* as the rest of the Nation, laying the blame of his miscarriage in it, on the want of Encouragement; and speaking disgracefully of the man which had given him most."

[1] " Cyp. Ang.," p. 343.

I had already hinted that the project practically failed for want of " Oyl."

Let us for a time disregard external matters and consider Laud's life at his own palace at Lambeth, now that he was settled there as archbishop.

He rose early, often by candle-light, and spent an hour or so in devotion and spiritual reading. Then he took a plain breakfast of bread and water. He was quite an exception in drinking this unintoxicating fluid at such an hour, as ale was then the usual beverage at breakfast. After his breakfast, he received his secretary and chaplain, and at ten o'clock he went to the service in his chapel, which was attended by his household of more than a hundred people, consisting exclusively of men. Not long after the morning service, came the great meal of the day, dinner ; so the lightness of Laud's breakfast was no proof of extreme asceticism. At the archiepiscopal dinner, open house was kept, and it was served in the hall, the archbishop and his more important guests, which often included members of the court, sitting at the cross-table at the upper end of the room. Mr Benson tells us [1] that Laud dined in his rochet, and wore it when out walking and at court, rarely taking it off, except in his study or garden, and he has doubtless good authority for saying so ; certainly in most of Laud's portraits he is thus represented and with a square college-cap on his head ; in the portraits of Bishop Andrews the same dress is worn ; but the bishops of the period do not appear to have invariably worn their rochets ; for in the frontispiece to Hackett's *Life of Archbishop Williams*, a black gown and square cap are given, and in two engravings, one of which will be noticed presently, Laud wears a black cassock and close-fitting black cap, although it is but fair to say that both represent him after his deposition.

After dinner, Laud commonly went to the Council or the Star Chamber, in his barge, his pike-bearers attending him.[2]

[1] " Cyp. Ang.," p. 158.
[2] The pikes are still at Lambeth. See Benson, p. 159, from whom I take most of this account of Laud's daily life.

If he did not leave the palace, he gave audiences. These frequently took place in the garden, if the weather permitted, or, if it did not, in the gallery, while he paced up and down for the sake of exercise. At about four or five o'clock, he went to Evensong in his chapel. After that, he took a time of quiet study, unless more immediately important duties demanded his attention. Then followed his supper, which he took in private, and, soon afterwards, he went to bed.

Laud's recreation is said by some of his biographers to have been music. Mr Benson maintains this opinion, chiefly on the strength of "a harp, a chest of viols, and a harpsico in his parlour at Lambeth," being mentioned in his will. He put an organ in each of the houses which he inhabited; but, as Mr Benson very fairly says, that he should do so is not surprising when we consider his liturgical inclinations.

While we are looking at him in his home, we may observe his small stature, his red and plump, if not exactly fat, face, with its high eyebrows, its moustache a little turned up at the ends, and its imperial, his hair, unlike that of most of the people about the court of Charles I., cut very short, his restless, jerky, imperious manner, and his hard, rasping, disagreeable voice. Probably his most striking features were his glittering, intelligent eyes, and his strongly-bridged nose—a nose with a good deal of decision of character visible in its not very pointed end.

So far as I can ascertain, he never took a holiday or allowed himself any recreation; on the other hand, such things would not be likely to be recorded in a concise, and rather irregularly kept, diary; nor would a contemporary biographer, such as Heylin, be likely to make any mention of them. We know, however, that he went to court, and the very anterooms of the great men whom he must have had constant occasion to visit were the scenes of what amounted to social gatherings, in which, while awaiting his turn for audience, he could talk politics, hear the freshest and raciest gossip, or discuss the latest poems of Milton, Ben Jonson, or Beaumont and Fletcher.

Unencumbered by a wife or family, he was free to concentrate all his thoughts and energies upon ecclesiastical and political affairs. If he had no wife, or child, or recreation, or hobby, properly so called, he had none the less plenty of variety of interest to pass his time and entertain him. His secular posts and appointments must have occupied him almost as much as his ecclesiastical, his correspondence with Wentworth and others was probably no less a pleasure and an amusement than a duty and a labour, and it is pretty clear that he enjoyed nothing so much as the exercise of power, of which he had an extraordinary share.

Perhaps his chief amusement was his garden in the front court of Lambeth Palace. Here he himself planted some fig-trees, and here a tortoise, about sixty years old, which had been given to him long before at Oxford, used to appear from its winter hiding-place at the first burst of spring, and crawl stiffly about. Mr Benson[1] tells us that he found, among a number of dusty relics in the palace, a tortoise-shell, on which was fastened a piece of paper, inscribed, " The shell of a tortoise which was put into the garden at Lambeth in the year 1633, where it remained till the year 1753," the remainder of the almost illegible writing appearing to imply that it then met with its death through some accident or negligence.

On one side of the garden were the great gates, destined to be assaulted by rioters some years later ; on the other were some high elms, under which Laud used to pace up and down when giving interviews to clergy or to statesmen ; and the middle of the court was covered with grass.

There are several engraved portraits of Laud, one of the best being the frontispiece in his *Troubles and Tryal;* but his face has been perhaps most faithfully presented to posterity by Vandyke, in the oil painting hanging in the guard-room, now used as the dining-room, at Lambeth Palace.

" Again and again,"[2] says Mr Benson, " I have heard people ask, 'And who is that very extraordinary-looking person ?' and, on being told who it is, say in a tone of incredulous bewilderment, '*That* Laud !'" As a criticism of the portrait, he presently adds :—" If faces betray character, this man had

---

[1] "Cyp. Ang.," p. 11.   [2] P. 8.

little of the saint about him." One of the least known, but most interesting, of his portraits, is an engraving by Marshall, in a very rare little book, or tract, called Laud's *Recantation*. In this he wears a sort of cassock and girdle, a ruff round his neck, and the plain black cap on his head, which is to be seen below the square college-cap in the pictures representing him in his rochet and lawn-sleeves. He wears a similar dress in the picture of his trial, in Prynne's *Breviate*. In Marshall's engraving there are the same raised eyebrows and turned-up moustaches as in the portrait in his *Diary;* but the stern, prosperous expression has given place to one of sorrow and regret, or, as a much abler critic than myself puts it, "great astonishment at the plight in which he finds himself." My readers, however, can judge for themselves, as a copy of it forms the frontispiece to this volume.

CHAPTER XIX.

WE left Laud in the peaceful dignity of his palace at Lambeth; we must now accompany him to the more stirring scene of the Star Chamber.

A certain William Prynne, the son of a farmer living between Clifton and Henbury (probably a sheep-farmer on Durdham Downs, and later an agent for a property near Bath, belonging to Oriel College, Oxford), and his wife, Marie (a daughter of Sherston, Mayor of Bath, and member of Parliament for that city for four years), became an undergraduate at Oriel, and afterwards a student at Lincoln's Inn. He inherited from £150 to £200 a year from his father—a good income in those days—and had every prospect of a comfortable, prosperous, and honoured life.

Unfortunately, he could not leave well alone; but must needs write and publish a book of above one thousand pages, called *Histrio-mastrix*, against theatres, balls, hunting, "Christmas-keeping," May-poles, bonfires, public festivals, the erection of altars in churches, "cringing and ducking to altars," "silk and satin divines," and the "barking," and "roaring," and "grunting" of choristers.

As a specimen of the style, I may quote the following extract from the part which treats of theatricals:—"God forbedd that any whoe have beene dipped in the sacred laver of Regeneracion, any that have been bathed, &c., should prove such desperate incarnate devills, such monsters of ympiety, such atheisticall Judases to their lord and Master, such perjured cutt throates to their Religion, such apostates or undeplored enimyes to their owne salvation, or such willfull bloody murtherers to their owne soules, as to approve or justifye or to practise these stage playes."

For publishing this "libellous volume," Prynne was summoned before the Court of High Commission in the Star Chamber; his trial lasted three days, and, on the fourth, the Court proceeded to pass sentence.

Lord Cottington, Chancellor of the Exchequer, began. Mr Prynne, he said, had published a volume of libels express-ing, in a manner, a malice[1] "against all mankind, and the best sort of mankind, against King, prince, peer, prelates, magistrates and governors, and truly in a manner against all things. But that which hath been more remarkable, is, his spleen against the church and government of it."

Lord Cottington's sentence was a very long one. When he came to the practical part, he ordered him to be disbarred, " and because he had his offspring from Oxford ('now,' with a low voice, said the bishop of Canterbury, 'I am sorry that ever Oxford bred such an evil member') there to be degraded. And I do condemn Mr Prynne to stand in the pillory in two places, in Westminster and Cheapside, and that he shall lose both his ears, one in each place; and with a paper on his head, declaring how foul an offence it is." "And lastly (nay, not lastly) I do condemn him in £5000 fine to the King. And, lastly, perpetual imprisonment."

The next judge fined him another £5000, and ordered him to "be restrained from writing, neither to have pen, ink, or paper; yet let him have," said he, "some pretty prayer-book, to pray to God to forgive him his sins."

The third judge fined him "£10,000, which is more than he is worth, yet less than he deserveth," and ordered him to be branded in the forehead and slit in the nose, as he feared that he might conceal the disgrace of his cropt ears by forcing " his conscience to make use of his unlovely love-locks on both sides."

Laud merely remarked that he was "sorrye that a man that hath been so prayerfull and had soe good breedinge should soe ill bestowe his labour to such haynous endes."[2] Yet it was with Laud that Prynne was most angry, and to whom he attributed his arrest, conviction, and cruel punishment.

---

[1] " State Trials," vol. i. p. 417.   [2] Official Summary of the Trial.

On the 11th of June 1634, Laud writes in his Diary :—
" Mr Prynne sent me a very Libellous Letter, about his Censure in the *Star-Chamber* for his *Histriomastrix*, and what I
said at that Censure ; in which he hath many ways mistaken
me and spoken untruth of me."

This letter, which is written from prison, where Laud had
obtained for him the favour of writing materials, is a very
long one ; it will be sufficient that I should quote its ending.[1]

" And thus desiring God of his infinite mercy to pardon, to
purge out all the venome, malice, and violence of your heart
against myself and others, and put bowells of mercy, pitty,
meekness, and affection towards good men into you, and to
give you grace unfainedly to repent of all your violent, unjust,
extravagant, oppressive, vexatious, despitefull courses and
proceedings which crye aloud for vengeance against you, and
will certainly end in misery, ruyne, if not in hell itself, if you
runne on madding in them, without restraint or feare, I
humbly take my leave, and rest Your Grace's oppressed one,
seeking, not grace, but justice from you,
                              " WILLIAM PRYNNE."

A letter written in such a tone was not very well calculated
to soften the heart of an oppressor, and Laud simply showed
it to the king, who commanded him to hand it to " Mr
Atturney *Noye*."[2]   Laud shall tell us what followed.   " *Junij*
17.   Mr Atturney sent for Mr *Prynn* to his Chamber ;
shewed him the Letter, asked him whether it were his hand.
Mr *Prynn* said ; he could not tell, unless he might read it.
The Letter being given into his hand, he tore it into small
pieces, threw it out at the Window, and said, that should
never rise in Judgment against him : Fearing, it seems, an
Ore tenus for this."

" Junij 18.   Mr Atturney brought him, for this, into the
Star-Chamber ; where all this appear'd with shame enough to
Mr *Prynn*.   I there forgave him, &c."

So far, so good ; but I must anticipate by saying that in

[1] " Documents relating to Wm. Prynne."   S. R. Gardiner, p. 56.
[2] Diary, p. 50.

1637, Prynne, with Bastwick and Burton, was again brought before the Star Chamber "for their Libells against the Hierarchy of the Church."

This time, something like twenty judges passed sentence upon him ; some adding penalties, others merely confirming, or expressing their approval of, the sentences already passed. Juxon, then Bishop of London, "condempnes the booke to the fyer." Lord Dorset says :—" This man wilbe affrighted at a three-cornered capp, sweate at a surplus, sighe to heare musicke, swounde to the signe of the crosse, yett will make noe conscyence to lye, forsweare, and perjure him selfe, and for the advantage of the common cause to rayle upon the Kinges estate, and instructe treason.   Hee is all purple within, all pryde, all mallyce, all spite."

Much time must already have been occupied by those sentences, yet when it came to Laud's turn he occupied two hours in delivering his judgment.   "Hee spake two howers out of a note booke prepard for that purpose,"[1] and he divided his matter into fourteen heads.   In the course of it, he contrived to give a side thrust at the Bishop of Lincoln's "book lately publisht, the Bishopp of Lincoln being present to heare it, when his Grace said the Bishopp was mistaken, and that as learned as himselfe were of that oppinion.   His Grace past no sentence, but he gave the lords thankes that did passe sentence upon those delinquents."

He was heard to remark to another of the Council, however, that there was still a good deal of Prynne's ears that would bear cropping, and that at his first execution, the hangman had merely cut away "the seams " ; an observation which Prynne, if he overheard it, would certainly consider ill-natured, as well as suggestive.   Although Laud, in neither sentence, assigned any actual bodily penalty to Prynne, he incurred his bitter hatred ; and Prynne may have believed, nor without reason, that while, as a bishop, he considered it more seemly to leave the sentencing to bodily pains to the secular arm, he took good care to instruct the secular arm as to the ghastly details.

---

[1] News Letter from C. Rossingham, 15 June 1637.

Undoubtedly Prynne was a very unsatisfactory character ; but, as he, rightly or wrongly, attributed all his sufferings, which were great and many, to Laud, it is scarcely a matter for surprise that he should have felt ill-will towards him.   It is true that John Selden said :—" Men cry out upon the high commission, as if only clergymen had to do with it ; when I believe there are more laymen in commission there, than clergymen.   If the laymen will not come, whose fault is that ?   So of the star-chamber, the people think the bishops only censured Prynne, Burton, and Bastwick, when there were but two there, and one spoke not in his own cause." [1]

On the other hand, another writer [2] says :—" The King and Queen did nothing direct against him (Prynne) till Laud set Dr Heylin (who bore a great malice to Prynne for confuting some of his doctrines) to peruse Prynne's book, &c.   The archbishop went with these notes to Mr Attorney Noy, and charged him to prosecute Prynne, which Noy afterwards did vigorously enough in the Star Chamber, &c."

The second sentence passed on Prynne had much in common with the first ; but, in effect, it was more severe ; for when he was in the pillory on the two first occasions, he promised the hangman five pieces of silver, if he would use him "kyndly," [3] so that official had merely snipped off a little of the rim of his ears, and performed the other dis-agreeable duties as mercifully, and with as much considera-tion for the comfort of his patient, as was possible under the circumstances.   After the operation was over, however, " Prin gave him but halfe a crowne, in six pences," instead of five shillings, which was the amount which the hangman had understood by Prynne's offer of five pieces of silver.   When Prynne was put into the pillory, four years later, the " haing-man was quitt with him."   He "burnt Prin," says the autho-rity above quoted, " in both the cheekes, and, as I heare, because hee burnt one cheeke with a letter the wronge waye " (owing, no doubt, to the sixpences instead of shillings), " hee burnt that againe ; precently a surgeon clapt a plaster to take

[1] Selden's " Table Talk," ed. 1892, p. 45.
[2] Whitelock, " Memorials," p. 18.   [3] S. P. O. Dom. vol. ccclxii. No. 42.

out the fire. The haingman hewed off Prin's cares very scurvily, which putt him to much paine, and after hee stood longer in the pillorye before his head could be gott out." The sixpences had probably something to do with this also.

I may mention, in passing, that several other prisoners were tried in the Star Chamber at the same time as Prynne. One of them was condemned by Cottington to stand in the pillory in St Paul's churchyard. "It is a consecrated place," exclaimed Laud. "I cry your grace's mercy," said Lord Cottington; "then let it be in Cheapside."[1]

The severities of the Court of High Commission, so far as they affected ecclesiastical and religious offences, were almost universally attributed to Laud. I will give a few examples of the cases of such a nature that came before it.

The Rector of Tretire with Michael Church, co. Hereford, was accused of having seldom read the Litany except in Lent, and of having omitted parts of the service, "as for example, when he came to the Psalms, or to one of the Lessons, he would leave reading and fall to expounding." "That done," he would go up to the pulpit and begin his sermon. In expounding, he inveighed by name against some of his parishioners with whom he was offended. For these, and sundry other irregularities, "the court pronounced him a man incorrigible," as, indeed, he appears to have been, "and ordered him to be deprived and suspended from his ministry."[2]

The Vicar of Poslingford, Suffolk, when preaching, "in his gesture" "feigns some man whom he aims at, throwing out his arm against the said party."[3] Augustine Moreland, of Stroud, Kent, gentleman, "was much given to excessive drinking, and at such times swore most desperate oaths and blasphemed the name of God."[4] The Court "ordered him to make acknowledgement at his parish church in certain words to be set down by the commissioners, fined him £500 to the King, and condemned him in costs. Lastly, he was committed to the gate-house till he gave bond with sureties

---

[1] "Celebrated Trials," vol. i. p. 420.
[2] "Cal. Sta. Pa. Dom.," 1634-5, p. 263.   [3] *Ib.*, p. 319.   [4] *Ib.*, p. 330.

to perform the order of the court." This was very different from the five shillings and costs usual for drunkenness, and what the police call "offull language," in these days.

One, George Gayre, appears to have been a Catholic, at whose house chalices and vestments had been seized ; for the Court made the following pronouncement :—"The massing-stuff and chalices ordered to be defaced and delivered to the owner if he will come into the court and require them." [1]

John Etkins, of Isham, was "charged with irreverent behaviour in wearing his hat during divine service, in causing £100 to be told over upon the communion-table" in payment for some land, "and in saying in the streets of Isham in scorn that a ploughman is as good as a priest. Fined £100, ordered to make a public submission in the church of Isham, and condemned in costs." [2]

The Vicar of Brigstock had resorted to the mean trick of causing "the clerk to lock the church door to keep in the whole congregation in the winter time to hear him preach until dark night." [3] I have only read the depositions, without taking the trouble of finding out what sentence was passed upon him. Certainly he deserved a heavy one !

We find a Sir William Hellwys brought up for deserting his wife and misbehaving himself. [4] "He was ordered to do penance, *more penitentiali*, in a white sheet," in the churches of the two parishes " where the greatest scandal had been given by him." He was also fined £500 and costs.

Trials before the Court of High Commission were by no means confined to the sterner sex. We have already seen how Lady Eleanor Davies was treated, and, on another occasion, Laud wrote to the king asking his leave to summon Lady Falkland before it. [5] And here we shall see how he treated converts to Catholicism. He wrote to the king :—

"Lord Newburgh has acquainted the writer that Mrs Ann and Mrs Elizabeth Cary, two daughters of the late Lord Falkland, are reconciled to the Church of Rome, not without the practise of their mother. Presumes his

[1] "Cal. Sta. Pa. Dom.," 1634-5, p. 322.   [2] *Ib.*, p. 268.
[3] *Ib.*, p. 415.   [4] *Ib.*, p. 553.   [5] *Ib.*, p. 159.

Majesty remembers what suit Lord Newburgh made at Greenwich, and what command his Majesty sent by Sec. Coke to the Lady, that she should forbear working on her daughters' consciences, and suffer them to go to their brother, or any other safe place where they might receive such instruction as was fit for them. The Lady trifled out of these commands, pretended her daughters' sickness, till now they are sick indeed, yet not without hope of recovery, for as Lord Newburgh informs the Archbishop they meet with some things there which they cannot digest and are willing to be taken again by any fair way. The Archbishop has taken hold of this, and according to his duty has done what he could think fittest for the present, but the greatest thing he fears is that the mother will still be practising, and do all she can to hinder. Prays his Majesty's leave to call the old Lady into the High Commission if he find cause so to do, and further as he was so is he still an earnest suitor that she might be commanded from Court, where if she live she is as like to breed inconvenience to his Majesty as any other."

Obviously there was not much "leaning towards Rome" on Laud's part.

If he was quite prepared to hold out the right hand of fellowship to the various Protestant Churches abroad, and to unite with them in one great Non-Catholic Church, he expected all their members, when in this country, to conform as much as possible to the Established Church of England.

A Walloon congregation had established itself at Maidstone, and Laud sent his vicar-general, Brent, to look after it. He reported to Laud [1] that he had seen the minister and " some of the principal of the Walloon congregation, to whom" he had "intimated that all the natives of their congregation must resort to the parish church of Maidstone, together with the English, to hear divine service and sermons, and to perform all duties of parishioners; and that as well minister as people of the same Walloon congregation which are aliens born shall have and use the Liturgy or Book of

[1] "Cal. Sta. Pa. Dom.," 1634-5, p. 366.

Common Prayer used in the English churches, as the same [is] or may be faithfully translated into French."

Some months later, we find Brent making his report to Laud of the French and Dutch ministers.[1] He has made them all promise that " they will obey his commands as much as possibly they can ; that is, they will repair often to the English churches to hear both divine service and sermons, and persuade their congregations so to do ; and say that they hope to induce them to receive the blessed Eucharist some times every year in the English churches also, and will do whatsoever else may be done without the utter dissipation of their own congregations." Presently he admits that he " could not get them to set down under their hands, because, as they said, they did not know what they should be able to persuade their several congregations unto."

A careful study of Laud's action in relation to the foreign Protestant Churches in England leads me to the conclusion that a rather mistaken view of it has been taken by several historians to whom I look up with the greatest respect. I almost tremble at the idea of questioning the opinion of that most charming writer, the late John Richard Green. In most respects his short summary of Laud's character is unsurpassed [2] :—" Cold, pedantic, superstitious as he was," " William Laud rose out of the mass of court-prelates by his industry, his personal unselfishness, his remarkable capacity for administration. At a later period, when immersed in State-business, he found time to acquire so complete a knowledge of commercial affairs that the London merchants themselves owned him a master in matters of trade. Of statesmanship he had none." And much else in the same style is excellent. But when he proceeds to say [3] that he aimed at " the severance of whatever ties had hitherto united the English Church to the Reformed Churches of the Continent," and that " in Laud's view episcopal succession was of the essence of a Church ; and by their rejection of bishops the Lutheran and Calvinistic Churches of Germany

---

[1] " Cal. Sta. Pa. Dom.," 1634-5, p. 575.
[2] " Hist. of the Eng. People," vol. iii. p. 157.   [3] *Ib.*, p. 158.

and Switzerland had ceased to be Churches at all," I cannot
follow him.   As we have already seen, Laud distinctly says [1]
that although the Lutherans had not retained the name of
bishops, they had retained "the Thing." "For instead of
Bishops they are called Superintendents."

Mr Green writes :—"The freedom of worship therefore
which had been allowed to the Huguenot refugees from France
or the Walloons from Flanders, was suddenly withdrawn ;
and the requirement of conformity with the Anglican ritual
drove them in crowds from the southern ports to seek toleration in Holland."

It is perfectly true that Laud pressed the descendants of
the members of the Dutch and French Churches, who had
settled in England, to conform to the Church of the country,
but not on the score of their having no bishops.   If we read
carefully through his address to the Lords "concerning the
Dutch and French Churches in England," we shall not find a
word about any want of apostolical succession.   His reasons
for desiring that they might be obliged to attend the Anglican
Churches were very different.   He says [2] that when they were
persecuted in their own countries, " it was honour and piety in
this State, when at the first way was given for those Churches,
both in London and some other parts of the kingdom " ; but
he conceives that it was never intended that if the descendants
of the members of those Churches remained in England and
obtained the privileges of British citizens, they should retain
religious exemptions denied to other British citizens, and con-
stitute "a Church within a Church"—observe that he does
not deny that each of the foreign bodies was a Church ; on
the contrary, he uses the very words commonly used by High
Anglicans when objecting to the existence of the Catholic
Church in England ; yet they never question its "Episcopal
Succession "—and he says that they would " in time grow to
be a kind of another commonwealth within this," and be "an
absolutely divided body from the Church of England established, which must needs work upon their affections, alienate

---

[1] "Hist.," p. 141.
[2] "Libr. Ang. Cath. Theo.," vol. vi. part i. pp. 25, 26.

them from the State, or at least made them ready for any
innovation that may sort better with their humour." He
suggested that if they must needs "continue as a divided
body from both State and Church, that they be used as
strangers, and not as natives. That is, that they may pay
all double duties, as strangers use to do, and have no more
immunities than strangers have, till they will live and con-
verse as other subjects do."

Moreover, when, in his trial for high treason, he was
charged with having "Trayterously endeavoured to cause
Division and Discord between the Church of England and
other Reformed Churches ; and, to that end, hath Suppressed
and Abrogated the Priveleges and Immunities, which have
been by his Majesty and his Royal Ancestors granted to the
French and Dutch Churches in this Kingdom,"[1] he replied—
"All which I did concerning those Churches, was with this
Moderation, that all those of their several Congregations, in
London, Canterbury, Sandwich, Norwich, or elsewhere, which
were of the second Descent, and born in *England,* should
repair to their several Parish Churches, and Conform themselves to the Doctrine, Discipline, and Liturgy of the Church
of *England,* and not live continually in an open Separation,
as if they were an *Israel* in *Egypt,* to the great distraction of
the Natives of this Kingdom."[2]

In proof of my contention that Laud's desire that the
members of the French and Walloon Protestant Churches
should conform themselves to the Church of the country did
not necessarily imply any objection to those Churches in
themselves, I may point to the custom of the Catholic Church
with regard to the members of local churches, with peculiar
rites and uses, but in communion with, and under obedience
to Rome, when they visit or take up their permanent abode
in other countries. I believe that I am correct in saying that
supposing, for instance, a party of miners from a country in
which the Slav rite is in use, were to come over to work in
the Cheshire salt mines—as indeed actually happened some
years ago—if one of their own Slav priests came with them,

[1] "Hist.," p. 374.   [2] *Ib.,* p. 378.

and were allowed the use of an altar, or a church, for the performance of his native rite, they would be instructed to attend his ministrations; but if no Slav priest were within reach, then they would be told to attend those of the ordinary Catholic priest of the parish. If, however, they were to settle for good and all in the country, and their children were to become British subjects, the Catholic Church would not allow a permanent Slav Church to be established in Cheshire under Slav priests, but would expect the descendants of the original settlers to conform themselves to the uses of their Catholic neighbours and fellow-citizens. Yet this would not imply the least question of either the validity of Slav orders, or the orthodoxy of the Slav liturgy or discipline, all three of which Rome fully recognises and approves. It is true that at Rome there is a permanent altar, or church, for every rite; but, as pilgrims from all countries go constantly to Rome, the centre of Christendom, the case is exceptional.

I do not pretend that such instances as the above are exact parallels to that of Laud and the foreign Protestant Churches in England; but I submit that there is enough in common between them to justify Laud's action towards the French and Walloon Congregations without the necessity of supposing that he objected to those churches in themselves.

Again, Mr Green wrote [1] :—" The same conformity was required from the English soldiers and merchants abroad, who had hitherto attended without scruple the services of the Calvinistic churches." [2] But Laud's wish appears to have been to have English chaplains attached to the regiments, and that their appointment should be in the hands of the two English archbishops. Certain " unconformable " clergymen, who had been turned out of their own livings or cures at home, had gone abroad and persuaded the colonels of English regiments to engage them as chaplains. Against such as these Laud waged a fierce war. " The several colonels in the Low Countries should entertain no minister as preacher to their regiments, but such as shall conform in all things to the Church of England established, and be commended unto

[1] " Hist.," p. 378.   [2] " Hist. of the Eng. People," vol. iii. p. 158.

them from your Lordships by advice of the Lords Archbishops
of Canterbury or York for the time being." " The company of
merchants residing there, or in other foreign parts, shall admit
no minister as preacher to them, but such as are so qualified
and so commended as aforesaid." It seems also that the English Protestants were singular in respect to their conduct in
Holland ; for Laud says [1] :—" It is to be observed that the
French and High German congregations in the Low
Countries do all observe the Liturgy of their own Mother
Churches ; only the English observe neither their own, nor
any other uniformity." When the English soldiers and
English merchants were observing " neither their own *nor
any other* uniformity," it did seem time that something should
be done to bring them into some sort of order, especially as
they were engaging, as preachers, disorderly and " unconformable " clergymen whom the English bishops would not
tolerate at home. It is well known that the nonconforming
clergy, who afterwards went to America and founded the
State of New England, went first to Holland, and that it was
Laud's energy, recorded above, which prevented them from
obtaining employment in the Low Countries. I make bold
to believe that these were the reasons, and not the want of
apostolical succession in the Lutheran and Calvinistic
Churches, which made Laud so anxious that English subjects
in Holland should have duly authorized English chaplains.

Laud's conduct towards the Foreign Protestants in England,
more especially towards those from the Palatinate, greatly
annoyed the Queen of Bohemia. Sir Thomas Roe had
written to her, that Laud was " an excellent man," [2] adding :
—" If your Majesty have no relation to him, I wish you
would be pleased to make one, for he is very just, incorrupt,
and above all, mistaken by the erring world. For my part I
do esteem him a rare counsellor for integrity, and a fast
friend, and one that hath more interest in his Majesty's
judgment than any man."

Elizabeth, Queen of Bohemia, replied [3] :—" For my Lord of

[1] " Lib. Ang. Cath. Theo.," vol. vi. part i. p. 25.
[2] S. P. O. Dom., vol. cclxxviii. No. 32.   [3] *Ib.*, vol. cclxxxiii. No. 36.

Canterbury, I am glad you commend him so much, for there are but few that do it. He hath indeed sent me sometimes a cold compliment, and I have answered it in the same kind. I have now written to him, at the entreaty of the Administrator, in the behalf of the poor preachers of the Palatinate."

As Mr Bruce says in his preface to the volume of the *Calendar of State Papers* for 1633-4 [1]:—"The Archbishop's watchfulness, it will be seen, extended to all persons and all classes. Churches of English people resident in Holland, chaplains of English regiments in the service of the presbyterian Hollanders, the formless and, as he esteemed it, irreverent Church of Scotland, and the churches in England of protestant refugees, who had fled hither for conscience sake, all came under his attention at once."

As to the Protestant refugees, he was disposed to tolerate a good deal, if they would but "receive the blessed Eucharist some times every year in the English churches also": it was even hinted that Catholics would not be much interfered with if they would do the same. Herein is shown the extreme anti-Catholic spirit of Laud; for, whereas the Catholic Church has ever guarded its Holy Communion with the greatest jealousy, restricting it exclusively to its own children, Laud endeavoured to press the communion of his Church upon everybody, whatever his faith and creed might be. The late Dean Stanley was blamed by High-Churchmen for admitting people, who did not believe in the Divinity of our Lord, to communion; yet the great champion of their own school, Archbishop Laud, would not only have admitted them, but would have exempted them from penalties in return for their compliance.

[1] P. xxiv.

CHAPTER XX.

PERHAPS there is nothing for which Laud is better known than his removal of the communion-tables from the body of the churches to the places in the chancels where the high altars had formerly stood.

As a protest against the sacramental teaching of the Catholic Church, the ministers of the new Church of England, in the latter part of the sixteenth century, had placed their communion-tables in the body of the church, without any coverings upon them, and allowed them to be put to many exceedingly queer uses.

Heylin tells [1] us that it was ordered in the visitation of the diocese of Canterbury, that the communion-table should " be placed altarwise, for it was urged that ' should it be permitted to stand as it before did, Church Wardens would keep their accounts on it, Parishioners would despatch the Parish business on it, Schoolmasters will teach their boys to write upon it, the boys will lay their hats, satchels and books upon it, many will sit and lean irreverently against it in sermon time, the Dogs will . . . and defile it, and Glaziers would knock it full of holes.'" " By which means he " [Laud] " prevailed so far, that of 469 Parishes which were in that Diocese, 140 had conformed to his Order in it, before the end of the Christmas holidays of the present year, 1635, without any great reluctancy in Priest or People."

This is a bold boast; but does it not seem wonderful that in the archdiocese of so determined a man as Laud, after he had occupied it two years, there should be 329 churches out of 469, in which the communion-tables were left in the body of the churches and *not* placed "altarwise," in direct defiance of his orders. Such a fact seems most inconsistent with our

[1] " Cyp. Ang.," p. 271.

ideas of Laud's autocratic rule! It is not an uncommon
thing, when some modern instance of lax ecclesiastical discipline is mentioned, to hear people say, "Archbishop Laud
would have made short work with a case of that kind!"
The 329 "table-wise" communion-tables make one inclined
to doubt it.

In his own days, however, Laud was considered over stern
in enforcing his favourite rubrics, or rather his interpretation
of them. Clarendon, who sympathised with him, did not
allow his action in the matter to pass altogether uncriticised.
[1] "The removing the Communion Table out of the body
of the Church, where it us'd to stand," says he, "and fixing
it to one place"—this implies what is well known, namely,
that it used to be moved about and only brought out when
the communion service was going to be celebrated—"in the
upper end of the chancel, which frequently made the buying
a new Table to be necessary, the inclosing it with a Rail of
Joyners work, and thereby fencing it off from the use of Dogs,
and all servile uses; the obliging of all Persons to come up
to those Rails to receive the Sacrament, how acceptable
soever to grave and intelligent Persons, who lov'd Order and
Decency (for acceptable it was to such) yet introduc'd first
Murmurings among the People (upon the very Charge and
Expence of it), and if the Minister were not a man of dis-
cretion and reputation to Compose, and Reconcile those
Indispositions (as too frequently he was not, and rather
inflam'd, and increas'd the Distemper) it begot Suits, and
Appeals at Law." Suits and appeals at law must have been
a good deal cheaper than they are now, if they cost less than
"Joyners work!" As to Laud, himself, Clarendon says that
"guided purely by his Zeal, and Reverence for the Place of
God's Service, and by the Canons, and Injunctions of the
Church, with the custom observ'd in the King's Chapel, and
in most Cathedral Churches, without considering the long
intermission, and discontinuance, in many other Places," he
"prosecuted this Affair more Passionately than was fit for
the season; and had Prejudice against Those, who out of

[1] "Hist. of the Rebellion," vol. i. p. 95.

fear, or foresight, or not understanding the Thing, had not the same Warmth to promote it."

In other dioceses, as well as Canterbury, there were constant wrangles about the moving of the communion-tables. An action was brought in the Court of Arches[1] against one of the proctors, the clerk, and the public notary of St Gregory's Church, "next the Cathedral of St Paul," for the offence of removing the communion-table "from its ancient and accustomed place in the middle of the chancel"—this was rather an exceptional case, as the table was usually, not in the chancel, but in the body of the church—"and placed the same altarwise along the east wall of the chancel." In about a fortnight there was an "Order of the King in Council made on debate of the difference which grew about removing the communion-table in St Gregory's Church, &c,"[2] "from the middle of the chancel to the upper end, there placed altarwise, in such manner as it stands in the cathedral and mother church, as also in all other cathedrals, and his Majesty's own chapel, and as is consonant to the practice of approved antiquity." It will be observed that there were two opinions as to ancient use on this point.

"The King took the book"[3] (containing an injunction of Queen Elizabeth) "into his own hand and read it, which was that, at Communion times, the table should stand in the body of the church, or chancel; the King declared that it was his mind that it should not stand in the body of the church, but middle of the chancel at Communion times. Dr Neyle or Neale being then Archbishop of York, said, if it please your Majesty, where I and Bishop Buckeridge have jurisdiction, we do so. Dr Laud stood up and said, I did not think that my Lord of York had been guilty of such a sin, and prayed God to forgive him;"—this was strong language, considering that Neale had long been one of Laud's friends and patrons;—"then he called on Dr Duck, a learned lawyer to speak, but he urging nothing material for its standing altarwise, the Archbishop affirmed that, upon his

---

[1] S. P. O., vol. ccxlviii. No. 18.

[2] "Cal. Sta. Pa. Dom.," 1633-4, p. 273.   [3] *Ib.*, 1641-3, p. 532.

reputation, the Communion Table was always called an
Altar in the primitive church" (as most undoubtedly it was,
for that matter), "and that the parishioners had fitted the
chancel up with pews to set themselves and their wives
above the Communion Table, but he would have none set
above God Almighty in his own house; then the King
said, refer it to the discretion of the minister and church-
wardens to take down at Communion times.   Laud said
that they would have it down to vex their minister, that they
would not kneel, and they were but a few Puritans, who,
when the example of the cathedral churches and your
Majesty's chapel was urged, said that though your Majesty
suffer idolatry in your chapel, they will not do so in their
church, &c."   On the next page it is stated that Laud said
that "when strangers came from beyond sea and saw the
table stand altarwise in Paul's and went but out at the door
and saw the table stand otherwise in St Gregory's, what a
disunion would they say was in the Church of England," a
remark which might possibly be made by strangers "from
beyond the sea" at certain varieties observable in different
Anglican churches even to-day.

Laud sent his Vicar-General, Brent, to make an archiepiscopal visitation in the diocese of Lincoln, of which his old
enemy, Williams, was bishop.   Williams stoutly objected,
and the matter was referred to Noy, the Attorney-General.

There is an entry in the *Calendar of State Papers*[1] of an
"Order or award of Attorney General Noy in a dispute
between Bishop Williams of Lincoln and Archbishop Laud.
Bishop Williams claimed an exemption of his diocese from
being metropolitically visited, and from the payment of
procurations, and also that if the Archbishop could of right
visit the diocese of Lincoln, he ought not to do so this year,
being the year of the Bishop's triennial visitation, and that if
he did, the archiepiscopal visitation should not interfere with
the Bishop's exercise of his ordinary jurisdiction.   The
Attorney General states at length the grounds and proofs on
all these points, and finally determines:—1. In favour of the

[1] 1633-4, p. 523.

Archbishop's right to visit. 2. That procurations ought of right to be paid to him on such visitation. 3. That he might visit when the Bishop is to make his triennial visitation. 4. He advised the Bishop to forbear to exercise jurisdiction ecclesiastical during the visitation metropolitical."

Laud, therefore, got the better of Williams on every point in dispute.

On one of these "visitations metropolitical," Laud's Vicar-General found that Williams had put the communion-table, which had been removed to the east end of the chancel and placed altarwise, back into the middle of the church.   Laud had it removed to the east end once again, and, as he could not touch Williams personally, he marked his displeasure by suspending his six archdeacons. [1]

I had just been reading (in the year 1893) several old accounts of the removal of the communion-tables from the bodies of the churches to the chancels, at Laud's command, when I happened to take up a religious newspaper [2] of the week, which showed how history repeats itself ; for therein I read :—" The following paper was read by the Rev. T. Davies, Vicar of St John's, Harbourne, Birmingham, on Sunday morning, before commencing the sermon.—Most, if not all, of the congregation will have observed on Sunday last that our communion-table has been removed some distance from the wall at the east end, and I feel it due to the congregation that I should briefly explain why this has been done. Originally, that is, at the Reformation "—there is something very fine in this, and a remarkable definition of ancient use, as well as of the Biblical phrase, " In the beginning "— " Originally, that is, at the Reformation, the tables generally stood in the body of the church, as the rubric before the communion service directs, and this, says the present Bishop of London, would be quite in accordance with the law. But in this church, as in many others, it is impossible to place it there.   Until the days of the Romanising Archbishop Laud, the table was placed as a table.   But he, anxious

---

[1] Mozley's " Essay on Laud," p. 171.
[2] *The English Churchman and St James's Chronicle*, January 12, 1893.

to substitute the altar of Romanism for the table of our
Protestant Church, had the table placed against the east wall
that it may there appear to be an altar. Its position there is
not, and never has been, according to the rubric. The faithful clergy of the Church of England have not hitherto desired
to alter its position, but since what is known as the Lincoln
judgment many of them have decided to place the table in
the body of the church where possible, and in other cases to
draw it so far from the east wall that it shall be to all intents
and purposes a table such as the Prayer Book directs. In
the recent judgments it was stated by the Archbishop and
the Privy Council, that all those ceremonies, bowings, kneel-
ings, making signs of the cross, &c., were ' meaningless,' and
we thank the Archbishop for the word." . . . " We do by
this action,"—*i.e.*, the removal of the communion table from
the east wall—" We do by this action most emphatically
declare that the Church of England knows nothing of an
altar, nothing of a sacrifice, except that of praise, and thanksgiving and service, that there is no shadow of sacerdotalism
attached to the office of her ministers," &c.

In the same newspaper it is stated that "the Rev. Basil D.
Aldwell, another tried champion of the Protestant cause, has
also moved the communion-table into the middle of the
chancel of St Luke's Church, Southsea, of which he is the
incumbent. Mr Aldwell now stands behind the table at
communion time, with his face towards the congregation."
So also does the Pope, when he says mass at the high altar
of St Peter's at Rome ; but that is apart from the question
with which I am dealing.

I will now dismiss the subject of the position of the communion-tables to notice another of Laud's reforms, not so
generally known, namely, the suppression of what were
then termed "non-kneelants." In many districts, where a
puritanical spirit prevailed, the congregation, in order to show
that they did not attribute anything supernatural to the bread
and wine in the sacrament, received it standing or sitting,
instead of kneeling. Laud gave orders that this custom should
be abolished. His Vicar-General writes from Ipswich, that

he has "suspended one Mr Cave, a precise minister of St Helen's, for giving the sacrament of the Eucharist to non-kneelants."[1] Again from Northampton :—" Mr Ball, the chief minister of the town, was accused to have given the sacrament of the Eucharist to non-kneelants."[2] Once more from Coventry :—" I suspended one Mr Moore, minister of Frankton, for administering the holy communion to non-kneelants."[3] " One Goodwin," he writes, " saith that to kneel at the receiving of the communion is idolatry."[4] Of this gentleman he has "taken order."

A petition was presented to Laud's Vicar-General by the rector of St Mary Bothaw, stating that the Lord Mayor, some fifty years earlier, had erected certain rows of seats whereby he had "so streightened the place that they have left no convenient room for placing forms for the more ready administration of the holy communion, so that the communi-cants receiving in the seats, where their boards to kneel against are set so shelving that they must of necessity rest upon their seats, it cannot well be discerned who kneel according to order or who do not."[5] On the other hand, at Boston, it was proved that the congregation were "con-formable," and that "many for want of room to kneel were forced to stand or sit at the receiving" of the communion ; but "if any of defendants have received otherwise than kneeling it was from no dislike of that gesture."[6]

The crime, as Laud considered it, of non-kneeling was not confined to the lower classes. " Sir Henry Vane also," writes Garrard to Lord Conway,[7] " hath as good as lost his eldest son, who is gone into New England for conscience' sake ; he liked not the discipline of the Church of England ; none of our ministers would give him the sacrament standing ; no persuasions of our bishops nor authority of his parents could prevail with him."

Stern as was Laud in enforcing his ecclesiastical injunc-tions, not a few clergymen dared to set them at defiance.

---

[1] "Cal. Sta. Pa. Dom.," 1635, p. xxxii. [2] *Ib.*, p. 35.
[3] *Ib.*, p. xxxix. [4] *Ib.*, p. xxxviii. [5] *Ib.*, 1634-5, p. 327.
[6] *Ib.*, p. 422. [7] *Ib.*, p. 385.

For example, in May 1634, a presentment to him was made against their minister, by the churchwardens and sidesmen of the parish of Holy Trinity, Shaftesbury, for various irregularities in the conduct of divine service, and for preaching against the Book of Sports, "in a most high kind of ' terrification,' as if it were a most dreadful thing, and near damnable ; if not absolute damnation, to use any recreations on the Sabbath or Lord's day." [1]

Nor did the laity show much inclination to please Laud by subscribing to his pet object, the repair of St Paul's. A correspondent, at Little Horsley, near Colchester, writes to Laud,[2] that it grieves his "spirit to see how dull and backward his neighbours near Colchester are in aiding the repair of St Paul's. A great parish near him very lately gave 6d., and some nothing at all, and the best gave not so much as was spent in persuading them." There is a deep note of pathos in the latter complaint! A certain Mr Ball, he says, 'did much hinder the service at the beginning," when a collection for St Paul's was being made. "Not so few as 100 were present straining courtesy who should make a beginning" by tendering a donation, when "'Marry,' said Ball, 'that will I !' and in a scornful posture threw 12d. upon the board, he being a great rich man. This was a pattern for the most there present, that do not hold it good manners to exceed their betters." And then the writer throws out the following significant hint :—"Although this will not be cause to question Ball ; yet he to enlarge his court and garden with a part of the churchyard will be worthy of an inquisition." He ends by saying that his only object in writing is to further "our loving lovely King's desire."

Others went further and roundly abused the archbishop. A Mr Parsons spoke of Laud as "that unsanctified rascal the Bishop of Canterbury." [3] One, Lodowick Bowyer, who had "slandered Laud," was condemned, in the Star Chamber, by Lord Cottington, in a sentence thus summarised [4] :—"£3000 fine, stand pillory here, in the palace, with a paper ; stand in

---

[1] "Cal. Sta. Pa. Dom.," 1634-5, p. 2.   [2] *Ib.*, p. 252.
[3] *Ib.*, 1633-4, p. 467.   [4] *Ib.*, p. 287.

Cheapside likewise ; at Reading likewise, with his cars nailed ; if he be quit from the felony to return to perpetual imprisonment in some house of correction. To this Lord Chief Justice Richardson added, to be ' whipt ; imprisonment in Bridewell ; burning in the face, R or L.' "

In the year 1634, an instrument attributed to Laud himself, but professedly " Charles R. Instructions for the most Reverend Father in God, our right Trusty, and right entirely Beloved Councillor *William* Lord Archbishop of *Canterbury,* concerning certain Orders to be observed and put in Execution by the several Bishops of his Province," [1] gave great offence to some of his episcopal brethren. These bishops had contracted a habit of leaving their dioceses to take care of themselves and living in London, so as to keep well in view in the hope of further advancement of some kind, now that Laud was putting clerics into various important posts hitherto occupied by laymen.

The first of these instructions ran :—" I. That the Lords the Bishops respectively be commanded to their several Sees, there to keep Residence ; excepting those who are in necessary Attendance at our Court."

It would appear, also, that some of them had been endeavouring to increase their incomes by cutting down timber ; for the second instruction enacts that they are not to " wast " their " Woods where any are left."

These " instructions," believed to have been suggested to the king by Laud, made him several enemies on the bench of bishops.

Nor did Laud hesitate to scold a brother bishop well, on occasion. Thus he writes[2] to Goodman, Bishop of Gloucester, who had written to him asking for a coadjutor, and hinting that he might perhaps resign his bishopric if the king would give him the livings which he held before he got it, or some others equally good :—" first, concerning a coadjutor, his Majesty thinks " " that it is a very unadvised notion." As to his intention " to petition his Majesty that he may resign his

[1] " Hist. of the Troub. and Tryal of W. Laud," p. 520.
[2] " Cal. Sta. Pa. Dom.," 1634-5, p. 208.

bishopric;" "to this the King commanded the Archbishop to
give answer: That he should be very well advised what he
did, for if Goodman tendered his Majesty a resignation he
would accept it"; but he makes it very evident that, in that
case, he must not expect to get a rich living instead of it.
Laud "will tell him plainly, that he is very ill advised to
think of resigning his bishopric." "And since Bishop Goodman knows that resigning his bishopric will not put off the
Bishop, it will be a fine contemptible thing for him, in a
settled church as this is, to bring himself and his calling
into such scorn. Therefore, once again the Archbishop prays
him to think no more of his resignations; but if he will need
do himself that wrong, the Archbishop prays Goodman to
trouble him no more with it."

It may be interesting, considering the present popularity
of the Oratorians in England, to remember that, shortly after
the year of which I am writing, an Oratorian Father was sent
from Rome to inquire into the state of affairs in England;
but "on no pretext whatever to allow himself to be
drawn into communication with the new Archbishop of
Canterbury." [1]

Laud's favour at court was no longer limited to the king.
"*Aug.* 30," he writes in his Diary,[2] in 1634, "*Saturday,* At
Oatlands the Queen sent for me, and gave me thanks for a
Business, with which she trusted me; her Promise then, that
she would be my Friend, and that I should have immediate
address to her, when I had Occasion." Possibly the queen
may still have cherished hopes of inducing Laud to become a
Catholic: if she did, they were vain; far from inclining more
and more towards the Catholic Church, he was becoming
more and more ambitious and hopeful for the welfare and
extension of the Established Church of England.

Heylin, in writing of the year 1634, says[3]:—"It was now
hoped there would be a Church of England in all Courts of
Christendom, in the chief cities of the Turk, and other great
Mahometan Princes, and in all our Factories and Plantations

[1] Barberini's Despatch of 13th March 1635.   [2] P. 50.
                        [3] "Cyp. Angl.," p. 260.

in every known part of the world, by which it might be rendered as diffused and Catholick as the Church of Rome."

The Church of England made Catholic, and the Archbishop of Canterbury its Pope! Such may have been a day-dream of Laud's.

Yet his wildest imagination could scarcely have realized the number of Anglican churches which now exist, not only in most of the countries known in his own time, but also in many since discovered. Certainly the Church of England has been "diffused": would to God that it had also been rendered "Catholick."

CHAPTER XXI

LAUD and Wentworth were in constant correspondence about ecclesiastical and other matters in Ireland. There is no doubt that they had a secret cipher, and various attempts have been made to explain it; but it has never been satisfactorily interpreted, and the chief difficulty in reading their letters is to determine when they are written in cipher and when otherwise.

Sometimes there can be no question about the use of cipher; as, for instance, when Laud writes :—" In the next place, you begin to be merry with your Heifer, and I wonder you have so little pity as not to let it rest when I have plowed with it " ; in other places it is more doubtful.

Laud is disgusted with the condition of Church matters in Ireland. One of the archbishops had no communion-table whatever in his chapel. " And truly," writes Laud to Wentworth, " I would wonder that a chapel should have never a communion table in it, save that I knew some divines are of opinion, that nothing belonging to the Sacrament is aught *extra usum*, and do therefore set the table aside in any corner (good enough for it) save only at the time of administration." [1]

So angry was he with the Irish bishops, that he tells Wentworth to "warn them," to " trounce " them, and to "give my Lord of Cashell a little of his Irish physic."

And truly there were some abuses which might well worry him. Bramhall writes to him [2] that he finds one parochial church converted into a stable, another into a nobleman's dwelling-house, the choir of a third into a tennis-court, while the vaults under the principal church in Ireland are con-

---

[1] " Lib. Ang. Cath. Theol.," vol. vi. part i. p. 551.
[2] See Baine's " Life of Laud," pp. 155-6.

verted into " tippling rooms for beer, wine, and tobacco," and
" so much frequented in time of divine service, that though
there is no danger of blowing up the assembly above their
heads, yet there is danger of poisoning them with the fumes."
He also says that, in the same cathedral, " the table used
for the administration of the blessed sacrament in the midst
of the choir," is " made an ordinary seat for maids and
apprentices."

In doctrine, also, Laud attacked the Irish bishops and
clergy. He imposed the thirty-nine articles upon them,
much against their will. It is difficult to realize that these
same Articles of Religion, which the modern ritualist clergy
speak of as " forty stripes save one," should have been
objected to as intensely Popish by the Irish clergy.

" Property worth £30,000 a year was actually refunded to
the Church in Ireland under Strafford's administration." [1]
It had been quite a common thing for a dignitary to hold
half a dozen or more preferments, and one bishop had leased
his palace to his son for fifty years.[2]

The correspondence between the English Archbishop and
the Lord Deputy in Ireland is not limited to ecclesiastical
and political affairs. Laud asks Wentworth to get him a
gown lined with the skins of pine-martens, which were then
common in Ireland, and tells him confidentially that he has
saved £13,000 in nine years. His income was now £6000
a year.[3] Occasionally he tries to say something funny in
his letters, and fails lamentably in so doing. " You
think," he writes, " to stop my mouth with some of your
hung beef out of Yorkshire ; which to your skill and commendation be it spoken, was the worst I ever tasted, and as
hard as the very horn the old Runt wore when she lived.
But I wonder you do not think of providing or drying
some of your Irish venison, and send that over to bray
too. Well, there's enough of this stuff." And, of a truth,
there is !

In one letter, Laud gently remonstrates with Wentworth for having married his third wife, and makes a poor

---

[1] Benson, p. 64. [2] *Ib.* [3] P. 66.

joke about his having himself taken in marriage official drudgery.

Wentworth was fond of writing about his children. " Nan, they tell me, danceth prettily. Arabella is a small practitioner that way also, and they are both very apt to learn that or anything that they are taught. Their brother is just now sitting at my elbow, in good health, God be praised." In a letter to Laud, from Dublin Castle, he writes : —" In good earnest, I should wax exceedingly melancholy were it not for two little girls that come now and then to play with me."

In their rule of Ireland, it is probable that neither Wentworth nor Laud fully realised the troubles which they were laying up for themselves, or that in a very few years a committee of both Houses of Parliament would print and publish a " Declaration against the Archbishop of *Canterbury* and the Lieutenant of *Ireland*," containing such words as these :— " That as they did reserve those of their Own Country who had been Incendiaries between the two Kingdoms, to be proceeded against in their Own Parliament, so they desired no other Justice to be done against these Two criminal Persons but what should seem good to the Wisdom of the Parliament." [1]

When Laud was being tried for high treason, he was accused of "procuring from the *King* such Impropriations in *Ireland*, as were in the *King's* Power, to the Church of *Ireland*." In his defence, he says of this :—" Which Mr *Nicolas* (in his gentle Language) calls ' Robbing the Crown.' *My Lords*, the Case was this. The Lord Primate of *Armagh* writ unto me, how ill Conditioned the State of that Church was for want of Means, and besought me that I would move *his Majesty* to give the Impropriations there, which yet remained in the Crown, for the Maintenance and Incouragement of able Ministers to Live among the People, and Instruct them. Assuring me, they were daily one by one begged away by Private Men, to the great prejudice both of Crown and Church. . . . And after long deliberation, the *King* was

---

[1] Clarendon's "Hist. of the Reb.," vol. i. p. 190.

pleased, at my humble Suit, to grant them in the way which I proposed. . . . And, *my Lords*, the increase of Popery is complained of in *Ireland*. Is there a better way to hinder this growth, than to place an Able Clergy among the Inhabitants? Can an Able Clergy be had without Means? Is any Means better than Impropriations restored? *My Lords*, I did this, as holding it the best Means to keep down Popery, and to advance the Protestant Religion. And I wish with all my Heart, I had been able to do it sooner, before so many Impropriations were gotten from the Crown into Private Hands."

If Laud was stern in reducing the Irish clergy to obedience to his orders as to doctrine and ritual, he did the best he could for them in the matter of emolument.

I will now recount an incident in his own country, to show how the king and the Church (as by law established) were ever the objects dearest to his heart. It entailed the petition of a royalist peer against a parliamentary squire, and an addition and improvement to a church, and therefore at once obtained his sympathy. I shall enter somewhat fully into the matter, as it is characteristic of Church disputes in the time of Laud, and it shows both that ecclesiastical litigation was carried on with bitter energy, and that appealing from one court to another in such cases is no new thing. In writing a life of so energetic an archbishop as Laud, one is tempted to quote many cases of this kind to illustrate the spirit and to show the condition of Church law in his time, and I shall dwell the longer on this particular instance, because I have determined that it shall be the only one which I shall notice at any length. It is also important from having been made the foundation of one of the charges against Laud at his trial for high treason.

In a northern corner of Shropshire lived two families— great families! as all Shropshire families always are and always were—the Corbets and the Needhams. They were very near neighbours and fiercely jealous of each other. At last they came to an open rupture about a little piece of land of the annual value of twelve shillings and sixpence. Now the parish church (Adderley church) was in the patronage of the Corbets, and the Needhams could not endure to pray in the nave, while their bitter enemy, the patron, was praying in the exalted atmosphere of the chancel. On one side of this chancel was a pew for the patron ; on the other was one for the rector. Perceiving how strained were the relations between the two great men in his parish, the well-meaning rector made the excuse of being a bachelor and requiring no pew, to place his own in the chancel at the disposal of the Needhams ; so for a time there was an armed neutrality.

On the accession of Charles I., Sir Robert Needham was made a peer, as Viscount Kilmorey, which increased the jealousy of Sir John Corbet. Worse still, the rector married, and although his wife allowed the Kilmoreys to continue to sit in her pew, they disliked being there simply as her guests. Lord Kilmorey then went to his bishop and asked his permission to rebuild his own private and domestic chapel, which had fallen into ruin. This was close to his own house, and he desired to be allowed to have service there instead of attending the parish church. The bishop was advised by counsel that the leave of the patron and the incumbent of the parish would be necessary to do this. Failing such leave, the bishop suggested that a proclamation should be made in the church to the effect that the chapel would be re-built, promising to grant a license unless an objection should be lodged. The proclamation was duly read, no objection was lodged, the license was granted, the private chapel was built, and, in 1629, it was consecrated by the bishop.

Eight months later, Sir John Corbet instituted a suit in the Court of Arches, on the ground that the rights of the parish church had been infringed, and a year later, the Dean of Arches annulled the consecration " in its plenary sense," but declared " the chapel to have been duly and validly consecrated ' for the celebration of the Lord's Supper, for Divine prayer, for preaching the Word of God therein purely and sincerely ; ' and, in that limited sense, he pronounced it valid."[1]

[1] " History of Shavington," p. 39.

To all intents and purposes, this was a victory for Lord Kilmorey; nevertheless, he deeply resented the decision, and at once gave notice of appeal. Shortly afterwards, he died; but the quarrel was carried on quite as fiercely by his son, the new Lord Kilmorey.

In due time a commission was appointed to hear the appeal. The commissioners met in a neighbouring parish church, and reversed the decision of the Court of Arches, declaring the consecration of the chapel valid in *all* respects.

The viscount, therefore, triumphed; but Sir John Corbet had another card to play. One of his footmen died (an Irish footman), and he persuaded the rector to let him bury him in the chancel, "in a shroud, and not coffined," about four feet above the place where the body of the late Lord Kilmorey lay.

The living Lord Kilmorey was furious. He took counsel's opinion, asking what remedy he could have; whether he should apply to the Earl-Marshal's Court, or to the High Commissioners, or to the delegates in the appeal in the Court of Arches, or to the Star Chamber.

The counsel consulted sent a long reply, ending with this very remarkable P.S., "Sir John Lambe is yesterday made judge of the Arches soe as if you have any interest in him he may doe yo' hono' better rights."

Lord Kilmorey, however, appealed to the Earl-Marshal, with whom he apparently had some "interest"; as he signs himself "Your Lord^ps very affeccionate frend." The Earl-Marshal ordered Sir John Corbet to dig up and remove the bones of his footman, and he also wrote to the bishop about Lord Kilmorey and Sir John Corbet, exhorting him "to endeavoure to reconcile them in love and friendshipp."

Lord Kilmorey had now got everything his own way; yet he sighed for fresh victories, and, not content with his private chapel, wanted to build an aisle or transept for himself in the parish church. Once again he asked counsel's opinion, writing to Noy, the Attorney-General, who replied :—"No man of the pish of what condčon soer may buyld an Isle or demolysh pt of ye church for ye purpose without consent of the byshop and the patron and the incumbent, and also of the pshioners."

Not long afterwards, fortune favoured Lord Kilmorey. Sir John Corbet, it was said at Laud's instigation, was imprisoned in the Fleet for joining in the famous Petition of Rights which he had read at the sessions in his own county.

Lord Kilmorey took this opportunity of appealing direct to the king, diplomatically ending his letter with the words, "if the lords grace of Canterbury your worthy metropolitan (upon reference to him) shall think fit."

Mr Harrod, in his *History of Shavington*,[1] says:—" The concluding reference to the Archbishop of Canterbury (Laud) makes it probable that this petition was prepared in view of the metropolitan visitation of the Archbishop, which was made in 1634-5. At all events, the Viscount then approached the Archbishop on the subject. Laud was the very man for the work. He would have no nice scruples about the legal rights of patrons, and would highly approve of the addition to the parish Church of a suitable family chantry."

In 1635, Laud gave Lord Kilmorey the license he desired for the erection of the aisle, in a long document,[2] beginning :— "GULIELMUS provideñ diõ Cant archiepus totius Angliæ primas et metropōnus ad quem omiñnis et omiñoda, &c."

Sir John Corbet was safe in prison, and could not, therefore, appear to object to the building of the transept, as patron of the living.

The transept, or chapel, which is a striking feature of Adderley church, was duly erected and was ready for use in 1637, when Lord Kilmorey wrote to the "principall secretary to the Reverend ffather in God the Lord Archbishope of Canterbury," saying that he had taken "a little more in bredthe and a greate deale less in length than" was allowed him, and asking Laud's leave to have it consecrated.

In reply, came a still longer document from GULIELMUS ; the transept was consecrated, and it was occupied by Lord

---

[1] P. 58.   [2] "Muniments of Shavington," § viii. v. 551.

Kilmorey for four or five years in peace. There were, none
the less, troubles ahead.

Sir John Corbet became a Member of Parliament, and
during his absence in London, his wife, who had neither
forgotten the quarrel nor forgiven the enemy who had got
the best of her husband, took the law into her own hands.
The parliamentary party were now getting into power, and
royalists like Lord Kilmorey were considered fair game. On
the 6th of March 1642, she had the courage to enter Lord
Kilmorey's transept, with her family and servants, and occupy
his seats throughout the service. Fortunately, the Kilmoreys
had a service that morning in their private chapel at home,
so no harm came of it.

On the 30th of the same month, however, there was a day
of General Humiliation, and Lord Kilmorey, after the service
in his own private chapel, went to the afternoon service at his
parish church. On going to his transept, he found four of
Sir John Corbet's servants sitting in it.[1] "The service was
proceeding, and a Psalm was being sung, so Lord Kilmorey
entered the chapel and quietly told the men to leave. They
made no reply, nor would they move from their position,
and Lord Kilmorey, who no doubt thought it well to be
well attended, sent in some of his people, with orders to
remove the men as quietly as possible. As they were armed,
and made a desperate resistance, this was impossible, and a
terrible *mêlée* ensued, but eventually the men were, with great
difficulty, dislodged, and the Kilmoreys occupied the pew to
the close of the service."

Nor was this the only battle. "On the 8th May, being
Sunday, about twenty men, armed with swords and staves,
took possession of the chapel and approaches, and kept out
the servants sent by Lord Kilmorey to take possession.
They remained there until Lady Corbet came, who, with her
family, seated herself in the chapel. The residue of the
servants placed themselves in the passage between the
church and the chapel, and kept out Lord Kilmorey's servants. In the afternoon, Lady Corbet came again, with at

[1] "History of Shavington," p. 70.

least forty men, all armed, and kept out Lord Kilmorey's servants from the chapel and from their seats in the body of the church." [1]

Lord Kilmorey then drew up a petition and sent it to Laud, begging him to assist him in recovering possession of his chapel. Laud, however, was then in the Tower; Sir John Corbet, as a Member of Parliament, was a privileged person, and, some four years later, the estates of Lord Kilmorey, who was an ardent royalist, were sequestrated.

As I said at starting, there is something more to be considered in this case with regard to Laud. It concerns accusations which were brought against him, at his trial for high treason. The charge ran thus [2] :—" That the said Arch-Bishop about Eight Years last Past, being then also a Privy-Counsellor to his Majesty, for the End and Purpose aforesaid, caused Sir John Corbet of Stoake in the County of Salop Baronet, then a Justice of Peace of the said County, to be committed to the Prison of the Fleet, where he continued a Prisoner for the space of half a year or more ; for no other Cause but for calling for the Petition of Right, and causing it to be Read at the Sessions of the Peace for that County, upon a just and necessary Occasion. And during the Time of his said Imprisonment, the said Arch-Bishop, without any Colour of Right, by a Writing under the Seal of his Arch-Bishoprick, granted away Parcel of the Glebe-Land of the Church of Adderley in the said County, whereof the said Sir Jo. Corbet was then Patron, unto Robert Viscount Kilmurry, without the consent of the said Sir John, or the then Incumbent of the said Church ; which said Viscount Kilmurry, Built a Chappel upon the said Parcel of Glebe-Land, to the great prejudice of the said Sir John Corbet, which hath caused great Suits and Dissentions between them."

In his defence, Laud made the following reply to these charges [3] :—" Sir John says, he *was sent for about Reading the* Petition of Right, *at a* Session, *in the Country, and that the Earl of* Bridgwater *should say, he was disaffected to the King.*

---

[1] "History of Shavington," and "Muniments of Shavington," § viii. v. 555-7.
[2] "Hist. of the Troub. and Tryal of W. Laud," p. 242.   [3] *Ib.*, p. 251.

This concerns me not in any thing.   He says, *That for this he was Committed, lay long in the* Fleet, *and was denied Bail:* But he says it was denyed by the whole *Board.*   So by his own Confession, this was the Act of the *Council,* not mine."

"For the Ile built by the *Lord Viscount Kilmurrye,* the Grant which I made was no more, than is ordinary in all such Cases . . . so there is nothing at all done to the prejudice of Sir *John's* Inheritance: For if we cannot Grant it by Law, then the Grant is voided by its own words."   These words were "*Quantum in nobis est, et de Jure possumus.*" "And whereas 'tis alledged, *That I made this Grant without the consent of*" "*the Patron, or the then Incumbent;* Sir *John* acknowledges, like a Gentleman, that I sent unto him for his consent, if it might be had."   [As the consent was evidently not given, it is difficult to see the force of this plea.]   "And this I foresaw also, that if I had denyed the *Lord Viscount* that which was not unusual ; then the Complaint would have fallen more heavy on the other side, that I made Persons of Quality in a manner *Recusants,* by denying them that conveniency which was in my power to grant.   So I must be faulty, whatever I do."

The fact that Lord Kilmorey was a royalist and that Sir John Corbet was a zealous supporter of the opposite faction is, of course, entirely ignored by Laud.

CHAPTER XXII.

I MUST now refer to Montague, whose antipathy towards the Church had apparently softened considerably since he wrote his *Appello Cæsarem*. He was now actually trying to negotiate a union between Anglicanism and Catholicism, with Panzani, the envoy from Rome. This action on his part would not much affect my memoir, were it not that he is stated to have assured Panzani "that the Archbishop of Canterbury was entirely of his sentiment, but with a great allay of fear and caution." Laud had his faults ; but fear and caution are not generally supposed to have been the most conspicuous. My quotations are taken from the *Memoirs of Gregorio Panzani*, translated from the Italian original, by the Rev. oseph Berington.

The interview with Panzani was of Montague's own seeking.[1] "When they met, he" (Montague) "immediately fell upon the project of an union." "He signified a great desire, that the breach between the two churches might be made up, and apprehended no danger from publishing the scheme, as things stood." Presently he said "that he was satisfied both the archbishops, with the bishop of London and several others of the episcopal order, besides a great number of the learned inferior clergy, were prepared to fall in with the Church of Rome as to a supremacy *purely spiritual:* That, for his own part, he knew no tenet of the Church of Rome to which he was not willing to subscribe, unless it were the article of *Transubstantiation*, which word, he had reason to think, was invented by pope Innocent III., after the council of Lateran was risen. He owned, he had some scruples concerning communion in one kind ; but as for particular points, he thought the best method would be to chuse moderate men

[1] " Panzani Memoirs," pp. 237 and following.

deputies on both sides, to draw up the differences in as small a compass as they could, and consider about them." He then suggested that such a committee, or congress, might be most conveniently held in France.

" Panzani modestly replied, that he did not know but his Holiness might approve of the scheme he had laid, but he could say no more to it till the motion were made, either by the king, or by some of the chief of the ministry in his name."

At parting, Montague told Panzani that " he would take the first opportunity to discourse the primate," Laud, " on the subject ; but insinuated he was a cautious man, who would make no advances unless he were well protected."

Panzani reported this interview to Rome. " The Italians were extremely pleased with it ; and it was a subject of great joy to understand that several of the Protestant bishops and clergy were ready to join with the universal church in the article of a spiritual supremacy." Panzani was ordered to tell Montague that " as for looking into particular controversies, or specifying the terms of communion, it was too soon to speak of those matters. At present, it would be more advisable to dwell upon generals ; and especially the Protestant bishops and clergy ought to examine the motives which first occasioned the breach from Rome, which being found human and unwarrantable, it would be their duty to come forward and sue for a reconciliation."

" Above all things, Panzani was advised never to favour the discussion of particular points." " The supreme point of a supreme judge " must be " first settled, for then other matters would come in of course." " In a word, authority and doctrinal points were the two capital objects." In " practices out of the limits of the *jus divinum*, which were disagreeable to the English nation, as it was in the power of the church to alter them, so they should meet with all the tenderness imaginable."

On their next meeting, Panzani complimented Montague, and told him that he was much admired in Rome for the steps he had taken. " The bishop, who was not a little vain, relished the compliment, and returned it, as far as was con-

venient, upon his admirers." It was then that he informed
Panzani "that the Archbishop of Canterbury was entirely of
his sentiment, but with a great allay of fear and caution."

Panzani now observed that he had orders not to "give encouragement that there should be any relaxation on the
Catholic side, as to the *credenda* or fundamentals of religion,
that the union designed was not only to be politic and
ceremonial, but real and in *unitate fidei*, without any mixture
of creeds.—The bishop assured him, that he aimed at a total
union."

" Montague then having occasion to mention his character
and priesthood said, he looked upon them as unquestionable.
—Panzani judging this to be too intricate a point, and knowing what exceptions some learned men made against it, would
not deliver his opinion, but passed to another matter."

The writer of the *Memoirs* then says " it was pretty plain
that there was a great inclination in many of the eminent
Protestant clergy to re-unite themselves to the see of Rome ; "
but that there was no united action among them, and that
they feared the king; "for they imagined the spiritual
supremacy was a prerogative he would not easily part with."
It was noticed, at court, that when Pope Urban, or Cardinal
Barberini, was mentioned, " he discovered an extraordinary
affection for them ; but his praises running mostly upon their
personal qualifications, and generous behaviour to the English nation," they could form no opinion as to whether he
merely wished to keep on a satisfactory diplomatic footing
with Rome, or desired a union with the Catholic Church.
One remarkable piece of evidence is given, that " Dr George
Leyburn assured Panzani, *in verbo sacerdotis* that the Archbishop of Canterbury encouraged the Duchess of Buckingham
to remain contented, for, in a little time, she would see England re-united to the see of Rome." If this is to be believed,
it is a very important incident in the life of Laud ! I do not
question Dr Leybourn's word; but may not the Duchess
have either misunderstood Laud, or unconsciously exaggerated in repeating what he said ?

At the next interview between Panzani and Montague, the

latter stated that there were only three Anglican bishops
who "could be counted violently bent against the church of
Rome, viz., Durham, Salisbury, and Exeter; the rest, he said,
were very moderate." These three bishops were Morton,
Davenant, and Hall.

At this conference, Montague again referred to the validity
of his own orders, maintaining that he derived them in direct
descent from St Augustin, the apostle of England, although
he admitted that Catholics "made little account of Protestant
ordinations.—Panzani managed as before, telling him, it was
a tedious, intricate controversy, the particulars whereof he
was a stranger to." Montague then said he had often heard
the king remark "that there was neither policy, Christianity,
nor good manners in not keeping a correspondence with
Rome," and he expressed his own desire to be selected for
that purpose. "'Then,' replied Panzani, 'the world would
immediately conclude, that you were going over to the
Church of Rome.'—'And what harm would there be in
that?' said the Anglican bishop."

Panzani next observed that the difficulties in the way of
union were very great; whereupon Montague "solemnly declared, that both he and many of his brethren were prepared
to conform themselves to the method and discipline of the
Gallican Church, where civil rights were well guarded; 'and
as for the aversion we discover in our sermons and printed
books, they are things of form, chiefly to humour the populace, and not to be much regarded.'"

This was, indeed, a candid admission, especially in the
mouth of a man who, in his "printed books," had accused
Catholics of "cosening tricks," called the Catholic "the
Roman exorbitant Church," described its miracles, and
visions as "hobgoblin stuffe," and stigmatised its priests as
"Beelzebub's attendants."[1] Such expressions, it seems, were
mere "things of form," only "to humour the populace, and
not to be much regarded."

Panzani's *Memoirs*,[2] in addition to their mention of the
fruitless overtures of Montague, state that "among those of

<hr />

[1] "A Gagg for the New Gospell."   [2] P. 248.

the episcopal order who seemed to desire an union, none appeared more zealous than Dr Goodman, of Gloucester, who every day said the priest's office, and observed several other duties as practised in the church of Rome." This Anglican bishop was a forerunner of the many modern ritualist clergymen who have said the divine office, or at least a portion of it.

Of the Anglican Bishop of Gloucester, I shall have a good deal to say, in direct connection with Laud, in a later chapter. It will be sufficient, here, to add that he died a Catholic.[1]

It is difficult to ascertain how far there was ever any real support given by the other Anglican bishops to Montague's proposals for union with the Church. Panzani received a letter of instructions from Cardinal Barberini, in which, after referring to some suggestions of Windebank, to the effect[2] "That the church of Rome should give up some of her articles, viz., communion in one kind, the celibacy of her clergy, &c.," he said that such ideas "would never please at Rome; that the English ought to look back upon the breach they had made, and attend to the motives that induced them to it; and that the whole world was against them as to the points mentioned."

It seems that Panzani had been accused of exceeding his commission, and he replied that certain priests had unfortunately excited by their action "the archbishop of Canterbury against the proposal." How far Panzani managed the matter to the best advantage seems doubtful. He was not on the best of terms with the religious orders, and it must be remembered, as it ought to be candidly admitted, that the very difficult question of the most advisable temporary ecclesiastical rule for the Catholics in England, now that the hierarchy was suspended in that country, had given rise to differences of opinion among good men, as difficult questions are ever apt to do.

Lingard, while admitting the authenticity of the Panzani

[1] Fuller's "History of the Church," p. 170. Also "Memoirs of Panzani,"
pp. 248 and 260.
[2] Panzani, p. 174.

Memoirs, which he has himself used to some extent, says[1] :—
"It appears plain that Charles had no idea of a re-union
between the churches ; and that, if Laud ever cherished such
a project, he kept it to himself. Panzani never saw him ; nor
is there anything in the correspondence except the assertion
of Montague, to make it appear that the archbishop was
favourable to it."

Laud's contemporary, friend, and biographer, Heylin,[2]
deserves to be heard on this matter, both as to the time
when Panzani was in England and also as to that of his
immediate successor, who was to carry on his work. "The
Pamphlet called *The Pope's Nuncio*, Printed in the year
1643, hath told us, 'That Panzani at his being here, did
desire a conference with the Archbishop of Canterbury,
but was put off and procrastinated therein from day to
day ; That at the last he departed the Kingdom without
any speech with him.' The like we find in the discovery
of Andreas ab Habernfield, who tells us of his *Con*,"—
Conn was the legate who succeeded Panzani in London—
"that finding the King's judgment to depend much on the
Archbishop of Canterbury, his faithful servant, he resolved to
move every stone, and bend all his strength to gain him to
his side, being confident he had prepared the means. For he
had had a command to make offer of a cardinal's cap to the
Lord Archbishop in the name of the Pope"—this is a more
than doubtful assertion—"and that he should allure him also
with higher promises, that he might corrupt his sincere mind ;
yet a fitting occasion was never offered whereby he might
insinuate himself into the Lord Archbishop, to whom free
access was to be impetrated by the Earl and Countess of
Arundel," (in another place Habernfield calls this lady "a
strenuous she-champion of the Popish religion "), "as also by
Secretary Windebank, all whose intercessions he neglected,
and did shun (as it were the plague) the company and
familiarity of *Con*. He was also solicited by others of no
mean rank, well known to him, and yet he continued im-

---

[1] " Hist. of Eng.," vol. vii. chap. v.
[2] " Cyp. Ang.," pp. 385 and following.

moveable." "And whereas," says Heylin, "some found a way
to help at last by making Windebank Internuncio betwixt him
and them, that only serves to make the matter rather worse
than better, there being a great strangeness grown betwixt
him and Windebank, not only before Con's coming into
the Realm ; but before Panzani had settled any course of
intelligence in the court of England."

Politically, Charles endeavoured to make capital of the
civilities shown by Rome through Panzani and Conn to
obtain the Pope's intervention on behalf of his nephew,
the Palatine ; and, on his own part, he sent Sir William
Hamilton to Rome, not only to endeavour to secure the
Holy Father's good offices on behalf of his sister's son, but
also to persuade him to favour and encourage a marriage
between her daughter and the King of Poland, as well as to
induce him to consent to the English Catholics taking the
oath of allegiance, either in its then form, or in some other
which would be acceptable to the English Government. On
the other hand, Panzani, to some extent, and, to a greater,
Conn, obtained Charles's promise that the English Catholics
should be relieved from the annoyance of domiciliary visits
from pursuivants. If Charles vacillated on this point, we
may fairly hope that Laud may have said a good word for
his Catholic fellow-countrymen ; for he was certainly no
great lover of pursuivants, as the following extract from an
old newspaper [1] will prove.

A certain priest was seen by a pursuivant, named Bray,
who "went about to apprehend him, but was abused by the
priest, who told him he had a protection from Sir Francis
Windebanke, of which the said Bray going to Lambeth to
complaine to the Archbishope of Canterbury, he would not
speake with him, but was answered that he could not attend
to such frivolous businesses ; whereupon the said Bray said, he
hoped to see better dayes. For which the Archbishop complained of him in the Star Chamber, and caused him to be
imprisoned fourteen weeks ; and when the said Mr Braye's

---

[1] *London's Intelligencer*, July 17, 1644. King's Pamphlets (British
Museum), No. 167.

wife petitioned him for her husband's release, he threw it away and said he would have nothing to doe with such priest-catching knaves. And afterwards before the setting High Commission Court openly threatened the other pursuivants, that if they employed the said Gray"—in the course of the accounts he is called Gray, Bray, and Braye—" in catching of priests, he would not only imprison them, but pull their coates over their eares. It was further alledged against him "—this was at Laud's trial for high treason—" that he had discouraged one Anne Hussey, who discovered a dangerous plot against the Kinge and kingdome. The plot was that a Jesuite declared, there were seven thousand in private pay to cut the throats of the Protestants, and that the King should be killed. He told her that she was mad, and hired by Londoners, and that she should be rackt."

On this ground I infer that when Charles yielded on the question of the pursuivant to Panzani or Conn, it may have been at Laud's advice. That very able judge, Lingard, however, on the strength of a MS. abstract of Conn's despatches, which was in his own possession, takes a different view.[1] Conn "was able," he says, " by his remonstrances on different occasions, to check the zeal of Archbishop Laud, who, through anxiety, as it was reported, to shake off the imputation of Popery cast upon him by the Puritans, sought to establish the belief of his orthodoxy by the rigorous enforcement of the penal laws."

That Laud was not supposed in Rome to have done much to alleviate the sufferings of Catholics may be gathered from the sworn testimony of a witness, to the effect that " the Honourable Sir *Lionel Tolmach* Baronet," related that when he was in that city immediately after Laud's execution, " a certain abbot" had observed "that the Greatest Enemy of the Church of *Rome* in *England* was cut off, and the *Greatest* CHAMPION of the Church of *England* silenced : Or in Words to that purpose." John Evelyn, who happened to be in Rome at the same time, testified that he was " in the Company of divers of the *English* Fathers," when the news arrived

[1] " Hist. of Eng.," vol. vii. chap. v.

of Laud's death, and that they "looked upon him as one that was a great Enemy to them, and stood in their Way."

The papal legate, although he was in England nominally on a purely private footing, became rather the fashion. He "resided at *London* in great Part,"[1] says Clarendon, "publickly visited the Court; and was avowedly resorted to by the Catholicks of all conditions, over whom he assum'd a particular jurisdiction; and was caress'd by the Ladies of Honour who inclin'd to that Profession."

Some direct communications certainly took place between Father Preston, a Benedictine Priest, and Laud's chaplain, Mr William Heywood, concerning one of the subjects of negotiation between Charles and Panzani—the approbation by Rome of the oath of allegiance. Some priests were of opinion that it was impossible that anything could be done in the matter; others thought something might, and among these was Father Preston. He writes[2] to the "Rev. and much respected Sir," Laud's chaplain:—"The Italian Oratorian [Panzani] sent hither from Rome, signified to me that some had informed him that I was printing a book in favour of the Oath, which would hinder the fair course then intended betwixt his Holiness and the King; for then he made show to procure of his Holiness some moderation or moderate declaration concerning the Oath, &c." "But now I perceive that they intend at Rome no such moderation concerning the Oath, and that deponibility, which is the only chief thing denied in the Oath, must not be meddled withal." Indeed, Preston had himself got into trouble by his efforts to please the king in the matter. "Our Procurator sent me word that the Pope's nephew our protector told him his Holiness and the Lords Cardinal were grievously offended with me." He sends some of his writings on the question for his correspondent "to peruse with your good leisure," and he would willingly have them printed, "if it may stand with my Lord Graces" [Laud's] "good liking," and he says

---

[1] "Hist. of the Rebellion," vol. i. p. 149.
[2] "Records of the Eng. Prov. S. J.," series 1, pp. 256-7.

"when you have perused them, I pray you acquaint my Lord's Grace."

So long as Rome left the question undecided officially, Preston stuck to his own opinion ; but when it had spoken, "he submitted, before being visited by any express censure or declaration."[1] Gee, the informer, in his list of priests says that "hee hath by one engine or another, of late seduced great multitudes to Popery," and the Jesuit writer, Brother Foley, says there is "every reason to hope that he died a martyr *in vinculis* for the faith."

This would appear to be the proper place to notice the interviews between Laud and a celebrated Benedictine monk. A young man, named John Jones, connected with the Scudamores of Kentchurch in Herefordshire, was an undergraduate with Laud at St John's, Oxford, where he became a Catholic.[2] He afterwards went to Spain, joined the Order of St Benedict, and eventually returned to England, as Father Leander of St Martin. My remarks about him are chiefly taken from a book[3] written by Dom. Bennet Weldon, a Benedictine monk, who was born less than thirty years after the death of Laud. Father Leander was "skilled in all the oriental languages," "an accomplished rhetorician, poet, grecian, and latinist." "He rendered the Catholic cause great services when upon the marriage of Charles I. with Henrietta of France there appeared an aurora of England's conversion, the Queen being Catholic and attended with a Chapel splendidly served by a great retinue of Priests, both Secular and Regular ; the King inclining and the famous Dr Laud, that renowned protestant archbishop of Canterbury (the best of them who have occupied that See since error hath prevailed in England), steering his course directly to the old and only Faith, guided and directed by his dear friend and old intimate acquaintance the R. F. Leander, to whom he gave a College in Kent. They had been colleagues together at Oxford, and not only this Reverend Father was so highly prized by Dr

---

[1] "Records of the Eng. Prov. S. J.," series I, p. 258.   [2] *Ib.*, p. 254, note.
[3] "A Chronicle of the English Benedictine Monks."   Ed. 1881, pp. 100-102.

Laud, but also by others of that heterodox misery, so that once in those most desperate times he had a special Royal Grant or leave to go into England. The last time he went he was called by the aforesaid good friend Dr Laud who wanted to confer with him about some points of controversy. But he had not been long in England when he fell sick and died the 27th of December 1635, &c." A modern Benedictine writer, the Rev. Dom. Edmund Ford says [1]:—" In 1634 Fr. Leander of St Martin, then president, came to England as the accredited agent of the Papal Court, to treat, among other matters, with his old college friend Laud about a union between the two Churches." Whether they ever actually discussed the subject seems doubtful; but Laud was charged at his trial with "holding correspondence" with "a Benedictine monke Father Leander." [2] For my own part, I cannot see, in any of the evidence adduced with regard to Father Leander, proof of Laud's having entered into any negotiations with a view to a union of the Anglican with the Catholic Church. Father Leander may have hoped to discuss the question of the reconciliation of the English with him ; possibly Laud may have even consented to talk the matter over with him, as an old college friend ; but I do not think that more than this can be made of the facts that I have been able to collect.

In discussing the subject of these attempts at an union of the Anglican with the Catholic Church, it may be well to consider the probable cause of their failure. Panzani attributed it chiefly to the absence of any concerted action on the part of the Anglican bishops and clergy, and the indifference exhibited towards the whole matter by the king and the Government.

It is but natural that we should ask ourselves whether the same difficulties would be likely to present themselves, were a movement to be set on foot for the same purpose, in our own days, by one or two of the Anglican bishops, with the

---

[1] " Notes on the Origin and Early Development of the Restored Eng. Ben. Congregation," p. 51.

[2] " Mercurius Civicus," July 1644.

tacit approval of many of the others, as well as the eager support of a large number of the clergy.

At first sight there would be several encouraging features connected with the question of such a re-union. The material advantages to the Catholic Church would be enormous. As to details, there are already several Eastern Churches united, or re-united, to Rome, which are allowed to continue to enjoy some of the principal *desiderata* claimed by Anglicans. I am not forgetting that the position of a schismatical Church, which had continued the use of a liturgy antecedent to its schism, is very different from that of a Church which deliberately altered and expurgated the liturgy of the Catholic Church in order to fit it to the tastes of some of the eldest-born children of the Reformation. Anglicans might reply that their Church had at least retained, and fondly clung to, much of the Catholic liturgy, and that they would gladly see it re-catholicized, if they might be permitted to use, as much as possible, the words and forms to which they have been accustomed since their childhood. On such questions as these, it would ill become the writer to express any opinion of his own ; should they ever present themselves in a practical form, loyal Catholics would be silent on the subject until Rome had spoken. My point, in the above remarks, has only been that it is not so much on the details of discipline, ceremony, and liturgy, that difficulties loom.

The doctrinal difficulty is, of course, a great one ; yet there are many Anglicans who hold most of the dogmas of the Catholic Church. If, however, it came to be a matter of uniting the whole body of the members of the Established Church of England to the Catholic Church, the doctrinal difficulty would assume such prodigious proportions as to appear to bar the way for once and for all. It is true that, in the days of Laud, various opinions were more or less tolerated within the sphere of the Anglican Church ; that it contained Arminians, Calvinists, and a rising school of which Hales and Chillingworth were the leaders, three parties which may be said to have been the forerunners of the High, the Low, and the Broad Church of to-day ; but, even allowing for a few variations of opinion among the members of the Arminian, Calvinistic, and free-thinking sections of Anglicanism, in Laudian times, what were these few schools of thought in comparison to the numberless divisions and subdivisions of parties in the Established Church at the end of the nineteenth century. Few things are more indefinite, at present, than the term a High-Churchman ; the very use of which provokes the question, "What *sort* of a High-Churchman?" For of High-Churchmen there are endless varieties.

The term Low-Church may mean almost anything, and there seems to be little that the term Broad-Church may not include. To unite the Established Church to the Catholic Church, all these varieties and sub-varieties would have to be satisfied, or at least to be reckoned with. Could we expect more concerted action among them, or their leaders, than that which was found in the period of Montague and Laud?

With regard to the attitude likely to be assumed towards a re-union movement by the sovereign, we should now have to substitute the word government for sovereign. Let us assume for a moment that the government encouraged such a movement ; that it supported a bill for its achievement ; that it went so far, if you will, as to make it a ministerial measure. This is a wild assumption, but let us make it. Well, even then, it is as likely as not, that, on the question of some amendment in committee, ministers might get beaten, and then—out goes the government, and good-bye to the Pope and re-union.

Long, however, before politicians could be induced to meddle with such a question, many hundreds of conflicting interests implicated in the possibility of re-union would be anxiously and suspiciously weighed by both Unionists and Radicals, and were either of those great parties to make up its mind to promote re-union—a most unlikely contingency— the very fact of its so doing would determine the other great party, *en bloc*, to oppose it to the very utmost of its power and ability. Charles I. may have been unstable ; but he was an immoveable rock in comparison with the constantly changing rule in Downing Street.

CHAPTER XXIII

THE year 1635 began in London with a remarkable frost. The Thames was frozen on the fifth of January and continued so until the third of February, when there was "a mighty Flood at the Thaw."

On the eighth of January, Laud married Lord Charles Herbert to a daughter of the Duke of Buckingham. Her mother, whom Laud had endeavoured to keep in the Established Church, by his conference with Fisher, brought her to the chapel door, but would not enter it, an action which must have been rather galling to the archbishop. Honours, however, continued to be showered upon him. On the fifth of February, he "was put into the great *Committee* of Trade and the King's Revenue"; on the fourteenth of March, he "was Named one of the Commissioners for the *Exchequer*, upon the death of *Richard* Lord *Weston*, Lord High Treasurer of *England*," and, on the sixteenth, he was "called" "into the *Forrain Committee*, by the King."[1]

In a former chapter I said that Laud made the impropriations in Ireland his special care; he looked after them even more eagerly in England. The Puritans conceived the scheme of buying up a large quantity of lay impropriations, with a view to obtaining ecclesiastical power in their own hands. They formed a committee of thirteen men, clergymen, lawyers, and citizens, for this purpose, and they despatched emissaries into different parts of the country to collect money. Laud heard of this plot and formed his own plans accordingly. He consulted with the king. The subject having been mooted, Cottington, Chancellor of the Exchequer, and Coventry, Privy Seal, had a dispute about the disposal of the benefices belonging to the king. Coventry claimed

[1] *Diary*, p. 51.

his share; Cottington refused to recognise that claim. While the two ministers were fighting, says Heylin, "Laud ended the difference by taking all unto himself." He advised the king "that many had served as chaplains in his Majesty's ships, and should have some reward given them for their services past. It was cold venturing upon such hot services without some hope of reward. He takes occasion, therefore, to inform his Majesty, that till this controversy be decided, he might do well to take these livings into his own disposal. Which proposition being approved, his Majesty committed the said benefices unto his" [the archbishop's] "disposal." Heylin goes on to say that "Cottington was not at all displeased at the designation . . . being more willing that a third man should carry off the prize from both, than to be overstepped in his own jurisdiction."

Lord Cottington was not always so well satisfied with Laud. On the contrary, if the two men found it the best policy to be apparently on good terms with each other, there was never much love lost between them. Cottington was even known to have gone so far as to "draw" the archbishop. I beg forgiveness for making use of this slang word.

It came about in this way. King Charles, who was very fond of hunting, wished to make a large park for red, as well as fallow, deer, between Hampton Court and Richmond, where he owned great pieces of waste land and some extensive woods; but here and there were a few farms which it would be necessary for him to purchase at a very high price, to carry out this scheme, and the wall which would surround the whole park would obviously add immensely to the expense. His best counsellors strongly advised him to abandon the scheme.

The owners of the small properties, intermingled among the woods and wastes, were by no means inclined to sell them, and when they saw that the wall, which was to enclose the great park, had been begun before the in-lying farms had been purchased, they feared that the enforesting of their lands would be compulsory, and they complained in loud terms. An outcry raised so near London soon became a

subject of gossip in the metropolis itself, and uncompli-
mentary things began to be said concerning the conduct of
the king in the matter. This was an additional objection to
the proposal in the minds of the king's advisers.

From the very first, Lord Cottington, as Chancellor of the
Exchequer, had protested strongly against the king's idea of
making this park, as a piece of unwarrantable extravagance,
especially at a time when the royal purse was in anything
but a flourishing condition. The price of the lands would
be enormous; the cost of a wall for so large a park would
be prodigious, and the discontent of the vendors, obliged to
sell against their wills, might possibly prove a still more
serious obstacle. Therefore, says Clarendon,[1] he "endeavour'd by all the ways he could, and by frequent impor-
tunities, to divert his Majesty from pursuing it, and put all
delays, he could well do, in the Bargains which were to be
made; till the King grew very angry with him and told
him ' He was resolv'd to go through with it, and had already
caused Brick to be burn'd, and much of the Wall to be
built upon his own Land :' upon which *Cottington* thought fit
to acquiesce."

Perceiving how obstinate the king was about his hobby,
and smarting from the scolding which he had just received
for trying to dissuade him, it occurred to Cottington that it
would be at least amusing, and possibly profitable, to entice
the archbishop into the trap into which he himself had fallen.
He knew that Laud was no less opposed than himself to the
foolish and expensive project, and that he would not be
likely to mince his words if interrogated upon the subject.

Accordingly, Cottington opened the question of the king's
project, in a conversation with Laud, who told the Chancellor
confidentially that [2] " He should do very well to give the King
good Counsel, and to withdraw him from a Resolution, in
which his Honour, and Justice was so much call'd in question ; " and he "spake with great warmth against " the king's
pet, but, as he thought, foolish whim.

Cottington did not say a word to imply that he had already

[1] " Hist. of the Reb.," vol. i. pp. 100-1.   [2] *Ib.*, p. 101.

done everything in his power to dissuade King Charles from his folly. Quite the contrary. He assumed a shocked and serious expression, and said, with a shake of the head, " that the thing designed was very Lawful, and he thought the King resolv'd very well, since the place lay so conveniently for his Winter Exercise, and that he should by it not be compell'd to make so long Journies, as he us'd to do in that season of the year for his Sport, and that no body ought to disswade him from it."

Laud was completely taken in. Instead of suspecting that Cottington was not speaking sincerely, as he well might have done, since he had been " inform'd " that Cottington " dislik'd " the scheme, he "grew into much Passion," and told him, in a rage, that " such Men as he would Ruin the King, and make him lose the affections of his subjects ; that for his own part, as he had begun, so he would go on to disswade the King from proceeding in so ill a Counsel, and that he hop'd it would appear who had been his counsellor."

Cottington was delighted. He had scarcely hoped " to see him so soon hot, and resolv'd to inflame him more." Speaking " very calmly," he said "that he thought a Man could not, with a good Conscience "—this was a sharp thrust— " hinder the King from pursuing his Resolutions, and that it could not but proceed from want of Affection to his Person, and he was not sure that it might not be High Treason."

This did not frighten Laud, who asked him "in great anger " " from whence he had receiv'd that Doctrine ? "

Cottington replied, with irritating coolness, that "they who did not wish the King's health could not love him ; and they who went about to hinder his taking Recreation, which preserv'd his health, might be thought, for ought he knew, guilty of the highest Crimes."

"Upon which the Arch-Bishop in great Rage, and with many Reproaches left him."

Laud pushed his way still further into the trap. On the very first opportunity, he told the king that " he now knew who was his Counsellor for making the Park," and, having given an account of his conversation with Cottington, abused him roundly.

For once in his life, Laud got laughed at and scolded by the king who was usually so obedient to his advice.

"My Lord," said Charles, "you are deceiv'd. *Cottington* is too hard" (sharp) "for you; upon my word he hath not only disswaded me more, and given more Reasons against this Business, than all the Men in *England* have done, but hath really obstructed the Work by not doing his Duty, as I commanded him, for which I have been very much displeased with him: you see how Unjustly your Passion hath transported you."

To be spoken to in such a manner, and to find that he had been—to use a vulgar phrase—"made a fool of" by Cottington was most humiliating to Laud, who cherished great resentment against the Chancellor of the Exchequer in consequence.

It was no doubt of this that Lord Conway wrote to Wentworth, in the November of the same year:[1]—"We say here in Court that there is a mortal quarrel between the Archbishop and my Lord *Cottington;* but *Cottington* hath gained in the King's Favour and the Bishop lost."

From time to time Laud's rancour towards Cottington manifests itself. "In this business" (*i.e.,* some legislation in respect to the privileges conceded to the soap-boilers, he says in his Diary[2]) "and some other of great consequence, during the Commission for the Treasury, my old Friend, Sir F. W."—probably Sir Francis Windebank—"forsook me, and joyned with the Lord Cottington: Which put me to the exercise of a great deal of patience."

The concluding paragraph of the first book of Clarendon's history is so pertinent to the period of Laud's life with which I am now dealing, that I cannot refrain from quoting a portion of it. "Whatsoever was the Cause of it, this excellent Man, who stood not upon the advantage ground before, from the time of his Promotion to the Arch-Bishoprick, or rather from that of his being Commissioner of the Treasury, exceed-

---

[1] "Strafford Papers," vol i. p. 479.   [2] Diary, p. 51.

ing provok'd, or underwent the Envy, and Reproach, and Malice of all Men of all Qualities, and Conditions ; who agreed in nothing else : all which, though well enough known to him, were not enough Consider'd by him, who believ'd, as most Men did, the Government to be so firmly Settled, that it could neither be Shaken from within, nor without, and that less than a general Confusion of Law and Gospel, could not hurt him ; which was true too ; but he did not Foresee how easily that Confusion might be brought to pass, as it prov'd shortly to be." [1]

Laud had that passion for stones, bricks and mortar, to which the clergy of " all denominations of Christians " are so much addicted. Three consecutive entries in his Diary [2] in the year 1635 afford examples of this.

" *Septemb.* 2. *Wednesday*, I was in attendance upon the King at *Woodstocke*, and went thence to *Cudsden*, to see the House which Dr *John Bancroft* then Lord Bishop of *Oxford* had there built, to be a House for the Bishops of that See for ever. He having built that House at my perswasion."

" *Septemb.* 3. *Thursday*, I went privately from the Bishop of *Oxford's* House at *Cudsden*, to St *John's* in *Oxford*, to see my building there, and give some directions for the last finishing of it. And returned the same Night, staying there not two Hours."

" *Septemb.* 23. *Wednesday*, I went to Saint *Pauls* to view the building, and returned that Night to *Croydon*."

In the same year, we find the Queen of Bohemia exercising her influence with Laud with a view to obtaining a bishopric for one of her chaplains.[3] " A worthy honest man has desired her recommendations to him. It is Dr Hassall, Dean of Norwich. She does not love to trouble him, or her other friends with recommendations, but this honest man for some years lived at the Hague, preacher in the English Church and she can answer for him, that he is a deserving man, and no puritan ; therefore she could not refuse to recommend him and entreats his Grace for her sake to prefer him when he shall have occasion." As in many other ladies' letters, the

[1] Diary, p. 102. [2] P. 52. [3] "Cal. Sta. Pa. Dom.," 1635, p. 327.

pith is in the postscript :—" P.S. She hears the Bishop of
Norwich is dead ; she says no more, but leaves all to the
Archbishop."

Laud replied [1] that he had " made Hassall Dean of Norwich
merely for the sake of the Queen of Bohemia, whom Hassall
had served at the Hague. . . . A fortnight before her letters
came, Hassall was with the Archbishop and he promised (if
it lay in his power) to help him to a better deanery, or something else to advance his means." [Hassall was evidently
a terrible place-hunter and beggar.] " After this, Hassall
brought him her letters, by the postscript whereof, he first
discovered his aim to be Bishop of Norwich, whereas Hassall
knows as well as the writer that the King "—*i.e.*, Laud—" will
make none bishops but such as he has some knowledge of
himself, as having been his own chaplain in ordinary or otherwise, &c. &c. . . . He would here end, being very unwilling
to make any complaint, but Hassall when he delivered him
her Majesty's letters, carried it so high upon his own merit
that he dares say had he done so to the writer's predecessor
he would soon have found he had done amiss. But the Archbishop will, for Hassall's reference to her Majesty, pass over
this, and do that which shall beseem him for Hassall, as he
may be able to prevail with his Majesty."

Not altogether an agreeable letter this for the Queen of
Bohemia to receive from Archbishop Laud, especially as she
was endeavouring, at that very time, to enlist his services and
influence with her brother, the King of England, on her own
personal behalf. In the same month that she received the
above letter, she wrote [2] to Laud, saying that her son, the
elector, was " desirous, for his first action, to show his respect
to the King his uncle, and go himself to kiss his hand and
give him thanks for his favours. Entreats the Archbishop to
give him his best counsel in all his actions and his favour in
his affairs." And then comes another P.S. " Had written
this when she received his from Mr Gordon. Gives him many
thanks for his favour to Dr Hassall for her sake, but is sorry he
behaved himself so ill as to give the Archbishop any offence."

---

[1] " Cal. Sta. Pa. Dom.," 1635, pp. 375-6.   [2] *Ib.*, p. 400.

It is pretty clear, here, that she felt her son's interests to be more important than those of Hassall, for whom she attempted no defence.

She writes more freely in recommending her son to Sir Henry Vane, on his visit to England.[1] " He is young *et fort nouveau*, so he will no doubt commit many errors, which Vane's good counsel may hinder him from. She fears damnably how he will do with their ladies, for he is a very ill courtier, therefore prays Vane to desire them not to laugh too much at him, but be merciful to him."

Among the many letters of Laud to the Queen of Bohemia, is a long one[2] in which he urges her to " demand of the Emperor the investiture of her son in a legal form." Certainly he spared no time or pains in advising her. In doing this however, he may have been acting chiefly at the bidding of his royal master, who strongly advocated a similar policy.[3]

After making many and strenuous objections, the queen acted on Laud's advice. Lord Arundel was sent by King Charles on an embassy to Vienna on her behalf. In a letter to Laud, " she said that though she would not dispute the king her dear brother's will in anything, she could not but regret the Viennese embassy." [4]

Into the merits of this question I have not space to enter ; I can only quote a few sentences to show the spirit of the correspondence between herself and Laud.

" I fear this last speech of mine," she says to him in one of her letters, " may make you think . . . that I would rather have my son restored by force than by treaty ; . . . it is all one to me by what ways he be restored, so he be so fully and honourably ; but indeed I do not think he will be restored fully, otherwise than by arms ; sixteen years' experience makes me believe it." [5]

Laud was, or pretended to be, dreadfully shocked at this.

---

[1] " Cal. Sta. Pa. Dom.," 1635, p. 435.   [2] *Ib.*, p. 415.
[3] Boswell's Dep., Feb. 18, March 6, April 20, 1635.
[4] Green's " Lives of the Princesses of Eng.," vol. v. p. 551.
[5] June 11, 1636, German Corresp.

He replies :—" You grant it *all one* to you by what way he be restored, so he be restored fully and honourably.   Under favour, good madam, not so.   For it cannot be all one to Christendom, nor to yourself to have him restored, be it never so honourably, by arms as by treaty.   It may be there is soldiers' counsel in this, madam ; but I am a priest, and as such, I can never think it all one to recover *by* effusion of Christian blood, and *without* it, provided that without blood right may be had." [1]

To this, perhaps rather priggish, letter of Laud's, the queen replies :—" I confess, as a woman and a Christian, I should rather desire it by peace, but I have lived so long amongst soldiers and wars, as it makes one to me as easy as the other and as familiar, especially when I remember never to have read in the chronicles of my ancestors, that any King of England got any good by treaties, but most commonly lost by them, and on the contrary, by wars made always good peaces. . . . I know your profession forbids you to like this scribbling of mine, yet I am confident you cannot condemn me for it. . . . All I fear is that you will think I have too warring a mind for my sex ; but the necessity of my fortune has made it." [2]

On this particular point, the woman got the last word !

A couple of years later, the queen and Laud were apparently of one mind about " the effusion of Christian blood," as well as her other affairs ; for she writes to him :—" The king my dear brother was pleased to write to me himself, that he doth approve of my son's intentions, and with so great a favour as the bestowing his money towards the levies. You may easily imagine how much contentment it brought to us both.   I am confident your good counsel did much contribute to this resolution of the king's, for which I shall ever be beholden to you.   Meppen is now rendered into my son's hands, the garrison there having sworn to him ; the levies are already begun ; I hope shortly he will be ready to go himself into the field." [3]

---

[1] June 26, 1636, German Corresp.   [2] Aug. 6, 1636, German Corresp.
[3] April 12, 1638, German Corresp.

R

There was no longer any question of the "cold compliments" passing between the queen and the archbishop,
which she mentioned in a letter to Roe in 1634; on the
other hand, she writes to him of another great ecclesiastic,
Cardinal Richelieu, "as this ulcerous priest." [1]

[1] Oct. 29, 1639, German Corresp.

CHAPTER XXIV.

THE re-appearance of the plague in London, made the spring of the year 1636 an anxious one in England; but, fortunately, the outbreak was less serious than that of 1603-4, mentioned in an earlier chapter, when over 30,000 people are said to have died of it in London alone, and still less so than that of about thirty years later, when upwards of 100,000 are reported to have perished. Political troubles were also gathering on the horizon; although it was attempted to conceal these by the splendour of the court and the pretended popularity of the king, hated as he was in reality by a large proportion of his subjects.

Loved, again, as was the queen among the few, she and her native attendants, more especially her chaplains, were objects of dislike and grave suspicion to the many. Yet everything, that could be, was being done to bring her charms and virtues into prominence before the country at large. Ben Jonson, Beaumont, Fletcher, and Waller were all engaged in promulgating her praises in verse; Rubens and Vandyke, the latter of whom married an English woman and lived at Blackfriars, painted portraits of her, while Inigo Jones was making her court picturesque by the scenery which he devised for her masques and ballets. Her tastes were imitated by the nobility. In the royal progresses, it became the fashion for the hosts who received the king and queen, to engage poets to compose special dramas for their entertainment, as was the case with the Earl of Newcastle when they paid him a visit at Bolsover Castle, in Derbyshire,[1] for which occasion Ben Jonson wrote complimentary verses to be recited before the royal guests.

The king was in reality more devoted to the arts than the

---

[1] " Hist. Coll. of Noble Families," by Collins, p. 26.

queen, although his people attributed his bent in that direction to her "evil" influence. He not only succeeded in bringing Rubens and Vandyke to England, but, with his own hand, wrote to Albano,[1] the famous painter of children —his popular picture of the Infant Saviour and St John is familiar to all who have visited Florence—asking him to come and live at his court in England. Daniel Mytens was one of his court artists, and Nicolas Laniere was not only employed to engrave for him, but also to choose works of art for purchase. As to Charles's poetical tastes, Milton sarcastically wrote of him (in his *Iconoclastes*) that he was actually so depraved as to be fond of Shakespeare. "I shall not instance an abstruse author, wherein the King might be less conversant, but one whom we well know was the closest companion of these his solitudes, William Shakespeare." [2]

Another poet, Drummond, had a slap at him, for his love of the arts. In his history of Scotland, when writing of "James the Third," he is evidently aiming at King Charles, of whom he says :—"It is allowable in men that have not much to do, to be taken with admiration of watches, clocks, dials, automates, pictures, statues ; but the art of princes is to give laws, and govern their people with wisdom in peace, and glory in war; to spare the humble, and prostrate the proud." [3]

A Puritan, again, after Charles's death, wrote of him as "squandering away millions of pounds on braveries and vanities, on old rotten pictures and broken-nosed marbles." [4]

Much as Laud undoubtedly influenced Charles in ecclesiastical affairs, I do not think there is any evidence to show that he did anything to encourage him in his taste for the fine arts, except in the matter of the repairs and adornments of St Paul's Cathedral. Laud sat for his portrait to Vandyke, and the picture now hangs in the palace at Lambeth—there is an excellent copy of it in Mr Benson's life of Laud—but

[1] " Academiæ Picturæ," p. 282.
[2] I quote from D'Israeli's " Life and Reign of Charles I.," vol. iii. p. 109.
[3] *Ib.*, pp. 106-7.
[4] " The Non-such Charles," his character, extracted out of divers original Transactions, Despatches, and the Notes of several public ministers, as well at home as abroad, 1651.

what artistic taste he possessed, personally, was chiefly in the direction of architecture, although his work at St Paul's and St John's may have been actuated rather by a desire for the advancement of the interests of his church and his college, than by any irrepressible exuberance of architectural genius.

The tastes in common between the king and his archbishop seem to have been chiefly religion and ecclesiastical matters, politics, and, on certain somewhat circumscribed lines, literature. On principle Laud was a king-worshipper; but he was also much attached to Charles as a man.

The features of Charles I. are probably better known than those of any other monarch in history. Different in many ways, his eyes, like those of Laud, were quick and penetrating. As they discussed their policy, each must have endeavoured to read the other with his glance, and so far there was much in common between them; but the round, plump, and rubicund face of the archbishop was in violent, and somewhat unbecoming, contrast to the long, narrow, pale features of the king; nor was there a less marked distinction between Charles's stuttering accents, and the decided, rasping voice of Laud. It is well to remember, when picturing to oneself the two friends, that Laud was the older by twenty-seven years. Both men were impetuous; but the king had most self-command; if neither of them was graceful, and both were hurried in their bodily movements, Charles was the most active; if neither was tall, the king was at least of moderate height, while the archbishop was diminutive. In point of character, Laud had one great advantage over his monarch—he always knew his own mind, whereas Charles often did not.

Most readers of English history must have contemplated the appearance of these two men who were so often in counsel together, and the share attributed to either in the misfortunes which were consequent from those counsels will have depended to a great extent upon the predilections of each individual student, some tracing every evil that befell Charles I. to the bad advices he received from Laud, others regarding Laud as a martyr to the follies of a weak and faithless monarch.

To be quite candid, I admit the difficulty of deciding how far Laud really influenced the conduct of the king. In ecclesiastical matters he most unquestionably did so very greatly, though even in these, there are evidences that Charles sometimes, if very rarely, took a line of his own ; in political affairs the extent of Laud's influence is very much more doubtful. That it existed, even that it existed to a very considerable degree, no honest observer of his times can deny ; yet it is open to an historian to assert that much of Charles's policy, commonly attributed to the suggestions of Laud, may more probably have been due to those of other ministers of the Crown.

Finance was the medium of one-half the troubles of Charles I., religion of the larger proportion of the other. If we allow that Laud was responsible for the latter, can we acquit him of all share in the former ? I fear it is impossible to do so ; but most certainly Charles's ruinous financial measures were not entirely the suggestion of his archbishop.

Both the Treasury and the king's private purse were woefully empty, and he and his ministers were at their wits' end for means to "raise the wind." Much money was brought into the royal exchequer by what was little else than a mere legal quibble, and one which was too technical to have been the work of the archbishop. The objects of this attempt to obtain funds were large landowners, who had hitherto considered themselves secure in tenure of the estates which they had inherited from their forefathers, but were now surprised to find themselves subjected to enormous so-called "fines." In those days, as in more modern ones, the proverb that "nothing is so safe as land" was proved to be subject to certain qualifications. "My Lord of Salisbury," writes Clarendon, "was fined £20,000 ; the Earl of Westmorland, £19,000 ; Sir Christopher Hatton, £12,000 ; My Lord Newport, £3000 ; Sir James Watson, £4000 ; Sir Robert Bannister, £3000, and many others smaller sums," [1] for encroachments on the forest of Rockingham alone. The commissioners of the Treasury had hunted up some ancient royal rights over certain forests ; and, although, in the course of five centuries, these rights had practically become obsolete, they revived them, and "the landholders were summoned to prove their titles, or otherwise to answer for their encroachments." [2]

Exactions were enforced by water, as well as by land. Noy, the Attorney-General, found among the documents at the Tower some old writs compelling the ports, under certain circumstances, to provide the king with ships ; and not only these, for there were other writs which obliged the maritime counties, as well as the actual ports, to contribute to their cost. This old tax was revived, and thereby "the King obtained a yearly supply of two hundred and eighteen thousand five hundred pounds " ; " a fleet of more than sixty sail annually swept the narrow seas, and the admirals, first the earl of Lindsay, afterwards the earl of Northumberland, received orders to sink every foreign ship which refused to salute the English flag." [3]

The success with the navy was made the stepping-stone to similar measures with the army. Laud's bosom friend, Wentworth, spoke thus on this subject in the Council. " Since it is lawful for the king to impose a tax towards the equipment of the navy, it must be equally so for the levy of an army ; and the same reason which authorizes him to levy an army to resist, will authorize him to carry that army abroad, that he may prevent invasion. Moreover, what is law in England, is law also in Scotland and Ireland." [4]

Admirable in logic, and, I am afraid, very Laudian in style !

A quiet, courteous, and, as was thought, retiring country gentleman, named Hampden, a rich Buckinghamshire squire of good family, had astonished his friends and acquaintances, some ten years earlier, by refusing to pay an assessment which he considered unjust, and going to prison rather than yield. In 1636, he again attracted the attention of his fellow-

[1] Clarendon's " Hist. of the Reb."   [2] Lingard, vol. vii. chap. v.
[3] Ib.   [4] Rushworth, ii. pp. 252-8 ; " Biblioth. Regia," pp. 246-250.

countrymen by resisting the tax for ship-money. His case was argued for twelve days, before as many judges, in the Court of Exchequer. " So strong," says Macaulay,[1] "were the arguments against the pretensions of the Crown that, dependent and servile as the judges were, the majority against Hampden was the smallest possible. Still there was a majority." The popularity of Hampden became extraordinary, and a spark had fallen upon a train of gunpowder which was to help materially in shattering the king and his Government, yet, outwardly, Charles seemed to be, for the time, triumphant.

In 1635 died one of Laud's many enemies, nor the least powerful. This was the Earl of Portland, Lord Treasurer, and as we have already seen, Laud took his place at the Board ; but, a year later, he persuaded the king to give the post to his old schoolfellow, William Juxon, Bishop of London. He says in his Diary [2] :—" No Church Man had it since *Henry* 7's time. I pray God bless him to carry it so, that the Church may have Honour, and the King and the State Service and Contentment by it. And now if the Church will not hold themselves up under God ; I can do no more."

Of this proceeding, Clarendon writes [3] :—"On a suddain the Staff was put into the hands of the Bishop of *London*, a man so unknown, that his Name was scarce heard of in the Kingdom, who had been, within two years before, but a private Chaplain to the King, and the President of a poor Colledge in *Oxford*. This Inflam'd more men than were angry before, and no doubt did not only sharpen the Edge of Envy and Malice against the Arch-Bishop (who was the known Architect of the Fabrick) but most unjustly Indisposed many towards the Church it self; which they look'd upon as the Gulph ready to swallow all the great Offices, there being Others in view, of that Robe, who were ambitious enough to expect the rest."

At the risk of being accused of overburdening my work with quotations, I will give part of what he says in the next

[1] " Hist. of Eng.," vol. i. chap. i.   [2] P. 53.
[3] " Hist. of the Reb.," vol. i. p. 99.

paragraph. "In the mean time the Arch-Bishop himself was infinitely pleas'd with what was done, and unhappily believ'd he had provided a stronger Support for the Church ; and never abated any thing of his Severity, and Rigour towards men of all conditions, or in the Sharpness of his language, and expressions, which was so natural to him, that he could not debate anything without some Commotion, when the Argument was not of moment, nor bear Contradiction in debate, even in the Council, where all men are free, with that Patience, and Temper that was necessary ; of which, They who wish'd him not well, took many Advantages, and would therefore contradict him, that he might be transported with Passion, which, upon a short recollection, he was always Sorry for, and most readily, and heartily would make Acknowledgment." In short, they doubtless nudged each other, and whispered the seventeenth century equivalent of :—" Now, I will get a rise out of old Laud ! "

We have seen how Cottington "drew" him, upon one occasion : it was not a solitary one. "No man," continues Clarendon, " so willingly made unkind use of all those Occasions, as the Lord *Cottington*, who, being a master of Temper, and of the most profound Dissimulation, knew too well how to lead him into a Mistake, and then drive him into Choler, and then Expose him upon the matter, and the manner, to the judgment of the Company ; and he chose to do this most, when the King was present ; and then he would Dine with him the next day."

Cottington would hardly have played these pranks upon Laud in the king's presence, unless he had reason for knowing that it would be entertaining to his Majesty, and it is far from impossible that, much as Charles respected Laud and trusted his advice, he may have been a little wearied of being constantly tutored by him, in which case it would be a relief to his feelings to see his pedagogue made sport of.

Of the " others in view," mentioned by Clarendon—that is to say, other ecclesiastics for whom high offices were intended, D'Israeli gives us some idea, in his *Life and Reign of*

Charles I.,[1] although he does not mention his authority. "An ill-natured rumour of the day made Wren, Bishop of Norwich, a Secretary of State; and Bancroft, Bishop of Oxford, Chancellor of the Exchequer." And he presently adds:—"This advancement of the ecclesiastics was never forgiven by the affronted nobility, nor even by the jealous lawyers: the lawyer Whitelocke is sore, and the courtier Clarendon murmurs." May, again, in his *History of the Parliament of England*,[2] says:—"The Archbishop by the same means which he used to preserve his clergy from contempt, exposed them to envy, and as the wisest could then prophesy, to a more than probability of losing all."

Laud was none the less on the eve of one of his greatest triumphs. His king and queen had consented to become his guests at Oxford. King, Church, and Oxford were the three things nearest to his heart, so that his delight at the prospect may well be imagined. Great preparations were made for the royal visit, and the great people in the neighbourhood were most liberal in sending provisions to assist Laud, as Chancellor of the University, in entertaining the king, queen, and court. Besides £155 in money, he received, as presents for the occasion, "7 stags, 63 bucks and does, 5 oxen, 74 wethers, 2 lambs, 1 calf, besides poultry innumerable, swans, pheasants, partridges, quails, turkeys, ducks, rabbits, and peafowl, fish, fruit, and even cakes, creams, and cheeses."[3]

He started from Croydon for the university town with not a little state, being accompanied by a retinue of between forty and fifty horsemen, "being all of my own," as he writes with evident pride.

Sir Thomas Roe had sent him an invitation to stay at his country house, on the journey, to which he replied that he[4] "will trouble him for the night, upon two conditions; that they will let him come as to a private lodging, and not trouble themselves with chargeable entertainment; and let him begone betimes in the morning without eating, for his thoughts

---

[1] Vol. iii. p. 69.   [2] P. 33.
[3] "Cal. Sta. Pa. Dom.," 1636, Preface, p. xxii.   [4] *Ib.*, 1636-7, Aug. 4, 1636.

will be full of business and will make him no good company for any of his friends."

The second night he stayed at Cuddeston, which seemed almost too near Oxford to be worth stopping at, but he may very likely have desired to enter the city with dignity, and as free as possible from travel-stains, although he writes[1] :— " I came privately into Oxford, in regard to the nearness of the King and Queen, then at Woodstock."

Garrard wrote to Lord Conway[2] :—" On Monday all repaired to St John's to pay their respects to Laud." " Courteous he was to all, but walked most and entertained longest my Lord Cottington." Was this returning good for evil, or was he rather afraid of him ?   " At one of the clock on the ringing out of the University Bell, all the students of quality waited on their Chancellor, Archbishop Laud, to meet his Majesty near two miles out of town, all on horseback and with footcloths."

The number of speeches to which the king had to listen on entering Oxford was extraordinary.   Laud writes[3] :—" The Vice-Chancellor made a very good speech," when the king reached Oxford from Woodstock.   As the procession passed St John's College, " Mr Thomas Atkinson made another speech unto them, very brief, and much approved of by his Majesty afterwards to me.   Within Christ Church Gate, Mr William Strode, the University Orator, entertained him with another speech, which was well approved.   Then the King accompanied his Queen to her lodging, and instantly returned and went with the Lords to the Cathedral."   Thither, of course, he had to go without his wife.   " There after his private devotions ended, at the West Door Dr Morris" (he was the Regius Professor of Hebrew), "one of the prebendaries, entertained him with another short speech, which was well liked, and thence his majesty proceeded into the quire and heard service."

The speeches were all very well in their way ; but there

---

[1] " Lib. of Ang. Cath. Theol.," vol. v. part i. p. 155.
[2] " Cal. Sta. Pa. Dom.," 1636-7, Sept. 14, 1636.
[3] " Lib. Ang. Cath. Theol.," part. i. pp. 148 and fol.

had been a lack of enthusiasm as the royal cavalcade passed in solemn state through the Cornmarket, past Carfax, and down St Aldate's, to Christ Church. "Though the streets were lined with scholars of all degrees, yet neither they nor the citizens made any expressions of joy, or uttered, as the manner is, ' *Vivat Rex.*" [1]

After supper, the royal party were entertained at Christ's Church with a play, which Laud admits, although "well penned," "did not take the Court so well"; while, in his already quoted letter to Lord Conway, Garrard says it was "fitter for scholars than a Court," adding that Lord Carnarvon pronounced it to have been the "worst he ever saw but one that he saw at Cambridge."

The next day, Laud had his royal master up betimes, in the cathedral, where there was "a service and a sermon," soon after eight o'clock. In the course of the morning there was convocation, at which "the two princes with divers lords, were pleased to be made Masters of Art; and the two princes names were by his majesty's leave entered in St John's College: to do that house honour for my sake," says Laud.

Then came the great event of the visit, the banquet given by Laud to his king and queen, with their court, in his own dearly loved St John's.

He says:—"They first viewed the new buildings,"—let it be remembered that the older part was not then at all ancient —"and that done, I attended them up the library stairs; where so soon as they began to ascend, the music began, and they had a fine short song fitted for them as they ascended the stairs."

The banquet was served in "the new library, built by myself." Crossfield remarks of this dinner that "the baked meats served up in St John's were so contrived by the cook that there was first the forms of Archbishops, then bishops, doctors, &c., seen in order, wherein the king and courtiers took much content."

After dinner there was a play at St John's. The windows of the hall, Laud tells us, were "shut," and candles were lighted. He "had the hall kept as fresh and cool,"—it was

---

[1] "Cal. Sta. Pa. Dom.," 1636, Preface, p. xxiv.

the 30th of August—"that there was not any one person
when the king and queen came into it." The play itself
"was merry without offence, and so gave a great deal of
content."

Of the royal visit to St John's College he writes : " I thank
God I had that happiness that all things were in very good
order, and that no man went out at the gates, courtier or
other, but content ; which was a happiness quite beyond
expectation."

That evening, after supper, at eight o'clock, there was again
a play at Christ Church. Fortunately, unlike its predecessor
of the previous evening, it was a great success. Even Garrard
admits this ! The subject was a Persian story, and the scenery
and decorations had been designed by Inigo Jones. Laud
writes that it was both "well penned and acted." "The
queen liked it so well, that she afterwards sent to me to have
the apparel sent to Hampton Court, that she might see her
own players act it over again, and see whether they could
do it as well as it was done at the university. I caused the
University to send both the clothes and the properties ; and
the play was acted in the November following. And by all
men's confession, the players came short of the University
actors. Then I humbly desired the King and Queen, that
neither the play nor stage might come into the hands and
use of the common players abroad, which was graciously
granted."

The next morning, Wednesday, at about nine o'clock, the
royal party and the court left Oxford. The total cost of the
two nights' entertainment was £2666, 1s. 7d.[1]

" I returned homewards, the Day after:" writes Laud in
his Diary;[2] " Having first entertained all the Heads of Houses
together."

Laud was now in the very zenith of the royal favour; the
king's and queen's visit to Oxford was a proof of it ; yet, six
weeks afterwards, he thinks it worth while to write in his
Diary :—" *Octob.* 14. *Friday* Night, I Dreamed marvellously,
that the King was offended with me, and would cast me off,

---

[1] "Cal. Sta. Pa. Dom.," 1636, Preface, p. xxx.   [2] P. 53.

and tell me no cause why. *Avertat Deus.* For Cause I have given none."

The poor man's nervous anxiety about the king's favour appears to have been almost a disease with him ; it seems to have been as great as that which he suffered concerning the favour of Buckingham during the life of that all-powerful statesman.

After all, in congratulating himself upon the royal visit to Oxford, and in reflecting that, as we say now, "everything went off without a hitch," Laud may have contrasted it with what he had heard of the visit which Queen Elizabeth paid to Oxford some seventy years earlier, and seven years before his own birth, when the students greeted her with loud cries of "Vivat Regina," as she drove up the Cornmarket, to which she replied "Gratias ago, gratias ago." He may have remembered hearing that, after a professor had made a Greek speech to her, at Carfax, instead of remarking to her attendants that she "much approved," she had replied in the same language ; that, although, like Charles I. and Henrietta Maria, she had been entertained with several plays, she had also spent long hours in the schools, listening to learned discussions on science, politics, and philosophy ; and that, instead of two nights, she had remained five at Oxford, leaving it on the sixth day, and reining in her horse on Headington Hill to turn round and exclaim : "Farewell, Oxford ! Farewell, my good subjects there ! Farewell, my dear scholars, and may God prosper your studies ! Farewell, farewell ! "[1]

Altogether, between the rumblings of distant thunder in the political atmosphere, the lack of enthusiasm for the monarch among the students and tradesmen, the attendance of a court who were bored to death by a play that had the slightest scholastic tendency, and the presence of a queen whose religion prevented her from attending any of the services in that very "churchy" city, King Charles's visit to Oxford was decidedly a less brilliant affair than had been that of Queen Elizabeth.

---

[1] Nicholl's " Progresses of Elizabeth," and Froude's " Hist. of Eng.," vol. viii chap. x.

CHAPTER XXV

LAUD appears to have been very well received by the Oxford dons when he went to their university to entertain the king and queen ; but a few months earlier there had been a slight strain in the relations between them and their chancellor. In 1635 he had endeavoured to establish his right of visitation at both Oxford and Cambridge, in the character of archbishop. So far as Oxford and his own personal influence were concerned, he had little to gain by maintaining it ; but he was a great stickler for the rights of office, and made it his duty to claim every prerogative pertaining to any post in which he had an interest, whether it was in his holding or in that of one of his subordinates, and of ecclesiastical privileges he was more jealous than of any other.

Both Oxford and Cambridge stoutly resisted the archbishop's claims to the right of visiting the universities, and the matter was debated, in 1636, before the king in Council.

Even in the Middle Ages, there had been some uncertainty with regard to the relations of the universities to the Church, and appeals to Rome on the question had not been unfrequent. It has been stated that no real archiepiscopal visitation of Oxford had ever taken place. Huber,[1] however, asserts that this "is an unfounded boast," and that instances occurred in 1276, 1284, and 1384. Sometime between 1394 and 1397, a Bull was put forth by Pope Boniface IX., in which the words were used :—" By the power of these presents we exempt, &c., from all jurisdiction, dominion and power of any Archbishops soever, as also of the natural [natorum] Legates of the said see ; likewise of all Bishops, and other ordinary Judges, as to contracts entered into, or excesses, crimes, and misdemeanours committed beneath the limits, &c."[2] This

---

[1] " Eng. Univ.," vol. ii. part ii. p. 485. [2] *Ib.*, p. 484.

Bull was revoked by Pope John XXIII., but confirmed, at least to some extent, by Pope Sixtus IV. Some authorities ascribe the Bull to Pope Boniface VIII.;[1] but the Bull of Pope Sixtus IV. ascribes it expressly to Pope Boniface IX.

When the Council met to try the question of the arch-bishop's rights, Laud, Chancellor of Oxford, stood at the king's right hand; on the left was Lord Holland, Chan-cellor of Cambridge; the Attorney-General represented Laud; the Recorder of London "spake for Cambridge"; " Sergeant *Thin* spake for the University of Oxford."[2]

The king decided in favour of the archbishop; but as Laud never made a visitation at either university in the character of archbishop, all this trouble seemed hardly worth the taking.

During the same year in which he triumphed over the two leading universities on this point, Laud had a vexation of a more private character. This was a letter from Sir Kenelm Digby announcing that he had joined the Church of Rome.

Kenelm was the eldest son of Sir Everard Digby, who had been attainted for his share in the conspiracy of the Gun-powder Plot. He was scarcely three years old when his father expiated his crime on the scaffold, and he says that from that father he "inherited nothing but a foul stain in his blood for attempting to make a fatal revolution in this state ";[3] not that this was strictly true, as some of Sir Everard's property, worth £3000 a year, was entailed, and the Crown failed in its endeavour to wrest it from his son.

Lady Digby was a Catholic; but Kenelm was taken from her—whether with or without her consent is not very clear —and placed under the tuition of Laud, who was at that time Dean of Gloucester. Laud held the Deanery of Gloucester from 1616 till 1620, and, as Kenelm Digby was born in 1603 and was sent to Oxford in his fifteenth year, he must have been put under Laud in his thirteenth or fourteenth year. It is needless to say that Laud brought him up as a Protestant.

---

[1] " Encyc. Brit.," 8th ed. vol. xxi. p. 454.   [2] Rushworth, vol. ii.
[3] " Private Memoirs of Sir Kenelm Digby."

He writes of the time when Kenelm joined the Church of England, as if that had been a voluntary matter : one would imagine that a boy of thirteen or fourteen would be a convert easily made in the hands of a strong-minded and determined ecclesiastic, like Laud, who would be certain to think that the rod and reproof gave wisdom. In the letter which Laud wrote to his former pupil, on receiving the news that he had become a Catholic, he says [1]:—" And whereas you say, that you have return'd into that Communion, who (*sic*) from your Birth had right of possession in you, and therefore ought to continue in it, unless clear and evident proof (which you say surely cannot be found) should have evicted you from it : Truly, Sir, I think this had been spoken with more advantage to you and your Cause, before your adhering to the Church of *England*, than now ; for then right of possession could not have been thought little. But now since you deserted that Communion, either you did it upon clear and evident proof, or upon apparent only."

Is there not something supremely absurd in writing in this strain to a man of thirty-three, and upbraiding him for seeing things in a different light, at that age, from that in which he had regarded them at thirteen, or thereabouts, especially as he was under the tuition of Laud himself at the earlier period, when a boy is naturally influenced by the opinions of older men ?

Before dealing with the rest of Laud's letter to Digby, it may be well to say that, although he only announced his return to the faith of his fathers to Laud in 1636, the author of the Introduction to his *Memoirs* believes that he really was reconciled to the Church some twelve or thirteen years earlier,[2] although he did not make it public until just before writing to Laud. This, with all humility, I should venture to doubt.

Three years before he wrote to announce his reconciliation, he had lost his wife, the famous beauty, Lady Venetia, daughter of Sir Edward Stanley ; when he "wore a long mourning cloak, a high cornered hatt, his beard unshorn,

---

[1] " Hist. of the Troub. and Tryal of W. Laud," p. 613.   [2] P. lv.

look't like a hermit, as signes of sorrowe for his beloved wife."[1] This is true enough ; for great is the contrast between the carefully curled locks, the twisted little moustache and small tuft beneath the lower lip, the clean shaven cheeks and chin, the richly patterned coat, and the splendidly embroidered lace collar, in his earlier portrait by Vandyke, and the wild locks, the unkempt, straggling beard, the plain, almost puritanical white collar, and the austere black garment in his later portrait by the same artist, as well as in another attributed to Janssen, both of which were painted some time after his wife's death. "To avoyd envy and scandall," says Aubrey, " he retired into Gresham Colledge, at London, where he diverted himselfe with his chymystry, and the professors good conversation."

His studious habits would recommend themselves to Laud ; so also would his devotion to his king, although the latter once led to consequences of which Laud would not approve ; for, having toasted King Charles as " the best king in the world," at a dinner given at a private house in France, a certain " French lord " at " those words seemed to laugh," when Sir Kenelm, " thoroughly moved in behalf of our Sovereign King Charles," challenged him to fight, and " ran his rapier into the French lord's breast till it came out of his throat again."[2]

It may be worthy of observation, in passing, that both Laud and another contemporary ecclesiastic who had much influence in mundane matters, namely, Cardinal Richelieu, did what they could to put down duelling. Laud imposed fines in the Star Chamber ; Richelieu contrived that sterner measures should be dealt by the judges. To such a point had duelling risen in France, that Louis XIII., in the course of twenty years, signed no less than eight thousand letters of pardon to duellists who had sent or received challenges."[3] Richelieu determined that this state of things should cease, and after the Comte de Chapelle and the Duc de Bonteville had fought a duel on the Place Royale in Paris, they were

---

[1] Aubrey's " Lives of Eminent Men."

[2] A very rare tract, entitled " Sir Kenelm Digby's honour maintained, &c."

[3] " Ency. Britt.," 8th ed. vol. xix. p. 163.

both tried and beheaded, a tragedy which had the effect of sending duelling out of fashion for a period in the French capital.

But I must return to Laud and his reply to Sir Kenelm Digby's letter announcing his return to the Catholic Church.

Whether Laud wrote more gently on account of the depression of spirits which hung over Digby for some years after the death of his wife, a wife of whom Ben Jonson wrote :—

> " In all her petite actions so devote,
>   As her whole life was now become one note
>   Of piety and private holiness " [1]

(although her morality had been more than questioned before her marriage), I cannot hazard an opinion; be this as it may, in some respects the letter of Laud to Sir Kenelm Digby might well serve as a model to Protestants when they write to upbraid a friend who has become a Catholic. I suppose that most converts, soon after their reception into the Church, receive a sheaf of letters couched in a very different spirit. I am, myself, the possessor of some choice specimens, although I have one, also written by an Anglican Bishop, which surpasses Laud's in kindness, consideration, good feeling, and charity.

In considering Laud's letter, too, we must remember his own temper and the temper of the times; nor should we forget that Kenelm Digby had been, in the first instance, induced to desert the Catholic for the Anglican Church by Laud himself, either directly or indirectly.

He begins [2] : " *Salutem in Christo.* Worthy Sir, I am sorry for all the Contents of your Letter, save that which expresses your Love to me." Then come some unimportant details as to the date and reception of another letter he had lately written to him.

The following paragraph begins :—" In the next place, I thank you, and take it for a great Testimony of your Love to me ; that you have been pleased to give me so open and

---

[1] " Eupheme."   [2] " Hist. of the Troub. and Tryal of W. Laud," p. 610.

clear Account of your proceedings with your self in this matter of Religion. In which as I cannot but commend the strict reckoning, to which you have called your self; so I could have wish'd, before you had absolutely setled the Foot of that Account, you would have called in some Friend, and made use of his Eye as a By-stander, who sometimes sees more than he that plays the Game. You write, I confess, that after you had fallen upon these troublesom Thoughts, you were nigh two Years in the diligent Discussion of this matter ; and that you omitted no Industry, either of conversing with Learned Men, or of reading the best Authors, to beget in you a right Intelligence of this Subject. I believe all this, and you did wisely to do it. But I have some Questions, out of the freedom of a Friend, to ask about it. Were not all the Learned Men, you conversed with for this Particular, of the Roman Party ? Were not the best Authors, you mention, of the same Side ? " And a few lines further on, he says :—" Why was I (whom you are pleased to Style one of your best Friends) omitted ? True, it may be, you could not reckon me among those Learned Men and Able for Direction, with whom you conversed : Suppose that ; yet your self accounts me among your Friends. And is it not many times as useful, when Thoughts are distracted, to make use of the Freedom and Openness of a Friend not altogether Ignorant, as of those which are thought more Learned ; but not so Free, nor perhaps so Indifferent ? "

There is something exceeding rich in the idea of Laud being called in to act the part of a disinterested bye-stander, on the question of remaining in or leaving the Church of England, as by law established. The principal argument used in the letter is that already quoted, namely, that if he left the Church of Rome for good reasons, those reasons still held good. This he harps upon, again and again, and repeats in different forms and language.

Further on he says :—" The Temper of your Mind (you say) arms you against all Censures, no slight Air of Reputation being able to move you. In this, I must needs say, you are happy. For he that can be moved from himself by the

changeable Breath of Men, lives more out of than in himself ;
and (which is a Misery beyond all expression) must in all
Doubts go to other Men for Resolution ; not to himself ; as if
he had no Soul within him.   But yet *post Conscientiam Fama.*
And though I would not desire to live by Reputation ; yet
would I leave no good means untried, rather than live without it.   And how far you have brought your self in question,
which of these two, Conscience or Reputation, you have
shaken by this double Change, I leave yourself to judge ;
because you say your first was with a semblance of very
good Reason.   And though you say again, That it now
appears you were then mis-led ; yet you will have much ado
to make the World think so."

And then came a passage for which all praise is due to
Laud.   Generally speaking, Protestants criticise severely the
time and the manner chosen by their convert friends for
seeking reception into the Church.   "There was trickery in
his mode of taking the step, or inconsiderateness towards the
feelings of others," says Newman.[1]   "They went too soon, or
they ought to have gone sooner.   They ought to have told
every one their doubts as soon as ever they felt them, and
before they knew whether they should overcome them or no."
Not so Laud !   He continues—

"The way you took in concealing this your Resolution of
returning into the Communion, and the Reasons which you
give why you so privately carried it here, I cannot but
approve.   They are full of all Ingenuity, tender and civil
Respects, fitted to avoid Discontent in your Friends, and
Scandal that might be taken by others, or Contumely that
might be returned upon your self.   And as are these Reasons,
so is the whole frame of your Letter (setting aside that I
cannot concur in Judgment) full of Discretion and Temper,
and so like your self, that I cannot but love even that which
I dislike in it."

Further on he writes :—"To the Moderation of your own
heart, under the Grace of God, I must and do now leave you
or matter of Religion ; but retaining still with me, and

[1] "Present Position of Catholics," p. 243.

entirely, all the Love and Friendliness which your Worth won from me ; well knowing, that all Differences in Opinion shall not shake the Foundations of Religion."

He concludes by saying :—"In the last place you promise yourself, That the Condition you are in, will not hinder me from continuing to be the Best Friend you have. To this I can say no more, than that I could never arrogate to my self to be your Best Friend ; but a poor yet respective Friend of yours I have been, ever since I knew you : And it is not Change, that can change me, who never yet left, but where I was first forsaken ; and not always there. So praying for God's blessing upon you, and in that Way which he knows most necessary for you, I rest. Your very Loving Friend to serve you *in Domino.*"

In a short postscript, he adds :—"I have writ this Letter freely ; I shall look upon all the Trust that you mean to carry with me, that you shew it not, nor deliver any Copy to any Man." (Laud kept a copy of it himself.) "Nor will I look for any Answer to the *Quæries* I have herein made. If they do you any good, I am glad ; if not, yet I have satisfied my self." And finally he apologises for making "a Volume of a Letter."

The tone and spirit of this letter are so excellent as to make me almost doubt whether even his friend and admirer, Clarendon, did not sometimes write a little too hardly of him.

The mutual promises of Digby and Laud to remain friends, in spite of the former's return to the Catholic Church, were no mere vain, conventional civilities. These two men had still much in common, as well they might, since Digby had "studied almost every branch of human science," and "as a philosopher," "an orator, a courtier, a soldier, his exquisite talents are alike conspicuous ;"[1] and, as one of his contemporaries said of him, "he was the magazine of all arts."[2] That they continued on a friendly footing is shown in a letter which Digby wrote to the Keeper of the Oxford University Archives, after Laud's death, in which he says :—"As I was one day waiting on the late king, my master, I told him of a

---

[1] Intro. to "Memoirs," p. lxxvi.   [2] *Ib.,* p. lxxviii.

collection of choice Arabic manuscripts I was sending after
my Latin ones to the University. My Lord of Canterbury
(that was present) wished they might go along with a parcel
that he was sending to St John's College : whereupon I sent
them to his Grace, &c., &c." " The troubles of the times soon
followed my sending these trunks of books to Lambeth-house,
and I was banished out of the land, and returned not till my
lord was dead, &c." [1]

A still greater proof of his good feeling towards Laud is to
be found in Laud's own writings. In his account of his trial,[2]
he says :—" My Servant, Mr *Edw. Lenthrop*, came to me and
told me, that the day before he met with *K. Digbye*, who had
the leave to go out of Prison (by the Suit of the *French
Queen*), and to Travel into France. But before he took his
Journey, he was to come before a *Committee*, and there (he
said) he had been. It seems it was some *Committee* about
my Business ; for he told Mr *Lenthrop*, and wished him to tell
it me, that the *Committee* took special notice of his Acquaintance with me, and Examined him strictly concerning me
and my Religion, whether he did not know, that I was offer'd
to be made a *Cardinal;* and many other such like things.
That he Answer'd them, That he knew nothing of any *Car-
dinal-ship* offer'd me ; And for my Religion he had Reason to
think, I was truly and really as I professed myself ; for I had
laboured with him against his return to the Church of *Rome :*
(Which is true, and I have some of my papers yet to shew.)
But he farther sent me word, that their Malice was great
against me ; though he saw plainly, they were like Men that
groped in the Dark, and were to seek what to lay to my
Charge."

And here we take leave of this clever and eccentric character, who was courtier, statesman, soldier, diplomatist, chemist,
Protestant, Catholic, Royalist, Parliamentarian, duellist, theologian, author, and philosopher, at one time or another.

It must not be supposed that because Laud wrote civilly to
Sir Kenelm Digby, on his conversion, and remained his friend
after it, that he was universally tender-hearted towards con-

---

[1] Aubrey's " Letters," No. 1.   [2] P. 209.

verts or old Catholics. On the contrary, he did all in his power to prevent conversions, as, indeed, one would expect that he should have done, if he honestly believed the Anglican to be the true Church of Christ. Who shall blame him? Even the late Cardinal Manning, a few years before his own conversion, being then an Anglican Archdeacon, persuaded a very young and recent convert to return to the Church of England, although both afterwards became distinguished ecclesiastics in the Church of Rome.

In respect to possible converts, Laud kept a specially sharp and anxious eye upon Oxford undergraduates, and made searching inquiries whether any of them showed signs of what are termed in these days, "Romish leanings." H once received information—I fear that he was not above employing spies—that a letter had been found, addressed to a Mr Fisher in Clerkenwell—this may have been the Fisher of Laud's controversy; unless, which is not impossible, the whole thing was a hoax—asking whether "he knows one or two, who for religion's sake are desirous to be entered in some order beyond the seas, especially that of fratrum minorum, or Jesuits." [1] The reply was to be directed "to one Richard Pulley" in St John's College in Oxford.

A Catholic recusant in Laud's own favourite college! This was very shocking.

He wrote at once to his vice-chancellor:—"If there be such a man as Pully here mentioned, be sure to make him fast;" and he was also ordered to inquire whether "any jesuits, or others, have lain hankering up and down thereabouts."

The vice-chancellor reported that there was a scholar of a name not unlike Pully at St John's. Modern undergraduates may be a little surprised at hearing how the vice-chancellor set about the delicate task of ascertaining this youth's religious views.

"I set a spy upon him," he says. "On Friday morning I took him coming from prayers in the quadrangle, where I might see how he behaved himself at citation. I instantly

[1] "Lib. of Ang. Cath. Theol.," vol. v. p. 180.

searched his pockets, took his keys of study and trunk from him, searched them (he staying in my lodging).   I looked over every book and paper; I found nothing that might give the least suspicion that he is inclined towards popery."

It might be supposed that this would more than satisfy Laud; but he replies :—" You cannot carry too careful an eye, either over Pullen or the rest; for certainly some are about that place to seduce as many as they can."   In the same letter, he admonishes his vice-chancellor rather sharply concerning another little matter connected with Popery.

Chillingworth was bringing out a book against the Catholic Church, and it was just then going through the Oxford press, which was under the control of the vice-chancellor.   Now a certain Jesuit, who went by the name of Knott (his real name was Wilson), intended to write a book in reply, called " A direction to N. N., being an admonition to Mr Chillingworth to attend to his own arguments."[1]   Laud, in his letter to the vice-chancellor, says that he has reason for believing that Father Knott is privately obtaining, from some workman at the Oxford printing-press, proof sheets of Chillingworth's book "as they are done."   " I know," he says, " the jesuits are very cunning at these tricks; but if you have no more hold over your printers, than that the press must lie thus open to their corruption, I shall take a sourer course, than perhaps is expected.   For though perhaps they go so cunningly to work, as that I shall not be able to make a legal proof of this foul misdemeanour; yet " (if) " I find that Knott makes a more speedy answer than is otherwise possible, without seeing of the sheets, I shall take that for proof enough, and proceed to discommission your printer, and suppress his press."

This was stern language and a stern threat to use to a vice-chancellor of the great University of Oxford, even from the pen of the chancellor himself.   He clearly kept his vice-chancellor well up to the mark in respect to any danger of Catholicising influences at Oxford; for three years later, that official wrote

---

[1] " Records of the Eng. Province, S.J.," series 1, p. 540.

to him [1]:—"We have an inn in the High Street called The
Mitre, which is the general rendezvous of all the recusants,
not in this shire only, but in the whole kingdom, that have
any business to Oxford.   Seldom are they there without
some scholars in their company, upon pretence or acquaintance."   "The host a professed papist."   "His house hath a
back gate towards Lincoln College, where most of the guests
privately enter, and is near neighboured by many recusants."
"I only give your grace the naked relation."

To this terrible revelation Laud replied—"I like it much
worse, because there is such a private back way to the inn
as you mention."   He says, however, that as the inn is under
the jurisdiction of the town authorities and not of the university, he has no power to interfere.   Nevertheless, he
proposes "to follow it close, till all be done which may be
done by law."

The vice-chancellor must have known as well as Laud
that he was powerless in the matter, and, as there was great
ill-feeling towards the university authorities on the part of
the town authorities, it would be as likely as not that the
latter would rather rejoice in anything calculated to annoy
Laud, and secretly, if not openly, encourage it.

It was not only at Oxford that the "Romish Recusants"
were disporting themselves and vexing the soul of Laud.
Great must have been his annoyance, in the year 1636, at
hearing of the brilliant success of the opening of the queen's
new chapel at Somerset House.[2]   Even the laying of the
foundation stone had been a grand affair; when "the plot
on which the chapel was to stand was very tastefully fitted
up in the form of a church; rich tapestry served for walls;
the most costly stuffs for roof; the floor strewed with flowers."
"At the further end was seen an altar, garnished with magnificent ornaments, with large chandeliers of silver gilt, and
with a great number of vases."   High mass was celebrated,
"while harmonious music ravished the heart.   The concourse

---

[1] "Lib. Ang. Cath. Theol.," vol. v. part i. p. 269.
[2] I take my account of it from Fr. Cyprien's "Memoirs of the Missions in
England of the Capuchin Friars, 1630 to 1669," Colburn's ed., pp. 308-314.

of people was so great, that it seemed as if all the inhabitants
of London had concerted to attend this noble ceremony.
Mass being finished, her Majesty was conducted by the
ambassador to the place where she was to lay the first
stone, &c., &c."

This alone must have been highly calculated to provoke
Laud, especially when such stringent laws were in force
against English Catholics ; but it must have been nothing to
his vexation when he heard the details, as he assuredly
would, of the opening of the chapel when built.

High Mass was celebrated "with all possible pomp and
magnificence " by the Bishop of Angoulême, and for the first
time "*pontifically*" in England "for about one hundred
years." " A multitude of Catholics thronged to receive the
Holy Communion from the hands of the bishop."

After dinner there were vespers, compline, and sermon,
and there was "a machine,"—there is a long description of
it, and it seems to have been an arrangement of decorations
and candles,—"which was admired by the most ingenious
person, to exhibit the Holy Sacrament, and to give it a more
majestic appearance."

"Those who were in the chapel had great difficulty to
leave it on account of the crowd of people who were bent on
forcing their way in." "The crush lasted so long that it
was impossible to close the doors of the church till the third
night," when the king desired to come to see it himself.
" Accordingly, he went thither, attended by his grand marshal,
the comptroller of his household, and some other gentlemen.
He admired the composition, kept his eyes fixed on it for a
very long time, &c."

Not only Catholics, but Protestants " never ceased coming
in crowds from all parts to behold this wonder." " From the
8th of December, the day consecrated to the immaculate conception of the Blessed Virgin, the queen with great prudence,
ordered the chapel to be left with all its decorations till
Christmas."

" From six o'clock in the morning there were successively
masses, and in general communions, till noon." The " con-

fessionals were surrounded by a crowd of penitents." " Persons were obliged to wait two or three hours before they could enter a confessional."

Imagine how galling it must have been to Laud to hear of all this at a time when he could not even induce a large number of the clergy in his own archdiocese to turn their communion-tables "altarwise," or some of the laity to kneel when receiving communion!

CHAPTER XXVI

IN the last chapter I showed that Laud was much put out at the prospect of a book by Father Knott, S.J., whom Oliver calls "a man of transcendent talents and vigour of intellect."[1] In the same year he was greatly worried about a book by another Catholic. This was that standard and beautiful work, *An Introduction to a Devout Life*, by St François de Sales. A greater contrast than that between the style of devotional writing of this saint and the style of Laud it would be difficult to imagine. How this worry came about Laud shall tell us for himself.[2]

"There was an English translation of a book of devotion, written by Sales, Bishop of Geneva, and entitled *Praxis Spiritualis sive introductio ad vitam devotam*, licensed by Dr Hayward, then my chaplain, about the latter end of November last; but before it passed his hands, he first struck out divers things wherein it varies from the doctrine of our Church, and so passed it."

Lingard says[3] that, among other alterations, he changed the word "mass," wherever it occurred, for "divine service."

"But by the practice of one Burrowes," continues Laud, ("who is now found to be a Roman Catholic,) those passages struck out by Dr Hayward were interlined afterwards (as appears upon examination before Mr Attorney-General, and by the manuscript copy), and were printed according to Burrowes's falsifications."

To call the restoration of the original, "falsifications," is really a magnificent piece of bare-faced casuistry! although, of course, the printer would be quite unjustified in making such a restoration under the circumstances. But to continue.

---

[1] "Collectanea S.J." [2] "Libr. of Ang. Cath. Theol.," vol. v. part i.
[3] Vol. vii. chap. v.

" The book being thus printed gave great and just offence, especially to myself."

In the account of his own trial[1] he says:—"The Complaint of Printing this Book came publickly into the *Star Chamber*. And then was the first time that I ever heard of it." "The whole thing," says he, "was a meer Plot of this Recusant, if not Priest, to have *Sales* Printed, with all his Points of *Popery* in him."

It is well to hear both sides in most cases, so we will read the evidence[2] of " Mary, widow of John Oates," who " attestes that her husband about seven years since printed part of a book intitled Francis Salis'" (Sale's) "Introduction to a Devout Life, licensed by Dr Haywood," (Hayward) "chaplain to Archbishop Laud, for the press. Finding some Popish passages not fit for the press as he conceived, Oakes carried the same to Haywood, who told him to go on and print the same, and he would bear him out therein. When the book was published exceptions were taken to these passages, and the book ordered to be burnt in Smithfield, which was done. Oakes was thereupon sent for and imprisoned about three weeks, and the fault put upon him and the publisher, as if they had put those passages into the licensed copy when Dr Haywood had purged them out, whereas in truth he commanded the passages to be put in and stand as they were in the copy brought to the press, which was proved before Sir Edward Deering at a Committee this Parliament."

Of this evidence, I would say in the first place that, at worst, it scarcely affects the reputation of Laud who, as he says, knew nothing about the matter until it came before the Star Chamber. Dr Haywood was the person whom it most concerned ; and even on his behalf it may be said that it was but second-hand evidence given through the widow of the actual witness ; yet she gives that evidence very plainly and straightforwardly. If Burrows, who appears to have been the publisher, was the author of the " falsifications," why did not Oates, or Oakes, lay the blame on him instead of on Dr Haywood ? Is it likely, again, that Burrows would have

[1] P. 363. [2] "Cal. Sta. Pa. Dom.," 1641-3, p. 550.

thought it worth his while to incur the penalties which would
certainly befall him, if he tampered with his employer's
"copy" before entrusting it to the hands of his printer.
And I would ask any fair-minded person to consider whether
a modern Catholic publisher or printer, if commissioned by a
Protestant to produce a garbled edition of a Catholic book,
would think that he could serve the interests of his own
religion by correcting it according to the original, in defiance
of the instructions of the editor, although he would be in no
danger from a Star Chamber?

The system of printing books by Catholics without all
their "Points of Popery in" them, unfortunately did not cease
with Laud's time.   I have often heard a Protestant say—" It
is remarkable how little mention a good man like ——"
(mentioning some Catholic writer) "makes of the Virgin ! So
unlike the modern Romanist writers !"   Whereas his books
are in reality full of allusions to Our Lady, of, what
Protestants call, "the most extravagant kind"; but they
have every one of them been carefully excised in the edition
" adapted to the use of English Churchmen."   If our books
are to be read at all, they ought to be read as their authors
wrote them.   In short, they should be read in the " falsified "
editions, as Laud would say ; that is, in the original.

As has already appeared by Mrs Oates's evidence, the
sequel of " Sale's " book was that Laud called in every copy
that could be laid hands on—some eleven or twelve hundred
in all—and had them publicly burned in Smithfield.

His zeal in this, and the other matters connected with
Catholicism, which I have mentioned in this and the preceding chapter, was probably stimulated by the "libels" that
were just then so freely promulgated against him, as an
abettor of Popery.

He writes to Wentworth,[1] boasting of the burning of *The
Devout Life*, and also of the arrest and trial of Father Morse,
a Jesuit priest, who had distinguished himself by his charity
in attending to the sick during the outbreak of a contagious
fever in St Giles's.   Indeed, he himself signed the warrant

[1] " Strafford Papers," ii. 74.

for his commitment to the Keeper of Newgate, on March 26, 1637. "Theis are to will and require you to receave into y^r custody the p'son of Henry Morse, a Romish priest, herewithall sent vnto yow ; and to keepe him safe prisoner vnder your charge in the prison of Newgate, vntill further order from this boarde. For which this shall be your Warrant. Dated at Whitehall, ye 26 of March, 1637 W. Cant"[1] (and other names).

When he was first arrested, Father Morse was shut up in a room by himself, and he "consumed the Blessed Sacrament, which he was at that time carrying to the dying, with all the reverence possible under the circumstances, though not fasting, to prevent Its falling into the hands of the heretics ; he also hid the pyx as well as he was able."[2]

No doubt he expected, nor without good reason, that searchers would come in presently and examine all his pockets and garments, and that, if they found the host, they would carry it off with his other effects. Possibly they might have "filed" it, as the lawyers for the plaintiff in a famous modern ritual case filed a wafer which had been received, but not consumed, at the communion-rails of a certain "high" church, and carried off and "put in" as evidence by one of their witnesses.

It is but fair to say that, at the earnest intercession of Henrietta Maria, who had supplied him with food and money when he was visiting the sick, Father Morse was respited by the king. No thanks to Laud for this! The discharge begins :—"Whereas at the instance of our deerest consort the Queene, wee have bene pleased to grant that Henry Morse," &c., "shal be enlarged, &c."[3]

Curiously enough, one of the charges against Laud, at his own trial, was "his holding correspondence with Papists and Jesuits, and amongst others . . . Henry Morse who had seduced five hundred and odd in Westminster,"[4]—a most groundless accusation.

---

[1] "Records of the Eng. Prov., S.J.," series 1, p. 606.   [2] *Ib.*, p. 578.
[3] S. P. Dom. Chas. I., vol. ccclxii. No. 6.
[4] *London's Intelligencer*, July 17 to 25, 1644.   Brit. Museum, King's Pamphlets, No. 167.

Laud was somewhat hard pressed to proceed against Father
Morse by the petition of the rector and church-wardens of St
Giles's-in-the-fields, who complained that people in their
parish who "before that tyme were Protestants, but in this
weeknes" [the outbreak of fever] were "p'verted by Morse
to the Romish Church" and "dyed soe." They humbly left
the "reformaçōn to your loᴾᴾˢ grave wisdomes."[1]

A few years later, Father Morse was again arrested, convicted of being a priest, hanged, drawn, and quartered; but
not before Laud's own head had fallen upon the scaffold.

Laud kept a sharp eye upon the queen's own private chapel.
Perhaps the accounts of that grand opening ceremony, the
crowded confessionals, and the communions at nearly every
mass from 6 A.M. till noon, may still have rankled in his
bosom. In 1636, Mr E. R. writes to Puckering[2]:—"One of
those two priests I mentioned in my last was clapped up by
my lord's grace" (Archbishop Laud), "because he preached
the sermon the Sunday before in the queen's chapel in Somerset House, that place being only allowed to the queen's chaplains, and not to any other priests, especially any English
priests. The other was committed for company; his fault
was his being a popish priest."

"His fault was his being a popish priest" is a remark very
much to the point, and shows that the law which made it a
criminal offence to be a priest was not allowed to lie dormant.
It also proves that the sufferings of such men were solely on
account of their religion.

Laud showed his anti-Papal zeal also against the laity,
as well as priests, in 1637. There is an entry in his
Diary[3]—"A great Noise about the perverting of the Lady
Newport: Speech of it at the Council: My free Speech there
to the King, concerning the increase of the *Roman* party,
the Freedom at *Denmark House*, the Carriage of Mr *Wal-
Montague*" [this was a converted son of the Earl of Manchester, who occupied several diplomatic appointments, and
eventually became abbot of the rich abbey of Pontoise—

---

[1] S. P. Dom. Charles I., vol. cccxxxi. No. 93.
[2] "Court and Times of Charles I.," vol. ii. p. 237.   [3] P. 55.

T

" Milord Montaigu, abbé de Pontoise "[1]—but he was more,
than abbé, being, as I said, abbot] " and Sir *Thoby Matthews*.
The Queen acquainted with all I said that very Night, and
highly displeased with me ; and so continues." This took
place in October. In December, he writes :—" I had Speech
with the Queen a good space, and all about the Business of
Mr *Montague*, but we parted fair." " Fair " sounds rather a
dubious footing on which to leave the presence of a queen ;
although the word may have meant more in those days than
it does at present.

Rushwood's account of the Sir Thoby Matthews, above mentioned, is not unamusing.[2] " Sir *Toby Matthew*, a Jesuit, of the
Order of Politicians, who was so vigilant that he never entr'd
a Bed, but only slept an hour or two in a Chair, imploy'd
himself Day and Night in Contrivances. This person was a
peculiar Plague to the King and Kingdom, thrusting himself
continually into the Company of his Superiors and others to
fish out their minds, which he imparted to the Pope's Legate,
to the Pope himself, or to Cardinal Barberini."

We come now to a difficult point in relation to Laud's
treatment of Catholics, namely, the question of how far he
influenced Wentworth in his harsh action towards them in
Ireland. It would be most unfair to saddle the memory of
Laud with every cruel oppression of Catholics practised by
Wentworth ; at the same time it must be admitted that
the Lord Deputy constantly consulted him with regard to
his management of ecclesiastical affairs in Ireland, and it is
difficult to put away the suspicion that he would be a good
deal guided by him in dealing with the Catholics in that
country, as well as with the Anglicans. At the very least,
Laud can scarcely have been ignorant that Wentworth, the
man who was perpetually inviting his advice and usually following it, was cruelly persecuting the Irish Catholic gentry.
In short, he was submitting those who were minors to the
same treatment to which Sir Kenelm Digby had been subjected many years earlier in England. He enforced to the
full the powers of the Court of Wards, by which a Catholic

---

[1] Notes to " Bassompierre's Embassy," pp. 6, 8.　　　[2] Vol. iii. p. 338.

ward, if a minor, was educated a Protestant, and, if he were not a minor, was not allowed to have possession of his property unless he would recant his faith by taking the oath of supremacy, which included the abjuration of several articles of the Catholic creed. Charles I. had bound himself to abolish this oppressive law in his contract of 1628. Wentworth, however, took good care that this contract should not be confirmed. Nay, he made this infamous law still more effective. "To elude the claim of the crown to the wardships," says Lingard, "and to prevent the necessity of suing out the livery of lands, the Catholics had been accustomed to alter the property of their estates, by long leases of some hundred years, and feoffments to secret trusts and uses. But such expedients were now rendered unavailable by an act passed at the suggestion of the Lord Deputy, which provided that all persons, for whose use others were seized of lands should be deemed in actual possession thereof, and that no conveyance of any estate of inheritance should be valid, unless it were by writing, and enrolled in the proper court." [1]

By this means, Wentworth hoped by degrees to make the families of the Irish landowners Protestant instead of Catholic. The matter, he says, "was a mighty consideration, for formerly by means of their feoffies in trust, their persons almost never came in ward, and so still lived from father to son in a contrary religion, which now, as they fall in ward, may be stopped and prevented." [2]

This was no empty boast. "Its consequence," he tells us, "appears in the person of the earl of Ormond, who, if bred under the wings of his own parents, had been under the same affections and religion his brothers and sisters are: whereas now he is a firm Protestant."

To enter upon the other ways in which Wentworth persecuted the Irish landlords, and deprived them of their property upon unjust pretexts, would demand more space than I can spare for such a purpose.

At the same time, it is due to Wentworth to say that he did not invent, suggest, or get enacted the Court of Wards in

---

[1] "Hist. of Eng.," vol. vii. chap. v.   [2] "Strafford Papers," i. p. 344.

Ireland.   That had been the handiwork of King James I.
It is true that Wentworth enforced its powers at a time when
they had been allowed to lie dormant ; but for that, as a
Protestant statesman, he might have defended himself with
a certain show of reason ; while he might have maintained
that if such were the law of the land, the Catholics ought
not to be allowed to set it at defiance by an evasion, even if
that evasion had been tolerated by his predecessor.

When, a couple of years later, Charles I., fearing that his
expedition against Cadiz might provoke Spanish retaliation
upon the coast of Ireland, wished to increase the Irish army,
he obtained £120,000 for this purpose from the Irish landlords, in return for certain concessions, one of which was that
Catholics should be able to sue the living of their landed
properties out of the Court of Wards, by an oath of civil
allegiance "made heartily, willingly, and truly upon the true
faith of a Christian,"[1] without any reference to religious
creeds.

Whether Laud recommended the king to agree to this,
does not appear ; let us hope that he did so, and it is not
unlikely ; but it greatly chagrined his brother archbishop,
Usher, of Dublin, who, when he heard that such a proposal
had been mooted, called together eleven other Irish Anglican
bishops, and with them declared in solemn synod "that to
permit the free exercise of the Catholic worship would be a
grievous sin, because it would make the Government a party
not only to the superstition, idolatry, and heresy of that
worship, but also to the perdition of the seduced people, who
would perish in the deluge of Catholic apostasy ; and that,
to grant such toleration for the sake of money to be contributed by the recusants, was to set religion to sale, and
with it the souls of the people whom Christ had redeemed
with his blood."[2]

To give Laud his due, he never wrote or spoke of Catholics
and their religion quite in this style.   Moreover, in one of
his letters to Wentworth,[3] he rather advises caution in the

---

[1] "Strafford Papers," i. p. 317.   [2] "Cyp. Angl.," p. 206.
[3] "Strafford Papers," vol. i. p. 479.

persecution of them, if not exactly from the highest motive. "My Lord, I am the bolder to write this last Line to you, upon a late Accident, which I have very casually discovered in Court. I find that notwithstanding all your great services in *Ireland*, which be most graciously accepted by the King, you want not them which whisper, and perhaps speak louder where they think they may, against your Proceedings in *Ireland*, as being over-full of personal Prosecutions against Men of Quality." "And this is somewhat loudly spoken by some on the Queen's side. And although I know a great Part of this proceeds from your wise and noble Proceedings against the *Romish* Party in that Kingdom, yet that shall never be made the cause in Publick, but Advantages taken (such as they can) from those and like Particulars to blast you and your Honour if they be able to do it."

If Laud occasionally worried Catholics, he was not without his own worries from other quarters.

We have had many instances, in our own times, of the fact that the no-Popery outcry of the puritanical party has not, as a rule, the effect of inclining the vilified Anglican ecclesiastics to, or even in the direction of, the fold of the Catholic Church; it may provoke them into becoming "higher"; but generally that is all.

In the year 1637, "libels," as he called them, were poured forth liberally upon Laud and his brother bishops. "A Short Libel" was "pasted on the Cross in Cheapside: that the Arch-Wolf of *Cant.* had his Hand, in persecuting the Saints, and shedding the Blood of the Martyrs."[1] "Another Libel" was "fastened to the North Gate of *St Pauls*. That the Government of the Church of *England* is a Candle in the snuff, going out in a Stench"; and "the same Day at Night my Lord Mayor sent me another Libel, hanged upon the Standard in *Cheapside*. My Speech in the *Star-Chamber*, set in a kind of Pillory, &c." Four days later, he writes "Another short Libel against me in Verse." A clergyman, a Bachelor of Divinity, had the effrontery to write of bishops as "Limbs of the Beast, even of Antichrist," as "Antichristian

---

[1] Diary, p. 54.

Mushrumps," as " Jesuited Polypragmatics," whatever they might be, and as " Sons of Belial " ; expressions for which he had to answer before Laud in the Star Chamber. Anagrams were the fashion in those days, and some puritanical wit made the pleasing discovery that, somehow or other, the letters of the name of William Laud would also spell[1] " Well, I am a Divel."   It was in this year that Prynne and his companions were tried before the same tribunal.   With these I have already dealt in a former chapter, but I should add that, after they had stood in the pillory, they were sent to prisons in different parts of the country, and that so strong was popular opinion in their favour, that the first part of their journey from London was more like the triumphal procession of heroes than the disgraceful conveyance of convicts to their places of punishment.   Laud himself wrote[2] that " thousands " of people assembled to see them pass by ; but, says Lingard, although all this " excited alarm in the breast of the Archbishop," " that alarm, instead of teaching him the impolicy of such cruel exhibitions, only prompted him to employ additional severity." [3]

The Catholic convert, Sir Kenelm Digby, in writing[4] of the cutting off of their ears on the pillory, said :—" The bloody sponges and handkerchiefs that did the hangman service in cutting off their ears " were picked up and treasured with great veneration by the Puritans, and, he continued :— " You may see how nature leads men to respect relics of martyrs."

A man of good family in Durham, John Lilburn, was put into trade in London, and one of the party of prisoners mentioned above, Bastwick, persuaded him to take the manuscript of a libellous pamphlet which he had written, called *The Merry Liturgy*, to Holland, where he got it printed, and then brought it back to England, together with a book called *The Vanity and Impiety of the Old Litany*, and other publications of a similar nature.   He dispersed these books, tracts, and pamphlets with the utmost secrecy ; but he

[1] Benson, p. 74.   From Lambeth Papers.   [2] "Strafford Papers," ii. 99.
[3] " Hist. of Eng.," vol. vii. chap. v.   [4] S. P. O. Dom., vol. ccclxix. No. 68.

was, as he says,[1] "treacherously and Judasly betrayed (by one that" he "supposed to be" his "friend") into the hands of "the pursuivant, with four of his assistants," and "committed to the Gate-house by Sir John Lamb, the prelate of Canterbury's chancellor."

He was tried in the Star Chamber, where he greatly scandalised Laud by refusing to take the oath, on the ground that it was "an oath of inquiry, and of the same nature as the high-commission oath; which oath" he knew "to be unlawful, and withal" he found "no warrant in the word of God for an oath of inquiry."

Laud happened at that moment to be standing with his back to him, and looking round over his shoulder, he peremptorily ordered him to pull off his glove, lay it on the book, and take the oath.

"'Sir,' replied Lilburn, 'I will not swear;' and then directing my speech unto the lords, I said, most honourable and noble lords, with all reverence and submission unto your honours, submitting my body unto your lordships' pleasure, and whatsoever you please to inflict upon it, yet I must refuse the oath."

"'My Lords,' said the Arch Prelate (in a deriding manner), 'do you hear him? he saith, with all reverence and submission, he refuseth the oath.'"

He "was cruelly whipped through the streets to Westminster," at the cart's tail, and was then placed in the pillory, in a place where the judges in the Star Chamber could see him through the windows, for two hours. He scattered a number of his libellous tracts from the very platform of the pillory, and, during his subsequent imprisonment, he wrote, and by some means managed to get published, a book entitled *Nine Arguments against Episcopacy.* He eventually became a captain in Cromwell's army; he fought at Edgehill; he was taken prisoner at Brentford, and only just escaped execution for high treason by an exchange of prisoners; he fought as a lieutenant colonel at Marston-Moor; he quarrelled with some of his fellow-officers and

---

[1] "Celebrated Trials," vol. i.

others among the Parliamentary party, including Cromwell himself; he was fined £7000 and banished, to come back to England and become a quaker and preacher, and at his funeral, in 1657, four thousand people were present.

One of the most unpopular measures instituted by Laud was the fruit of his desire to put a stop to the publication of books directed against his own school in the Established Church. He was intent, says Heylin, " upon [1] keeping down the *Genevian* Party, and hindring them from Printing and Publishing any thing which might disturb the Churches Peace, or corrupt her Doctrine. To this end he procured a Decree to be pass'd in the *Star-Chamber*, on *July* 1 *Anno* 1637." "By which Decree it had been Ordered, That the Master Printers from thenceforth should be reduced to a certain number ; and that if any other should secretly or openly pursue that Trade, he should be set in the Pillory, or whipped through the Streets, &c."; and that no books or prints should in future be published even by the "said Master Printers," until they had been "lawfully Licensed, either by the Archbishop of Canterbury, or the Bishop of London, or certain other authorities mentioned." Also that "every Merchant, Bookseller, or other Person, who shall Import any Printed Books from beyond the Seas, shall present a true Catalogue of them to the said Archbishop or Bishop for the time being, before they be delivered, or exposed for Sale, &c."

One of the first books seized, under the power of this decree, was the little Genevan edition of the pocket Bible, with footnotes.[2] Two entire editions were confiscated at the Hague. On this account, Laud was accused of having deliberately opposed the circulation of the Holy Scriptures, with about as much reason as the same accusation has often been brought against the Catholic Church. In either case it was, of course, not the Holy Bible itself, but the garbled translation, or else the notes appended, to which exception was taken.

The notes [3] in "The *Genevian* Bibles," says Heylin, "did not only teach the Lawfulness of breaking Faith and Promise

[1] "Cyp. Ang.," pp. 340 and 341.   [2] Benson, p. 79.   [3] "Cyp. Ang.," p. 342.

when the keeping of it might conduce to the hurt of the Gospel : but ranked Archbishops, Bishops, and all men in Holy Orders, or *Academical Degrees*, amongst those *Locusts* in the *Revelation*, which came out of the Pit." Naturally Laud did not wish to be compared to a locust, in the Revelation, coming out of the Pit. The notes of the same Bible advocated "the murthering" of kings, "if they proved Idolaters." Nevertheless, this arbitrary curtailment of· the liberty of the press has not been generally considered a diplomatic measure, on the part of Laud, by political critics of his history.

Upon Laud was thrown the whole odium of another national annoyance. This was the exodus of a number of Puritans to America, to avoid his persecution, and their settlement in the place they called New England. It was said that Laud "in his own Person, and his Suffragans, &c., &c.," "had caused divers Learned, Pious and Orthodox Preachers of God's Word to be silenced, suspended, deprived, degraded, excommunicated, or otherwise grieved and vexed without any just cause ; whereby, and by divers other means he had hindered the Preaching of God's Word, and caused divers of his Majesties Subjects to forsake the Kingdom"[1] and settle in New England.

Heylin says that " *New England,* like the Spleen in the Natural Body, by drawing to it so many sullen, sad, and offensive Humours, was not unuseful and unserviceable to the General Health : But when the Spleen is grown once too full," and so on, and so on, " it both corrupts the Blood, and disturbs the Head, and leaves the whole man wearisom to himself and others." For this reason, it was actually contemplated, by Laud, he goes on to say, " to send a Bishop over to them, for their better Government " ;—mark especially what follows—"and back him with some Forces to compel, if he were not able to perswade Obedience. But this Design was strangled in the first Conception, by the violent breakings out of the Troubles in *Scotland*."

Yet, when we think with pity of the narrow escape of the

[1] "Cyp. Ang., p. 346."

exiles for conscience sake, in New England, from a persecuting bishop, backed up by an army of soldiers, it is well to remember that they not only practised barbarous cruelties upon the native Indians soon after their arrival in their adopted country ; but that, in a few years, they caught three Quaker women, who had landed in New England, stripped them to the waist, flogged them through eleven towns, and drove them through frost and snow a distance of eighty miles, and that they hanged three Quakers and one Quakeress,[1] for no other offence than their religion.

[1] " Ency. Brit.," 8th ed. vol. xviii. p. 719.

CHAPTER XXVII

A MUCH more important personage than any of the so-called "libellers" described in the last chapter, was to be brought before Laud in the Star Chamber in the year 1637. The archbishop was to have the pleasure of lecturing, in that tribunal, a brother bishop, a future archbishop, an enemy, and a man of religious and political views very different from his own.

When Williams, Bishop of Lincoln, lost his post of Keeper of the Great Seal, he had assumed the role of a popular, liberal and democratic, if not republican, bishop. Retiring to his own diocese, he had lived there in considerable splendour and become quite a hero among those who bore no good will towards the king and the court. He was vain, imperious, hot-tempered, and no respecter of persons. In appearance, his portrait represents him as high-shouldered, small-eyed, with a pointed chin and nose, and a disagreeable smile. It does not look a sincere face ; but it is a shrewd one.

Clarendon tells us that[1] "he did not always confine himself to a precise Veracity, and did often presume, in those unwary discourses, to mention the person of the king with too little reverence." And he says that "he would frequently, and in the presence of many, speak with too much Freedom, and tell many stories of Things and Persons upon his own former experience."

Nor was it only against the king and the court that Williams felt ill-will and talked gossip. "He did affect to be thought an Enemy to the Arch-Bishop of Canterbury ; whose Person he seem'd exceedingly to contemn, and to be much displeased with those Ceremonies and Innovations, as

[1] "Hist. of the Reb.," vol. iii. p. 345.

they were then called, which were countenanced by the
Other ; and had himself published, by his own Authority, a
Book against the using those Ceremonies, in which there
was much good learning, and too little Gravity for a Bishop."

It will be remembered that, even if it be true that Williams
recommended Laud for a bishopric, he certainly quarrelled
with him afterwards. It will also be remembered that the
quarrel was patched up, after some sort of fashion. That the
nominal peace was not very sincere is shown by the remarks
of Clarendon which I have just quoted ; and when a man of
Laud's temperament heard that Williams was not only abusing him but, still worse, making fun of him, he must have
been irritated to the last degree.

D'Israeli [1] says that " Laud cruelly persecuted Williams for
a contemptuous jest." Considering Williams' attempts to
prejudice Laud in high quarters, when he was himself in
power, and his attacks with his pen on both Laud and his
ecclesiastical policy when he fell into disgrace, I do not think
that this is a very just accusation. At the same time, I am
not prepared to deny that Laud may have felt sensations of
inward satisfaction, when Williams was summoned in the
Star Chamber "for contriving and publishing False Tales and
News to the scandal of his Majesty's Government, and for
revealing some things contrary to the Duty of his Place, and
Oath of a Privy Counsellor." [2]

So little was the prosecution expected by the Bishop of
Lincoln, that when the summons was presented to him by
" Mr Attorney's Clerk," " he said somewhat merrily to him,
' You mistake the party ;' quoth he, ' this bill belongeth to
the Earl of Lincoln, and not to the Bishop.' The messenger
replied, ' If it please your lordship to peruse it, you shall find
it concerns the Bishop only.' " [3]

The Attorney-General, in prosecuting, did not soften his
language in deference to the Right Rev. Father in God, whom
it was his business to attack. " Here," said he, " was a heap

[1] " Life and Reign of Charles I.," vol. iii. p. 74.
[2] Rushworth's " Historical Recollections," vol. ii.
[3] Mr Pery to Lord Brooke, " Court and Times of Ch. I.," vol. ii. p. 196.

of offences tending to the subversion of Justice, and labouring, tampering, suborning and sending away the King's
Witnesses, to suppress the Truth, and to cause Retracting a
Scandal rais'd against the Proceedings of the Sessions, and
an Aspersion cast upon Sir *John Mounson:* These are great
crimes in themselves, much more in a Bishop; if not reme-
died, will draw the same Infamy on this Nation as it did
upon *Greece, Dare mutuum Testimonium.*"

This speech of the Attorney-General's cannot have been
other than very pleasant hearing to Laud. Quite as delightful
to the archbishop's ears must have been the opening sentences
of Lord Cottington's judgment. Laud himself knew what it
was to be worsted by Cottington, and he would all the more
relish the spectacle of his enemy writhing in the hands of the
same tormentor.

Lord Cottington said that "the Well-head from whence all
these foul Streams flow'd was very small, and the Bishop's overthrow was of his own seeking: he was sorry a Person so great,
wise and well-experienced, and who had sat there himself,
should come to be censured for such foul Offences."

Very agreeable, too, to Laud, must have been the concluding portion of Lord Cottington's judgment, when he sentenced
the Bishop of Lincoln to be fined "£10,000 to the King, to
be imprison'd in the *Tower* during the King's pleasure,
suspended from all Ecclesiastical Functions, *ab officio et
beneficio,* &c., &c."

When it came to Laud's own turn to pass sentence on
his brother bishop, it may have been that he felt a little
nervous; for Laud had nerves, like other men, although
excessive nervousness has not generally been considered one
of his most characteristic attributes.[1]

"The Archbishop began with his great sorrow, that a
Person of the Bishop of Lincoln's Profession, one so wise,
discreet and understanding, of such excellent Parts natural
and acquired, of such Wisdom, learning, Agility of Memory
and Experience, should be guilty of such Offences as deserved
the Censure of this Court; that after he had been overtaken

---

[1] I quote from the long account of the trial in Rushworth, vol. ii.

in one Error in the first Cause he should now fall into a worse by obnoxious and Criminal ways ; that when some question was made of his Loyalty and Discretion in words only, he should by unlawful means seek to justify his Words and Actions."

But it would not do to appear to be rejoicing over a fallen foe ; so Laud assumed for a moment the part of a sorrowing friend. " He said he had been five times upon his Knees to the King on his behalf." [Would Williams, himself a fibber, be very likely to believe this ?] " The Bishop" of Lincoln " by his Letters, acknowledged that his main hopes rested on him " (the archbishop), " yet for all this he was but coarsely us'd and ill requited by him."

This was a private and personal matter, which had nothing to do with the case before the Court, and it was a grievous mistake on the part of Laud to introduce it, more especially in delivering his judgment.

By and bye, Laud could not resist the opportunity of showing himself off. He must needs become historical, biblical, and classical, at poor Williams' expense. " He wished he," Williams, " had been as free from Passion as St Cecilia." " As for the Charges and Defences in the Cause, for him to repeat them, would be but *dictum dicere ;* that though this matter be not perhaps subornation of Perjury, yet tampering, threatening, deterring, affrighting, corrupting, silencing, or absenting of Witnesses, are *ejusdem naturæ* and foul Crimes ; and if this be suffer'd, it will destroy the Interest of *meum et tuum*, and subvert all Right and Justice."

Bearing false witness " took its birth in Hell, and came in with two Sons of Belial, in the Devil's Name." " This Engine, fetch'd from Hell outfac'd the God of Truth, for false Witnesses were found out against Christ himself."

The Romans made a law against false witnesses, " that the guilty Person should be thrown down a steep high rock, *e monte Tarpeio*, or *e saxo Tarpeio*, and have his Bones dash'd to pieces."

All this must have been very interesting to poor Williams.

" In the second part of the Decretals, a Suborner of Witnesses, if he brought a false Testimony (though compel'd thereunto by his Lord and Master), was to be excommunicated during his Life."—This was a pretty direct thrust at his bishop-victim.—"A heavy Burden (though in these looser times little set by) to be bereav'd of the Communion of Saints, and of being a Member of Christ's Body."

Williams was reputed to "set little by" such matters as membership of any particular church ; so this delicate hint would be well understood.

As to a bearer of false witness, "Aristotle terms him one *qui pietatem non curat.*" The great philosopher was made the medium of some more lecturing, and presently Laud said :—"the Bishop is a miserable man"!

"In the first Council of Macedon, seventeenth canon, a perjur'd Person is ranked with Murderers ; nay, the Suborner and Procurer of false witnesses is worse than a Manslayer, for he destroys two souls at once, his own and that of him who sweareth."

Even this was not enough. "In the seventeenth Council of Agatho," "a Tamperer with false witnesses was to be put to death."

I have only given a fraction of Laud's long judgment, the deliverance of which evidently afforded him keen enjoyment. Bishop Hacket says of it[1] :—"Then comes in the Archbishop with a Trick, to Noise up the Bishop with some Praise, that it might push him in pieces with a greater Censure, That when he thought upon this Delinquent's Learning, Wisdom, Agility in Despatch, Memory, and Experience, that accompanied him with all these Endowments, he wondred at his Follies and Sins in this Cause. O Sins by all means ! for by dioptrical Glasses some find Blemishes in the Sun." "So upon this matter his Grace took up no less than a full Hour to declaim against the horrid Sin of Perjury." "The Auditors thought he would never make an end." But, as he pithily observes, "It was Williams's turn now to suffer Episcopal Disgrace and Declension ;" "it was *Canterbury's* not long after."

---

[1] "Scrinia Reserata," pp. 125-6.

Williams spent some years in the Tower. While there, he is said by Clarendon[1] to have given his friends and admirers a very mendacious account of his trial, as well as of some secret offers which he pretended were made to him. He also put forth a statement " impeaching the credit of Kilvert " (one of the principal witnesses against him), " who had been informed against for perjury, and was living in adultery ' under my Lord Graces nose.' "[2]

" It had once been mention'd to Him, whether by Authority, or no, is not known, ' that his Peace should be made if he would resign his Bishoprick, and Deanery of *Westminster*' (for he had That in Commendam), ' and take a good Bishoprick in *Ireland*'*;* which he positively refused ; and said, ' he had much to do to defend himself against the Arch-Bishop Here ; but if he was in *Ireland*, There was a Man (meaning the Earl of Strafford) who would cut off his Head within one month.' "[3] He long outlived Laud, became eventually Archbishop of York, and died of a " Squinancy."[4]

The greater part of this chapter has been devoted to showing how stern Laud could be to a Broad-Church bishop ; I must admit that I fear personal enmities may have had quite as much to do with the bitter feeling, which existed between these two Anglican dignitaries, as theological, and I am about to show that he could be very kind if firm to a Broad-Church ecclesiastic on occasion.

" The ever-memorable " Hales, as he has been called, had written a tract on schism, in which he not only showed a contempt for ecclesiastical authority, but dealt with it in a spirit of sarcasm. Although privately printed, a copy, somehow or other, fell into the hands of Laud, who immediately sent for its author.

Poor Hales arrived at Lambeth at about nine o'clock on a summer's morning, most probably in considerable trepidation. Laud took him into his garden, and, pacing up and down, gave him his mind on the subject of the unlucky tract. Hales afterwards confessed to Heylin that he had had a terrible

[1] " Hist. of the Reb.," vol. iii. pp. 346-8.   [2] " Cal. Sta. Pa.," 1637, p. 262.
[3] *Ib.*, p. 348.   [4] " Scrinia Reserata," p. 227.

time of it. " He had been ferreted from one hole to another, till he was resolved to be orthodox and declare himself a true son of the Church of England, both for doctrine and discipline."

Nor was the ferreting soon over. When they, or at least Laud, had been talking for some time, the bell rang for prayers, when the archbishop took his victim with him through the door from the garden into the chapel. The service being over, he led him forth by the same portal into the garden and went at him again till dinner-time. Having then fed him, he took him once more into the garden and lectured him again till four o'clock.

But, in all this, Laud did nothing but argue out the points in dispute ; he evidently allowed Hales to have his fair share of the controversy ; for, says Heylin :—" In they came, highly coloured and almost panting for breath ; enough to shew that there had been some heats between them not then fully cooled."

Opposite as were Hales's views to Laud's, the archbishop recognised his talent and his powers as a conversationalist as well as a listener ; he may have also flattered himself that he had to a great extent converted him to a better state of mind ; at any rate, instead of summoning him as a heretic before the High Commission, he made him one of his chaplains, and afterwards persuaded the king to give him a canonry at Windsor.

In the year 1637, we hear once more of our old acquaintance, Lady Eleanor Davies, in connection with one of Laud's pet works, the railing-in and the adornment of communion-tables.[1] " It seems that the cathedral church of Lichfield is lately very beautifully set out with hangings of arras behind the altar ; the communion-table itself set out in the best manner, and the bishop's seat fairly built. This lady " [Lady Eleanor Davies] " came one communion day in the morning with a kettle in one hand and a brush in the other, to sprinkle some of her holy water (as she called that in the kettle) upon

[1] Mr E. R. to Sir T. Puckering, Bart., " Court and Times of Ch. I.," vol. ii. p. 259.

these hangings and the bishop's seat, which was only a composition of tar, pitch, sink-puddle, water, &c., and such kind
of nasty ingredients, which she did sprinkle upon the aforesaid things."

For this performance, she was shut up in a lunatic asylum.
After all, may there not have been "a method in her madness"? for she hated Laud and all his works, and anything
that he had enjoined, whether it were hangings of arras, communion-tables set out in the best manner, or anything else,
was odious to her. He had introduced many Popish practices
into the Reformed Church ; but not holy water ; so she
determined to do this for him.

Unorthodoxy in religion was not the only offence towards
which Laud turned his attention ; immorality was a crime
which he took an equal delight in punishing. In the year
1627, Lady Purbeck, the wife of Viscount Purbeck, was convicted before the High Commission at London House of
adultery, and was ordered, by the twenty commissioners
present, to do penance, barefooted, in a white sheet, in the
church of the Savoy. Such a performance was not at all to
the taste of her ladyship, and she determined to avoid it. As
Laud says,[1] "she withdrew her self, to avoid the Penance."
Who can wonder? As a matter of fact, she disguised herself
—not in a white sheet, but in a man's clothes,[2] and joined her
paramour, Sir Robert Howard, at his house in Shropshire,
where she lived, says Laud, "avowedly with him," and had a
family.

While these two wicked people were living in the country,
they were left unmolested ; but, "at last, they grew to that
open boldness, that" Sir Robert brought Lady Purbeck
"up to *London*, and lodged her in *Westminster.* This was
so near the Court, and in so open view ; that *the King* and
the Lords took notice of it, as a thing full of Impudence,
that they should so publickly adventure to outface the
Justice of the Realm, in so fowl a business."

One day, when Laud was at court, the king took him

---

[1] " Hist. of the Troub. and Tryal of W. Laud," p. 146.
[2] Lingard's " History," vol. vii. chap. v.

aside and told him of this scandal, "and added, that it was a great Reproach to the Church and Nation"; worse still, says Laud, he said that "I neglected my duty, in case I did not take order for it." Laud replied that Lady Purbeck was the wife of a peer of the realm; but that now he knew his Majesty's pleasure, he would do his "best to have her taken, and brought to Penance, according to the Sentence against her."

He was as good as his word. "The next day," he continues, "I had the good hap to apprehend both Her and Sir *Robert;* and by Order of the High-Commission-Court, Imprisoned her in the *Gate-house,* and him in the *Fleet.*" He took care not even to let them be in the same prison.

"The *Sunday* sevennight after, was thought upon her to bring to *Penance.* She was much troubled at it, and so was he." Sir Robert, therefore, "dealt with some of his friends," one of whom, "with Mony, corrupted the Turn-Key of the Prison (so they call him) and conveyed the Lady forth, and after that into *France* in Man's Apparel (as that Knight hath since made his boast)." That knight, however, remained a prisoner in the Fleet, and although Laud could not prove him to have been the means of contriving Lady Purbeck's escape, "in the next sitting of the *High-Commission,*" he "Ordered him to be close Prisoner till he brought the Lady forth." After being in prison for three months—for the lady remained abroad—Sir Robert was liberated, on his own bond of £2000, never to admit Lady Purbeck again into his presence.

It would seem that, while living in France, Lady Purbeck repented of her sin and became a Catholic. "My Lady *Purbeck* left her Country and Religion both together," writes the Rev. Mr Garrard to Wentworth,[1] "and since he will not leave thinking of her, but live in that detestable Sin still, let him go to their Church for Absolution, for Comfort he can find none in ours."

Again, a Mr E. R. writes to Sir R. Puckering[2]:—"The

---

[1] "Strafford Papers," vol. ii. p. 73.
[2] "Court and Times of Charles I.," vol ii. p. 242.

last week we had certain news that the Lady Purbeck was declared a papist ; and that she had engaged their Majesties of France and the Cardinal Richelieu to move the King of England for her pardon, and that she may come over. They do undertake it, and to that purpose they have sent instructions hither to their ambassador extraordinary, who is very zealous in the business. The lady hath written a long letter of three sheets to her majesty, the story of her life from her very childhood to her conversion, humbly desiring her majesty to intercede for her pardon. She hath also written to the Duchess of Buckingham and to some other of the great ladies, to take off (*sic*) my Lord's Grace of Canterbury. It is said she is altogether advised by Sir Kenelm Digby, who indeed hath written over letters to some of his noble friends of the privy council, wherein he sets down what convert this lady is become, so superlatively virtuous and sanctimonious, as the like hath rarely been either in men or women : and therefore he does most humbly desire their lordships to farther this lady's peace, and that she may return into England, for otherwise she does resolve to put herself into some monastery. I hear his majesty does utterly dislike that the lady is so much directed by Sir Kenelm Digby, and that she fares nothing better for it."

But this is not the end of the story ; for not only did the lady escape her penance, but Sir Robert applied for damages for false imprisonment, when the Long Parliament was in power, and was awarded £1000; that is to say, £500 from Laud, and £250 each from Martin and Lambe, who were judges in the Court.[1] Laud writes :—" I payd it, to satisfie the Command of the *House:* but was not therein so well advised as I might have been, being Committed for *Treason*."

Our divorce courts might be less popular if the delinquents were made to stand, barefooted and in white sheets, in the churches in one or more parishes in which they had given scandal, as in the days of Laud. Among Laud's papers is also a form of penance and reconciliation for renegades or

---

[1] Lingard's " Hist.," vol. vii. chap. v.

apostates,[1] which one would imagine must have been an obstacle calculated to stand much in the way of the return to the fold of a lost sheep.

After various preliminaries, including the penitent's formal excommunication, both in his own parish church and in the cathedral of his diocese, he is to appear, on a Sunday, in "the porch of the church, if it have any, if none, yet without the church door, if extremity of weather hinder not, in a penitent white sheet, and with a white wand in his hand, his head uncovered, his countenance dejected, not taking particular notice of any person that passeth by him." He is to kneel and say to people going into the church :—"Good Christians, remember in your prayers a poor wretched apostate, or renegado." A judicious N.B. is appended :—"Order must be taken that boys and idle people flock not about him."

On the second Sunday he is to be allowed to stand inside the porch, and when the *Te Deum* has been sung, one of the church-wardens is to bring him into the church and place him on the west side of the font, where he is to kneel until the end of the second lesson, when he is to read a long act of contrition and then go back to his place in the porch.

On the third Sunday he is to stand in his sheet "near unto the minister's pew." "The clergyman is to take no notice of him until just before the Apostle's creed, when he shall publicly put the offender in mind of the foulness of his sin, and stir him up to a serious repentance, advising him that a slight and ordinary sorrow is not enough for so grievous an offence."

The penitent is then to read a long confession, and the minister an exhortation to the congregation to forgive him. Then the penitent is to read another long form, begging for absolution, which the minister is at once to administer. After this, the clergyman is to kneel, facing eastward, and the penitent in his sheet is to kneel behind him. More, and very long, prayers are to be recited, and finally, the white sheet is to be taken off the repentant sinner, and the minister is to inform him that he may be admitted to receive the sacrament "upon any communion-day following."

[1] " Lib. Ang. Cath. Theol.," part v. vol. ii. pp. 373 and following.

When we reflect that this ceremony did not seem a likely
bait to win back a " renegado," it may be well to remember
that, in those times, the civil disabilities of a formally excommunicated person were so inconvenient, so many, and so great,
as to make life scarcely worth living, and that it may have
been desirable, for purely temporal reasons, to go through the
form of this tedious penance.

The marvel is that, with all these severities, bold tricks
were sometimes played in churches.   Several are mentioned
in the course of this volume, and not long after the date of
the present chapter, when the king and Laud went solemnly
to thank God for the judges' decision that he could levy ship-
money, someone actually bribed the leading chorister to sing,
instead of the proper psalms for the day, the lxxxii., which
contains the words, "How long will ye give wrong judgment?"
" They will not be learned nor understand, but walk on still
in darkness," and " Ye shall die like men : and fall like one of
the princes."   The judges " were very angry and Canterbury
put the youth in prison for not saying who gave him the
money." [1]

[1] Transcript from Papal Registers relating to Eng. Brit. Mus., Add. MSS. 15,
390, 1638, tom. vii., fol. 74.

CHAPTER XXVIII.

WE shall now have to concentrate our attention for a time on Scotland, a country from which a cloud arose that was to sweep England with the storm in which Laud was to perish.

When Charles had returned from the North in 1633, he had brought with him unfading memories of the opposition which he had experienced in the Scottish Parliament, and he left behind him disloyal feelings among his subjects no less bitter; these were still further increased by his ill-advised, and practically fruitless, prosecution of Lord Balmerino.

It was over ecclesiastical affairs that the storm was to burst. The king's father, James I., at Laud's suggestion, had induced the General Assembly, much against its inclination, to authorise the drawing up of a code of ecclesiastical law and the preparation of a liturgy in the year 1616. This liturgy was composed, and, after the king himself had altered it a little with his own pen, it was sent back to the Scotch bishops; but so strong was the feeling in the country against it, that it did not come into general use; neither did the so-called "Canons of the Assembly of Perth." Indeed James was much annoyed with Laud for having proposed the use of a liturgy for Scotland at all, and still more for urging that it should be enforced upon the unwilling people. "He feared not mine Anger," said he to Williams,[1] "but assaulted me again with another ill-fangled Platform, to make that stubborn Kirk stoop more to the English Pattern. But I durst not play fast and loose with my Word. He knows not the Stomach of that People."

Some time after his son Charles I. had come to the throne —in 1629, in fact—the matter was revived, it is generally believed at Laud's suggestion, albeit he denied it at his trial.

---

[1] "Scrinia Reserata," p. 64.

The accusation ran [1] :—" He hath maliciously and Trayterously Plotted, and endeavoured to stir up War and Enmity betwixt his Majesty's two Kingdoms of England and Scotland ; and to that purpose hath laboured to introduce into the Kingdom of Scotland divers Innovations both in Religion and Government, all or the most part tending to Popery and Superstition."

In Laud's reply, he says :—" Nor did I labour to introduce into the Kingdom of *Scotland* any Innovations in Religion or Government." Presently he mentions " that *Service-Book*," and says he will " set down briefly what was done."

" Dr *John Maxwel*, the late Bishop of *Ross*, came to me from *his Majesty*, it was during the time of a great and dangerous Fever, under which I then laboured." " The Cause of his coming was to speak with me about a *Liturgy* for *Scotland*. At his coming I was so extream Ill, that I saw him not." " When I was able to sit up, he came to me again, and told me it was *his Majesty's* Pleasure, that I should receive Instructions from some Bishops of *Scotland* concerning a *Liturgy* for that Church ; and that he was imployed from my Lord the Arch-Bishop of St *Andrews*, and other Prelates there about it. I told him that I was clear of Opinion, that if *his Majesty* would have a *Liturgy* setled there, it were best to take the *English Liturgy* without any variation, that so the same *Service-Book* might be established in all *his Majesty's* Dominions."

King Charles, on this point, " inclined to my Opinion " ; but, " afterwards, the *Scottish* Bishops still pressing *his Majesty* that a *Liturgy* Framed by themselves, and in some few things different from ours, would relish better with their Countrymen. They at last prevailed with *his Majesty*, to have it so, and carried it against me, notwithstanding all I could say or do to the contrary. Then *his Majesty* commanded me to give the Bishops of *Scotland* my best Assistance in this Way and Work. I delayed as much as I could with my Obedience ; and when nothing would serve, but it must go on, I confess I was then very serious, and gave the

---

[1] " Hist. of the Troub.," &c., p. 167.

best help I could." "And I do verily believe, there is no one
thing in *that Book*, which may not stand with the Conscience
of a right Good *Protestant.*"

I commend this expression of the great founder of High
Anglicanism, as some will have him to be, to my ritualist
friends. "A right Good Protestant!" There is an honest,
genuine ring in these words, which they may well take to
heart. Whether a liturgy, which had rather more in common
with the Roman Missal than the Anglican, would relish better
with the Scotch Presbyterians, was at least doubtful. That
adopted varied but little from the present curious *Communion
Office of the Church of Scotland*, which first uses the prayer of
consecration and *afterwards* prays that the "Creatures of
Bread and Wine" "may become the Body and Blood of
Christ." A very dubious criticism upon the efficacy of the
consecration! An invocation, from which this was probably
copied, occurs in the Missal; but, of course, before instead of
after the consecration. Even in our own times, the Scottish
Liturgy has been regarded from different points of view.
Dean Stanley wrote[1]:—"The Scottish Prayer-Book (with one
exception, that of the words of administering the Eucharistic
elements) was, not as is often erroneously supposed by both
sides, more Roman and less Protestant than the English,
but in all essential points was more Protestant and less
Roman."

I see no reason for doubting Laud's account of the matter;
but, whether the Scottish Liturgy was a little "higher" or a
little "lower" than the Anglican, does not affect the point
that Laud, from first to last, did all in his power to thrust *a*
liturgy upon the Scotch.

A little further on, Laud continues, in his written account
of his defence at his trial[2]:—"And here I take leave to
acquaint the *Reader*, That this was no new Conceit of *His
Majesty*, to have a *Liturgy* framed, and *Canons* made for
the Church of Scotland: For he followed his Royal Father

[1] "Lectures on the History of the Church of Scotland." By Arthur Penrhyn
Stanley. 1872. P. 43.
[2] "Hist. of the Troub.," &c., p. 170.

King *James* his Example and Care therein, who took Order for both at *the Assembly of Perth*, An. 1618."

Exactly, and, if Hacket and Williams are to be believed, his Royal Father, as we have already shown, declared that Laud himself had "assaulted" him with this "ill-fangled Platform," not understanding "the Stomach of that people"; and so ill-advised did James consider it that he practically allowed the whole matter to fall into abeyance.

The visit of Charles I. and Laud to Scotland, for the coronation, in 1633, was the precursor of decided action on their part in respect to ecclesiastical matters in that country. It took some time to complete the new liturgy, and when it was ready, the king, who, be it remembered, was not legally the head of the Church in Scotland, as he was in England, enjoined its use, as well as that of the Book of Canons, by "his authority royal."[1]

James was quite right when he implied that Laud did not understand the Scotch. They had been in the habit of boasting "that they were not, as the ministers in other churches, fettered and shackled with forms and rubrics,"[2] says Lingard; and the moment that the obligatory use of the new liturgy was announced, there was an uproar, not only among the people, but from the pulpits. So great and loud was the outcry that the bishops themselves trembled for the probable result of the using of the new prayer-book, or "the buke," as it was called in the North; and even in the South of England certain misgivings may have been experienced.

At last, it became known in Edinburgh that on a certain day the new liturgy would be used for the first time in the high church, which had been made the cathedral. The bishop and the dean, accompanied by the lords of the Council, and the judges and magistrates, went thither in solemn state. The building was crowded, the devout female sex being very strongly represented.

The dean nervously began to read the service, and was not set at his ease by the groans, which gradually developed into hisses, that arose from the congregation. A small fraction of

---

[1] "Bib. Regia.," pp. 136, 138; Balfour, ii. 224.

it, however, was more orthodox, and even ventured to repeat the responses. "Ane godly woman," Balfour, who did not sympathise with High-Churchism, tells us in *Stonicfield Day*, " when sche hard a young man behind sounding forth *amen* to that new composed comedie, sche quicklie turned her about, and after sche had warmed both his cheeks with the weight of her hands, sche thus shot against him the thunder-bolt of her zeal :—' False thief,' said sche, ' is there na uther pairt of the churche to sing mess in but thou must sing it at my lugge ? ' "

Other ladies yelled out that " the mass was entered, that Baal was in the church." Nor did the poor dean, who was reading the service, escape personal remarks. He was " a thief, a devil's gett, and of a witche's breeding." Neverthe-less, in spite of these and other opprobrious epithets, he stuck to his post and read away manfully at his " divine service."

Finding that barking produced no effect, a valiant old Scotchwoman thought the time had arrived for biting. Stealthily taking in her hand the stool on which she had been sitting, she hurled it at the head of the unhappy dean. It was a very fair shot ; it is true that it just missed its mark, but it flew within a few inches of the dean's nose.

He winced. The bishop observed it and boldly took the place of honour, believing that the dignity of his office would be respected, and began to read. He could scarcely hear his own voice for the loud cries of " fox ; wolf ; belly-god "— this was an ungraceful allusion to his corpulency. Presently a stool, deftly flung, almost grazed his ear. " Neither," says Balfour, " could that lubberly monster with his satine gown defend himself by his swollen hands and greasy belly, but he had half a dissen seck fishes to a reckoning." Clasped Bibles now began to hurtle through the air in the direction of the " satine gown." Worse still, there were unmistakable symp-toms of riot from without as well as within. Stones came crashing through the windows, amidst cries of " A pape, a pape, anti-christ, stane him ; pull him down."

The magistrates had by this time turned most of the

---

[1] " Hist. of Eng.," vol. vii. chap. v.

rioters out of the church, and the doors were locked ; but the storm of stones through the windows increased, and it vented its force in the direction of the bishop, who thought it high time to beat a retreat.

The service, between one minister and another, was got through somehow, and the bishop was not sorry to leave his cathedral for his lodgings in the High Street. On his way thither, he was followed by a crowd of "godly women." He hastened his steps, and just succeeded in reaching his door before they caught him. To his disgust, they came into the house after him. He ran upstairs: they ran after him. A party of stalwart women soon had him in their close embraces, and carrying their Right Reverend Father in God down his own staircase, they took him through the door and delivered him to the crowd of she-saints waiting in the street, who rolled him in the muddy gutter.

At the afternoon service, ladies were excluded, and it was performed in moderate quiet ; but when the bishop started for it, his appearance in the street was more than the "gude weiffes" could resist, and they greeted him with a volley of stones. Fortunately, Lord Roxburgh hurried him into his carriage and drove him to a safe asylum at Holyrood, followed, however, the whole way, by a crowd of shrieking women and showers of stones.

Edinburgh was not the only city in which strong exception was taken to the new liturgy. In a synod at Glasgow, a Mr Annan had spoken favourably of "the buke" in his sermon. " At the outgoing of the church," says a contemporary writer,[1] " about thirty or forty of our honestest women, in one voice before the bishop and magistrates, fell a railing, cursing, scolding, with clamours on Mr Annan." "He is no sooner in the street at nine o'clock, in a dark night, with three or four ministers with him, but some hundreds of enraged women of all qualities are about him with neaves, staves, and peats, but no stones. They beat him sore. His cloak, hat, and ruff were rent. However he escaped all bloody wounds, yet he was in great danger even of killing."

[1] Baillie, 8.

The news of the result of attempting to force a liturgy upon the Scotch reached Laud, the man who was reputed to be the author of it, early one morning.

It was not calculated to put him into a good humour. He was intensely irritated, and he started for Whitehall to attend the Council, brooding over the failure of one of his favourite projects. On his way thither, he met Archie Armstrong, the court jester. A fool, whether real or pretended, was not a character suited to the taste of so matter-of-fact a man as Laud, and this particular jester was specially odious to him ; for it is said [1] that at a banquet at which the archbishop was present, Archie had volunteered to say grace, which he proceeded to do in the following words :—" Great praise be to God, and little *laud* to the Devil." When, therefore, Laud met the court jester—the last but one in English history, according to Dr Doran—on his way to the Council, his already exasperated nerves were still further irritated. There was no escape, however, and he was obliged to pass close to the fool. Archie, in his motley, cap, and bells, bowed mockingly before the little archbishop in his rochet and lawn sleeves. " News from Scotland, your Grace," said he. " *Who's the fool now ?* "

This was more than Laud could endure. Boiling over with passion, he went at once to the king and complained of the insult which had been offered to him by his jester. Although Archie had been in his service since he ascended the throne, as well as in that of his father, King James, before him, King Charles gave orders for his dismissal then and there. Archie pleaded the privileges of his coat, but all in vain, as the following order, dated Whitehall, 11th March, 1637, will show : —" It is this day ordered by His Majesty, with the advice of the board, that Archibald Armstrong, the King's fool, for certain scandalous words of a high nature, spoken by him against the Lord Archbishop of Canterbury, his Grace, and proved to be uttered by him, by two witnesses, shall have his coat pulled over his head, and be discharged the King's service, and banished the court, for which the Lord

---

[1] " History of Court Fools," by Dr Doran, p. 204.

Chamberlain of the King's Household is prayed and required to give order to be executed. And immediately the same was put in execution."

A writer in "Phœnix Britannicus"[1] says that he afterwards met Archie in Westminster Abbey in a suit of black, and sympathised with him over the loss of his brilliant jester's coat. "'Oh,' quoth he, 'my Lord of Canterbury hath taken it from me, because either he or some of the Scots bishops may have the use of it themselves. But he hath given me a black coat for it; and now I may speak what I please, so it be not against the prelates, for this coat hath a greater privilege than the other had.'"

Laud had lost Archie Armstrong his place at court and his means of livelihood, while he himself remained in royal favour; but, as a matter of fact, the archbishop was on the eve of the downfall which was to end in his execution, whereas the ex-clown had already amply feathered his nest, and, after retiring to his native place in Cumberland, marrying, and living in wealth and comfort to a good old age, he died a natural death, very many years after the heads of the king who dismissed him and the prelate who accused him had fallen on the scaffold.

It was long before matters showed any symptoms of mending in Scotland. Laud had himself chosen and nominated several of the Scotch bishops, with whom he kept up a correspondence, and he may have been misled by their reports. The Archbishop of St Andrews advised the suppression of "the Buke." After that first terrible day of its introduction, he said :—"The labour of thirty years is lost for ever in one day"; but the younger bishops of Laud's selection were in favour of fighting the matter out. The Lord Treasurer of the Scottish Council, the Earl of Traquair, was supposed to have sympathised with Laud, and to have made things no better by his want of tact.

On the other hand, Laud, in his letters to Wentworth, accuses him of blundering, if not of treachery, and Heylin, in enumerating the causes of the failure of the attempt to

[1] I quote from "Court Fools," p. 207.

enforce the use of a liturgy in Scotland, writes[1] :—" That which appears first is the confidence which *Canterbury* had in the Earl of Traquaire, whom he had raised from the condition of a private Laird to be a Peer of that Realm, made him first *Treasurer Deputy* (Chancellor of the Exchequer we should call him in *England*), afterwards Lord *Treasurer* and Privy Counsellor of that Kingdom. This man wrought himself so far into *Laud's* good liking, when he was Bishop of London only, that he looked upon him as the fittest minister to promote the Service of that Church, taking him into his nearest thoughts, communicating to him all his counsels, committed to his care the conduct of the whole Affair, and giving orders to the Archbishops and Bishops of *Scotland*, not to do any thing without his privity and direction. But being a *Hamiltonian Scot* (either originally such, or brought over at last) he treacherously betrayed the cause, communicated his Instructions to the opposite Faction from one time to another, and conscious of the plot for the next days tumult, withdrew himself to the Earl of Morton's house of Dalkeith to expect the issue."

Lingard's reply to this accusation is much to the point, be its value what it may[2] :—" The failure of every measure prescribed by Charles induced the prelatic party to accuse Traquair of treachery ; his best justification will be found in the conduct of his opponents, who pursued him with unrelenting hatred, as their most vigilant and most dangerous enemy."

I do not think that Laud would have laid blame on another unjustly, had he been aware that he was doing so ; the blame again, in this instance, may have been due ; but, in cases of failure, there is a great temptation to account for the want of success of one's own "admirable plans," on the score of the clumsy, or the dishonest, executions of some one to whom they have been entrusted.

The Scottish Council suspended the use of the book ; King Charles sent a messenger to reprove that Council, and commanded the renewal of its use. A second time it was

---

[1] "Cyp. Ang.," p. 328.　　　[2] " Hist. of Eng.," vol. vii. chap. v.

suspended, and again did Charles order its enforcement. An angry crowd hung about Edinburgh protesting against " the Buke," and the authorities became alarmed. The petitioners kept increasing in numbers, and formed committees, under the name of the Four Tables, representing the nobles, the gentry, the clergy, and the burghers, to promulgate their opinions, and to deal with the authorities on the subject. The Tables demanded the revocation by the Government of the book of canons, of the liturgy, and of the Court of High Commission. The affair was beginning to wear the look of a rebellion, the more dangerous because men in the position of Lord Rothes, Lord Balmerino, Lord Lindsay, Lord Lothian, Lord Loudon, and other influential magnates, were supporting it.

Traquair condemned the Tables as unlawful, but offered to pardon all who should at once return peaceably to their homes. This order was publicly read and posted. The petitioners were prepared for it, and the herald had no sooner finished his task, than they read a counter-order which they had drawn up themselves, and affixed it to the market-cross.

A still stronger measure was adopted by the Puritan petitioners. They formed " a Covenant," a vow, by which all the subscribers were to bind themselves, " by the great name of the Lord their God," to defend the king ; to maintain the true religion ; and to resist everything that might be contrary to it, *i.e.*, to the opinions of the Tables. There were committees all over Scotland, and they summoned everyone who valued the true Gospel and the discipline of the Kirk, to sign the Covenant.

A great fast was held in preparation, and on a certain day all the faithful who were within reach were ordered to meet at the Church of the Grey Friars. After an exciting address from Lord Loudon, the whole congregation rose, and with outstretched arms swore to observe the Covenant. The enthusiasm spread from the capital to the provincial towns, from the towns to the villages, and from the villages to the most remote hamlets and huts in the Highlands. In most places the Covenant was readily and eagerly subscribed, and

where the will was wanting, compulsion was used.[1] " You
could not have chused but laugh to have seen the pipers
and candle-makers in our town committed to the town-jail by
our zealous Mr Mayor ; and herdmen and hiremen laid in
the stocks up and down the country, and all for refusing to put
their hand to the pen, as a thousand have done, who cannot
write, indeed ; " and the author quoted says that " you would
have laughed better to have seen the wives in Edinburgh,"
who could not write, holding up their hands as a sign of swearing to the Covenant, "as soldiers do when they pass a muster."

Charles resolved to put down the Covenant by force.   He
sent the Marquess of Hamilton to Scotland as his Commissioner, with a promise that the book of canons and the liturgy
should not be pressed upon the people in any other than a
fair and legal manner, and that the High Commission should
be put upon a footing less likely to be offensive, and that all
who had signed the Covenant should be pardoned, provided
they would at once renounce it.

Hamilton soon returned to London with a despairing report of the attitude of the Covenanters, and after making a
second visit to the North, he came back in a yet more discouraged state of mind.   Charles thought it wiser to temporise:
he sent Hamilton to Scotland a third time, with orders to
command the people to renounce the Covenant, at the same
time suspending the liturgy, the book of canons, and the High
Commission, and summoning a Parliament for the following
year, as well as a free Assembly of the Kirk for an earlier
date.   Soon after he had started, Charles wrote to Hamilton :—
" Your chief end being now to win time; that they may commit more follies, until I be ready to suppress them." [2]

The leaders of the Covenanters were not deceived by this
ruse ; for they were privately informed, on what appeared
good authority, that Charles was only endeavouring tem-
porarily to pacify them, while he was preparing an army with
which to enforce every obnoxious measure which he had for
the moment withdrawn, and they were much encouraged by

---

[1] Dalrymple, ii. 25. (I quote from a note of Lingard's.)
[2] Lingard, vol. vii. chap. v.

communications from puritanical Englishmen, who proposed to emigrate to the northern land of the pure Gospel, if the Scotchmen would but be firm. "*Anno* 1638, *April* 29," writes Laud,[1] "The Tumults in *Scotland*, about the Service-Book offered to be brought in, began *July* 23, 1637, and continued increasing by fits, and hath now brought that Kingdom in danger. No question, but there is a great Concurrence between them, and the *Puritan* Party in *England*. A great aim there to destroy me in the King's Opinion." Again, he writes to Wentworth, a couple of months later[2] :—" The *Scotish* Business is extream ill indeed, and what will become of it God knows, but certainly no good, and his Majesty has been notoriously betrayed by some of them."

The Covenanters issued a formal protest in reply to the Royal Proclamation, and it became evident to both sides that a crisis was imminent.

The General Assembly met in due time, the election having been successfully manipulated by the supporters of the Tables. Hamilton attended, in his office of Royal Commissioner, and, after having been opposed on every point, he rose from his seat, in tears, and dissolved the Assembly, taking the opportunity, not only of denouncing the treasonable conduct of the Covenanters, but also of blaming the ambition and even the immorality of some of the Scottish bishops.

The Assembly was not going to be dissolved at the command of the representative of the Crown ; on the contrary, it continued to sit, and in a more determined frame of mind than ever. At this point, the hitherto doubtful Earl of Argyle joined it, and a resolution was passed that in spiritual matters the Kirk was independent of the king and the civil power ; "the buke," the canons, and the High Commission were condemned ; Episcopacy was abolished ; the bishops and their clergy were excommunicated, and a day of national thanksgiving was proclaimed for the merciful deliverance of Scotland from the yoke of Prelacy and Popery.

Both countries, England and Scotland, immediately began to prepare for war.

---

[1] Diary, p. 55.   [2] "Strafford Papers," vol. ii. p. 185.

CHAPTER XXIX.

COMPARISONS have often been made between the great
ecclesiastic who virtually ruled France, at the period of
which I am writing, and the subject of my biography; perhaps a life of Laud would scarcely be complete without
one.

Certain characteristics and certain accidents of fortune
were common to both men. Each was the son of far from
wealthy, if well-to-do, parents; there, however, the similarity
in their beginnings ended, as Richelieu was a man of old
family, and Laud was of comparatively low birth. Both were
born during the latter part of the sixteenth century; both
were exceedingly ambitious; both became ecclesiastics, both
became bishops,—real or otherwise,—both used their clerical
positions as stepping stones to political power; both, in time,
ruled the rulers of their country; both made many bitter
enemies; both men died within the same decade.

I think it will be pretty generally admitted that, as a
statesman, Richelieu was immeasurably superior to Laud;
as a man, in respect to disposition, honesty of purpose, trust-
worthiness, and general good feeling, and apart from the
right or wrong of the religions professed by either, I venture
to think that the palm should be given to Laud.

One great distinction between the conduct of the two men
was their treatment of the Calvinists, whom both hated.
Laud never spared them; Richelieu, stern and severe as he
was in many matters, treated them with, for those times,
considerable tolerance. It is true that he instigated the
siege of La Rochelle, and that he crushed the power of the
Huguenots as a political body; but the cause of his so doing
had been the unwise action of Henry IV., in making the
Huguenots an *imperium in imperio* by establishing their

political status in the Edict of Nantes; and even when he had reduced the power of the Protestants as to matters connected with the State, and had razed their fortifications and castles to the ground, he neither demolished their churches nor interfered with them in the practice of their religion. He not only adopted an opposite policy to that of Laud in his treatment of the Calvinists, but actually gave the Calvinistic Scottish Covenanters assistance in their struggle against Laud.

In matters concerning his Church, Laud was absolutely uncompromising; so also, in religious matters, was Richelieu; but he sent the Marquis de Cœuvres with a Swiss army against the Papal troops, when they were protecting the communication of the Spaniards with the German Empire through the passes of the Alps.

Laud was not made a bishop (so-called) until he was forty-eight; Richelieu was consecrated bishop at the age of twenty-three; Laud was deposed and executed; Richelieu, although he fell at one time into temporary disgrace, was in the plenitude of his power at the time of his death.

Honestly and disinterestedly as Laud served his country, he never secured for it a fair province like Lorraine, nor humbled mighty enemies like Spain and Austria, nor built a palace like the Palais Royale and presented it to his king, nor founded an institution like the French Academy; on the other hand, Laud's ambition was more moderate, his self-esteem was humility in comparison with Richelieu's vanity, and his persecution of his personal enemies was somewhat less cruel; yet Richelieu, on his deathbed, when asked by his confessor if he forgave his enemies, replied that he had never had any, except those of the State; he never oppressed the people with exorbitant taxes or subsidies—a point on which Laud had the reputation of having given questionable advice; if Richelieu punished severely, he rewarded generously; and his disposal of ecclesiastical dignities was generally based rather on the virtue and learning of the recipients than on the question of the party to which they belonged, which, I fear, is more than could always be said of Laud.

I must now describe the manner in which Richelieu's influence came to be used adversely to Laud's policy and interests, and to do this some apparent digression may be necessary.

Richelieu was deeply interested in the Thirty Years' War, in which, after first making a treaty with Gustavus Adolphus, and assisting him with money, he joined openly in 1635, and endeavoured to turn to the aggrandisement of France. One contemplated move in his game was to seize the maritime towns of the Spanish Netherlands, and in order to do so, he desired to make sure of the neutrality of England. Accordingly, with a view to ascertaining the disposition of the English Crown and Cabinet, he sent Count D'Estrades to England, armed with private instructions, in the year 1637.

He was well aware that he himself was not in the best of favour, at that time, with the Queen of England, whose mother, Marie de Medicis, he had lately quarrelled with ; but he told D'Estrades to assure her of his good will and his anxiety to serve her interests.

D'Estrades carried two letters in his pocket for Henrietta Maria—one from Richelieu, the other from her brother, the King of France. If he found that he could soothe her animosity towards the cardinal, he was to present the former, if not, the latter only. He soon found that to induce her to trust Richelieu would be impossible, so he gave her the letter from Louis XIII., which implored her to do all that lay in her power to persuade her husband, King Charles, to guarantee his neutrality. She replied to D'Estrades that she "never intermeddled in affairs of this nature," but, to please her brother, she promised to mention the subject to the king, and she asked D'Estrades to come to see her again the same day, at five o'clock in the afternoon.

He returned punctually at that hour, and was at once received by her Majesty. She was in a very bad humour, and told him that she had broached the matter in question to her husband, and had got a scolding for her pains. D'Estrades "had been the occasion of her suffering a severe reprimand for having proposed to the King to remain neuter while the sea-ports of Flanders were to be attacked." He would be able, however, to judge of the king's disposition in the matter for himself, as his Majesty wished to see him at six o'clock.

The prospect of this audience was not very agreeable ; but, to the surprise of D'Estrades, King Charles received him graciously enough.

The ambassador plunged into his business forthwith, assuring Charles that if he would guarantee his neutrality, the cardinal would not only take care to further his interests at the Court of France, but endeavour to induce Louis XIII. to help him in suppressing his own rebellious subjects.

Charles replied that he wished always to remain a friend to his brother-in-law, the King of France ; but that there could be no friendship between them if he would be expected to do anything dishonourable, or injurious to the interests of his people. If the ports of Flanders were to be attacked by France, the English fleet would be in the Downs ready for action, and on board it would be an army of 15,000 men. He was much obliged to the cardinal for his offer to keep his own subjects in order for him, but that he would prefer to do for himself.

Richelieu had been fully prepared for the possible contingency of such an answer from Charles to his overtures, and he had instructed D'Estrades as to what he should do in that event. If Charles should guarantee a strict neutrality, he was to be rewarded by help in some form against the Scotch Covenanters ; if, on the contrary, he should refuse to be neutral, his neutrality was to be practically assured, by assisting the Scotch Covenanters to attack him, and thus divert his army from the south to the north. Therefore, D'Estrades at once put himself into communication with two of the leading members of the Scotch Covenanting party, then in London, and communicated with Richelieu, who sent to Edinburgh his chamberlain, the Abbé Chambres, or Chambers, as he called himself when he reached Scotland, accompanied by a confidential page of his own, who happened to be a Scotchman. Richelieu gave the Covenanters material help, by procuring the release of six thousand stand of arms, which had been purchased by them and seized by the States of Holland, and by presenting their commander-in-chief, General Leslie, with a hundred thousand crowns.

Matters were now, therefore, reduced to this absurd position, that a Catholic bishop and cardinal was assisting a puritanical army, whose chief cry was "No-Popery," while the army which it was attacking, on the ground of its encouragement of Popery, was under the patronage of a Protestant archbishop ; nor is it altogether unlikely that the absurdity of the situation may have amused Richelieu himself, who would consider one party quite as Protestant as the other.

In his attempts to influence King Charles, Richelieu failed ; but he was successful in considerably hampering him, for the sake of the interests of France, and it is to be feared that, in view of the same interests, he helped to foster complications in England,[1] as well as Scotland, so that the great French ecclesiastic intentionally, and the great English ecclesiastic unintentionally, both helped to bring about the overthrow of that unfortunate monarch, Charles I.

Wentworth did not take the movements of Richelieu into calculation, when he wrote[2] to the Lord High Admiral, of the threatened war with Scotland, that it happened, "in some Rispects, in a very ill Conjuncture of Time and affairs" :— "And yet there is some Good in this Evil, in regard all our Neighbours are so soundly together by the Ears one with another, as admits them no Leisure to look so far Northward, or Boldness to move his Majesty to declare himself a Party on either Side, where now he is upon a Neutrality." "And on the other Side, without Assistance from abroad, the gallant Gospellers shall not by God's Blessing be able to bear up their rebellious Humours against their King or bring other than their own Ruin upon themselves." He thought himself very clever and a great diplomatist ; yet at least one of his neighbours was not so soundly " by the Ears " with the others, but that he had leisure to plot against his Majesty of England and to laugh at Wentworth and Laud.

---

[1] Lingard, vol. viii. chap. i.   [2] "Strafford Papers," vol. ii. p. 190.

Macaulay[1] says :—" Charles and Laud determined to force on the Scots the English liturgy, or rather a liturgy which, wherever it differed from that of England, differed, in the judgment of all rigid Protestants, for the worse"; and he calls it "a step, taken in the mere wantonness of tyranny, and in criminal ignorance of public feeling." In the next paragraph he says :—" For the senseless freak which had produced these effects Wentworth is not responsible," and a footnote directs the reader to "see his letter to the Earl of Northumberland, dated July 30, 1638," the very letter of Wentworth's from which I have just been quoting.

Lord Macaulay is quite right, strictly speaking ; for Wentworth expressly says :—" Indeed in this matter of *Scotland*, I was utterly resolved to decline meddling or giving any counsel at all further than I should be commanded and required thereunto by his Majesty ; and hitherto I have kept myself intire on that Foot, not a Syllable writ on that Subject, &c.," and he mentions "that unhappy Principle of State, practised as well by his Majesty as by his blessed Father, of keeping secret and distinct all the Affairs and Constitution of that Crown" (of Scotland) "from the Privity and Knowledge of the Council of *England*, in so much as no Man was intrusted or knew any Thing, but those of their own Nation, which was in effect to keep them two Kingdoms still."

This proves Macaulay's accuracy ; at the same time, I must admit that, until I had read the whole letter for myself, I inferred from his words that he intended to imply that the letter, in some way, showed that Wentworth objected to the "senseless freak" of Charles and Laud, in forcing a liturgy on the Scots ; and knowing Wentworth's sympathy with Laud in ecclesiastical matters, I was puzzled ; this was an error on my part, but one into which others might possibly fall ; I hasten, therefore, to show that, although, as Macaulay very truly says, Wentworth was in no way directly responsible for the enforcement of the liturgy, far from objecting to it, he heartily sympathised with it.

I will quote one or two passages from this very letter in

[1] "Hist. of Eng.," vol. i. chap. i.

proof of this. " I have read the late Proclamation, penned
with all Moderation, as likewise their Protestation, the
sauciest and most unmannerly Piece my Eyes ever went
over, which will to Posterity remain the first Fruits of their
Rebellion, and the Scandal of the reformed Churches." " I
am clear in Opinion this is such an Insolency, as is not to be
borne by any Rule of Monarchy, but must be thoroughly
corrected, &c." After describing his plan for the campaign, he
says :—" I should hope his Majesty might instantly give his
Law to *Edenborough*, and not long after to the whole Kingdom ;
which though it should all succeed, yet at the Charge of that
Kingdom would I uphold my Garrison at *Leith*, till they had
received our Common Prayer Book, used in our Churches of
England without any Alteration." He implies here a wish for
the use of the English rather than the Scottish liturgy, but in
this he only shows himself at one mind with Laud.   " The best
Part of the *Irish* Army might be drawn down into *Ulster*,
close upon *Scotland*, as well to amuse those upon that Side as
to contain their Countrymen amongst us in due Obedience."
The Clergy of *England* and *Ireland* would be instructed to
preach to the People against their Disorders and Rebellions,
as they do most impudently against the Common Prayer
Book, and Ceremonies of our Church."

I have entered into this matter at some length, lest any
other reader should fall into my own mistake, of inferring
from Macaulay's words that Wentworth was out of sympathy
with Laud in his endeavours to introduce a liturgy into
Scotland. I may add that Mr Gladstone writes :[1]—" There
seems to have been established a thorough community of
soul between them ; and it might be hard to show any single
point of action or opinion on which they differed."

At his own trial for high treason, Laud said in his defence[2] :—" I ever advised the" (Scotch) " Bishops, both in
his Majesty's Presence, and at other times, both by Word
and by Writing, that they would look carefully to it, and be
sure to do nothing about it but what should be agreeable to
the *Laws of that Kingdom*. And that they should at all

[1] Romanes' Lecture.   [2] " Hist. of the Troub., &c., of W. Laud," p. 169.

times be sure to take the Advice of the *Lords of his Majesty's
Council* in that Kingdom, &c." "Which Course if they have
not followed, that can no way reflect upon me." Again he
says:—"In a *Letter* of mine after my last coming out of
Scotland, thus I wrote to the late Reverend Arch-Bishop of
S. *Andrews, Septemb.* 30, 1633, concerning the *Liturgy:*
That whether that of *England,* or another were resolved on,
yet they should proceed Circumspectly; *Because his Majesty
had no intendment to do any thing, but that which was
according to Honour and Justice, and the Laws of that
Kingdom, &c.*"

It may be replied that this defence, made by Laud when
he was being tried for his life, was probably exaggerated, if
not untrue. To prove the contrary, I will quote from his
correspondence with Wentworth some years before the very
idea of his impeachment had been mooted.

I must apologise for my length on this point; but it
seems my duty, in writing a life of Laud, to give evidence
for my belief that the strong things which have been said
about his share in enforcing a liturgy, *nolens, volens,* upon the
Scotch, are subject to very considerable modifications.

In November 1638, Wentworth wrote to Laud[1]:—"It
was ever clear in my Judgment, that the Business of *Scotland* so well laid, so pleasing to God and Man"—this shows
that he approved of the introduction of a liturgy into that
country—"had it been effected, was miserably lost in the
Execution, yet could never have so fatally miscarried, if
there had not been Failure likewise in the Direction, occasioned either by over-great desires to do all quietly without Noise,"—possibly he meant by this the king's reservation
on the subject to his English advisers, himself and Laud
included,—" by the State of Business misrepresented, by
Opportunities and Seasons slipped,"—it was then four years
since the king's visit to Scotland,—"or by some such like.
Besides, it sometimes falls forth, that out of an Easiness and
Sweetness of Nature some Men insensibly suffer Opposi-
tions." By this "sweetness of nature" he doubtless meant

[1] "Strafford Papers," vol. ii. p. 250.

the king's, and he goes on to explain that those who give way to such a disposition, often "difficult their own Affairs and discourage their own Party most extremely, &c." In the next paragraph, he presently says :—"Therefore God Almighty guide his Majesty's Counsels, and strengthen his Courage. For if he master not them," there will be danger that "this Affair" (the affair of the use of the Anglican liturgy, be it observed) "tending so much and visibly to the Tranquility and Peace of his Kingdom," and "to the Honour of Almighty God," may lead to serious trouble.

To this Laud replied,[1] that the errors were "all Errors about the Execution not the Direction." One of them, he said, was "a great one ; but I could not help it. For such of the Bishops of *Scotland* as were trusted with it were all for the quiet Way, and that fitting his Majesty's Disposition, I was not able to withstand it, and indeed must have been thought very bold, had I taken upon me to understand the Course of that Church and Kingdom better than they."

By "the quiet Way" Laud probably meant the introduction of the new liturgy, without allowing the country and the Council to know much about it until it was actually sprung upon them. One cannot conceive that he meant the opposite of introducing it under armed force ; for, in that case, a body of soldiers would have been required both within and without every kirk in Scotland. He goes on to say :—"But the main Failure in the Direction, if I mistake not, was, that all the Lords of that Council were not more thoroughly dealt with by the King, and their Judgments more thoroughly sifted before any thing had been put to Execution."

It is needless to say that the majority of "the Lords of that Council" would not have recommended the forcing of a liturgy upon their fellow-countrymen.

Wentworth took a very grave view of the situation. In his reply to Laud,[2] he wrote about the "insolent and peevish Covenanters," and asserted that it behoved "his Majesty to buckle himself roundly and severely to the Discipline of these rebellious Assumptions and Attempts, which otherwise

[1] "Strafford Papers,",vol. ii., p. 264.   [2] *Ib.*, p. 271.

certainly will never rest, till they lay on their rough Hands and even captivate Sovereignty itself."

This proved to be but too accurate a prophecy ! It will be observed that both Wentworth and Laud had now begun to find serious fault with the policy and behaviour of their pet king, and to admit that he did not always act upon the advice of either. What is even more remarkable is that two men, who depended so much upon the royal favour, should run the risk of sending letters to each other from England to Ireland, and *vice versa*, in which such opinions were freely expressed, not in cypher, but in ordinary characters. The discovery of one of the letters, which I have lately quoted, if it had got into the king's hands, would probably have led to the disgrace and fall of one, if not both, of these royal favourites.

CHAPTER XXX

LAUD'S own account, in his Diary, of the troubles in Scotland, in 1638 and 1639, are so short, and at the same time so descriptive, that I do not hesitate to quote freely from them.

In 1638, he writes [1] on "April 29. The Tumults in *Scotland*, about the Service-Book offered to be brought in, began *July* 23, 1637, and continued increasing by fits, and hath now brought that Kingdom in danger."

"Maij 26. *Saturday, James* Lord Marquess *Hamilton* set forth, as the King's Commissioner, to appease the Tumults in *Scotland*. God prosper him, for God and the King."

"*Novemb.* 21. *Wednesday*, The General Assembly in *Scotland* began to sit."

Now observe the length of its session. "*Novemb.* 29. *Thursday*, The Proclamation issued out, for dissolving the General Assembly in *Scotland*, under pain of Treason. *Decemb.* 20. They sate notwithstanding, and made many strange Acts, till *Decemb.* 20, which was *Thursday*, and then rose. But have indicted another Assembly against *July* next." With these events we have already dealt.

In 1639, he writes [2] on "*March* 27. *Wednesday*, Coronation-day, King *Charles* took his Journey *Northward*, against the *Scottish* Covenanting Rebels. God of his infinite Mercy bless him with Health and Success."

He is silent as to his own efforts in assisting the king's army; but there is evidence of them in a letter which he wrote to his suffragan bishops, in which he says [3] :—"In this Case of so great danger both to State and Church of England, your Lordships, I doubt not, and your Clergie under you, will not only be vigilant against the close Workings of any Pretenders in that kind : but very free also to your Power

---

[1] Diary, p. 55.   [2] P. 56.   [3] "Cyp. Ang.," p. 357.

and Proportion of means left to the Church, to contribute towards the raising of such an Army, as, by God's Blessing and his Majestie's Care, may secure this Church and Kingdom from all intended violence." " These are to pray your Lordship to give a good Example in your own Person, &c." " And I hope also your Lordship will so order it, as that every man will at the least give after the Proportion of 3s. 10d. in the Pound, of the valuation of his Living, or other Preferment, in the Kinge's Books." " Your Lordship must further be pleased to send a List of the Names of such as refuse this service."

While Laud was urging his bishops and clergy to contribute towards the army for the North, his old friend, Sir Kenelm Digby, with Walter Montague, against whose " carriage," since he had become a Catholic, Laud had lately declaimed at the Council,[1] " likewise dispers'd the Letters among the Roman Catholics to this effect: That the happy Moderation they live under, being to be ascribed to the Queen's Protection and Intercession, they doubt not but the occasion of expressing their Gratitude will be joyfully embraced by every one ; that they have already by their former Letters endeavour'd to prepare them to a cheerful Assistance of his Majesty in his Journey to the Northern Parts. They recommend to them the Nomination of some of the ablest and best dispos'd in every County, both to solicit and collect such voluntary Contributions."

If plenty of money was subscribed, ill use was made of it. Looking through the accounts of letters written from men with the army, in the *Calendar of State Papers*,[2] we find a state of things which puts into the shade the modern blunderings for which we always blame our own authorities whenever we go to war.

There are some who " think all this business too long, too costly, and too troublesome." A letter-writer tells his correspondent that " our soldiers " " lay last night and were fed yesterday worse perhaps than your dogs." ." Never till now was an army heard of without sutler or victualler till this ; it

[1] Rushworth, vol. iii. pp. 20 and foll.   [2] 1639, pp. 270-283.

is true they are paid, but they cannot eat money." "Well, God amend it all! but it is very scurvy, and we begin to have our factions and our fooleries already." There was treachery, too, in the camp. "A sycophantical rascal" in the king's army, "stole six great horses, is gone into Scotland and turned Covenanter." "Here is another fellow, one Sir [John] Hay, the Clerk Registrar, who has frequent access to the King. This trout, for all his hypocritical and asinine aspect, is thought no honester than he should be, and to wish well to the holy cause as the most puritanical varlet in the company."

"Our men grow sick with lodging *sub dio ;* above 100 are sick of the small-pox in Sir Thomas Morton's regiment." "Last night we were here in great affliction for fear of the miscarriage of our troops." "Here is great complaint made in town of somebody's indiscretion."

Perhaps the most extraordinary ill-management and want of discipline in Charles' army was when his soldiers, whom he was taking to Scotland to enforce High-Church doctrines and ceremonies, were [1] "so ill principled, or so ill perswaded, that in their marchings through the Country they brake into the Churches, pulled up the Railes, threw down the Communion Tables, defac'd the Common Prayer Books, tore the Surplices, and committed many other Acts of outragious insolence."

Letters of this period mention the virulence of some of the Scotch ladies against those of their own kith and kin who take the side of the king against the Covenanters. Hamilton's own mother is waiting her opportunity to shoot him, and has had some silver bullets cast for the purpose.

"Here [2] is great talk of my old lady, Marchioness of Hamilton ; of her case of pistols at her saddle, for she leads her own troop of horse, and is in the field, and her case of dags at her girdle. Her silver bullets are not forgotten for her own son and my Lord General, and how the ladies and gentlewomen, by her example, do all practise their arms, in which new kind of housewifery they are very expert. Of the form of their, I mean the women's, imprecation and curse, every one talks, and certainly but too true, wishing their husband's

---

[1] "Cyp. Ang.," p. 426. [2] *Ib.,* p. 282.

and children's flesh to be converted into that of dogs, and their souls annihilated, is the word, or " [and ?] "damned the meaning, if they refuse to come into the covenant, or ever consent to admit of the bishops."

Strong opinions were not wanting on the opposite side. Sir James Douglas wrote to Windebank[1] :—" The Act of the present Assembly abrogating and annulling Episcopacy as unlawful in the Church of Scotland was sent up to his Majesty four days since. Episcopacy orthodox in England, heretical in Scotland. Lord God have mercy on my soul." If Sir James had lived now, he might have said something partly to the same effect. Strongly as Laud had urged the clergy to contribute towards the expenses of the war against the Covenanters, when Charles had condescended to ask the advice of his counsellors, after Hamilton's first return from Scotland, he argued earnestly in favour of peace ; much to the annoyance of the king, who reprimanded him for his pusillanimity. The majority of the Council were more anxious to keep in the good graces of their sovereign, and confirmed him in his resolution.

It is needless for me to describe how this first war between King Charles and the Covenanters ended in a sort of ill-defined compromise and truce, without any very serious fighting. Laud, as he admitted at his trial, maintained that the king might have obtained better terms. " There arose,"[2] he writes, "a debate at the" (Council) " *Table*, about these Affairs, and *the Pacification ;* and I said that I did often wish from my Heart that *His Majesty* had kept the Army which he had at *Barwick* together but Eight or Ten Days longer : And that I did not doubt, but that if he had done so, he might have had more Honourable Conditions of his *Scottish* Subjects."

Further on, he says :—" And for the *Pacification,* I shall say thus much more : Though I could with all my Heart have wished it more Honourable for *the King*, and more express and safe for my Brethren of the Clergy ; yet all things Considered, which were put unto me, I did approve it.

[1] " Cyp. Ang.," p. 454.
[2] " Hist. of the Troub., &c., of W. Laud," p. 170.

For before the *Pacification* was fully agreed upon, *His Majesty* did me the Honour to write unto me with his own Hand : In this Letter he Commanded me, all delay set apart, to send him my Judgment plainly and freely what I thought of the *Pacification ;* which was then almost ready for conclusion. I in all Humility approved of the *Pacification*, as it was then put to me ; and sent my Answer presently back, and my Reasons why I approved it."

Clarendon more than agrees with Laud in thinking that Charles ought to have made better terms with the Scots, and instead of approving the "Pacification," as the best course under the difficult circumstances, he condemns it roundly.[1] " The Mischief that befel the King from this wonderful Attonement cannot be express'd, nor was it ever discover'd what prevail'd over his Majesty to bring it so wofully to pass : all Men were asham'd who had contributed to it." " The Factions and Animosities at Court were either greater, or more visible, than they had been before." " The King himself was very Melancholick, and quickly discern'd that he had lost Reputation at home and abroad." As to his coun- sellors, every man was "shifting the blame from himself, and finding some Friend to excuse him : and it being yet necessary that so Infamous a matter should not be cover'd with ab- solute Oblivion, it fell to Secretary *Coke's* turn (for whom nobody cared) who was then near fourscore years of age, to be made the Sacrifice." " This unhappy Pacification kindled many Fires of Contention in Court and Country, though the Flame broke out first in *Scotland.* On the other side the *Scots* got so much Benefit and Advantage by it, that they brought all their other mischievous Devices to pass, with ease, and a prosperous Gale in all they went about."

It is probable, therefore, that Laud did not speak of this " Pacification " in stronger terms than the rest of his party.

In another part of his History,[2] Laud writes :—" From the Publishing of this *Service-Book*, to this *Pacification*, I was voyced by the Faction in both *Nations*, to be an *Incendiary*, a Man that laboured to set the two *Nations* into a bloody

---

[1] " Hist. of the Reb.," pp. 124 and foll.   [2] P. 76.

War: Whereas, God knows, I laboured for Peace so long, till I received a great check for my labour."

In October, the king met with a distraction from his Scottish affairs. A Spanish fleet had been discovered in the English Channel by De Wit, the commander of the Dutch squadron, who gave chase, in which he was joined by Van Tromp. It seemed as if the Spaniards could not escape, when Charles, seeing, as he thought, a tempting opportunity of earning money wherewith to raise an army to keep the Scots in order, offered to take the Spanish fleet under his protection and convey it safely to the coast of Flanders, and from thence to a port in Spain, for a payment of £150,000.[1] The terms were gladly accepted; but the Free States were too quick for the negotiators, and ordered De Wit and Van Tromp to attack immediately. Twenty-three of the Spanish ships ran ashore, and twenty which put out to sea were either destroyed or captured by the enemy.

Laud's account of this misadventure runs as follows[2] :—
"Oct. 11 and 12. *Friday and Saturday*, The *Spanish* Navy was set upon by the *Hollanders* in the *Downs*. The Fight began to be hot, when they were past *Dover*. They were in all nearly sixty sail. The *Spaniards* suffered much in that Fight, not without our dishonour, that they should dare to begin the Fight there. But this is one of the effects of the *Scottish* daring."

It was much more to "our dishonour," because Charles had undertaken to protect the Spanish fleet and failed to do so, although, according to Lingard, Pennington, who was in command of the English fleet, with orders to prevent hostilities, lay within sight of the battle, an idle spectator. To all intents and purposes, he probably was one; but Van Tromp wrote to the Comte de Charost :—" As far as we can judge, the fire of the English was intended rather for a feint than from passion ; " so he seems to have at least opened fire.[3]

In this affair, the influence of the great French ecclesiastic gave trouble to the master of the English archbishop, for

---

[1] Lingard, vol. vii. chap. v.   [2] Diary, p. 56.   [3] Griffet, xxi. 233.

Cardinal Richelieu "had desired the Prince of Orange 'to give orders to his admirals to engage the Spanish Fleet in the Downs, notwithstanding the protection which the King of England seemed inclined to give them.'"[1]

Owing to Charles's indecision, Richelieu obtained for nothing from him the neutrality, in the matter of the Spanish and Netherlandish fleets, which he had offered to purchase at a great price, and while the well-meaning Laud was helping to make his master more unpopular, and gradually to bring about his ruin, the wily French bishop was not only managing the domestic policy of his country with admirable skill, but directing its foreign diplomacy with consummate tact and foresight.

In reply to Charles's angry remonstrance, the Dutch ambassador made a reluctant apology, pretending that the Spaniards had fired the first shot, which he admitted might possibly have been accidental, but was, in that case, misunderstood. King Charles accepted this lame apology, and endured the disgrace of the event.

The ambassador, to use a modern diplomatic phrase, "departed from accuracy of statement," for D'Estrade's Correspondence with Cardinal Richelieu shows that Van Tromp had orders to attack the English fleet, as well as the Spanish, if it should attempt to defend the latter. Before this order had been given, or decided upon, some member of the States-General had expressed a fear of anything which might lead to a rupture between Holland and England, when it was at once and insolently replied that King Charles dared not quarrel with them.

Even D'Israeli admits[2] that "the state of his affairs no longer admitted of an expostulation by his own navy; what was just and glorious in 1637 was no longer so in 1639. The mind of Charles was now too deeply engaged in military preparations against his own revolting subjects, while his Exchequer was so utterly exhausted that it became for him a

---

[1] "Life and Reign of Ch. I.," D'Israeli, vol. iii. p. 427 ; also D'Estrade's Correspondence with Cardinal Richelieu.

[2] Vol. iii. p. 435.

direful necessity to look to the help of his people, to gather
the reluctant alms of their loyalty, or to submit once more to
the dubious results of that new master of Sovereignty—the
Parliament."

The assistance given by Cardinal Richelieu to the "revolting subjects" had obviously effected the object he had aimed
at—the neutrality of Charles in naval battles between the
Dutch and the Spanish.

The alternative of a Parliament was gradually becoming
more and more necessary, and on "*Decemb.* 5. Thursday," in
1639, we find Laud writing[1]:—"The King declared his Resolution for a Parliament, in case of the *Scottish* Rebellion.
The first Movers to it were my Lord Deputy of *Ireland*"
(Wentworth), "my Lord Marquess *Hamilton*, and my self."

Here we have Laud, who hated parliaments, advising the
king to summon one, after an interval of eleven years, only,
no doubt, because, as Macaulay says, "to impose fresh taxes
on England in defiance of law would, at this juncture, have
been madness. No resource was left but a Parliament, &c."
Nevertheless, Laud adds to the entry in his Diary above
recorded :—"A Resolution Voted at the Board, to assist
the King in extraordinary ways; if the Parliament should
prove peevish, and refuse, &c."

From his Diary, his letters to Wentworth, his pacific
counsels with regard to Scotland when the liturgy had been
rejected, and other symptoms, Laud seems, at this time, to have
been dejected, out of spirits, and even nervous. Certainly he
had much to make him all three, and he may have been the
more disposed to yield, both to his own personal depression and the force of circumstances, owing to his ill health.
Three days before the king decided, "in case of the *Scottish*
Rebellion," to call a Parliament, Laud writes : — "My
Chyrurgeon in trust, gave me great and unexpected ease in
my great Infirmity. But after, the weakness continued."

We know little as to the "chyrurgeons" and physicians who
attended Laud. It would be interesting to know whether Dr
Harvey, the discoverer of the true theory of the circulation of

---

[1] Diary, p. 57.

the blood, ever attended him. As he was physician extraordinary to James I., and afterwards court physician to
Charles I., it is not unlikely. Harvey's services to Charles I.
were of a practical nature; for he was in personal attendance
upon the king at the battle of Edgehill.[1]

In all his political troubles Laud was not forgetful of his
beloved Oxford, for, in the year 1639, he sent 576 manuscripts,
about a hundred of which were Hebrew, Arabic, and Persian,
to the university library, having already sent more than 700
volumes.

He had contrived to get on good terms again with the
queen, and so far as his favour at court was concerned, he
had no cause for uneasiness.

It was decided that, before the English Parliament assembled, Wentworth should go to Ireland and appeal for
pecuniary and military assistance to the liberality of the
Parliament of that country.[2] Before he started, the king
created him Earl of Strafford and made him Lord Lieutenant
of Ireland. The Irish Parliament dared not oppose him, but
at once voted large subsidies, and, after ordering a levy of
eight thousand Irish soldiers, he returned to London to assist
at the English Council.

On April 13, 1640, "The Parliament sat down, called about
the Rebellion of Scotland," Laud tells [3] us. Again,[4] "At that
time it sat down, and many tumultuary Complaints were made
by the *Scots* against the Bishop and Church Government in
England, and with great vehemency against my self. All this
while the *King* could get no Money, to Aid him against the
Scottish Rebellion. At last, after many Attempts, Sir *Henry
Vane* told the *King* plainly, that it was in vain to expect
longer, or to make any other overture to them. For no
Money wou'd be had against the Scots."

Then he says that the king called "all his Lords of
Council" to meet at 6 A.M. in the Council Chamber. All the
peers, except two, "concurred to the ending of that Parliament"; yet the blame of it was laid chiefly upon Laud, and

[1] "The Origin and Growth of the Healing Art," Bardoe, p. 384.
[2] "Clarendon Papers," ii. 82.   [3] Diary, p. 57.   [4] "History, &c.," p. 78.

notices were "set up in divers parts of the City, animating
and calling together *Apprentices* and others, to come and meet
in St *George's* Fields, for the Hunting of *William the Fox*,"
or, as would now be said, to "draw Laud," for "the Breach,"
i.e., the dissolution, "of the Parliament." The archbishop
fortunately got warning of the night on which the sportsmen
intended to pay him a visit for this purpose, "and by the
Advice of some Friends," he "went over the water, and lay at"
"his Chamber in *White-Hall* that Night, and some other
following."

In his Diary,[1] he says :—"*Maij* 11. *Munday-night*, At Mid-
night my House at [*Lam*]*beth* was beset with 500 [of] these
Rascal Routers. [I] had notice, and stren[gthened] the House
as well as I could ; and God be [thanked, I had] no harm,
t[hey continued] there full two hours : Since I hav[e—for]tified
my House as well as I can ; and hope all may be safe, &c."
"My deliverance was great ; God make me thankful for it."

He was evidently terribly frightened, as well he might be ;
for it is not unlikely that the mob and rabble would have
given him a bath in the Thames, if they could have caught
him.

The punishment of at least one of the hunters of "William
the Fox" was severe. Laud writes :—"*Maij* 21. *Thursday*.
One of the Chief being taken, was Condemned at *Southwark*,
and Hanged and Quartered on *Saturday* Morning following,
Maij 23."

---

[1] P. 58.

CHAPTER XXXI

THIS, perhaps, may be the most fitting place to make a break in the continuous history of Laud, and interpose a chapter concerning certain persons with whom he was connected, or whom he influenced, within the space of a few years preceding the date of the last chapter.

Laud took a great interest in an attempt—the only attempt, so far as I can ascertain—to institute a kind of spurious religious life in the Anglican Establishment during the first half of the seventeenth century.

The St Benedict of the modern monasticism was one Nicolas Ferrar, a man nineteen years younger than Laud, and the son of a highly respected London merchant. His portrait by Cornelius Janssen shows us a handsome but rather effeminate countenance. Even as a little child he had been of a religious turn of mind, and the favourite books of his boyhood are said to have been the Bible and Fox's *Book of Martyrs*. He was a clever lad, and distinguished himself at Cambridge. When he left it, he went to Holland in the suite of King James's newly-married daughter, Elizabeth, afterwards Queen of Bohemia. He remained on the Continent about five years, making Venice his head-quarters; but he travelled a good deal in different countries, and wandered about Spain, chiefly on foot. While abroad he collected books, old prints of biblical subjects, and curiosities. On his return to England, proposals were made that he should accept a professorship at Cambridge; but he took up law instead, and became counsel to the Virginia Company. In 1624 he became a Member of Parliament; but in the same year he made up his mind to give up the world and live a religious, or semi-religious, life.

For this purpose, he purchased a property in Huntingdonshire, called Little Gidding. There, a half-ruined manor-house, with a building which had once been a church, but was then a barn, stood in an almost deserted village. He sent workmen to repair them sufficiently for use, though in great simplicity ; and, for a community, he enlisted his mother, his sister, Mrs Collet, and her husband—whether his monastery contained nurseries does not appear—his married brother and his son and other relations to the number of thirty or forty in all.

Ferrar himself was to be a sort of prior to the establishment, and, being a layman, he felt some diffidence at the prospect of such a situation; he did not want to be a clergyman ; yet he thought his position as a layman would be anomalous ; and in his perplexity he consulted Laud, who was at that time Bishop of St David's. Now, at that particular period, lay teachers and preachers were only too common, and they went by the name of lecturers. These lecturers were a thorn in the flesh to Laud. The idea of the proposed religious community, however, was pleasing to him, and he advised that the difficulty should be overcome 'by his ordaining Nicolas Ferrar a deacon, and a deacon only. His advice was followed. As Laud had been Archdeacon of Huntingdon, it is not unlikely that he may have recommended Ferrar to buy Little Gidding, which must have been formerly under his jurisdiction.

When it became known that Ferrar had received ordination, his friends, who were many and influential, offered him preferment ; but he refused all such offers, stating that he had only received deacon's orders so as to be legally qualified to give spiritual assistance to those living in the establishment which he proposed to found.

There is evidence that Laud not only made Ferrar a deacon, but took a keen interest in his pseudo monastery.

A short notice of this precursor of modern Anglican religious houses may not be out of place here, especially as Laud ordained its founder, and, as I shall show by-and-bye, endeavoured to advance his son in learning and royal favour. I take my account of it chiefly from Professor Creighton's article on Nicholas Ferrar in the *Dictionary of National Biography*, the notice of Ferrar in Chalmer's *General Biographical Dictionary*, Mr Benson's *Archbishop Laud*, Mozley's Essay on Laud, *Nicholas Ferrar: His Household and Friends*, Edited by Rev. T. T. Carter, and Rushworth's account of King Charles's visit to Little Gidding.

Everybody in the establishment was supposed to be taught a trade; although, judging from the length and frequency of their devotions, they would seem to have had little time to learn them, and still less to practise them. Education was one of the leading works of the community, and children were received free of charge. Visiting the sick and helping the poor were also among the principal occupations of these good people, and they kept alms-houses for widows. Their chief duty, however, was prayer. Bishop Horne wrote that "through the whole four and twenty hours of the day and night, there was no portion of the time when some of the members were not employed in the performing that most pleasant part of duty and devotion."

The whole establishment rose at four; at five, there were prayers in the oratory; at six, "the psalms of the hour"— Ferrar's psalms for the hour; he had divided them after a fashion of his own—with a portion of the Gospel and a hymn; at least they used to read some Gospel until Mr Ferrar had completed "his Concordance," and, after that, this Concordance was substituted for the Gospel. Judging from the little that I have seen of it, it must have been most dreary reading, and it was a curious book to choose as part of a devotional office. At half-past six, the whole community set off for the church to recite *Mattins*. They marched in procession, according to a prescribed order, two and two, Mr Ferrar bringing up the rear in his surplice. Caps and gowns were worn by most of the men, and both males and females wore a uniform. On entering the church, every one "made a low obeisance," and then went to his, or her, allotted place, except Mr Ferrar, in his surplice, who made one genuflection on entering the building, another when a little way inside the church, and a third before ascending the reading-desk. Having finished *Mattins*, the psalms of the hour and a hymn were said. Then followed breakfast. At ten, the whole party went to church again for the Litany, and at eleven they dined. After dinner came reading from the Scriptures and Fox's *Book of Martyrs*. I would specially call the attention of the superiors of modern Anglican sisterhoods, and religious houses for men, to their daily use of that edifying Martyrology. After Fox there was recreation until one o'clock, from which hour till three there was "instruction." At four, all went to church again for *Evensong ;* at five, or sometimes six, there was supper, and from supper till eight there were "diversions." Then came prayers, and, after prayers, bed—but not for everybody ; for there were the Night Watches to be kept, and doubly kept too, a certain number of men watching at one end of the house, and of women at the other. A watch lasted four hours, and during that time the watchers, it is said, repeated the whole book of psalms, verse and verse about ; but possibly this may be an exaggeration. Mr Ferrar, who slept in a frieze gown on bare boards, rose at one o'clock, to pray and meditate, and people from outside used to come in to listen to him.

It may surprise modern High-Churchmen to learn that the communion service was only celebrated once a month in this Anglican monastery, when the clergyman from a neighbouring parish came over to officiate, and Mr Ferrar acted as deacon.

Such a community was certain to provoke unfavourable remarks among those without, and Ferrar admitted that these were a constant mortification to him. "They were abused," [1] says Chalmers, "by some as Papists, by others as Puritans," and a treatise was written upon *The Arminian Nunnery*. On the other hand, they obtained the episcopal approval, not only of Laud, but also of his extreme opposite, Williams, Bishop of Lincoln.

Many people went to see the place for themselves, among others George Herbert and Crashaw, the poet, who later on became a Catholic, a priest, and a canon of Loretto ; but the

---

[1] P. 227.

little community was also honoured by two visits from royalty itself. In 1633, on a royal progress, the king and court went out of their way in order to see the Little Gidding establishment; an event which must have somewhat interfered with the recitation of "the psalms of the hour," the reading of Fox's *Book of Martyrs*, and such like monastic avocations. Charles was much pleased with a work which Ferrar had engaged a professional to teach his community, called "pasting-printing," or the making of "diatessarons." This consisted in cutting out selected texts from two printed copies of the four Gospels, so as to make a continuous narrative, and pasting them in a book, with pictures to illustrate them, and binding them in coloured velvet, with gold lace. Charles was delighted with the book, and honoured it by scribbling notes on the margin, an evil trick to which he was much addicted. Before leaving, he desired Nicholas Ferrar's nephew and namesake, the son of his brother John, a lad of about one-and-twenty, to come up to London and present himself to Laud.

The king's invitation was responded to some time afterwards, and before going to court, Nicholas went to Lambeth, as he had been bidden, to present himself to the archbishop. On being ushered into his presence, he knelt down, kissed his hand, and reverently asked his blessing. "My Lord embraced him very lovingly, took him up, and after some salutes, began to talk very kindly to him, and promised to take him the next day to the king at Whitehall." Nicholas had brought with him some books, executed by the community at Little Gidding in their "pasting-printing" style, as an offering to his Majesty, and Laud expressed himself much pleased with them, promising to let the king know beforehand that he might expect a present.

On the morrow, young Nicholas met the great archbishop at Whitehall, and followed him nervously into the presence-chamber.

Charles was standing by the fire, talking to some of his court. "What," said he to Laud, "have you brought with you those rareties and jewels you spoke of?"

"Yes," replied the archbishop, "here is the young gentleman and his works," and, taking Nicholas by the hand, he led him up to the king.

A case, which the lad had brought with him, was then opened, and eight richly-bound volumes were taken out of it. Charles was delighted and even the courtiers expressed their admiration. One of the books contained the Gospel in eight languages. Another was a Concordance. When the king had looked at it he said to Laud :—"You have given me a right character of the work, truly it passeth what I could have wished." And after making a long, bombastic oration, he concluded by saying :—"It shall, I assure you, be my companion in the daytime, and the sweetest perfumed bags that can lay under my pillow at night." Then he made a very characteristic speech to Laud :—"I know that they" (the Ferrars) "look for none, nor will they receive any reward. Yet let them know, as occasion shall be, I will not forget them." It is but fair to add that he promised to send Nicholas to Oxford at his own expense, and he ordered him to dine that morning with the younger lords, in the palace.

As soon as he had left the presence-chamber, the king, himself a stutterer, turned to Laud and said that it was a great pity that the boy stammered. Laud respectfully ventured to differ from his Majesty ; for if the youth had had the free use of his own tongue, the chances were that he would not have acquired a familiarity with so many written ones.

Lord Holland recommended that he should be made to try the effect of talking with pebbles in his mouth ; but Charles said that that was a useless remedy ; he had tried it for his own stammering, and had derived no benefit from it whatever. In his opinion, singing was the only thing that could cure stammering, and young Ferrar, he told Laud, must be taught to sing.

Besides bringing presents for the king, Nicholas had brought a book illustrated with coloured pictures for Prince Charles. The boy was much pleased with it, and so also was the little

Duke of York, who envied his brother his brilliantly coloured present. "Will you not make me such another fine book? Do!" said he to Nicholas. "Most certainly, your Grace," was the reply. "One shall be made without fail." Then came the childlike inquiry, "But how long will it be before I have it?" "Very soon," answered Nicholas. "Yes, but how long will that be? Tell the ladies at Gidding to be very quick."

The next day Nicholas left London and took leave of Laud at Lambeth. The archbishop reminded him of the king's promise to pay for his education at Oxford, and informed him that it was his Majesty's great wish to have a polyglot of the New Testament in twenty-four languages. He thought Nicholas might in time be capable of such a work; that he should have a good education given him at Oxford, and every opportunity of learning more languages, as well as the help of all the learned linguists whom the king could secure. This polyglot Testament was to be the labour of his life.

The lad knelt down, took the archbishop's hand, and kissed it. This pleased Laud, who "took him up in his arms"—he must have been very diminutive, considering how small Laud himself was—"laid his hand upon his cheek," blessed him, and prayed for him that God would "increase all graces in him, and fit him every day more and more for an instrument of His glory here upon earth, and a saint in heaven." As he took his leave of him, he said, "God bless you! God bless you! I have told your father what is to be done for you after the holidays. God will provide for you better than your father can. God bless you and help you!"

King Charles's great polyglot was never to be made; for a few months after his visit to London young Nicholas Ferrar died. The next time that the king visited Little Gidding Laud was a prisoner in the Tower.

I need not enumerate the writings of Nicholas Ferrar, he founder of the religious house at Little Gidding; they were not many, but I may observe that he wrote one for Archbishop Laud, a Harmony of the Mosaic Law, and that it is at present among the manuscripts of St John's College, Oxford.

It may be added that the end of the Little Gidding establishment for prayer, praise, and good works, was to be plundered and looted by the soldiers of the Parliament.

But, before dismissing the matter of the Ferrar family and their Anglican convent, I must say something of one who was thrown in the way of both, as well as of Laud. Indeed, like Nicholas Ferrar the elder, he consulted Laud at a critical period of his career, and upon much the same question.

George Herbert was only a year younger than Nicholas Ferrar, and, like him also, passed a brilliant career at Cambridge. Long before he fell under the influence of Laud, he had attracted the notice of Laud's model bishop, Lancelot Andrewes. He was a very finished classical scholar, and he especially distinguished himself by his Latin versification. In 1619 he was installed Public Orator at Cambridge, and his duties brought him into contact with King James, his court, and the great Buckingham himself. Like Nethersole, who had held the appointment before him, he hoped to obtain still higher offices, and his many opportunities of paying compliments to great and influential personages in his orations, seemed to pave the way to advancement. He was somewhat divided, however, between two opinions, asking himself whether he should seek " the painted pleasures of a court life, or betake himself to a study of divinity."

While he was yet in this state of indecision, he received an offer which might well have influenced him ; not from Laud, who eventually settled his mind as to which course to follow, but from one of Laud's greatest enemies, Williams, Bishop of Lincoln. It came in the form of a presentation to the prebend of Layton Ecclesia, which was attached to an estate at Leighton Bromswold, Huntingdonshire, a place only a couple of miles from Little Gidding, where his Cambridge acquaintance, Nicholas Ferrar, had just set up his ascetic establishment. He at once offered the prebend to Ferrar, who refused it, but advised Herbert to restore the ruined church, giving money for the purpose, in addition to advice. Herbert, who was far from well off, collected more money towards the same object among his friends, and the two men became very intimate over the work. Yet Herbert did not feel prepared to undertake the duties of a benefice.

In addition to the influence of Ferrar, he fell also under that of the good-looking and religious-minded Dr Donne, who was, like himself, a poet, and of whose effusions Chamberlain wrote to Carleton [1] that they contained " curious conceits, but much piety." Herbert and Donne wrote verses to each other, and conversed about spiritual things. " Betwixt this George Herbert and Dr Donne," says Izaak Walton in his life of the latter, "there was a long and dear friendship, made up by such a sympathy of inclinations, that they coveted and joyed to be in each other's company."

A threat of consumption induced him to resign his post of Orator to the University of Cambridge, and he retired to the house of his brother for a time, fell in love, and got married. Soon afterwards, in the year 1630, Charles I., at the request of Herbert's cousin, Lord Pembroke, presented Herbert to a rectory in Wiltshire. Again he hesitated ; but he went to Wilton to thank his relative for his kindness. Just at that time the king happened to be at Salisbury, and with the king was Laud, who was then Bishop of London.

Lord Pembroke, anxious that his cousin should not let slip this good opportunity which he had been at such pains to obtain for him, went to Laud, asked him to use his influence in endeavouring to induce George Herbert to take " priest's order," so-called, and to accept the living. Accordingly, he took Laud to Wilton. There he met George Herbert, and drew him into conversation ; he led him into the great gallery, and paced up and down, after his wont, as he talked to him.

George Herbert was handsome, if somewhat too aquiline in the nose, refined-looking, graceful in figure, and charming in manner ; yet he was free from all pride, as well as from the swagger which was only too common among the courtiers of the period, and he was a scholar and highly cultivated.

The Anglican clergy were not in those days remarkable

---

[1] " Cal. Sta. Pa.," 1623-5, p. 168.

for either their breeding or their refinement, and to lead into
their ranks a member of one of the best families in England,
as distinguished for his acquirements as for his genealogy,
and as charming as he was cultured, seemed to be a step that
might be of untold importance to the Church whose interests
Laud had so much at heart.

As the event proved, it was of even greater importance
than he imagined. He convinced his recruit that he had
a call to the ministry, and that it would be sinful to refuse to
obey it, and a messenger was hurried off to Salisbury to
summon a tailor to supply him, forthwith, with clerical
garments; for, although he "had been made Deacon some
years before,"[1] he seems to have still worn the gay dress of
a courtier. In his new "canonical clothes," George Herbert
went to Dr Davenant, Bishop of Salisbury, on April 26th,
1630, and was by him, on the same day, "inducted into
the good, and more pleasant than healthful, Parsonage of
Bemerton; which is a mile from Salisbury."

Laud was thus the means of enlisting into the ranks of the
clergy of the Church of England one who was to become
the model of those refined and cultivated scions of good
families that have done so much to grace the Anglican
establishment for the last two hundred and sixty years.
Perhaps it would be no great exaggeration to say that Laud
did few, if any, greater services to the Church of England
than that of persuading George Herbert to enter its
ministry.

This is not the place to enter upon the question of Herbert's literary merits, or demerits, to enumerate his works,
beginning with the little manuscript volume of verse which
he dedicated to his friend—his "most entire friend and
brother"—Nicholas Ferrar, a book of which good old Izaak
Walton tells us that twenty thousand copies had been sold
in 1670, or to give a history of his life, which, by the way,
lasted only three years after his institution to his rectory;
but I would venture to point out that, by his example, he
did that for his Church which Laud failed to do. May we

---

[1] Izaak Walton's "Life of George Herbert," Bullen's ed. p. 291.

not indeed ask whether her poets have not, as a class, done more for the Anglican Church than her preachers or her canonists? To mention no others, who can estimate the influence of Keble in the nineteenth, Ken in the eighteenth and seventeenth, and George Herbert in the seventeenth centuries, upon their co-religionists.

I would go further still, and say in the words of Cardinal Newman[1] :—"It is sometimes asked whether poets are not more commonly found external to the Church than among her children; and it would not surprise us to find the question answered in the affirmative. Poetry is the refuge of those who have not the Catholic Church to flee to, and repose upon; for the Church herself is the most sacred and august of poets." "She is the poet of her children; full of music to soothe the sad and control the wayward—wonderful in story for the imagination of the romantic; rich in symbol and imagery, so that gentle and delicate feelings, which will not bear words, may in silence intimate their presence or commune with themselves. Her very being is poetry; every psalm, every petition, every collect, every versicle, the cross, the mitre, the thurible, is a fulfilment of some dream of childhood, or aspiration of youth. Such poets as are born under her shadow, she takes into her service; she sets them to write hymns, or to compose chants, to embellish shrines, or to determine ceremonies, or to marshal processions; nay, she can even make schoolmen of them, as she made of St Thomas, till logic becomes poetical." And of what a list of poets she can boast, from Dante downwards! It would not have surprised Newman to hear the question he mentions answered by some in the affirmative, but I think that the true reply must certainly be in the negative.

I must now notice another character with whom Laud was brought into contact, namely, Lucius Cary, Viscount Falkland, whom Mr Matthew Arnold described as a "martyr of sweetness and light."[2] No phrase is more identified with

---

[1] "Essays, Crit. and Hist.," vol. ii. pp. 441 and foll.
[2] "Mixed Essays," p. 326.

that writer's name than "sweetness and light"; yet it is not so original as some may suppose; for when he used it in Falkland's case, he had evidently been studying Clarendon, who writes of the same person as one of "inimitablé sweetness and delight in conversation." "Sweetness and delight" may have suggested the modern rendering of "sweetness and light."

Falkland was a great friend of Laud's two *protégés*, Chillingworth and Hales, who more or less shared his freethinking views, and were ever welcome at his manor-house of Great Tew, some ten or twelve miles from Oxford. He made certain Oxford men free of his house; they came when they liked, they stayed as long as they liked, and he only knew, by meeting them at meals or in his gardens or hall, whether they were at any particular time his guests. Nor was he limited to men of his own theological opinions for friends; Sir Kenelm Digby, Ben Jonson, Waller, Selden, Hobbes and others swelled the list. I do not claim that Laud ever ranked in it: on the contrary, Matthew Arnold says that Falkland "disliked Laud."[1] "He had a natural antipathy to his heat, fussiness, and arbitrary temper." Perhaps Laud disliked him less than his mother and brothers, who became Catholics; but it is probable that he was more or less worried, from different theological directions, by the whole family, which, between sweetness and light on the one hand, and Popery on the other, sorely tormented his soul.

[1] "Mixed Essays," p. 215.

CHAPTER XXXII.

I MUST go back a year to describe how Laud had anxieties in connection with ecclesiastical affairs abroad, as well as at home, and I will take, as an example, the case of a Mr Johnson, one of his clergy, who was acting as the Queen of Bohemia's chaplain at the Hague. It will serve also as a specimen of Laud's correspondence with his clergy. The clergyman in question wrote to Laud[1] that his "halcyon days" of "peace with all" were "disturbed by those who rejoice in all troubles," and that he had "tasted of the malice of some Scottish spirits," who said that he was an Arminian. Laud replied[2] that he heard a much worse accusation against him, namely that he "had commended the Socinian writers for their rational and clear expression of themselves. And though it be one thing to commend the style of an author and quite another to commend the matter; yet, in that place, and in these dangerous times, and where there is justly conceived so much jealousy of the increase of the Socinian party, being a most desperate and dangerous heresy," Johnson "did extremely ill in any sort to commend their writings, and thereby give any probable occasion to strangers to think that either" he "or any else in the Church of England were inclinable to that foul heresy, and the most dangerous that ever spread itself since the beginnings of Christianity." He then ordered Johnson to "take some discreet way to stop this suspicion"; for if it were to "once break out into public, the scandal" would "be too heavy," and, he adds, "I shall be driven to recall you thence, which being done upon such an occasion will utterly lose you in the Church, and for my part I shall account myself very unhappy to have meddled with you." "And I hereby further require you, upon your

[1] "Cal. Sta. Pa.," 1639, p. 35. [2] *Ib.*, pp. 41-42.

canonical obedience, to abstain from giving any the like offence hereafter." He also said, somewhat sadly:—" The times are so injurious to me, that every man's error with whom I have to do is cast upon me."

Laud made inquiries as to the truth of the reports of Johnson, from a man at Amsterdam, named John le Maire, who wrote [1] in reply that " Dr Johnson utters himself 'in his discourses, as well at the table as in conference with men of great knowledge, sustaining boldly that the heresy of Faustus Socinus is ' vera et solida theologia,' and that the arguments of our chiefest divines ' pro divinitate Christi ' are ' futilia, straminea,' which abominable opinion makes great discontent and mourning among the ministers of this country, &c."

Then more correspondence took place between Laud and Johnson, in which the latter endeavoured to explain that he had been entirely misrepresented. Laud replied [2]:—" You must give me leave to tell you two things. First, that mistaking or no mistaking, it is a very ill-favoured accident, both for yourself and the Church of England, that such a rumour should be raised and spread. Secondly, that the words which you are said to have spoken, as they are related to me, are very desperately foul in themselves, and cannot be salved by any pretence of being mistaken." Then he admits that the Queen of Bohemia and other great people are " all satisfied that the whole business was a misunderstanding," and that he hopes he did not speak the words as they were related to him ; and he says he " will rest satisfied for the present as they do, provided that the business die so and be quieted. But if it rise again, and make any distemper in that church at their synods or otherwise, you must then give me leave to take more care of the Church of England than of you. And I heartily pray you to make this a sad warning to yourself for your future conversation."

Looking homewards, again, we find the vice-chancellor writing to worry him, as Chancellor of Oxford, about disputes between the town authorities and the university.[3] " The mayor pretending the statute of Edward I. for his night

---

[1] " Cal. Sta. Pa.," 1639, p. 76.   [2] *Ib.*, p. 223.   [3] *Ib.*, pp. 272-4.

watch." This civic night watch trenched upon the duties and privileges of the proctors and their bull-dogs. " That statute appoints the watch to stand at the gate, where had they kept themselves the proctors had not questioned them ; but when they took the boldness to walk the streets, to examine scholars of all conditions, to enter houses and search what company there, then they thought it high time to appear and stand up in defence of their own authority and the privilege of the University. Your Grace having been proctor long since cannot but know that the night walk has of old belonged to the University, &c."

Again, although knowing " that upon his Majesty's return " (from Scotland) Laud would have his " hands full of great business, and that time is precious to " him, the Archbishop of York writes[1] to enlist his assistance against " a blasphemous heretic " who, before the High Commission itself, had " avowed and maintained his damnable blasphemous heresies and opinions," yet escaped without censure.

The Bishop of Bristol also writes[2] to Laud complaining of a case, at the assizes at his cathedral town, in which one, Davis, was found not guilty. The bishop had seen the judge beforehand and expressed his desire " that a matter of this high nature might not be slighted nor slubbered over, but carried at least with severity, so as *metus ad omnes.*" Apparently, "the judge did his part copiously, gravely, and with semblance of great severity." He asked the prisoner what he thought of bishops, and Davies replied that they were appointed by Christ for the government of his Church ; and he knelt down and prayed for them. The bishop's " conceit upon the whole matter is this, that the whole carriage of the business was a mere scene, wherein the judge acted his part cunningly, the jury plausibly, *populo ut placerent,* and the prisoner craftily, that he might no longer resemble Davis, *qui perturbat omnia.*"

The Bishop of Exeter adds his complaints, in a long letter to Laud,[3] against the " heady and ignorant opposers of government and good order," who should be " chokingly convinced

[1] "Cal. Sta. Pa.," 1639, p. 455.   [2] *Ib.,* p. 460.   [3] *Ib.,* pp. 526-7.

and seasonably checked." He thinks it would be "seasonable, safe, and happy to employ the spiritual sword against them."

Laud was to have trouble with a bishop in the spring of the year 1640. "*Maij* 29. Friday,"[1] he writes, "The Convocation sate after the ending of the Parliament till Maij 29, and then ended ; having made in that time 17 Canons ; which, I hope, will be useful to the Church." Among the rules laid down in these canons was one that, four times every year, every clergyman in England should "instruct his parishioners in the divine right of kings, and the damnable sin of resistance to authority."[2] There were also some very intolerant enactments against Socinians, Separatists, and Catholics. That against the latter greatly annoyed Dr Goodman, Bishop of Gloucester, the bishop, already mentioned, who was in the habit of reading the Divine Office. This bishop, in a sermon preached before the king, had spoken very strongly on the subject of the Real Presence in the Eucharist, and his doctrines thus expressed had caused considerable sensation and comment. The king himself doubted their soundness, and appointed a committee to consider and report upon the matter.[3] The committee were inclined to treat it leniently, "howsoever," "they thought it very fit that Dr Goodman should be appointed to preach again before His Majesty, for the better explaining of his meaning." The affair was in this manner passed over without any more serious consequence than making Goodman suspected of Popish inclinations. But when the bishops, sitting in Convocation, in their very first canon, enacted "Proceedings against the *Papists*,"[4] a canon which was so framed as to be "very express for the use of all good and Christian means, to bring them out of their Superstitious Errors, and to settle them in the Church of *England*," "this *Canon* would not down with my Lord of Gloucester," h:ɔ nly member of Convocation who made any objection to it.

Laud says that in the morning of the day on which the

---

[1] Diary, p. 58.   [2] Lingard's "Hist.," vol. vii. chap. v.
[3] See Hook's "Lives of the Arch. of Cant.," vol. xi. p. 121.
[4] "History, &c., of W. Laud," p. 81.

canon was to be subscribed, Goodman crossed the river to
Lambeth, called on him, and gave vent to "great expressions
of his dislike to this Canon." Laud "gave him the best
Counsel" he "could, that he would keep himself out of that
scandal, which his refusing to Subscribe would bring, both
upon his Person, his Calling, and the Church of *England*, in
these broken times especially. But" Laud "fell so short of
prevailing with him," that Goodman told him "plainly, *He
would be torn with wild Horses, before he would Subscribe that
Canon :* And so" they "parted."

"The hour of Convocation drew on ; and" the bishops "met
to *Subscribe the Canons.*"

Now, according to ancient custom, Convocation ought to
have risen with the Parliament ; but Charles, being anxious
to get a grant of subsidies from the clergy voted to him by
the bishops, contrived to get some of the judges to declare
that it was quite legal for Convocation to continue to sit.
Laud himself told the king [1] his fears that such a course
"would be excepted against in all likelyhood by divers, and
desired his *Majesty* to Advise well upon it." The king replied,
"that he had spoken with the Lord *Keeper*, the Lord *Finch*,"
—an "obsequious lawyer," says Lingard, who had only very
lately been made Lord Keeper—"about it, and that he assured
him it was Legal." This nettled Laud, who wrote :—" I confess, I was a little troubled, both at the difficulties of the Time,
and at the Answer it self ; that after so many Years faithful
Service, in a business concerning the *Church* so nearly, his
Majesty would speak with the Lord *Keeper*, both without me,
and before he would move it to me : And somewhat I said
thereupon, which pleased not ; but the Particulars I do not
well remember. Upon this, I was Commanded to sit, and
go on with the *Convocation*." This is the first occasion on which
we meet with any mention of friction between King Charles
and Laud.

We will return to the subscription of the canons, and see
what use Goodman made of the doubtful legality of Convocation sitting when Parliament had risen. When it came to his

---

[1] "History, &c., of W. Laud," p. 79.

turn, he objected that Convocation "had no Power to make
Canons out of *Parliament* time, since the Statute H. 8. It
was then told his Lordship, that" Convocation, on the present
occasion, "had the *King's* Power according to that Statute."
Laud adds: "This was but a pretence to disgrace our Proceedings, the better to hide his unwillingness to subscribe that
Canon against the *Papists;* as appeared by that Speech,
which he had privately used to me that Morning, and with
which I publickly charged him upon this occasion, that he
spake the words unto me." Surely this looked like a breach
of confidence on Laud's part!

Laud quotes a number of precedents of Synods and
Councils in the Catholic Church, for about a page, and then
says that when Dr Goodman would neither affirm nor deny
" that *Canon* against the *Papists*," he, " with the consent of
the *Synod* suspended him. Divers of my Lords the Bishops
were very tender of him, and the Scandal given by him.
And *John Davenant* then Lord Bishop of *Salisbury*, and
Joseph Hall then Lord Bishop of *Exeter*, desired leave of the
House (and had it) to speak with my Lord of *Glocester*, to
see if they could prevail with him. They did prevail; and
he came back and Subscribed the *Canons*, in open *Convocation.* But I told him: Considering his Lordship's Words, I
did not know with what Mind he Subscribed; and would
therefore according to my Duty acquaint his *Majesty* with
all the Proceedings, and there leave it."

Convocation being ended, Laud tells us that he " did
acquaint his *Majesty* with my Lord of *Glocester's* Carriage."

" His *Majesty*," he says, " having other Jealousies of this
Bishop besides this, resolved to put him to it. So his Lordship was brought before the *King*, and the *Lords* in *Council;*
and restrained to his Lodging, and a *Writ ne exeat Regnum*
sent him."

Now mark especially what follows:—" But this *Writ* proceeded not for any thing said or done by his Lordship in the
Convocation, but upon other information which his *Majesty*
had received from some *Agents* of his beyond the Seas."

The king sent him to prison; but he did not stay there

long, for he acknowledged his fault before the Lords of the
Council, and he seems [1] to have taken " the Oath injoyned in
the sixth *Canon*, for preserving the Doctrine and Discipline
of the Church of *England*, against all *Popish* Doctrines which
were thereunto repugnant." Of this oath he afterwards repented; for, as I said in a preceding chapter, he died a
Catholic.[2] " In the time of his last Sickness," says Heylin,
" he declared himself to be a Member of the Church of *Rome*,
and caused it so to be expressed in his last Will and Testament, that the news thereof might spread the further, and his
Apostacy stand upon Record to all future Ages. A Scandal
so unseasonably given, as if the Devil himself had watched
an opportunity to despite this Church." [3] Dean Hook [4]
quotes the editor of the Clarendon State Papers, as remarking [5] that " within a year he conformed again "; but neither
the *Panzani Memoirs* nor *Cyprianus Anglicanus* make any
mention of his relapsing after having been received into the
Church ; and Heylin would pretty certainly have crowed
loudly over such an event had it actually taken place. The
acknowledgment of his having become a Catholic in his will,
too, would almost certainly have been revoked, had he
returned to the Anglican Church.

It was the archbishop's duty to publish the seventeen new
canons ; and when he did so, in order to propitiate the
Puritans and the mob that supported them, of whom he had
by this time become thoroughly afraid, he appended a letter,
signed by himself and the Bishop of Rochester, in their
characters of judges, of the High Commission, ordering the
arrest and production before that Court, not only of all
priests and their harbourers, but also of any person in whose
possession might be found Catholic books, of everyone who
had been, or was suspected of having been, present at mass,
of all who had been baptized by priests, and of every boy who
had been at, or was about to be sent to, a Catholic seminary.[6]

[1] " Cyp. Ang.," p. 418.   [2] " Memoirs of Panzani," pp. 248 and 260.
[3] " Cyp. Ang.," p. 419.   [4] " Lives of the Archbishops," vol. xi. p. 123.
[5] Vol. ii. pp. 17 and 18.
[6] Despatch from Rosetti Luglio, 27 ; N. S. Lingard's "History," vol. vii.
chap. v.

This order, on the part of Laud, greatly alarmed the English Catholics, who had been accustomed to look upon him as a somewhat harmless and only half-hearted enemy, and they applied for relief to the queen. Although she had been on excellent terms of late with Laud, she was too wise to appeal to him directly in the matter, but took into her confidence Windebank, who was probably, by this time, already half-converted. They went together to her husband, and reminded him respectfully of the assistance which he had lately received towards his army against the Covenanters, from his Catholic subjects, in the shape of a free and gratuitous present of £14,000, and represented to him that Laud's action might well have the result of alienating every Catholic Englishman from his loyalty to the king. Charles was frightened, and sent for Laud. Again there was an unpleasantness between the monarch and his archbishop; the king reprimanded Laud for his officiousness, and commanded him to be very careful, in such critical times, not to offend any of his subjects, whether Catholic or Protestant.

Considerable ridicule was brought upon Laud in the year 1640 by a stringent oath which he drew up and required to be taken by a large number of people, consenting to whatever ecclesiastical measures might be imposed by the " Archbishops, Deans, Archdeacons, &c." It was spoken of as the "et cetera oath," and Mr Gardiner says that it " turned the laugh against Laud." [1]   It was generally looked upon as being as ridiculous as it was vague and dangerous, and in the October of the same year, by the king's orders, Laud suspended it.

Among the State Papers are some notes for a speech by Sir Thomas Framston " against Archbishop Laud demonstrating the unconstitutional character of the [et cetera] oath and canons approved by the late Synod." [2]   " I find," he says, " by this oath he doth advance himself in point of Government of the Church above the King, and without his leave; 2nd above the Parliament; 3rd above the law."

---

[1] "Dictionary of National Biography," Article on Laud.
[2] "Cal. Sta. Pa. Dom.," 1641-3, pp. 529-30.

" Must the King judge ? No. Must the Parliament judge ? No. Must the rubric and confirmed Canons judge ? No. Then let [us] inquire who is made judge by the Canons." And he argues that the et cetera oath was so framed that the Archbishop of Canterbury should be the supreme judge—"the Patriarch of England ; and this he says, if we well please, we may call him Metropolitan or Patriarch, in his late book [*margin*, page 171, line 28 *Relat. contra* Fisher]."

The Scots were again giving trouble. In August news arrived that the Scottish army had crossed the English border and, as Laud says, " His Majesty took his Journey towards the *North* in haste." On the twenty-fourth of September, he writes :—" A great Council of the Lords were called by the King to *York*, to consider what way was best to be taken to get out the Scots."

Charles found it absolutely necessary to obtain assistance from the nation, and, of the two evils, he preferred an assembly of Lords to a Parliament with its House of Commons. Twelve of these very Lords, however, signed a petition, representing the grievances under which the nation was suffering, and begging him to summon a Parliament, at once, as the only safe remedy. Presently, another, in a similar tone, reached York, signed by ten thousand Londoners, and the majority of the peers urged him to consent. After much hesitation, the king gave way. In the meantime, negotiations were opened by the peers at York with the Covenanters, a meeting taking place between the representatives of both at Ripon.

Poor Laud was much deserving of pity in the year 1640. He was thoroughly frightened, being, at last, fully alive to the danger threatened by the puritanical party ; he had had at least two disagreeable scenes with the king, who, till this year, had almost invariably treated him with respect and affection ; his nerves had been quite unstrung by the attack upon his palace at Lambeth ; they had been still further shaken by a shower of stones with which he, together with several other members of the High Commission, had been received, on emerging from one of its sittings in October ; and

his health, never very good, was giving way. It was enough
to alarm him when, on [1] "the *High Commission* sitting at St
Paul's, because of the Troubles of the Times," very "near
2000 *Brownists* made a Tumult at the end of the Court, tore
down all the Benches in the Consistory; and cryed out, they
would have no Bishop, no High Commission."

There were other disquieting symptoms. He writes in his
Diary:—" *Sep.* 21, I received a [Letter from] *John Rockel* a
M[an both by] Name and Person [unknown] to me. He
was [among the] *Scots*, as he tra[velled through the] Bishoprick of [Durham] he heard them [inveigh and] rail at me
[exceedingly, and that] they hoped Shortly [to see me, as the
Duke was] Slain by [one least] suspected. His Letter [was
to] advise me to look to my self." I copy the brackets as
they are placed in the old edition of his Diary.

Laud's terrors were fomented by his superstition. On
October 27th, he writes in his Diary:—"I went into my
upper study, to see some Manuscripts, which I was sending
to *Oxford*. In that Study hung my Picture, taken by the
Life;"—Can this have been his portrait by Vandyke now at
Lambeth palace?—"and coming in, I found it fallen down
upon the Face, and lying on the Floor, the String being
broken, by which it hanged against the Wall. I am almost
every day threatened with my Ruine in Parliament. God
grant this be no Omen."

In his *History*, also, he mentions the troubles of that time.[2]
The seventeen new canons "at their first Publication"
"were generally approved in all Parts of the Kingdom; and
I had Letters from the remotest Parts of it, full of Approbation: Insomuch, that not my self only, but my Breth'ren
which lived near these Parts, and which were not yet gone
down, were very much Joyed at it. But about a Month
after their Printing, there began some Whisperings," and then
he describes how ill-feeling against the canons rapidly spread,
"Till at last, by the practise of the *Faction*, there was
suddenly a great alteration, and nothing so much cryed
down as the *Canons*. The comfort is, *Christ* himself had

[1] Diary, p. 59. [2] P. 8.

his *Osanna* turned into a *Crucifige* in far less Time. By this means the Malice of the Time took another occasion to whet it self against me."

Laud was now on the very eve of his fall, and he seems to have been aware of it. Wearied out, and with ruin staring him in the face, he may well have recalled the words of his contemporary, Bacon :—" The rising unto place is laborious ; and by pains men come to greater pains." " The standing is slippery, and the regress is either a downfall or at least an eclipse."[1] Alas, it was to be "a downfall" in Laud's case.

[1] Bacon's Essay, " On Great Place."

CHAPTER XXXIII.

"In November 1640," says Lord Macaulay, "met that re-nowned Parliament which, in spite of many errors and disasters, is justly entitled to the reverence and gratitude of all who, in any part of the world, enjoy the blessings of constitutional government." [1]

Laud announces the fact in periods less rounded. "*Novemb.* 3. *Tuesday*, The Parliament began: the King did not ride, but went by Water to *Kings Stairs*, and through *Westminster-Hall* to the Church, and so to the House." [2]

Heylin says that [3] "entring the Church at the Little door which openeth towards the East, he was received by the Sub-Dean and Prebendaries under a Canopy of State, and so conducted to the place where he heard the Sermon; the performance of which work was commended by his Grace of *Canterbury* to the Bishop of *Oxon*."

We have had plenty of opportunities of observing how fond Laud was of preaching before the king at state functions of this kind, and I am inclined to attribute his having "commended" the task to a friend on this occasion to the condition of his nerves.

It is likely enough that Charles doubted whether he would receive a very loyal welcome if he rode in state through the streets to open Parliament, and feared to run the risk of a cold reception, which might become a matter of common gossip and thus increase his unpopularity.

He must have met his Parliament with very serious mis-givings, and he made a short but conciliatory speech from the throne. Nevertheless, it by no means pleased everybody. Heylin tells us [4] that "the Commons were not more willing

---

[1] "Hist. of Eng.," chap i.
[3] "Cyp. Ang.," p. 430.

[2] Diary, p. 59.
[4] *Ib.*, p. 430.

to hear that his Majesty was resolved to cast himself wholly
on their good affections, than many zealous Patriots seemed
to be troubled at it ; knowing how ill it sorts with Kings when
they have no way to subsist, or carry on their great Designs,
but by casting themselves wholly on the love of the People.
These on the other side were no better pleased with hearing
his Majesty call the *Scots* by the name of *Rebels.*"   Indeed,
on this particular point, "the displeasure went so high, that
his Majesty finding into what condition he had cast himself,
was fain to call both Houses before him within two days
after, there to Explain, or rather to Retract so harsh a Title,
calling them afterwards by the name of his *Subjects* of *Scotland*, as he used to do ; which gave the Commons such a
sense of their Power, and of his Compliance, that they resolved
to husband both to their best advantage."

The day after the assembling of the Parliament, Convocation was opened at St Paul's.   It was saddened by the news
of the death of the Archbishop of York, Dr Neile.   To Laud
himself the death of this faithful friend must have been a
great blow, and a most disheartening one at such a critical
moment and in his state of extreme depression.   The first
business of Convocation, after the hearing of the sermon in
the choir of St Paul's, was to elect a prolocutor, and then an
adjournment was made to Westminster.

After the usual formalities—the protestation of the sub-
dean and prebends, &c.—and the presentation of the prolocutor in Henry Seventh's chapel, the archbishop "in an
eloquent but sad Oration, bemoaned the infelicities which he
saw hanging over the Church." [1]   Although no business of
importance was transacted that day, a sign of the times was
given, when a clergyman from the diocese of Worcester proposed a motion, " That they should endeavour (according to
the *Levitical* Laws) *to cover the Pitt which they had opened*,
and to prevent their Adversaries intention by condemning
such offensive Canons as were made in the last Convocation." [2]
Nothing, however, came of it.

Other troubles began to thicken for Laud and his friends.

---

[1] "Cyp. Ang.," p. 431.   [2] *Ib.*

Wentworth, now Earl of Strafford, who had been with the army in the North, was well aware that, in their Remonstrance, the Scots had complained against him for calling them traitors and rebels, and for his energy in endeavouring to thwart them in every possible way. This knowledge had been confirmed by a private warning that it would be more prudent for him either to return to Ireland, where he was popular with the army, or to go abroad until the threatened storm of popular ill-will should have passed over, and his friends, among whom may have been Laud, judging from Heylin's intimacy with their advice, recommended him not to fear lest his absence, should an impeachment take place, might be regarded as an acknowledgment of guilt, " where Partiality held the Scales, and Self-ends backt with Power, and made blind with Prejudice, were like to over-ballance Justice."

Strafford was inclined to listen to their advice, but the king desired his assistance in London, and assured him that " not a hair of his head should be touched by the parliament " ; so he braved his enemies, and came up to the metropolis to take his seat in the House of Lords. Even as he entered the House, he was followed closely by Pym, who went into the House of Commons and immediately made a speech, in which he declared him to be the " principal author and promoter of all those counsels which had exposed the kingdom to so much ruin." It was a remarkable speech ; nor was the speaker a man devoid of talent. Sprung from a wealthy Somersetshire family, he had been at Pembroke College, Oxford, and then studied for the law. He had become a Member of Parliament early in life, and had soon proved himself to be a bold and able debater.

So great was the influence of his declamation against Strafford that the House of Commons concurred in his desire for the impeachment, and he went, accompanied by the majority of the members of that House, to the Bar of the House of Lords for that purpose. There he was quite at home, for he had stood at that Bar both to impeach Buckingham and to arraign Mainwaring.

Strafford was in consultation with the king when Pym and

his companions entered the House of Lords. On hearing of
what was taking place, he hurried to the House, and was
about to take his usual seat, when there were loud cries that
he must withdraw. After an interval, a messenger recalled
him into the House, where he was informed that he must
kneel at the Bar, and then the Lord Keeper told him that,
as he had been impeached by the Commons, the House had
committed him to the custody of the Black Rod until he
should have cleared himself of the imputation of guilt.

It was thought by some people that, on this occasion,
Strafford did not exhibit his usual nerve or decision of
character. In fact, when Pym had impeached him, he showed
no fight at all, and, although no particular act of treason had
thus far been brought home to him, he was forthwith committed to the custody of the Black Rod. This took place a
week after the opening of Parliament, and a fortnight later
he was sent to the Tower.

Laud writes[1] :—" It is thought (and upon good Grounds)
that the *Earl of Strafford* had got Knowledge of the Treason
of some Men, and that he was preparing to accuse them.
And this Fear both hastened and heated the proceedings
against him. And upon *Dec. 4,* being *Friday*, his Majesty,
at the great Importunity of some Lords of his *Council,* gave
way that his *Council* should be examined upon Oath in the
Earl of Strafford's Case ; and I (with others) was examined
that very Day. There were great Thoughts of Heart upon
this Business, and somewhat vapoured out at Men's Tongues ;
but the thing was done."

Laud clearly disapproved of it, and considered the king
weak in yielding on this point. In the next paragraph he
tells us why he thought so much eagerness was shown to examine the Lords of the Council. It seems that, " after the
breaking up of the late *Parliament,* Sir *Hen. Vane,* at the
private *Committee* concerning the *Scotch* Affairs," instead of
merely " setting down the Heads of the Several Businesses
then Treated of," had " Writ down " in full " what every Man
said at the *Committee.*" Worse still, " by a cunning con-

---

[1] " History," p. 85.

trivance between his Son" and "himself, this Paper, or a Copy of it was delivered to some Members of the *House of Commons;* and in all probability, was the Ground of that which was done against the Lord *Strafford*, my self, and others, and the Cause, why the *King* was so hard pressed to have the Lords and others of his *Council* examined, was, that so Sir *Henry Vane* might upon Oath avow the Paper which his Son had seen and shewed; and others be brought to witness as much (had Truth, and their Memories been able to say as much) as his Paper."

With regard to the "cunning contrivance" between Sir Henry Vane and his son, both its authors were brought to book. This they had fully expected, and were equally prepared for. Clarendon gives a long and amusing description of what took place,—the virtuous indignation of the father, and the, if possible, more virtuous, although respectful, wrath of the son, and he ends by saying [1]:—" This scene was so well acted, with such Passion and Gestures, between the Father and the Son, that many Speeches were made in commendation of the Conscience, Integrity, and Merit, of the Young Man, and a motion made, ' That the Father might be enjoyn'd by the House to be Friends with his Son:' but for some time there was, in Publick, a great distance observ'd between them."

Most likely there had been some exceedingly free speaking at the private committee upon " the *Scotch* Affairs," and many things may have been said by both Laud and Strafford, which they never intended to be divulged in public; things, moreover, which would be exceedingly dangerous to their liberty, and even to their lives, when known to their enemies.

Strafford had not long been under arrest, when the king took a most unpropitious step, so far as Laud's interests were concerned, by the release of his enemy, Williams, Bishop of Lincoln. There can have no longer been any question of Charles having shaken himself free from the influence of Laud, when he could do such a thing as this. Like Laud, the king was frightened, as well he might be, and the two

---

[1] "History of the Reb.," vol. i. p. 230.

instances we have lately seen of his disapproval of Laud's proceedings make it appear that he was half inclined to attribute some of his own troubles to the want of tact of his archbishop.   On the 17th of November, Williams was received, and conducted into Westminster Abbey, by six bishops.[1]   Having entered the abbey, he officiated, the day being one of humiliation and prayer.   He afterwards took his seat in the House of Lords.

The reinstatement of Williams was a serious danger to the High-Church party ; but on the very day that he entered the abbey with so much pomp, another ominous event took place, close by, at St Margaret's, Westminster.   "The Minister Officiating the Second Service at the Communion-Table, according to the ancient Custom, was unexpectedly interrupted by the naming and singing of a Psalm, to the great amazement of all sober and well-minded men." [2]

Williams was not the only prisoner, sentenced by Laud, who was liberated.   The House of Commons also set free Bastwick, Prynne, and Burton, who arranged to meet on their journey back to London, and were triumphantly escorted by thousands "of the Puritan Faction," carrying "Bays and Rosemary in their hands."   Prynne had not reached London many hours before he was admitted to a private conference with the Bishop of Lincoln, nor can it be doubted that such a meeting boded no good to Laud, who had preached a long sermon to each, when passing sentence upon them, at their respective trials.

This interview took place early in December, and on the eleventh appeared the notorious "Root and Branch Petition." [3] It complained of "the Growth of Popery and increase of Papists, Priests and Jesuits in sundry places, but especially about London since the Reformation ; the frequent venting of crucifixes and Popish pictures both engraved and printed, and the placing of such in Bibles."

But it was against the Established Church that the petition

[1] " Cyp. Ang.," p. 435.   [2] *Ib.*, p. 439.
[3] Rushworth, iv. 93 ; Gardiner's " Const. Doc. of the Puritan Revolution,"
pp. 67 and foll.

more directly asserted itself, pointing out "the great conformity and likeness both contrived and increased of our
Church to the Church of Rome, in vestures, postures, ceremonies, and administrations, namely as the bishop's rochets
and the lawn-sleeves, the four-cornered cap, the cope and
surplice, the tippet, the hood, and the canonical coat; the
pulpits clothed, especially now of late, with the Jesuits
badge" (I.H.S.) "upon them in every way."

Then there was the superstitious "standing up at the *Gloria
Patri* and at the reading of the Gospel, the praying towards
the East, the bowing at the name of Jesus, the bowing to the
altar at the East, the cross in baptism, the kneeling at
communion."

Moreover, there was "the turning of the Communion Tables
altarwise, the setting images, crucifixes, and conceits over
them, the tapers and books upon them: the reading of the
second service at the altar, and forcing people to come up
thither to receive" (communion) "or else denying the sacrament to them; the turning the altar to be a mercy-seat, or
the place of God Almighty, which is a plain device to usher
in the mass."

The bishops, of course, were railed at also, nor altogether
illogically. "The offices and jurisdictions of archbishops,
lord bishops, deans and archdeacons, being the same way of
Church Government, which is in the Romish Church," . . .
"the same arguments supporting the Pope which do uphold
the prelates, the overthrowing the prelates, which do pull
down the Pope; the other Reformed Churches, having upon
their rejection of the Pope cast the prelates out also as
members of the beast, &c."

It was for this reason, said the petitioners, that "the prelates
here in England, by themselves or their disciples, plead and
maintain that the Pope is not Antichrist, and that the Church
of Rome is a true Church, hath not erred in fundamental parts,
and that salvation is attainable in that religion."

All these crying evils the petitioners wished to be eradi-
cated, "root and branch."

The House of Commons were turning their attention

towards the iniquities of another of Laud's friends. Secretary
Windebanke had signed warrants for the protection of several
Catholics, and for the discharge of others in prison.   It is true
that he had signed them all at the orders of the king, and
that, for his greater security, he had even obtained a written
pardon from the king himself; but Charles, unnerved and
demoralized, was very anxious to escape the odium of these
transactions.   Windebanke, therefore, escaped to France,
eventually became a Catholic, and died abroad.

In the middle of December, things looked more threatening every day and every hour for Laud.   He tells [1] us that
"there arose great and violent Debates in the *House of
Commons* against the *Bishops*, and particularly their *Votes in
Parliament.*"   On the 16th, a vote was taken against the
canons, as contrary to law, the rights of Parliament, and the
property and liberty of the subject, and as containing " matters
tending to Sedition."   " I," writes Laud, "was made the
Author of all, and presently a *Committee* put upon me to
inquire into my Actions and prepare a *Charge.*   The same
Morning in the *Upper-House*, I was Named as an *Incendiary*,
in an Accusation put in by the *Scottish Commissioners :* For
now by this Time they were come to the *Article* of the
Treaty, which reflected upon me.   And this was done with
great noise, to bring me into Hatred with the People, especially the *Londoners ;* who approved too well the Proceedings
of their Brethren the *Scots*, and debased the Bishops and the
Church Government in *England.*"

He cannot have failed to see for himself that the crisis
was at hand.   Ballads were "cried about *London-Streets*,"
abusing and deriding him.   Some of these were brought
both into the House of Commons and the House of Lords ;
and it was ominous that while the peers and the commons
handed them from one to the other and laughed at them, no
steps were taken to suppress them.

On the 18th of December, a direct accusation of high
treason was made against him in the House of Commons ;
but no particular charges were made ; these, it was said,

[1] " Hist.," p. 86.

should be drawn up in due time. Among the speakers was a member named Grymstone, who said :—" Look upon him as hee is in his Highnesse, and hee is the stye of all pestilent filth, that hath infected the State, and Government of the Church and Common Wealth."[1] What is now termed " Parliamentary Language " had not been invented in those days.

Denzell Hollys was chosen to convey the message to the Bar of the Upper House. As soon as he reached it, he impeached Laud for the crime of high treason ; he had hardly done so, when the Scottish Commissioners brought up the distinct charges they had promised against him, as an incendiary between the two nations.

I have several times said that, within the last few months, Laud's nerves had been considerably shattered ; yet, in the face of this double attack, he rose from his seat with his old courage, energy, and temper. It seemed that, when the battle really began, he forgot his fears and rushed eagerly into the fray. He not only indignantly protested his own innocence, but began angrily to arraign his accusers. His well-known irritable voice had regained all its wonted warmth, when a chill was given to its jarring tones by the cold incisive orders of the Earl of Essex, and Lord Saye and Sele, that he must submit himself to the House, which, without hearing his proffered defence, committed him, like Strafford, to the custody of the Black Rod.

Maxwell, the Gentleman Usher, whose prisoner he had now to consider himself, permitted him to return, in his own company, to his palace at Lambeth, in order that he might get, as he says,[2] " a Book or two to Read in, and such Papers as pertained to my defence against the *Scots.*" What follows is pathetic. "I stayed at *Lambeth* till the Evening, to avoid the gazing of the People." And again,[3] " When I was gone to *Lambeth*, after some little discourse (and sad enough) with my Steward, and some private Friends, I went into my chappel to Evening Prayer. *The Psalms* for that day[4] gave me much comfort, and were observed by some Friends then

[1] " Canterburie's Doome."   [2] Diary, p. 60.
[3] *Ib.*, p. 74.   [4] Psalms 93 and 94.

present, as well as by my self. And upon the Comfort I then received, I have every day since (unless some urgent Business prevented me) Read over both these *Psalms*, and, God willing, purpose so to do every day of my Life. Prayers being ended, I went with Mr *Maxwell*, as I was commanded; Hundreds of my Poor Neighbours standing at my Gates to see me go, and Praying heartily for my safe return to my House: For which, I blessed God, and them."

There is no passage more eloquent, in the whole of Mr Benson's graceful *Life of Laud*, than that [1] which treats of these events:—" I know of few authentic scenes which combine such tragic and pathetic elements—the long, restless day spent in the well-known house, musing over the sudden snapping off of all designs and treasured conceptions. It is not probable that he anticipated death, but it is certain that he expected to be sequestrated from his Archbishopric. We may stop to wonder a little over the thoughts of the busy self-willed man at such a crisis—so sure that he had been doing God's work, and yet so irresistibly arrested; and then the familiar household routine not even interrupted; the anxious wonderings and confabulations of chaplains, secretaries, and domestics; the silence in the corridors, and evening chapel as the day closed in; and the little active figure, the centre of so much life, moving to his place for the last time, almost broken down; then the barge ordered as usual, and the crowd gathering at the gates—perhaps the only people in England who felt a spark of love for the hard lonely man."

[1] P. 120.

CHAPTER XXXIV.

WITH Laud safe in custody (although in the private house of Maxwell, for the time being), his deadly enemy, Prynne, set to work with renewed vigour.

In order to comfort Laud, "a Parliament Man of good Note, and Interested with divers Lords," sent word to him, three days after his arrest, that, in consequence of his patience and "moderate Carriage" since his commitment, the peers were not now "so sharp against" him as they had been at first, and they were now determined *only* to turn him out of his archbishopric and the king's Council. Very cold comfort, indeed, did the poor man consider this well-intended message. "So I see," he says,[1] "what Justice I may expect; since here is a Resolution taken, not only before my Answer, but before any Charge was brought up against me." He would have considered this resolution trivial enough, and much to be desired, had he been aware of the real resolution of his enemies, which was to have his blood.

Meanwhile, he was well-treated and rather liked than otherwise under the roof of his jailer, Maxwell, where "he gained so much on the good opinion of the Gentlewoman of the House, that she reported him to some of her Gossips, to be one of the goodest men, and most Pious Souls, but with all one of the silliest fellows to hold talk with a Lady that ever she met with in all her life." Laud was not at all a "lady's man," although he was accustomed to the society of queens and princesses.

To wait an indefinite time, a prisoner in a private house, tried the patience of a man of a naturally impetuous, and habitually active temperament. Nothing happened. Each weary day and anxious hour passed without any charge being

---

[1] Diary, p. 60.

376

lodged against him. It must have seemed, as he had written half in jest, that his persecutors really intended to punish him, not only untried, but unaccused.

Laud was not kept at the king's expense at the Gentleman Usher's; for in fees and for his "Dyet," he was charged twenty nobles a day, and his bill, after being there two months and a half, came to £460, 13s. 4d.;[1] and, as he says, "Mr Maxwell had it all, without any Abatement."

At last the charges were prepared, and Laud was conducted to the House of Lords to hear them. Pym, Hampden, and Maynard carried them up from the Commons to the Lords, says Rushworth;[2] but Laud himself writes on Friday, February 26th[3]:—"This day I had been full ten weeks in restraint at Mr *Maxwell's* House. And this day, being *St Augustin's* day, my Charge was brought up from the House of Commons to the Lords, by Sir *Henry Vane* the Younger." (This was the Vane, who, he said, had made "a cunning conveyance" with his father in divulging what had been spoken in "the private *Committee* concerning the *Scotch* Affairs.") The charge "consisted of fourteen Articles."

The articles were read to him at the Bar, by "the Clerk of the Parliament." He at once made a short, but dignified reply, especially to a charge of encouraging the Catholic religion, "as if," says he, "I should profess with the Church of *England*, and have my Heart at Rome, and labour by all cunning ways to bring *Romish* Superstition in upon the *Kingdom*. This (*my Lords*) I confess, troubles me exceedingly; and if I should forget my self, and fall into passion upon it" (here the old familiar Laud comes out!); "I should but be in that case which St *Jerome* confessed he was in; when he knew not how to be patient, when Falsehood in Religion was charged upon him."

Having noticed some of the charges, he ended his speech, which was not intended to be a formal reply to them. His regular trial had yet to begin. For the present he was ordered to be committed to the Tower; but, for his con-

[1] "Hist.," p. 145.   [2] Vol. iii., pp. 195-199, &c.   [3] Diary, p. 60.

venience, his removal thither was deferred until the following
Monday. (It was now Friday.)

During the two intervening days, he cannot have looked
forward to his journey to the Tower with feelings altogether
devoid of dread. On the Friday afternoon, he sent his
steward to the Lieutenant of the Tower to arrange for his
lodging there "with as much convenience as might be."
When the Monday came, Maxwell had duties, as Gentleman
Usher, which prevented the journey to the Tower being made
very late in the evening, as Laud had specially wished, so as
to escape publicity; failing this, "Noon, when the Citizens
were at Dinner, was chosen as the next fittest time for
Privateness."[1] Maxwell, he says, "carried me in his Coach."
"All was well, till I passed through *Newgate Shambles*, and
entred into *Cheapside.*" (A place in which so many of
Laud's prisoners in the Star Chamber had been made to
stand in the pillory!) "There some one Prentice first
Hollowed out, more and" ("and more," is put in the margin)
"followed the Coach (the Number still increasing as they
went) till by that time I came to the *Exchange*, the shouting
was exceeding great. And so they followed me with Clamour
and Revilings, even beyond *Barbarity* it self; not giving over,
till the Coach was entred in at the *Tower-Gate.* Mr *Maxwell*,
out of his Love and Care, was extreamly troubled at it; but I
bless God for it, my Patience was not moved: I looked upon
a higher Cause, than the tongues of *Shimei* and his Children."
Or, as his biographer, Heylin, called them, "the Raskle
Rabble." It ought not, however, to be forgotten that Laud
had been very glad that Prynne, Burton, Bastwick, and others
should be exposed to the "Tongues of *Shimei* and his Children."

His imprisonment created a great sensation, not only in
England, but also on the Continent, and the very worst fears
were expressed as to the probable outcome of it. Grotius
sent his friend Pococke, an Oriental scholar, to offer him his
sympathy, and to beseech him to make his escape, assuring
him that if he would seek a refuge on the Continent, he would
be gladly welcomed.[2]

[1] "Hist.," p. 174.   [2] "Cal. Sta. Pa. Dom.," 1644-45; Preface, p. xxii.

To this the archbishop replied[1]:—"I can by no means be persuaded to comply with my friend Grotius's advice. An escape, indeed, is feasible enough ; yea, it is, I believe, the very thing which my enemies desire; for every day an opportunity for it is presented to me, a passage being left free, in all likelihood for this very purpose, that I should endeavour to take advantage of it ; but they shall not be gratified by me in what they appear to long for. I am almost 70 years old, and shall I now go about to prolong a miserable life, by the trouble and shame of flying? Besides, whither should I fly? . . . No, I am resolved not to think of flight, but, continuing where I am, patiently expect to bear what a good and wise Providence hath appointed me, of what kind soever it may be."

The very day that he was taken to the Tower, a committee was named in the House of Lords to examine into " Innovations in Doctrine or Discipline, introduced into the Church without Law since the Reformation." To Laud's intense indignation, it was to consist of ten earls, ten barons, and ten bishops ; so, as he writes, "the *Lay Votes* will be double to the *Clergy.*"

These ten clergy, or rather the other nine besides himself, were summoned in a letter by Laud's foe, Williams, Bishop of Lincoln, who wrote with his "best Wishes" "in *Christ Jesus*" to say that they were to attend "as Assistant in that *Committee*," and to help their lordships to find out what was " behoveful for the good of the Church and State." They were to "prepare" their "Thoughts, Studies and Meditations accordingly," and he recommended them "to God's protection," signing himself their "very loving Friend and Brother."[2] A copy of this got into Laud's hands and must have annoyed him excessively.

The poor prisoner "setled" himself in his "Lodging in the *Tower*," where, he says, "I pass my weary time as well as I can." After his active life, this must have been a most unwelcome change. When he had been there a fortnight, someone told him an anecdote, which he records as follows.[3]

---

[1] "Cal. Sta. Pa. Dom.," 1644-45; Preface, p. xxii.   [2] "Hist.," p. 175.   [3] *Ib.*

"On *Saturday*, *Mar.* 13, Divers Lords dined with the Lord
Herbert, Son to the Earl of *Worcester*, at his new House by
Fox-Hall in *Lambeth*. As they came back after dinner, three
young Lords were in a Boat together, and St *Paul's* Church
was in their Eye. Hereupon one of them said, he was sorry for
my Commitment, if it were but for the building of St *Pauls*,
which would go but Slowly on there-while. The Lord *Brook*,
who was one of the three, replyed, *I hope one of us shall live
to see, no one stone left upon another of that building.*"

This was not very consoling news ; for it showed that
others, besides the " Raskle Rabble," felt ill-will both towards
Laud and the church which he so greatly loved.

Three weeks after Laud had been imprisoned in the Tower,
a great trouble befell him in the trial of his bosom friend,
Strafford, in Westminster Hall ; it lasted about three weeks,
with a few intervals, and Laud says that "the Earl got all
the time a great deal of Reputation by his Patient, yet
Stout and clear Answers."[1]   The popular feeling against
him was, nevertheless, tremendous, and the names of all the
members of the House of Commons who opposed the bill of
attainder, "were Pasted up at the *Exchange* under the Title
of Straffordians."

Laud's anxiety as to the fate of his friend must have been
still further embittered by the very shilly-shallying conduct
shown by the king in the matter ; for Charles's faithlessness
threatened danger to his own life, as well as to Strafford's.
When the trial had been proceeding for about ten days, the
king went into the House of Lords and declared to the
members of both Houses that he had been present at each
day's hearing, and had listened to all the evidence and all
the arguments with the greatest care, and had come to the
conclusion "that his Fault, whatever it were, could not
amount to *Treason ;*" he added that he would never be
able to wrong his honour or his conscience by passing a bill
finding him guilty of treason ; but that if they would " proceed by way of *Misdemeanour*," "he would concur with them
in any sentence."

[1] "Hist.," p. 176.

It must have gone to Laud's heart to put on paper his disapproval of this conduct of the king, who had formerly obeyed him so implicitly, and whom he had loved with such devotion for so long a time ; but he would speak the truth and he proceeds :—" This displeased mightily, and I verily think it hastened the *Earl's* Death. And indeed to what end should *the King* come voluntarily to say this, and there, unless he would have abode by it, whatever came ? And it had been far more *Regal* to reject *the Bill* when it had been brought to him (his Conscience standing so as *his Majesty* openly professed it did), than to make this Honourable Preface, and let the *Bill* pass after."

How he must have wished that he could have been at the side of Charles to prevent his doing this stupid thing, as he flattered himself he had prevented his doing many a stupid thing in the past !

The mob was trying to intimidate the king, his court, and the Lords ; " Citizens of *London* and Prentices came down in Multitudes to *the Parliament*, called there for Justice, and pretended all Trade was stopp'd, till Justice was done upon the Earl of *Strafford*." Nor were they by any means unsuccessful. " Upon *Sunday, May* 9, *the King* was so laid at, and so frighted with these Bugbears, that if Justice were not done, and *the bill* passed for the Earl of *Strafford's* Execution, the Multitude would come the Next Day, and pull down *White-Hall* (and God knows what might become of the King himself), that these fears prevailing, *his Majesty* gave way, and *the Bill* passed ; and that Night late, Sir *Dudly Carlton*, one of the Clerks of the *Council*, was sent to the *Tower*, to give the Earl warning that he must prepare to Dye the *Wednesday* Morning following."

It is much to Laud's honour that he gives no further details of the king's weakness and faithlessness on this occasion, if he knew them, which he probably did. It is almost needless to say that every reader of English history is aware of the pitiable condition of vacillation, fear, and distress, in which the king spent that Sunday ; of the warning by Juxon —who was to succeed Laud in the Archbishopric of Canterbury and to attend Charles himself on the scaffold—that he ought on no account to shed innocent blood by consenting to the bill; of the sinister advice of Williams, Bishop of Lincoln, to the effect that whatever the king's private and individual opinion might be, he was bound to concur in that of his two houses of Parliament; and of the grave representations which were made to his Majesty of the dangers which would threaten himself and his family in the case of his rejecting the bill which would forfeit the life of his devoted friend and faithful servant.

Strafford, says Laud, "received the Message of Death with great Courage, yet Sweetness; (as Sir *Dudly* himself after told me :)." On the Monday morning, he sent for the Bishop of Armagh, who went to see Laud, when he left Strafford, and told him "that he never knew any Layman in all his Life, that so well and fully understood Matters of *Divinity*, as the *Earl* did, and that his Resolutions were as firm and good."

Laud then says that Strafford made "two Suits to his *Majesty*," the first that he might " Dye privately," the second that he might be respited till the Saturday. Charles sent both requests to the houses of Parliament, and both were refused.

And now Laud relates a circumstance which, had "the Church" been the Catholic Church, might have obtained for Strafford canonisation as a martyr.

"The *Earl* made these two Suits; in the mean time one Offer was made to him. It was this, That if he would employ his Power and Credit with *the King*, for the taking of *Episcopacy* out of the *Church*, he should yet have his Life. His Christian Answer was very *Heroical;* Namely, That *he would not buy his Life at so dear a rate.*"

For the next part of the account of Strafford's end, so far as it related to Laud, I must refer to Heylin.[1] The night before the execution, Strafford sent for the Lieutenant of the Tower and asked whether it would be possible that he might see the archbishop. The lieutenant replied that he had no power to grant his request without an order from Parlia-

---

[1] "Cyp. Ang.," p. 450.

ment. Then Strafford said that, if the interview were permitted, the lieutenant would be welcome to be present and
hear every word that passed between them; "for it is not a
time for him to plot Heresie, or me to plot Treason."

The lieutenant pleaded his inability and begged his lordship
to send a petition at once to the Parliament for the favour.

"No," answered Strafford, "I have gotten my despatch
from them, and will trouble them no more; I am now
Petitioning an Higher Court, where neither partiality can
be expected, nor Error feared." And then, turning to the
Archbishop of Armagh, who was present, he said that he
would tell him what he should have spoken to the archbishop, and would ask him to convey the matter to him.
"You shall desire the Archbishop to lend me his Prayers
this night, and to give me his Blessing when I do go abroad
tomorrow; and to be in his Window, that by my last
Farewel I may give thanks for this, and all other his former
Favours."

When Laud received this message, he said, "That in conscience he was bound to the first, and in duty and obligation
to the second; but he feared his weakness and passion would
not lend him eyes to behold his last Departure."

Strafford was undoubtedly Laud's greatest friend, and, now
that the king had shown his faithlessness, the loss of such a
friend would be so much the greater. It was only natural
that he should dread the last farewell, especially under such
trying circumstances.

The next morning dawned, and the hour arrived for
Strafford to leave his chamber and walk towards the scaffold.
As he drew near the window of the room which he was informed was that of the archbishop, he said to the Lieutenant
of the Tower:—"Though I do not see the Archbishop, yet
give me leave I pray you to do my last observance towards
his Rooms."

Almost at that moment the figure of Laud was seen behind
the iron bars of the window. Strafford immediately knelt
down and exclaimed, "My Lord, your Prayers and your
Blessing."

Laud's hands appeared between the bars, and his trembling voice was heard, blessing Strafford and praying for him. Then, in a second, all was silent, and the dark window was vacant: the poor, over-wrought old man had fallen back, overcome with grief.

Strafford, who had risen from his knees, perceived that his old friend was no longer at the window, and may have suspected the cause. Reverentially bowing down again, he cried out, so that Laud should hear him :—" Farewel, my Lord, God protect your Innocency."

The archbishop heard him and made another effort. He was just able to say " that he hoped by God's Assistance, and his own Innocency, that when he came to his own Execution (which he daily longed for) the World should perceive he had been more sensible of the Lord *Strafford's* Loss, than of his own: And good reason it should be so (said he) for the Gentleman was more serviceable to the Church (he would not mention the State) than either himself, or any of all the Church-men had ever been."

Heylin calls this, and not unjustly, " A gallant Farewel to so eminent and beloved a Friend."

Laud's account of this scene is much shorter. " As he passed by," he says,[1] " he turned towards me, and took the Solemnest leave, that I think was ever by any at a distance taken one of another; and this in the sight of," Lord Newport, Constable of the Tower, the Bishop of Armagh, Lord Cleveland, the Lieutenant of the Tower, " and divers other Knights and Gentlemen of Worth. Besides, though during the time of both our Restraints, and the nearness of our Lodgings, we held no Intercourse with each other; yet Sir *William Balfore*, then Lieutenant of the *Tower*, told me often what frequent and great expressions of Love the *Earl* made to me."

His description of the execution is dry and practical[2] :— " The *Earl* prepared himself: And upon *Wednesday* Morning, about Ten of the Clock, being *May* the Twelfth, he was Beheaded on the *Tower-Hill*, many Thousands beholding

[1] " Hist.," p. 179.   [2] *Ib.*, pp. 177, 178.

him. The Speech which he made at his End, was a great
Testimony of his Religion and Piety, &c." All this is a little
prosaic; but presently he becomes more animated at the
thought of his lost friend, and adds:—"Thus ended the
Wisest, the Stoutest, and every way the Ablest Subject,
that this Nation hath bred these many Years. The only
Imperfections which he had, that were known to me, were
his want of *Bodily Health*, and a Carelessness (or rather
Roughness) not to oblige any: And his Mishaps in this last
Action were, that he groan'd under the Publick Envy of the
Nobles, served a Mild and a Gracious Prince, who knew not
how to be, or to be made great;"—observe here how Laud
had lost confidence in, as well as respect for, Charles—
"and trusted false, perfidious and cowardly Men in the
Northern Imployment, though he had many Doubts put to
him about it."

Clarendon gives a longer, a more eloquent, and a more
critical summary of the character of Strafford; but, perhaps,
the best part of it is the conclusion, in which he says[1]:—"In
a word, the Epitaph which *Plutarch* records that *Sylla* wrote
for himself, may not be unfitly applied to him, 'That no man
did ever exceed him, either in doing good to his Friends, or
in doing Mischief to his Enemies; for his acts of both kinds
are most notorious.'" Excellent, again, is the passage in
which he says of him:—"Of all his Passions, his Pride was
most predominant: which a moderate exercise of ill Fortune
might have corrected and reform'd; and which was by the
hand of Heaven strangely Punish'd, by bringing his Destruction upon him by Two Things that he most despised, the
People and Sir *Henry Vane*."

Of Strafford's affection, Laud never harboured a doubt;
but, to his intense distress, others did so and more; for he
heard that "most notorious untruths" on this point "were
swallowed and believed by the most." "They delivered to
the World, that the Earl of *Strafford* drawing near to his
End, when he saw no Remedy, but he must Dye, fell into
great and passionate Expressions against me; that I and my

---

[1] "Hist. of the Reb.," vol. i. p. 260.

Counsels had been the Ruine of him and his House ; and that
he cursed me bitterly." Few, if any, of the many troubles
which befell Laud in the course of his long confinement in the
Tower of London, can have given him as much pain as these
" untruths " concerning his relations to his best, his dearest,
and his most faithful friend.

CHAPTER XXXV

LAUD was keenly sensitive, especially for a man who had for
so many years held prominent public positions. He constantly complains of "libels" both in his Diary and his History. Even in prison he laments that, not only libels, but
" *Ballads* against me were frequently sung up and down the
Streets. And (I thank God for it) they were as full of Falsehood as Gall. Besides, they made base Pictures of me;
putting me into a Cage, and fastning me to a Post by a Chain
at my Shoulder, and the like."[1] When one thinks of the
equanimity with which—let us say—cabinet ministers endure
the thousands of " base Pictures " which are " made " of them,
one can scarcely forbear a smile at the serious evil which
Laud considered such things to be. He goes on to say that
" divers of these *Libels* made Men sport in Taverns and Ale-
houses; where too many were as Drunk with Malice, as with
the Liquor they sucked in."

Among the "libels" published at this period is one which
was scarcely suited to an ale-house. It is entitled *The Recantation Of The Prelate of Canterbury : Being his last Advice to
his Brethren the Bishops of England: To consider his Fall,
observe the Times, forsake their Wayes, and to joyne in this
good work of Reformation. London, Printed* 1641. I have
used a copy of its frontispiece for my own. It is very serious
and heavy fooling, so much so, that it might almost deceive
a reader into fancying that it is what it pretends to be. It is
partly in prose and partly in verse. I will give a specimen
of each.

" Though I have hitherto deckt my self with a kinde of
Majesty, and Grace, in my Prelaticall pride arrayed with
Splendor, and taught the gazing times to hide my faults,

---

[1] " Hist.," p. 180.

giving my Plots good Fortune, yet behold, an ungratious light (sudden as a Tempest at Sea) hath discovered my nackednesse, and publisht my shame; I am vile, and abased, trode down, and hid in the dust; Judgment and Justice take hold on me, and cast abroad the rage of their wrath, which will certainly extend their terrours to you" (the rest of the bishops), "if you forsake not these wayes, whose going down are to the chambers of death."[1]

He is made to give "the world's estimation" of himself in the following lines[2] :—

> " Sp'rit of Delusion, Church and State
> Have found this wrapt in thy black fate :
> Thou roarest forth the Canon law,
> And trembling madst them stand in aw,
> And both the Scepters swaya'st, but now
> Thy Mitre tumbles from thy brow.
> Thy maske is torn, and we do see
> The flames of thine adulterate eye,
> 'Twas from the North was heard the voice
> Making all England to rejoyce,
> Which first betrayed thee to thy shame,
> And did display thy stinking fame :
> With tyrant Laws, and Iron rod,
> Thou mad'st the prouder Mountains nod,
> And Cædars reel, Thence thou wouldst try
> The Artick Pole, and reach the Skie,
> But thence great terrours, lightnings, thunder
> Did teare thy throne, thy selfe asunder,
> And drown'd thee in eternal night
> Proud and counterfeited light."

A more serious evil shortly befell him in "a Tertian Ague, which," he says, "was Comfortless in a Prison." It was fortunately of short duration, and then he was restored to his usual state of health, "the only Comfort" he had "in this time" of his "Affliction."

And here I may observe, that with the exception of this short attack of ague and a strain in his leg, which laid him up for a long time, Laud's health, and certainly his nerves, appear to have improved during the four years which he

[1] P. 4. [2] P. 18.

spent in the Tower, in spite of the anxieties which he underwent there.   At sixty-eight, after a very active life, the
beneficial effects of the rest and quiet of the old fortress seem
to have more than counteracted the evil consequences of the
disgrace, solitude, and threatening prospects of his imprisonment.   It should be remembered that the surroundings of
the Tower of London were very different then from what
they are now; instead of the densely packed population, of
a low class, which at present half-encircles it, and the filthy
Thames, the overgrown Billingsgate market, and the prodigious modern dockyards in its neighbourhood, a few houses
here and there in the open fields, markets and dockyards on
what would now be called very diminutive scales, and the
comparatively clean river did little to pollute the atmosphere
of the fine old building, standing out conspicuously by itself.
Even in these days, officers quartered at the Tower do not
find much fault with it on the score of insalubrity, and in the
seventeenth century, its best "lodgings," as they were called,
probably offered not unhealthy places of retirement for over-
worked old gentlemen, while the Tower gardens afforded
them sufficient opportunities of getting fresh air and moderate
exercise.   Certainly, many lived there to considerable ages,
and, had it not been for the executioner's axe, very likely
Laud might have become an octogenarian in his prison.

In June 1641, knowing that he was charged with treason
by the civic authorities of Oxford, for his proceedings in the
regulation of that city in his own name, as chancellor, he
sent to the king, through the Bishop of London, to say that
although he had answered all the complaints which had been
made against him in the matter, he considered it "requisite"
that he should "Resign the *Chancellorship* of that place."
He gave "*His Majesty* such Reasons, as he approved," for
his doing so; and it is not impossible that this ready approval
of his Majesty may not have been altogether gratifying to
him.

"The truth is," he says,[1] "I suffered much by the Clamours
of the Earl of *Pembroke*, who thought it long, till he had

[1] "Hist.," p. 181.

that place, which he had long gaped for: And after the
Cloud was once spread over me, spared me in no Company;
though I had in all the time of my Prosperity observed him
in *Court*, more than ever he deserved of me."

To have to give up to an enemy a post which he had held
so long and with so much pride, in his dearly beloved Oxford,
must have been a cruel blow!

The same autumn, King Charles "rode away Post into
Scotland." There were no consultations with Laud before
he made important expeditions now, and his former mentor
seemed to have his misgivings as to what foolish things his
old pupil, with no tutor to look after him, might be guilty of.
He says "there was great Scanning about this Journey." I
may add, however, in the words of Laud himself, "What the
King did in *Scotland*, hath no Relation, for ought I yet hear,
to this poor Story of mine."

In September 1641, Laud had the great misfortune to
lose his old factotum. He says of this trouble, "my Ancient,
Loving, and Faithful Servant, and then my *Steward*, after he
had served me full Forty and Two Years, dyed, to my great
both loss and grief. For all my Accounts since my Commitment, were in his Hands." Of his death, just at a time
when he himself was in such trouble, he writes:—"So true
it is, that Afflictions seldom come single."

True indeed; for another was treading on the heels of the
one just mentioned.

There was a parliamentary recess, during which the Judge
of the Prerogative died. This post was in the gift of the
Archbishop of Canterbury, and Laud promptly appointed
a certain Dr Merricke. Then a "Dr *Duck* missing his hopes
of this *Office*, by his own absence and default, and finding
me under this thick Cloud, hoped to have wrested this *Office*
out of my Hands, and his to whom I had given it," says
Laud. "This was one of the basest, and most ungrateful
parts, that ever Man played me." Duck tried to oust Merricke by law, and herein he failed; but Williams, who had
now been made Archbishop of York, induced the Lords to
sequester Laud's right of jurisdiction as archbishop until

such a time as he should be either acquitted or convicted of the charge of high treason which had been brought against him, and, further, that " concerning these Ecclesiastical Benefices, Promotions, or Dignities, that " were " in his disposing, he " should present for approval to the House of Lords the names of such persons as he proposed to appoint to them. Laud thought this " very hard " ; but really, in the case of an archbishop awaiting his trial for high treason, it was only what should have been expected. He appears to have forgotten that Abbot's jurisdiction was for some time sequestered, when he was archbishop, and that he himself had had the principal hand in administering it.

" The day on which the Houses " of Parliament met again, says Macaulay,[1] " is one of the most remarkable epochs in our history. From that day dates the corporate existence of the two great parties which have ever since alternately governed the country." " During some years they were designated as Cavaliers and Roundheads. They were subsequently called Tories and Whigs ; nor does it seem that these appellations are likely soon to become obsolete." Nevertheless, we have had Conservatives and Liberals, and Caves of Adullam and Fourth Parties, as well as Unionists and Separatists, since then, and of Tories and Whigs we now hear little !

When the king returned from Scotland, he was received in London " with great State and Joy, and Sumptuously Entertained." In old days, Laud would have been one of the first men he would have seen and confided in ; now, Laud was under lock and key at the Tower and the king made no sign to him. Still, Laud writes that his good reception " made divers Men think, there would have been a Turn in the present business " ; and this, of course, might have meant saving Laud's life, and possibly even a restoration of his dignities ; but it was not to be. " What it might have proved," he writes, " if the *King* would have presently and vigorously set himself to vindicate his own Just Power, and leave them their Antient and Just Priviledges, is not I think

[1] " Hist. of Eng.," vol. i. chap. i.

hard to judge. But he let it cool, and gave that which is truly the *Malignant Faction* (but call others so) time to underwork him, &c." The fact was, he would appear to imply, that Charles had not got himself at his elbow now; so what could be expected?

It is amusing to read that Williams, who had but lately got out of the Tower and got Laud into it, and had succeeded in getting himself made as good an archbishop as his rival, was suddenly sent back to prison in that very same Tower, and, like Laud, for high treason. Both these deadly enemies, therefore, were locked up in the Tower at the same time, and both on charges of high treason. It was fortunate that there were good thick walls between them.

Nor was Williams sent alone; nine other bishops were sent to the Tower with him; so that there were, in all, eleven bishops in the Tower, including two archbishops. Besides this formidable array, there was a sort of "overflow meeting," as it is the fashion to say in these days, at the house of Maxwell, which Laud had left but a few months earlier; for here a couple more bishops, old and infirm bishops, were prisoners. Heylin, as might be expected, writes of the incarceration of Williams with the greatest satisfaction.[1] "The Archbishop of *York* was now so much declined in favour, that he stood in as bad termes with the Common People, as the other" [Laud] "did. His Picture cut in Brass, attired in his Episcopal Robes, with his square cap upon his head, and Bandileers about his Neck, shouldring a Musket upon one of his shoulders, &c." "Together with which a book was Printed, in which he was Resembled to the *Decoy-Duck* (alluding to the *Decoyes* in *Lincolnshire* where he had been Bishop), restored to Liberty on design, that he might bring more Company with him at his coming back, and a device Ingraven for the Front of the Book, which represented the conceit; and that not unhappily. Certain I am that our Archbishop in the midst of those sorrows seemed much pleased with the Fancy, whither out of his great Love to wit, or some other self-satisfaction which he found therein, is be-

[1] "Cyp. Ang.," p. 460.

yond my knowledge." It can hardly be beyond the knowledge of posterity that it was the "self-satisfaction which he
found therein" which pleased Laud, and that his gratification
did not proceed purely from "his great Love to wit."

The offence committed by these delinquent bishops—I
write of the twelve, of course, and not of Laud—had been
that they had had the audacity to present a "Petition and
Protestation" to the king, asserting that they had "been at
several times violently Menaced, Affronted, and Assaulted
by multitudes of People, in coming to perform their service
to" the House of Lords; that they had been "chased away
and put in danger of their lives"; and that they dared "not
sit to Vote in the House of Peers" unless his Majesty would
"secure them from all Affronts, Indignities, and Danger in
the Premises." Nor were their fears " built upon Fancies and
Conceipts, but upon such Grounds and Objects, as " might
"well terrific Men of great Resolution and much Constancy."
Yet they were "called upon, by several and respective Writs,
under great Penalties, to Attend in *Parliament*," and give
their votes. All they begged for was to " be protected from
force and violence." As a guarantee of their good faith, they
further protested that they did "abominate all Actions and
Opinions tending to *Popery*."

So far, so good; unfortunately they added that "all Votes,
Resolutions, and Determinations" passed during "their forced
and violented absence" from "the said Honourable *House*,"
were "in themselves null." This was more than the House
of Commons could endure, and it there and then impeached
the dozen bishops for high treason.

The nervous " Head of the Church " bore the imprisonment
of so large a portion of his bench of bishops with praise-
worthy indifference; but there is a point at which a worm
will turn, and in Charles's case it was a hint that the Commons
contemplated an impeachment of the Queen.

Four days after the bishops had been sent to the Tower,
the Attorney-General, at the king's command, appeared at the
Bar of the House of Lords—a hard-worked tribunal of late—
and impeached Pym, Hampden, Holles, Stroud, Lord Kim-

bolton, and Haslerig[1] for high treason. Instead of ordering them at once into custody, the House of Lords appointed a committee to search for precedents. This maddened Charles, who, on his own responsibility, sent a serjeant-at-arms to demand the persons of the impeached members in the Lower House. The Commons, instead of sending the five members, sent a message to say that they required time for mature deliberation. At this, the king was still more angry, and, the next day, he went, in a rather melodramatic fashion, to the House of Commons in person, accompanied by his guards and a number of officers with drawn swords to seize his prey. The objects of his vengeance, however, had avoided a scene, by the very simple method of absenting themselves, and Charles was placed in a ridiculous position, for getting into which he was condemned by friends as well as foes.

The Commons adjourned for a week, and then the five impeached members came to the House by water, with an escort of two thousand sailors in boats, while eight pieces of cannon were mounted, and detachments of the trained bands were placed on each bank of the river for their defence. On landing they were received by four thousand mounted horsemen, and, amidst shouts of joy and the music of military bands, they walked in procession to the House of Commons, the populace execrating the king in shouts and screams as they passed Whitehall.

This complete defeat of the king must have been sad news to Laud, and it left him little hope of escape from the block and the axe.

He writes that the king and queen had gone to Dover, and that her Majesty had resolved to " go into *Holland*, with her young Daughter the *Princess Mary*, who the Year before was Married to the *Prince of Aurange* his Son. But the true Cause of this intended Journey, was to be out of the Fears, Discontents and Dangers (as she conceived) of the present Times."

The question now presents itself whether Laud, in spite of the dignified protest against all idea of attempting an escape,

---

[1] Lingard, vol. vii. chap. vi.

which he is said to have sent to Grotius soon after he had
been taken to the Tower, did not, later on, wish that he, too,
could take a "journey" to the Continent, and get clear away
from " Fears, Discontents and Dangers." Who could blame
him if he did? Windebanke had fled abroad, so had Cottington, so also had Lord-Keeper Finch; why should not
Laud do the same—if he could?

It may be worth while to notice here a passage from Lingard, which has some bearing on this matter[1]:—" There is
however, some reason to believe that, in the solitude of his
cell, and with the prospect of the block before his eyes, he
began to think more favourably of the Catholic church. At
least, I find Rosetti inquiring of Cardinal Barberini whether,
if Laud should escape from the Tower, the pope would afford
him an asylum and a pension in Rome. He would be content with one thousand crowns—' il quale, quando avesse
potuto liberarsi dalle carceri, sarebbe ito volontieri a vivere e
morire in Roma, contendandosi di mille scudi annui.' Barberini answered, that Laud was in such bad repute in Rome,
being looked upon as the cause of all the troubles in England, that it would previously be necessary that he should
give good proof of his repentance; in which case he should
receive assistance, though such assistance would give a colour
to the imputation that there had always been an understanding between him and Rome. ' Era si cattivo il concetto, che
di lui avevasi in Roma, cioè che fosse stato autore di tutte le
torbolenze d'Inghilterra, che era necessario dasse primo segni
ben grandi del suo pentimento. Ed in tal caso sarebbe stato
ajutato; sebene saria paruto che nelle sue passate resoluzioni
se la fosse sempre intesa con Roma.'—From the MS. abstract
of the Barberini papers made by the canon Nicoletti soon
after the death of the cardinal."

To put a right interpretation upon these exceedingly important letters is not very easy. Did Rosetti speak on his
own authority only, or on that of Laud himself, when he
asserted that he would " be content with one thousand
crowns" as a pension? It reads as if he had had better

[1] " Hist. of Eng.," vol. viii., note at the end of chap. i.

grounds than his own expectations when he wrote so decisively.

Then, why a pension? A pension presupposes past services. What services had Laud ever rendered to the Pope? Barberini himself notices this point, when he says that "such assistance would give a colour to the imputation that there had always been an understanding between him and Rome." It may be replied that Barberini does not deny that there had been some such understanding. To this, on the other side, it might be answered that Barberini distinctly states that he "was in bad repute in Rome, being looked upon as the cause of all the troubles in England," and that, before any help could be given to him, "it would previously be necessary that he should give good proof of his repentance." Even to this a counter reply is open. Barberini says that if "he should give good proof of his repentance," "he should receive assistance." Now, why should he receive assistance? Is it usual to give pensions to repentant heretics and persecutors of the Church? Converts would be expensive at a thousand crowns a head, and much more at a thousand crowns a year for the rest of their lives. It is very noticeable, too, that not a word is said on either side about any question of his conversion. Altogether, it might be maintained, with some colour, that this correspondence leads to the supposition that, at one time or another, if not from time to time, the authorities at Rome came to some understanding with Laud that, in return for certain benefits on their part, (whether monetary or otherwise, or whether personal or otherwise, there is nothing to show), he should contrive to control the persecution of Catholics in England, which the laws of that country enjoined, within the narrowest possible limits; that he had fulfilled his promise faithfully up to a certain point ; but that, when the Puritans and Covenanters had raised an outcry against him for his toleration of Popery, he had become alarmed and had permitted, and even perpetrated, cruel proceedings against Catholics in England, and that it was for this offence that he must give good proof of his repentance, before he could receive an asylum and

a pension for his former services. Those who choose to hold
such a theory, might not unreasonably refer to the story of
the offers of a cardinal's hat, as tending to prove that overtures were made to him by Rome, that he may have been
told that if he would become a Catholic, he would be made
a cardinal, and that even if he would suppress the persecution of the English Catholics he should be well paid for so
doing.

Another thing in favour of the advocates of such a theory
is that Cardinal Barberini undoubtedly sent money, in order
to obtain relief for the Catholics in England, through other
channels. Henrietta Maria, in 1641 or 1642, applied for
assistance in the troubles of her husband to the Pope, asking
him for a grant of a hundred and fifty thousand crowns out
of the treasury in the Castle of St Angelo,[1] and promising in
return that the king should forthwith abolish the penal laws
against Catholics in Ireland, and, as soon as possible, against
those in England also. The Holy Father knew a little too
much of Charles to be tempted by the offer of such a bar-
gain, and replied that the papal treasury was a trust which
could only be applied for the benefit of Catholic princes,
nor even in their case except where their interests coincided
entirely with those of the Church; but Barberini (his nephew),
in conveying the refusal, gave the queen a present of thirty-
five thousand crowns out of his own purse, hoping thereby
to induce her husband to show favour to the poor persecuted
English Catholics.

Looking at the matter from every point of view, the relations of Laud to the Roman authorities cannot, on the
evidence at present available, be at all definitely ascertained.
I cannot find any certain proof that he ever gave signs of
an inclination to become a Catholic, and I should not like
to think that he took anything in the shape of a bribe for
tempering his zeal against the "popish recusants"; at the
same time, it must be admitted that, in spite of his declama-
tions against their errors and their "unconformableness," his
angry attempt at a refutation of Father Fisher's explanation

[1] Lingard's "Hist.," vol. vii. chap. vi.

of the Catholic position, and his protest on the scaffold itself
that he had "always lived in the Protestant religion" and
was about to die in it, he acted, on the whole, and except in
a few aggravated instances, far more leniently, and with much
greater toleration towards the Catholics than towards those in
his own Church who held certain views which were different
from his own and transgressed what he considered to be its
laws, and the question remains whether he did so from purely
disinterested motives. It is true that in those days little was
thought of accepting a bribe ; but, while I have done all in
my power to do ample justice to the opposite point of view,
from my own it appears that Laud was probably quite
guiltless of having been influenced in his conduct towards
Catholics by any presents, or income, or pension received
from Rome ; and I have come to this conclusion, not so much
from any evidence on this particular point, as from a study
of the man's whole life and character, with which any such
conduct would have been exceedingly inconsistent.

The backsliding of the king—King Charles the Martyr !—
was a perpetual sorrow, as well as danger, to Laud in his
prison. On his very journey to Dover, to get the queen safe
out of the country, the king sent a message to both Houses
of Parliament, in which these words occurred [1] :—" Concerning
the Government and Liturgy of the Church, *his Majesty* is
willing to declare, that he will refer that whole Consideration
to the Wisdom of his *Parliament*, which he desires them to
enter into speedily, that the present Distractions about the
same may be composed, &c." To refer the government of
the Church and the liturgy of the Church to the greatest
enemies of both, was practically to sacrifice his Church in
order to save his own head, and, if possible, his crown on the
top of it. Well might Laud write, " So here they are made
Masters of all, and in a time of great exasperation against the
Clergy and the *Bishops*." The latter, too, were at that time
turned out of the House of Lords ; so they could not vote
in any legislation which might take place about ecclesiastical
matters.

[1] " Hist.," p. 188.

The very day that this objectionable message was sent by
the king, an order was issued by the House of Lords that
" the Twelve Bishops might put in Bayl if they would."
They had now been imprisoned more than six weeks in the
Tower, and " They were glad Men, procured their Bayl, and
went out of the Tower." This order for their release on bail
" was known to the *House* of *Commons* " well enough ; but
they pretended to be ignorant of it and did nothing to prevent the twelve bishops from walking out of prison. When,
however, they " were sure the *Bishops* were come forth and
gone to their several Lodgings, they sent a Message to *the
Lords*, that they desired *the Bishops* might be presently re-
manded to safe Custody, or else they might and would Protest against their Lordships for Breach of the Privileges of
their *House :* Because being Impeached by them, *the Lords*
had Bayled them, without acquainting them first with it in a
Parliamentary way."

The Commons, therefore, had waited until the bishops had
actually been set at liberty on the order of the Lords, on purpose to let the latter put themselves, as the Commons held,
in the wrong ! As Laud writes, " though the *Bishops* had a
great Indignity and Scorn put upon them ; yet that which
was put upon *the Lords* was far greater."

Instead of showing firmness, the Lords, following the example of the king, lost courage and yielded, " and the poor
Bishops were brought back again to the *Tower* the next
Morning." And there we must leave them for the present,
merely remarking that they were kept in prison, from first to
last. " just eighteen weeks." [1]

I will end this chapter by observing that, as if there were
not already troubles enough with Scotland, a rebellion broke
out in Ireland, of which Laud writes :—" The Irish pretended
the *Scots* Example, and hoped they should get their Liberties,
and the Freedom of their *Religion*, as well as they."

[1] "Cyp. Ang.," p. 466.

CHAPTER XXXVI.

ONE Sunday, Laud received a visit at the Tower from a member of the House of Commons, Mr Edward Hyde, who was many years later to become Lord Clarendon and to write much about him in his *History of the Great Rebellion.* They were sitting together in Laud's bedroom, when a message was delivered that a Mr Hunt desired an interview with him. Leaving Hyde in the inner room, Laud went into his sitting-room, where he found "a tall Gentleman" waiting for him. This man began by saying that, although he was unknown to the archbishop, he came to do him a "service in a great Particular," and gave his assurance that he had come purely on his account, not having been sent by any statesman or member of Parliament, and with no wish for any reward, but solely and only in the hope of being able to be useful to his grace. Laud "wondred what the matter should be." Presently his tall visitor "drew a Paper out of his Pocket" and gave it him to read. It contained four articles drawn up against him, all of them, he says, "touching my near Conversation with *Priests*, and my endeavour by them to subvert Religion in *England*." Mr Hunt told him that they had not yet been presented to the House of Commons, but probably soon would be. They were signed "by one *Willoughby*," who, Mr Hunt said, "was a Priest, but now turned." Laud asked Mr Hunt what service he hoped to render him by showing him this paper. Mr Hunt replied that he left the archbishop to consider that for himself, and again repeated his statement that his motives were purely disinterested. At this Laud grew angry, and told him that Willoughby "was a *Villain* to subscribe such a paper," and that he might present it to the Parliament whenever he pleased.

400

Then, he tells us,[1] " I left him and his Paper, and returned to
Mr *Hide* into my Bed-Chamber.   There I told him, and my
Servant Mr *Richard Cobb*, all that passed : And they were
glad I gave him so short and so harsh an Answer, and did
think as I my self did, that it was a Plot to intrap me.   After
they were gone, I sat thinking with my self, and was very
Sorry that my Indignation at this base *Villany* had made
me so hasty to send *Hunt* away, and that I did not desire
Mr *Lieutenant of the Tower* to seize on him, till he brought
forth this *Willoughby*.   I am since informed, that this *Hunt*
is a Gentleman that hath spent all or most of his Means :
and I verily believe this was a Plot between him and *Willoughby* to draw Money from me to conceal the *Articles ;* in
which way had I complyed with him, I had utterly undone
my self."

A meaner trick to try to extort money from the poor old
man, in his trouble, could hardly be imagined.

A fortnight later, a physical misfortune befell him.   A
tendon of his right leg " brake asunder," as he was walking
up and down a large room, of which he had the use, before
he went to dinner.   He was walking at the time " upon plain
Boards, and had no uneven step nor slip, not so much as a
turning of" his " Foot aside upon any chink.   This *Tendon*,
or part of the main Sinew above" his " Heel, brake just in
the same Place where" he " had unhappily broken it before,"
fourteen years earlier.   The consequent " Lameness continued two whole Months, before" he " was able to go down
Stairs to take any Air to refresh" himself ; and it was long
after even that date that he " received any competent Measure
of Strength."

While he was laid up, he was worried by orders from the
Parliament as to the disposal of his preferments.   In being
forced to submit, he felt that he was not only yielding a
trust, but that his power was being taken away from him in
every sense.

At last the poor lame prisoner thought he would try
to go to church.   " I made a shift between my Man and my

---

[1] " Hist.," p. 190.

Staff," he says,[1] "to go to Church. There preached one Mr
Jostin.[2] His Text, *Judg.* 5, 23, *Curse ye Meroz*, &c. To
pass over what was strangely Evil throughout his Sermon,
his Personal Abuse of me was so foul and so palpable, that
Women and Boys stood up in the Church, to see how I
could bear it: And this was my first Welcome into the
Church, after my long Lameness." He then says that he
bore it very well, adding " God forgive them."

After this he, personally, " had some quietness " ; but none
the less " all things grew higher and higher between the King
and the *Parliament*, to the great Dammage and Distraction
of the Kingdom." Laud might well say this. The king and
his Parliament were, in fact, actually at war ; while he " had
some quietness," the royalist and parliamentary troops were
in bloody conflict, and at least a thousand men were laid
dead at the single battle of Edge Hill.

It was not so long since Charles had reprimanded Laud for
endeavouring to propitiate the Puritans by an exhibition of
stern measures upon the Catholics ; but in the early part of
this ill-fated civil war, the king paraded his own Protestantism
by ordering two priests to be put to death at Tyburn and a
couple more at York.[3] But I am writing a life of Laud, and
not a history of England ; so I cannot follow Charles I. in
his battles or describe his policy, further than it relates,
directly or indirectly, to the subject of my memoir.

The clash of arms in the field does not seem to have
affected Laud so much as the seizure of his own arms at
Lambeth palace by " Captain *Royden* and his Company, by
Order of *Parliament*," on the 19th of August. They arrived
at Lambeth about " seven of the Clock in the Evening,"
" stayed there all Night, and searched every Room, and
where any Key was not ready, brake open Doors: And the
next Morning they carried my Arms away in Carts to *Guild-
Hall, London ;* and I was sufficiently abused all the way by
the People, as my Arms passed. They gave out in *London*,
there were Arms for Ten Thousand Men ; whereas there was
not enough for Two Hundred. And the Arms I bought of

---

[1] " Hist.," p. 196.　　　[2] Jocelin.　　　[3] Lingard, vol. viii. chap. i.

my Predecessor's Executors; only some I was forced to mend, the Fashion of Arms being changed."

Within three months another unwelcome visit was paid to "my House at *Lambeth.*" The callers were two members of the House of Commons, this time, accompanied by some musketeers. They searched, not for weapons, but "for Mony," and walked off with £78, which they took from the archbishop's official receiver, stating that it was required "for the Maintenance of *the King's children.* God of his Mercy look favourably upon the King, and bless his *Children* from needing any such poor Maintenance."

Once again, before the year was out, visitors arrived at "Lambeth-House," in the shape of "Souldiers," who, as Oxford undergraduates would term it, "made hay" in Laud's chapel, and "offer'd violence to the Organ." Just before Christmas, says Heylin :[1]—"*Leighton* the Schismatick, who had before been sentenced in the Star-Chamber for his libellous and seditious Pamphlets, came with an Order from" the Commons "to dispossess the Souldiers of their quarters there, and turn his house into a Prison."

I must return now to September, when, says Laud,[2] "*the Bishops* were voted down in the *House of Commons.*" "And that Night there was great Ringing," which he himself could not have failed to hear from his chambers in the Tower, "and Bonfires in the City; which I conceive was cunningly ordered to be done by Alderman *Pennington*, the new *Lord Mayor*, chosen in the room of Sir *Richard Gurney*, who was then in *the Tower.*"

On the tenth of the same month, the bishops were "Voted down" by the Lords also; whereupon Laud writes:—"So it seems I must live to see my Calling fall before me." That he would leave the Tower "by any other door than the door of death,"[3] he had long ceased to hope; but to see the Anglican episcopacy appear to fall before him was a bitter sorrow.

In October it was resolved "That all Rents and Profits of all *Arch-Bishops, Bishops, Deans* and Chapters, and other De-

---

[1] "Cyp. Ang.," p. 467.   [2] "Hist.," p. 196.   [3] "Cyp. Ang.," p. 467.

linquents, should be Sequestered for the Use and Service
of the Common-Wealth." There was something specially
cutting in the words "and other Delinquents." By this
ordinance Laud says :— "All the Profits of my *Arch-
Bishoprick* were taken away from me, and not one Penny
allowed me for Maintenance."

A further discomfort came, in a few days, in the form of an
order that no prisoner in the Tower should keep more than
two servants, or speak to anyone, except in the presence of a
warder. He "humbly besought the *Lords*," on account of
his age and infirmities, to allow him to have a cook and a
butler, in addition to two servants who attended him in his
rooms—rather a liberal allowance, one might suppose, for a
prisoner ; but it was granted.

Ill-tidings now followed each other rapidly. News came
that his own "Cathedral Church of *Canterbury* was grossly
Prophaned ; yet far worse afterward."

In January 1643, "the *Bill* passed in the *Lords House* for
abolishing of *Episcopacy*. God be merciful to this sinking
Church." Even a little revenge in the midst of such troubles
was sweet. It will be remembered that Lord Brook, when
some one had praised Laud for restoring St Paul's Cathedral,
had said he hoped to live to see the time when one stone of
it should not be left standing upon another. He was a bitter
enemy to the Church, and to the very name of episcopacy.
Well, this wicked man, to Laud's evident satisfaction, met
with his deserts. He was just going to order an attack on
the close of Lichfield Cathedral, and was "taking view of the
place, from a Window in a House opposite to *the Close*," with
the "Bever" of his helmet raised, to get a better view, and
naturally thinking "that a Musket at such a distance could
have done him but little harm ; yet was he Shot in the left
Eye, and killed Dead in the place without speaking one
word." He adds with gusto :—"This great Enemy to
Cathedral-Churches died thus fearfully in the Assault of a
Cathedral. A fearful manner of Death in such a Quarrel !"
And then, recalling Lord Brook's after-dinner remark about
himself and St Paul's Cathedral, he says :—" That Church

stands yet, and that Eye is put out that hoped to see the Ruins of it."

A stranger to Laud came to the Tower one day and told him a most alarming piece of gossip—namely, that he was to be sent to *New England*. This would indeed have been falling out of the frying-pan into the fire. Considering the gentle manner in which the New-Englanders had treated the Quakers—women as well as men—what would they not have done to Laud, who was reputed among them to have been the primary cause of their exile and all their woes? A couple of months after he had heard this rumour, " it was moved in the *House of Commons*, to send " Laud "to *New England;* but it was rejected. The Plot was laid by *Peters*, *Wells*, and others of that Crew, that so they might insult over "[1] him.

A petty annoyance was the seizure of his furniture and other effects at Lambeth, and their public sale. Although the sum they realised in no way affected him, it appears to have mortified him to hear that they were sold ." scarce at a third of their worth." A more serious matter to his own personal comfort was an order issued on the very day of what would now be called the sale of the " Laud Collection," to the effect that he was not to go out of his chambers without his " Keeper, so much as to take the Air." He sarcastically calls the first of these annoyances "an Exemplary piece of Justice," the other " of Mercy."

" Much about this time," he received another letter from his Majesty. Letters from Charles were no longer written in a tone of affectionate banter. The missive in question required him " that as oft as any Benefice or other Spiritual Promotion whatsoever should fall void in " his gift, he " should dispose it only to such as *his Majesty* should name unto him." In old days, his Majesty used to ask him, on the contrary, to name clergymen for the benefices and spiritual preferments, including bishoprics, in the royal gift ; but, at any rate, by this letter the king was trying to get the better of the Parliament, which would be some comfort to Laud ; for the letter proceeded to order that " if any Command lay

[1] " Hist.," p. 203.

otherwise upon " Laud " from either, or both *Houses of Parliament*," he " should then let them fall into Lapse, that " the king " might dispose of them to men of worth."

There were suspicions, as Laud points out a little later, that the Parliament knew this letter had been written ; and a few days after he had received it, an "Ordinance of both Houses" of Parliament was handed to him requiring to " give no benefice, or Spiritual Promotion now void, or to be void at any time before " his " Trial, *but with leave and Order of both Houses of Parliament."*

On the 31st of May 1643, " A Search came betimes in the Morning into *the Tower* upon all the Prisoners, for Letters and other Papers." Laud thought that the real object of this search was for his own papers, and that the Commons specially aimed at finding out whether Laud had received any letter about the disposal of his preferments from King Charles. He was the more convinced that the search was intended for himself, personally, by learning that " all other Prisoners had their Papers re-delivered them before the Searchers went from *the Tower* "; whereas his own were " carried to the *Committee."*

So far as Laud was concerned, his " implacable Enemy, Mr *Pryn*, was picked out (as a Man whose Malice might be trusted) to make the search upon " him. " And he did it exactly."

No sooner were the gates of the Tower opened in the morning, than the search-party entered them. Prynne, armed with his search-warrant, proceeded at once to Laud's rooms, and commanded the warder in charge of them to open the doors. Leaving two musketeers beside the doorway, as " centinels," he marched upstairs " with three other, which had their Muskets ready cocked."

Laud was in bed, and he must have been very much astonished when his door was thrown open and his " implacable Enemy, Mr *Pryn*," walked into the room with his three musketeers. Perhaps he may have fancied that one of his most vivid, unpleasant, and ominous dreams was upon him. Presently, he says, he thought upon his " Blessed Saviour,

when Judas led in the Swords and Staves about him."
Judas, in this case, however, showed no inclination to offer a
kiss ; there was no question whatever of betrayal ; nor could
Prynne's worst enemy accuse him of ever having been one
of Laud's disciples ; so, altogether, the comparison was not
very apt.

I will give the description of the interview in Laud's own
words.[1] " Mr *Pryn*, seeing me safe in Bed, falls first to my
Pockets to rifle them ; and by that time my two Servants
came running in, half ready. I demanded the sight of his
Warrant ; he shewed it me, and therein was Expressed, that
he should search my *Pockets*. The Warrant came from the
Close Committee, and the Hands that were to it, were these.
*E. Manchester, W. Saye and Seale, Wharton, H. Vane, Gilbert
Gerard*, and *John Pim*. Did they remember when they gave
this Warrant, how odious it was to Parliaments, and some of
themselves, to have the *Pockets* of Men Searched ?" For the
moment he appears to have forgotten the complaisancy with
which he heard of the rifling of the pockets of an Oxford
undergraduate, whom he had ordered to be watched on
account of his Popish inclinations. "When my *Pockets* had
been sufficiently ransacked, I rose and got my Cloathes about
me, and so half ready, with my Gown upon my Shoulders, he
held me in the Search till past Nine of the Clock in the
Morning. He took from me Twenty and One Bundles of
Papers, which I had prepared for my Defence ; and the two
Letters before named, which came to me from his *Gracious
Majesty* about *Chartham* and my other Benefices ; the
Scottish Service-Book, with such Directions as accompanied
it ; a little Book, or *Diary*, containing all the Occurrences of
my Life ; and my *Book of Private Devotions ;* both these last
written through with my own Hand. Nor could I get him to
leave this last ; but he must needs see what passed between
God and me : A thing, I think, scarce ever offer'd to any
Christian. The last place which he rifled, was a Trunk which
stood by my Bed-side. In that he found nothing, but about
Forty Pound in Money for my necessary Expences (which he

[1] " Hist.," p. 205.

meddled not with), and a Bundle of some Gloves. This Bundle he was so careful to open, as that he caused each Glove to be looked into; upon this I tendered him one pair of the Gloves; which he refusing, I told him he might take them, and fear no Bribe, for he had already done me all the Mischief he could, and I asked no Favour of him: So he thanked me, took the Gloves, bound up my Papers, left two *Centinels* at my Door (which were not dismissed till the next Day Noon), and went his way." Finally, Laud, as usual on such occasions, expresses his thankfulness for the patience which God gave him during this trying scene; as usual, too, it reads rather like a veiled piece of self-praise.

It was quite a relief to him when the Parliament formally sequestrated his archbishopric; for it had gone sorely against his conscience to be forced by the Commons to appoint men, whom he considered unfit and unworthy, to benefices which fell to his disposal; whereas now his responsibility entirely ceased.

He had to listen to another very disagreeable sermon at church, in the Tower, from a preacher whose name he could not learn. "In his Sermon," says he, "after he had liberally railed on me, he told the Auditory, that Mr *Pryn* had found *a Book* in my Pocket, which would discover great things." "This is Zealous Preaching! God forgive their Malice."

In the same month, Laud was greatly scandalized by the publication of the names of the "Synodical Men," who were to sit in committee for the reformation of the Anglican Church and its liturgy. They were not at all men to his taste —"A great, if not the greater part of them, *Brownists*, or *Independents*, or *New-England-Ministers*, if not worse, or at the best refractory Persons to the Doctrine or Discipline, or both, of the Church of *England* Established by Law, and now brought to Reform it. An excellent Conclave! But I pray God, that befal not them, which *Tully* observes fell upon *Epicurus, Si quæ corrigere voluit, deteriora fecit;* He made every thing worse that he went about to mend. I shall for my part never deny, but that the *Liturgy of the Church of* England may be better; but I am sure withal it may easily be made worse." Then he says that this Synod should re-member that the authorised Convocation of English prelates and clergy still existed, and that there could not be two lawful ecclesiastical Synods in the same nation and place at the same time. "Belike we shall fall to it in the Donatists way : They set up *Altare contra Altare* in *Africk ;* and these will set up *Synodum contra Synodum* in *England."* It may be worth noticing that both Laud's and Newman's minds were directed to the Donatist schism ; but with different consequences.

Not very long before this declamation against the new liturgy-reformers was written, Laud had been engaged in writing a defence of his own attempt at liturgy-making, and this seems a proper time to notice it. While in the Tower, he had been considering the accusations lodged against him for his share in framing the Scottish Prayer-Book. Without going into this matter at any length, or following him into wearisome details and quibbles, I think it may be interesting to give some expressions of his which bear upon the doctrine he held on the Real Presence in the Eucharist.[1]

It had been objected that the words ordered in the prayer of consecration, in the liturgy for Scotland, "that they may be unto us the Body and Blood of thy most dearly beloved Son," occurred also in the Roman Missal. Laud replied that he could wish with all his heart that the words "ut fiant nobis" "were the worst Error in the *Mass."* For, says he, the words "that they may be unto us, the Body and Blood of Christ," imply that the consecrated elements "*are to us,* but are *not Transubstantiated in themselves,* into the Body and Blood of *Christ,* nor that there is any *Corporal* Presence, in, or under the *Elements."* And again, "The true Sense, so well signified and expressed, that the words cannot well be under-stood otherwise, than to imply not the *Corporal Substance,* but the *Real,* and yet the Spiritual use of them." He evidently believed that the body and blood of Christ were present to the receiver of the elements; but not in the elements themselves ; a very common, perhaps the most

[1] "Hist.," p. 121.

usual, Anglican theory, but not what would be considered in these days a very "high" one. This opinion of his was further confirmed in the same manuscript, when he wrote [1] :— "They say *there are, which teach them, that* Christ *is received in the Sacrament* Corporaliter, *both* Objectivè, and Subjectivé. For this Opinion, be it whose it will, I for my part do utterly condemn it, as grosly Superstitious." On page 124, he also condemns the theory, put forward now by many advanced High-Churchmen, that there is any sacrifice in the eucharist, except "the Sacrifice of Praise." It is a "Commemoration and a *Representation* of that great Sacrifice offered up by *Christ* himself: As Bishop *Jewel* very Learnedly, and fully acknowledges." The name of Bellarmine, the well-known Catholic controversialist, who had died only a few years earlier, having been mentioned, Laud says :—"If *Bellarmin* go farther than this"—as of course he knew well enough that he did—"he is Erroneous." His feelings as to the eucharist are obviously implied again when, in contrasting the Catholic with the Anglican liturgy,[2] he says :—"'Tis one thing to Offer us *his Body*, and another to Offer up *the Memorial of his Body.*"

All that Laud would admit, in respect to the Real Presence, was that the receiver was made a spiritual partaker of Christ's body and blood. Thus he writes to Fisher [3] of "the faith of the church of England, that in the most blessed sacrament the worthy receiver is by his faith made spiritually partaker of the true and real body and blood of Christ truly, and really, and of all the benefits of his passion. Your Roman Catholics add a manner of this his presence, transubstantiation, which many deny ; and the Lutherans a manner of this presence, consubstantiation, which more deny." Referring to this passage, his Jesuit critic, T. C., not unfairly, I think, says [4] :—"He understands such a belief of the English Protestants *real presence,* as carries with it an express denial both of Transubstantiation and Consubstantiation in the Sacrament." I write under correction ; but I imagine that this

---

[1] P. 123. [2] P. 115.
[3] "Conf. with Fisher," Oxford ed., p. 241. [4] "Lawd's Labyrinth," p. 308.

would be considered rather low eucharistic teaching by High-Churchmen of the present day.

In forming an opinion as to the orthodoxy of Laud's views from a modern High-Church standpoint, it is well to bear in mind his doctrine on the question of intention. Among Catholics it is held that three things are necessary for the validity of a sacrament, namely, the matter, the form, and the intention, and I imagine that Anglicans of the High-Church school would say as much, although they might use those terms with a more or less modified meaning ; but Laud distinctly denies that " this intention of either bishop or priest " is " of absolute necessity to the essence of a sacrament, so as to make void the gracious institution of Christ." [1]

On the preceding page he says :—" Your council of Florence had told us, that three things are necessary to every sacrament ; the matter, the form of the sacrament, and the intention of the priest which administers it, that he intends to do as the church doth. Your council of Trent confirms it for the intention of the priest." He is treating of the possibility of a pope's not being validly ordained ; but exactly the same argument would apply to every sacrament. Perhaps he may have felt the necessity of discarding the doctrine of intention, owing to the certainty that some of the early bishops of the Anglican establishment had no intention of ordaining priests, or consecrating bishops, and consequently that, if intention were necessary, at least a large number of Anglican ordinations must be invalid. In support of his theory of the needlessness of intention, he quotes a Neapolitan bishop ; but the author of *Lawd's Labyrinth* proves [2] that this bishop, Cardinal Catharinus, meant nothing of the kind. Neither the matter nor the form were very certain in some of the early Anglican consecrations of bishops, and little seemed left to give the slightest colour of a sacrament to them when Laud calmly repudiated the value of intention, and absolutely taunted Fisher about the "error" held by his Church, in maintaining that " a sacrament is not perfectly given, if he

---

[1] "Conf. with Fisher," Oxford ed., p. 229.   [2] P. 285.

that administers it have not *intentionem faciendi quod facit ecclesia*, an intention to do that which the church doth by sacraments."

Should it, however, turn out that modern High-Anglicans are of one mind with Laud on this question, I would humbly apologise for misrepresenting them.

CHAPTER XXXVII

MR PRYNNE was not long in producing before the world one of the treasures he discovered among the papers which he had laid hands upon in Laud's rooms at the Tower. It appeared in the form of a tract, bearing on its title page the words, "It is ordered by the Committee of the House of Commons in Parliament, concerning Printing, this first day of August, 1643. That this Book, Intituled ROME's MASTER-PIECE, be forthwith Printed by Michael Sparke, Senior." The full title was "Rome's Master-Piece: or, The Grand Conspiracy of the Pope and his Jesuited Instruments, To Extirpate the Protestant Religion, Re-establish Popery, Subvert Laws, Liberties, Peace, Parliaments; By Kindling a Civil War in Scotland, and all his Majesty's Realms, and to Poison the King himself, in case he Comply not with them in these their execrable Designs." This plot was said to have been revealed to Andreas ab Habernfield by an apostate priest, who "having known the vanities of the Pontifician Religion," "felt his conscience to be burdened," and appears to have relieved it by telling lies to the Protestants. "This good man" having told his story to Habernfield, who is said to have been a chaplain to the Queen of Bohemia, Habernfield repeated it to Sir William Boswell, English Minister at the Hague; Boswell then wrote about it to Laud, and Laud told King Charles. Prynne's object in getting this correspondence published was to show that although several well-known characters were named as concerned in the plot, namely, the Duchess of Buckingham, Lady Arundel ("a strenuous she-champion of the Popish Religion"), Lady Newport, Montague, Digby, Winter, Lord Arundel, Windebank ("a most fierce Papist"), and Porter, the Groom of the

Bed-Chamber, neither Laud nor the king instituted "any Prosecution of the Conspirators."

The greater part of the correspondence printed in this pamphlet took place in 1640, and Habernfield's letters read very like hoaxes. They state "that a certain Society hath conspired, which attempts the Death of the King (and Lord Archbishop), and Convulsion of the whole Realm." Habernfield wrote to Laud that when the "good man," *i.e.,* the apostate priest, "related to me the Factions of the Jesuits, with which the whole Earthly World was assaulted," "my Bowels were contracted together, my Loyns trembled with horrour, that a pernicious Gulf should be prepared for so many thousands of Souls." As to Laud himself, he wrote : —"How many Rocks, how many Scillas, how many displeased Charibdes appear before your Grace, in what a dangerous Sea the Cockboat of your Grace's Life, next to Shipwrack, is tossed, your self may judge ; the Fore-deck of the Ship is speedily to be driven to the Harbour." He signs himself, not at all inaptly, "Your Grace's most Observant, and most Officious *Andrew Habernfield.*"

Laud wrote an account of the matter to Charles, saying : —"The Business (if it be) is extream foul. The discovery thus by God's Providence offered, seems fair." And he professes that "with the labour or indignation" produced by it, he "fell into an extream faint Sweat." Judging, however, from the fact that neither the archbishop nor the king proceeded to take any steps against the alleged conspirators, it would seem that, on their calmer judgment, both of them came to regard the affair in the light of a mare's nest and certainly there is not a grain of evidence in Habernfield's letters in support of his assertions. Even in his letters to the king, Laud appears to have had some doubts of the authenticity of the story. In asking Charles to keep the affair secret for the present, he says :—"This Information is either true, or there is some mistake in it : If it be true, the persons which make the discovery, will deserve Thanks and Reward ; if there should be any mistake in it, your Majesty can lose nothing but a little silence."

As Charles and Laud were, according to Habernfield, the chief people endangered, one would have thought that the publication of the correspondence by their enemies would have only proved to the nation that neither of them had shown any inclination, or favour, to Popery. The object of the Commons, however, may have been to reveal Habernfield's statement that Con had been informally received as a Papal Legate in London.[1]

Laud writes[2] that the publishing of the pamphlet was " to drive the People into headlong mischief."

It is difficult, if possible, to believe that designs were ever framed by any of the people named in the " Master-piece" against the persons of either Charles or Laud ; that they were entertained by either the Pope or Cardinal Barberini, who were also stated to be in the plot, is much more unlikely, nor is it probable that any plot to murder either Laud or Charles was ever contemplated by even a small party of English Catholics. Without doubt a " Plot to Extirpate the Protestant Religion," and to " Re-establish Popery," existed, as it exists now, in exactly the same sense that a plot to extirpate one religion and establish another exists wherever, and whenever, missionaries go to a country to introduce their own religion and substitute it for the religion held by the majority of the inhabitants of that country.

As to Laud's relations with Con, further evidence is now available. Con wrote to Rome :—" Canterbury told the Queen he could not visit me without raising a storm." " Canterbury spoke of me, saying I was bitter because he could not visit me." " Canterbury urged the King to renew edicts against the Queen's chapels and to stop the growth of Popery. Was only way of quieting the affairs in Scotland to make laws against the Catholics." " Canterbury is following his old artifices. He shows himself the head of the Anglican Church, and is as much a Puritan as a Catholic. In London

---

[1] " Hist.," p. 585. " Master Cuneus did at that time enjoy the Office of the Pope's Legat." Again, " Cuneus smelling from the Archbishop, most trusty to the King, that the King's mind was wholly pendulous (or doubtful), &c."

[2] *Ib.*, p. 209.

many reports are spread of the negotiations between Canterbury and myself; but as I have written, though I would willingly make use of him to undo the schism, still he changes so much in what he says. Of his nature he is timid, ambitious and inconstant."[1] As a matter of fact, Con would have made a good witness for Laud at his trial !

To add to the sorrows of Laud's imprisonment, news arrived in the spring of 1643 that his dear old native town of Reading, after a siege of ten days, had surrendered to the parliamentary forces under the Earl of Essex, who had a force of eighteen thousand men. The only comfort we hear of his receiving, about this time, was the news (already noticed in an earlier chapter) that Sir Kenelm Digby had borne witness, in examination before a committee of the House of Commons, that Laud " laboured with him against his return to the Church of *Rome*," and that he believed Laud to be, what he professed to be, a Protestant, accompanied by a kind message from Sir Kenelm himself. But this was a single good incident among many that were unfavourable. The queen was impeached in the House of Lords by Pym, in the name of the Commons, and Waller, the poet, who had privately advocated the formation of a third party to mediate between the king and the Parliament, was arrested, together with several who sympathised with him, and he only " saved his life by the most abject submission. ' He seemed much smitten in conscience : he desired the help of Godly ministers.' "[2] Two of his companions were executed.

" Then came the *Covenant*, that excellent Piece of . . . ,"[3] as Laud writes, which was a new oath taken by the members of the House of Commons, in which they all swore " never to consent to the laying down of arms so long as the papists, in open war against the parliament should be protected against the justice thereof, but according to their power and vocation, to assist the forces raised by the parliament

[1] Transcript from Papal Registers relating to England, &c., 1637-8. Brit. Mus., Add. MSS. 15,390.
[2] Lingard, vol. viii. chap. i.   [3] " Hist.," p. 210.

against the forces raised by the king." It was ordained
that not only M.P.s, but every man should swear the same
covenant in his parish church.[1]

This oath was much more than a mere protestation. It
was a covenant between the English and the Scots, between
the Puritans and the Presbyterians. It provided "that all
endeavours should be used for the preservation of the
Reformed Religion in the Church of *Scotland*, both in
Doctrine, Worship, Liturgy, and Government; and for
bringing the three Kingdoms to the nearest Conjunction,
and Uniformity in Religion, Confession of Faith, Form of
Church Government, *Directory* for Worship and Catechism."
There was also to be an "extirpation of *Popery*, Prelacy,
that is, Church Government, by Arch-bishops and Bishops,"
&c., "and all other Ecclesiastical Officers depending on the
Hierarchy, Superstition, Heresie, Schism, Profaneness, and
whatsoever should be found contrary to sound Doctrine, and
the power of Godliness."

The extirpation of archbishops threatened the complete
ruin of Laud, and afterwards came a passage that, as Heylin
says,[2] "seems to have been made to no other purpose but
to bring the Archbishop to the Block." It makes the
covenanters swear "that they should with all diligence and
faithfulness discover all such as have been, or shall be
Incendiaries, Malignants, or evil Instruments, by hindering
the Reformation of Religion, dividing the King from his
People, or one of the Kingdoms from one another, or making
any Faction or Parties amongst the People contrary to this
League and Covenant, that they may be brought to publick
trial, and receive condign punishment, &c." If Laud's name
had been mentioned among them, the object of these words
could scarcely have been plainer. Heylin says[3] that certain
people "with no unhappy curiosity observing the number
of words which make up this Covenant, abstracted from the
Preface and Conclusion of it, found them amounting in the
total to 666, neither more nor less, which being the number
of the Beast in the Revelation, &c., &c., may very justly

[1] Lingard, vol. viii. chap. i.   [2] "Cyp. Ang.," p. 478.   [3] *Ib.*, p. 479.

intitle it to so much of *Antichrist*, as others have endeavoured to confer on the Popes of Rome."

When the news of this covenant reached the king, he
interdicted all his subjects from either imposing or taking it,
but his proclamation "came out too late to hinder the taking
and enjoying of this *Covenant*."[1] Two days after the members
of Parliament and the Assembly of divines took it in St
Margaret's Church, Westminster, "it was administered with
no less solemnity to divers Lords, Knights, Gentlemen,
Colonels, Officers, Souldiers, and others residing in and
about the City of *London*." On the Sunday following, it
was "enjoyned to be taken" in all the churches and "Chappels
of *London*, within the *Lines of Communication*, by all and
every the Inhabitants within the same, as afterwards by all
the Kingdom in convenient time. Prosecuted in all places,
with such cursed rigour, that all such who refused to subscribe the same, and to lift up their hands to God in testimony that they called him to witness to it, were turned out
of house and home, as they use to say, not suffered to
compound for their Goods or Lands till they had submitted
thereunto. A terrible and a woful time, in which men were
not suffered to enjoy their Estates without betraying themselves to the King's displeasure, and making shipwreck of a
good conscience in the sight of God."

Meanwhile, Charles was no less eager than the covenanters
in proclaiming his Protestant orthodoxy. On one occasion,
when Archbishop Usher was just going to give him communion, he rose and said to him, in a loud enough voice for
the whole congregation to hear [2] :—" My Lord, I have to the
utmost of my soul prepared to become a worthy receiver ; and
may I so receive comfort by the blessed sacrament, as I do
intend the establishment of the true reformed Protestant
religion, as it stood in its beauty in the happy days of Queen
Elizabeth, without any connivance at popery." [This almost
sounded like a hit at Laud.] "I bless God that in the
midst of these publick distractions I have still liberty to
communicate ; and may this sacrament be to my damnation,

---

[1] "Cyp. Ang.," p. 479. [2] Rushworth, v. 346.

if my heart do not joyn with my lipps in this protestation."
Who, then, was ever a stronger Protestant than Charles I.?
It was no question of the Church of England, the English
Church in its continuity from the early British Church, which
always, as we are now told, opposed Rome, or the English
Catholic Church *versus* the Roman Catholic Church; but
"the true reformed Protestant religion"! and might the
sacrament, which he was then and there about to receive, be
to his damnation, if his heart did not join with his lips in this
his solemn declaration of Protestantism.

Pennington, Lord Mayor of London, was now made Lieutenant of the Tower, and the day after he took possession of
it, which was a Sunday, Laud had to endure listening to a
sermon from a preacher who wore a buff coat under his gown,
and told the congregation that those who died in the cause
of the Parliament "were all Blessed," "with much more such
stuff."

Laud had now been long in prison awaiting his trial, and
in October 1643 he writes:—"By this time *Mr Pryn's*
malice had hammer'd out something." Ten additional
articles were brought against him by the Commons on the
24th, and he was required to answer them in writing in six
days. He at once sent to the Lords to ask for longer time,
for money out of his own sequestrated estate "to fee" his
"councel, and to bear the necessary Charge of" his "*Trial;*
for *Councel,* and for a Solicitor, and some Servants to attend"
his "Business." The Lords gave him all he asked for except
the money, as to which they referred him "to the *Committee*
of Sequestrations." The latter desired him to appear "*in
Formâ Pauperis.*" On this and other questions he sent
several petitions to the Houses of Parliament.

His trial had been delayed by the alarm felt by the Parliament at some of the king's successes; but when the parliamentary troops were reported to be getting the best of the
war, the Commons took heart and proceeded fearlessly
against the archbishop. In short, as Heylin puts it [1]:—"And
thus the business was drilled on, hastned, or slackned, as the

[1] " Cyp. Ang.," p. 482.

Scots advanced in their expedition; and as the expedition prospered in success and fortune, so was it prosecuted and advanced to its fatal Period. For understanding that the *Scots* were entred *England* and had marcht victoriously almost as far as the Banks of the River *Tine*, they prest the Lords to name a day for the beginning of his Tryal, who thereupon fixed it upon Tuesday the twelfth of March next ensuing."

But I am anticipating. In the previous November, he was summoned to the Bar of the House of Lords, in order to put in his claims for the assistance of counsel and fees to pay them with. What he [1] "spake *to the Lords* was this: ' That I had no Skill to judge of the Streights into which I might fall by my *Plea*, which I had resolved on, being left without all assistance of my *Councel*, in regard to the nature and form of *the Impeachment*, that was against me."

When he had put in his written answer—" *All Advantages of Law against this Impeachment saved and reserved to this Defendant, he pleads* Not Guilty *to all, and every part of the Impeachment, in manner and form as 'tis Charged in the Articles:* " he humbly besought their Lordships " to take into their Honourable Consideration," his great years, " being Threescore and ten compleat," pleading that his "Memory, and other Faculties, by Age and Affliction," were " much decayed," and that he was suffering from the effects of his " long Imprisonment, wanting very little of three whole Years, and this last year little better than close Imprisonment." Then he thanked the Lords for assigning him counsel ; at the same time expressing a doubt whether, as his " *Councel* were most ready to obey *their Lordships* in all the Commands laid upon them," they would advise him " without Offence." The charges against him were " so interwoven, and left without all distinguishment, what is intended as a Charge of *Treason*, and what of *Crime and Misdemeanour:* That to remove these Doubts," he " had humbly besought *their Lordships* twice for distinguishment, &c.," and his " Prayers were " " that having (not without much difficulty) prevailed upon " his " *Councel*

---

[1] " Hist.," **212.**

to attend ; *their Lordships* would be pleased to hear them speak in this very perplexed Business."

His counsel were heard, and so far induced the Lords to " think upon the distinguishment " that they " seem'd some-what better content, that they had gotten so much." He adds, with evident pride :—" Not long after this, I heard from good Hands, that some of *the Lords* confessed, I had much deceived their expectation ; for they found me in a Calm, but thought I would have been stormy," anticipating that " Choler and Indignation might thrust forth." If they had expected anything of the kind, they had been foolish enough to forget that it is one thing to be a judge—especially in such a tribunal as the Star Chamber—and quite another to be a prisoner.

Twice, again, within the next couple of months, he had to appear at the Bar " at the *Lords House*," to put in his answers, before his regular trial began. On the last occasion (it was the 22nd of January) " the *Thames* was so full of Ice, that he could not go by Water. It was Frost and Snow, and a most bitter day." He went " therefore with the *Lieutenant* in his Coach, and twelve Warders with Halberts went all along the Streets." He " could not obtain either the sending of them before, or the suffering them to come behind, but with the Coach they must come ; which was as good as to call the People about " him. " So from the *Tower-gate* to *Westmin-ster*," he " was sufficiently railed on, and reviled all the way. God forgive the misguided People." Coming back, however, " the Tyde serving " him, he " made a hard shift to return by Water."

On the 28th of December 1643, " one Mr *Wells*," a New-England minister went to the Tower, obtained, through the son of the Lieutenant, an interview with Laud, " and in a boisterous manner demanded to know " whether he had repented or not. Laud fancied that he had never seen the man before ; but, when he hinted as much, Mr Wells cor-rected him, reminding him that when he had been a clergy-man in Essex, Laud, then Bishop of London, had suspended him. By degrees, Laud " recalled the Man to " his " Remembrance, and what care " he " took in Conference with him at *London-House*, to recall him from some of his turbulent ways ; but all in vain." This probably meant a sound and violent rating. Now Mr Wells was taking care to recall Laud from some of his turbulent ways, telling him in conclusion that he " went about to bring Popery into the Kingdom, and " he hoped he should have his " Reward for it." But the last word was with Laud, who writes :—" When I saw him at this heighth, I told him, he and his Fellows, what by their Ignorance, and what by their Railing, and other boisterous Carriage, would soon actually make more *Papists* by far, than ever I intended ; and that I was a better *Protestant* than he, or any of his Followers." A proud, nor unfounded boast ! " So I left him in his Heat," he says. He tells us nothing of his own temperature.

We now approach Laud's trial. To deal with it at length would require a separate volume. Laud's own account of it fills more than two hundred folio pages. So many are the details of his past that are brought to light in it, that to take the trial alone, and write fully upon it, would be one way, nor altogether a bad way, of writing a life of Laud. I have rather worked in the opposite direction, referring occasionally to Laud's account of his trial for particulars on this point or on that, in the course of my attempt to write his biography.

It was an exceedingly long trial. " Mr *Pryn* was trusted with the providing of all the *Evidence*, and was *Relater* and *Prompter*, and all : Never weary of anything, so he might do " Laud " mischief." The counsel employed by the Government against the prisoner were Serjeant Wilde, Browne, Maynard, Nicolas, and Hill ; but the last named " was Consul-*Bibulus*," and did not speak at the Bar.

Laud was convinced, and with reason, of the strong general feeling that he must be sacrificed. " A Man of good Credit " told him that " a *Parliament*-Man " " was pleased to say " that Laud was now an old man, and that it would be a happy thing, both for himself and the Parliament, if God would be pleased to take him away ; but Laud writes that he was certain that " if Age, or Grief, or Faintness of Spirit had

ended " his days, there would have been an outcry " against
this hard Chance, that should take away so guilty a Person
from Publick Tryal." When a friend of his bemoaned his
case to "another *Parliament*-Man (of whom " he " had deserved very well)," and said he was a good man, " The *Parlia-*
ment-Man replyed, *Be he never so Good, we must now make*
him Ill for our own sakes." During the trial itself, again,
" some Citizens of *London* were heard to say, that indeed "
Laud " answered many things very well : But " he " must
suffer somewhat for the *Honour of the House.*"

CHAPTER XXXVIII.

I YIELD to none in my admiration of the courage with which Laud met his judges and his accusers at his trial; yet I cannot but admit that he may have been, to some small extent, buoyed up all through it by the thought that he had a signed and sealed pardon from the king in his pocket, in case he should be condemned to death. Clarendon says[1] that "the Chancellor of the Exchequer, who had always a great Reverence and affection for him, had spoken to the King of it," [his trial] "and proposed to him, 'that in all events, there might be a Pardon prepared, and sent to him, under the Great Seal of *England;* to the end, if they proceeded against him in any form of Law, he might plead the King's Pardon; which must be allow'd by all who pretended to be govern'd by the Law; but if they proceeded in a Martial, or any other extraordinary way, without any form of Law, his Majesty should declare his Justice and Affection to an old faithful Servant, whom he much esteem'd, in having done all towards his preservation that was in his power to do.' The King was wonderfully pleased with this Proposition; and took from thence occasion to commend the Piety and Virtue of the Arch-Bishop, with extraordinary Affection; and commanded the Chancellor of the Exchequer, to cause the Pardon to be prepared, and his Majesty would Sign and Seal it with all possible secrecy; which at that time was necessary." This project was carried out, and the pardon, "Sign'd and Seal'd with the Great Seal of *England*," was "carefully sent, and deliver'd into the Arch-Bishop's own hand, before he was brought to his Trial; who receiv'd it with great joy, as it was a Testimony of the King's gracious Affection to him, and care of him, without any opinion that they who endeavour'd

[1] Vol. iv. p. 573.

to take away the King's Life, would preserve his by his Majesty's Authority."

When Laud showed the pardon to his counsel, they made certain technical objections to it, so he sent it back to the king by the same messenger, and "it was perfected accordingly, and deliver'd safely again to him, and was in his hands during the whole time of his Trial."

I will endeavour to keep my account of this celebrated trial for high treason within reasonable limits ; but I should not be doing justice to the subject unless I gave some idea of the articles of impeachment. I will, therefore, quote a summary of them from *Celebrated Trials, and Remarkable Cases of Criminal Jurisprudence. From the Earliest Records to the Year* 1825 : and the reader can glance through it, or not, as he pleases.

These articles were sent in two divisions. The first were :—

" 1. That he had traitorously endeavoured to subvert the laws, and introduce arbitrary government.

" 2. That he had denied the authority of parliaments, establishing an absolute power, not only in the king, but in himself and other bishops, above and against the law.

" 3. That by threats and promises to the judges, he had perverted the courts of justice, and deprived the king's subjects of their rights.

" 4. That in his own courts he had sold justice, and taken bribes.

" 5. That he had caused divers canons to be made, contrary to the king's prerogative, and the laws ; established an unlawful authority in himself, and successors ; and endeavoured to confirm his exorbitant power by a wicked oath.

" 6. That he had assumed a papal and tyrannical power.

" 7. That he endeavoured to subvert the true religion, and introduce popish superstition.

" 8. That he abused the trust his Majesty reposed in him, procuring the nomination of persons to ecclesiastical preferments, which belonged to others, preferring persons that were popishly affected.

" 9. That his own chaplains, to whom he committed the

licensing of books, were popishly affected, which had occasioned the publishing of divers superstitious books.

" 10. That he endeavoured to reconcile the churches of England and Rome, and countenanced the establishing a popish hierarchy in the kingdom.

" 11. That he had caused several orthodox ministers to be silenced, and deprived, and many loyal subjects to forsake the kingdom.

" 12. That he had abrogated the privileges granted the French and Dutch churches in this kingdom, endeavouring to cause discord between the Church of England and other reformed churches.

" 13. That he had laboured to bring divers popish innovations into the kingdom of Scotland, in order to create a war between the kingdoms of England and Scotland, and advised his Majesty to subdue the Scots, forcing the English clergy to contribute to that war; that he had censured the pacification as dishonourable, and so incensed his Majesty, that he entered into an offensive war with the Scots.

" 14. That, to prevent his being questioned for these traitorous proceedings, he endeavoured to subvert the rights of the parliament, and to cause divisions between his Majesty and his people ; for which they impeached him of high treason."

The second set of articles comprised the following :—

" 1. The first additional article charges, that in the 3rd and 4th year of the king, he caused the parliament to be dissolved, and aspersed the members, affirming they were factious Puritans, and commended the Papists.

" 2. That for ten years past he had endeavoured to advance the power of the council-table, the canons of the church, and the king's prerogative above the laws.

" 3. That to advance the ecclesiastical power, he had hindered the granting writs of prohibition to the ecclesiastical courts.

" 4. That a judgment being given against one Burley, a parson, for non-residency, he had stayed execution by applying to the judges, and said, ' He would never suffer a judgment to pass against a clergyman, by nihil dicit.'

" 5. That he had caused Sir John Corbet, a justice of peace, to be imprisoned, for causing the petition of right to be read at the sessions of the peace ; and, during his imprisonment, granted away part of the glebe lands of Alderley" [Adderley] " belonging to the said Sir John ; and prevented the execution of a judgment, which Sir John had obtained, and procured him to be committed by the council-table, till he submitted to their order.

" 6. That divers sums being given for purchasing impropriations, he had caused the same to be overthrown in the Court of Exchequer.

" 7. That he had harboured and relieved Popish priests, who had traduced the 39 articles.

" 8. That he had said, a blow must be given to the church before it could be brought to conformity.

" 9. That in May 1640 he caused the convocation to be held, after the dissolution of the parliament, where canons were made, contrary to law and the privilege of the parliament, and a dangerous and illegal oath formed, approving the doctrine and discipline of the established church, and promising not to consent to any alteration in the government of the church by archbishops, bishops, deans, archdeacons, &c. Which oath he had taken himself, and caused other ministers to take ; and imprisoned the bishop of Gloucester, for refusing to subscribe the said canons, and take the oath, till he submitted.

" 10. That a resolution being taken at the council-table for assisting the king by extraordinary means, if the parliament should prove peevish, the archbishop wickedly advised his Majesty to dissolve the parliament in 1640, and it was thereupon dissolved ; and soon after he told his Majesty, ' that he was now absolved from all rules of government, and at liberty to use extraordinary ways for a supply.' " [1]

Now the evidence given in the foregoing portion of the present volume should be sufficient, I think, to convince the reader of three things ; the first, that a great part of the above charges were utterly unfounded ; the second, that a

[1] " Celebrated Trials," vol. ii. pp. 26-28.

large proportion of the remainder were grossly exaggerated ; the third, that there was a certain residue of true accusations which, in the hands of the kind of judges who were to try Laud, might be used for ruinous, if not fatal, purposes.　This being the case, it became of the utmost importance to him to ascertain which of the offences charged in the articles were held to be high treason, and which mere misdemeanours, and for this reason, as we saw in the last chapter, he " besought *their Lordships* twice for distinguishment."

At last the day came, and the little old man, still rather lame, hobbled to the Bar of the House of Lords, dressed in his black gown and white ruff, without his rochet, and wearing his close-fitting black cap on his head.　As he looked up the long hall, with its tapestried walls, within which he had so often acted a prominent part, he observed that the benches on either side were very scantily occupied.　Instead of being set at his ease by seeing an array of judges that was numerically far from formidable, he was filled with dismay ; for he knew that the larger the number of peers present, the stronger would have been the majority in his favour.

He had only just become " settled at the Bar," when Serjeant Wilde rose to open the case for the prosecution.　If Laud had little personal knowledge of Wilde, he had " had a Character given " him " of this Gentleman, which " he forebore to express.　Still, he was conscious that he himself had been a member of the august body which was to try him, and he probably comforted himself with the reflection that, for this reason, he would be treated with respect and courtesy, if with severity.

When he had passed sentence on Williams, had he not begun with compliments ?　Whatever might come later in the Serjeant's speech, the opening would be flattering.　A contemporary writer informs us that Serjeant Wilde spoke " with abundance of elegancy."

" This great cause of the Archbishop of Canterbury," he began,[1] " after a long and painful travail, is now come to the Birth."　And then he explained the reasons of the long

---

[1] " Canterburies Doome."

delay, amounting to three years and as many months. Having disposed of these preliminary details, he proceeded to the business in hand. "If all the oppressions, all the pernicious practices and machinations, which have been in each time to ruinate our religious laws and liberties, were lost, I think here they might be found again to the life."

Then he enumerated some of the prisoner's crimes. He "laboured a Reconciliation with Rome." (I am quoting now from Laud's own account.[1]) He "maintained *Popish* and *Arminian* Opinions:" he "suffered *Transubstantiation, Justification by Merits, Purgatory*, and what not, to be openly preached all over the Kingdom:" he "induced Superstitious Ceremonies, as Consecrations of Churches, and Chalices, and Pictures of *Christ* in Glas-Windows": he "held Intelligence with Cardinals and Priests, and endeavoured to ascend to Papal Dignity ; Offers being made " him "to be a Cardinal." He "caused *Sermons* to be Preached in *Court* to set *the King's* Prerogative above the Law." Presently he went on (I refer now to Prynne's account [2]) :—" Had they been faults of common frailty, error or incognitancy, which this man had committed, we should gladly have stepped back, and cast a cloak over them ; but being so wilful, so universal, so comprehensive of all the evils and miseries which now we suffer, the sin would lie upon our own heads, if we should not call for justice."

After going on in this strain, for a time, he said :—" That which of itself is so heinous is much more enhanced and aggravated by the quality of the person : a church-man ; a great prelate ; a great man in great trust ; " and " a man endued with so great gifts of nature "—here Laud may have been reminded of his own sentence on Williams—" and favour from His Majesty, and for all these to be perverted to a contrary end, even to the destruction of the public, and the ruin of the womb that bare him, how deep a dye do these impose upon his foul crime." [3]

" Here was treason in the highest pitch and altitude " (I am quoting now from *Celebrated Trials* [4]); " even the betray-

---

[1] " Hist.," p. 221.   [2] " Canterburies Doome."   [3] *Ib.*   [4] Vol. ii. p. 30.

ing the whole realm, and the subversion of the very foundations." " Churchmen in all ages, were the archest seedsmen
of mischief, and the principal actors in all the great distractions that had happened ; and as they meddled with temporal things, heterogeneal to their calling, God was pleased
to smite with blindness, and infatuate their councils, of which
this prelate was an instance ; who, employing his time in
state affairs, became the author of all the illegal and tyrannical proceedings and innovations in religion and government, and indeed, of all the concussions and distractions
that had happened in church and state. And when by the
magnanimity of former princes, and the wisdom of their ancestors, they had shaken off the antichristian yoke ; and when
they had seen such bloody massacres, plots, and prosecutions
at home and abroad, in order to introduce it again ; that this
man should go about to reduce them to those rotten principles of error and darkness again, it could not be expected
but the people should be ready to stone him."

" To conclude." (I quote from Prynne.[1]) " Naaman was a
great man, but he was a leper. This man's leprosy hath so
infected all, as there remains no other cure but the sword of
justice, which we doubt not but your Lordships will so apply,
that the Common Wealth shall yet live again and flourish."

The rodomontade of this Serjeant Buzfuz of the seventeenth century greatly affected the prisoner against whom it
was directed. " I was much troubled," he writes, " to see my
self, in such an Honourable Assembly made so vile." Nevertheless, he braced himself up and said :—

" *My Lords*, my being in this Place, and in this Condition,
recalls to my memory that which I long since read in *Seneca;
Tormentum est, etiamsi absolutus quis fuerit, Causam dixisse.*
'Tis not a grief only, no, 'tis no less than a Torment, for an
ingenuous Man to plead Criminally, much more Capitally, at
such a *Bar* as this ; yea, though it should so fall out, that he
be absolved. The truth of this I find at present in my self :
And so much the more because I am *a Christian ;* And not
that only, but in *Holy Orders ;* And not so only, but by God's

---

[1] " Canterburies Doome," p. 53.

Grace and Goodness *preferred* to the greatest Place this Church affords ; and yet now brought, *Causam dicere*, to Plead, and for no less than Life, at this Great Bar. And whatsoever the World thinks of me (and they have been taught to think more ill, than, I humbly thank *Christ* for it, I was ever acquainted with ;) Yet, *my Lords*, this I find, *Tormentum est*, 'tis no less than Torment to me to appear in this Place to such an Accusation. Nay, *my Lords*, give me leave, I beseech you, to speak plain Truth : No Sentence, that you can justly pass upon me (and other I will never fear from *your Lordships*), can go near me as *Causam dixisse*, to have pleaded for my self, upon this occasion, and in this Place. For as for the Sentence (I thank God for it) I am at St *Paul's* Word : *If I have committed any thing worthy of death, I refuse not to die :* For I bless God, I have so spent my time, as that I am neither ashamed to live, nor afraid to die. Nor can the World be more weary of me, than I am of it : For seeing the Malignity which hath been raised against me by some Men, I have carried my Life in my Hands these divers years past. But yet, *my Lords*, if none of these things, whereof these Men accuse me, merit Death by Law ; though I may not in this Case, and from this Bar *appeal unto Cæsar ;* yet to *your Lordships* Justice and Integrity, I both may, and do Appeal ; not doubting, but that God of his Goodness will preserve my Innocency."

Laud's greatest enemies could not fairly deny that this opening of his defence was dignified and pathetic, and as free from bombast as from cringing servility. He went on to say that the charge against him was divided into two " main Heads, the *Laws* of the Land, and the *Religion* by those Laws established."

As to the laws of the land, he made a very good case for himself for having been "as strict an Observer of them all the Days of" his " Life, so far as they" concerned him, " as any Man." His defence in the matter of religion was longer; for he knew very well that it was here that the danger lay. It was on his freedom from any inclination to Catholicism that he placed most stress. " My Lords," he

said, " I am as Innocent in this business of *Religion,* as free
from all *Practise,* or so much as thought of *Practise* for any
alteration to *Popery,* or any way blemishing the True *Protestant Religion* Established in the *Church of England,* as I
was when my Mother first bare me into the World."[1]   Again
he says :—" If I had any purpose to blast the True *Religion*
Established in the *Church of England,* and to introduce
Popery ; sure I took a very wrong way to it."   Then he
said that he " stayed as many that were going to *Rome,*
and reduced as many that were already gone," as any
" Bishop or other Minister " in England.   He gave the names
of about twenty people, whom he had either induced to
leave the Catholic Church after joining it, or to refrain from
joining it when they were on the point of doing so.

Thus ended the first day of his trial.   He then left the
Bar and " went patiently into the little Committee-Chamber
at the entring into the *House.*"   Thither a Mr Peters, a
clergyman whom Laud had never before seen, but of whom
he had heard more than enough, followed him " in great
haste, and began to give " him " ill Language," telling him
that " he, and other Ministers, were able to name Thousands,
that they had converted."   Peters was in such a "choler"
that one of Laud's counsel " stepped between " them, and
reproached him for his " uncivil Carriage " towards the archbishop " in his Affliction."   Mr Peters revenged himself by
going shortly afterwards to a church in Lambeth and preaching against Laud, saying " that a great Prelat, their Neighbour
(or in words to that effect), had bragged in the *Parliament-
House,* that he had Converted Two and Twenty ; but that
he had Wisdom enough, not to tell how many Thousands
he had Perverted."

" After a little stay " in the " Committee-Chamber," Laud
received his " Dismission for that time, and a Command
to appear again at Nine in the Morning."   He must have
spent, from first to last, a good deal of time in this chamber ;
for he tells us that although nine in the morning was his
" usual Hour to attend," he " was seldom called into the

---

[1] " Hist.," p. 225.

House till two Hours after." Worse than this, on one
occasion, he writes[1]:— "After some Hours Attendance, I
was sent back again unheard, and Order'd to come again
on *Thursday*," and on another, " I was again brought to the
House, made a sufficient scorn and gazing-stock to the
People ; and after I had waited some hours, was sent back,
by Reason of other Business, unheard." Twice again he
mentions that he "attended the Pleasure of the House some
Hours," and " was remitted without Hearing " ; and he complains of " the Charge which this frequent coming put " him
to. " I did not appear any day but it cost me six or seven
Pound. I grew into want." [2]

Besides its expense, " this frequent coming " was attended
with other annoyances. We find him writing[3] that "the
Landing place at *Westminster* was not so full of People ;
and they which were there, much more civil towards me
than formerly. My Friends were willing to perswade me,
that my Answer had much abated the edge of the People,
saving from the violent and factious Leaders of the Multitude,
whom it seems nothing would satisfie but my Life (for so
I was told in plain terms, by a Man deeply interested in
them ;) when I presently saw *Quaterman* coming towards
me, who, soon as he came, fell to his wonted Railing, and
asked aloud, *what* the Lords *meant, to be troubled so long and
so often, with such a base Fellow as I was, they should do well
to Hang me out of the way.*"

Before dealing with Laud's trial in detail, it may be well
to consider some of the public events which had recently
taken place, or were to take place in the course of it.

The great ecclesiastic in the neighbouring kingdom, whom
Laud is believed by some historians to have emulated, if not
imitated, was no more. Cardinal Richelieu had died when
he was at the summit of his power, just at the time that death
was threatening Laud when power had fallen from his grasp.
Again, when Laud's master, Charles I., had lost the control of
the kingdom which he had ruled in so despotic a manner for
many years, a youthful king, who was to become remarkable

---

[1] " Hist.," p. 281.   [2] *Ib.*, p. 281.   [3] *Ib.*, p. 354.

as the embodiment of extreme monarchical pretensions, had
ascended the throne of France, in the person of Louis XIV.
In England, a very different character was rapidly rising to
distinction during the progress of the trial of Laud.   Oliver
Cromwell was to be the means of destroying the king who
had not, perhaps, been so faithful to Laud as Laud had been
to him.   In the middle of Laud's trial, Cromwell crushed the
power of the royalists in the North of England at the battle
of Marston Moor.   Each piece of news, as it reached Laud in
the Tower, must have increased his hopelessness.   Perhaps
the most cruel blow of all may have been the abolition of his
beloved *Book of Common Prayer.*

It was while Laud's trial was going on that the great party
of Independents attained its extraordinary supremacy in
England.   Their very existence as a predominant power
would have been fatal to Laud's liberty, if not to his existence.

Meanwhile, the appearance of the streets of London had
greatly changed.   The smart cavaliers and gay royalist troops
were no more seen, and in their place were round-heads,
whigs, high-peaked hats, black capes, " godly " ministers, and
the sombre uniforms of the parliamentary soldiers.   The
" raskle rabble," as Heylin called it, was allowed to go
pretty much where it liked, and peers and peeresses, and
country squires and their wives and daughters were little
thought of or respected.   It is true that the wild ruffianism
and immorality that usually accompany revolutions were
absent, and that sermons, which are rarely tolerated in any
shape on such occasions, were the favourite entertainment of
both soldiers and civilians ; but it was none the less evident
that London was in the stern presence of what has been well
named by Clarendon " The Great Rebellion."

CHAPTER XXXIX

AN account of the trial of Laud might be written in more than one way. His biographer, Heylin, might be quoted to the effect that his persecutors found [1] "more difficulty in it than was first lookt for," as his defence "gave such a general satisfaction to all that heard it, that the mustering up of all the evidence against him would not take it off. To prove the first branch of the charge against him, they had ript up the whole course of his Life, from his first coming to *Oxford*, till his Commitment to the Tower; but could find no sufficient Proof of any design to bring in *Popery*, or suppress the true Protestant Religion here by Law Established. For want whereof, they insisted upon such Reproaches as were laid upon him when he lived in the University, the beautifying of his Chappel Windows with Pictures and Images, the Solemn Consecration of Churches and Chappels, &c., &c.; " "the care and diligence of his Chaplains in expunging some offensive passages out of" certain books; "the preferring of many able men to his Majesties Service, and to advancements in the Church;" "and finally the Piety of his endeavours, &c."

Or another contemporary writer might be chosen as the authority to follow, and we might "begin with his owne Kennel at Lambeth"[2] and show how it was proved by his accusers that "no chappell in Rome could be more idolatrous;" that he had taught his clergy to make " low bowings or duckings to the Altar;" and that "he likewise introduced Gaudy Romish Copes into his Chappell." Next we might "pursue and trace this Romish Fox from his chappell and public, to his Study and private devotions." "Having hunted this Popish Vermin from place to place in his own kennel, and

---

[1] "Cyp. Ang.," p. 491.   [2] "Canterburies Doome," pp. 59 and foll.

bolted him out thence," we might follow him "from Lambeth across the Thames to the Kings own Royal Chapel at Whitehall," and see what was proved against him, at his trial, concerning his misdoings there ; we might "in the next place pursue this Romish Reinold unto our Cathedrall Churches, where hee began his Popish Innovations very early ;" and last of all we might "so fully uncase this *Romish Fox*, as notwithstanding all his shifts and subterfuges to evidence him the most *Pestilent Jesuiticall underminer and subverter* of the *established doctrines of the Church of England*, the Archest *advancer* of the *Erroneous Positions* of the Church of *Rome*, that ever breathed in our *English Ayre*."

A third method would be to work entirely from Laud's own account of the trial, which is much the fullest. I propose to make the latter the basis of my report; but freely to use materials from various convenient sources and to make my story as short as I can.

First I will quote from Clarendon.[1] " They accused him ' of a design to bring in Popery,' and of having ' correspondence with the Pope,' and such like particulars, as the Consciences of his greatest Enemies absolv'd him from. No Man was a greater, or abler Enemy to Popery ; No Man a more resolute and devout Son of the Church of *England*. He was prosecuted by Lawyers, assign'd to that purpose, out of those, who from their own Antipathy to the Church and Bishops, or from some disobligations receiv'd from him, were sure to bring Passion, Animosity, and Malice enough of their own, what evidence soever they had from others. And they did treat him with all the rudeness, reproach, and barbarity imaginable ; with which his Judges were not displeased. He defended himself with great and undaunted Courage, and less Passion than was expected from his Constitution ; answer'd all their objections with clearness, and irresistible reason ; and convinced all impartial Men of his Integrity, and his detestation of all Treasonable Intentions. So that though few excellent Men have ever had fewer Friends to their Persons, yet all reasonable Men

---

[1] " Hist. of the Reb.," vol. iv. p. 572.

absolv'd him from any foul Crime that the Law could take notice of, and punish."

I will now give a short summary of some of the evidence brought against him in the course of his trial.[1]

Alderman Atkins deposed that when he was prosecuted before the Council about ship-money, Laud was more violent against him than anybody else.

Sir Henry Vane swore that when the last Parliament rose, the archbishop said to the king that "now he might use his power."

It was deposed that when someone had denied the king's proclamation to be of equal force to a statute, his grace had replied :—" Whosoever falls upon it shall be broken; but upon whomsoever it falls, it shall grind him to powder."

The imprisoning of Burton, Prynne, and Bastwick were laid to his charge, as also was that of Sir John Corbet.

A witness named Ask swore that he had protected some players who had been found at a tavern at an unreasonable hour of the night, and that he had threatened Ask himself for not coming to receive the sacrament at the communion-rails.

A Brownist named Grafton deposed that he had been imprisoned and fined £50, owing to the archbishop.

Witnesses deposed that Laud had censured, deprived, and imprisoned a good clergyman named Huntley; that he practically took a bribe by making Sir Edward Gresham give half a bond of £200, which the Court assigned to him, towards the repair of St Paul's; that he got the men of Chester fined £1000 for feasting Prynne, and then, for the bribe of two hogshead of sack, had the fine reduced to £200; that he brought Sir Richard Samuel before the High Commission simply for doing his duty as a magistrate in punishing some clergymen; that he had summoned some other magistrates for holding their sessions in a part of the church at Tewkesbury; that he had illegally extorted from the king a patent for appropriating the fines inflicted by the Court of High Commission to the repairing of St Paul's;

---

[1] Chiefly from " Celebrated Trials," vol. ii.

that he had presented a blind man to a living ; that, making himself a universal law-giver, he had illegally altered the statutes for cathedrals and the University of Oxford ; and that he had assumed papal power by allowing himself to be written to as *Sanctitas tua, Spiritu sancto effusissime plenus,* and *Summus Pontifex.*

Further evidence was produced in a Bible found in his study with the five wounds of our Lord represented upon the cover, a Missal, and some other Catholic books ; and it was shown by depositions that there was an *Ecce Homo* among the pictures in his gallery and a painting behind the communion-table in his chapel.

It was proved that he had caused very many communion-tables to be placed altar-wise ; that he had consecrated communion plate ; and that, on the other hand, he had passed heavy sentences in the Court of High Commission upon a clergyman who had preached against images, as well as upon another who had removed a representation of God the Father from a church window at Salisbury.

Sir Henry and Anthony Mildmay gave evidence that he was hated in Rome by one faction and loved by another, and that there was a strong opinion that there had been a considerable improvement in the prospects of a reconciliation between the Anglican and Catholic Churches since he had been in power.

Other witnesses swore that, on hearing that a clergyman whom he had driven out of his benefice had gone to New England, he said that his arm should reach him even there ; that he had suppressed the English Bible with Geneva notes, and had also suppressed, or tampered with, other religious books ; that he had said in the Star Chamber that the altar was the greatest place of God's residence on earth, "greater than the pulpit" ; and that he had stated "that the Church of Rome and ours, were all one, that we did not differ in fundamentals, but circumstances, that Rome was a true church, &c."

Another accusation was that he had had "intelligence" with the Pope through a Franciscan Friar named Santa

Clara, and had given him rooms at Oxford. As this matter
has not yet been noticed in these pages, I may take this
opportunity of saying that, among the State Papers, are his
notes on this subject, in which he states that this man "was
setting out a book about the Articles of the Church of England," and "his desire was to have his book printed here."
" I gave him this answer : That I did not like the way which
the Church of Rome went concerning Episcopacy ; and howsoever that I could never give way that any such book from
the pen of any Romanist should be printed here ; and that
the Bishops of England are very well able to defend their
own cause and calling, without calling in aid from Rome,
and would so do when they saw cause." [1] He only gave
him rooms at Oxford, at the request of the king, in order
that he might have the use of the library.

Many passages out of his Diary, which I have already
noticed, as well as events which I have recorded, were put
in and sworn to as evidence.

Although Laud had the assistance of counsel, he conducted his own case in the House of Lords, except on some
purely technical points, and, when he had returned to the
Tower, he carefully wrote out an account of each day's
defence. Perhaps he may have made up his mind that his
judges were determined to condemn him to death, whatever
might happen, and he may have come to the conclusion that
the best he could hope for would be to be acquitted by
posterity, when his own history of his trial should be read
by future generations.

Many of the charges brought against him were so frivolous
that he was able to reply to them without difficulty and even
to hold them up for derision. In respect to not a few of the
remainder, he answered that the actions of other men, and
even those of the Star Chamber, the Council Table, the
Court of High Commission, and Convocation were unjustly
attributed to himself, personally, when he had had nothing
to do with them, or else exclusively laid to his charge when
he had only shared in them with several others.

[1] " Cal. Sta. Pa. Dom.," 1641-3, p. 542.

Laud showed no want of courage in addressing his judges. For instance, when replying to a charge of saying that certain churchwardens, who refused to turn a communion-table, which was placed "table-wise," "altar-wise," "deserved to be laid by the Heels for the Contempt of their Bishop"; he said [1] :—" Under Favour, *my Lords*, I spake Truth." Again, in defending himself for having been the means of causing a man named Adams to be excommunicated, he said [2] :—"I cannot but think he well deserved it." Yet again, when dealing with an accusation that he had had a pew taken down which "was set above the Communion Table" in a London church, he said [3] :—" I confess to your Lordships, I could never like, that Seats should be set above the Communion Table : If that be any Error in me, be it so."

Now and then he would give a slap to a witness. A Mr Wheeler had given evidence of an offensive passage in one of his sermons, and of this he spoke [4] as follows :—" I cannot but be sorry to hear it from Mr *Wheeler's* own Mouth ; that he was so careful to write this Passage, and so ready to come to witness it against me ; considering how many Years I have known him, and how freely he hath often come to my Table, and been welcome to me ; yet never told me, this Passage in my Sermon troubled him. It seems some Malignity or other laid it up against this wet Day."

Mr Nicholas, one of the committee appointed to manage the evidence against him, said " 'Tis Blasphemy to give that Title (Sanctitas) in the Abstract, to any but God." [5] Laud replied that it had been given to many bishops besides himself (to say nothing of its not having been applied exclusively to Popes), " clean through the Primitive Church, both *Greek* and *Latin ;* " and he added that he " must tell Mr *Nicholas*, that 'tis a great Presumption for him, a Lawyer, and no Studied Divine, to Charge *Blasphemy upon all the Fathers of the Primitive Church.* 'Tis given to *St Augustine* by *Hilarius* and *Enodius*, and in the Abstract." And presently he said :—" According to Mr *Nicolas* his Divinity, we shall

<hr/>

[1] "Hist.," p. 262.   [2] *Ib.*, p. 267.   [3] *Ib.*, p. 272.
        [4] *Ib.*, p. 273.   [5] *Ib.*, p. 284.

learn in time, to deny *the Immortality* of the Soul. For *Immortality* in the Abstract is applied to God only, 1 *Tim.* 6, who only hath *Immortality*. Therefore, if it may not in an under and a qualified Sense, by Participation, be applied to the Creature, the Soul of Man cannot be *Immortal*." It seems strange that a man who could see the force of this argument should not be able to understand the inferior worship or homage paid by Catholics to saints.

But to return to Mr Nicholas. On another day of his trial, Laud said that " Mr *Nicolas* was up again with *Pander to the Whore of* Babylon, and his other foul Language," and he went on to prove that one of Mr Nicholas's "zealous Witnesses against the *Whore of Babylon*," was not a particularly moral character in his own private life, and he implied in language which would not be tolerated in the present day, that he would do well to remember that there were other places besides Babylon in which all people were not quite so immaculate as might be desired.

A Mr Pincen bore witness that Laud, in the Court of High Commission, had declared that the clergy were now "debased." To this Laud answered [1] :—" Truly, *my Lords*, if I did say thus (which is more than I can call to Memory) I spake truth ; they were debased."

Laud was accused of treason and assuming Papal power in forbidding marriages in the chapel of the White Tower at the Tower of London, the witness being " Sir *William Balfore*, *then Lieutenant of the Tower*. He says, that *I did oppose those Marriages*. And so say I. But I did it for the Subject of *England's* sake. For many of their Sons and Daughters were there undone. Nor *Banes* " (Banns) " nor *Licence*, nor any means of fore-knowledge to prevent it. Was this ill ? " [2] Later he writes :—" Then he tells the Lords, *that in a Discourse of mine with him at* Greenwich, *about this business, I let fall an Oath*. I am sorry for it, if I did. But that 's no *Treason*." And by-and-bye, he girds himself up for a thrust at his tormentor, saying :—" And *his Majesty* having Graciously taken this Care for the Indemnity of his Subject, I troubled

[1] " Hist.," p. 287.   [2] *Ib.*, p. 295.

my self no more with it: My aim being not to cut off any Priviledges of that Place, but only to prevent the Abuses of that Lawless Custom. And if *cui bono* be a considerable Circumstance, as it uses to be in all such Businesses, then it may be thought on too, that this Gentleman the Lieutenant had a considerable share for his part out of the Fee of every Marriage. Which I believe was as dear to him as the Priviledge."

He is delighted to have a laugh at his old enemy, Prynne, too [1] :—" I pray in all this curious Search (and Mr *Pryn* here, and all along spared no pains), why were no Prayers to the *B. Virgin* and the Saints found, if I were so swallowed up in Popery?" He loses his temper with Prynne, on another occasion, about the stained glass windows in his chapel. Prynne had said that " *he had taken a survey of the Windows* at Lambeth. And I doubt not his diligence." [2] " He says, *the Pictures of these Stories* are in the *Mass-Book*. If it be so, yet they were not taken thence by me. Arch-Bishop *Morton* did that work, as appears by his Device in the Windows. He says, *the Story of the day of Judgment was in a Window* in atrio, *that must not come into the Chappel.* Good Lord, whither will Malice carry a Man?"

He is severe, again, upon some clergymen who said he had unjustly suspended them. Of one he observes [3] :—" He says, *that his Patron took away his Benefice.* Why, *my Lords,* he had none; he was only a *Curate,* and, God knows, unfit for that." Of another:—" He says, *That I sent to Sir* Nath. Brent *to Suspend him.* That is true, but it was when he would neither Obey, nor keep in his Tongue."

One of the charges led to a curious defence, which has an important bearing upon his views concerning apostolical succession. I will quote his own words [4] :—" The First Charge is, *That I* deny them to be a Church" (*i.e.,* the French and Dutch Reformed Churches): " For they say, that I say *plainly in my* Book *against* Fisher, *that* No Bishop, no Church." And then he says that " Mr *Nicolas* added, *that this was seconded by Bishop* Mountague's *Book, which Mr*

Pryn (carefully) *witnessed was found in my Study, and Licensed by Dr* Braye": who was one of Laud's deputies. Observe now what Laud says on this point: — "He" Montague, "adds this Exception, that none but a Bishop can ordain, but *in Casu Necessitatis*, which is the Opinion of many Learned and Moderate Divines." That is to say, when a priest is urgently required, and no bishop can be obtained to ordain him, a simple priest can do so. It is a case of necessity. It might very rarely happen, but, were it to do so, the thing might be done. Verily, necessity is the mother of invention! He makes this further comment:— "Yet this is very considerable in the Business, whether an inevitable Necessity be cast upon them, or they pluck a kind of necessity upon themselves."

It would be very wrong, he evidently means, for any one to go purposely out of reach of bishops in order to have the excuse of ordaining a priest on the ground of "inevitable Necessity," and thus "pluck a kind of Necessity"; but if a shipwrecked crew and one clergyman were to be cast on a desert island, and the clergyman were to find himself dying he might ordain a successor, who would be able to celebrate the eucharist for them just as well as any other in the world. It is needless to say that this is a tremendous admission. Of course, the strictest Catholic theologian would admit that a shipwrecked crew, on a lonely island, could unite together in prayer and worship; that, if they had women with them, they could marry, as, *in Casu Necessitatis*, such marriages would be valid; for the man and woman, and not the priest, perform the sacrament in every marriage; and that if they had children, they could themselves baptize them, as any man, or woman, for that matter, can baptize *in Casu Necessitatis;* but no Catholic would for a moment allow that any but a bishop could ordain a priest in *Casu Necessitatis;* for the Catholic Church does not make two and two equal to five in *casu necessitatis.* For instance, where there is no priest, no host can be consecrated, and where there is no consecrated host there can be no sacramental communion; but the Church teaches her children that they can make spiritual communions wherever they may be, and one of her saints compares sacramental and spiritual communions to gold and silver vessels; she teaches that, where no priest can be obtained, a good act of contrition gains forgiveness of sin; she claims, by the power of the keys, to grant enormous spiritual blessings to those who devoutly make certain short ejaculations, wherever they may be, and more especially at the hour of death; and she lays enormous stress on the doctrine that the desire for sacraments, where they cannot be had, may obtain the graces of them; but she never pretends that any but bishops can consecrate bishops or ordain priests, or that any but priests can make bread and wine into the body and blood of Christ, even in the most extreme *casu necessitatis.*

It is but fair to Laud to say that, in mentioning the question of the validity of ordinations by others than bishops, *in casu necessitatis,* he observes that his accusers said he disliked the idea of it; but he does not deny the doctrine; indeed he appears to imply that orders so given would be valid, provided the necessity were "inevitable," and not "plucked."

It is very far from my purpose to deny that Laud believed in either apostolical succession or the real presence, *as he understood them;* on the contrary, in that sense, he was an ardent champion of both; but I do most emphatically deny that he believed in what Catholics understand by those terms, or anything at all approaching it, and I more than doubt whether he believed in what modern High-Churchmen mean when they make use of them, although this is a somewhat "unknown quantity," and a point on which I write under a possibility of correction.

One day, when Laud came to the Bar of the House of Lords, he was surprised to see [1] "every Lord present with a New Thin Book *in Folio* in a blue Coat." He adds:—"I heard that Morning that Mr *Pryn* had Printed my *Diary,* and Published it to the World to disgrace me. Some Notes of his own are made upon it. The first and the last are two

---

[1] "Hist.," p. 411.

desperate Untruths, besides some others. This was the Book then in *the Lords* Hands, and I assure my self, that time picked for it, that the sight of it might damp me, and disinable me to speak : I confess I was a little troubled at it."

When he did speak, and it was the occasion of a recapitulation of his defence up to this point, he referred to the fact of his judges having his private Diary in their hands. After complaining that his very pockets had been searched, and his Diary, nay, his very prayer-book taken from him, he declared that he was[1] "thus far glad, even for this sad Accident. For by *my Diary* your Lordships have seen the Passages of my Life : And by my *Prayer Book* the greatest Secrets between God and my Soul : So that you may be sure you have me at the very bottom : Yet blessed be God, no Disloyalty is found in the one ; no Popery in the other." This was something to be thankful for !

[1] " Hist.," p. 413.

CHAPTER XL

LAUD'S recapitulation, from which I gave an extract at the end of the last chapter, need not be discussed at length in these pages. It began [1]:—"*My Lords*, my Hearing began *March* 12, 164¾, and continued to the end of July. In this time I was heard before *your Lordships*, with much Honour and Patience, Twenty Days, and sent back without Hearing, by reason of *your Lordships* greater Employments, Twelve Days. The rest were taken up with providing the Charge against me."

Some of the points of his recapitulation were not devoid of sarcasm.

"*All the late Canons* have been charged against me ; and the Argument which is drawn from thence, must lie thus : The Third of these *Canons* for suppressing the Growth of *Popery*, is the most full and strict *Canon* that ever was made against it in the Church of *England :* Therefore I that made this *Canon* to keep it out, am guilty of endeavouring to bring it in."

Next he refers to his having "reduced to *the Church of England* as many that were gone to *Rome*, as I believe any Minister in *England* can truly say he hath done :" "where the Argument lies thus : I converted many from *Popery*, and setled them in the Religion established in *England ;* Therefore I laboured to bring in *Popery ;* which out of all doubt can be no sober Man's way."

Then he refers to the already mentioned " Rome's Master Piece " revealed by Andreas ab Habernfield, by which, he says, it appeared that he had been in danger of his life " for stiffly opposing the bringing in of *Popery ;* and that there was no hope to alter Religion in *England*, till " he " was taken out

[1] " Hist.," p. 412.

of the way." "And then," he says, "the Argument against
me lies thus: There's no hope to bring in *Popery*, till I am
taken out of the way; therefore I did labour to bring it in.
Do not these things, *my Lords*, hang handsomely together?"

"Lastly, There have been above Threescore Letters and
other Papers, brought out of my Study into this Honourable
House; they are all about composing the Differences between
the Lutherans and the Calvinists in Germany." "Then the
Argument will be thus: I laboured to reconcile the *Protestants* in *Germany*, that they might unanimously set themselves against the *Papists;* therefore I laboured to bring
Popery into *England.*"

He then reminds the Lords of something which had been
said against him at the Bar by his prosecutors—"That *they
did not urge any of these particular Actions as Treason against
me; but the Result of them all together amounted to Treason.*
For answer to which, I must be bold to tell *your Lordships*,
That if no particular which is charged upon me be Treason,
the Result from them cannot be Treason." "*The Result*
must be of the same Nature and Species with the Particulars
from which it rises. But 'tis confessed no one of the Particulars are (*sic*) Treason: Therefore neither is the Result that
rises from them." "Neither can the Body of a Bear, and the
Soul of a Lion result into a Fox: nor the Legs of a Bull, the
Body of a Horse, and the Head of an Ass, result into a Man."
And then he proceeds to prove that, not only in nature, but
also in morality and law, the same rule holds good. He
ends by thanking their lordships for the "very Honourable
Patience" with which they had heard him "through this long
and tedious Tryal," by treating them to a quotation from St
Augustine, and by saying:—"And under that Providence,
which will, I doubt not, work to the best to my Soul that
loves God, I repose my self."

We travel quickly from the sublime to the ridiculous in
Laud's autobiography. Half a dozen lines below the quotation just made, he continues[1]:—"On *Wednesday, Septemb.*
4, as I was washing my Face, my Nose bled, and some-

---

[1] "Hist.," p. 421.

thing plentifully, which it had not done, to my remembrance, in Forty years before, save only once, and that was just the same Day and Hour, when my most Honourable Friend *the Lord Duke of Buckingham* was killed at *Portsmouth*, my self being then at *Westminster*. And upon *Friday*, as I was washing after Dinner, my Nose bled again. I thank God I make no superstitious Observation of this or any thing else ; yet I have ever used to mark what and how any thing of note falls to me. And here I after came to know, that upon both these Days in which I bled, there was great agitation in the *House of Commons*, to have me Sentenced by Ordinance ; but both times put off, in regard very few of that House had heard either my Charge or Defence."

And this was the man who found fault with Catholics for being superstitious !

In reply to Laud's recapitulation, a Mr Brown made " a Summ or Brief of the Charge which was brought against " him, during the recital of which Laud " possessed " his " Soul in Patience ; yet wondring at the bold, free, frequent, and most false Swearing that had been against " him.

Three weeks later, he writes [1] :--" Mr *Nicolas* made a great noise about me in the House, and would have had me presently Censured in the House ; and no less would serve his turn, but that I must be *Hanged*, and was at *Sus. per Coll.* till upon the Reasons before given, that if they went on this way, they must Condemn me unheard ; this violent Clamour ceased for that time."

At last one of Laud's own counsel, Mr Hern of Lincoln's Inn, got up to defend him, and " delivered his *Argument* very freely and stoutly, proving that nothing which " Laud " had either said or done according to this Charge is Treason, by any known Established Law of this Kingdom." His speech was very dry, very technical, very abrupt, very jerky, yet very wordy. Its entire drift was upon the legal question whether the charges against his client, even if proved, amounted to high treason. He maintained the contrary.

[1] " Hist. " p. 422.

To Laud's intense annoyance, on the first of November a warrant was delivered to the Lieutenant of the Tower commanding him to be brought to the Bar of the House of Commons. "I knew no Law or Custom for this," he writes;[1] "for though *our Votes*" (those of the bishops), "by a late Act of Parliament, be taken away, yet our *Baronies* are not : And so long as we remain *Barons*, we belong to the *Lords House*, and not to the *Commons*. Yet how to help my self I knew not." The House of Lords had risen when he received notice to be at the Bar of the Commons the very next morning ; so it was too late to petition his compeers for any privilege. He adds, with practical sense, "And should I have under any Pretence refused to go, Mr *Lieutenant* would have carried me."

He had no sooner taken his stand at the Bar of the House of Commons, than the Speaker informed him that an Ordinance had been already drawn up to attaint him of high treason ; "but, that they would not pass it, till they had heard a Summary of the Charge which was laid against" him, and that he "was sent for to hear it also." Laud then begged that his counsel and solicitor "might stand now by" him. This request was refused. Upon this, Mr Brown got up, and "delivered the Collection and Sum of the Charge against" him ; "much at one with that which he formerly made in the *Lords House*."

The moment that Mr Brown sat down, the Speaker called upon Laud to reply there and then. Against this, Laud humbly protested and begged for time. Ten days were granted to him.

When the day and hour arrived for him to make his answer, he stood at the Bar of the House of Commons and began as follows[2] :—"Mr *Speaker*, I was here *Novemb.* 2. It was the first time that ever I came within these Doors : And here then you gave me the most uncomfortable Break-fast that ever I came to ; namely, That this *Honourable House* had drawn up an *Ordinance* against me of High Treason ; but that before they would proceed farther, I should hear the Sum of the Charge which was against me ; which was the

[1] "Hist.," p. 432.   [2] *Ib.*, p. 433.

cause I was sent for then. And to give my Answer to that
which was then said, or rather mistaken in saying and inferring, is the cause of my coming now." He proceeded to tell
his judges that he hoped if he should say anything un-
advisedly, he might be given "liberty to re-call and expound"
himself; and then he said :—" Favourably consider into what
Straits I am cast, that after a long and tedious Hearing, I
must now come to answer to a Sum, or *Epitome* of the same
Charge; which how dangerous it may be for me, all Men
that know *Epitomes*, cannot but understand."

In referring to the charge reported to the Commons against
him by Mr Brown, he spoke as graciously of that lawyer as he
could [1] :—" This worthy Gentleman hath pressed all things as
hardly against me, as the Cause can any way bear: That was
his Duty to this *Honourable House*, and it troubles me not.
But his Carriage and Expressions were civil towards me, in
this my great Affliction ; And for this I render him humble
and hearty Thanks ; having from other Hands pledged my
Saviour in Gall and Vinegar, and drunk up the Cup of the
Scornings of the People to the very bottom." He had
evidently not forgotten the opening speech for the prosecution from the lips of Mr Serjeant Wilde !

Considering that he was standing before the tribunal of the
House of Commons—and we must bear in mind of what kind
of men its members for the most part consisted—Laud spoke
very boldly on one point, Mr Brown had stated that he had
complained that many of the witnesses, who had been produced against him in the House of Lords, were Separatists—
not Home Rulers ; but, as we should now say, Dissenters—
and it was certain that many Separatist M.P.s were at that
moment sitting in judgment upon him. Thereupon Laud
said :—" I did indeed complain of this, and I had abundant
Cause so to do. For there was scarce an active Separatist in
England, but some way or other his Influence was into this
Business against me. And whereas, the Gentleman said, *the
Witnesses were some Aldermen, and some Gentlemen, and Men
of Quality.* That's nothing ; for both Gentlemen, and Alder-

[1] " Hist.," p. 434.

men, and Men of all Conditions (the more's the pity), as the
Times now go, are Separatists from the Doctrine and Discip-
line of *the Church of England* Established by Law.   And
I would to God some of my Judges were not."

He then went through all the charges which had been
brought against him, and gave an answer to each, much as
he had done in the House of Lords, but more briefly, as the
time at his disposal was very limited.

He objected to his trial before the Commons on the ground
that that House was going to try him only upon Mr Brown's
report, " or a Hearsay," and not upon oath.   He " most humbly
desired " that his counsel might be heard upon the " point of
Law," whether even the charges brought against him, " if
proved (which " he conceives " they are not "), made him
guilty of high treason.   He also wished for the assistance
of his counsel, because his infirmities were " many and great,
which Age and Grief " had " added to those which " were
" naturally in " him.   He mentioned his " full four years
durance," and made an urgent appeal to the Speaker.

" I humbly desire you to take into consideration, my Calling, my Age, my former Life, my Fall, my Imprisonment,
long and strict.   That these Considerations may move you." [1]

" *Mr Speaker*, I am very aged, considering the Turmoils of
my Life ; and I daily find in my self more Decays than I make
shew of ; and the Period of my Life, in the Course of Nature,
cannot be far off.   It cannot but be a Grief unto me, to be
at these Years thus Charged before ye : Yet give me leave to
say thus much without Offence, Whatsoever Errors or Faults
I may have committed by the way, in any of my Proceedings,
through Human Infirmity ; as who is He that hath not
offended, and broken some Statutes too by Ignorance, or Mis-
apprehension or Forgetfulness, at some sudden time of Action ?
Yet if God bless me with so much Memory, I will die with
these Words in my Mouth: *That* I never intended, much less
endeavoured the subversion of the Laws of the Kingdom ;
nor the bringing in of Popish Superstition upon the true
Protestant Religion, Established by Law in this Kingdom."

[1] " Hist.," p. 439.

To make his long speech before the Commons was all he could do. "I was exceeding faint," he says,[1] "with speaking so long; and I had great pain and soreness in my Breast for almost a Fortnight after; then, I thank God, it wore away."

Two days after his reply to Mr Brown, he attended at the Bar of the House of Commons to hear that lawyer's "reply to his reply." It "had some great Mistakes in it; but else was for the most part but a more earnest Affirming of what he had delivered." Laud "conceived" that he was not intended to make a counter-reply, but that Mr Brown was to have the privilege of "the last Speech." "Therefore," says he, "being dismissed, I went away: And I was no sooner gone, but the *House* called for the *Ordinance* which was drawn up against me, and without Hearing *my Councel*, or any more ado, Voted me guilty of *High Treason*."

Three days afterwards, this Ordinance was presented to the House of Lords. There and then, says Laud, "the Earl of *Pembroke* began more fully to shew his canker'd Humour against me; how provoked, I protest I know not, unless by my serving him far beyond his Desert. There, among other coarse Language, he bestowed (as I am informed) the *Rascal* and the *Villain* upon me."

The business of the Ordinance against Laud was then discussed and adjourned several times, for a fortnight, when the Lords appointed a committee to examine the notes they had made during his trial in their own House. "The Earl of *Northumberland* on the Wool-Sack during the Debate, which lasted some days. When their own Notes failed, they called to Mr *Brown*, Clerk of their *House*, for his."

In yet another fortnight, December 16th, there was "(the Times considered) a very full *House of Lords;* about Twenty present, and my Business largely debated, and ready to come to the Question." What Laud implied, in saying "the Times considered," was that most of the peers had left London, either to support the king in person, or to levy troops for him among their tenants and retainers.

"I wish," he goes on, "with all my Heart it had, while the

[1] "Hist.," p. 441.

House was so full. But the *Earl of Pembroke* fell again into
his wonted violence : And asked *the Lords* what they stuck
at ? And added ; what, *shall we think the House of* Commons
had no Conscience in passing this Ordinance ? *Yes, they knew
well enough what they did.* One of the Wits hearing this
Excellent Passage of *the Earls ;* Protested, If ever he lived
to see a Parliament in *Bedlam*, this Prudent Earl should be
the Speaker, if he were able to procure him the Place."

The subject was then adjourned to the next day. There
were only fourteen peers present on this occasion ; they
voted Laud guilty of endeavouring to subvert the laws and
overthrow the Protestant religion, and declared him to be
an enemy to parliaments. " Then it being put to the Judges,
whether this were Treason or no ; the Judges unanimously
declared, that nothing which was charged against " him " was
Treason, by any known and established Law of the Land."

On Christmas Eve, the Lords and the Commons had " a
Conference " on the matter, when the former stated that they
had given the whole affair their most careful consideration,
and were quite unable to find the prisoner guilty of treason ;
therefore they begged that the arguments which had been
previously laid before them by Laud's counsel might be
answered.

" Then came *Christmas-Day*," Laud tells us,[1] and a most
Solemn Fast kept on it, with as Solemn an *Ordinance* for the
due observance of this Fast, and against the manner of keeping of that day in former Superstitious Times. A Fast never
before heard of in *Christendom*." There can have been little
object in instituting this fast on such a day, except to annoy
the more orthodox Anglicans, of whom Laud was, at that
time, chief !

After the conference between the Lords and the Commons,
Mr Serjeant Wilde told some friends that he wondered that
the peers should " so much distract their judgments."

On hearing this, Laud wrote :—" To see how good Wits
agree ! Surely, I believe he was of the *Earl of Pembroke's*
Councel, or *the Earl* of his, they jump so together. It seems

---

[1] " Hist.," p. 442.

in these Mens Opinions, the *House of Commons* can neither Err in Conscience nor Judgment. Howsoever, that *House* thought it fit *the Lords* should be satisfied, that I was by Law guilty of High Treason. And to that end sent up a Committee, *Jan.* 2, 1644 "—he must have meant 1645—" to make proof of it to their Lordships. At this Meeting two Judges were present, *Justice Reeves*, and *Judge Bacon.* The Managers of the business against me were three Lawyers, Mr *Brown*, *Serjeant Wild*, and Mr *Nicolas.* Neither my self nor any of *my Councel* there. What will this effect upon *the Lords*, Time must discover, as it doth the effect of other *Eclipses.* And thus far I had proceeded in this sad History by *Jan.* 3, 1644 " (1645). " The rest shall follow as it comes to my Knowledge."

These were the last words written by Laud in his History. A note in italics is added by his editor[1] :—" *Next day, the Arch-Bishop receiving the News that the* Bill of Attainder *had passed in the* House of Lords, broke off his History, and prepared himself for Death."

We hear something of the place where, and the manner in which, he received the information that he was to die, from Heylin.[2] " The passing of the Ordinance being signified to him by the then Lieutenant of the *Tower*, he neither entertained the news with *Stoical Apathy*, nor wailed his fate with weak and womanish Lamentations (to which Extremes most men are carried in this case) but heard it with so even and smooth a Temper, as shewed he neither was ashamed to live nor afraid to die."

There is some difference of opinion among historians as to the number of peers who passed the Ordinance for Laud's attainder ; some put it at " not above fourteen," [3] others say that only seven were present—the Earls of Kent, Pembroke, Salisbury, and Bolingbroke, Lord North, Lord Grey, and one other unnamed.[4] Clarendon says that the number was " not above twelve." [5] Heylin gives the same names as those

---

[1] " Hist.," p. 443.
[2] " Cyp. Ang.," p. 496.
[3] " Celebrated Trials," vol. ii. p. 43.
[4] *Ib.*, footnote.
[5] " Hist. of the Great Reb.," vol. iv. p. 572.

quoted above with that of " Lord *Bruce* (better known by the
name of the Earl of *Elgin*)" ;[1] but he adds "that the said
Lord *Bruce* hath frequently disclaimed that Action, and
solemnly professed his detestation of the whole Proceedings,
as most abhorrent from his nature, and contrary to his known
affections."

Clarendon's brief account[2] of the passing of the Ordinance
may be worth recording. "When they had said all they
could against Him, and he all for himself that need to be
said, and no such Crime" (as treason) "appearing, as the
Lords, as the Supreme Court of Judicatory, would take upon
them to judge him to be worthy of death; they resorted to
their Legislative Power, and by Ordinance of Parliament, as
they call'd it, that is by a determination of those Members
who sate in the Houses (whereof in the House of Peers there
were not above twelve) they appointed him to be put to death
as guilty of High Treason. The first time the two Houses
of Parliament had ever assumed that Jurisdiction, or that
ever Ordinance had been made to such a purpose; nor
could any Rebellion be more against the Law, than their
Murtherous Act."

---

[1] "Cyp. Ang.," p. 494.   [2] "Hist. of the Great Reb.," vol. iv. p. 572.

[This may not be an inappropriate place in which to quote Carlyle's opinion
of Laud. " Poor Laud seems to me to have been weak and ill-starred, not dishonest ; an unfortunate Pedant rather than anything worse. His ' Dreams ' and
superstitions, at which they laugh so, have an affectionate, loveable kind of
character. He is like a College Tutor, whose whole world is forms, College-
rules ; whose notion is that these are the life and safety of the world. He is
placed suddenly, with that unalterable luckless notion of his, at the head not of a
College but of a Nation, to regulate the most complex deep-reaching interests of
men. He thinks they ought to go by the old decent regulations ; nay that their
salvation will lie in extending and improving these. Like a weak man, he drives
with spasmodic vehemence towards his purpose ; cramps himself to it, heeding no
voice of prudence, no cry of pity : He will have his College-rules obeyed by his
Collegians ; that first ; and till that, nothing. He is an ill-starred Pedant, as I
said. He would have it the world was a College of that kind, and the world *was
not* that. Alas, was not his doom stern enough ? Whatever wrongs he did, were
they not all frightfully avenged on him."—*Lectures on Heroes. The Hero as
King.*]

CHAPTER XLI.

On Tuesday, the 6th of January, in the year 1645, it was ordered that William Laud, sometime Archbishop of Canterbury, should be hanged, drawn, and quartered on the following Friday. Laud immediately sent to the Lords the king's pardon which, as already stated, he had for some time had in his possession, "which he pleaded, and tender'd to them, and desired that it might be allow'd,"[1] together with a petition, in which he prayed that, if die he must, the manner of his execution might be changed to beheading, and that Dr Stern, Dr Heywood, and Dr Martin might be allowed to attend him, "before and at his Death, to Administer Comfort to his Soul."[2]

The next day, Wednesday, "the Lords, at a Conference, acquainted the *Commons*"[3] with their reception of this pardon and petition, and they were read in both Houses. After a very short debate, the Commons declared the pardon to be of no effect, as the king had not the power of pardoning a prisoner condemned to death by the Parliament. The House of Lords agreed to the alteration in the mode of execution, and to his receiving the ministrations of the three clergymen he had selected; but the House of Commons gave a point blank refusal to the petition *in toto*, with the single exception of permitting Dr Stern to visit the prisoner, provided that one, or both, of two "Godly Ministers" of their own choosing were invariably present while Stern was with him.

Wednesday, therefore, must have been a miserable day to Laud; there were only forty-eight hours, or less, of life before him, and the horrible and disgraceful death of hanging, being cut down while yet alive, having his bowels roughly torn

---

[1] Clarendon, "Hist.," vol. iv. pp. 573-4.
[2] Rushworth, par. 3, vol. ii. p. 834.   [3] *Ib.*

out by the executioner and burned before his eyes, if he
should have life enough left in him to see it done, and then
to have his naked body hacked to pieces, as if it were that of
a pig in the hands of a butcher, in the presence of an immense
crowd, was the prospect before him at the end of it.   In the
meantime, there would be a canting, covenanting, "unconformable" minister in his room, whenever he wished to confess to, or receive spiritual comfort from, his own chaplain.

He made, however, another attempt to soften the rigour of
his sentence, by sending a petition to the Parliament, praying
that, as a divine, as a bishop, as one who had had the honour
of sitting in the House of Lords, and of being a member of
the king's most Honourable Privy Council, he might not be
exposed to such an ignominious death, and that he might die
at the block.   On the Thursday, within four-and-twenty
hours of his execution, to his great relief he was told that the
Commons had relented, and that, instead of being hanged,
drawn, and quartered, he would have his head cut off on the
following morning.   He spent his time, during the interval,
beyond what was required for sleep and the taking of food,
partly at his devotions, and partly in writing out a speech
which he intended to deliver on the scaffold ; for he was not
only anxious to say the right thing at such a time, which he
might fail to do, from nervousness or distractions, if he trusted
himself to make an extempore address, but also to be able to
hand to his chaplain a written paper containing the very
words he had used, so that no garbled report of them need be
tolerated.   It was a sad sermon to have to prepare ; but he
evidently bestowed very great care and trouble upon it.

Heylin says [1]:—"So well was he studied in the Art of
Dying (especially in the last and strictest part of his Imprisonment) that by continual Fastings, Watchings, Prayers,
and such like Acts of Christian Humiliation, his Flesh was
rarified into Spirit, and the whole man so fitted for Eternal
Glories, that he was more than half in Heaven, before Death
brought his bloody (but Triumphant) Chariot, to convey him
thither."

[1] "Cyp. Ang.," p. 496.

I hope that it may have been so; but it is not always easy for the biographer of Laud to steer between eulogiums of this kind from the pen of Heylin and the angry abuses of Prynne, who describes the "transcendent Hainousnesse" of "the boldest and most impudent Oppressour that ever was."

The warrant for his execution was brought to the Tower by Sheriff Chambers on the evening of Thursday, January 9th. He now devoted himself to prayer, and begged the prayers of others, especially those of Dr Holdsworth, who had been a fellow prisoner in the Tower for a year and a half; although they had had no intercourse during that time.

Shortly before his fall from power, Laud had shown many symptoms of nervousness, if not of abject fear; but throughout his trial, and still more at the time of his execution, although worn out with anxiety and sorrow, he displayed admirable courage.

On the Thursday evening, says Heylin,[1] " after he had refreshed his Spirits with a moderate Supper, he betook himself unto his Rest, and slept very soundly, till the time came, in which his Servants were appointed to attend his rising. A most assured sign of a Soul prepared." This, I venture to think, is a somewhat bold assertion; for the sleep of many a modern murderer, on the night preceding his execution, has been better than, at least, the apparent preparation of his soul.

Laud got up early on the Friday morning, and, as might have been expected when he had only a few hours to live, began his prayers. Perhaps Mr Benson may be right in saying [2]:—" I do not think we are justified in saying more than that he was a prayerful man, but more liturgically than contemplatively. I do not think he went to his prayers for light and leading," " but that he looked upon them as a bounden duty and as a source of comfort." The prospect of immediate execution, however, is said to be a wonderful stimulant to devotion when a man has any faith at all.

It was observed that the day of Laud's death, the tenth of January, was the feast day of his namesake, William (Saint

[1] "Cyp. Ang.," p. 496.   [2] P. 207.

William), Archbishop of Bourges, who had fought as zealously
against the Albigenses as Laud had fought against the
Puritans and Covenanters;[1] but no notice was taken of the
fact that the French William, Archbishop, was a remarkably
devoted servant to the Pope, and that, unlike the English
William, "he refused to have recourse to the civil power
against" "impenitent sinners."[2]

Laud continued in prayer until Pennington, the Lieutenant
of the Tower, accompanied by other officers, came to conduct
him to the place of execution on Tower Hill. The distance
to be walked was not very great, perhaps between two and
three hundred yards in all; but it may have seemed quite
long enough when, after passing through the gates, beyond
the precincts of the Tower, and turning to the right, the procession wended its way amidst the dense crowd assembled to
see the execution. Any sort of execution is a pleasure to a
mob, and to see the head of an Archbishop of Canterbury
chopped off was a treat to look upon for which, what modern
reporters call, "every coign of vantage," would be eagerly
seized.

As Laud paced slowly on, surrounded by officials and
soldiers, through the tightly packed mass of spectators, "some
rude and uncivil People reviled him as he pass'd along, with
opprobrious Language, as loth to let him *go to the Grave in
Peace*; yet it never discomposed his Thoughts, nor disturbed
his Patience."[3]

The outward surroundings, apart from his guard with their
pikes and the soldiers with their muskets, must have looked
far less stern than the thick walls and embattlements of the
Tower in which he had been imprisoned for some years,
and the row of ordinary houses, with their pointed gables,
which we find represented in most old pictures of Tower Hill,
would give a peaceful and civilian appearance to the unen-
closed piece of ground to which the party was progressing on
that fine January morning; but presently an ugly, square
erection, with a single railing round it, came into view, and

[1] Benson, p. 158.   [2] Butler's "Lives of the Saints," vol. i., January 10.
[3] "Cyp. Ang.," p. 496.

Laud saw before him the scaffold and the block. Within six weeks that scaffold was erected for no less than five executions—Sir Alexander Carew's, the Hothams' (father and son), Laud's, and Lord Maguire's.

Poor old fellow! He walked with great courage up to the forbidding structure, ascended the steps, and stood upon the boarded floor. "As he did not fear the frowns," says Heylin,[1] "so neither did he covet the Applause of the *Vulgar Herd;* and therefore rather chose to read what he had to speak unto the People, than to affect the ostentation either of Memory or Wit in that dreadful *Agony;* whether with greater Magnanimity than Prudence, I can hardly say. As for the matter of his Speech, besides what did concern himself and his own *Purgation*, his great care was to clear his Majesty, and the Church of *England*, from any inclination to *Popery.*"

As Laud's speech on the scaffold is long, I shall take the liberty of quoting Mr Benson's rendering of it into modern spelling.

"'Good People, this is an uncomfortable time to preach; yet I shall begin with a text of Scripture, Hebrews xii. 2, "Let us run with patience the race that is set before us; looking unto Jesus, the Author and Finisher of our faith, Who for the joy that was set before Him endured the Cross, despising the shame, and is set down at the right hand of the throne of God."

"'I have been long in my race; and how I have looked unto Jesus, the Author and Finisher of my faith, He best knows. I am now come to the end of my race, and here I find the Cross, a death of shame. But the shame must be despised, or no coming to the right hand of God. Jesus despised the shame for me, and God forbid that I should not despise the shame for Him.

"'I am going apace, as you see, towards the Red Sea, and my feet are upon the very brink of it: an argument, I hope, that God is bringing me into the Land of Promise; for that was the way through which He led His people.

[1] "Cyp. Ang.," p. 496.

"'But before they came to it, He instituted a passover for them. A lamb it was ; but it must be eaten with sour herbs. I shall obey, and labour to digest the sour herbs, as well as the lamb. And I shall remember it is the Lord's passover. I shall not think of the herbs, nor be angry with the hands that gather them ; but look up only to Him who instituted that, and governs these : for men can have no more power over me than what is given them from above.

"'I am not in love with this passage through the Red Sea, for I have the weakness and infirmity of flesh and blood plentifully in me. And I have prayed with my Saviour, *Ut transiret calix iste*, that this cup of red wine might pass from me. But if not, God's will, not mine, be done. And I shall most willingly drink of this cup as deep as He pleases, and enter into this sea, yea, and pass through it, in the way that He shall lead me.

"'But I would have it remembered, good people, that when God's servants were in this boisterous sea, and Aaron among them, the Egyptians which persecuted them, and did in a manner drive them into that sea, were drowned in the same waters, while they were in pursuit of them.

"'I know my God, Whom I serve, is as able to deliver me from the sea of blood, as He was to deliver the Three Children from the furnace. And (I most humbly thank my Saviour for it) my resolution is as theirs was : they would not worship the image which the king had set up, nor will I the imaginations which the people are setting up. Nor will I forsake the temple and the truth of God, to follow the bleating of Jeroboam's calves in Dan and in Bethel.

"'And as for this people, they are at this day miserably misled : God in His mercy open their eyes, that they may see the right way. For at this day the blind lead the blind ; and if they go on, both will certainly fall into the ditch.

"'For myself, I am (and I acknowledge it in all humility) a most grievous sinner many ways—by thought, word, and deed ; and yet I cannot doubt but that God hath mercy in store for me, a poor penitent, as well as for other sinners. I have now, upon this sad occasion, ransacked every corner of my heart ; and yet I thank God I have not found among the many, any one sin which deserves death by any known law of this kingdom.

"'And yet hereby I charge nothing upon my judges : for if they proceed upon proof by valuable witnesses, I or any other innocent may be justly condemned. And I thank God, though the weight of the sentence lie heavy upon me, I am as quiet within as ever I was in my life.

"'And though I am not only the first Archbishop, but the first man, that ever died by an Ordinance in Parliament, yet some of my predecessors have gone this way, though not by this means : for Elphegus was hurried away and lost his head by the Danes ; Simon Sudbury in the fury of Wat Tyler and his fellows. Before these, St John the Baptist had his head danced off by a lewd woman ; and St Cyprian, Archbishop of Carthage, submitted his head to a persecuting sword. Many examples great and good ; and they teach me patience. For I hope my cause in heaven will look of another dye, than the colour that is put upon it here.

"'And some comfort it is to me, not only that I go the way of these great men in their several generations, but also that my charge, as foul as it is made, looks like that of the Jews against St Paul (Acts xxv. 8) ; for he was accused for the law and the temple, *i.e.* religion ; and like that of St Stephen (Acts vi. 14) for breaking the ordinances which Moses gave, *i.e.* law and religion, the holy place and the law (verse 13).

"But you will say, Do I then compare myself with the integrity of St Paul and St Stephen ? No : far be that from me. I only raise a comfort to myself, that these great saints and servants of God were laid at in their times, as I am now. And it is memorable that St Paul, who helped on this accusation against St Stephen, did after fall under the very same himself.

"'Yes, but here is a great clamour that I would have brought in Popery. I shall answer that more fully by and by. In the mean time, you know what the Pharisees laid against Christ Himself, "If we let Him alone, all men will believe on Him *et venient Romani*, and the Romans will come,

and take away both our place and nation." Here was a
causeless cry against Christ, that the Romans would come :
and see how just the judgment of God was. They crucified
Christ for fear lest the Romans should come ; and His death
was it which brought in the Romans upon them, God punishing them with that which they most feared. And I pray God
this clamour of *venient Romani* (of which I have given no
cause) help not to bring them in. For the Pope never had
such an harvest in England since the Reformation, as he hath
now upon the sects and divisions that are amongst us. In
the mean time, " by honour and dishonour, by good report
and evil report, as a deceiver and yet true," am I passing
through this world.

"'Some particulars also I think it not amiss to speak of.

"'1. And first, this I shall be bold to speak of the King,
our gracious Sovereign. He hath been much traduced also
for bringing in of Popery ; but on my conscience (of which
I shall give God a present account), I know him to be as
free from this charge as any man living. And I hold him to
be as sound a Protestant, according to the religion by law
established, as any man in the kingdom ; and that he will
venture his life as far and as freely for it. And I think I do
or should know both his affection to religion, and his grounds
for it, as fully as any man in England.

"'2. The second particular is concerning this great and
populous city (which God bless). Here hath been of late a
fashion taken up to gather hands, and then go to the great
court of the kingdom, the Parliament, and clamour for
justice ; as if that great and wise court, before whom the
causes come which are unknown to the many, could not or
would not do justice but at their appointment ; a way which
may endanger many an innocent man, and pluck his blood
upon their own heads, and perhaps upon the city's also.

"'And this hath been lately practised against myself ; the
magistrates standing still, and suffering them openly to proceed from parish to parish without check. God forgive the
setters of this ; with all my heart I beg it : but many well-
meaning people are caught by it.

"'In St Stephen's case, when nothing else would serve, they stirred up the people against him (Acts vi. 12). And Herod went the same way: when he had killed St James, yet he would not venture upon St Peter, till he found how the other pleased the people (Acts xii. 3).

"'But take heed of having your hands full of blood (Isai. i. 15); for there is a time best known to Himself, when God, above other sins, makes inquisition for blood. And when that inquisition is on foot, the Psalmist tells us that God remembers; but that is not all: He remembers, and forgets not the complaint of the poor, *i.e.* whose blood is shed by oppression.

"'Take heed of this: "It is a fearful thing to fall into the hands of the living God"; but then especially when He is making inquisition for blood. And with my prayers to avert it, I do heartily desire this city to remember the prophecy that is expressed in Jer. xxvi. 15.

"'3. The third particular is, the poor Church of England. It hath flourished, and been a shelter to other neighbouring Churches, when storms have driven upon them. But, alas! now it is in a storm itself and God only knows whether or how it shall get out. And, which is worse than a storm from without, it is become like an oak cleft to shivers with wedges made out of its own body; and at every cleft, profaneness and irreligion is entering in. While (as Prosper says) men that introduce profaneness are cloked over with the name *religionis imaginariæ*, of imaginary religion; for we have lost the substance, and dwell too much in opinion. And that Church, which all the Jesuits' machinations could not ruin, is fallen into danger by her own.

"'4. The last particular (for I am not willing to be too long) is myself. I was born and baptised in the bosom of the Church of England, established by law: in that profession I have ever since lived, and in that I come now to die.

"'What clamours and slanders I have endured for labouring to keep an uniformity in the external service of God, according to the doctrine and discipline of this Church, all men know, and I have abundantly felt. Now at last I am accused of high treason in Parliament, a crime which my soul ever abhorred. This treason was charged to consist of two parts—an endeavour to subvert the laws of the land ; and a like endeavour to overthrow the true Protestant religion, established by law.

"' Besides my answers to the several charges, I protested mine innocency in both Houses. It was said, Prisoners' protestations at the bar must not be taken. I must, therefore, come now to it upon my death, being instantly to give God an account for the truth of it.

"' I do therefore here, in the presence of God and His holy Angels, take it upon my death, that I never endeavoured the subversion either of law or religion. And I desire you all to remember this protest of mine for my innocency in this, and from all treasons whatsoever.

"' I have been accused likewise as an enemy of Parliaments. No ; I understand them, and the benefit that comes by them, too well to be so. But I did dislike the misgovernments of some Parliaments many ways, and I had good reason for it ; for *corruptio optimi est pessima.* And that being the highest court, over which no other hath jurisdiction, when it is misinformed or misgoverned, the subject is left without all remedy.

"' But I have done. I forgive all the world, all and every of those bitter enemies which have persecuted me ; and humbly desire to be forgiven of God first, and then of every man. And so I heartily desire you to join in prayer with me.

"' O eternal God and merciful Father, look down upon me in mercy, in the riches and fulness of all Thy mercies. Look upon me, but not till Thou hast nailed my sins to the Cross of Christ, not till Thou hast bathed me in the blood of Christ, not till I have hid myself in the wounds of Christ ; that so the punishment due unto my sins may pass over me. And since Thou art pleased to try me to the uttermost, I most humbly beseech Thee, give me now, in this great instant, full patience, proportionable comfort,

and a heart ready to die for Thine honour, the King's
happiness, and this Church's preservation.   And my zeal
to these (far from arrogancy be it spoken) is all the sin
(human frailty excepted, and all incidents thereto) which is
yet known to me in this particular, for which I come now to
suffer; I say, in this particular of treason.   But otherwise,
my sins are many and great.   Lord, pardon them all, and
those especially (whatever they are) which have drawn down
this present judgment upon me.   And when Thou hast given
me strength to bear it, do with me as seems best in Thine
own eyes.   Amen.

"'And that there may be a stop of this issue of blood
in this more than miserable kingdom, O Lord, I beseech
Thee give grace of repentance to all blood-thirsty people.
But if they will not repent, O Lord, confound all their
devices, defeat and frustrate all their designs and endeavours upon them, which are or shall be contrary to the
glory of Thy great Name, the truth and sincerity of
religion, the establishment of the King, and his posterity
after him, in their just rights and privileges; the honour
and conservation of Parliaments in their just power; the
preservation of this poor Church in her truth, peace, and
patrimony; and the settlement of this distracted and distressed people, under their ancient laws, and in their native
liberties.   And when Thou hast done all this in mere
mercy for them, O Lord, fill their hearts with thankfulness, and with religious dutiful obedience to Thee and
Thy commandments all their days.   So, Amen, Lord Jesu,
amen.   And receive my soul into Thy bosom.   Amen.

"'Our Father, which art in heaven, Hallowed be Thy
Name.   Thy kingdom come.   Thy will be done in earth,
As it is in heaven.   Give us this day our daily bread.
And forgive us our trespasses, As we forgive them that
trespass against us.   And lead us not into temptation;
But deliver us from evil: For Thine is the kingdom, and
the power, and the glory, For ever and ever.   Amen.'"

CHAPTER XLII.

ONE feature of Laud's speech upon the scaffold deserves especial attention, and that is the manner in which he said all he could in favour of his king, and endeavoured, if possible, to save him. His conduct, in this matter, towards Charles contrasts very favourably with Charles's towards himself from the time of his arrest. I am not imputing any blame to the king in respect to the actual execution, which he was powerless to prevent at the time it occurred ; for Laud was then in the hands of the Parliament, with whom Charles was at war ; but, in the earlier days of his archbishop's imprisonment, it is not unfair to think that he might have made greater efforts on his behalf. Again, even if it were impossible that he could do anything to save him, it might have been expected that we should find some records of communications and kind offices between two men who had been such intimate friends, even if it might have been a dangerous step for Charles to visit Laud personally in the Tower. Let all credit be paid to the king's memory for sending his old servant a free (and, as it proved, useless) pardon ; but it would have been pleasanter to have read of other acts of kindness and recognition besides this. Not a word, on the other hand, can be said against the faithfulness of Laud to his master, and at the very last he made a valiant defence of his king's Protestantism and freedom from Popery—his "gracious Sovereign," who "hath been much traduced also for bringing in of Popery" ; but on his conscience, of which he is on the very point of giving an account, he knows him "to be as free from this charge as any man living," and holds "him to be as sound a Protestant, according to religion by law established, as any man in the Kingdom," feeling certain that he would "venture his life as far and as freely for it."

Perhaps, in his prayer, we cannot altogether defend Laud from what is vulgarly called " playing to the gallery," when he beseeches God to give repentance " to all blood-thirsty people," and, if they will not repent, " to confound all their devices," and " defeat and frustrate all their designs and endeavours "; and again, when he prays for " this distracted and distressed people," and tells his Maker confidentially that he is not guilty of treason. All this was carefully written out beforehand, and was probably intended partly for God and partly for the mob.

When he had finished reading his speech, Laud handed it to his chaplain, Dr Sterne, and observing that a man, named Hinde, had kept taking notes of it as he uttered it, he begged him to let him have no wrong done him by the publication of an imperfect edition. " Sir," replied Hinde, " you shall not. If I do so, let it fall upon my own head. I pray God have mercy upon your soul." " I thank you," answered Laud. " I did not speak with any jealousy as if you would do so, but only, as a poor man going out of the world, it is not possible for me to keep to the words of my paper, and a phrase might do me wrong." [1]

He then began to prepare himself for the axe, and as he took off his coat he said :—" I will put off my doublets, and God's will be done. I am willing to go out of the world ; no man can be more willing to send me out, than I am willing to be gone."

A great many officials and others had been allowed to come on to the scaffold, and they had the bad taste so to press round the archbishop, to see how he was bearing up, that he had scarcely sufficient room to disrobe himself ; whereupon he begged that he might at least have space enough given him for his death. " I thought," " there would have been an empty scaffold, that I might have had room to die. I beseech you let me have an end of this misery, for I have endured it long," said he.

A space was then cleared immediately round him. This enabled him to see the boards of the scaffold, when, to his

[1] Benson, p. 151.

annoyance, he perceived, on looking down through the chinks between them, that, in addition to the people upon the platform, there were others beneath it, even almost under the very block itself, who probably hoped thereby to have a choice view of some of the more ghastly details of the execution. He begged that either the spaces between the boards might be filled up, or that the people beneath the scaffold might be removed, " Lest my innocent blood should fall upon the heads of the people," said he.

In the meantime, the crowd kept jeering at the disgraced archbishop, who took no notice whatever of the uproar ; but a certain Sir John Clotworthy, an Irishman, determined to worry the poor victim at the point of death. He had succeeded in obtaining admission to the scaffold, and, standing close to Laud, he said :—" What is the comfortablest saying which a dying man would have in his mouth ? " " *Cupio dissolvi et esse cum Christo,*" answered Laud. " That is a good desire," went on Sir John, " but there must be a foundation for that divine assurance "; to which Laud replied :—" No man can express it ; it is to be found within." The Irishman was not yet satisfied. " It is founded upon a word," said he, " and that word should be known." " That word," responded Laud, " is the knowledge of Jesus Christ, and that alone."[1] But he saw that the man had not done ; so " he turned away to the executioner, as the gentler and discreeter person ; and, putting some money into his hand, without the least distemper or change of countenance, said, ' Here, honest friend, God forgive thee, and do thine office upon me with mercy.' "

Then he knelt down, and, as soon as he had done so, the executioner asked him to give him a signal when to strike. He replied that the sign should be his using the word, " Lord, receive my soul " ; but " first," said he, " let me fit myself."

Kneeling opposite the block, but not leaning down upon it, he prayed as follows :—

" Lord, I am coming as fast as I can. I know I must pass through the shadow of death, before I can come to see

---

[1] Benson, pp. 152-3.

Thee. But it is but *umbra mortis*, a mere shadow of death, a little darkness upon nature : but Thou by Thy merits and passions hast broke through the jaws of death. So, Lord, receive my soul, and have mercy upon me ; and bless this kingdom with peace and plenty, and with brotherly love and charity, that there may not be this effusion of Christian blood amongst them, for Jesus Christ His sake, if it be Thy will."

Having said this prayer loudly enough for those standing near him to hear, he bent down and fitted his neck on to the block. Then he prayed for a short time ("to himself," as Heylin expresses it [1]), inaudibly, and presently said aloud, "*Lord receive my Soul*," when, immediately, "the Executioner, who very dexterously did his Office," "took off his head at a blow."

His body was put into a leaden coffin and carried to the Church of All Hallows, Barking, which was close to the scene of the execution. A large number of people accompanied it, and at its burial the liturgy, which had just been abolished, was duly used. Therefore, his very funeral itself was an act of high treason. His body lay in the church of All Hallows, at Barking, for about eighteen years, and was then—it was after the Restoration—removed to the chapel of his dearly beloved St John's College, Oxford, where it was placed beneath the communion-table.[2]

Malicious people said that he had purposely painted his face, on the morning of his execution, in order to prevent his paleness making him look as if he feared death. This, explains his great biographer, was a base calumny ; there was no paint whatever on his face, and yet it sustained its ruddiness even until he knelt at the block itself. Very probably ; but it may be well to remember that there is such a thing as eczema, which would give a colour more permanent than paint. Heylin describes [3] his countenance as "chearful and well-bloudied, more fleshly, (as I have often heard him say) than any other part of his body."

---

[1] "Cyp. Ang.," p. 503.   [2] Benson, p. 156 ; also Heylin.
[3] "Cyp. Ang.," p. 507.

Laud's death presented the ghastly and horrible comedy of the execution of a man for spreading and encouraging a religion in which he did not believe, and against which he had perpetually protested. From a Catholic point of view, he had the honour of martyrdom thrust upon him, and its merits offered him, only to suffer its pains without obtaining its merits; as he died abusing the faith for which he was put to death.

It is not improbable that, at this point of my story, non-Catholic readers may feel some curiosity as to the opinion of a Roman Catholic biographer upon the question of the destination of Laud's soul, when the fatal axe had severed his head from his body.

Our theologians would, I believe, say, that granted the very worst interpretation of Laud's life,—an interpretation which I, for one, am not in the very least inclined to put upon it—from the Catholic standpoint it would be possible, I do not say probable, that during the fraction of a second in which the sharp-edged iron was falling through the air, he might have made such a perfect act of contrition as to save his soul;

> " Between the saddle and the ground
> He mercy sought and mercy found."

but, without supposing such an extreme case as this, there is a far more likely issue. I may convey my meaning by making the following quotation from a book which the late Cardinal Manning wrote of as " one of the most complete and useful Manuals of Doctrine, Devotion, and Elementary information for the instruction of those who are seeking the truth ; and not for them only, but for those who have inherited it." In a chapter headed " Things that Catholics do *not* believe," the author writes : —" Catholics do *not* believe that Protestants who are baptized, who lead a good life, love God and their neighbour, and are *blamelessly* ignorant of the just claims of the Catholic Religion to be the only one true Religion (which is called *being in good faith*), are excluded from Heaven, provided they believe that there is one God in three Divine persons;[1] that God will duly reward the good and punish the wicked; that Jesus Christ is the Son of God made man; who redeemed us, and in whom we must trust for our salvation; and provided they thoroughly repent of having ever, by their sins, offended God. Catholics hold that such Protestants who have these dispositions, and, moreover, have no suspicion of their religion being false, or have not the means to discover, or fail in their honest endeavours to discover, the true Religion, and who are so disposed in their heart that they would *at any cost* embrace the Roman Catholic Religion if they knew it to be the true one, *are Catholics in spirit* and in some sense within the Catholic Church, without themselves knowing it. She holds that these Christians belong to and are united to the '*soul*,' as it is called, of the Catholic Church, although they are not united to the visible *body* of the Church by external communion with her, and by the outward profession of her faith." [2]

What follows, however, must be given its due measure of serious consideration. " Very different is the case of a person who, having the opportunity, neglects to learn from genuine, trustworthy sources what the Catholic Religion is and really teaches, *fearing*, that were he to become convinced of the truth of the Catholic Faith, he would be compelled by his conscience to forsake his own religion and bear the worldly inconveniences attached to this step. This very *fear* shows a want of good faith, and that he is not in that *insurmountable ignorance* which could excuse him in the sight of God, but that he is one of those of whom it is said in Psalm xxxv. 4, ' *He would not understand that he might do well.*' "

Now that we have seen Laud's own head cut off, it may be well to consider how far he contributed to the decapitation of others. There appears to be little doubt that his proceedings,

---

[1] A footnote says :—"A believer in one God who, without any fault on his part, does not know and believe that in God there are three divine Persons, is, notwithstanding, in a state of salvation, according to the opinion of most Catholic theologians." To go further than this and explain the reasons given by theologians for their belief in the salvation of "the honest savage" would be beyond the scope of a Life of Laud.

[2] " Catholic Belief," by the Rev. J. F. Di Bruno, pp. 219, 220.

and more still his advice, led to events which brought about, or helped to bring about, the executions of both Charles I. and Strafford.   It is possible that, had Laud never existed, they might none the less have met their deaths in the same manner and under similar circumstances; yet it is difficult to study Laud's relations to those unfortunate men without coming to the conclusion that his friendship, policy, and advice had something to do with the fall of both.

Whether Buckingham would have become a victim to the spite of his many enemies, if he had not died from the blow of an assassin, no man can say; if he had, it may be a question whether in his case, also, Laud would not have had a share in increasing his unpopularity and effecting his overthrow.

Turning from individuals to institutions, a hostile historian of Laud might plausibly argue that, by encouraging the king to dispense with a Parliament, by urging him to the most arbitrary, if not unjust, actions, and by causing him to make enemies among his nobility and gentry with severe punishments for offences against ecclesiastical laws, he unintentionally but most effectively gave a blow to monarchical government in this country from which it has scarcely yet fully recovered.   I am not myself prepared to go to such lengths in criticising his secular policy; but I should hesitate to accept a brief on the opposite side.

As to the institution with which he was more directly concerned, the Established Church of his country, it appears to me, as an outsider, that the result of his endeavours was to bring the whole fabric down about his ears.   He lived to see the abolition of its bishops, as well as that of its liturgy, and its government placed in the hands of its bitterest enemies.   His Anglican admirers boast that it grew again from his ashes to a greater size than it had ever attained before, and that it flourished in proportion to the sacrifices which he made for it.[1]   It would appear, according to this theory, that, as the

---

[1] "He obtained hold of the helm.   He gave to the Anglican polity and worship what was in the main the impress of his own mind.   He then sank to the ground in that conflict of the times, which he had made and helped to exasperate.   But

Christian Church rose in all its greatness from the death of
its founder, so the Established Church of England sprang into
a new and more vigorous life owing to the death of Laud. I
venture to think that the two cases are not exactly parallel.
It is quite certain that Laud reduced his Church to confusion ;
it is, at best, uncertain whether his death contributed in any
perceptible degree to its resurrection. Its doctrinal advancement in the early part of the seventeenth century was due
rather to Andrews than to Laud ; its restoration in the latter
half of that century was to a large extent the work of the
temperate and judicious Juxon.

Again, writing as an outsider, I may say that I think Laud
certainly did do one thing for the Church of England, which
was to demonstrate the dangers of its authorities assuming
very marked, decided, and aggressive religious " views," and
it may be that, by the warning of his sad example, he practically founded that race of moderate, "safe," non-extreme,
compromising, and colourless bishops for which his Church
has been so celebrated since his death.

I anticipate that in addition to unfavourable criticisms on
account of my dulness and my unblushing practice of the
literary vice commonly described as " book-making," I shall
incur the censures of High-Churchmen for representing Laud's
" views" concerning apostolical succession and the eucharist
as very different from theirs. My defence must be that, from
the evidence which I have been able to obtain on the subject
and have produced in the foregoing pages, I honestly imagine
them to have been so. On the other hand, I readily admit
that I am not very conversant with the High-Church doctrines of this particular moment. Moreover, I gratuitously
volunteer the opinion that, had Laud lived now, it is not
impossible that he might have rejoiced at the development
of ritualism and have "levelled-up" his views to the times.

Perhaps I may be fairly open to criticism for having dwelt
so little upon Laud's Erastianism, and I may as well state

his scheme of Church polity, for his it largely was, grew up afresh out of his
tomb, and took effect at the Restoration."—Romanes' Lecture, 1892. By the
Right Hon. W. E. Gladstone, M.P.

candidly that the cause of my hesitation in doing so has been that I have felt some doubts whether he would have been such a keen advocate for kingly rule in ecclesiastical affairs, had not the particular king with whom he had most to do been singularly subservient to ecclesiastical rule.   In short, during Laud's prosperity, he told the king what to tell him to do, and then, if complaints were made, he said to the complainers that it had been the king's doing.   James I. had not sympathised with Laud's high views, and at the risk of offending him, Laud tried, nor altogether without success, to elevate those of James ; but he did not pander to the religious opinions of the " Head of the Church," and consequently never fully obtained James's confidence.   I do not deny that Laud was an Erastian ; nay, I clearly perceive his Erastianism in many details of his history ; but, to my mind, this is one of his characteristics to which somewhat undue prominence has been given, and I feel pretty certain that it was never his intention that the Established Church of England should be governed so much by Car. Rex as by Guil. Cant.

I must pause in my own criticisms on Laud to notice two or three which were passed immediately after his death by his contemporaries.   One of them consists of a poem of ninety lines, entitled an " Elegy upon the life and death of Bishop Laud of Canterbury."   It begins [1] :—

> " Can Britain's Patriarchal Peer expire,
> And bid the world good night, without a choir
> Of Saints to sing his requiem, and toll
> A blessing bell unto his dying soul ?
> Shall he steal to his rest thus ? and not have
> A blazing star to light him to his grave ;
> Nor warning ' Pace !' no volley—shot of thunder
> From Heaven's artillery, to strike with wonder,
> To ring alarums in the world's dull ear
> And rend the universe with panic fear."

The thing is too long to quote at length : I will only give a few lines, taken here and there.

---

[1] " Cal. Sta. Pa. Dom.," 1644-5, Preface, pp. xxiii.-v.

" How sweetly went'st thou hence ; thy fluent tongue
Warbling thy [own] swan-like *expedicum :*
Where such a concourse rolled, as they had been
To hear the raptures of some seraphim."

(Thou) " didst press
And trample death, with such undauntedness
As if thou meanst to spurn at Fate and spit
Defiance in death's face, and welcome it."

" Thy scaffold was thy Church, and we may please
Term it, a chapel (as some do) of Ease ;
There pouring forth thyself to Syon's King,
Thyself wert both high priest and th' offering ;
An offering to the Almighty, since thy late
Sad decollation doth conduplicate
Thy triumphs with thy Saviour ; who didst list
And Canonize thee an Evangelist.
Thus hast thou left us, only to lay down
And change thy mitre for a glorious crown."

All the poetry written about him, at the time of his death,
was not quite in the same tone.   Here is a verse from another,[1]
written just before his execution :—

" Take with you Bishop La[u]d
That's Canterbury
Trotting upon a jade
Soon to the ferry.
Advance ye Charon
With a good freight,
When ye are every one
To his boat brought."

Here is yet another[2] :—

" My little Lord [Laud] methinks it's strange
You should induce so great a change
In such a little space ;
You that so proudly th' other day
Did rule and the King's country sway,
Must trudge to know the other place ;
Remember now from whence you came
And that the grandsires of your name
Were dressers of old cloth ; "

[1] "Cal. Sta. Pa. Dom.," 1644-5, p. 280.   [2] *Ib.*

" Within six years six ears have been
Cropt off [most] worthy men and grave
For speaking what was true ;
But if the subtle head and ears
Can satisfy these six of theirs
Expect what is your due.
Poor people of late have felt your rod,
Give Laud to the Devil and praise to God
For freeing them from thrall ;
Your little Grace for want of Grace
Must lose the Patriarchal place,
And have no grace at all."

After such quotations as these, I feel it incumbent upon
myself once more to vindicate my hero from the charge of
Popery. I can see no reason for doubting the sincerity of
his ardent professions of Protestantism in his speech on the
scaffold. From the earliest times of the Anglican Church
Establishment to this very moment, High-Churchmen have
been accused of being in league with Rome, of furthering the
interests of Rome, of being Romanists at heart, and, for the
most part, very unjustly. People of every school of thought
except their own, and most of all Catholics, see how illogical
is their position ; but they are blind to it themselves. They
believe themselves to be in the Catholic Church ; they acknowledge " Roman " Catholics to be a branch of the Church, or a
sister Church, or a local Church ; but only as a rotten branch,
as a fallen sister, or as a local establishment which has no
business away from home. Catholics would be as eager as
they are themselves to clear Anglicans of " Romanism." A
good Puritan, who had an intense personal love of his
" Saviour "—a form of piety which has much in common with
the Catholic devotion to the Sacred Heart—may have been
quite as " near to Rome " as Archbishop Laud, or even very
much nearer, for that matter ; just as, to-day, an Evangelical
clergyman, preaching true contrition, may be really, but
unknowingly—how angry he would be if he did know—
united to the " soul " of the Roman Catholic Church, while a
Ritualist, with a Roman chasuble on his back and a golden
thurible full of the very choicest incense in his hand, may be

exceedingly foreign to it. But this neither of the great parties in the Anglican Church ever recognises or realises.

As in the nineteenth century, so also in the seventeenth, the Anglican Church, as a body, did not know either what it was, or what it wanted. True, it had its creeds, it had its articles of religion, it had its liturgy; but then, as now, some of its ministers interpreted them in one way, some in another; its various parties attributed its origin to very different sources; this section of its clergy stating that it was Protestant, that section that it was Catholic, a third section that it was not exactly one or the other, yet partly both; and, with regard to its wants, some maintained that its best interests lay in a higher ceremonial and an increasing conformity to the ancient usages of the Catholic Church, while others asserted that its only hope rested in the eradication of the last vestige of the papal rags. These divisions of the Anglican Church have ever been in conflict since her foundation, and have prevented it from knowing its own mind, its beginning, its ends, or its wants. In one of the throes of this perpetual agony, Laud fell. He was devoid of that spirit of compromise which is the very essence of the Church to which he belonged; he failed to appreciate the comprehensiveness which some of its modern bishops declare to be one of its greatest beauties, and, unlike High-Churchmen of our own time, he tried to insert the thick end of the wedge where he ought to have applied the thin.

Possibly Laud might have succeeded better if he had had a judicious and a popular wife to soothe his feelings when ruffled, to laugh him out of his little idiosyncrasies, and to counteract his own unconscious efforts at making himself unpopular. With Catholic priests the case is very different; their whole position is apart from that of the parson, and their duties differ as much from his as do their doctrines. It is true that the Catholic Church allows its priests, in certain localities and under certain rites, to marry, and that there are married Catholic priests at this moment—in the Lebanon, for instance —but it is not found, as a rule, to be a satisfactory arrangement, and a married clergy would not be liked by the laity

Life of Archbishop Laud. 479

any more than by the clerical authorities at Rome. In parson-dom, on the other hand, a clergyman is but half-fledged until he is a married man, and it may be that if Laud had had a sensible wife, she might have prevented the abolition of episcopacy and the decapitation of her husband.

I can find nothing in the writings of any unprejudiced historian of Laud, or in any unbiassed contemporary evidence, to lead me to consider him other than a well-meaning man ; my readers, I hope, will agree with me in believing him to have been an honest one ; nor can there be two opinions on the question whether he put the interests of the Church to which he belonged, and the king whom he served, before his own. Ambitious he was, without doubt, but his love of power was much more strongly developed than his love of place ; and if he loved wealth, he used it generously enough in assisting in the improvements at St John's College, the repairs of St Paul's Cathedral, the enrichment of the Bodleian Library, the erection of alms-houses in his native town of Reading, in other works of charity, and in his hospitalities at his palace of Lambeth and elsewhere.

He certainly did not owe his successes in life to the charms of either his appearance, his manner, or his voice ; he was no great orator, and his literary style was stiff and ungraceful, although he lived in the days of such prose writers as Bacon, Clarendon, Hobbes, Burton, Brown, and Chillingworth, and of such poets as Shakespeare and Milton ; neither did he win his way in the world by the subtilty of his tact or the brilliancy of his statesmanship, in both of which he was singularly deficient ; but he obtained respect and confidence in high places by the certainty with which he knew his own mind, by his immense power of will, and by his unwavering honesty of purpose.

It is true that, as Clarendon and others say of him, he was generally anything but obsequious to great people, that he was often rude to them, and that he never hesitated to get them punished if he caught them tripping ; but he chose a few mighty potentates, almost worshipped them in word and work, and was prepared to sacrifice everybody else's interests,

and even his own, to theirs. We may observe the first symp-
tom of this in his consenting to marry his earliest great
patron, the Earl of Devonshire, against his own conscience,
and more still in his conduct towards Buckingham, Charles I.,
and Wentworth.

If Anglicans should ever think of canonizing Laud—I
once read a little book in which such an idea was mooted—
they will find an *Advocatus Diaboli* ready made in Prynne.
The question of Laud's personal sanctity would be a delicate
one for a writer professing a different religion to enter upon ;
but if it should be said that his period was not one remarkable for Christian holiness, or that his piety was remarkable
for his times, I would reply that he lived in the days of that
great mystic, St Teresa, of St Charles Borromeo, of St
Aloysius, of St John of the Cross, of St Philip Neri, the
founder of the Oratorians ; of St Camillus of Lellis, the founder
of a great order of men-nurses ; of St Rose of Lima, the first
canonized saint of America; of the charming St Francis of
Sales ; of his disciple, St Jane Francis of Chantal ; of St Peter
Claver, "the Apostle of the Negroes"; of the gentle and
charitable St Vincent of Paul, and of many others, while,
close at home, he may have almost seen some of the lately
beatified English martyrs pouring forth their blood for their
faith. "And," I can imagine my readers saying, "he poured
forth his own for his faith." Nay, he was made to pour it
forth for encouraging "Romanism," whereas he died professing himself the best of Protestants.

Let us not dispute over this. He died a brave man, I hope
a good one, and, take him all in all, he may be said to have
been an historical character of whom "conformable" people
have every reason to feel proud, while even "Romish
recusants" may admire him as a well-intentioned, straightforward, and manly Englishman.

THE END.

INDEX.

2 II

ARCHBISHOP LAUD

www.ingramcontent.com/pod-product-compliance
Lightning Source LLC
Chambersburg PA
CBHW032004110726
47901CB00004B/960